# LOTTE

## PETER KRÜGER

Steinkrug

First published in Great Britain in 2025 by Steinkrug
an imprint of Steinkrug Publications Ltd

1

A CIP catalogue record for this title is available from the British Library

Paperback ISBN  9780954097769
eBook  ISBN  9780954097776

Printed by Biddles Books Ltd.
Paper used is FSC certified and all materials in the book are from sustainably managed forests.

Steinkrug, an imprint of Steinkrug Publications Ltd
20 Leaden Hill
Orwell, Royston
SG8 5QH   UK

www.steinkrugpublications.co.uk

It took the Stasi thirty nine years to gather sufficient information on the citizens of the DDR to fill the 100 km of files now held in the German Federal Archives

Facebook could have done this in under twelve hours

# Part One

Tricks

# 1

## If Only Erich Honecker Had Been A Better Shot

May 2019

Is it possible to betray a country which no longer exists? The person who had asked now stood on the other side of the street. As spies go, he did not strike me as a particularly good one, evidenced by the innocent purchase of a lottery ticket resembling a dead-letter drop.

'It is anomalies that give people away, Lotte. Lack of attention to detail, small things even the cleverest agent might miss.' This according to Hubert Hüber, who had started calling me Lotte around the time I dropped the *Comrade* and *Oberleutnant*. That was fifty years ago in another life, in that country which no longer exists. 'Loose threads... Find one and keep picking at it and even the best cover story unravels.' This attempt to educate or impress a novice agent came to mind while I sat outside the small café next to Templin Stadt railway station, waiting to see what the man, who kept glancing at the piece of paper in his hand, did next.

A breeze brought from the Baltic a memory of winter and the promise of summer. The sun was a little too bright for someone who had only got two hours sleep the previous night, explaining the sunglasses – so, now who looks like the spy? Suspicious too was the length of time I had sat making a show of reading a newspaper and pretending to drink the coffee which was now cold. The intention had been to catch the 10:32 train to Berlin. During the forty-five minutes since the train left without me, far from finding the courage to make the journey, I was now on the point of walking back to my car and driving home. But then, distracted by the man across the street, I was back in a world where a waitress would report anyone acting oddly, such as sitting outside her café half an hour before it opened, especially if she had spotted an audio tape in their shoulder bag. Today she would merely insist the suspected spy had a nice day, which as early as Christmas 1989 had already become almost as tedious as a knock on the door by the Stasi.

At first I thought the man across the street was looking in my direction, but then realised he was watching a young woman in her twenties, bounce past; at least parts of her were bouncing. He had obviously failed to notice the slightly overweight woman in her mid-sixties with a pageboy hairstyle, fashionable for a few months when she was a teenager, who looked like she chose her clothes by sticking a pin at random in a two-year-old Queller catalogue. An unflattering description by a writer who used me as a character in one of her books; quite what I did to upset her was never made clear. The novel contained a great deal of embarrassing sex and a series of grisly murders. In real life the only person I have slept with is my husband, and as we are both now over sixty most of our time in bed is spent asleep. As for murders there have been just two, only one involving substantial bleeding and described by someone, rather flippantly I thought, as a freak shaving accident.

My attention was still on the man across the street, who I am calling Rolf, not his real name – but neither is Lotte mine – both have been changed to protect the unfortunate, or the fortunate, this is the former East Germany after all so sometimes it is difficult to decide which you are. Rolf had just left the supermarket, but was not carrying a shopping bag. He was a tall slim man in his seventies,

4

upright and alert with an air of self-importance, dressed in a suit instead of the jeans and anorak he was wearing the last time we met. The suit looked new, and the hair washed and trimmed as befitting someone about to become one of the richest men in Brandenburg. Or maybe he thought it was better people believed he was already wealthy rather than receive the unwelcome attention a particularly unusual lottery win would attract.

The memory of the young girl clinging onto the back of a motorbike, speeding through the streets of Berlin, blonde hair trailing behind her and long elegant fingers gripping the rider's leather jacket, evaporated after catching sight of my reflection in the café window. The hair was shorter now, and Auburn, according to the label on the bottle. Why my fingers also also seemed shorter than I recalled was something of a mystery, perhaps one of those things lost in translation when you reinvent your past. And the sunglasses really did make me look like a spy so I replaced them with the pair I usually only wore indoors. Larger, with heavier frames to disguise my piggy eyes and rounded face. This suggestion care of my sister Ursula: not the most subtle of people.

Then the dramatic development I had half expected. Rolf stepped off the pavement into the path of a car which was accelerating away from the traffic lights at the roadworks next to the level crossing. The man behind Rolf grabbed his arm, preventing what could well have been a serious accident. The squeal of tyres and the car's blaring horn would have distracted anyone observing the old man. They would have missed the 'kiss' – the covert passing of information to a contact – and failed to notice the neatly folded piece of paper in Rolf's hand. His left hand, perhaps revealing his state of mind, or simply facilitating a less obvious transfer of the message to a co-conspirator.

A cloud of dust drifted across the street from the roadworks. When it cleared, Rolf was standing on his own again, but still holding the note, at least until he spotted me. Then, maybe consumed by guilt or realising the importance of what was written on it, he pushed the scrap of paper into his trouser pocket. What was the point of doing that? I already knew the code, or at least the first three numbers, 4, 7 and 11 – the other three were in a back issue of *Neues Deutschland*.

The numbers had come up during a conversation with Rolf the previous month. He had come to me after the death of his mother. Grief counselling is not my speciality and I tend to deal with other forms of loss – status, privilege and direction. A lot of my patients are from the corporate sector, most in Berlin where I rent a room in a colleague's practice for five or six days a month. The rest of my time is spent working from my home in Gehrden, a small village a short distance from Templin.

'Most of the people I know whose parents have died are over it in a year. It just seems to stay with me. Some days I can't think of anything else.' Rolf's hands hovered in front of him then gently patted his knees. 'So, can you help?'

Was he asking for help or doubting my ability to provide it? Or maybe that was just me. Oddly enough, I'm more comfortable with high-powered businessmen and politicians than ordinary members of the public.

'Perhaps we can start by you telling me about your family, your earliest memories of your mother,' I said, doubting Rolf's problem was especially unique.

'I remember very little about anything that happened before my father died. He was captured at the end of the war, taken to a camp in Siberia and never returned.' Thirty years after the Wende and Rolf was still reluctant to say out loud his father had been killed by the Russians. 'My mother remarried in 1950 when it became obvious he would not return.'

'And you have brothers and sisters?'

'Just one brother, or rather a stepbrother. He was born in 1951.'

'Are you close?'

'No, we rarely speak – there is very little contact. None since my mother's death.' We then spent the next two sessions travelling down a blind alley guided by the assumption Rolf grew up in a family from which he felt excluded. That his mother associated her first son with

6

the loss and grief of her first marriage and now, with her death, the last chance to become part of her new family had slipped from Rolf's grasp. Then midway through the third appointment he removed his glasses and wiped the lenses with a handkerchief taken from his jacket pocket.

'You are left-handed,' I said. The impact was surprisingly dramatic; he fumbled with his glasses which almost slipped from his grasp and hurriedly pushed the handkerchief back into his pocket. It took some time for him to regain his composure.

'Yes, it was still regarded as a taboo when I was young. My mother made sure I used my right hand for writing before I went to school.'

'How did she do that?'

'Punished me.'

'Punished how?'

'Physical, striking me. Sometimes she tied my left hand behind my back. But mostly just shouting. She had quite a temper.'

'Can you remember what she shouted?'

Rolf fell silent and was visibly upset. 'That I was useless, would never amount to anything, that she wished I had never been born ...' He seemed close to tears again but this time leaving his glasses in place and staring at the window rather than confront this troubling aspect of his relationship with his mother. The blinds were kept drawn specifically to prevent troubled minds escaping. 'Sometimes ... sometimes she said at least she had one son who was normal.'

My exaggerated wince was to convey sympathy and prise open this fissure from which all that troubled Rolf about the death of his mother would flow.

'There was nothing I could do to please her. My degree in mathematics and my job as a statistician with the government counted for nothing, while my brother could do no wrong.' Rolf shrugged and shook his head. 'Then of course the Wende and she felt vindicated.'

'How?'

Another shrug and resigned shake of the head. 'The job with the ministry ended and her son with a mathematics degree ended up counting tins of beans in a supermarket.'

Tell me about it. There was a temptation to empathise. To tell him about the professor of psychiatry at Humbolt University banned from practising and forced to take up nursing, dispensing medication to mental patients on the night shift in a regional mental hospital. And her husband, just a couple of promotions away from being the DDR's minister of technology, reduced to tinkering with cars and repairing agricultural machinery. And while some of us had regained much of what we lost, we still found ourselves wondering *if only*.

In Rolf's case, his insight into the behaviour of East Germany's consumers proved invaluable and his time as a stock controller was short. However, his steady rise through the management hierarchy of one of the country's leading supermarkets merely provided another chapter of Rolf's life that his mother could denigrate. 'In her opinion I would fail for a second time in my life.'

'Do you feel you failed?'

He hesitated before answering. Up until then his hand had been a little too close to his mouth for someone who was being completely honest but now it was resting on the arm of the chair. 'No, in fact since I retired, they keep inviting me back, mostly when there is a new marketing campaign.'

This seemed familiar, wringing a person out before finally dumping them on the scrapheap, as I had frequently warned my husband and been chastised for being cynical.

'Will I ever be free from baked beans?' Rolf laughed, and this was good, suggesting he was no longer dwelling on the negative.

'You will have to meet with your mother again,' I suggested, jumping a couple of chapters in the bereavement counselling handbook. 'Choose a place you are familiar with. Perhaps the table you sat around as a family when you were young. You list everything you have achieved, your inventory of successes ...'

'I think there are laws regarding digging up bodies, even your relatives.' Rolf smiled, but then adopted a more thoughtful expression. 'I think I know where you are going with this. I'm just not sure it will work.' Opinion is divided on whether it is helpful if patients have done their own research. Fortunately, it appeared Rolf's mind was not completely closed to the idea of a virtual meeting with his departed nemesis.

'Obviously your mother will not be able to respond. So, you can divide up everything that once connected you. She can take with her all her negativity, and you can keep all your positive achievements.'

Did this work? Did Rolf even hold that meeting? I would never know for sure, but he seemed far more relaxed during the most recent and, hopefully, final session. To assess his progress, I asked what he had planned for the next month. It seemed his former employer was hosting a group marketing event and had asked Rolf to sit in on some of the panel discussions. And there was a reunion of former employees of the DDR's department of statistics.

A moment's hesitation as he bit his lip in attempt to hide a smile. Eventually he relented and confessed. 'Oh, of course two weeks from now I will win the lottery.'

'Sorry?'

'The lottery, six out of forty-nine. I am going to win the jackpot. Madness, I know.'

'I'm not sure *madness* is a word to use lightly when speaking to a therapist.' By now any semblance of professional conduct on my part had evaporated.

'I know it's crazy ...'

'Crazy is not much better.'

Rolf burst out laughing. 'I realise that. Consider how many times the numbers one, two, three, four, five, six have come up. Never. In fact, if they did, the jackpot would be worthless because of how many crazy people choose those numbers every week.' This was Rolf the statistician, rather than Rolf the denigrated son speaking. 'It's irrational because the lottery is a tax on the daft. It's the government clawing back some of the money wasted trying to teach children basic mathematics. So, what are the chances of one, two, three, four, five, six coming up twice? Infinitely small, but that's exactly what is going to happen on the twenty-sixth of May.'

'So, seven weeks from now the winning numbers will be one, two, three, four, five, six? I must write that down,' I said, picking up my pen and notebook.

'No, no, they will be four, seven, eleven...' Rolf stopped abruptly, having noticed I was indeed taking notes. Presumably he was unwilling to share this potential fortune.

I realised he was serious and maybe the last ten sessions had achieved nothing. 'Interesting, perhaps you could tell the whole story from the beginning.'

'Well, all this came about because Erich Honecker was such a poor shot.'

Actually, *whole story* did not mean the earth cooling, fish walking on land, an asteroid killing all the dinosaurs right up to an East German woman being elected chancellor of Germany and all the improbable events leading up to Rolf discovering a way to predict winning lottery numbers. But this was my last appointment for the day, it was only 2:30 and raining and so no sunbathing outside until my husband got back from Berlin, and who would not be just a little intrigued?

Rolf continued with what seemed like a well-rehearsed monologue. 'It was May nineteen seventy-nine, a hunting party in Joachimsthal arranged by the ministry of trade. Some bigshot from Moscow had been invited and Honecker was there, of course. Well, this wild boar wandered out of trees next to the lake. Honecker took aim and missed. Missed by a long way because, apparently, you could see the splash when the bullet hit the water. No one else was prepared to fire, not even the Russian, not wanting to show up the chief. The wild boar disappeared into the forest and no one knew what to say. Then someone decided to break what had become an embarrassing silence by saying how well the economy of East Germany was doing and suggested that at some point it would overtake those of countries in the West. Honecker leapt on this, suggesting someone should work out the date when this miracle would happen because it would raise the spirits of young people who were becoming disenchanted with the apparent lack of economic progress. No one present knew how serious Honecker was about this but equally no one was prepared to take the chance he was not.'

'You were there with Honecker?'

'No.'

'So how did you know any of this happened? Because it's news to me.'

Rolf leaned forward as if taking me into his confidence. 'Well, the following week,' Rolf was almost whispering at his point, 'my boss told me what had happened, and I said anyone who thought the DDR would overtake the West any time before the end of the next century must be an idiot. Then he tells me he was the idiot and now needed someone equally stupid to come up with the figures to prove it, and have them on his desk by the end of the next day. I made some predictions based on all of East Germany's industry eventually performing as well as Zeiss, and Robotron becoming a serious player in the European computer market. And maybe industrial unrest would cripple industries in Spain, Britain, Italy and even West Germany. The date I came up with was the twenty-fifth of May two thousand and nineteen. I prepared a report and sent it to the editor of *Neues Deutschland* and thought that would be the end of it. But later that week someone I knew from university, who now worked on the paper, phoned me to say a heap of rubbish with my name on it had landed on his desk. He suggested we meet up to discuss it, and we did. He wanted to know why it was me and not my boss who was credited with coming up with the date. That was obvious of course, my punishment for suggesting he was an idiot. Neither of us wanted to make ourselves look stupid so my friend tried to persuade the editor to ignore the report. Unfortunately, he had also heard about the hunting trip and Honecker's interest.'

'So, it was published.' I noticed Rolf did not mention the name of the journalist – perhaps he thought I might contact him suggesting we each shared a third of Rolf's fortune.

'Yes, although it was hardly front-page news. There was a strike at the Fiat factory in Milan and this was the main business story that day with the report mentioned as an aside, as I had highlighted industrial disputes as one reason East Germany's economy would overtake those of countries such as Italy. Even so, the journalist was angry at having to write something his readers would laugh at, and not because it was satirical. That was the problem, because it was common knowledge he wrote, under an assumed name, for *Eulenspiegel*.'

'And he got away with that. Rather unusual.'

'It was rumoured he had contacts within the Party and also abroad. He received news about industrial disputes and new technology long before it was picked up by the HVA. In fact the Stasi tried hard to find out who his source was. Anyway, until one of his stories upset someone in Moscow he could do pretty much what he liked. As a joke he also put the date in the report above that week's lottery results.'

'Well, you certainly have quite a memory.'

'Not really, I was just clearing out a cupboard and found the copy of the newspaper. At first I couldn't remember why I'd kept it, but then saw the article about my report and it came back to me. The Lottery results were ringed with a pen and I remembered laughing about it with my girlfriend.' The number of people who might be sharing Rolf's lottery win was growing. 'That's the thing, I stumbled on it by chance which makes it harder to ignore. In my place you would buy a ticket, wouldn't you?' He asked.

'I admit the money would be useful.' I replied, immediately regretting having done so.

'Although technically it would be wrong.' Rolf continued. 'Cheating the laws of chance, and the DDR because had I bought a ticket in nineteen seventy-nine the winnings would have contributed to East Germany's GDP. I could hardly have taken a trip to

Disneyland or gone shopping in West Berlin but a week in Rugen would have been nice and perhaps I would have bought a tractor for a collective farm.' Rolf laughed. 'Or at least that is what I would have told the TV and local party boss. Now of course it will all be for the benefit of Wessies. They've stolen so much from us, so why shouldn't I keep this piece of good luck to myself?'

'Interesting you should feel guilty about betraying a country which no longer exists.' *Guilty* is another word not used lightly, or unnecessarily, during the healing process.

A little over a month later it was guilt, and betrayal, on my mind while sitting outside the café watching Rolf, who was now talking to the young man whose stone cutting machine had been responsible for that cloud of dust. Rolf gripped the plastic barrier separating pedestrians from road-making equipment and piles of building material. There was an exchange shouted above the noise of a jackhammer which, given Rolf's age, and the fact both men laughed, perhaps included a reference to the Berlin wall.

The young man lifted the visor from his face and pointed along Dargersdorfer Strasse where there was a tobacconist which sold lottery tickets, and this was most likely where Rolf was headed as I stood on the platform of Templin Stadt station waiting for the train to Berlin.

# 2

# The Man Upstairs

Five weeks earlier

Tripping while crossing the veranda, I stumbled into the crowded room like an actor with stage fright pushed in front of an audience. Hoping it would make me feel less vulnerable, I glanced back through the French doors to signal that outside lay something responsible for my apparent clumsiness. Not that anyone acknowledged my presence; most were too preoccupied with eating and drinking or engaged in conversation, some in small groups, others seated on chairs and settees, all of which looked both modern and expensive. Everyone was talking loudly, almost shouting as if to drown out the noise from the room above. It was what was causing this noise, a scraping sound then banging and screaming, I had felt compelled to question. However, my enquiries were ignored. Had I been in possession of some form of ID and not arrived at the house wearing just shorts and a tee-shirt, my enquiry would have carried more weight. There was a feeling of not belonging, of being powerless and borderline naked in a room full of people who were fully dressed.

From the room above came the sound of fighting, possibly a punishment beating or an interrogation, torture even, except now there was an absence of shouts or screams. In front of me a flight of stairs and to my right a door to another room. It was through this door that a man of indeterminate age – he had his back to me – disappeared as I was about to start climbing the stairs. It was also at this point someone spoke to me although either I could not hear them or do not remember what they said.

Expecting the décor to be the same throughout the house I was surprised to find myself in the doorway of a white tiled room. There was a sharp intake of breath on seeing in the centre of this room a man tied to a chair. Although barely recognisable due to the injuries to his face and neck, this person was known to me although I was uncertain from when or where. He had obviously sustained a beating and my inclination was to help him but I held back when a door to my left opened and a large and somewhat aggressive man, both taller and stronger than me, stepped into the room. He was wiping his hands, and I noticed there was a crescent-shaped smear of blood on the door of what I assumed was a bathroom.

The interrogator kicked the chair, tipping it and the prisoner onto the floor. Totally unnecessary in my opinion as it was obvious from the amount of his blood already pooled on the tiles, the severity of the bruising on the upper body and face, and the fact he was no longer breathing that this man was dead.

'Please stop,' I shouted and, despite immediately realising how pathetic this sounded, stepped forward. Intending to do what? Because this person was obviously beyond my help.

'This has nothing to do with you, Lotte.' Someone had grabbed my right arm and it was apparent how little I knew about the layout of the house. There must have been a second staircase because beside me stood the man who had left the room downstairs at the same time as me. His voice I recognised, his face I did not, but we must have met before because how did he know my name?

'It has everything to do with me,' I replied.

'So, you know this person?' he asked. 'I mean, *really* know this person?'

Looking back at the injured man on the floor, because the voice in the darkened corner of the room had caused me to doubt myself, I saw a third person: a stocky woman in a white coat, the sort worn by laboratory technicians, clinicians and assistant interrogators apparently, was in the room. She leaned over the body and cut the ropes tying it to the chair. The long-blade knife used to do this was replaced with exaggerated care on the stainless-steel tray beside the array of instruments used during the interrogation, including the one responsible for the cut on the man's neck.

'Please be careful with him,' I said as the interrogator and his female assistant grabbed the body by its feet and dragged it out of the room. Stepping back to let them pass I turned to the person standing in the shadows and ask for help. This not forthcoming and I followed the body on its journey down the stairs.

Shock or disgust – it is difficult to describe which I felt. Both perhaps, because no one registered the slightest surprise when the bruised and bloodied body was dragged through the room and out of the door. The dead man's head bumped on the three steps leading from the veranda to the garden and I now remembered it was one of these which had caused me to stumble when entering the house. Perhaps the enormity of what I was witnessing had caused me to become distracted by this somewhat trivial detail. Some of the people standing in small groups in the garden I had previously seen inside the house, and they cared as little about a bloodied body being dragged across the lawn as the sound of someone beaten to death above their heads. 'Will someone help me, please?' A shortness of breath caused my voice to sound strangled.

Then I remembered being out here in the garden before entering the house, speaking to the man who had just been killed. I had asked him something but got no reply. Then someone had told me to stop bothering him. That stocky woman, who then led the man away. At that time, it seemed unlikely she intended to harm him. 'This is all your fault,' she said now as the body was dragged towards a gap in the trees.

'Be careful with him,' I said for a second time.

'Stay where you are, the woman said while pulling at the body.

Ignoring her, I kept walking towards the trees. Voices from the garden grew fainter, replaced by others, younger and less restrained. Shouts and laughter echoed through the trees. The path gave onto a small strip of sand at the edge of a lake. The laughter had come from teenagers in a boat who ignored both me and the couple who were now collecting stones and putting them in the dead man's pockets.

It was only when the body was laid at the end of the small jetty which extended out into the lake that I recognised who this was. But too late because he was now being swung back and forth: three times before being let go, rising into the air and then plunging into the water. There was hardly a splash, although a boy in the boat was pointing to where the body had entered the water. Seemingly oblivious to me shouting at the end of the jetty, the young man manoeuvred the boat towards where bubbles were still rising to the surface.

There were footsteps behind me. It was the man who had been standing in the shadows during the beating. It was unclear how I knew this, because, too engrossed in the young people's search for the body, I did not take my eyes off the water. Perhaps it was his voice although I cannot recall him speaking. Below me there was something in the water. The reflection of the sun, or even the moon, because I am not sure if all this happened during the day or the night. I felt faint. I wanted to call out but was gasping for breath. The white disk, if not a reflection, must have been something below the surface, a face. It was, and my first thought was it was rising up through the water, but then realised I was falling. The person who had been standing behind me must have pushed me into the water.

'Mice?'

I was sat up in bed, my clothes wet, but from sweat rather than a swim in a lake. There was someone beside me, lying propped up on one elbow. Where I was, and who was asking me questions, only became apparent when my husband Herman said, 'You kept saying *mice*. I think you were dreaming.'

'Not about mice.'

'Was it the same dream?'

'Yes,' I whispered. My throat felt sore, probably from shouting. Perhaps this was still a dream, a nightmare which would only end if I escaped from this room and the person asking all these questions.

After three minutes sitting on the toilet in the bathroom taking deep breaths, my heart rate began to slow. Reaching for the glass on the shelf below the mirror I caught sight of myself looking much like anyone would after spending fifteen minutes grappling with torturers and murderers and then drowning in a lake. The glass slipped from my fingers and bounced around in the sink like the clapper in a bell before surrendering to the inevitable and shattering into small pieces. It was one of these pieces which cut my finger when I picked it up. The second reel of the nightmare was loaded into the projector and momentarily the image of a man cutting himself shaving flashed through my mind: he swore, and wiped the blood from his neck and was gone almost as quickly as he appeared, slamming the door to my subconscious where he had resided since I was a child.

'I can cancel tomorrow's meeting, tell them to rearrange it for Monday.' Herman said as I crawled back into bed, and I recalled the first time his arms were wrapped around me, and I felt his breath on my neck while drifting off to sleep. That was after a party in Leipzig, the summer of 1971.

'The big man who was talking to me just then, what's his name?' I had shouted, trying to make myself heard over the Rolling Stones' *Street Fighting Man*. Asking because the boy who towered over fellow researchers, physically and intellectually, had rescued a young girl hopelessly out of her depth.

Ursula put her mouth close to my ear. 'That's Herman, the person I told you about, the one helping Roland restore the Volkswagen

Beetle. I'll introduce you.' Which she did, and never one to miss a chance to embarrass her younger sister, Ursula said, 'Hi, *big man*, this is Lotte.' And for the next forty years, to his annoyance, the nickname stuck, and I felt guilty for taking my anger and frustration out on my longtime protector. He could quite easily have spent the night in Berlin after the end of his four-day trip to Britain, especially as he was needed back there in the morning.

'I'll be OK.' I said.

'Is it one of your patients? Someone with an unsavoury past?'

'No, they have all gone. Dead by now I should think.' Although Herman was getting uncomfortably close to the truth. 'Anyway the dream has nothing to do with that.'

'Well, if it's that one about the house full of people standing by while a person is beaten to death it sounds rather like someone has been offloading guilt. It's not someone who thinks they should have tried to stop the Stasi grabbing people off the street and torturing them?'

'My last patient had issues with his late mother. Mind you when it came to torture it sounded like she put the Stasi in the shade.' I laughed, not at this but Rolf's story about the lotto ticket. I would have liked to retell it to Herman, not least because it would have brought the discussion about the dream to a close.

'Dreams are not like that, they're not nuanced or metaphorical. If you fall asleep listening to a radio program you can find yourself immersed in the narrative, but mostly they are personal. And anyway, I started having this dream when I was a child.' Sometimes I regretted describing my dreams to Herman.

My nightmares were like jigsaws. The origin and provenance of most of the pieces were known. But always there was something new to contemporise and provide context. Some were disjointed; others, like this one, seemed complete and so the reference to mice had been strange, a piece of the puzzle I knew belonged somewhere but seemed not to fit.

'And now it's back ...' Herman was a great one for pointing out the obvious.

'Yes, it's back,' I interrupted. 'I remember an engineer telling me a problem that goes away on its own comes back on its own.' Pulling his arms around me, I pushed myself back against the person who was going to protect me while I stared at the blind over the window, all there was between me and the complete darkness only those of us living in the part of Germany referred to as the *Far End of the Milky Way* experience. This problem had not come back on its own. It had been helped on its way by someone who hopefully was now in a hotel far away and not standing, silhouetted in the moonlight, beside the lake at the other end of the village.

# 3

# Going Bananas in Netto

April 2019

We had planned to spend the day in Neuglobsow, arriving in time for lunch then in the afternoon cycle around Stechlinsee. Thursdays were kept clear, set aside for research. Herman had been due home after two days in Britain, dealing with the fall-out from Brexit for the company he worked for, Schulenberg Electronics.

'Another crisis,' he complained, despite enjoying every minute of it. On this occasion the crisis necessitated Herman flying to Munich for a meeting at Schulenberg's headquarters instead of back home via Berlin. So, our one-day break was postponed. Fortunate perhaps because the weather on the day was not as advertised on TV. True it was sunny and unseasonably warm, but rain clouds stalked the countryside soaking unsuspecting villages. So far Lychen had been spared and it was there I was doing the weekly shop and afterwards intended to meet Dagmar, a friend from my nursing days, for lunch at the Mühlenwirtschaft.

Supermarkets I still find overwhelming and sensory overload kicks in somewhere between the vegetable aisle and the fish counter. But this was Netto, so no need to choose from twenty varieties of olive oil. Even so, I probably seemed distant while struggling to remember what was written on the list, compiled while on the phone to Herman the previous evening but then left on the breakfast bar in the kitchen.

A bunch of bananas landed in my shopping trolley. 'Grab as many of these as you can carry, people will be queueing down the street when news gets around these are on the shelves.' The man now standing beside me said.

My first thought was this was one of my patients, but most would have been reluctant to converse with their therapist in public. And would any be so crass? The well-worn trope, a reference to the shortage of fresh fruit in the former East Germany, had become somewhat tired. As well this person, dressed in a knee length black jacket and carrying a walking stick, spoke with a foreign accent.

'It's Lotte isn't it? I was passing through Lychen and thought I recognised you.' He was vaguely familiar – the accent was English. 'I'm Paul, Paul Anweiler. We met at a party in Rethen in August nineteen seventy-five. You were my cousin Erich's girlfriend.' He placed a packet of sandwiches next to the bananas in the trolley then held out his hand, and caught unawares, I shook it.

'It is anomalies that give people away.' This was the first time, for more years than I could remember, that Hubert Hüber's advice came to mind; later, it would become obvious why.

Ignoring the unwanted attention from the person now pretending to take a sudden interest in the price of potatoes, I pushed the trolley along the aisle. But he followed me. 'Can we have lunch?' he asked. 'There is something I need to discuss with you.' His eyes were a piercing blue and assuming his thick white hair was once blond, he might well have been the English student I met forty years earlier. The scarring above the left eye could have come later and failing eyesight the reason he now wore glasses.

My stalker was behind me as I waited while an elderly couple loaded their shopping on the conveyor belt at the tills. He took a Ritter Sport bar from the rack strategically placed to persuade shoppers with a chocolate addiction to part with a few euros. Marzipan, but then he changed his mind and replaced it, taking a hazelnut bar instead. 'The tyranny of choice. How are you coping with that in East Germany?'

'An Ami,' the elderly man in front of me muttered to his wife, mistaking the Englishman for an American.

Seeming to ignore the remark, the target for the old man's ire dropped the chocolate bar into my trolley and picked up a packet of contraceptives, which I found disconcerting to say the least, although thankfully he kept it in the palm of his hand. After scratching at the packet with a coin he waited until the old man was distracted then reached past me and slid the contraceptives under a cabbage on the conveyor. The packet was the last item the cashier picked up. It seemed the old man decided arguing over how it got into the couple's shopping would prove more embarrassing than letting the young girl scan it. Except of course, the damaged barcode meant the packet of contraceptives was held up for everyone to see while the cashier typed in the product code. A stupid prank of the sort a student might play, and not always for fun.

After paying for the shopping and, to my annoyance, bananas which would give me stomach cramps and tuna sandwiches I would only eat if desperate, I pushed the trolley out of the shop. The bar of hazelnut chocolate I rather hoped the Englishman would forget to take with him.

'My name is not Lotte, or Charlotte even, and I have never heard of your cousin Erich or been to a party in Rethen,' I said, slightly louder than I would have liked because with the sun shining in my face I felt at a disadvantage. Despite shielding my eyes with my hand, I felt I was shouting in the dark. 'In fact, I don't think there's such a place as Rethen.' Doubt is sometimes better than an outright denial but, in this instance, I might have introduced slightly more than was credible.

My attacker – a slight exaggeration but this did feel like an act of aggression – turned and stood aside as if giving me permission to return to the carpark. 'It is just north of Müncheberg, halfway between Berlin and the Polish border,' he said, walking beside me. 'You should call your friend and tell her something important has come up.'

How on earth did he know about my lunch with Dagmar? Still trying to process this, I noticed a van parked close to my VW Polo, its side door open causing the words *Fresh Fruit* to become separated from *and Vegetables*. Another reference to the DDR, this one more sinister than bananas. Vans such as these were used by the Stasi to grab people off the street and transport them to either Stasi headquarters or the prison in Hohenschönhausen. They helped maintain an element of surprise because until becoming a reluctant passenger in one, a person was usually unaware they were under surveillance. Also, their use disguised the number of people in the penal system and, according to some, gave the impression there was a plentiful supply of fruit and fresh vegetables in East Berlin.

After packing away the shopping, and returning the trolley, I came back to my car to find the man claiming to be Paul Anweiler sitting in the passenger seat. I eased myself slowly into the narrow space between the driver's door and the van, relieved to get behind the wheel without being abducted. Feeling slightly more confident, I went on the attack. 'I'm going to phone the police.' There was no attempt to grab the mobile phone when I took it from my coat pocket.

'And tell them what?'

'About that for a start,' I said, tilting my head towards the van. 'That stupid piece of Stasi theatre.'

'That will be long gone when they get here.'

I turned and took a picture of the van with my phone then dialled 110, although held back from pressing send, hoping a demonstration of intent would persuade this man to get out of my car.

'Of course, you know there's an elderly couple in Rostock who have spent forty years wondering how their son ended up dead in a hotel room in Vienna.'

'What the hell are you talking about?'

'Just thought you might want to know how I'm going to explain being here in your car when the police turn up. My guess is they will be none too pleased. They tend to regard investigating murders as their job.' Watching my hand, he waited, maybe thinking I might actually place the call. 'It has taken you and Herman a long time to rebuild your careers, repair everything the West Germans destroyed. Would you throw all that away for the sake of lunch with an old friend?' Lychen's luck finally ran out. Rain hammered on the roof of my car and turned the carpark into a sea of mist. A young woman dashed towards her car, one hand pushing a trolley, the other holding the collar of a raincoat pulled over her head. 'There is a place next to the lake, do you know it?' Anweiler asked.

He was referring to the Strand café, a fortunate choice as it would be embarrassing to arrive at the restaurant where Dagmar was waiting for me with this man in tow. Starting the car and putting it in gear I deleted the emergency call then phoned Dagmar. I told her a patient was having an emotional crisis and needed my help. As it would turn out this was not so far from the truth.

'You said you were passing. On the way to where?' I asked, hoping to gain some advantage by taking control of the conversation. 'Were you halfway between London and Moscow and decided to drop into Netto in Lychen to buy a packet of sandwiches? You owe me two euros fifty for those, by the way.'

'Your expenses will cover that.'

'I'm sorry, what expenses?'

But he ignored the question. 'I'm visiting farms. This morning it was one near Eberswalde and this afternoon another in Dossow, it's a small village just south of Wittstock.'

'Thank you for the geography lesson but I know where Dossow is.'

'But not Rethen.'

'So, what do you do? Your day job when you are not kidnapping people?'

'I work for a bank in Köln, it's considering investing in farms here in the East.'

'Good luck with that, the Dutch got here ahead of you.'

He just shrugged. 'There's always something that gets missed, owners who held out but are now thinking of retiring or just need money for new equipment.' His attention wandered; he was looking across the lake which had just come into view.

How much of his story made sense? Well, at some point the walking stick had been pushed into the earth to a depth of around fifteen centimetres, some of the sandy soil which stuck to it fell off when he dropped it onto the back seat of my car. There was also dust on his shoes and his navy-blue chinos, which looked well-worn and far less expensive than his jacket. The left-hand cuff of his shirt was slightly frayed but the watch responsible for causing the damage was absent. Had he dressed down to disguise the fact he was just another robber baron from the West?

I turned off Templiner Strasse into Garten Strasse. 'Roads still a work in progress, I see,' he said as my car rumbled over the cobbles.

'The bank?' I asked, ignoring his derogatory comment about the former East Germany.

'Sorry?'

'The name of the bank you work for.'

'You won't have heard of it.'

'Try me.'

'K and S, or Köhl and Strasse Investments for those with an attention span longer than that of a gnat.' He was still staring at the lake. Shadows, cast by clouds in a paint-by-numbers sky, raced across the water and periodically one of the small boats on it was lit up in a pool of sunlight. 'In Glasgow they say if you see three people in a boat the one sat in the middle is dead.'

Later, with more time to consider why he chose that moment to say this, it was apparent what he was doing. His prisoner had come to terms with having a stranger in her car, let her guard down, relieved it now seemed after buying her lunch he would most likely continue on his way to Dossow, or wherever he was headed, and then be out of her life forever. So, time to strike, and the anticipation of being free of Paul Anweiler was overshadowed by the fear of what might have happened to my husband. Herman had planned to leave Edinburgh for Heathrow the previous afternoon for a meeting with someone from Schulenberg UK. Then he was flying to Munich for a meeting at the company's head office. Anweiler saw me look at my watch. I was wondering if my husband got to Heathrow or if, instead, his body had been dumped in the sea, which was impossible because I had spoken to Herman the previous evening. Even so I was now trying to remember where my husband was when he called.

'You have to be somewhere?' Anweiler asked when I looked at my watch for a second time.

'Templin station to meet my husband.'

Anweiler raised an eyebrow and smiled to himself. I knew this game well and on occasions, played it myself, but never before on the losing side. It even had a name: Zersetzung

The steps leading up to the terrace of the Strand cafe would appear twice in the dream that woke me in the early hours of the next morning. The banker from Köln peered through the café's door then said, 'I think we'll dine alfresco, it will be more private.' He went inside and emerged with a handful of serviettes to wipe the rainwater from two chairs and the top of a table. Then he hung his walking stick on the handrail at the edge of the terrace, slumped into one of the chairs and massaged his back, which appeared to be causing him pain. The waiter seemed surprised we chose not to eat inside, insisting another rain shower was on its way.

Just salmon with rice and a bowl of salad, a glass of mineral water, no starter and no plans for coffee or a dessert; I wanted this charade over as quickly as possible. 'I need to be in Templin to pick up my husband,' I said for a second time, after the waiter took my order, inadvertently revealing that the story about Glasgow gangsters had hit home. 'So, Mr Anweiler, if that's who you really are, please explain yourself.'

'Paul, please,' he replied, then ordered schnitzel, French fries, salad and a coffee without even a glance at the menu. In doing so he betrayed a vulnerability obvious when I had met the young student in 1975, one he had, by accident or design, incorporated as part of this false persona he had created. However, I knew something he obviously did not: that for forty-four years Paul Anweiler's body has been at the bottom of a lake in that small village just north of Müncheberg.

'Yes?' he asked, his questioning look a response to mine.

'Nothing,' I said, shaking my head.

Thrusting a hand into his jacket pocket, he took out a mobile phone which must have been on vibrate because there was nothing audible to suggest someone had contacted him.

'Had I wanted to have lunch with someone who can't go thirty seconds without checking their phone, I've got four grandchildren to choose from.'

Paul smiled and placed his phone on the table. 'OK. Certain people I know have a problem with the idea the next Prime Minister of Britain might be an unreconstructed Marxist.'

'You're a banker so I imagine everyone you know has a problem with Marxists.'

'It's nothing to do with economics or finance. Markets dictate government policy and as for trying to escape the narrow confines of neoliberalism while squeezed between the EU and US, well, the best of luck with that.'

The café door opened, and Paul glanced over my shoulder. Another trick: applying pressure when a person senses someone standing behind them. 'The real concern is security,' he said, still looking past me. 'Whether people who mean Britain harm believe there is something embarrassing in Geoffrey Cathcart's past they can exploit.'

'Based on what evidence?'

'You know very well. The Stasi file with his code name on the cover.'

Dismissing this with a shake of the head, I feigned a sudden loss of interest, turning my attention instead to the boat on the lake.

'The file does not exist. It never did according to German Federal Archives.' I said. 'A request was submitted and a search made but nothing was found.' The door to the restaurant creaked open and rather than continually feeling the need to look over my shoulder I moved my chair around the table. One weapon less in Mr Anweiler's armoury. Also, discussing Geoffrey Cathcart would be easier without Paul looking into my eyes to work out if I was telling the truth.

'Really, you are well informed. But you can't actually believe the Federal Archive? Even I ended up with a file...' Paul, not wanting to be overheard, stopped speaking mid-sentence and picked up his mobile phone as the waiter placed cutlery on the table together with a jug of water and two glasses.

After assuring the waiter that condiments were not required Paul picked up where he left off: '...and all I did was spend two weeks sampling my family's homemade schnapps and sunbathing in their garden.'

'Perhaps it was what you did on the rare days you were sober and upright the Stasi thought was suspicious.' The pretence of not being the person he claimed to have met in 1975 was dropped simply because he deserved a slap; admittedly a somewhat feeble one.

'There was a world of difference between the odd visit to the Pergamon Museum and secret lunches with a colonel in the KGB, partying with peace activists and spying on visitors from the West, which I guess is why the Stasi also had a file on you.' Retaliation came as quick as that, and it seemed Paul had access via his mobile phone to information I previously assumed was considered sensitive and not made public.

There was a long and embarrassing silence until the food arrived, during which my host studied his mobile phone. 'How is the salmon?' he asked when I started eating.

'Fine,' I replied, grudgingly. There was no point in asking what he thought of the schnitzel; from the way it was torn apart and shovelled into his mouth he obviously did not care.

A couple leaving the café lingered on the terrace, taking in the view of the lake.

Paul had glanced at the couple and was now speaking softly. 'What if sometime in the nineteen fifties a pastor living in Hamburg decided to leave the freedom and safety of the British Zone and move with his young family to East Germany? An odd decision and one which would intrigue someone in British Army Intelligence who might see some advantage in maintaining contact with a member of an organisation which attracted East German citizens opposed to communism.' I must have looked puzzled but even so he pressed on with the story. 'So a file was created, and despite remaining largely empty had an account of that initial contact. Fifty years later the file is about to be destroyed when someone with a sharp eye for detail spots the pastor's daughter is about to become the Chancellor of Germany. So now not only was the file kept, it was considered highly secret and inquisitive journalists from Germany visiting the British national archive at Kew are told *sorry, no such file exists.*'

'Well, if the Cathcart file has been put beyond reach, your friends are trying to prove a negative,' I said without lowering my voice, having decided against whispering like a gossiping housewife. Paul looked somewhat nervously at the couple now taking photographs of the lake, café and each other, and, in truth, probably had better things to do than eavesdrop on a fantasist. I was tempted to ask how long Paul had been experiencing these delusions, give him one of my cards and suggest he make an appointment.

'These are not my friends, just people I know, or more accurately people I'm known to. The file might be beyond reach but, thanks to the Stasi's obsession with crossing every *T* and dotting every *U*, evidence of its existence is in the public domain. It would be relatively simple to remove someone's file, less easy to delete every reference to it in numerous other files in the Stasi archive.' Paul leaned closer. 'Yours and mine, for example,' he said. Pleased that he now had my undivided attention, he sat upright and swallowed a mouthful of coffee. He turned in his chair to see what the couple were photographing and then sat staring at them. If the intention had been to make them feel uncomfortable it worked, because the man put the camera in the rucksack he was carrying and took out a map. Paul's paranoia was contagious because I too now thought the couple's behaviour suspicious and wondered if studying the map was another excuse to remain on the terrace.

'There would have been reports from informers all along Cathcart's route through East Germany as well as records of him entering from West Germany and exiting into Poland. Cathcart was riding an East German-made motorbike and the Stasi would have realised he could quite easily disappear into a forest and be impossible to follow by car. Cathcart might have chosen the motorbike because it would attract less attention. However, the garage owner who filled it up with petrol thought it prudent to report a customer riding a motorbike with a foreign number plate, as did someone who noticed it parked outside a shop. Cathcart's route through East Germany took him close to Soviet and East German military bases. This was someone open about his opposition to nuclear weapons, travelling through one of the most militarised countries in Europe. Also, he was in contact with East German peace activists. So, what did the Stasi think? Here was someone genuinely opposed to nuclear weapons, in which case he was a potential threat to East Germany's Soviet overlords. Or maybe he was a spy, collecting information while at the same time burnishing his reputation as a left-wing activist to gain the trust of the anti-war and disarmament movements in the UK. My guess was the Stasi never discovered the truth, but a lot of information was collected while they tried and there was a physical repository for it, a very thick file.'

'Perhaps it was shredded, did you think of that?'

'Well, if it was, someone has created a time bomb.'

'In what sense?'

31

'People with a lot of time on their hands are feeding strips of paper into a machine which slowly rebuilds files the Stasi thought they had destroyed. If Cathcart's file has been shredded, hopefully it will be another five years before it is reassembled. Presumably by that time he will have retired from politics. Still, a shredded file is the second-best scenario.'

'The first is?'

'The BND have inherited it and won't release it for fear of kicking off a mud-slinging contest in which some of the brown stuff sticks to a number of German politicians. But even this is not ideal. There could be heavy hints of the file's existence if Cathcart is Prime Minister while Brexit negotiations are still under way.'

'Of course, Vladamir Putin may have taken a copy home as a souvenir of his days in Dresden.' Why I suddenly felt the need to contribute to this madness was something of a mystery.

'Putin makes mischief with lots of things and has damaged the credibility of Russia's intelligence agencies. Any story coming out of the Kremlin about Cathcart will be seen for what it is, malicious mischief based on rumours and conspiracy theories. It might play well on social media and in the tabloid press for a week or so but would be relatively easy to contradict.'

'But it could be used to blackmail your new Prime Minister.'

Paul shrugged, drained the last of his coffee, which must have been cold by now, then picked up his phone. 'True, and the Americans would stop sharing security information. And what would other countries think of Britain if its Prime Minister appeared at the best misguided and at the worst predisposed to placing the interests of other countries ahead of his own?' This he said almost as an aside while scrolling through information on his phone. 'Which is why it would be helpful to know if there is any mention in his file about the meeting in nineteen seventy eight with members of the East German peace movement. Perhaps something that confirms he knew the group had been infiltrated by the Stasi, evidence that he was not being totally naive when talking to a potential enemy.'

'Interesting, but what has that got to do with me?'

'Well, to begin with, you were at the meeting.' This seemed to confirm that Paul, or someone he knew, had access to my Stasi file.

'And what makes you think I was interested in the peace movement? I had a good job and so did my husband; we were comparatively well off. Why would I have put that at risk?'

'The same reason you turned up at the party in Rethen.'

'Sorry, you've lost me.' I pushed the plate of half-eaten salmon to one side, placed my elbows on the table and rested my chin on my hands. 'You've got fifteen minutes to explain what you want because I've got better things to do than listen to this rubbish.'

Paul leant back in his chair and gave the appearance of gathering his thoughts, then suddenly his elbows too were on the table and his face close to mine. 'There are three tapes, recordings made during Cathcart's visit: one of a meet-and-greet event with someone from the government, part propaganda, part tourist information. Another of his stay in a hotel, most likely care of Poland's SB. The third during the meeting with peace activists. This is the one I'm interested in, because it was used by the Stasi to determine whether Cathcart was the genuine article or a British agent. It was handed to a psychiatrist along with background information collected in Britain and then was supposed to be returned along with the report which was added to Cathcart's file. Except...' Paul sat back and again watched the couple on the other side of the terrace still studying their map and occasionally pointing to the trees on the other side of the lake. Although, this time, I suspected the pause was for dramatic effect.

'Except the third recording never made it back to the Stasi. A tape was returned but it was not a recording of the meeting. Instead, in the Stasi archive, or the vault of whoever took possession of Cathcart's file, is the recording of a psychological assessment of a young girl caught shoplifting. Now you can imagine what the young psychiatrist must have thought when she discovered her error. Would the Stasi accept this was an honest mistake, or would they suspect criminal intent? As paranoia was rife in the Stasi, most likely the latter, especially given the psychiatrist's numerous contacts with visitors from the West and trips abroad. Maybe a reprimand, but quite possibly a loss of employment, interrogation, then prison for a very long time. Or maybe she would just disappear, ashes returned to relatives years later. So, she hid the tape away, along with that Kaftan, a pair of jeans and any other evidence suggesting she was anything other than a model citizen. All the time in the back of her mind was the fear she might end up strapped to a chair in the basement of Hohenschönhausen prison and beaten until she confessed. Then her body dumped in a forest or thrown into a lake.'

Another pause while I absorbed this. Paul rested his arm on the railing, studying me, waiting for a reaction. When one was not forthcoming, he looked out over the lake and those three men in the boat.

Without making eye contact he pressed on. 'Then comes November nineteen eighty-nine and the problem just goes away, but instead of disposing of the tape she keeps it hidden. Lucky, because now it can be used to produce a transcript of her meeting with Cathcart. It might even confirm the Stasi regarded the future Prime Minister as neither useful, nor an idiot. I assume you still have the typewriter and maybe even a few spare sheets of the paper you used when writing reports for the Stasi. You'll need a reel-to-reel tape recorder but I'm sure you can buy one on eBay.'

This was much like listening to Rolf's story about the lottery results. Usually when talking to patients it was possible to remain grounded and view their experiences objectively. As far-fetched as Paul's story sounded, I now felt trapped within it.

'Well?'

'Sorry, you lost me somewhere between the sublime and the ridiculous,' I said, hoping this would buy me time to think. 'What, exactly, are you asking me to do?'

'Simply transcribe the tape and sell it to a journalist as an extract from Geoffrey Cathcart's file.' At this point I laughed out loud. The couple finally folded their map and left. If they had been hoping to learn something they missed the best bit of the story.

'You really are crazy. There is no tape and, if anything you said was true, why would I be stupid enough to talk to a newspaper?'

'Because there are people prepared to pay a lot of money to ensure Geoffrey Cathcart is no longer a security threat. Your share would be 250,000 euros and you can keep whatever the journalist pays for the story. I'd suggest you ask for 80,000 euros and accept 50,000 when it's offered.'

'You work for a German bank – why are you running errands for Britain's security service?'

'Because I want to stay working for a German bank. Not running this errand, as you call it, would result in life becoming difficult for the bank I work for. Perhaps even losing its license to trade in the City of London. Also, I have dual nationality so my British passport could be taken away without rendering me stateless – another inconvenient implication of Brexit. Three years away from retiring, I'd rather not lose my job, pension and share options.'

'But if I refuse, what then? Putting aside for the moment the tape you're talking about does not exist.'

Paul had a pained expression on his face as he rubbed the back of his neck. 'Well, as you are a German citizen, Britain's spooks only have access to you through me, but they could tip off *Bild* or *Stern* about the tape a few weeks ahead of the general election. The British press would pick up the story guaranteeing Cathcart's party loses or, even if it doesn't, Cathcart is forced to resign as prime minister. You will be exposed as having worked for the Stasi and the information trail will lead back to me. We both lose control of the narrative, I lose my job and you kiss goodbye to yours, your husband's career and 250,000 euros.

'As for the tape not existing, I can understand why you might have blocked out something so traumatic.' One last look at his mobile phone. 'Anyway, time's up.' He took an envelope from his inside jacket pocket and pushed it across the table. 'There are instructions and enough to cover your expenses, including the sandwich. Don't go online and start Googling anything related to Cathcart, me or K and S Investments, at least not from home. If you want to carry out any background research, do it in Berlin, preferably in a cyber-café close to a university. I'll contact you sometime next week.' He stood up, shook my hand and went into the restaurant, presumably to pay the bill.

The envelope was brown, sealed at one end and thick, as though it might contain folded paper. Rather than leaving it on the table, which in retrospect would have been for the best, I picked it up and dropped it into my shoulder bag.

Instead of driving back to Templin, I returned to the carpark next to Netto, turned off the car's ignition and sat in silence, repeating *think* to myself over and over again. The vegetable delivery van had gone. If it had been driven to the Strand Cafe to collect Paul, why had I not passed it? Just an hour and a half earlier I was merely a housewife out shopping, someone who, over the years, had become complacent and no longer constantly looking over her shoulder. *Think of this as a game you can only win by understanding what motivates the opposition.* More advice from Hubert Hüber, who believed the game was infinitely simpler if your opponent was motivated by fear rather than material gain. Interestingly, Paul had used both as an inducement. Even so, risk and reward were out of proportion and there were other solutions to Herr Anweiler's problem.

Perhaps lunch was merely to buy time for the person in the van. There were two routes I could take when returning to Gehrden, however both would involve travelling along the short stretch of tree-lined road north of the village. It was into one of the trees that, two years earlier, a middle-aged woman crashed her car. The road had been dry, the weather clear and it was assumed she had been distracted by a call on the mobile phone found lying in the passenger footwell.

The vegetable delivery van seems to come from nowhere. I swerve to avoid it, my car mounts the verge then slams into a tree. The gloved hand of the van's hooded driver reaches into the pocket of my blood-soaked coat and takes my phone. Their other hand is pressing the buttons on a second phone, mine rings twice and then is dropped onto the passenger seat. The last thing I remember before everything goes black is someone taking the envelope from my bag. The only witnesses to my meeting with Paul would be the waiter and the couple with the map who confirm I seemed upset and left in a temper. They might have assumed the man I had lunch with was my husband. But the police would discover Herman was on a train from Berlin so perhaps the mystery man was my lover. Could the couple identify the man? He was dressed in Chinos and a jacket much like every other businessman in Germany. The registration number and make of his car? *Sorry, we didn't see him arrive, and he left on foot.* Was that how it would play out? It seemed I was at least two moves behind in a game that had started without me.

# 4

## Sex Was Better in The DDR

Summer 1991

It was the end of my first week at the hospital and my car was low on petrol, so I stopped off at the garage on the outskirts of Gehrden. Usually, it was the owner manning the pump but on this occasion a mechanic in the workshop ducked out from under the car he was working on, wiping the oil from his hands with a rag, or at least, some of it because later I discovered his handprint on the roof of my Lada. The athletic-looking man with unkempt brown hair and tanned face walked slovenly across the forecourt. He remained silent and distant while filling the car; only after returning from the garage's tiny office with my change did he speak.

'You've moved into Habicht's place?'

'Yes.' I replied and the mechanic sucked air through his teeth, shook his head and walked away.

The next time the mechanic filled the car Herman was driving and he managed to prise a sentence out of him. 'Well done,' I said as we drove away. 'That's what passes for a conversation in Gehrden.'

'Oh, Joachim... he's OK. Just keeps himself to himself.'

Now having learnt his name I used it when visiting the garage again, although the most I got out of Joachim was an enquiry about the car Herman was restoring.

So two years later, after being allowed to practise as a therapist again, I was taken aback, perhaps because he did not seem the sort of person to seek help, when Joachim turned up at my door and asked. 'Would it be possible to talk?' But then I recalled that his wife, who once ran the village shop but was now the assistant manager of a supermarket in Templin, had been particularly inquisitive after news went around the village that the woman from Berlin had given up nursing and was providing counselling.

After fifteen minutes listening to Joachim, I realised the move to Gehrden two years after the Wende was much like walking into a theatre halfway through a play. It was almost impossible to catch up with the plot of the drama which began in Gehrden at the end of November 1989, especially as so many of the original cast had left for a new life in the West.

'My father was a writer,' Joachim said in response to a question about growing up in the village. Perhaps he noticed my surprise. 'I doubt you've heard of him.' I had not. 'His works were banned and he was excluded from the Authors Association, for distorting the history of the DDR for personal glorification, apparently. He wrote fiction, for goodness' sake, what did they expect? Anyway, he was no Stefan Heym, was unknown outside of East Germany and so instead of exile in the West he ended up here.'

'You never thought of being a writer yourself?'

'No, I wanted to be a scientist or an engineer. But that didn't happen. Part of my father's punishment was his children being denied a place at university.' This crazy thinking was something which annoyed Herman when he worked for VEB Mikroelektronik and frequently said East German industry paid the price of choosing a generation of engineers who grew up surrounded by empty beer bottles rather than books. Not an opinion it had been wise to express openly, even after the policy of denying higher education to anyone with parents regarded as bourgeois was reversed.

'Did you feel any resentment towards your father when you were not allowed to continue your studies?'

'Some of the books written by well-known dissidents seem rather tame today. You wonder what all the fuss was about, whether it was worth it.' A roundabout way of saying yes. 'Anyway, I was quite happy with what I had here in Gehrden.' This may have been true but his awareness of a world beyond the village was also apparent. It was also clear that while Joachim never made it to university, he had not given up on studying.

'You say *what you had here in Gehrden,* what do you mean by that? The garage is still trading, it's a Volkswagen dealership. Not bad for a small village.'

'Volkswagen are just testing the water. Learning about the East German market where any mistakes won't be noticed. If they fail, we close. If it works out, they'll move away, probably sign up a dealer in Templin. Either way, Gehrden Motors will only last another two years at the most. And the work isn't what it was. We used to repair cars.' A smile for the first time as he reminisced. 'I could build a car from scratch, we even had a machine shop for making parts. Today I just plug a computer into the engine and it tells me which part has failed. A monkey could be trained to do that. The only interesting part of the job is talking to potential customers. The boss hasn't got a clue about West German cars.'

'Perhaps you should turn the problem on its head. If Volkswagen are here to learn about the East German market, you should see this as an opportunity. You are the one teaching them. That's what your wife did, isn't it?'

'Yes,' And another hint of the resentment he attempted to suppress. One I was familiar with as the gender balance within my own family was disrupted on numerous occasions following the Wende. First when I became the main, in fact sole, breadwinner after we left Berlin. Herman was relaxed about this at first; less so, however, after a series of unsuccessful job interviews. Mine was the mirror image of changes experienced by most women, including my sister. Free childcare ended when unemployment rose, and women were no longer needed to fill a gap in the labour market. We all knew East German politicians were as misogynistic as their West German counterparts and the equality of women in the DDR was the result of expedience rather than enlightenment. This made it harder for Herman as an unemployed man in a society which had become more male-orientated.

The conversation veered towards Joachim's relationship with his wife and stumbled into an area he was obviously uncomfortable discussing, because he blurted out: 'Sex was better in the DDR.' Which taken out of context sounds rather amusing and even, at the time, made Joachim smile.

'So why not concentrate on the part of the job you enjoy?' I suggested to avoid further embarrassment. 'Persuade your boss to hire a trained monkey while you have a go at selling cars?'

'I'd rather stick to what I'm doing.'

'Well, if you want to continue getting your hands dirty, you can always do it as a hobby.'

'What, like Herman? That Steinmetz was a lucky find, although I'm not that interested in Western cars.'

'I've seen plenty of Trabants parked next to the garage that no one seems to want.' Joachim laughed and shook his head.

'Really, are you serious? I don't know if you've noticed, but the car has become a joke.'

'I seem to recall it always was.'

'We used to joke about the Trabant because you could poke fun at it without getting locked up, really we were mocking the Communist Party. But after the Wende Wessies saw the shortcomings of the car as another excuse to laugh at us. Ironic really because there's plenty of jokes about West German cars.'

'Really?'

'Yes. In fact, there's one you should appreciate. If you think your life is pointless, remember there is someone in Bavaria spending all day fitting indicators to Audis.'

'I admit that's amusing.'

'Anyway, I've got to get back to work.' Joachim said getting to his feet. 'How much do I owe you?'

'Nothing, this was just an exploratory chat. If you want to talk again, I can arrange a series of weekly or monthly sessions.'

'OK then.' He said, meaning he had no intention of coming back. 'If there is anything I can help you with, let me know.'

Twenty-five years seemed a long time to wait before calling in this favour, and to be honest there had been numerous times in the past that Joachim had come to my rescue, and now hopefully would do so again. 'Joachim,' I whimpered, after the receptionist transferred my call to his office. 'The brakes on my car have just failed.'

# 5

# Soap

The van was in the entrance to a field close to where the sun shone in a driver's eyes as they emerged from the forest. An ideal place to pull out and force a car to swerve and hit one of the trees at the side of the road. It was the van which had been parked at the supermarket in Lychen. While no longer advertising fruit and vegetables, but promising instead to deliver high-speed broadband, the Berlin registration was the same. Clearly, I had been expected, just not arriving in the cab of a breakdown truck.

'A strange place to park,' muttered the mechanic under his breath as, through the rear-view mirror, I watched the van race off in the direction of Lychen, most likely to pick up the man who had taken me to lunch.

Prominent in the row of cars in front of Gehrden Motors was a black Trabant; the only one chained to a metal pole which was concreted into the ground. At weekends people travelled to Gehrden to take selfies with the most famous car in Brandenburg.

'Technically it's not a Trabant.' This according to my husband who checked the provenance of every spare part when renovating his Steinmetz. 'It has an Audi instead of a Volkswagen engine. The suspension is made by Honda, the body is fibreglass, and the Trabant didn't have roll bars, wide rim wheels and air intakes sticking out of the bonnet.' Rarely mentioned was the original Trabant only having a top speed of 107km/h, whereas the one customized by Joachim achieved twice this speed and was faster than Herman's Steinmetz.

*Wessies may have given us the Porsche but only an Ossie can drive past one in a Trabant at two hundred and fifty kilometres per hour.* This headline paraphrasing P J O'Rourke appeared in a classic car magazine. The Porsche in question was a police car parked beside the motorway when Joachim returned from a car show in Berlin. A framed copy of the article hung on the wall in his office alongside photographs of Gehrden Motors in the 1970s. The person in overalls perched on the bonnet of a Wartberg looked as happy and confident as he did now, sitting behind a desk wearing a blue striped shirt, jacket hung on the back of his chair.

'Sorry to be a bother,' I said. 'But I was just leaving the carpark and the brakes failed. Luckily there was nothing coming.'

'Look on the bright side, the fault might be too expensive to fix and Herman will have to buy you a new car.' Joachim pushed a brochure across the desk. 'I can get you a special price on a new Polo.'

'We can't afford a new car.'

'Not even with Herman's new job?'

'How do you know he's been promoted?' Obviously, Herman had told him, which was slightly annoying as I had only found out the previous weekend. Despite, or perhaps because of, the rivalry over their cars, the two men were close. They spent a lot of time at Templin car club racing on the former Soviet airbase. The souped-up Trabant proved a publicity triumph for the garage as pictures of it sporting a VW logo appeared in both tabloids and broadsheets. Both Joachim and the car received a mention on national TV news. While Joachim had feared the exposure would bring Volkswagen's experiment with Gehrden Motors to a premature end, marketing executives and engineers from the company began dreaming up excuses to visit the garage and Joachim received an invitation to attend a meeting in Wolfsberg, suggesting he brought the Trabant. Next to the article was a photograph, taken from an office window, of a crowd of people in the carpark below standing in a circle around Joachim, who appeared to be midway through a sales presentation. 'They say the whole engineering department stopped work for the day.' This was probably an exaggeration; more believable was Joachim explaining to Volkswagen engineers that a Lada – coincidently the car he persuaded me to part with as it needed confining to the dustbin of history – coped better with East Germany's pot-holed roads than the VW Polo – the car he convinced me, despite being second hand, was the future. At the time I suspected its previous owner in the Hünsruck region of West Germany was a farmer and, given the strange smell when I turned on the heater, had used it to transport chickens to the market.

Closer examination of the photograph revealed Joachim had exchanged his overalls for a suit. 'Is that a mobile phone you're holding?' I asked, putting on my reading glasses.

'No, it's a fob. The Trabant has got central locking, which everyone found amusing except it wasn't the Trabant they were laughing at, the joke was all those pointless features the West have been adding to cars. As well, after that, no one treated me like a lesser person because I hadn't spent all my life up to nineteen eighty-nine thinking up ways to escape from East Germany.'

'So, you didn't mention your tunnel.'

Joachim smiled, only too pleased to provide the punchline for one of his favourite stories. 'You mean the one I spent ten years digging only to find myself in Poland? Geography was never my subject.'

The mechanic stood in the doorway. It was difficult to look at him without being reminded of that comment all those years ago about a trained monkey. 'It's done, do you want to have a look?'

Perhaps Joachim assumed that while he checked the computer readout, I would browse the sales brochure and be seduced by the idea of owning a new car. Instead, my attention returned to the photograph of the man selling his modified Trabant, and himself, to the engineers at Volkswagen. I wondered what his father would have thought of this performance. *Distorting the history of the DDR for personal glorification* came to mind. The person in that photograph was, in part, my creation. My suggestion Joachim renovated a Trabant facilitated his escape from the past. A past, following that encounter in Lychen, it felt I would be forever trapped in with my suitcase packed and standing at the entrance to the tunnel, Joachim at the other end calling for me to hurry up. *Sorry Joachim too much baggage, you go on without me.* How many of my patients over the years have left me feeling like that? This was exactly the state of mind which caused people to do something stupid, like agreeing to buy a new car.

Joachim and the mechanic returned and I caught the end of a conversation which, at the time, made little sense. '... well, it didn't stop the Reimanns' four by four ending up in Minsk,' said the mechanic as he lowered my car to the floor.

'I wish I could tell you it was a write off, but it seems fine,' Joachim said, sinking down into the chair behind his desk.

'That's a relief, money won't stretch to a new car.'

'But I bet Herman gets that seven series BMW he keeps talking about.'

'Probably, it's a long-time ambition of his.' Herman's mind had been set on owning one since we took our first tentative steps into West Berlin two days after the border crossings were opened in November 1989. 'Anyway, I saw you on TV again last week,' I said, hoping changing the subject would stop me ruminating. 'In your Trabant with that weather girl.'

'Was the weather warm enough to fold down the roof of your open-top car? A bit of a shoe in, but good publicity. We were supposed to be driving a Golf but the program's editor remembered the Trabant.'

'Well, you seemed to enjoy it.'

'In a way, but it always was a bit like a clown's suit, funny just once. But can't complain, it still brings in the customers. We sold three Golf GTIs the week after that weather forecast, and there's another classic car someone now wants renovating.' I envied the ease with which Joachim could ground himself in the present.

Despite having no intention of buying a new car I felt it polite to take the brochure and even turned its pages as Joachim walked me back to my car. 'Lotte, a new Polo is what you need, something to help you relax and take the stress out of life, feel protected, or simply look fantastic.'

'Is that so?'

'Well, that's what it says on page fourteen,' Joachim replied. 'So, I'm guessing Volkswagen's marketing department has recruited one of your ex-students.'

Parked next to my Polo was a white van with a Gehrden Motors logo on the door. 'How long would it take to replace the sign on that?' I asked.

'Why, are you thinking of changing professions?' In fact, it was delivering fruit and vegetables and installing broadband I had in mind. Joachim peeled off the logo, turned it through 180 degrees and then threw it back onto the side of the van where it stuck upside down. 'Magnetic, want me to get you one? *Lotte, building confidence and conservatories.*'

'How was your day?' Herman asked when he climbed into the car.

'Spent it shopping. Oh, and there was a slight problem with the car,' I added, because Joachim was bound to mention the suspected brake failure next time he spoke to Herman. 'How was your trip?'

'OK,' Herman sighed, 'but I'm getting too old for this.'

As we got out of the car a Doberman threw itself at the front gate of the house opposite. It growled and then began barking. For some reason it had taken a dislike to Herman. Its owners, the Reimanns, suggested the dog disliked men, although it had no problem with the one who drove their car away in the middle of the night.

'Quiet, Brutus!' Mrs Reimann shouted, which only served to further antagonise the dog. 'You still having problems with your broadband, then?' She called across the road. 'Only I noticed you had the engineer here again today.'

'No, our telephone is OK,' I insisted, now realising how the van driver filled their time between intimidating me in Lychen and the attempted ambush.

'I'm not sure which is crazier, her or the dog, and what was all that about our broadband?' Herman asked.

'I don't know, I've been in Lychen and then in the garage talking to Joachim while the car was checked.' Of course, there was that key word missed in Mrs Reimann's observation. *Again,* suggested a previous visit by someone in the guise of a telephone engineer and this should have alerted me to the planning that went into that chance encounter in Netto.

'There are some presents for you, nothing particularly original, I'm afraid,' Herman called out, as I was in the kitchen transferring clothes from his suitcase into the washing machine. I had already discovered the mug with a Scottish flag on it and a tartan patterned tin of biscuits. 'They were given to me by someone at Edinburgh University.' Although, presumably, the box of matches came from the hotel Herman stayed in. This was added to those in the bowl on the breakfast bar – a pointless collection of souvenirs, as neither of us smoked.

'It's still the same shitshow,' Herman said, rubbing one eye as I picked up the TV remote and turned off the news he was obviously not watching. 'Less for us than them. Brexit will be commercial suicide for Britain.' An opinion Herman had expressed numerous times since asked to manage Schulenberg Electronics' withdrawal from EU-funded research it was undertaking with British universities. It had been suggested that having been involved in the sale, post-Wende, of what remained of Robotron and VEB Elektronik, Herman was well qualified for the job. This he had found particularly depressing, resulting in weeks dwelling on failure and missed opportunities.

Eventually, I persuaded him to list all he had achieved since asked to manage an obscure EU project. My husband was about to be promoted to the board of Schulenburg Electronics and he sat on a government committee advising on how Germany's hi-tech sector could benefit from Britain's decision to leave the European Union. He had regained much of what was lost after 1989 but, thanks to me, this was now under threat.

The next morning, despite waking up screaming about rodents, I felt it had been right not to burden Herman with my problems. He would have cancelled his trip to Berlin, and I needed a day alone to think, especially after it was pointed out I had bought the wrong brand of coffee. And there had been a sickening sinking feeling on discovering in place of the Glanz Meister washing up liquid, which usually stood next to the sink, there was a bottle of Herr Klee. A practical joke of a type which was all too familiar and few regarded as amusing; not those who played them and certainly not the victims.

# 6

## Frederick The Great

November 1974

The entry in my diary for Thursday 14<sup>th</sup> November 1974 mentioned seeing a truck delivering lignite to a house in Brunobaum Strasse as I walked to Karl-Maron S-Bahn Station. This marked the end of a respite between hot summer breezes carrying pollution from the south and a sulphurous mist blanketing Biesdorf as it did each Autumn, particles of soot attaching themselves to tiny droplets of water which hung in the air and burned my throat. When younger I would spend my school holidays in the countryside recovering from what was dismissed as a mild breathing problem. However, on that particular day the chance of an asthma attack was not uppermost in my mind; I had been asked to attend a meeting with members of a research group from Potsdam University.

Professor Heinz Pohl was a fragile man, prematurely bald with a face pitted by smallpox, his pointed nose looked thin enough to use as a paperknife. He supervised my research in the psychology department of Humboldt University and sat opposite me on the train to Potsdam driving me crazy by constantly flicking the clasp of the briefcase on his lap. 'God knows what these people are thinking, the Neuen Palais for heaven's sake,' he scoffed. 'I think Janowitz has delusions of grandeur.'

It did seem strange not to hold the meeting at The Academy of Law in Golm. Neither was it clear, to me at least, why either of us had been invited to the meeting. 'Most likely to fill some empty chairs,' Heinz suggested. 'Best just sit and listen, speak when you are spoken to and even then, be careful what you say. Agree with everything but commit to nothing.' In retrospect it would have been wise to heed his advice.

The grandeur of the Neuen Palais suggested a meeting regarding something of national importance. Less impressive was Karl Janowitz's welcome address, which was interrupted by a short, but nevertheless formidable, middle-aged woman. Frau S was the guardian of the personal possessions of Frederick the Great, of which very few were evident. There was, however, a long highly polished table with a row of chairs along each side. 'We are in the process of recovering the remainder from the Netherlands.' She felt this was more important than anything Janowitz had to say. It conjured up the image of Frau S entering Amsterdam at the head of a column of trucks and personally demanding the return of everything the Kaiser smuggled out of Germany at the end of the first world war. She was probably disappointed when, as a gesture of goodwill, the Dutch government agreed to simply hand everything back.

For now, only the table was original and Frau S circled it slowly, occasionally stooping to check it for scratches. We were informed any damage discovered after the meeting would be blamed on those present. 'This table survived bombing by capitalist imperialists.' Although Frau S omitted to mention, this was due to it being locked in a warehouse somewhere in the Netherlands during the second world war, had it not been the Red Army would have carted it off to Moscow. 'So, I expect you to treat it with care, no briefcases on the table, all pens and other implements to stay on the mats provided. The same goes for cups. The coffee jug is to stay over there.' Frau S pointed to a refreshment bar on the far side of the room. It was next to this, apparently, Frau S would be sitting for the duration of the meeting despite Janowitz arguing he had concerns regarding security. 'The room is closed to the public this morning, so your meeting will be private.' Frau S obviously did not regard herself as a security risk.

As for privacy, there were already people outside pressing their faces against the window. Had Frau S lived in the eighteenth century, she would have probably insisted Frederick the Great did not wear his riding boots inside the palace. Everyone attending the meeting, Janowitz included, was forced to swap their shoes for outsized dual-purpose slippers which both protected and polished the marble floors.

'OK, shall we start?' Janowitz's lips curled upwards, but the smile was forced and not reflected in his eyes. 'First, thank you to Professor Pohl for coming all the way from Berlin and bringing one of your students,' he said with his eyes remaining fixed on Heinz. 'As you know I am project leader on the Zersetzung program. And on my right is Erwin Müller, who works with me at the academy.' The top half of Müller's face was hidden behind glasses which appeared to have been made from two discarded television screens. He was overweight, seemed tired, and instead of acknowledging our presence when introduced, rubbed his chin and stared up at the ceiling. After removing his glasses, which he dropped onto the folder in front of him, he pinched the bridge of his nose as if struggling to stay awake. 'Hubert Hüber, HVA and Domestic Security liaison on my left, you already know.' I did not but assumed it hardly mattered as none of what Janowitz said was directed at me.

So far, my attempt to remain invisible had been successful – no easy task as there were only six of us around the table. Hüber was, unlike the two men beside him, immaculately dressed; his suit looked as if it had been purchased in the West. Despite an attempt to hide his age with a well-trimmed beard and cropped hair, I guessed he was in his late fifties. The only other female at the table was a dowdily dressed girl in an olive-coloured skirt and grey blouse. She had the cheerful demeanour of a new recruit at the academy and still keen, her pen already poised over a notepad ready to record the minutes of the meeting.

Finally, Janowitz acknowledged my presence. 'Lotte, you are familiar with Andreas K.' I was, but then Andreas was well known to most of the students, as well as the staff, of Humboldt University. 'How would you describe him?' Heinz had suggested I was merely a passive observer, and my participation would be minimal, now I was expected to contribute despite not knowing the purpose of the meeting.

'Well, he's ...' was all I managed before stuttering and then falling silent.

'In your own words,' suggested Müller. Who else's words would I use? Or maybe I was expected to repeat campus gossip. If so, there would be three very disappointed people as Andreas and I moved in different circles.

Then Hüber said. 'Your impression as an impartial observer, try to think of Andreas as a member of one of your study groups.' While *Charismatic* was all I had to offer Müller seemed pleased with the answer. He replaced his glasses and opened the file lying on the table in front of him; this file presumably contained the information the Stasi held on Andreas. Janowitz nodded and Hüber scribbled a short note.

'Charismatic,' repeated Janowitz. Andreas K, the Che Guevara of Humboldt University, was indeed charismatic. But beyond that? The three men looked at me expectantly. The girl in the olive-green dress used the silence to check back through her notes.

'In much the same way as a rock star in the West is charismatic.' Pohl had come to my rescue, except his attempt to save me failed. He merely replaced an embarrassing silence with his equally embarrassing theory. 'A dramatic increase in the number of births after the second world war has created a large cohort of young people, half male, half female but these young women are reaching sexual maturity ahead of young men. In the West this has resulted in sexual frustration of teenaged females which is partially satisfied by the adoration of older males, such as Elvis Presley and the Beatles, this adoration manifesting itself as a form of mania. Of course as more males reach sexual maturity, this phenomenon becomes less prevalent. Even so, it is interesting that more females than males attend Andreas K's meetings.'

'You're saying if East Germany had more rock stars, Andreas K would no longer be a problem,' suggested Müller.

'I don't think we can make direct comparisons between the demographics of East Germany and that of the West, remember we have lost a large number of young people due to migration.'

Ouch. I did not expect this to go down well and was correct.

'Well, Professor Pohl, while I find your theory interesting, in the DDR we encourage young people to redirect any adoration of vacuous pop stars towards serious minded political leaders.'

Janowitz had decided he had remained silent too long. 'You find that amusing?' he asked me as I had smiled at the thought of teenage girls tearing off their underwear and throwing it at Erich Honecker at the end of one of his two-hour long speeches. In truth, as derided as Pohl's theory was, the East German Communist Party had belatedly, after Honecker became its leader, encouraged home-grown rock stars. However, this was probably a compromise too far for those across the table.

'In my opinion he is loyal, a dedicated Marxist.' This embellishment of my description of Andreas K should have ended with a *but* because, recalling one of his rants, which electrified the audience in the university's refectory, I understood why Janowitz and Müller were interested in this particular student. It had been a monologue few could have ignored, mapping out a vision of a Democratic German Republic, the path it would follow from socialism to communism, an uncompromising journey for a generation in a hurry and hungry for change. No more kowtowing to the West, East German workers used as cheap labour by West

German companies; instead an emphasis on equality, so an end to gated communities and privileges for party members.

More to the point, and no doubt this had brought him to the attention of the Stasi, Andreas openly and loudly expressed the view that progress in East Germany had stalled because dialectic materialism was not possible in an authoritarian state which prohibited criticism in any form. 'There is an urgent and overwhelming need for change,' he would tell his audience. 'The train is about to leave the station and only the committed should be on it.' Unfortunately, I was now sat facing three of Andreas's unwanted passengers.

'It's not that we doubt Herr K's commitment, nothing he has said or done suggests his interpretation of Marxism is incorrect or at variance with that of the Party.' Janowitz put both elbows on the table and folded his hands together, casting his eyes downwards as if he too was reading from a copy of Andreas's file. 'I do not think, and comrade Müller agrees with me on this,' and apparently comrade Müller did, because he nodded in advance of discovering exactly what he was in agreement with, 'that our journey from true socialism to communism is quite as straightforward as some young people like to believe. There has to be a degree of realism, pragmatism and yes, unfortunately, in some cases compromises. A simplistic message is often compelling, especially to young people, such as yourself Lotte, those keen to make their mark on the world.'

Was I being accused here? Was this a less than subtle threat? Janowitz's hands were back on the table. He picked up a pen and tapped it on the file. 'Those of us older, and wiser, have seen the tragic results of raising people's expectations above what it is practical, or possible, to deliver. And we have detected in Herr K hints of nationalism. His criticism of our aid for comrades in other countries, the victims of colonialism in Africa and Vietnam, those oppressed by capitalists in West Germany, striking miners in Britain, smacks of the isolationism which often goes hand in hand with fascism.

Communism or even true socialism in East Germany will not become a reality while we are surrounded by imperialists and capitalists.'

Müller, still nodding, picked up where Janowitz left off. 'Through his tutors we have attempted to persuade Herr K to moderate his behaviour, so far to no avail. We are now considering a different approach and for this we would like both you and Professor Pohl to help.' Looking to my left, I noticed Heinz was as despondent now as during the train ride from Berlin. 'You have our assurance this involves nothing more than producing a report highlighting any change in Herr K's behaviour in the coming weeks. Not necessarily what he does, we are not expecting you to inform on him but merely note any change in how he interacts with other students.'

Was I supposed to agree at this point? If so, the opportunity to do so passed.

'Professor Pohl...' Janowitz opened another of the buff folders piled up in front of him and turned his attention to Heinz, who was as surprised as me by this abrupt change of tack. 'I understand you studied under Kurt Gottschaldt who has now left East Germany to take up a post at Göttingen university. Are you still in contact with him?'

'No,' Heinz replied firmly.

'And what is your opinion of Professor Gottschaldt's approach to psychology?'

There was a short, and no doubt in the mind of Janowitz, incriminating delay before Heinz answered. 'Well, his belief that science and politics should remain separate were controversial from a Marxist viewpoint.'

'Obviously, professor, but did you agree with it?'

'No.'

'Did you totally, or only partially, disagree with Professor Gottschaldt's approach?'

Before Heinz could answer, Müller joined the attack. 'Professor Pohl, have you ever discussed Gottschaldt's past or present work with your students, either collectively or on a one-to-one basis?' Müller slowly removed his glasses for effect but given how far away we were sitting, and the sunlight streaming into the room behind us, Heinz and I must have now appeared to Müller as merely a pair of blurred silhouettes.

My throat was dry, and nerves shredded, so I decided to leave the table and begin the lonely and painfully self-conscious journey in search of something to drink. After just a few steps I realised my mistake and that it would now be assumed Heinz had indeed talked of his former tutor with one of his students, and that student had been me. Also, I heard a chair scrape on the floor and realised someone else had left the table. Glancing over my shoulder I saw Hubert Hüber was just a few paces behind me.

Hüber caught up with me and we arrived at the refreshment counter together. He lifted one of the jugs and held it over a cup. 'Tea or coffee, I'll just pour some of this brown liquid and you try to guess which it is.' There was the briefest of smiles before he became distracted by a sightseer, hands cupped over their eyes, peering at us through one of the windows. 'What a complete farce this is.' And I got the feeling Hüber was uncomfortable being stared at by a member of the public. He smelled of cigarette smoke but there were no nicotine stains on his fingers – I later discovered this was down to his use of a cigarette holder which at that moment would have been as incongruous as the outsized fluffy slippers he was wearing. The eye was drawn to these and I noticed that his stance was now radically different from earlier when he had greeted Janowitz and Müller as they entered the room. Then Hüber stood with his feet apart and shoulders tensed as if about to throw a punch. Janowitz, outwardly at least, had seemed oblivious to what was obviously an attempt to intimidate him. While Hüber's gait now suggested someone whose authority had been recognised and accepted, he was still unhappy being stared at by the person outside and he glared at the onlooker, perhaps hoping this would encourage them to move on. It did not. Instead the tourist held up a camera and started taking photographs.

57

'My God,' muttered Hüber, turning his back to the window and, at the same time, shielding me from the camera. 'It will be your turn next,' he said, looking back at the table where Heinz was still being questioned by Janowitz and Müller. 'But don't worry, their influence and ability to do you harm decays exponentially in proportion to how far you are from Golm, isn't that correct?' This to Frau S, still seated beside the refreshment bar. While she pretended not to hear, I noticed a smile punctuated her continued indifference to everything save her beloved highly polished furniture.

Hüber leaned forward, his mouth close to my ear because this was not for Frau S but me. 'This is merely politics, two men trying to retain control of something they believed they invented but you, I, and Professor Pohl, know they did not. These are people who believe everyone in the country is either greedy, bored or frightened. They haven't the resources to feed the first, the intellect to inspire the second so fear is their only means of control. Well, the best of luck with that, don't you agree?'

Was I supposed to agree? I turned to walk away but Hüber grabbed my arm. 'Not yet, wait. And ignore them the first time they call your name – make Janowitz raise his voice.'

'Lotte, we need to ask you a few questions!' Janowitz asked for a second time and Hüber was correct because by raising his voice Janowitz had now set the bar higher for the level of aggression he could demonstrate during my interrogation. This began with him making it clear he already knew a great deal about me.

'Born in Wiessensee in nineteen fifty-two, mother a nurse, your father a teacher until nineteen forty-two then joined the army.' Janowitz was reading from one of the pieces of paper spread in front of him. Presumably Müller also had a copy. A great deal of research had been carried out into the past life of a student Heinz suggested was chosen at random.

'Awarded the Iron Cross.' For the first time Müller demonstrated something other than indifference. 'He died in nineteen sixty-two. When you were ...' There was a pause while Müller pretended to struggle with basic maths, giving time for the memory of peering around the door into a tiled room where a paper-white body lay on a trolley to become fully developed in my mind. '...ten years old.'

'Yes, ten,' I said. 'Just, ten.' Hoping both Janowitz and Müller understood that not only did I realise what they hoped to achieve but was familiar with the techniques they were employing, although doing so clumsily and transparently.

'Suicide, his body was discovered in Weissensee itself.' Müller again.

'Suspected suicide.' I corrected.

'It says here the pockets of his coat were filled with stones.' The image of the mortuary faded, replaced by that of an empty boat drifting on a lake shrouded in mist and with ice around its shoreline. I fought back the tears. Müller had discovered an open wound and pushed the pen he had been rotating between his fingers into it, and maybe I would have broken down and cried had not something else, further down the page, caught his eye. 'Tell me about the party in Leipzig you attended last year.'

'Sorry, which one?'

'The party at which you met your boyfriend Herman, that is his name, am I correct?' This line of questioning was too important for Müller because Janowitz took over. Either that or the roles of the two men had become blurred in this botched hardman – softman style interrogation.

'Yes.'

'And you are now engaged.'

'Yes.'

'I believe there was a serious incident at that party.'

'An altercation.'

'A little more than an altercation. Someone was seriously injured. There was a report in the local newspaper.' Janowicz held up the cutting from the *Sächsische Zeitung*.

'That happened after Herman and I left the party.'

'Yes, you left to spend the night with a boy you met for the first time just a few hours earlier.' That did not sound good then, or several years later, when the subject came up during a conversation with my daughter.

'It was not like it sounds.' I said to Inge

'What was it like, mother? Please tell, because all I did was stay out until two AM. I didn't jump into bed with a boy I met in a bar.' Inge protested loudly. So perhaps not a *conversation* – *shouting match* would be more accurate.

'It wasn't a bar, Inge, it was your Uncle Roland's and Aunt Ursula's apartment. Their engagement party. It got rowdy, one of Uncle Roland's friends had rather too much to drink and wouldn't leave me alone.' His name escaped me, all I remember about him was his large, pointed nose. Ursula called him Beaky Boy, and this, like Herman's nickname *Big Man*, stuck. Beaky Boy's seduction technique was based on public humiliation to erode a girl's confidence. He homed in on me after discovering I was studying psychology and claimed loudly, so everyone heard even above the music, that in the future computers would be so advanced they would be better equipped than myself to understand the human mind. In fact, there would be microprocessors almost as powerful as my brain. It was at this point Herman came to my rescue with a comparison of the number of transistors making up Intel's most advanced microprocessor and the number of synapses in the brain. When Beaky Boy proved unwilling to accept the limitations of something called Moore's law, Herman turned to me and said, 'I think you will have people on your couch until you retire.' And for some reason I felt when that day came here was the person I would like to retire with.

'Yeah, right, love at first sight.' Inge said. 'This is the one, so off to his apartment and straight into bed. What happened to the *wait and find out if this is the right person before doing something you regret* that you keep telling me about.' She had a point, but back then Beaky Boy refused to give up. Having lost the argument he became aggressive, as people tend to do after too much to drink. Every word he uttered was nodded into my face, psychology was not actually a science he suggested. But then Herman intervened again, asked me if I wanted to dance, which I did not but this was preferable to having my eyes pecked out by Beaky Boy. Halfway through our second dance Herman suggested we found somewhere quiet to talk. The plan was to visit a nearby cafe but, unfortunately, it had closed.

'And daddy's apartment just happened to be nearby. How very convenient.' Inge said. Not nice having my daughter suggest what I regarded as a romantic evening began with me being picked up in the street like a hooker. Even so I pressed on with my explanation.

Roland and Herman had been sharing an apartment in a building half of which had been destroyed during the bombing of Leipzig. 'That one is at the end of our hallway.' Herman had said, pointing up at a door four floors above, set in a wall still covered in wallpaper. There was only one bed in the apartment as Roland had already moved his to the rooms he now shared with Ursula.

'Really, and you believed him.' Inge sneered.

I was hoping Herman would have done more at this point than smile. Instead, he carried on reading his newspaper.

The plan was for me to have the bed and Herman to sleep in the bath, but he was six foot and the bed was big enough for two and we shared it. And we slept facing away from each other. Well, to start with at least, but best not to tell my daughter that. At about three in the morning I got up for a pee and tiptoed out of the room so as not to wake Herman, but the door at the end of the hall was stuck. Pushing against it woke Herman who reminded me this was the door we had seen from the street below. The hope was this anecdote would take Inge's mind of what may, or may not, have happened when her parents returned to the bedroom.

What might have happened if that door had opened flash through my mind when recalling that evening. Freud thought dreams about falling indicate a person is on the verge of giving way to their sexual urges. Although Freud thought most dreams had something to do with sex. Herman and I woke in each other's arms. No need for Inge to know that, although I suspected her Aunt Ursula had already dropped some very heavy hints.

'Sorry, mother, can we go over that last bit again? This time I'll write it down and read it back to you next time you threaten to ground me.' Who would ever have thought it was harder to explain yourself to your daughter than two members of the Stasi?

'Actually, we are more interested in what happened at the party after you left, the incident which resulted in someone ending up in hospital.' Janowitz became impatient or maybe was merely feigning impatience. Herman and I had only discovered, while having breakfast at the café which had been closed the previous evening, that police were called following the incident at the party.

'You missed all the excitement,' a breathless Ursula had said after rushing into the café with Roland in tow.

'Excitement? A disaster more like,' Roland corrected her. 'Some jerk banged on the door to complain about the noise, said if we didn't turn the music down, he'd call the police.'

Ursula took up the story. 'Then Beaky Boy, who was really drunk by then, told him to get lost. There was an argument, and Beaky Boy punched this guy in the face.'

'So, an interfering block warden gets a bloody nose. Serves him right. It's his word against yours.' Herman still looked tired from the previous night. Ursula had noticed – she looked at me and smiled.

'What's the worst that can happen?' Herman said.

'Not a block warden, one of Leipzig's highest-ranking members of the SED. And Beaky Boy has managed to break his jaw.'

While Herman was taking this in Ursula leant across the table and whispered in my ear. 'Is he to scale?'

'What are you talking about?' I asked.

'The *big man*. Are all the parts, you know, big?'

'I've no idea.' But she must have noticed my cheeks go red. Meanwhile Herman and Roland were discussing the implications of a key member of VEB Mikroelektronik's development team ending up in prison.

'So, your boyfriend, now your fiancé, defended a person who attacked a politician.' Janowitz was making the sort of incident the police deal with most Saturday evenings sound like a political uprising. Both Herman and Roland disliked Beaky Boy and admitted he had been in the wrong. Their argument was that sacking him and putting him in prison would delay the launch of the microprocessor they were working on by at least six months and have a knock-on effect for Robotron, which intended to use the device in its new computer.

'It seems your future husband was prepared to put personal advancement ahead of political considerations,' insisted Müller.

'No, he was merely pointing out the economic damage which would result from the incarceration of an engineer with a unique set of skills.' It was difficult to sound as convincing as Herman had when defending someone I had found both obnoxious and objectionable. Beaky Boy was released from custody but, because the politician refused to drop the charges, he was rearrested when development of VEB Mikroelektronik's microprocessor was completed. Possession of banned items imported from the West, including Rolling Stones and Beatles recordings, bootleg films and a book of poems by Allen Ginsberg, all of which actually belonged to Roland and Herman, were added to the charges against Beaky Boy, who was sentenced to two years in prison. Herman did not see his former colleague again until the winter of 1981; he was working as a toilet attendant in Berlin, having been prohibited from returning to engineering.

'It was embarrassing,' Herman said. 'I didn't know what to say, so just left a twenty mark note on the plate as I left.' However, Beaky Boy's time as a toilet attendant was short and he was allowed to move to the West in exchange for a payment of 60,000 Deutschmarks by the West German government. Beaky Boy finally returned to East Germany in 1990 as part of a team of consultants from Frankfurt: 'It will take more than twenty marks to flush this shit away,' he'd said after explaining, with the help of a PowerPoint presentation, that while some parts of East Germany's electronics industry might have a future with its new owners, others, unfortunately those Herman had spent almost twenty-five years building up, did not.

Little did I realise at the time that every response I gave to Janowitz's and Müller's questions, diligently written down by the young girl at their side, would one day be read back to me by a group of people with radically different ideas of what constituted an appropriate and ethical application of psychological research. Nothing I had said or agreed to up to this point was embarrassing or incriminating. Unfortunately, what came next was.

# 7

# Zersetzung

Perhaps Janowitz and Müller were not as incompetent as they first appeared; they were both experienced psychologists after all. That said, experienced engineers, including Herman's father, designed the Baade 152, East Germany's first and only passenger airliner, and that crashed in flames. In fact, one might have suspected it was the wreckage of an airliner blazing in the grounds of Neuen Palace, not the sun, responsible for the heat on my back and blinding light reflected off every polished surface in the hall. Janowitz and Müller seemed not to understand that bright lights used during an interrogation are shone into a prisoner's eyes, not those of the person asking the questions.

'Would it be possible to close the shutters on the windows?' Janowitz shouted to Frau S.

'No,' came the terse reply from the far end of the room. The perception of Janowitz in the eyes of those around the table was at rock bottom and still sinking.

'You are familiar with Hans Leibnitz.' Janowitz was reading from a file, presumably mine.

'Yes.' Frau S had dismissed his last question with a one-word answer, so I gave it a try.

Janowitz cleared his throat. 'You interviewed him in the February of this year.'

'He had sought help from his doctor and was referred to a psychiatrist. I sat in on one of the sessions and his case was included in a study on trauma.'

'Now according to your file...' – Janowitz was shielding his eyes from the sunlight – 'er, here it says Leibnitz... he was tortured by the Gestapo during the Second World War.'

'Yes.'

'I'm sorry, could you elaborate?'

'Well, at first it was assumed the trauma was due to the torture itself, but it transpired Hans struggled to come to terms with the guilt he felt after betraying his comrades.'

'It appears he held out for quite some time... Where is it now? Oh yes, over a week and a half.' Janowitz turned his chair and was no longer looking in my direction. Even with the page held below the table he sounded like a five-year-old learning to read. 'You say here... *He memorised his cell... each brick in the wall... the door and tiled floor. Then... then when taken to be tortured he mentally rebuilt the cell ... around him ... and imagined he was still safe inside it.* But ultimately this did not work.'

'No, he became mentally and physically exhausted, mostly due to the pain and lack of sleep, and was unable to maintain the illusion.'

'Now I am not suggesting there is any connection between the barbarity of the Gestapo and our Zersetzung program.' In the coming years there would be many who felt there was, especially those who fell victim to it. 'You are familiar with the Zersetzung program, I take it.' He turned to Hüber, seeking confirmation. Apparently, I was.

'Yes. It is a technique the Stasi plans to employ to sow distrust within dissident groups,' I replied, to remove any element of doubt.

'In your opinion would it be possible to counteract this technique in much the same way as Leibnitz held out when interrogated?'

'Sorry, when he was interrogated by whom?' I asked, hoping Janowitz would unwittingly reveal the Stasi were aware the techniques they employed were strikingly similar to those once used by the Gestapo.

Müller jumped in. 'We would rather you didn't get smart with us,' he snapped.

'Well?' Janowitz persisted.

'It might be possible for a group to collectively build a protective wall around themselves, possibly by ascribing all the strange things that happened to something akin to a mythical creature such as a kobold.' I resisted the temptation to point out the kobold in this instance would be the organisation he worked for.

'And you think this would work?'

'It would require cohesiveness and trust, for individuals to resist the temptation to exploit the attack on Andreas to increase their own status within the group. More important would be identifying the attack before it eroded that cohesiveness and trust, which would be difficult if the attack was subtle.' This prompted Hüber to take a fountain pen from his pocket and write a note on a piece of paper which he then folded, presumably to prevent either Janowitz or Müller from seeing what he had written.

'Interesting,' Janowitz said as he flicked back three pages in my file, and I wondered why so much information had been collected on someone still only twenty-three years old. 'Now, Professor Pohl claims he never discussed Gottschaldt with any of his students. Did anyone else discuss his work with you?'

'On occasion, yes.'

'Who?'

'I really can't remember.'

Janowitz paused and turned to Müller who shook his head. Perhaps this was a line of questioning to pursue at a later date.

'Have you read any of his work, his books or journals?' Janowitz continued.

'They would be difficult to ignore at Humboldt.'

'Fortunately you don't refer to any of his work in your research, so you won't be required to rewrite your thesis as some of your colleagues have been asked to do.'

'Explain what you believe is the Marxist approach to social psychology.' Müller's question caught me off guard and I felt both he and Janowitz were attempting to force me into a corner.

'It is one based on group dynamics, the dialectic relationship between the individual and the group.'

'Which is the answer I would expect a first-year student in your faculty to give. Now please tell us what you now believe after three years exposed to the thoughts and musings of tutors and colleagues.'

'Well, there seems to be a growing consensus it is time for a new approach based on dialectic materialism.' While this would later become the accepted approach, for now it was still – especially in the Academy of Law, it seemed – regarded as tantamount to heresy.

'And this consensus is where? Within the ministry of education, here in the Academy of Law or amongst your fellow students at Humboldt University? Do you feel, like Andreas K, we are all dragging our feet? Perhaps you are also one of the young people in a hurry to abandon social realism and embrace true communism.' Müller waited for a reaction, but there was none from a person now persuaded, by a pair of middle-aged men in outsized bedroom slippers and blinded by light, that Andreas K had a point. And maybe this was exactly what Janowitz and Müller intended.

'So, you might be tempted to warn Andreas K Zersetzung was being used to curb his disruptive influence. Perhaps pass on what you learned from speaking to Hans Leibnitz and help Andreas K resist attempts to make him see sense.'

It was unclear how I could have done this without Andreas and his colleagues asking where I had come by this information. Guessing Janowitz realised this, I did not respond. How my silence was recorded by the girl in olive green would remain a mystery until her badly punctuated transcript of the meeting was read out to members of the committee of enquiry which decided I should receive a lifetime ban from either carrying out further research into psychology or practising psychiatry.

'Well, I think that is everything,' said Hüber, although it was clear neither Janowitz or Müller agreed, and both seemed annoyed, having been denied the opportunity to land the final punch. 'Thank you for coming today,' Hüber continued, ignoring the discomfort of his colleagues. 'I hope you both have a pleasant journey back to Berlin.'

For Heinz, the return journey to Berlin appeared almost as fraught as the one to Potsdam. I, on the other hand, was merely confused. Even more so when the professor suggested we left the train at Blankenfelde and take the shuttle to Marlow. We waited until everyone else had left the station, then Heinz said, 'OK, let's find somewhere quiet to have lunch.'

That somewhere was not a café or restaurant, but a park bench a short walk from the station. Heinz took a tin box, containing his lunch, from his briefcase. 'Hüber is the one to worry about, the other two are just jerks,' he said under his breath, as if talking to himself. 'If he had his way, Andreas would be taken to Hohenschönhausen prison and made to disappear, his body dumped in a forest. And if Stalin was still alive Hüber would have Andreas taken to Moscow, put on trial and executed. Do you want one of these?' Heinz packed lunch looked like something a mother prepared for a schoolchild – two sandwiches, one ham, one cheese, an apple and bar of Schicht Nougat. Heinz was a fussy eater and the joke in the department was if anyone wanted to study compulsive obsessive behaviour they would not need to search far for a suitable subject. I refused Heinz's offer. It seemed we had both lost our appetite.

A woman pushing a pram stooped to pick up a child's toy which lay on the ground. Had the child thrown the toy out of the pram, or did the woman drop it herself providing an excuse to remain within earshot? Heinz must have suspected the latter and waited until the woman moved on before speaking again. At the time it seemed he was being paranoid; later I became equally cautious, suspecting anyone loitering close for no apparent reason.

'Fortunately for Andreas, the DDR desperately needs western currency.' Heinz paused while using his tongue to dislodge a piece of nougat stuck to the roof of his mouth. 'And West German companies will only continue trading with us, and its government lend us money, if we stop locking up and beating dissidents. Ironically the very thing Andreas complains about is keeping him from getting his legs broken by the Stasi. So, it's psychological instead of physical thuggery from now on, and fingers crossed no one in West Germany realises its equally brutal.' Heinz rolled his bottom lip and shrugged. 'Or perhaps they do know, and just don't care.'

'That doesn't explain why we were invited to Potsdam.'

'Janowitz regards the Zersetzung program as his own and, to some extent, he is right. But the Academy of Law lacks the resources to implement it. So, a power struggle as Hüber transfers control of the program to Normannenstrasse. We were there to show he has access to people who understand how the technique works and can monitor its effectiveness. Of course, Janowitz and Müller tried to discredit us. Welcome to the wonderful world of Stasi politics.' Heinz chewed a mouthful of bread and ham.

'Aren't you worried?' I asked.

Heinz shrugged. 'Why, do you think I should be?'

'Those accusations about Kurt Gottschaldt sounded serious.'

'Not really, Janowitz and Müller have very little influence outside the Academy of Law.' Which is what Hüber intimated. 'I doubt if either have contacts within the SED. And you need those these days. As you discovered, the approach to psychological research can go out of fashion very quickly. Who knows how much longer Pavlovian psychology will be in vogue? One thing I can tell you, the party may claim psychoanalysis is bourgeois and narcissistic but if the wife of some high-ranking politician comes knocking on your door asking if you can help them through an emotional crisis, it's time to dig out those books by Sigmund Freud you're hiding.'

The woman with the pram had turned around and was headed back our way. 'Come on, time to go.' Heinz said, hurriedly re-wrapping the remains of his lunch and pushing the tin box into his briefcase as he got to his feet.

'So, all that about monitoring Andreas's behaviour was rubbish,' I suggested as we returned to the station.

'Oh, yes. They will probably forget all about it.' Unfortunately they did not.

It started two weeks later with what one might easily dismiss as a practical joke. Someone replaced the photograph of Andreas's girlfriend he kept by his bed with that of a student who often flirted with him. Instead of the next meeting of young revolutionaries hearing Andreas's thoughts on the East German Government's relationship with the West, the Soviet Union, Czechoslovakia and Hungary, they were treated to a very public row between him and his girlfriend. She sought solace with her friends, and a few days later I noticed her in the company of an economics student long seen as Andreas's rival. A rumour started that this student was responsible for exchanging the photograph. By then Andreas was arriving late for meetings, complaining he had been told the start time or location had changed. Each time Andreas failed to turn up in time, someone else stepped in to chair the meeting. Over time his dominance of the group was diminished to the point where a rift opened up and there began a long and destructive argument regarding policy and direction, which eventually resulted in the group splitting into two opposing factions.

Looking back was there a point when I could, or should, have intervened? Would Andreas have believed me if I had? Would he have trusted the word of someone outside his immediate circle bearing in mind he had already become paranoid? Perhaps now, over forty years later, I am still making excuses for doing what most people did back then and looked the other way. In fact, not only did I turn a blind eye, but documented the decline and fall of Humboldt University's young revolutionary.

Perhaps, after all these years, Andreas K had decided to exact revenge, possibly following some unrelated crisis in his life. A web search revealed he was now a member of the Links Party; his speeches and articles betraying an unswerving commitment to the ideology he preached during his youth. He studiously avoided any mention of the Stasi, save for pointing out its reputation overshadowed what was achieved during forty-five years of socialism and was now used by West German media *as a stick to beat those impertinent enough to suggest there were aspects of life in East Germany superior to anything capitalism has offered in exchange.* So, it was unlikely it was him who changed the coffee and washing up liquid in my kitchen, or asked Paul Anweiler to do it on his behalf.

*Anomalies and inconsistencies.* These gave an agent away, and sometimes betrayed intent, and I should have searched the house for anything else changed or, more importantly, hidden.

# 8

# The Elephant in The Room

May 2019

Most of the people who came to me in the 1990s with Wende-related issues had by now largely come to terms with life in a reunited Germany despite many still identifying as East Germans. Ironically, those least equipped to cope with all that came after November 1989 were those who for years dreamed of reunification and believed it offered a solution to all their problems, including those unconnected to the way of life in the DDR. When the dream fell short of what had been advertised on the banned West German TV, watched in secret and anticipation, now being constantly told *What's not to like about freedom and consumerism* was of little compensation for those with no job or whose pensions were suddenly worthless.

Now it was the sons, daughters and even grandchildren of the Wende generation seeking therapy. One was Jurgen B, visiting my practice in Gehrden the day after my own life had been turned upside down. The nightmare the previous evening was still on my mind, as was being pounced on while shopping, the incident on the way home from Lychen and having my house broken into. Had it been possible to contact the patient, I would have cancelled an appointment which was as pointless as it was cynical.

Jurgen B was 18 and had been arrested for his part in beating up a man he assumed, incorrectly, was an asylum seeker. Jurgen claimed it was he who was attacked and while there was evidence this might have been the case, it was the middle-aged German of Turkish birth, and not Jurgen, who ended up in hospital. The incident began after Jurgen, rather than step into the road, pushed his way between a couple walking towards him on a narrow pavement. Jurgen claimed he failed to appreciate positioning himself between the man and woman might have been interpreted as a threat or an insult. According to a witness it appeared Jurgen believed the pavement belonged to Germans and the *fucking migrant* should step to one side and let him pass.

Now the cynical part – my contribution prior to Jurgen's court appearance in two weeks' time, during which he would admit to overreacting and claim he succumbed to peer pressure, the influence of a bad crowd he no longer associated with. It would be pointed out he had already attended an anger management session, hence him sitting in my consulting room while his mother waited outside in her car. There would be no report, no mention of me at the trial because, despite having my license to practise psychotherapy reinstated, best not to have the prosecution at Jurgen's trial looking too closely at my CV.

'Fickle, aren't they? Nineteen eighty nine they were cheering and standing at Brandenburg gate handing us money. Then they sold everything off and are now handing the money to any foreigner who turns up at Munich railway station with a hard luck story.' Jurgen adjusted the collar of a 1970s-style roll neck sweater partially hiding a more fashionable tattoo, at least fashionable within the circles Jurgen moved in.

It was difficult to remain objective and not be judgemental. I thought of my two children; they witnessed their parent's lives fall apart but, if anyone, they blamed us and not some innocent stranger.

And now I had four grandchildren who in ten years' time would be the same age as Jurgen. They would grow up in households in which the Wende, and all the perceived, and real, injustices that followed, were a distant memory. So perhaps Jurgen's generation was unique, a disaffected, but nevertheless vocal, and sometimes violent, minority.

'Sorry, what do you mean by fickle?'

'What I said,' he sneered and now was the time to trip him up.

'And what did you feel when the border with West Germany was opened?'

'Don't be stupid. I wasn't even born in nineteen eighty-nine.' This was the short-tempered Jurgen he was trying hard to suppress. But his response was more violent than I expected, and my mind went back to the previous day. If as suggested I had information which, if made public, would embarrass someone rich and important, or even the future Prime Minister of Britain, it might be better if I was silenced, and perhaps Jurgen had been sent to do just that. The fact he was seeking the help of a psychotherapist meant pleading temporary insanity would minimise the time he was incarcerated; 250,000 euros would compensate for the short time spent in an institution. On the other hand, how many hitmen employ their mothers as getaway drivers?

'Stupid,' Jurgen repeated, because I was not giving him my full attention.

'Sorry, I realise that, but you must have discussed it with your friends and your parents.' An attempt to identify who had, and possibly still was, responsible for Jurgen's worldview.

*Yeah right, the usual cop out, blame the parents. You know there's more to it than that.* This from one of my particularly combative students a few weeks later when we were discussing this and other cases. As well as now having a licence to practise psychotherapy again, I had been allowed to return to my post at Humbolt University.

The doorbell rang, not a good point to interrupt the session so I waited, hoping whoever was stood outside would go away. They did not but rang again then hammered on the door with their fist.

The delivery driver, with a parcel at his feet, explained he needed a signature. Something Herman had bought online – my name on the label so presumably he had used my eBay account. Jurgen's mother was watching me drag the box over the doorstep. She was probably more familiar with the word *fickle* and the events of 1989 than her son, perhaps it should have been her sitting in my consulting room. The cause of Jurgen's bitterness was, at a guess, the result of his parents not realising how their own disappointment with life in the new Germany was absorbed and interpreted by their son.

*Yeah right blame the parents.* But if my student was right, and Jurgen's parents were responsible for their son's alienation, perhaps we should ask why they themselves still seemed so disoriented? Perhaps it was the result of all the years East Germany defined itself spiritually as what it hoped to become. At the same time, the country it measured itself against in material terms, West Germany, feared any spiritual identity would reawaken the ghost laid to rest in 1945. Hardly surprising the Wende had, for many, been a bewildering journey into an uncertain future. That particular observation would have been omitted from any report, even had one been submitted to the court, it was in fact a paragraph from a paper on identity in a reunited Germany written by my argumentative student.

'Can I help you with that?' Jurgen stood behind me. He did not wait for a reply but stooped to pick up the parcel, revealing the tattoo on his neck. The box contained something heavy and Jurgen groaned and breathed heavily when carrying it into the consulting room.

Some weeks later when Jurgen B appeared on TV, his face hidden behind the folder containing his indictment, Herman joked, 'Are they prosecuting people for dressing as nineteen sixties pop stars now.'

'The roll-neck sweater is hiding the cross and eagle tattooed on his neck.'

'And you know that how?' So, I told him about my session with Jurgen which had been mainly taken up with him talking about his relationship with his parents which broke down around the time he bonded with an increasingly supportive group of like-minded and equally disaffected teenagers. He received a custodial sentence in Mecklenburg's prison for adolescents, a short one in view of the assurance that his current anger management training would continue once released. Perhaps he kept that promise and sought help – if so, it was not from me. A relief as even the short time spent with Jurgen brought back memories of a troubled relationship with my own children.

On a Saturday afternoon in July 1991, roughly where the courier was now standing with that parcel, a simmering argument with my son Peter and daughter Inge exploded into a screaming row. During the two-hour drive to Gehrden, Herman had pretended to be oblivious to the snide comments of two children resenting having to leave Berlin for our new home in the countryside, most of which had been aimed at me. They interpreted their father's silence as tacit approval, and the protests continued. There was however a moment's silence after the car's engine was turned off and we all sat staring at our new home, a silence of an intensity two children who grew up in Berlin had probably never experienced before.

'We seem to have travelled back in time to the nineteen seventies,' Peter said, having become increasingly despondent during the journey through near empty villages, the car bouncing along pot-holed roads flanked by dilapidated houses, abandoned factories and run-down farms. Now standing on the weed-choked drive in front of a house with brickwork exposed through holes in the rendering, he seemed lost for words. Inge claimed she and her brother were being exiled for a crime they had not committed, and asked how long I expected her to live in this prison. She was 12 and Peter 13, both old enough to realise what a vibrant city Berlin had become for a young person.

The assurance that Gehrden was only two hours from the capital was no consolation. In theory it was, but the train ride was along a single track with a passing point at Zehdenick where drivers stood gossiping while passengers patiently waited, except of course an ever-impatient Peter. On one of our rare family trips back to the place my son and daughter would always refer to as home, Peter leaned out of the window and shouted, 'Are you getting back in here and taking this train to Berlin? Because much longer and I will be old enough to drive it myself.' His father, perhaps unwisely, sided with the other passengers and told Peter to behave himself, and the gulf between them grew a little wider and closer to becoming unbridgeable. It was clear Peter had no interest in technology and after he abandoned a career in electronics, the rebellious son and unemployed father came to view each other as failures.

In retrospect it was clear Peter only enrolled at university so he could return to Berlin – his real passion was music and art. With a group of friends, he acquired, or at least occupied, a former warehouse in which to hold raves. This developed from an ad hoc meeting place into a moderately well-known venue. It was eventually purchased by a West German media company and after Peter married, he and his wife moved to Wittenberge and purchased a small hotel on the banks of the Elbe. 'Just an *e* away from somewhere significant,' he once remarked, comparing the town to Wittenberg further south along the river.

Inge took an even stronger dislike to her new home the moment she got out of the car. 'All my friends are in Berlin so why have we come here?'

Possibly the worst thing a mother could have said at this point was, 'Don't worry, you'll make new friends.' How many times have I told parents over the years sometimes a little empathy helps. Unfortunately, my relationship with my children, and husband, was moving ever closer to the tipping point at the end of a catastrophe curve.

'There was nothing wrong with the ones I had already,' Inge replied. 'And, anyway, where are all these new friends supposed to come from?' she said, scanning the horizon. Inge had a point; our arrival in Gehrden created only a small, 4-person blip in the village's population, which had fallen each year since 1989.

'Last one out turns the light off,' she said.

'What light?' Peter added.

Further disappointment came when Peter and Inge discovered their school was an hour away on a bus which collected small groups of children from villages in the area and transported them to Templin. I gave up asking if they had made any friends as new acquaintances often disappeared when their parents migrated west. Inge left home when she was 18 and went on to study medicine, met and married a chemist, then moved to Hannover.

The important thing was to keep Herman on side. It was partially for his benefit we left Berlin. A network of former associates resembled a version of LinkedIn for the discarded and despondent. He applied for numerous jobs but was too closely associated with companies and a government department perceived to have failed as the result of outdated ideas and poor management. When a property developer made what we felt was a stupidly large offer for our house next to the Kleine Müggelsee, and I was offered a post in a mental hospital a few kilometres from Templin, it was time to make a move.

'This person Habicht, he wasn't with the Russian army by any chance?' Herman asked as I stood beside him in an empty kitchen.

'He promised me he was leaving all the furniture.' This was not exactly true.

'The apartment my daughter has found us in Hamburg is fully furnished so we won't need to take any of this with us,' Edgar Habicht had said as he ran his hand along the top of a sideboard, while showing me around the house. The devil was in the detail hidden within this verbal small print.

'Well, I hope Roland gets here with the furniture we've kept, or we'll be eating off the floor.' This may well have been the final straw, or perhaps it was Peter and Inge demanding to know, as I emerged from the house, why they should pay for their mother's stupid mistake.

'Look, we've moved here because I've taken a shit job I wouldn't have accepted in a thousand years because someone needs to put food on the table and at this moment no one else seems capable of doing it. So, I would be grateful if all of you would give it a rest,' I said, with no regard as to how my children would view this not-so-oblique criticism of their father, the person they looked up to and respected and, for as long as they could remember, the family's main provider and protector. Now I had intimated he was no longer head of the family but merely another sibling. In this respect perhaps Jurgen's mother and I were not as different as I would have liked to believe.

Jurgen placed the parcel in the corner of my consulting room, and this was where my husband had found me that afternoon following the argument with Peter and Inge, sitting on the floor and crying.

'The people who live across the road have invited us for tea and cakes.' Herman looked around the room, trying to think of something positive to say without sounding sarcastic. 'An alcove, what was inside it?'

'A cupboard and shelves for cutlery and plates,' I answered, standing up and wiping my eyes on my sleeve. 'I think this was a dining room.'

'Not very practical, too far away from the kitchen.'

'Habicht didn't strike me as a practical person.'

Mr Reimann was a short square-shouldered man, with rounded face and hooded eyes, and appeared to have a problem relaxing because when we entered his garden he was sitting bolt upright in a garden chair. Only when he stood up to shake hands was it apparent there was a problem with his back. His handshake was firm and after crushing my fingers he folded both arms across his chest.

'You've arrived at an interesting time,' he said. 'Manufacturing has been turned on its head and now it's the farmer's turn. You'll need to keep your wits about you.' I would soon discover, as well as deceiving me regarding the furniture, Edgar Habicht had omitted to mention a potential problem regarding the ownership of land at the rear of our new house.

Mrs Reimann had one arm draped over the back of her chair. She tilted her head forward to peer over the sunglasses resting near the tip of her nose when she spoke. 'An interesting time indeed, I work in the council offices in Templin,' she said, pushing back the shoulder-length brown hair which had fallen over her face. This remark too should have given me cause to read again the document I had signed when handing the cheque to Edgar Habicht.

While Herman and Mr Reimann were mourning the demise of manufacturing in East Germany – until it closed, Mr Reimann had been the manager of the village's wood mill, now he sold agricultural equipment – I helped Mrs Reimann fetch trays of tea, soft drinks and cakes from the kitchen. This involved squeezing past a large, and familiar looking, wardrobe in the hallway. My surprise at seeing it there must have been apparent.

'That was Habicht's, a strange man, even stranger after his wife died. We wouldn't have bothered with it, but he was practically giving it away.' This sorry story continued after we sat at the table drinking tea and eating one of Mrs Reimann's home-made cakes.

'He took everything out of the house and told people they could have anything they wanted for just a few marks,' explained Mr Reimann. 'Everything that was left he put in a pile and set fire to. I thought most of it was rubbish but needed a cupboard in the garage for my tools.'

It seemed the furniture had been disposed of out of spite and later it would become clear why Habicht had done this. However further embarrassment for the Reimann's was avoided because Roland had arrived with the van carrying the few possessions retained after selling our house in Berlin, including shelves large enough to hide that alcove.

Jurgen was back on the chair in my consulting room when I printed off an invoice for the fifty euro he, or more likely his mother, would pay for the forty-minute session. After he left I opened the parcel, which had been sent from Holland but rather than car parts or computer equipment contained the reel-to-reel tape recorder Herr Anweiler had promised the previous day. This must have been ordered in advance of the lunch in Lychen. There was also a receipt from a retro electronics store in Amsterdam showing I paid for the recorder using my PayPal account which, I found after checking on my computer, had received a payment from an email address I did not recognise. This payment matched the amount paid for the recorder. Clearly someone had hacked into the account.

I must have sat behind my desk staring into space for at least ten minutes. Only when the phone rang did my mind return from wherever it had wandered; probably somewhere quiet where I could think. Or maybe I had been back at the Strand Café in Lychen going through sentence by sentence everything that was said.

'Yes, I'm sure I can fit you in next week. I'm afraid I haven't got my diary to hand at the moment. Would it be possible to phone you later this afternoon with some dates and times?' After the somewhat irritated patient hung up my eyes fell on the brass elephant that stood on top of the shelves in front of the alcove, and I wondered why it was facing the door.

'I wish you'd stop doing that. You're teasing the poor girl.'

'I'm not, just checking she is doing her job,' Herman told me when turning the elephant so it faced into the room. He knew Maria our cleaner was superstitious and would turn the ornament around when she cleaned the room, which she did without fail every two weeks. Except this was not her week so someone else had put the elephant back in the correct position. Which, after that story about a tape being hidden in a suitcase with all my 1970s memorabilia, suggested the shelves had been moved to gain access to the alcove.

There was dust on my fingers after running them along the edge of my desk, but none when I did the same with the shelves. Someone had cleaned them hoping it would be less obvious the ornaments on it, including the elephant, had been removed and then replaced.

Whoever had been in the house, most likely that person in the van, had little time to find what they were looking for. Presumably Anweiler was monitoring the burglar's progress – was why he had kept checking his phone and sending texts. Even so it would have taken some time to discover where the suitcase was hidden. What was it Mrs Reimann had said about the broadband engineer being at the house *again*? An earlier visit then, one I would have never been aware of because there had been time to replace everything exactly where it was found. Time to photograph each room. But not on the second occasion, hence the assumption the elephant faced the door. Unfortunately asking Mrs Reimann if she could remember the date of the broadband engineer's previous visit would alert her to there being a problem.

There had been numerous occasions on which the house was empty, mostly when Herman was abroad and I was in Berlin, either at the practice or the university. But one in particular came to mind, an appointment booked a week in advance but then cancelled as Herman and I were already on the way to Berlin. All communication was by mobile phone. It was a woman, no name provided, very apologetic when explaining a crisis prevented her travelling to Berlin, paid in full by bank transfer. Unfortunately, most of the information regarding this appointment was stored in the head of the practice's receptionist along with TV schedules and exhaustive accounts of holidays and evenings spent clubbing with her friends.

However the cancelled appointment was some time ago which, like the parcel and hacked PayPal account, suggested a great deal of planning had gone into the previous day's chance encounter. I wondered if Andreas K ever realised the size of the machine responsible for all those seemingly trivial incidents. At least I understood what was happening to me, although I was not sure this helped.

*Best not to over think this one, Lotte*, Hüber had told me a long time ago, so long ago I was not sure in what context. Perhaps I was doing just that. The envelope I had been given at Lychen was now in my desk drawer. Until now I had decided I would not open it and if approached again would hand it, still sealed, to the police and to hell with the consequences. If all this was as described to me the previous day then it was something the German security service should know about.

I slit open the envelope and took out the sheet of paper inside it.

*Transcribe again the recording of Geoffrey Cathcart's meeting with peace activists you retained in 1978 using your Erika typewriter and the stationery you kept for the work carried out for the Ministerium für Staatssicherheit. Please put the index number on the reel of tape at the top of each page.*

*Enclosed is part payment to cover any expenses incurred before our next meeting.*

This was madness, but while re-reading the letter a hundred-euro banknote slid onto the desk. Others followed after I upended the envelope. The *part payment* was 5,000 euros.

The alcove had not seen daylight for twenty-seven years. Roland and Herman assembled the shelves because both could see I was upset and perhaps thought having at least one piece of furniture in the house would make me feel better, help me get over being short-changed by Habicht. The alcove, with the shelves standing in front of it, was an ideal hiding place for a suitcase containing a detailed record of the part of my life best forgotten.

Inside the suitcase was a pair of flared jeans, a Kaftan and a tarnished pendant with the word *modern* engraved on it. Hidden under the Kaftan was a collection of diaries from a time when it was unwise to commit your thoughts to paper. Beside the diaries lay a flat square cardboard box approximately fifteen millimetres thick. On this was written *Sabine J 9ᵗʰ July 1975*. Inside it was a reel of tape with a yellowing label: *Brückenbauer Tonband 3 1978 MfS XV/(xxxx)/78*. Sitting cross legged on the floor I stared at the tape. The clothes and the diaries made sense. Interviewing Sabine, a light-fingered shoplifter, I vaguely remembered but not retaining a recording or ever having an envelope of blank paper with *Staatssicherheitsdienst* stencilled on it.

Herman was taking me out for dinner that evening and had already texted to say he was on his way home. There was an appointment that afternoon and the patient to call back. The Cathcart tape mystery would have to wait until after the weekend. I selected one of the diaries at random and placed it in my desk drawer along with the envelope containing the 5,000 euros. There had been something odd about the way the diaries were stacked in the suitcase, in date order, but with the older ones on the top. They had clearly been removed and then replaced; why someone had done this only became apparent much later. The suitcase and the tape recorder were returned to the alcove and then the shelves pushed against the wall. The elephant was stood on the shelf, first facing away from the door. Then, for some reason, I changed my mind and turned it through a hundred and eighty degrees.

# 9

## Hoppegarten

Gerde Eppelmann's house was a short walk from the S-Bahn station. Like many in Hoppegarten, it was once used as a weekend retreat. People came here to escape the bombs during the second world war and, as by 1945 a third of Berlin's houses were uninhabitable, it was where many stayed. A local shopkeeper had mentioned that Gerde appeared stressed, nervous, withdrawn and increasingly reluctant to socialise. How Professor Pohl learned of this was not clear when he suggested Gerde, widowed in 1942, might be an ideal subject for research into psychological problems linked to experiences during the second world war.

The house was well maintained, unlike others in the street, at least those visible because, that day, like the rest of Berlin, Hoppegarten was enveloped in mist. After tripping on the second of the steps leading up to Gerde's veranda I began coughing and fearing an asthma attack took the inhaler from my pocket. Before I had the chance to press the bell, the front door opened.

'Yes?' This was not the woman I expected, no dark shadow beneath her eyes from sleepless nights, not pale and shabbily dressed. Not the woman who rarely ventured further than the shop a street away where someone took it on themselves to alert the authorities as to the depths to which Frau Eppelmann had sunk. Instead, the lazy stare of a woman resembling a 1920s film star with permed silver hair, flat to her head with a single curl over her forehead and a tanned face made more striking by high cheekbones. There was a cigarette between the fingers of her right hand; her left hand still held the door.

'Frau Eppelmann?' I asked. She turned her head and looked at the nameplate next to the doorbell.

'So, you can read, or was that a lucky guess?'

Coughing again and unable to respond I took a letter of introduction from my briefcase and handed it to Frau Eppelmann.

'Humboldt University, Department of Psychology. Yes, I spoke to your professor on the phone. And now you've travelled across Berlin to die on my veranda.' Then something behind me caught her eye, because she was no longer staring into my face but looking over my shoulder. 'Did you come by car?' she asked.

'No, by train.' I managed between wheezes.

'So not with those two men over there.'

This puzzled me as I thought the road was deserted when I walked from the station.

'Don't look,' she snapped as I began to turn my head. 'Just come inside.' She pushed the door open and stood back to let me pass. 'Are you ill?' she asked, noticing the inhaler in my hand as I stepped into a well-furnished room, modern and stylish, the chairs, tables and cupboards all Scandinavian imports.

'No, I suffer slightly from asthma and the smoke today isn't helping.' *Slightly* was something of an understatement, having already used my inhaler twice that morning. Without comment Frau Eppelmann crushed her cigarette into a large cut glass ashtray.

As I sat at one end of a long, low, settee. Frau Eppelmann pulled a chrome-framed office chair from under a desk, turning it so she could sit facing me.

'It was felt you might be experiencing difficulties recently.'

'Really, what sort of difficulties?'

'Well...' I took a notebook from my briefcase and read what the shopkeeper had told someone he may or may not have realised was a Stasi informer. Frau Eppelmann quickly became impatient with the long pauses between sentences while I caught my breath.

'No dear, let me help you. I am not about to go insane, but if I do it will be the fault of the person who, noticing the work carried out on my house, is consumed with envy and instead of spending a little time repairing his shabby little shop is wasting it gossiping about me to his other customers.' Frau Eppelmann stared at me expectantly. Unfortunately, I could not think of a response. Ignoring me for a moment she looked around the room, her gaze lingering on a painting of buildings, the centre of Berlin as it looked in the 1930s. Next there was a brief glimpse at a collection of photographs above the fireplace. Then, once again, her attention was all mine.

'Do you work, Frau Eppelmann?'

'That's a stupid question, of course I work, how do you expect I live?' Another pause. Her hand fidgeted slightly; she was missing that cigarette. 'I write, nothing creative or controversial in case you, or whoever sent you, are wondering. Just descriptive pieces for our brochures.' This could possibly explain the postcard from Leningrad on the mantelpiece. 'By the way, you can call me Gerde,' she added as an afterthought.

'Your husband, what ...'

'My husband is dead. At the bottom of the Atlantic since nineteen forty-two. If there is a box on that form you are filling in don't bother putting a tick next to *Wakes up screaming at night after dreaming about drowning or has an irrational fear of taking a bath or swimming in the sea.*'

If there had been, I would have put a question mark. 'You were living here in Hoppegarten during the war.'

'Our house in Friedrichshain was destroyed in a bombing raid in the autumn of nineteen forty-four, so like a lot of people left homeless I moved into someone's garden house. The owner had been taken prisoner in France and probably stayed in the West. His wife died in one of the raids.'

'So, you were here on your own when the war ended.'

'Yes, here when the Red Army arrived, which is next on your list and the subject you are pussyfooting around.' Silence again but no sign of emotion beyond irritation.

'Were you raped?' I blurted out, but then there was no easy way to ask the question.

'Lotte, some say it was just a hundred thousand, some say it was a million, others it was almost everyone. Not for nothing they call the Treptow Park Memorial the tomb of the unknown rapist.' I stopped writing, wary of committing any of this to paper and it was quite possible this is what Gerde intended. 'If you were living with a man then it was possible to hide in the cellar. Alone, not so easy because the house would be searched and eventually you were found. If you were lucky not by Mongolian soldiers, who were the worst. Or by someone whose family had been wiped out by Nazis and was looking for revenge. After all, if all you had in the world was a shack and a goat and you discovered the people who had travelled a thousand kilometres to destroy both lived like this...' Gerde waved her hand around the room, 'well, it's no surprise what we got.' Again she was silent, biting her lip and rubbing her fingers. Had my chest not felt so tight I would have suggested she smoked.

'One day there was a knock at the door and eight Russian soldiers stood there.' The recollection came unprompted. 'Each had an armful of tins of food they had found in a half-destroyed canning factory. They just pushed past me and piled all the cans on the table. I couldn't understand what they were saying. You never knew what to expect. Sometimes they took all the lightbulbs, would send them back home with a note telling their families to hang them from the ceiling and they will fill the room with light. It was best to let them believe this, if you explained they would need switches and wires they would probably tear the house apart and take those as well. Suddenly all the soldiers stood to attention because an officer had followed them into the room, he took a can opener out of the drawer and bowls out of the cupboard. None of the cans had labels so he opened them and emptied them into the bowls. Some contained fruit, others meat. It was the first proper meal I had eaten in weeks.

'As they were leaving the officer noticed some mouldy bread in a bin. He told me to lay it out on the veranda and let it dry in the sun. The next day he brought the soldiers back. They put the dried bread in sacks and tied a label on each one with their address written on it. Later I was told this was only done to maintain morale. Most of the sacks were delivered to empty or burned down farmhouses.' Gerde stood up abruptly. 'Well, that's enough of that. I'm sure you have sufficient for whoever sent you.' I had not and it seemed to have been a wasted journey. 'Would you like a coffee or tea before you go?' she asked.

'Yes, that would be nice, thank you.'

'Oh, and by the way, when you write your report, mention the person worried I'm about to drown myself is holding back chickens so he can sell them at double the price,' Gerde said over her shoulder while walking through to the kitchen.

Now alone in the room I took a closer look at the photographs on the mantelpiece. One was of Gerde and her late husband who was wearing a navy uniform. In the other she was sitting on the veranda holding a baby.

There were voices in the kitchen – not an argument but a difference of opinion all the same. Gerde was talking to a young man, presumably her son. Suddenly they both started talking in Russian. Perhaps they thought I would not understand what was being said. They were wrong. Gerde was being chastised for letting me into the house and told by her son if he had realised how much trouble it would cause he would have left the briefcase where he'd found it.

The postcard with a picture of a cathedral in Leningrad had neither a stamp nor address, only a telephone number on the back. Puzzling over the photograph of mother and child I failed to notice the dispute in the kitchen was over.

'That was my son Thomas.' Gerde stood behind me holding a tray.

'He lives with you?'

'No, he is married now but sometimes calls in for lunch. Are you married?'

'No, I have a boyfriend but no plans for a serious relationship.'

'I know it seems an odd thing to say but perhaps I was fortunate my husband never returned.' Gerde was obviously avoiding the more final *died*. 'For many women it wasn't just their treatment at the hands of the Russians.' Again, *treatment*, not *rape*. 'It was how they were viewed by their husbands. Some were understanding, some were not. Some women committed suicide, more than a few with their husband's encouragement.' Then just as it seemed Gerde would succumb to the despair maliciously ascribed to her, she lifted herself up. 'Well if you do get married we might be able to help with your honeymoon.' She gave me a Reisebüro brochure and pointed out the cities and resorts she had visited.

'Actually, it is possible I will be attending a conference in Vienna next year.' Something Professor Pohl sprung on me after that meeting in Potsdam.

'Really? I'm afraid I can't help you with that.' Which was true, but not because there were no holidays in Austria listed in Reisebüro's brochure.

Even so, there was the feeling of having missed something obvious as Gerde showed me to the door. 'If you are travelling back to Berlin on the S-Bahn,' she said, 'you might meet Thomas, he's a ticket inspector. You'll recognise him, that's assuming you really are returning by train.' The engine of the car still parked across the street had started and Gerde must have assumed this was in anticipation of me getting into it.

It was only when sitting on the train that it became apparent what Gerde meant when she said I would recognise her son. A man in his thirties with large bushy eyebrows and resembling a younger Leonid Brezhnev stood towering over me.

'Ticket please, fräulein,' he said, then after studying the ticket for a short while, handed it back. There were cuts and grazes on his knuckles and a bruise over his left eye. 'I overheard you talking with my mother.' He stood back to let a passenger pass, then moved closer again. 'You look shocked so I'm guessing your maths is not good.' Thomas, because this was obviously who he was, leaned forward so his mouth was close to my ear and whispered, 'Tell whoever sent you, if anyone bothers my family again they will end up with more than bruised ribs and a broken nose.' Then he patted my shoulder and moved along the train to the next passenger and was immediately transformed into someone far more jovial.

The next day I was still annoyed with Professor Pohl. Even had Gerde Eppelmann been as traumatised as suggested, this was not a topic for discussion at a conference in the West. The alternative, youth crime in the DDR, seemed just as inappropriate. In fact, I was wondering how a paper claiming there was no evidence of psychological problems in East Germany might be received in Vienna. The morning was spent talking to an eighteen-year-old girl who had stolen an item of clothing, a tee-shirt, from the clothes shop where she worked.

'Sabine, do you ever watch West German TV?' This line of questioning had been suggested by Professor Pohl, an indication of the desperation to have his department represented at the conference the following year. 'Don't worry, you won't be in trouble if you say yes. Look, your name will not appear in my report.'

She looked at the writing pad on which I had referred to her as Fraulein J then nodded and stared at her feet. 'Sometimes,' Sabine grudgingly admitted.

'And do you think it truly shows how everyone in the West lives?'

Eventually we got past shrugs and ventured deeper into the territory of unsated desires and unrealistic expectations. In many ways Sabine was symptomatic of one of the fundamental problems East Germany faced. In the eyes of the rebellious Andreas, the party's experiment with consumerism was doomed to failure; for him even the fashion magazine Sibylle was a compromise too far. He claimed it objectified women – although I suspected this was for the benefit of his mostly female audience rather than something he felt passionately about. In reality, with a growing number of young people prepared to risk watching West German television, the state had little choice but to offer an alternative to what capitalists were selling. Here the anti-fascist barrier was of little help because it merely prevented young people travelling to the West and discovering for themselves not all that glitters is gold.

'Do you believe, from what you see on West German television, your life would be better in the West than here in the DDR?'

'Of course it would,' Sabine replied emphatically.

'So let them travel to the West,' Andreas insisted. 'Let them discover everything the West is offering is based on a lie. A few weeks of exploitation by capitalists and they will be back.' Except given the chance to do that Sabine would not return; like a moth attracted to the lights of West Berlin she would spend the rest of her days mindlessly banging her head against the neon signs and brightly lit shop windows on Kurfürstendamm.

By the time Sabine was 28, apart from in one small area of the DDR where the signal from West German broadcasters was weak – the so-called *valley of ignorance* – the law against watching television was being widely flouted. As Sabine and her friends travelled to work on the bus or U-Bahn they would openly discuss the previous evening's episode of the US soap opera *The Denver Clan*. At 32 she was able to experience Western consumerism first hand and despite West Germany parting with a fortune to honour a cheque it never expected anyone would cash, along with many others she was probably disappointed.

For now, however, I was intrigued by the pendant hung around the teenager's neck; plated brass made to look like silver. I imagined a committee, probably made up of men all aged over forty, deciding if this example of mindless consumerism was an appropriate way for a teenager to express themselves. No doubt they decided against allowing young people to have their name engraved on the pendants; partly due to a lack of resources, but also out of fear some might choose a politically inappropriate slogan instead of their name. Required was a word that might appeal to fashion-conscious young people, like Sabine. Which was why she had ended up wearing a pendant with the word *Modern* on it.

Perhaps this never happened, but even so the DDR convincing itself a partial embrace of Western-style consumerism might work was rather like believing it was possible to become slightly pregnant. Something I had given some thought to as my period was two days late. The Party's attitude to consumerism – which went in and out of fashion faster than the previous season's clothes – created a minefield for both sociologists and psychologists. There was a real danger my explanation for the root cause of Sabine's thievery might prove as controversial as suggesting that, while rescuing us from the Nazis, our Russian Comrades amused themselves by raping our mothers. In less than a week someone would accuse me of planning to do just that.

# 10

# Lotte By Gaslight

A week later

'You seem nervous, Lotte.' And I was because Normannenstrasse 20, headquarters of the DDR Ministry of State Security, was not somewhere people went to relax. 'So, it appears you are thinking of leaving East Germany. Was it something we said or did?' Hüber muttered as he studied my application for a visa. His rank was Lieutenant Colonel but this seemed out of kilter with all outward indications of his position in the Stasi's hierarchy. At the meeting in Potsdam when the question of resources for Müller's and Janovitz's research was discussed, the head of Working Group E and the AGE program, was mentioned. Hüber spoke of Patrick Herman as if he was a subordinate rather than a superior or a colleague. The same was true when the three men were gossiping about Paul Kienberg who had recently been awarded a law degree by the university. It seemed unlikely Hüber held a position more important than the head of Department Twenty.

Hüber's office in Building One at Normannenstrasse was even more perplexing because next to it was another occupied by his secretary and beyond that a conference room with a large window looking out on the courtyard at the rear of the building. It was in this room I sat facing someone who must have had more important matters to deal with than a request by an academic to speak at an overseas conference. 'Not planning to take up a post at Göttingen University, I hope.' Hüber grinned and I recalled Professor Pohl's grilling in Potsdam.

'I have the opportunity to present a paper at a conference in Vienna.'

'Vienna, charming city, I spent a few years there after leaving university. If you get permission to go you must visit the Altstadt and the café Frauenhuber. No relation,' he laughed, but then returned from wherever his reminiscing had taken him to read the rest of my application. 'But it says here you don't intend going until next year.'

'I won't have finished my research in time for this year's conference.'

'And the content of your paper will depend on whether it can be presented in the West or only suitable for an audience here in the DDR. Presumably you wish to know in advance whether you have our permission to attend rather than waste time producing something which will never see the light of day. Like, for example, the case of a traumatised woman in Hoppegarten and her experiences at the hands of brave soldiers who liberated our country. That would certainly be well received in the West where people are convinced our Soviet comrades were all rapists and who are apparently unaware who fed the population of Berlin in 1945 while the rest of Europe was starving.' Hüber dropped my application into the in-tray on his desk. 'Don't worry, I'm sure we can work something out.' He then stared at me until convinced I was sitting uncomfortably.

'What made you decide to study psychology?'

At a loss how to answer this I remained silent. Possibly I shrugged – if I did there was no mention of doing so in that diary I took from the suitcase. It just seemed the sort of thing I would have done to avoid appearing terrified, which I definitely would have been at the time.

'You mentioned your father died when you were twelve, suicide.'

'Suspected suicide,' I insisted yet again.

'But they took his body back to St Joseph's.'

'It was close to the lake, but I'm not sure that was where he was being treated.'

'What was he being treated for? Can you remember?'

'He had problems with his arm.'

'Oh yes, he was wounded at Stalingrad, awarded the Iron Cross.' Clearly Hüber had being doing some research. 'Shame he never got the chance to wear it in public, he must have been brave.'

'Unlucky was how he saw it. A factory used as a command post was hit and he and two other soldiers were sent into the building to look for survivors. My father wondered why all the snipers were firing at him but then realised he was carrying a high ranking general. He was hit but still managed to get himself and the General to safety.' This was the story much as my father told it, not to me but to former colleagues, those who survived the Russian prison camps or, like my father, were wounded and evacuated on one of the last flights out of the besieged city. Hüber winced at the description of the scar on my father's wrist, another on his lower arm, a third on his bicep, a fourth on his shoulder and the final one on his neck; wounds from a single bullet which he coughed into his hand after reaching safety. 'The medal was my father's reward for an unintentional act of bravery, although I think he would have preferred to have a fully working arm and never have suffered the trauma of fighting at Stalingrad.'

Ursula and I were told not to talk about our father's demons: not to mention the time he stood motionless in the garden, gazing into the distance, resembling the snowman he helped us build, until our mother helped him into the house. According to her, only my father's body had been injured, his mind was undamaged, and we should ignore the moods. Was Hüber telling the truth? Was my father's body, after it was found floating in the Weissensee, taken to St Joseph's mental hospital because he was being treated for shell shock? Was it there I had been left, sitting on my own, while my mother identified his body? There was the sound of someone walking along the corridor outside of Hüber's office and for a moment there was a distant memory of trolleys with squeaking wheels, footsteps, doors swinging open then slamming shut, and catching sight of a body covered in a green cloth, only its lifeless paperwhite face visible.

'Perhaps there you have the answer.'

'Sorry?' But there was no need for Hüber to repeat the question because perhaps he was right and my decision to study psychology was the beginning of a search for answers and maybe even assuage guilt as, for some reason, there was the feeling I'd failed my father, not provided the help he needed. There were even times, especially during my teens, I suspected in some way it was me who was responsible for his death.

'Actually, there is something you may be able to help me with.' Hüber had one elbow on his desk and was massaging his chin. 'Tell me everything about your visit to Frau Eppelmann, between you tripping on the steps in front of her house to being accosted on the S-Bahn by that gorilla of her son.'

Which I did, describing the interior of Gerde's house, including seemingly unimportant details such as the postcard of Leningrad. Although as he seemed disappointed I could not remember the telephone number written on the back, perhaps the postcard was more important than I had thought. On the S-Bahn no one would have heard Thomas threaten me, and as that reference to a missing briefcase suggested he was mixed up in something serious, I merely pointed out Thomas seemed particularly unfriendly, even for a ticket inspector.

We both sat in silence. Hüber tapped his lips with his forefinger, indicating he suspected my account was not complete.

'So, let's change the story slightly.' Hüber spoke slowly. 'Take part of it and turn it through one hundred and eighty degrees, because I suspect a small lie on Frau Eppelmann's part may point to a much bigger one. What if instead of the officer following his men into the house he entered first? Did anything you were told, or Frau Eppelmann omitted to tell you, suggest this might be the case?'

'The only thing that struck me as odd was the officer not asking for a can opener or bowls to put the food in and, according to Frau Eppelmann, he did not search the drawers and cupboards looking for them. Perhaps the soldiers ransacked the kitchen and she omitted this detail, but it meant the soldier's visit sounded less dramatic and, given she perceived my presence as a threat, it was in her interest to shock me. If her account was correct then the officer already knew where the can opener and bowls were kept, and most likely had been in Frau Eppelmann's kitchen on other occasions.' Given Thomas's Slavic appearance, I suspected the officer might also have been familiar with Gerde's bedroom.

'Exactly, Lotte, because perhaps this was not a raiding party but a friend and his comrades dropping by for lunch. Not unusual in those days for a woman to seek the protection of a Russian officer until normality returned and women were safe from unwanted attention. However, that postcard on the mantelpiece points to a permanent arrangement. Which would be unusual as such relationships are frowned on and as a rule members of the soviet military are no longer allowed to fraternise with East Germans. So, very interesting.' Hüber placed both hands behind his head.

'You have probably heard stories about life in Berlin after the war.' Hüber had relaxed and I presumed the interrogation was over. 'And you have been told Russian soldiers were confined to barracks to put an end to robbery and attacks on German civilians. This was one reason; the other was a little too much camaraderie between Germans and Russians. The Soviet military feared that as the standard of living in East Germany was higher than in Russia, soldiers would return home with aspirations which could not be met. And there were concerns on our side too. A friendly Soviet officer, such as Frau Eppelmann's boyfriend, and a small platoon of men could open doors, in some cases kick them in, as Berlin's local politicians vied for power. At the same time an influential local party official could prove useful should a Soviet commander want control of a part of Berlin which, despite the destruction of the city during the war, contained untold riches, not just abandoned food canning factories. The result was our sector, like the one controlled by the Americans, starting to resemble nineteen twenties Chicago. So, the puzzle is, how is it some thirty years later Frau Eppelmann's friend is still roaming the streets of Berlin unhindered? Minus his small army of course, at least we hope so. Ordinarily, he would be on the next train to Moscow, so one suspects he is no ordinary soldier and quite likely a high-ranking member of the KGB.' Hüber shuffled in his chair. I too suddenly felt a little uneasy. 'Now, was there anything during your conversation with Thomas that might indicate who his father is?'

'To tell you the truth, Herr Hüber... sorry, Comrade...'

'Hubert, please.' The unexpected informality saw me offer up the rest of the story.

'I'm afraid I concentrated less on what he said than the way he said it. He told me someone else would get their nose broken if they didn't stop harassing his mother and talked about finding a briefcase. It didn't make a lot of sense.'

'Actually, it was Thomas who was harassed.' Hüber said. 'Someone here as enthusiastic as they were incompetent took some files home. Not usually allowed, but apparently there was a report to finish. Unfortunately, the briefcase containing the files was left on a train where it was found by Thomas. As it was the end of his shift, he took the briefcase home intending to hand it into the lost property office the next morning. However, discovering what it contained, I'm guessing he contacted his father. We don't know that for sure, but there is reason to believe he did, and given the files belonged to the HVA and contained information on foreign politicians and businessmen, his father no doubt advised him to bring the briefcase straight here.

'The next morning Thomas turned up and asked to speak to the briefcase's owner, assuming correctly, believe it or not, its loss had not been reported. The most sensible course of action would have been to thank Thomas and give him a few marks for his trouble. Instead for some inexplicable reason the agent accused him of stealing it. This was Thomas's day off so he wasn't wearing his uniform and the story about him being a ticket inspector may have sounded far-fetched. The agent probably assumed here was just another Ivan bastard who spent his childhood languishing in an orphanage. Thomas was thrown into the Magdelene pending his transfer to Hohenschönhausen prison, this despite the discovery he was indeed a ticket inspector and, like he said, had found the briefcase. Perhaps someone thought they could get him to admit being in possession of state secrets and planning to blackmail a member of the Stasi. Thomas made things worse for himself by asking if his interrogator was familiar with the works of Franz Kafka at which point it was thought he might be a member of a dissident group.

'Meanwhile Thomas's wife wondered why her husband had not returned and telephoned her mother-in-law to ask if he was visiting her. After being told about the briefcase, Frau Eppelmann senior assumed the worse. I'm guessing she called the number on the postcard and somewhere in Karlshorst a telephone rang on the desk of someone influential because people in this building panicked when he enquired after Thomas. Within minutes the young man was collected from his cell, apologised to profusely and had a large amount of money thrust into his hand. The owner of the briefcase claimed there were no hard feelings and offered to shake Thomas's hand. Not a good idea because the agent ended up flat on his back with a broken nose.'

'So, if you knew all that why make up a story about a worried shopkeeper?' I asked. 'I'm assuming it was you who persuaded Professor Pohl to arrange my visit to Gerde Eppelmann.'

Hüber raised his hands. 'Guilty as charged. Although a shopkeeper did have concerns about Frau Eppelmann's welfare.'

'Her lifestyle, actually.'

'That may be true but we were not entirely sure who was supporting that lavish lifestyle. It was quite likely someone more senior than the person in KGB Headquarters who enquired after Thomas, so thought it best to tread carefully.'

'*Not entirely sure*, meaning you have a good idea.'

'A suspicion.'

'Well, I'm sorry I wasn't able to help.'

'Oh, but you did, believe me. In fact...' Hüber flipped open his diary. 'Would it be possible for you to come back tomorrow? The meeting will be here, I'm afraid; unlike the Academy of Law, we don't have access to palaces.'

The diary I took from the suitcase, when looking for the tape, contained accounts of that visit to Frau Eppelmann's house in Hoppegarten, being questioned afterwards and two further meetings at Stasi headquarters. Reading it while seated at my desk I recalled my first encounter with Hüber in the autumn of the previous year, when Professor Pohl and I travelled to Potsdam. After pulling the shelves away from the wall for a second time I took the rest of the diaries out of the suitcase. There were twenty-seven in total, covering the period from my father's death to 1993, the year I set up my psychotherapy practice. The earliest diaries were thin school exercise books, each page filled to the edges with tiny writing, up to three days per page. In the first one were drawings: one of my father, with me holding his hand; the snowman we built in the garden and the empty boat on the lake – images from the mind of a troubled child, talking to her older self all those years later. With Herman came a supply of hardback notebooks from VEB Mikroelektronik's stationery store, but less time to put pen to paper, so several blank pages in each.

A lot happened in my life in 1974 and 1975, hence the interest in these two diaries. In total the meetings with the Stasi took up less than twenty pages. The rest were filled with the *will he, won't he* and *should I, shouldn't I* musings of a young woman in love with the man she would eventually marry. More entries mentioned late periods than fears of becoming too involved with the Stasi and it seemed Inge may have been right – her parents *were going at it like rabbits*.

However, there were pages of the mundane: train times, names of cafés and restaurants where Herman and I arranged to meet and addresses where parties were held. Ignoring all these left just those twenty pages, and reading these in isolation, with everything else merely faded memories, it was clear a common thread ran through all my encounters with Hubert Hüber.

Why had Hüber taken an interest in my application for a visa? Why had he begun to act like my case officer? Why did this not alert me to the possibility I had somehow become a person of interest to the Stasi? Perhaps I did have my suspicions. At the end of the entry describing one of the meetings, I wrote *Remember Andreas K?* Maybe a reminder to submit an update on the student's current state of mind. Or maybe suspecting my involvement in the Zersetzung program was not as tangential as Hüber led me to believe. Had it crossed my mind that the visit to Frau Eppelmann might have been part of the psychological warfare the Stasi was waging on a member of the KGB?

*Lotte, how could you have been so naive?* I asked myself when reading the entry for the following day

# 11

# One Small Favour

In Potsdam a pair of academics behaved like thugs but at this meeting, facing me across the table in one of Normannenstrasse's conference rooms, were two thugs attempting to pass themselves off as academics. One was seated either side of Hubert Hüber.

'Lotte, on my right is Comrade Weidel from the HVA and on my left Comrade Steuernagel, from the domestic security division.'

'Werner, please,' Weidel insisted, the informality at odds with his manner and appearance. Like Hüber he was well dressed and, no doubt if challenged, would insist purchasing a suit, tie and shirts abroad, rather than in East Germany, was an unfortunate necessity if one worked in the foreign intelligence department. He was thick-set, broad-shouldered with black, neatly trimmed hair, and maintained eye contact long enough to make me feel uncomfortable.

While Weidel's lingering, finger-numbing, vice-like grip was designed to give the impression that here was someone both strong and confident, Otto Steuernagel's limp, effeminate handshake suggested someone weak and out of their depth. But both men's appearance and demeanour were confected. Would you notice

Steuernagel while waiting for a train – the man with tired eyes, wire-rimmed glasses and unkempt collar-length brown hair standing at the far end of the platform, or even pay him any heed if he was sitting at the next table in a restaurant, pretending to read his newspaper while eavesdropping on you and your friends? Would you suspect he was a member of the Stasi as he moaned about the weather, or how long it took to get served? Would you suspect it was him co-ordinating the movement of the surveillance team watching your every move? More worryingly, from my point of view, he would pass for any one of the students at the university who styled themselves on John Lennon.

The conference room had neither the intimacy of Hüber's office nor the grandeur of Neues Palais, although, as in Potsdam, the size of the room was excessive given there were only four of us around the table. 'The sensitivity of this operation dictates that the number of people involved is kept to a minimum,' Hüber explained. Had this been to make me feel special, a member of a select team? If so, it failed. 'First some background information for the benefit of our guest.' Copies of the file slid across the table in my direction were passed to Weidel and Steuernagel.

'I thought Kasimir Malevich's art was frowned upon in the DDR?' I said, struggling to make sense of the heavily redacted text. Weidel smiled and Hüber laughed.

Steuernagel however was not amused – either he lacked a sense of humour or, more likely, had no interest in abstract art. 'Let's press on,' he said. 'As Comrade Hüber pointed out, this is an extremely sensitive matter.' *Extremely*, so the meeting was only minutes old and already the level of sensitivity had been escalated.

Hüber looked in my direction and smiled. 'Well, the Anweiler family, at least the East German part, is your area, Otto,' he said. 'So perhaps, for the benefit of our guest, you can fill in some of the information hidden by all those black rectangles she mentioned.'

I wondered if this was an oblique reference to the joke that went over Steuernagel's head.

'Certainly, Comrade Hüber.'

Steuernagel's formality seemed to amuse both Weidel and Hüber and the icy stare I received from time to time was possibly his attempt to get at least one person in the room to show him a modicum of respect.

Steuernagel seemed reluctant to do as Hüber asked, unless of course some of what was hidden in my copy of the report was also redacted in his. 'Heinrich Anweiler, builder, fought in the first world war and the beginning of the second. Wife Maria, died in nineteen forty-five, Heinrich died ten years later.' Then he paused and for some reason left out the fact that the eldest of Heinrich's two sons, Klaus had been trained as an engineer. 'In nineteen forty-three Klaus joined the army.' Steuernagel continued. 'The other brother Wilhelm was too young to fight and when the war ended, like his father, began working as a builder. He is now nominal head of the small company run by Wilhelm's son, Hans Anweiler.

'Klaus surrendered to the American Army at the end of the second world war and was handed over to the British. Until the Autumn of nineteen forty-five he worked on a farm in Bremen but then was moved to a camp in Belgium. As the stated aim of some members of the German army after surrendering had been to join with the Americans and British to drive the Red Army out of Germany, it was felt wise not to release whole regiments of prisoners of war. Instead, they were kept in the camps.' Steuernagel appeared to be enjoying himself and I suspected he spent his free time reading novels about the second world war. 'Interestingly, just before the British left Greece and the Americans moved in, Klaus Anweiler, along with the rest of what remained of his regiment, was transferred to Britain. Klaus was not released until nineteen forty-eight. It could be the Amis told the British it would be unwise to release anyone who had detailed knowledge of the Greek communist resistance movement it was now fighting.'

Steuernagel moved onto the next page, studying it for a while before continuing, perhaps trying to work out what had been redacted in my copy of the document and what was appropriate to read out from his. 'Around this time the East German Security service received a request from our Soviet comrades regarding the whereabouts of Klaus. Enquiries were made with members of the Anweiler family who insisted Klaus was missing, presumed dead. Quite why they lied was unclear. Perhaps they assumed if we knew he was still alive we might pressure them to persuade him to work for us.' From what I learned during my short time working for the Stasi, anyone in the Anweiler's position had reason to be concerned.

'Eventually Klaus was tracked down. However, by then, with one notable exception our Soviet Comrades were less persistent.' In my copy of the document the name of this comrade had been redacted. 'Perhaps like us this person had come around to the idea that someone assimilated and integrated into British society, and with relatives here in the DDR, might be pressured to part with information of interest to the Soviet Bloc. Which I understand, Comrade Weidel, is what your department did.'

'Precisely, Otto.'

Steuernagel obviously interpreted Weidel's reluctance to refer to him as Comrade as a slight, realising the HVA officer was using every opportunity to belittle him. 'Contact was made.' Weidel said, 'And, presumably, this would have been coordinated with pressure on his family applied by your section here in Berlin.' He paused, waiting for a response, but Steuernagel remained silent. 'I understand you have been unable to find any record of this.' Weidel said eventually.

Steuernagel pulled himself upright in a failed attempt to disguise a damaged pride. He was about to offer an explanation, but Weidel robbed him of the opportunity. 'As a result, this time Klaus disappeared again and, as far as we could tell, cut all ties with his brother. But then, in nineteen seventy-one, as if by magic, he reappears, arrives at Friedrichstrasse railway station with a British passport, is reunited with his brother at the old family home in Gladowshöhe. That goes well because neither we or the KGB throw him in prison, cart him off to Moscow or put him to work in a uranium mine, and so next year he returns, this time by car, with the rest of his British family, with one notable exception, causing all manner of havoc on the way. And what did your department do about that, Otto?'

Steuernagel remained silent and it was left to Hüber to explain. 'Nothing, apparently.'

'Nothing, and why was that?' It was clear Weidel knew the answer and he was merely venting his frustration with Steuernagel.

'Because they were Anweilers, protected by God on high,' Hüber replied, looking at me but talking to Weidel, then added as an afterthought, 'For the moment, at least.'

'Don't bank on it, Hubert, what the British Anweilers get up to on this side of the anti-fascist barrier is not the HVA's concern, it's the responsibility of the domestic security department, isn't it, Otto? So perhaps you should tell Lotte that part of the story.'

Otto puffed out his cheeks and adjusted his glasses then leaned forward and sat hunched over the file in front of him, flipping back and forth between two pages before finding what he was looking for. 'Usually, Klaus and his family stay in Gladowshöhe for two weeks.'

'Sorry where is this?' I asked studying my copy of the file, to show I was still awake and taking an interest.

Steuernagel glared at me. 'Page seven,' he snapped. Weidel, it seemed, had also been a page behind, but Steuernagel appeared not to notice and continued translating the secrets in the file into a staccato story edited for a person without the necessary security clearance. 'On the last day of the visit there is a large family reunion, too big for the brothers' three-bedroom house so held in a former hunting lodge in Rethen, a village north of Müncheberg, and by all accounts a lavish affair.' Otto turned to Hubert. 'How much more of this does the frauline need to know?

It was tempting to request he addressed me as *Comrade Frauline,* but I thought better of it.

'Everything, if you want Lotte to help us,' Hüber insisted.

'Very well,' Steuernagel replied as though I was not in the room. 'We are not sure when this began. We do know that during Klaus Anweiler's visit in nineteen seventy three his brother's neighbour went on holiday in the Harz mountains. The next year, also during Klaus's visit, this neighbour spent a week in Odessa. Questioned about this it transpired on both occasions they had won a holiday in a competition. An entry form had been dropped through door, they filled it in and returned it to Reisebüro der DDR and, a week later, the tickets arrived along with two weeks' spending money.

'Initially we thought this might be the Anweilers wanting some privacy or possibly additional rooms, but their guests rented rooms in a nearby hotel. More puzzling was that while for most of the time the neighbouring house was empty, on occasion it received a visitor.' Again, Steuernagel turned to Hüber. 'Does Lotte need to know who this visitor was?'

At last, I have a name; although still it was tempting to annoy Otto by insisting on *Comrade Lotte*.

'I don't think so. Suffice to say someone is taking what could, at some point, prove an unhealthy interest in Klaus Anweiler.'

'OK, moving on then,' Steuernagel continued, visibly relieved. 'This year's visit looks to be much the same. Two weeks with Wilhelm and his wife, various friends and relations dropping in, the neighbours appear to have won a two-week expenses-paid holiday on the Black Sea and presumably the hunting lodge in Rethen has been booked for the big reunion.'

'Perhaps you should go upstairs and check,' Weidel suggested.

'That's not funny.' But apparently it was, because both Weidel and Hüber obviously found Steuernagel's discomfort amusing.

'Despite what you are suggesting, this year is different,' Weidel had taken the baton from Steuernagel, 'and there will be an extra guest at the party. Paul Anweiler who, coincidentally, like his cousin Hans, builds houses is this year forgoing his annual holiday in Bern with a young Swiss lady called Christina, who he has been visiting each year since he was sixteen years old. Instead, he will be spending two weeks with his long lost and previously ignored relatives here in East Germany. Putting aside the possibility he might have tired of the Alps and has an overwhelming desire to breathe the fresh air we enjoy here in Berlin, we should ask: why now?'

Hüber did not answer but instead came up with a question of his own: 'Was the person with the Anweiler family when they collected their visas from our London embassy really Klaus's son? Because from what I'm reading here there are so many anomalies one suspects he may not be.' Presumably the document Hüber was reading had far fewer sentences redacted than mine. 'Firstly, how in a country not renowned for social mobility did the son of a building worker get into one of its top universities? Second, the timing is interesting, and this should interest you, Lotte, because it appears the university in question had its equivalent of our Andreas K and in nineteen sixty-eight a left-wing activist, David Cathcart, almost succeeded in turning it into an educational commune under worker and student control. Of course this failed, and one suspects Cathcart may have fallen victim to something not dissimilar to our Zersetzung program.'

(I should point out the Cathcart Hüber referred to was not the same person whose name was on the document in the suitcase hidden behind the bookcase in my consulting room. David Cathcart was the brother of Geoffrey Cathcart, the man who four decades on looked likely to become Britain's next prime minister.)

'Sorry, going back a bit.' I said, then asked. 'At what age did Klaus Anweiler join the army, and did he volunteer or was he called up?' This, I thought, was a timely question and asked it because we were about to move onto the next chapter in Steuernagel's story. I had not expected the response would be a pin-dropping silence.

'Is that at all relevant?' asked Steuernagel eventually.

Hüber came to my defence. 'The fact Lotte asked it suggests it is,' he snapped and then, with Steuernagel put in his place, added, 'However, perhaps it is best that we leave all the questions to the end. Also, I must point out those notes you are making, Lotte, will not leave this building.'

Steuernagel, not one to be sidelined turned on Weidel. 'Was any attempt made to recruit Cathcart?'

'Feelers were put out, but he wasn't interested.'

'Why not'?

'You have to remember this was nineteen sixty-eight, not an easy time for the HVA. After we backed the crushing of the uprising in Czechoslovakia, East Germany was regarded by even the most dedicated socialist in the West as an unreformed Stalinist stooge of Moscow. Only with the hosting of the tenth World Festival of Youth did that change and even then most members of Britain's so called far left who attended were at best champagne socialists or worse, members of the British Secret Service.'

'Which do you to suspect Paul Anweiler is?' Hüber asked.

'Well, we are hoping Lotte will help us find that out,' Weidel suggested, although exactly how I was expected to do this was still a mystery and at this point did not realise it would involve direct contact with the Anweiler family. 'Although we already suspect the person claiming to be Paul Anweiler is either a plant or, if the real thing, has been recruited by Britain's Secret Service.'

'Evidence?' asked Steuernagel.

'Timing and behaviour,' Weidel responded. 'He arrives at the university after David Cathcart's attempted putsch. Outwardly he appeared to show little interest in politics although he did join the university's Conservative Society. But at the same time he befriends students close to one of the radical Marxist professors involved in Cathcart's attempted putsch.'

Did this mean the HVA was also in close contact with Cathcart's former disciple? I was about to ask but then remembered – *no questions until the end*.

'You will see from the report in front of you Anweiler arrived at the college with a substantial collection of books, almost exclusively by socialist and Marxist authors, including a copy of Marx's *First International and After*. Also in his room were novels by Camus and

Sartre which he purchased from the college bookshop. It appeared very few of these books had been read.'

How did the HVA gain access to Anweiler's room? The answer was halfway down the first page of the report – a comment passed on by a fellow student, name redacted, although *Tricksy*, which, as I assumed it was a nickname rather than a codename, had not been blanked out. Was it him, or more likely her, who had taken the photograph of Anweiler lounging in deckchair, trouser legs rolled up and with a knotted handkerchief on his head?

'Yes, interesting isn't it, Lotte?' Weidel said, noticing my interest in another photograph, this one of Paul Anweiler sitting on a park bench with a young woman, the two students pretending to ignore each other.

'Anweiler acting the part of a character from a popular comedy programme called *Monty Python's Flying Circus*.' Weidel held up the photograph of the young Anweiler in the deck chair, explaining the TV programme was the work of privileged members of Britain's ruling class and most of the jokes were at the expense of the country's oppressed proletariat. Not quite the way it was viewed by students at Humboldt who had seen the copy of *Fliegender Zirkus*, filmed with a home movie camera when it was broadcast on West German television. Roland and Herman also had a copy which had been lost when Beaky Boy was arrested and the police searched their apartment. 'So either Anweiler is naive and doesn't realise he is being treated as a figure of fun or...?' Weidel looked to me for an explanation.

'Or he realises this will endear him to fellow students who believe their embrace of Marxism will appear stronger and more credible if they have welcomed someone working class into their circle of friends.'

'Precisely Lotte, and we believe it is someone in that circle of friends Anweiler is attempting to gain access to.'

'And that's it? That's why you believe Anweiler is not who he seems?' Steuernagel asked.

It was Hüber rather than Weidel who answered. 'I think there is more to it than that. Something the HVA was reluctant to commit to paper, isn't that correct, Werner?'

'Yes, after Paul Anweiler applied for a visa, we became concerned, given the risk the visit might involve, and carried out some low-level surveillance, just two of our agents following him when he was not in college. Most of his free time he spent with his girlfriend who was a nurse in a hospital in central London.'

'Not Tricksy?' I asked.

'No..., no, not Tricksy,' replied Weidel as he scanned a page of the report in vain for the name which someone had forgotten to redact. 'He usually visited the nurse every Wednesday and Friday evening.' As nurses usually work rotating shifts this was the first thing which struck me as odd. 'The journey was by bus seventy three from South Kensington to Central London. On one occasion it was observed the person sitting next to Anweiler initiated a conversation. She remarked how cold and lonely London seemed, then told Anweiler she missed her horses at home in Texas where her family owned a ranch. But at least her job was interesting, because she worked in the US embassy logging radio communications from all across Europe.' Hüber scoffed and even I realised how amateurish this attempt at entrapment appeared. 'All of this conversation was quite audible to our agents, apart from a remark by Anweiler as the girl got off the bus at Park Lane, the closest stop to the US embassy.'

'That's amazing,' whispered Steuernagel.

'Too good to be true,' said Hüber.

'Which means it was not.' Weidel now looked pleased with himself. 'Most people at our embassy are followed and, on this occasion, we suspected at least two of the other passengers on the bus were members of Britain's domestic security service MI5. So, this little performance could well have been purely for our benefit and the young lady was no more an intelligence gold mine than Lotte here. One would have thought that given his father's experience, Anweiler would have quickly worked out what was going on, but according to our agents he seemed relaxed about the incident. That changed, however, when he got off the bus near Oxford Circus. Suddenly he became incredibly surveillance-aware. He stood for some time pretending to look in a shop window but instead was watching the reflections of people on the opposite side of the street. Then, after moving on, a small notebook fell to the ground when he took a handkerchief from his pocket. After retracing his steps, he picked up the notebook but instead of continuing his journey he walked off in another direction. At this point it was impossible to follow him without being spotted. Our agents did however notice he caught another bus, this one headed towards a place called the Elephant and Castle.'

'And what do you suspect he was doing at the Elephant Castle?' Steuernagel asked.

'Elephant *and* Castle,' Wiedel corrected Steuernagel, 'Part of London named after a public house. But he could have got off the bus at any point en route. Discovering where would have taken a lot more resources than London was prepared to make available. We are trying to keep this low key, no more than the cursory checks normal on someone applying for a visa. It's best not to draw attention to the potential risk posed by Anweiler's visit. Which means we won't be asking our agent in Bern to find out if the real Paul Anweiler is hiking in the mountains with his Christina while his doppelganger spies on us here in Berlin. Instead, we will have to rely on insights from Lotte.'

While desperate to intervene at this point, I remained quiet while Weidel shared more intelligence, which even he admitted was low grade and second hand and, presumably, came via Tricksy. 'How likely is it that someone, a student and one with family connections here in East Germany, is offered the chance to work for a defence contractor during his summer vacation excluding, of course, the two weeks he will spend with his relations here?'

Steuernagel frowned and tapped his copy of Paul Anweiler's file with a pencil. 'Certainly, a lot of work has been put into making this person appear a useful catch. Catch being the appropriate word in this case, because we could end up with a double agent in the most dangerous place imaginable.' I got the feeling Steuernagel had been rehearsing that line as a prelude to including me in the conversation. 'Young lady, you had some questions about Klaus Anweiler. You wanted to know if he volunteered to fight or was called up.'

'Yes, it's something a person of Paul Anweiler's age might be starting to question, especially if his interest in socialism is serious and his friendship with students of similar political persuasion is genuine. If one of your agents befriends Paul Anweiler during his visit perhaps it is something they could ask. It might encourage him to open up or, if he is an imposter and Klaus Anweiler isn't his father, throw him off balance.' For the second time there was a stony silence save for footsteps in the corridor outside.

Hüber drew a breath. 'I'm not sure you understand, Lotte. There are no other agents. Comrade Steuernagel is all we have got. He can offer some support, but you are the one who must get close enough to Paul Anweiler to ask questions.'

'I can't possibly do that.'

'Don't worry, this isn't a honey trap,' Hüber reassured.

'Obviously,' added Steuernagel.

'Well, thank you very much,' I snapped.

Weidel smiled and got to his feet. 'Hubert, are we done here because I have another meeting. Hopefully this has been of some help. Keep me updated.'

I think what he meant was *goodbye, good luck, and please don't bother me again*.

'Thanks, Werner. I'll do that.'

Then Weidel hesitated. 'There is just one other thing. It may be nothing, but you ought to know. A week after Paul Anweiler applied for a visa, he joined his university's gun club and apparently had been practising on its rifle range.'

For a moment Hüber's calm façade evaporated and there was genuine fear in his eyes.

'My god,' muttered Steuernagel. 'Is it possible...?'

Hüber caught my eye, an involuntary glance. 'We will discuss this later,' he said to Steuernagel.

Hüber too was now gathering the papers on the desk and preparing to leave. 'Sorry if you misunderstood what we are asking you to do,' he said. 'You will be engaging with Anweiler on an intellectual level, nothing else.'

'Just how does someone with a degree in psychology engage at an intellectual level with a building worker, or even someone pretending to be a building worker?'

'Oh, dear that's a very bourgeois attitude, if you don't mind me saying,' Steuernagel sneered as he reached across the table. 'Please hand me your notebook.' After I did, the first page containing my notes was torn out. 'As you were told, nothing discussed in this room leaves the building.' Which was not quite true because five hours later, everything I managed to remember would be recorded in my diary.

As I reach the door Hüber took hold of my arm. 'There are a few things we need to discuss in my office.'

## 12

# There's Something You Should Know About the Anweilers

'Don't pay Steuernagel too much attention Lotte' Hüber said almost as an aside as his secretary handed him a telex. 'He turned a page in his career and discovered a full stop where he expected a comma. Which reminds me, can I have that notebook you were using?'

Sitting behind the desk in his office, Hüber held the notebook so the light from a desk lamp skimmed the first page which he tore out before checking the second. Convinced it was clear of impressions, he handed the notebook back. 'I was intrigued why you squeezed your account of the meeting onto a single page and pressed so hard with your pen.' I felt slightly embarrassed although, at the same time, pleased to have at least outwitted Steuernagel. 'Time for coffee I think, or would you prefer tea?' he asked, picking up the phone. 'I'm not sure we have anything to compare with what Frau Eppelmann offered you.'

'Coffee will be fine, thanks.'

Hüber sighed and slumped forward. 'The Anweiler family... Soon we will have enough evidence to arrest the whole lot. No trial, just take them out into the forest and shoot them.' He pulled himself up and stared at me. 'Don't worry,' he said, noticing I was visibly shocked. 'The painful reality is we are stuck with these people. Nuclear missiles could rain down and reduce Berlin to a wasteland, but the Anweilers would survive, probably prosper, they are builders, after all.'

A secretary appeared in the doorway and took Hüber's order for coffee. Then began an attempt to soothe and reassure. 'This will be straightforward, like your trip to Hoppegarten, only hopefully without being chased by a bear. You will attend the Anweilers' party in Rethen, a guest of Erich Anweiler. You're to be his girlfriend for the afternoon. Erich will agree to this rather than have us pursue issues regarding his recent behaviour, particularly jokes regarding members of the SED. I only mention this because it will help you prepare for your brief relationship which, knowing Eric, is unlikely to extend beyond your arrival at the party.'

'I still think there will be a problem passing myself off as the girlfriend of a builder.' Hüber appeared to ignore this. 'Sorry to appear bourgeoise,' I added, hoping to elicit a response, which it did not because the secretary arrived with the coffee. When she had closed the door Hüber opened a desk drawer and took out a packet of biscuits.

With the coffee, cream, sugar and a plate of chocolate biscuits carefully arranged on the desk, Hüber finally spoke, but not to address my concerns regarding the Anweilers' party. 'There seems to be the impression in West Germany, no doubt encouraged by its government and the media, that East Germany is some sort of third world country. As a result, food parcels flood through the border each day.' He picked up one of the biscuits, which I recognised as a Leibnitz. 'However, there comes a point where this supposed generosity can be regarded as merely another component in a propaganda exercise designed to undermine the recipient's faith in socialism. That is why those charged with manning the anti-fascist barrier take certain items from parcels.'

This was the most bizarre explanation I had ever heard for the petty larceny of border guards. Hüber was studying me closely trying to gauge my reaction. There must have been one, most likely surprise.

'Cynical maybe, but everyone knows it happens, after all your friends bring books and records, even films, into the country. Of course, you are merely educating yourself on life in the West; gratification and abuse of privilege doesn't play any part in this illegal activity. However sometimes our border guards overstep the mark, then we are forced to intervene.'

'Obviously an awkward position to find yourself in. Very nice coffee by the way, also from the West by any chance?' I asked, smiling at Hüber as I took a sip from my cup.

He laughed out loud and shook his head. 'Seriously though, you will be meeting people for whom the rules you and your friends bend on rare occasions do not apply. At exactly eight am on the day before the party, members of the Anweiler family will present themselves at various border checkpoints in Berlin. Each will be allowed through because it is assumed the rest of the family is still here in the DDR. One will travel in a van, the rest on foot. Once in the West of the city they will meet up, and after a visit to a bank to draw out a substantial amount of money, will spend the day shopping and sightseeing. Just before midnight they will split up and present themselves at the same checkpoints through which they left in the morning.' My amazement at the Anweilers' audacity must have been obvious.

'Yes, if you or I tried something like that there would be serious questions but strangely enough reports from border checkpoints are never correlated because written on the index cards of members of the Anweiler family is *Refer to head of domestic security*. As neither you nor your boyfriend have that degree of protection it's best you forgo any shopping trip on the Ku Dam if you want to experience the delights of Vienna next year. There are other activities the Anweilers are free to engage in but, at the same time, also services they are compelled to provide to maintain the level of protection they enjoy. So, during the party, please concentrate on our visitor from Britain and his interaction with other members of the Anweiler family. Ignore anything irrelevant in your peripheral vision.' He seemed relieved to have got this off his chest and I suspected the person protecting the Anweiler family was several pay grades above Hüber.

'Just one other thing you should be aware of. There has been less time than we would have liked to plan this operation. A few months ago, Paul Anweiler was taken ill, and it seemed unlikely he would be coming to Berlin or travelling anywhere come to that. Try to get him to talk about his health.'

'You think Paul Anweiler is staying in Britain and Klaus is bringing someone else?'

'It is possible. But now onto more practical matters. Sabine J, the light-fingered young shopworker you interviewed recently.' Hüber had certainly been doing his homework. 'She is probably the sort of girl who moves in similar circles to Eric. Conceivably he might meet her one evening during the week and invite her out to a party at the weekend. There's the basis for a credible story should any of the Anweilers ask what you are doing at the party. And no doubt you gathered enough information on her to pass yourself off as a somewhat truculent teenager.' As unappealing as the thought of doing this sounded, Hüber had a point. 'Just remember, while you are at the party you will see certain things we would prefer you ignored. Your task is to assess whether Paul Anweiler is the genuine article and if he is benign or means us harm.' The second time Hüber had mentioned this, and then another reference to my notebook, which was still on the desk. 'And anything you commit to paper should be restricted to that. What the rest of the Anweiler family are up to is solely our concern.'

Hüber took a bite from a biscuit and closed his eyes. 'I sometimes wish I had relatives in Hamburg. Perhaps they would send me a Mercedes Benz. It would be nice to have a car with a personalised number plate.' Another sip of coffee and then a long pause before whispering under his breath. 'God, how I detest the Anweilers.'

The Stasi employed two levels of surveillance; one you were aware of, the other you were not. Two men sitting in a car parked near a house you were visiting, or a person walking the same pace as you on the other side of the road, was merely harassment. Anything more serious, the prelude to a trip to prison in a grocery van for example, involved at least twelve people and was almost impossible to spot. So, it was oddly reassuring when, after leaving Karl Maron Strasse S-Bahn station, the engine of a Lada started as I began the half-kilometre walk home. The car was driven by Otto Steuernagel and beside him in the passenger seat was an overweight middle-aged man.

During one of their nerdier discussions about cars, Herman and Roland debated the purpose of brake lights which could be turned on by flicking a switch on the dashboard, rumoured to be fitted to cars driven by members of the Stasi. A feature Herman considered pointless if you were following someone, and pointed towards members of the Stasi spending too much time watching the Bond movies they routinely confiscated.

The Stasi's engineering department built a version of the Trabant with a large infrared emitter built into the passenger door. This enabled someone under surveillance to be photographed in secret at night without the need for a flash. The first time this was used the car burst into flames when the camera's shutter was pressed. The fact Steuernagel had been chosen to test the technology should have alerted him to the fact he was regarded as dispensable.

Most likely Steuernagel's Lada had numerous other technical features, some totally unnecessary and equally ill-conceived, and potentially lethal to the occupants, as an infrared emitter. So, the car's presence was of less concern than Hüber's assurance the two men inside it would be ready to intervene at a moment's notice should anything untoward happen during my afternoon with the Anweilers.

My mother's house was already in sight when a large truck turned into our street and parked itself at an angle in front of the Lada. Steuernagel and his oversized colleague climbed out of their car and remonstrated with the driver who ignored their order to *get the hell out of the way*. It was entertaining to watch the two men getting increasingly angry, not quite so amusing, however, when I turned back and found my path blocked by a man holding open the passenger door of a large black limousine. 'Get in if you please, Lotte,' the man said softly and politely. Had I turned and retraced my steps to where Steuernagel was still shouting, my abductor would have been powerless to stop me. But, perhaps, it occurred to me someone else might leap from the car and grab me if I tried to escape. This would have provided the basis for a student research project on the flight or fight mechanism. An experiment to determine why sometimes people neither fight, or run away, but instead end up sitting in the front passenger seat of a car speeding past their house and screeching around the corner at the end of the street.

'You know who I am?' the driver asked.

'Sorry, no,' I lied, because apart from being shorter and having grey hair the resemblance between father and son was striking.

'I'm Nikolai Shetlov.' He took his hand off the steering wheel to shake mine and the car swerved across the street, mounted the pavement and clipped the fence in front of someone's garden. 'Sorry about that,' he said when the car was back on the road and almost under control. 'I don't usually drive myself, I'm an important guy in the Russian army, but you probably worked that out. I would have worn my uniform, but I thought snatching you off the street would be scary enough, am I right?' His right hand was still off the steering wheel and he took a packet of cigarettes from his pocket, shook two out, put them in his mouth and lit both. While he did this the car snaked along the road. Shetlov handed me one of the cigarettes. 'This will calm your nerves,' he said.

'I very much doubt it,' I said, trying to find something to hold onto. 'And I don't smoke, I have a problem with my breathing.'

He threw both cigarettes out of the car window. 'Pity that looked pretty damn sexy when Humphrey Bogart did it in a movie,' he said, then shrugged. 'Then I guess Bette Davis didn't have asthma, did she?'

'Where are we going?' I asked.

'There's a restaurant in Werneuchen because I sometimes eat there while waiting for my flight to Moscow.'

'I thought you lived in Leningrad.' A guess based on that postcard in Gerde Eppelmann's house.

'I do.' And then he was silent, and I spent the rest of the journey to Werneuchen watching the farmland and forest of Brandenburg slip by and, as the road became progressively more pitted the further we got from Berlin, avoided saying anything that might distract Shetlov and result in the car ending up on its roof in a field.

'We're closed, can't you read the sign?' shouted the square-shouldered man with his back to us behind the bar of the restaurant.

'Sorry to hear that, Karl because I was looking forward to a plate of bratwurst and potatoes and a glass of your somewhat watery beer.'

A surprised Karl spun around. 'Nikolai, how are you? Good to see you again, are you coming or going?' There was a shaking of hands and grasping of shoulders falling just short of an embrace.

'Neither, Karl, I just need somewhere quiet to talk to my friend here.'

This was a relief although did not entirely rule out me being bundled onto a Moscow-bound flight and spending my last few days alive in the Lubyanka. It was clear Karl knew better than to enquire who I was and, as Shetlov did not introduce me, had decided it was prudent to ignore me.

'You will eat something too,' Shetlov suggested as we sat at a table next to the window looking down on Berliner Allee where his car had already attracted the attention of a group of children.

'Is there a menu?' I asked.

'If you're not having bratwurst, I can do cold chicken and potato salad,' Karl said, and I shrugged and then nodded. Had Shetlov not kidnapped me, by now my mother would have been cooking dinner. Strange that I should be more concerned about her worrying where I was than what Shetlov had in mind.

123

'So, Lotte, your father was at Stalingrad. Iron Cross, fortunately without killing any of my comrades,' Shetlov said once Karl was out of earshot. 'I was lucky, I missed that and joined later when the Nazis were losing and on the run. Was halfway through my studies at university when I was asked to join the Red Army as an intelligence officer. If you could read, you joined the GRU; if you could read and write you joined the MGB and if you could do neither they made you a commissar. By the way, if you are looking for a joke to break the ice at a party in Moscow, that probably isn't it.' So, still the implication this was merely a stopover on my journey east.

'I had travelled, was familiar with various cities in Europe. I spent most of my time tidying up after the fighting was over. My brother wasn't so lucky. Mind you, he was itching to fight, one of those boys concerned the war would be over before they proved themselves a man. I was supposed to look out for him. A crazy idea but as we were fighting in the same part of Europe my parents thought I could do this.' It was some time, during which there was a long ponderous stare out of the window, before Shetlov continued with his story. 'I was in Romania when my brother was killed but only discovered how he died the following year while stationed in Austria. He had been with a rifle division in Hungary and fighting to the west of Budapest, near a village called Lucfalva. The eighteenth of December nineteen forty-four, it should have been an easy battle.' The telling of the story was becoming increasingly staccato. 'Just dislodging a five hundred strong Waffen SS reconnaissance division, mostly made up of soldiers who had never seen combat. But its commander had spent the previous evening scouting the area and preparing an ambush. My brother's division took heavy casualties but managed to destroy all but fifteen of the enemy. Then, he and seven of his comrades ran out of ammunition and surrendered.'

The food arrived, as did a glass of beer, a quarter of which Shetlov drank in three gulps. 'Would you like something to drink?' Karl asked.

'Coffee, if that's possible.'

'Anything is possible, isn't that true, Nikolai?'

'Yes, one day a Russian will walk on the moon, Karl.'

'If there were women on the moon you would be there already,' Karl said as he returned to the bar.

'Careful, the Stasi will find out you've been listening to western imperialist jokes on Radio Free Europe.'

Karl merely shrugged and I was wondering how to give the impression none of what I was hearing would be reported.

'My brother and his comrades fell victim to the logic of war. Fifteen Germans now had eight enemy prisoners. If they encountered another ten of our boys, and at that point the war was mostly being fought by teenagers, they would have then been outnumbered. So, the Germans killed them, and to save ammunition, they did it by hand, an empty cartridge case hammered into the back of the neck.' Had Shetlov been more composed at this point he might have noticed me swallow hard and the colour drain from my face. Instead, he fumbled in his pocket for that packet of cigarettes. 'I'm sure you've grown out of your asthma,' he said putting a cigarette in his mouth and holding a struck match between his thumb and nicotine-stained finger, stared at me as if asking my permission to light it. 'Of course you haven't, that's stupid, please excuse me.' He waved the match out, then stood up and left the restaurant.

Karl placed a cup of coffee in front of me. 'The real stuff, thank your friend for that,' he said then he too left to join Nikolai outside. Shetlov pulled hard on his cigarette. Karl took a packet of his own from his shirt pocket and swapped a lit cigarette for the one Shetlov was smoking. I watched through the window what appeared to be a discussion about the relative merits of each man's smokes. This most likely included how much they cost, given these two men would have remembered the time when cigarettes were the principal currency in Berlin. Shetlov was briefly distracted by a plane which had taken off from the airfield and was about to disappear into the low cloud over the town. The sight of the aircraft seemed to prompt a discussion and, given Karl was asking all the questions, and Shetlov was doing most of the nodding, I suspected the subject was the KGB officer's personal life.

It was interesting, and informative, watching Shetlov from a distance. Karl was perfectly at ease talking with this person whose mere presence would normally, with good reason, strike fear into most Germans. Only then, for the first time since climbing into his car, my heartbeat slowed, and I no longer felt on the point of throwing up. One could only imagine how much information Shetlov was gleaning through the cultivation of this innkeeper as one of his closest friends, which I guessed was exactly what Karl assumed he was.

'I'm sure your father never knew who shot him.' A far calmer Nikola Shetlov had returned to the table and stabbed his fork into the bratwurst on his plate. I too now felt relaxed enough to enjoy the chicken and potato salad. 'Mostly war is an anonymous impersonal affair, bombs dropped from the sky and guns fired from a thousand metres away. But my brother was killed by one of fifteen people who were not so difficult to track down. Three had died in the battle of Berlin, fighting their way through Red Army lines, hoping the Americans would help finish what Hitler started. One was wounded but somehow escaped while being treated by a Red Army medic, would you believe. He now lives in West Germany along with two of his six comrades who spent time in prisoner of war camps. Four others returned to East Germany.' Shetlov had run out of fingers so closed his hand and opened it again then carried on counting. 'Two died after being put to work in a uranium mine, two were transferred to a prisoner of war camp in Siberia where one died.' 'So, one soldier unaccounted for.' He said holding up his thumb. 'According to his family dead but actually transferred to Britain from a camp in Belgium and then simply disappeared. But recently he has visited his old home here in Berlin. Just a pity he now has a British passport.' Shetlov picked up his beer. 'He thinks he is untouchable, perhaps he is.' He contemplated this for a short while then drained his glass.

Perhaps Klaus Anweiler was indeed untouchable, but I suspected Shetlov intended to put this to the test, most likely with the help of an East German woman working for the DDR Reisebüro. Because I suspected she arranged for the house next to Willhelm Anweiler's to be empty when Klaus visits his brother. I imagined Shetlov sat in the garden of this empty house considering what to do about the man he held responsible for his brother's death.

'I feel my brother needs...'

'Avenging?' I prompted; the response was a cold hard stare.

'Justice was the word I was looking for.'

'If Klaus Anweiler is actually guilty.'

'What does it matter if he was the person pinning my brother to the ground, the one holding the cartridge case or the one hammering it into his neck ...' The fork with a piece of chicken on it which I had been about to put in my mouth was laid back on the plate. 'I'm sorry,' Shetlov said, massaging his forehead as if trying to erase the image of his dying brother, 'I should not be troubling you with this, I'm sorry.' He frowned and for a few moments was silent while we both ate.

'You know about the briefcase Thomas found on the train.' The Shetlov consumed by a desire for revenge had gone, and the cool, calm and jovial KGB officer had returned to take his place.

'Yes,' I replied.

'And do you believe in coincidences?'

'No, they are usually the result of the mind attempting to find a pattern within a collection of unconnected and random events.'

Shetlov laughed. 'Unconnected and random events, I like that. OK, so what do you know about Paul Anweiler, Klaus's son?'

'A little.'

'A little? I think by now you know quite a lot. Did you know someone tried to kill him?'

I thought back to the meeting earlier that day, separating what had been said from what could be learned from reading unredacted parts of Paul Anweiler's file, guessing the latter was the limit of Shetlov's knowledge. 'I think he may have been hospitalised,' I said.

'He was, after an evening out with friends, slightly worse for drink, when someone in a subway station in Kensington accused him of being drunk and waved an umbrella at him. His friends thought nothing of this, in fact treated it as a joke. They mistook his illness the next day for a hangover. Anweiler knew different and was quick-thinking enough to dig the small pellet out of his leg with a knife. Even so ...'

'But he is still alive.'

'Yes, he is. Now what if I told you that he was rushed to hospital on the eighteenth of December.'

'The same date your brother was killed.' There was suddenly what felt like a cold draught on the back of my neck.

'Precisely. The number of times, after hearing Klaus's son was coming to East Germany, I considered ending his life. After all there was no point in killing his father. He had already enjoyed the thirty years I have spent without my brother, nothing will bring that back. But kill his son and Klaus Anweiler too will experience thirty years of grief. And to do this on the same day of the year my brother died, a week before Christmas, would ensure Klaus knew who was responsible for the death of his son.' Shetlov studied me intently, then finished the last of his bratwurst, broke a bread roll and wiped it around his plate. 'So, now you are thinking it was me sent an assassin to kill Paul Anweiler, aren't you? Be honest.'

Shetlov did not give me the chance to answer. 'Of course you do, along with everyone else. My comrades in the KGB and the Stasi. I tell you, Lotte, even I started to believe it.' The briefest of laughs, not much more than a snort, then he stared down at the empty plate, gathering his thoughts. He spoke softly as if concerned what came next should not be overheard even by someone as trusted as Karl. 'The KGB may no longer have friends in Bucharest, but I have a few from my time there in 1944. Romania was sending medical students for training in British hospitals. I took a guess at the poison which was used on Anweiler and sent the antidote via a diplomatic bag to a young doctor starting her three months' training at the hospital where Paul Anweiler was treated.' This story seemed too far-fetched to be true, but had it been a lie, what did Shetlov gain by telling it? 'Ironic, isn't it?' he continued. 'Had I not been planning to kill Paul Anweiler, he would probably be dead.' Then, catching Karl's eye, and without asking if I wanted a dessert, he ordered apple cake for both of us and more coffee.

'Another of those strange coincidences,' Shetlov said, whispering because I was about to be told something too secret even for the restaurant's walls. 'A briefcase is left on an almost empty S-Bahn train near the end of its journey, ensuring the only person likely to find it was the ticket inspector, Thomas. You have met, yes?' Shetlov was unwilling to acknowledge the young man was his son. 'He would have returned it the same day to the person who lost it, but when he looked inside, the name on one of the files was Paul Anweiler. This was a name he had heard mentioned and so he brought the briefcase to me. Now I'm thinking this is exactly what the person who left that briefcase on the train wanted Thomas to do.'

Our desserts arrived. Karl had provided a small jug of cream for the coffee, half of which Shetlov poured onto his apple cake.

'So why was Thomas arrested, why accuse him of stealing it?' I was thinking out loud, unintentionally confirming the depth of my involvement in this real or imagined conspiracy.

'I hear you are involved in the Zersetzung program, the Stasi making people like your university friend more paranoid than they already are, if that is possible. Trying it out on the KGB would be a serious mistake.'

'If they are then it sounds like it's working,' I said, and Shetlov found this amusing.

'I like you, Lotte, you're clever.' Although, temporarily at least, he decided the apple cake was more interesting than an outspoken psychology graduate. He gulped down the coffee and suddenly appeared in a hurry. While chasing the last piece of apple cake around the plate with a fork he beckoned Karl to the table and asked for the bill. Karl insisted there was no charge, so Shetlov took three notes from his wallet which he folded and slid under his coffee cup while getting to his feet. There was a brief, whispered exchange with Karl at the bar as I stood waiting by the door. As the conversation ended Shetlov's eyebrows suddenly rose, and he tapped Karl's arm with his forefinger. Presumably the information Karl passed on to his Russian friend was worth the thirty marks waiting for him on the table.

'Look after yourself, Karl, and best wishes to Lena and the kids,' Shetlov shouted across the restaurant as he ushered me out of the door.

'You too, Nikolai, and tell Gerde and Thomas to drop in next time they are passing through.' Passing through to where I wondered? Then I remembered all those places Frau Eppelmann suggested Herman and I spend our honeymoon.

'I will take you to Neuenhagen S-Bahn station,' Shetlov explained as we travelled south on the Berliner Ring. 'If you change trains at Biesdorf it will confuse anyone waiting for you at Karl Maron Strasse. I assume you are going home.' I had forgotten about Steuernagel and the fat man. 'Mind you, I don't think those guys are difficult to confuse. After all, instead of standing arguing with the truck driver, one of them should have followed you on foot. They didn't because the truck driver distracted them by picking a fight. It's not as if he was one of our top agents, just someone who moves furniture for us. So not the Stasi's best, do you think?'

'Definitely not.'

'So, you know these people?'

'I encountered one of them before.' Although this was all I was prepared to divulge, in part because too much had happened in a short space of time but mostly because I was exhausted.

Shetlov's car was parked a hundred metres from Neuenhagen S-Bahn station when he gently shook me awake. As I opened the door to get out, he said, 'Remember, these people may not be clever but even stupid people can cause a lot of damage.' I had one foot on the road and was pulling the strap of my bag over my shoulder. 'One other thing I should have mentioned. There was a file in the briefcase Thomas found with your name on it. You take care, Lotte.'

Shetlov's car drove away in the direction of Hoppegarten, leaving me momentarily paralysed by the implication of his final remark.

'The Stasi are parked outside, they been there nearly three hours,' Mother said, pulling back the curtain to check the car was still there. Whatever Steuernagel and the fat man were discussing, it must have been interesting because I managed to get into the house without them noticing. I smiled and waved when they saw me at the window, at which point Steuernagel shook his head, started the car and drove away at speed. 'You shouldn't do that.' Mother was right because she might now guess it was me they were interested in and not Frau Klink next door, who apparently had been *shooting her mouth off again*.

'And you're late,' Mother said, following me into the kitchen.

'A few of us went to a restaurant to celebrate someone's birthday.'

'So, you've eaten.' She sounded disappointed so instead of disappearing into my room I sat with her in the kitchen.

'Are you alright, you seem distant?' Mother asked after, apparently, having to repeat herself three times before receiving an answer. But my mind was elsewhere in a world where the Stasi, KGB and a young man I had yet to meet were playing an unusual, and probably very dangerous, game. Too tired to think and too worried to sleep, neither reading nor watching television took my mind off everything that had happened since leaving home that morning.

Then the telephone rang. 'It's Herman for you,' Mother said, returning to the settee, glancing at the television, muttering *rubbish* and then hiding behind her newspaper.

'Hello, how are things?' Then before I could reply, 'Are you still OK for the weekend?' Herman sounded hesitant, perhaps concerned I had changed my mind.

'Of course I will be there, Friday evening, straight after work.' And then after talking for half an hour during which my day was dismissed in a single sentence – *Dealing with some difficult people* – I said goodnight first to Herman, and then my mother, and went upstairs to my bedroom. Sleep proved elusive so I sat in bed writing my diary, the last paragraph describing everything I expected from my visit to Herman's home in Müggelheim.

# 13

# Not In My House

'Would it be possible to sail closer to the shore?'

'You won't get the full experience of being on a lake if we do,' Herman replied. Unfortunately, it was that *full experience* I had issues with.

My knowledge of this part of Berlin was sketchy. There was a school outing when I was thirteen; a round trip which took in the Spree and Müggelsee on a boat far larger than Herman's cruiser. Although we had been expected to produce a map of the route, mine was not particularly accurate and possibly copied from one drawn by a friend. I did, however, recall the Gosener Kanal opening onto Seddinsee, it was this expanse of water we were now about to cross.

The weight of water below me, when I caught sight of the piece of metal attached to a rope used as a makeshift anchor, caused me to recall Hüber's remark about the stones discovered in my father's pockets when his body eventually rose to the surface of the Weisensee. And a conversation with my tutor at the university about suicide as a response to fear, came to mind, the suggestion this was the last desperate attempt by someone completely overwhelmed to take control of their life by ending it.

'How old is this boat?' I asked Herman, hoping he would change his mind about sailing it across the lake, which he did not.

'My father bought it in the nineteen thirties but stopped sailing it during the war when he could no longer get the fuel. When he returned from Russia it was in a bad shape. We worked on it together when I was in my teens, but I only got the engine fixed after he died.'

Then, figuratively and literally, we entered choppier waters. 'How did your father end up in Russia?'

'He was an aircraft and radar engineer and at the end of the war was taken to Moscow to work on the Soviet Union's jet aircraft program with Brunolf Baade, the person who designed the DDR's passenger jet.'

'I thought most of Germany's aircraft engineers went to America?'

'Could have happened.' Herman did a poor imitation of an American accent. 'We could be darn well sailing off the coast of California right now.' He pushed the throttle forward and the cruiser sped up. I felt spray from the bow on my face. 'A lot of the engineers he was working with did just that,' he shouted over the roar of the engine. 'They left before the Red Army arrived, but he was still in Werneuchen retrieving equipment he had been working on.'

'It's strange you should mention Werneuchen,' I said as the expanse of water widened.

'Why's that?'

'It came up in a conversation with someone recently.'

'Someone who worked there?'

'No, someone who uses it when they fly back to Moscow.'

'A Russian!'

'Don't sound so surprised, even our Soviet comrades have emotional problems.' I recalled something Shetlov had asked. Did I believe in coincidences? Well, yes, of course – never underestimate the mind's ability to find patterns where none exist. Faces in the clouds of information we process each day. But at that very moment, this particular coincidence was proving difficult to dismiss as pure chance, especially as Herman's father had spent time in Moscow.

Were some of the people he met while there now in contact with his son? I was starting to appreciate how Andreas must have felt when strange unexplained things began happening, and I wondered how long before I was no longer capable of rational thought. So far, the weekend had taken me on a different path than I envisaged, beginning with my arrival in Müggelheim the previous afternoon.

'I hear you intend to work as a psychiatrist.' Herman's mother remarked during the first of numerous strained conversations with my future mother-in-law. A polite person might have added, *That's interesting*. Instead, she asked, somewhat caustically, 'Is there really any call for that these days?' Before I could explain there was, another slap. 'And Herman tells me you live in Biesdorf. When I worked there it was a nice part of Berlin.' Suggesting it had gone downhill since.

We had been sat in a lounge which more closely resembled Frau Eppelmann's than my mother's. Even so there was some evidence of the financial hardship which accompanied widowhood and perhaps the bitterness I detected was that of an ageing woman unable to maintain the lifestyle she had previously enjoyed. Also, my presence may have reminded her that one day she would be living there on her own. Ironically, in later years, it would be my income that helped maintain what my sister referred to as a lakeside villa.

Herman had steered the boat back towards the edge of the lake, perhaps noticing I sounded nervous when I asked. 'What did your father do when he came back from Russia?'

'Carried on working in the aviation industry and helped design the electronics and navigation system for the Baade 152.' This was East Germany's first, only, and ultimately failed attempt to build its own passenger airliner. There were models of the Baade 152, and a Russian jet fighter, on the desk in his father's study where Herman now worked when home at weekends.

Herman was silent, deep in thought during the thirty minutes it took to travel the length of Seddinsee. Once past Schmöckwitz we were close enough to the shore again to hear the shouts and screams of the children playing at the water's edge. 'Have you ever been to the Schmetterlingshorst?' Herman asked.

'Yes, a long time ago, when I was very young with my mother and...' There, almost did it again, mentioned my father. Still, another ghost might have been company for one invited on board by his son. 'I remember being disappointed there were no butterflies.'

'The collection was destroyed in a bombing raid in 1943.' As on that first night in his bomb-damaged apartment in Leipzig, no evidence that anti-western propaganda influenced Herman's view of the second world war. 'We'll try this place instead,' he said, turning the boat towards one of the mooring points in front of the Gaststatte Marianluste. Perhaps he thought the absence of butterflies at the Schmetterlingshorst was a deal-breaker.

A tour boat had just deposited a large group of tourists on the jetty. Some walked into the forest but enough wandered into the restaurant to ensure it took forty minutes for the waiter to bring the food we ordered. Herman had chosen wild boar, chips and salad and was amused when the Gulaschsuppe I ordered bore an uncanny resemblance to an Eintopf. Less so when a plate of chicken and Pomme Fritz was placed in front of him. He called after the waiter, who was retreating at speed towards the kitchen. 'This isn't what we ordered,' Herman said, but when he picked up the plate to hand it back, I grabbed his wrist.

'Do you want it or not?' asked the slovenly young man with a complexion like the surface of the moon, who was gazing out of the window at another boat disgorging day trippers.

'It will be fine,' I replied.

'But it's not what I ordered,' insisted Herman. And you asked for Gulaschsuppe,' he said, stating the blindingly obvious.

'Yes, but if you're hungry, you'll eat it.' And I made a start on the Eintopf in case Herman persuaded the waiter to relieve me of it. 'Your chicken would have ended up in front of someone who had been waiting almost as long as us to get served. You would go to the bottom the list and still be sitting here when it got dark. And possibly end up with nothing because by then they will have run out of chicken as well.'

'It's still not right.'

'No, it isn't. Unfortunately, you'll probably starve to death before you can change it.' That Herman seemed so naive and unfamiliar with dining out in Berlin was a surprise. He ate greedily, obviously uncomfortable with his surroundings.

'So, no dessert or coffee... And no tip for the waiter,' I said as we climbed back in the boat. Herman was not amused. The plan, as explained to me over breakfast, was for a round-trip similar to the ones made by tour boats. Not something I had been looking forward to given this would inevitably have meant sailing across the Müggelsee. My first thought after starting the return trip across Seddinsee was we were headed home because Herman was annoyed. Perhaps, now realising being so far away from the shore made me nervous, he had chosen the route out of spite. But instead of entering the Gosener Kanal we sailed down a narrow waterway which opened out onto a lake to the south of Schmöckwitz, finally mooring at a landing stage in front of what appeared to be a mansion.

'Are you sure we don't need a reservation?' I asked as we stood waiting inside the door.

'Of course not,' Herman assured me as we were handed a menu each.

'We can sit outside in the beer garden if you like or stay in here.' It was clear which Herman preferred so we followed the waiter to a table with a view out over the lake.

'But we have just eaten,' I reminded him.

'But no coffee or dessert,' he said, smiling while he studied the menu. Herman chose apple strudel and cream and a glass of beer followed by a coffee. Still somewhat disoriented I plumped for the same except mineral water instead of beer. It was then a middle-aged man, who was sitting at another table with a woman who, I presumed, was his wife, caught Herman's eye. The two men acknowledged each other with a smile. The man leaned across and whispered something to the woman then she too acknowledged our presence. Obviously, this was one of Herman's regular haunts and I now felt lunch at the Marianluste had been under sufferance. I also wondered if Herman had thought it was the sort of place a person like me would usually eat. Was this second stop compensation for what he regarded as a truly awful experience, or a less than subtle way of highlighting the difference between his world and mine?

'How is it you got a place at university?' A question I felt needed asking.

'What do you mean?'

'Well, your father was ... I mean ...'

'Considered bourgeois by virtue of his profession, education and privileges.'

Suddenly I felt self-conscious, reluctant to look up from the table, fearing the couple still watching us might be wondering what sort of people Herman was fraternising with these days.

The waiter arrived with the apple strudel, and I thought Herman would use the interruption to spare my embarrassment and change the subject; he did not. 'Working on a high-prestige project, my father came into contact with well-connected people in the party. Some of them were in the room when ways to improve education in East Germany were discussed.' I could hear in the back of my mind Andreas's voice and the claim East Germany's leaders were merely destroying one elite and replacing it with another.

In retrospect, Herman's belief that people who grew up surrounded by books were more useful to companies such as Mikroelektronik than those who spent their childhood surrounded by empty beer bottles was not something that developed over time, but an idea inherited from his father.

'It is only natural for a father to want what's best for their children,' Herman said after gulping down the beer which no doubt tasted better because he was not having to drink it while surrounded by factory workers on their day off.

'You're right. I'm sure if my father had been alive, he would have done the same.' A thought as unwelcome as it was unpleasant came to mind. 'It's ironic really, but had he lived I might have been denied a place at the Humboldt.'

'Let's change the subject,' Herman said, and laid his hands on mine, an attempt to reassure which might have succeeded had it not reminded me of how Hüber used physical contact to do much the same following my mauling by Wiedel and Steuernagel. Looking back, after years of explaining to women the subtle, and sometimes not so subtle, techniques boyfriends and husbands employed to manipulate them, I now realise Herman, while the intent was far less sinister than Hüber's, had nevertheless spotted a weakness and was exploiting it. Except, of course, in this case it was a two-way street.

Talking about seduction, which I think we are, as we sailed back along the Gosener Kanal I asked for a turn at piloting the boat. Once at the controls I steered the boat towards the bank, gently, to ensure Herman did not take back control. Even so, he felt compelled to stand behind me, his hands over mine on the wheel. I pushed my body back against his and bowed my head pretending to study the dashboard.

'So, what is this one?' I asked, pointing at one of the dials. Predictably, Herman kissed me on the back of the neck after explaining it was simply a temperature gauge. There were blankets in a locker for cold days which on that warm afternoon found a better use spread on the floor of the boat.

The Berliner Stadtwald was both beautiful and peaceful. With its engine stopped, the boat drifted, the only sounds the breeze in the trees, tapping of woodpeckers and water lapping against the bank. No other boats and so an opportunity for the physical contact which we guessed, correctly, would be out of the question back at the house.

Herman's mother was in a sulk, having expected us to return in time for afternoon tea on the lawn. She even appeared to blame me for the midges biting her after the sun went down. When Herman mentioned encountering family friends, his mother seemed horrified her son had been seen in the company of a clearly unsuitable young woman. Dinner was a painful affair.

'It must have been hard for your mother, bringing up two children after your father's death.' It is unclear why people feel the need to state the obvious, other than to reinforce a feeling of superiority. In this case it was possibly punishment for seducing her son.

What was the catalyst for the nightmare? It could have been any number of things that happened during that week or even that day. It started with the snowman my sister and I built in the garden with my father's help. Next it was that large piece of metal in Herman's boat, only instead of it being used as an anchor, two faceless men tied it around my ankles and I was being pulled to the bottom of the lake. Then I woke, but not in the spare bedroom of Herman's house but in a white tiled room. And so, the multilayered, episodic dreaming continued, only ending when daylight found me struggling to free myself from a duvet which had tied itself in a knot around my legs.

My future mother-in-law was particularly frosty at breakfast. It was some time before she could bring herself to speak. 'What you two get up to when you are in Leipzig is your own affair, but I would rather you behaved when you are under my roof and you both kept to separate rooms. This isn't a large house and sound carries.' It took a few moments to work out why she had pointed this out. I got there a few moments ahead of Herman. 'It's nothing to smile about.' But we both did. 'Either of you, and I would ask you to have a little respect.' This last remark aimed at me.

Perhaps unsurprisingly Herman found the incident more embarrassing than I did. He apologised as we set off for a cycle ride around the Müggelsee. 'All I can say is your mother must have had an interesting sex life.' I told him, which he probably found equally embarrassing.

'I'll explain it was only you dreaming,' he said, although I made him promise not to do this until after the weekend as although it was unlikely his mother would apologise, had she done so it would have been impossible to keep a straight face.

Sunday was spent doing what some on the shoreline must have done the previous day; speculating what might be happening in the seemingly empty boats drifting past. By mid-afternoon we had circumnavigated the Müggelsee and spent the rest of the day relaxing on the beach.

At some point during that weekend I decided that when, or if, Herman asked me to marry him, I would say yes. His house, despite being haunted by a witch – our son Peter's description of his grandmother, not mine – became a refuge. Over time I stopped noticing Herman's sense of entitlement and privilege, perhaps because, once we were married, it gradually permeated my life. This would prove problematic for both of us in the years during the Wende although Herman adjusted far more easily than I did.

I never did discover how Herman's mother felt about me taking her son and becoming the new lady of the house. There were only two months between the first heart attack, after which we moved in temporarily to care for her, and the second, which killed her. So our children were raised in the house Herman always regarded as home. And, strange as it may seem, while that nightmare returned from time to time, it never did so during all the years we lived in that house. For that I probably have Herman's mother to thank.

# 14

# Dömitz

May 2019

'I'm thinking of visiting Peter and Dorothea while you're away.' But I was competing for Herman's attention with the business section of the Frankfurter Allgemeine. 'Are you listening?'

'Yes, Peter and Dorothea are visiting.' Not a bad guess.

'That's not what I said. I'm going to Wittenberge.'

'When?' Herman said, lowering the newspaper.

'While you're away.' This was frustrating, made even more so by the deceit on my part, so I took the newspaper from Herman, folded it slowly then laid it on the table.

'Sorry, I was somewhere else. Goodness knows how I'm supposed to do all this. The EU thing is still up in the air and now there is the move to the new office in Aldershof.' Like most husbands, Herman focussed on major issues: whether we should place tariffs on Chinese imports and who Union Berlin should put in goal for its game against Bayern Munich, leaving me to deal with the trivial, such as buying us a new house and making sure we have enough money in the bank.

'Aldershof?' This was news to me.

'Yes, the company wants a bigger presence here in Berlin, which reminds me, the developer touting for the work is holding a party in a few weeks. A boat trip around Berlin, you'll enjoy it,' he said. 'It will make a nice break.' Perhaps a reference to me also seeming distracted of late, something he had commented on more than once. 'Wives and partners included, according to Anweiler Construction.'

A moment earlier, despite a glass of orange and two cups of coffee I still felt weary after a difficult day and another sleepless night. But the mention of Anweiler Construction jolted me awake as the trip to Wittenberge was cover for a clandestine meeting with the person who may, or may not, have been Paul Anweiler. What was it Nikola Shetlov asked? 'Lotte, do you believe in coincidences?'

Herman was about to pick up the newspaper again but looked at me and changed his mind. Instead he slowly turned his head and gazed out of the window across the open countryside at the rear of our house which, after we moved to Gehrden, in winter he compared to the Russian Steppes and in summer the Sahara desert. 'I think it might be time to retire,' he said, avoiding eye contact, as he often did when deceiving me, and himself.

'Well, you are sixty-five,' I reminded him, not sure why I entertained this nonsense, although it had been preferable to discussing my trip to Wittenberge which, in any case, Herman showed little interest in because I would be staying in the hotel owned by his estranged son.

'True, but most of the projects I'm working on won't be finished for at least another two years.' So, no intention of stopping work any time soon.

'Someone else will have to finish them.' I was not going to let him off that easily. Herman frowned and I recalled what Paul Anweiler said about my husband rebuilding his career. All that had been lost in 1990 was almost within his grasp; no way was he about to give up now.

The wheels of Herman's suitcase left two tramlines on the gravelled drive. 'Knock them dead, big man,' I said, giving him a playful punch on the chest and, because Frau Reimann was watching from across the road, a squeezed backside, which earned me a kiss on the forehead and a hug.

'Take care and good luck in Wittenberge.' Was it too much for him to send his regards to his son? Apparently, it was. Herman climbed in the car and was gone.

For a moment there was that same sinking feeling experienced before we were married, when the train for Berlin pulled out of Leipzig Hauptbahnhof after one of our weekends together. I wandered slowly back into the house, arms folded across my chest to defend against a growing feeling of guilt. I seemed to remember there were times, when Herman was standing on the platform waving me goodbye, that I felt I should have been more honest and open with him. Unfortunately, it was not possible then and neither was it now. Again, thanks to the Anweiler family, I was deceiving the person I loved. No longer prepared to do this I would return the money and take my chances with the tabloid press. Although if this was really what I intended to do, why travel to Dömitz? Why not simply put the envelope in the post?

Rather than leaving for Wittenberge immediately, the day was spent at home. That way when Herman phoned in the evening, he was not left with the impression I had set off as soon as his back was turned – another indication of my state of mind at the time.


'So how was your day?'

'Quiet,' I replied,' I had a few things to sort out before I went to see Peter.'

'I thought you were already there.'

'No, like I said, I had some catching up to do.'

Thankfully Herman did not press this but, instead, told me about Schulenberg's plan to add another glass and metal box to Berlin's skyline.

The catching up that I had been unwilling to discuss involved reading and re-reading my diary entry describing the afternoon of the

Anweiler party, which was incomplete and ended abruptly. A mystery which, while playing on my mind for many years, stopped troubling me around the time those dreams stopped.

There were also other, more practical, matters to deal with. While Dömitz was close to Wittenberge, it was not on the route one would usually take. The story that my car broke down necessitating an overnight stay in Dömitz would not ring true. Herman was unlikely to question why I was a day late reaching Wittenberge, but even so I would be happier in my own mind to have an excuse which sounded credible. My car would have to experience a problem somewhere else along the route suggested by Google. Not so close to Wittenberge that Peter would come to my rescue or within the range of Gehrden Motors, who would send a pickup truck. Pritzwalk seemed ideal although I eventually settled on nearby Heiligengrabe. Next was working out what time I should leave home to reach a garage around an hour before it closed for the day then check there was a hotel nearby.

Should I return the tape? My inclination was to get shot of it but eventually, while packing my suitcase the next morning, I changed my mind, intending to deny any knowledge of it and hoping to convince Paul I had still not discovered where it was hidden.

'I kerbed it while driving through Wittstock and now it doesn't seem to be driving correctly.' The mechanic peered under the wheel arch of my car, then fetched a light connected to a length of cable.

'Yes, the roads are terrible,' he said, bending down to search for the non-existent damage. Ironically the streets of Wittstock had been in remarkably good condition. 'It seems OK but I will take it for a test drive.' He took the ignition key, temporarily blinding me with the light as he did so.

'Could you check the brakes as well please?' I asked as he climbed into the car. He did this and discovered the brakes and suspension were, like the rest of the car, in perfect working order.

'How much do I owe you?' What I had not bargained for was the mechanic taking pity on a damsel in distress.

'That's OK, there's no charge,' he replied, although I managed to convince him my fictious company would reimburse me, so we settled on thirty-five euro and I paid with my credit card. The same card was used to pay for dinner and book a room, which would remain empty, at the Hotel Zum Erbhof. This, on the remote chance that Herman helped me out with the monthly accounts, would provide documentary evidence backing up the story of a night marooned in the wilds of Western Pomerania.

The Dömitzer Hafen hotel was a converted warehouse overlooking the harbour where the Elde flowed into the Elbe. The email I had received gave no clue as to whether the man who insisted on a meeting was also booked into the hotel. It seemed inappropriate to ask when I checked in.

'Ah yes, one night, K and S Investments, and you are Ute Lorenz,' said the neatly dressed young man, his jacket colour co-ordinated with the decor of the hotel.

'I am not, I think there has been a mistake.' I probably sounded somewhat irritable and aggressive. There was a furious burst of typing on the computer's keyboard followed by a short pause while the machine responded.

'Ah yes, I see now.' Although what he saw remained a mystery as did, for now, the identity of Ute Lorenz.


Amongst the not-so-trivial tasks delegated to the woman of the house, well ours at least, was planning the family holiday. Taxing, to say the least, given Herman's expectations were high before the Wende and even higher in the years after. 'By any chance did you spot the words *retro* or *ostalgie* in the brochure when you booked this?' I would be asked if my husband discovered the taps were old and dripping or any part of the décor was brown or beige. We had both travelled outside East Germany before 1989, Herman attending trade shows and visiting high tech companies in the West, me as a delegate at conferences in Austria and Scandinavia. The difference being, before the Wende, Herman went on his own and was entertained by the companies he visited while I was always part of a delegation watched over for the duration of the visit. Our differing experiences of what lay outside the DDR became apparent when Ursula, worried our marriage might be headed for the rocks, suggested Herman and I took a holiday. 'You two need some time on your own, go somewhere exciting, leave Inge and Peter with me.'

'You are joking,' I'd replied, fearing I would spend the rest of the year trying to turn the children back into normal people. Even so, we accepted my sister's offer and headed for the airport.

'You haven't said where we are going.' I had assumed it was a surprise, that is until we were standing at a computer terminal displaying a list of last-minute summer breaks. Two hours later we were on a flight to Sicily. 'Shouldn't we have filled in some forms?' I asked remembering the labyrinthine bureaucracy when I travelled to Vienna, Helsinki or Stockholm.

'Don't worry, it's fine.'

It was OK for him, closing his eyes after eating his complimentary packed lunch and half of mine – I had lost my appetite – then washing it down with a plastic glass of white wine.

'There was this boy, Rudolf, who lived on our street, something of a fanatic.' I said. 'He'd been a Thälmann pioneer until the age of thirteen, then he joined the FDJ. They said if you dropped a sweet paper anywhere in Biesdorf, Rudi would catch it before it reached the pavement. In nineteen sixty-eight he collected so many tin cans and bottles they gave him a prize, a week's holiday on the Black Sea. Except after arriving at the airport he accidentally got on a plane to Prague. As he was in Czechoslovakia unofficially there was no way he could get permission to board a flight back to Berlin.'

'So, what happened?' Herman had merely been polite, less interested in my story than grabbing a few minutes sleep before we changed planes in Rome.

'Well, instead of a holiday on the beach, Rudi spent a week in a hotel in Prague then, when the Russians invaded to oust Dubcek, he was thrown in prison because there were rumours the East German army was massing on the border.'

'Well, I doubt Germany is about to invade Italy so we should be OK.'

The temperature at Catania airport was forty degrees but when confronted by uniformed customs and border police, it was not only the heat, but memories of that fear I once felt when someone either abroad or in the DDR studied my passport and visa, that caused me to break into a sweat. The first two nights we stayed in a hotel called The Palace which looked nothing like any palace I had seen before. Then we travelled by train to Palermo for three nights in the Villa Igiea with a reception which brought to mind the grandeur of Neues Palais in Potsdam. Convinced there had been a mistake, I insisted Herman checked the itinerary. It was the Schröders, the late-middle-aged couple sitting at the next table as we dined out on the terrace, who solved the mystery as to why the holiday was so cheap.

'Beirut, Lockerbie, and now the Gulf War ... American tourists are staying away, especially from anywhere here on the Mediterranean. So, some really good deals for the rest of us,' explained Mr Schröder.

'We've been coming for the last four years,' Mrs Schröder added.

'Yes, I noticed the US pavilion at Hannover has been rather empty since nineteen eighty-eight,' said Herman, and he and Mr Schröder, who once worked for a company which manufactured computer equipment used by supermarkets, spent an hour reminiscing about their respective visits to the annual trade show.

Mrs Schröder, like me, had probably heard these stories numerous times before and mistook my exhaustion, the result of a combination of heat and sensory overload, for boredom. 'Is this your first holiday in the West?' she asked, then without waiting for an answer, added, 'You must find all this very exciting.'

Thankfully less exciting than Vienna, my first trip abroad. So far, no dead bodies in the hotel. Just how was it Herman had so little difficulty engaging with Wessies, while seconds from stepping out of his shadow I had fallen victim to Mrs Schröder's preconceived idea that East Germans were people to be patronised or pitied?

'You're too sensitive,' insisted Herman when we got back to our room.

'Really? *You must try the donkey cart ride around the city, you'll love it.* Why, because it will make me feel at home? Oh yes, I forgot, we haven't got cars in East Germany, only horses.' Looking into the bathroom mirror, I lifted the hair from my forehead. 'No, it's not there, I thought I might have *Ossie* tattooed on my forehead. Perhaps not using the right knife and fork gave it away.'

'This looks fun, come and try it.' Behind me Herman was stepping into a large sunken bath.

After stripping off I joined him. 'There is something odd about the Schröders. I'm sure they were at the airport in Berlin before we left.'

'They probably were and chose the same last-minute deal as us. Or do you think they are Stasi and Mr Schröder has stolen all that technology that's appearing in our supermarkets from Robotron and sold it to Mannesmann and IBM?' Herman whispered in my ear as he slid his arms around my waist and pulled me close. He was right of course; while *Ossie* may not have been tattooed on my forehead, it was imprinted in my mind, and I had fallen victim to the very thing I later encouraged my patients to guard against. He was also right about the bath – it was fun.

Herman would have approved of the junior suite of the Dömitzer Hafen Hotel. We would have probably had as much fun on the low king-sized double bed in a room with an uninterrupted view of the sky and the tops of trees stretching to the horizon as in the sunken bath in the Villa Igea. Unfortunately, it was not possible to share a description of it with him when my mobile rang and he asked, 'So how is Wittenberge?' Not *How is Peter the prodigal son*, by the way.

'Never made it. There was a problem with the car. A garage is sorting it out, but I'm stuck in Heiligengrabe for the night.' I said while sitting cross-legged on that king-sized bed trying to convince the person who made love to me in Sicily I was in a hotel eighty kilometres away

'Are you OK?'

'Fine, I've booked into a small hotel. It's not too bad, look.' I texted a picture taken earlier while having dinner.

'Well, at least the car isn't a write off?' Puzzled by this I looked at the picture again and realised my Polo, which I had intimated was in the local garage, was visible through the window of the restaurant.

*Loose threads, Lotte, find one and keep picking at it, and even the best cover story unravels.*

Having said goodnight to Herman I read again the description in my diary for 1975 of that first encounter with the man I was meeting the following day.

# 15

# It's Our Party – You'll Cry If We Want You To

August 1975

My German teacher accused me of including verbose, flowery, grandiloquent but largely irrelevant descriptions in my essays simply to increase the word count. He would have been pleased with the entry in my diary for 23rd August 1975 which was a prosaic *Hot* followed by *thankfully* in brackets.

Had Sabine attended a garden party on a summer's afternoon, I guessed she might go dressed in the peach-coloured shorts, sandals and white tee-shirt she wore when I interviewed her. Even the pendant engraved with the word *Modern* was included as part of my disguise although, unlike Sabine, I did not intend putting it in my mouth when under stress.

At twelve-fifteen in the afternoon I was standing at the corner of Hönower Strasse and Zandergeise Strasse just north of Mahlsdorf S-Bahn station, well away from both my home in Biesdorf and Treptow where Erich Anweiler had an apartment. Unfortunately, Erich did not own a car. This I only discovered when he arrived on a small motorbike: ideal for navigating the streets of Berlin but unsuited for the roads outside the city. So much for Hüber's claim every detail had been checked.

The car containing Otto Steuernagel and the fat man appeared shortly after Erich arrived, parked on the opposite side of the street and waited for us to set off. Sabine had probably never travelled on the back of a motorbike. Had she done so, a thick pair of trousers and a coat might also have gone missing from the shop where she worked. My hands and legs were frozen, hair blew into my face and pushing it from my eyes meant letting go of Erich, causing the motorcycle to swerve across the road. We came to a halt after passing a sign for Rüdersdorf. Steuernagel's Lada sped past, coming to a halt 150 metres along the road.

'I think we're lost,' Erich said, unzipping his jacket.

'If you think we are lost, then we are lost.' He climbed off the motorbike and took a map from his pocket. 'You have been to Rethen before, haven't you?' I said while he unfolded it.

'Yes, but not along this road.'

'I'm not sure you should be standing here reading a map. Not this close to a Soviet base.'

Erich scanned the horizon. 'Are we close to one?'

'Everywhere in East Germany is close to a Soviet base. Now put the map away and let's get going. When I tap you on the left shoulder take the next left turn, the right shoulder, take the next right. Got that?'

Erich nodded and we set off again. Steuernagel shrugged as we rode past.

What should have been a one-and-a-half-hour journey took almost two, travelling into Müncheberg, then out again on Eberswalder Strasse, then turning right after the railway station and into uncharted territory. Despite studying a map the previous evening, it was unclear exactly where in Rethen the Anweilers were holding their party. The road into the village was well maintained, loose parts of the motorbike no longer rattled, the rumble of cobbles and thump of potholes ceased. Then I saw a Mercedes and a white sticker with *GB* on the large grey limousine parked next to it. Puzzled by the first three letters of the limousine's number plate, *MFS*, I forgot to tap Erich's shoulder, and he drove on for almost a quarter of a kilometre. While we retraced our route back to a house resembling an Alpine chalet, I tried to work out why someone from Britain appeared to be driving a car belonging to the Stasi.

A young woman dressed in jeans and a white blouse, having seen us arrive, left a group of people stood on the lawn at the rear of the house to greet Erich and his girlfriend for the afternoon. She had shoulder-length blond hair, pale blue eyes and a soft mouth and I was surprised her voice was quite so harsh. 'You look frozen,' she said, looking me up and down, then snapped at my ersatz boyfriend. 'Erich get ...' But then turned to me again. 'Sorry, I don't know your name.'

'Lotte,' I said, extending a numbed hand which was shaken firmly.

'I'm Petra, Erich's sister.'

'Please to meet you ... Petra.' I hesitated slightly before saying her name to give the impression she was a complete stranger, not someone I recognised from the photograph in her Stasi file which, like those of the rest of her family, I had read one afternoon while sitting in the office next to Hüber's.

'Don't just stand there, Erich, get Lotte something to drink.' But it seemed my fling with her brother was almost over.

'Beer or wine?' Erich asked while looking across the garden to where other members of his family were standing.

'Have you any tea?' I replied.

'Sure,' Erich said with a shrug, and walked off towards the house leaving me alone with Petra, putting flesh on the bones of the still-shivering shopgirl using information gleaned from conversations with Sabine. Meanwhile after stopping several times to laugh and joke with other guests, Erich had climbed the steps at the rear of the house, crossed the veranda and disappeared through the opened French windows.

Eventually, when it was clear Erich would not be coming back, Petra suggested we also went into the house. I formulated a question, something along the lines of *This is a nice house, do you live here?* but never got the chance to ask it. A grey van turned off the road and parked close to where Erich's motorbike was leant against a tree. The driver climbed out and slid open the side door from which another three men carrying shoulder bags emerged, caps pulled down over their eyes as if fearing they would be recognised. Within seconds all four men had disappeared through the side door of the house.

Petra took hold of my arm, perhaps to distract me. 'We have visitors from Britain, I'll introduce you,' she said, leading me across the lawn. I glanced over my shoulder, still trying to understand what I had just witnessed, but then remembered the warning to *ignore anything unusual in my peripheral vision*.

Inside the house Erich stood at a makeshift bar. It was difficult not to compare his behaviour with Herman's or think of other places I would rather have spent that afternoon. Petra shrugged. 'My God, Erich,' she muttered, as much to herself as me, then waved her hand dismissively at plates of food arranged on a long cloth-covered table. 'Help yourself,' she said. 'And there is wine, tea and coffee.' But no mention of beer, perhaps due to the look on my face while watching Erich gulping from a bottle like a newborn lamb.

A colour TV set was showing an old black-and-white film broadcast from the West. The screen was mounted in a cabinet with doors resembling a piece of antique furniture. 'Do you watch *Tatort*?' Petra asked as I poured a cup of tea and put a slice of chocolate gateau on a paper plate.

Was this a trick question, because *Tatort* was only broadcast on West German TV? 'Only I think the detective in this film is Götz George who plays Joachim Siedel,' she said, standing to one side so I got a better view of the screen. 'Hans says it isn't.'

'Götz George wasn't mentioned in the titles,' said the young man I already knew was Petra's husband. Hans Anweiler was medium height with the gait of a boxer and was wearing jeans and a blue tee-shirt, which made me feel slightly less out of place in a room full of people in formal dress.

'Maybe he wasn't so famous when this was made. What do you think, Lotte?' Petra asked.

At the mention of my name Hans shook my hand. 'You're Erich's friend,' he said, as if this was something to be pitied. Although I was glad there were no more questions about Tatort. I wondered how many hours Sabine spent watching West German TV, and if I should have tried to appear more knowledgeable. However, even my alter ego would have found the black-and-white film on the television of less interest than the pile of clothes, all of them imported from the West, on the table beside it.

'Presents from our relatives,' according to Petra when she registered my sudden interest.

There was a noise from overhead, in one of the rooms upstairs. A dull thud followed by the sound of something dragged across the floor. 'What was that?' I immediately regretted asking, remembering I was only there to determine if a guest from Britain was the genuine article.

'Mice,' Petra whispered, as if only half believing this herself, her mood suddenly changing as she turned up the volume of the television to drown out the noise overhead.

Hans seemed just as defensive. 'Perhaps Lotte would like to meet the rest of the family,' he said to Petra. In other words: *Get her out of here.* I just had time to pick up some grapes and a peach before Petra escorted me out onto the veranda.

'Father, this is Lotte, Erich's friend,' Petra said as we eased ourselves past one of the two men at the top of the steps leading down to the garden. Regarded as an appendage of Erich, himself treated even by his relatives as something of an outsider, I felt uncomfortable introduced to an Anweiler several years my senior. But, this time, an embrace of sorts.

Wilhelm Anweiler was keen to include me in the conversation with the man facing him, who I recognised as Klaus Anweiler. Even without access to his file I would have guessed Klaus was Wilhelm's brother; there was the same prematurely receding hairline, narrow face, piercing blue eyes, thin lips and high cheekbones. Oddly, however, neither man seemed entirely at ease with the other, and the raised voices created the impression Wilhelm and Klaus were about to exchange blows.

'Isn't that right, Lotte?' Wilhelm had lowered his voice but only slightly, and I was sure he could still be heard by guests both inside the house and those stood on the lawn.

'I'm sorry?' Is what right I wondered, although soon found out.

'Will Russia invade Afghanistan to stop Daoud moving closer to Iran and the US?' I was puzzled as to why Wilhelm thought a young girl who worked in a clothes shop might have an opinion on this. Fortunately, it appeared a response was not required.

Klaus said, 'Well, that won't be possible if what you say about the Soviet Airforce running short of fuel is true. Which I must say I doubt.'

'They definitely are short of fuel,' confirmed Wilhelm. 'Two months ago, they cut training flights to one day a week. Even so, there is a tank regiment here in Berlin ready to move to the Afghanistan border.' OK I was only Erich's girlfriend, a shop assistant with zero interest in the Soviet military or international affairs. Even so, given that I might repeat what was just said to someone more knowledgeable, this was dangerous talk on Wilhelm's part.

Feeling increasingly uneasy consulted on a subject about which Sabine would have known little if anything at all, I was relieved when Petra came to my rescue. 'Lotte works in a clothes shop.' I would have preferred a little more support from Wilhelm's daughter-in-law, but she walked down the steps to join her husband, who had dragged himself away from the television set and was circulating amongst the guests in the garden. The fact I might spend more time reading fashion magazines than newspapers seemed not to have sunk in, and Wilhelm persisted in attempting to draw me into the debate with his brother.

'You're a young person, you must have some interest in politics. What about Vietnam?' Wilhelm turned to Klaus. 'I'm sure now he is studying in London, Paul is protesting against the war.'

Klaus shook his head. 'Too busy catching up after his illness.' Mention of Paul appeared to remind him his immediate family was sitting around one of the picnic tables in the garden. 'We'll talk later,' he said, descending the steps and walking across the lawn, leaving me alone with Wilhelm, who I felt might know more about me than I would have liked.

'Where is the shop?' Wilhelm asked when Klaus was far enough away not to hear.

'It's in Ahrensfelde.' The shop where Sabina worked was actually in Lichtenberg, but there was a reason for relocating it to a small town outside the city. 'On Lindenberger Strasse, do you know it?' And a last something I thought might be worth a try, after studying Wilhelm's file, actually worked.

Wilhelm's whole demeanour changed. A shadow was cast over the face of the previously confident, jovial middle-aged man and behind it hid a frightened boy in his early teens. 'I was there once, a long time ago at the end of the war,' he said slowly, as if tiptoeing over broken glass. 'A lot of us children along with old men from our village were forced into the Volkssturm. I wasn't even old enough to join the Hitler youth, still they expected me to fight. It was a lost cause, old men and children defending Berlin against the Red Army. We spent two days retreating towards the city. A member of the Waffen SS, still recovering after being wounded, was forcing us to keep fighting. We did manage to destroy a Russian tank with a Panzerfaust.' Willelm animated his story with an imitation of an explosion. 'That was just outside of Ahrensfelde, where you work. The Russians destroyed Blumberg Manor, and the Wehrmacht blew up the railway lines. So, we were trapped and our leader decided we should make a stand near the station. He found a box of grenades and was showing us how to use them.'

It was unlikely I would ever need to blow up a Russian tank with a grenade, but Wilhelm felt I ought to know how it was done. 'Pull out the pin, hold the arm straight behind the head remembering not to let go until you've swung your arm forward.' Then Wilhelm smiled. 'On no account let go too early, and let it fall on the ground behind you. Which he did and we all ran like hell, while our crazy leader looked for the grenade in the rubble. Then boom!' Another imitation of an explosion. I would have preferred Wilhelm left me to imagine body parts raining down on the road and the burned-out car behind which he was hiding, but received a graphic description of this as well.

'The dust had cleared.' Wilhelm had now calmed down a little, his mood lightened slightly. 'We were surrounded by soldiers, and I thought, *This is it*. But then the officer asked me, in German, *What have you come dressed as, little boy?* Asked where I lived, and it turned out the officer was Polish but grew up on a farm just outside Gladowshöhe. Not only that, he remembered my uncle and aunt from his schooldays, before his father returned to his ancestral home near Lublin after the Nazis came to power. What were the chances of that?'

(Well, a few weeks ago I was speaking to a man who could have probably told Wilhelm; after all they do say life is a lottery.)

'The officer told me to take off my fancy dress costume and go home to my mother. Back in Gladowshöhe we loaded a handcart with a few possessions and food then headed west. We almost reached the Elbe but Russian soldiers turned us back.'

Then silence for a few moments because I suspected Wilhelm found the next part of the story too harrowing to tell out loud, although, given the expression on his face, I imagined it was playing out in his head. When he spoke it sounded less rehearsed. Less like the account of the incident in Ahrensfelde which he had recalled many times, once to a workmate who was a Stasi informer, which is how it ended up in Wilhelm's file and why I moved Sabine's workplace. A cruel trick perhaps, but a well-judged one in my opinion; I needed a way to connect with the Anweiler family and, after reading his file, it was clear Erich's help would not extend beyond getting me to the party, and he had only just managed to do that.

When Wilhelm spoke again he did so slowly, hesitantly and almost in a whisper. 'My parents were ill and Klaus ... well, Klaus was missing, so just me and my sister looking after the family.' Another pause and Wilhelm began tapping his half-empty glass with his finger.

'I made trips into Berlin to find food, until one day, travelling home on the roof of a crowded train with a sack of potatoes, a spark from the engine set the carriage on fire. Our mother died later that year. We took her body out into the forest and buried it in an unmarked grave.'

Silence, and I regretted causing Wilhelm to relive dark and disturbing events from his past on such a bright sunny day. During my childhood, my father's memories of Stalingrad only resurfaced when there was snow on the ground. The voices of people in the house and the garden faded into the background and all I could hear was the breeze which was bending the tops of pine trees in the forest and the tap tap tap of Wilhelm's fingernail on the side of his glass.

There was part of his story Wilhelm did not share: what happened after a Russian officer knocked on the Anweilers' door asking after his brother. For this I relied on what came to light during the meeting with Hüber, Weidel and Steuernagel. Even this had me wondering how much attention any of the three men had paid to copies of the documents in Wilhelm's file.

Wilhelm's father Friedrich had already been informed by the Red Cross that Klaus had been taken prisoner and in the autumn of 1946 was moved from a camp in Belgium to one in Britain. In 1948 Klaus wrote to his father informing him he was about to be released and would return home to Berlin. This was the last letter Klaus wrote to his father and future letters sent by Friedrich to his son went unanswered.

Presumably missed at first, by those under orders from Soviet Military Intelligence to monitor any communications between Friedrich Anweiler and Klaus, was the possibility his other son

Wilhelm might be acting as a go-between. Only then did suspicion fall on letters Wilhelm sent to an old school friend now living in Bavaria updating this *friend* on current events in Gladowshöhe. Then it was discovered this friend lived at the same address as Klaus's former commander. One of the early letters sent by Wilhelm would have mentioned Russian soldiers arriving at the house looking for his brother, a warning to Klaus not to come home.

Rather than stopping or interfering with any future correspondence between Wilhelm and Klaus, or even the presents exchanged each Christmas, it was agreed by both the Stasi and the Soviets to let it continue, which they both did until 1971, building up a picture of Klaus and his family who, it appeared were now living somewhere in Britain. Even then letters between the two brothers were still being routed through an address in Bavaria so it was assumed the British Secret Service remained ignorant of the communication. As far as I was concerned, this was only relevant in respect to how much Wilhelm had learned about his nephew Paul during those twenty years, and the possibility they too might have been in contact with each other. However, the opportunity to find out now passed.

'It's proving tougher than we thought, I think we'll need Hans.' Standing behind me was one of the men who had climbed out of the van parked beside the house. He was sweating and appeared frustrated and impatient, out of place amongst the guests who by and large were relaxed and enjoying themselves. Perhaps aware of this discontinuance, the interloper avoided eye contact and stayed in the doorway as if hoping to remain invisible. Meanwhile Wilhelm returned from the dark place my reference to Ahrensfelde had taken him. 'Don't bother Hans with that, I'll do it,' he said.

'Guard this with your life,' Wilhelm told me, balancing his glass of beer on top of the railing which ran the length of the veranda. Then he accompanied the uninvited guest into the house. They weaved their way between the tables stopping only for a brief exchange with Erich, already unsteady on his feet and swaying as he spoke, and to pick up cake and sandwiches. Then both men walked along the hallway into which light poured from a window in the front of the house. I watched two silhouettes pause for a moment, conversing while looking back into the room, suspecting they were talking about me before climbing the stairs.

With Wilhelm having left to assist with whatever was happening upstairs, any insights into the life and career of his nephew would only be gained from Paul Anweiler himself. However, Paul was talking, or rather arguing, with his cousin Hans.

'The problem with state ownership is no one gets to choose where they live.' Paul Anweiler was sitting on the edge of a table, arms folded across his chest, but otherwise appearing relaxed.

'And in capitalist Britain you get to choose which crumbling tower block you are crushed to death in when it collapses after someone's gas cooker explodes.' Hans had the same defensive stance when talking to his cousin as he adopted with me. He had spent five years as a truck driver and trusted enough to make frequent deliveries to the West. For some reason in my copy of his file certain details regarding these trips were redacted. Hans joined the family business and took over the day to day running when his father began experiencing prolonged periods of ill health which, from what I had read and now seen, were probably the result of wartime trauma.

Holding a coin between his thumb and forefinger, Hans asked Paul. 'How much do people pay in capitalist Britain for the privilege of living in the slums you are building for the working class? Because this is all I pay each week to live in my modern central heated apartment,' he said, holding the Ostmark in Paul's face. 'Which, by the way, doesn't have water dripping through the ceiling because the pipework in the flat above has been stolen. We have a person in each block who keeps the thieves out.'

'And reports you for watching West German TV and keeps a record of who you invite for dinner.' Again I recalled what Hüber had said about ignoring much of what I overheard.

The two young men dispensed with references to capitalism and communism as the argument became personal. 'But you'll never own your apartment.'

'And you don't own your house. It's owned by a bank. You pay them a stupidly huge rent which you won't be able to afford come the next financial crisis because you'll have no job. Then the bank takes your house away and you will be living on the street.'

'Well, at least I have the freedom to live where I want.'

'So, I expect the next house you build will be next to Buckingham Palace.' Members of both the German and British sides of the Anweiler family found this amusing.

Even Paul smiled, perhaps not at his cousin's quip but at a thought that had obviously crossed his mind. 'And if you asked the person who owns this place,' he said, tilting his head towards the house, 'he would be happy for you to move in for an Ostmark a month?'

'Keep your voice down,' Klaus suggested to his son and everyone's eyes were turned everywhere except on me.

But Paul ignored his father's advice. 'Ten years from now you'll still be paying to live in your apartment. But I will own the one I've built.'

Hans glanced at Petra, who frowned, looked at Paul and shook her head. The discussion became less aggressive; perhaps Paul had belatedly heeded his father's advice or more likely took his cue from Petra. Talk then was less about politics than the economics and practicalities of house building, with Hans using a food tray to demonstrate how East Germany's prefabricated apartment blocks were constructed. Then Paul explained why one built in London to a similar design seven years earlier had collapsed.

'I can't believe someone would simply cut bolts off to make the panels fit. If that happened here someone would find themselves in prison,' Hans said. Then I noticed Klaus's wife sat alone and apart from other members of the Anweiler family.

'Hello, my name is Lotte.' I said, sitting next to Mrs Anweiler.

'I'm sorry, I don't speak German,' she said, and my conversation with Paul's mother ended there because while I could speak English fluently, Sabine's only option of a second language at school had been Russian.

There came a thud from an open window on the first floor of the house, and someone calling out, obviously in pain. Looking up I caught sight of the man who had left the party with Wilhelm. He pulled the open window to and closed the blind. I was reminded of Professor Pohl's comment regarding Hüber's half-hearted commitment to Zersetzung, and his suspicion the Stasi officer still preferred physical over psychological torture. Was he only pretending to adhere to party policy and continuing to use the methods he trusted, and maybe enjoyed employing, and doing this in secret? All he would need were people willing to assist him in exchange for certain privileges, and the people around me appeared privileged indeed.

# 16

# Sinking Without Trace

When Wilhelm rejoined the party, his right hand, in which he held the glass of beer I was supposed to have been guarding on pain of death, was crudely bandaged with a handkerchief. Did the person beaten suffer more because I forced Wilhelm to recall those wartime experiences? More puzzling, and worrying, was why the other guests ignored what was happening above their heads. Perhaps no one noticed because they were all struggling to make themselves understood in a second language and heard above a cacophony of voices, music and the sound of a television turned up to full volume. It had only been by chance I spotted those men climb out of the van. Maybe Hüber's warning that things happened in Rethen it was best to ignore made me overly aware of anything suspicious or unusual.

It seemed the Anweiler family was using their annual reunion as cover for something sinister. The visitors from England would have been familiar with the use of physical violence as a means of control; truncheon-wielding policemen suppressing dissent, charging on horseback, like medieval knights, into crowds of demonstrating students or striking workers. Could it be, the reservations Professor Pohl expressed after the meeting in Potsdam were well founded, and

Zersetzung would have little impact on the way police suppressed dissent.

Andreas, the rebel and thorn in the side of the East German Communist Party, would not, despite what Hüber suggested, be spared pain like that inflicted on the person upstairs by Wilhelm and his associates. My thoughts turned to escape, getting as far away from this house, Rethen and my hosts as possible. Given the amount of beer poured down his throat, the chance of Erich being able to stand upright, let alone ride a motorbike, was remote.

An alternative was slipping away unnoticed, walking along the road to where Steuernagel had parked his car. While this would get me safely back to Berlin it would mean coming up with a credible excuse for leaving the party early. There was another option – a path through the trees used as a shortcut from the house to Rethen railway station. The trains to Müncheberg were infrequent but I could hide in the forest to ensure the least time possible was spent waiting on the platform. The only person likely to alert Steuernagel if I disappeared was Erich and even he would not be stupid enough to approach a member of the Stasi in his current state.

'Thanks for looking after my beer,' Wilhelm said, then lowered his voice. 'Can't be too careful, not with all these Englishmen about, so just to make sure, I spat in it before I left.'

'That's a coincidence.' Paul Anweiler now stood by my side. 'So did I.'

Wilhelm was back to his old self, confidence restored, although no more talk of politics, army manoeuvres or global conflict. He sat himself down on a bench and began telling jokes to anyone who would listen; none of these stories appropriate within earshot of a Stasi officer or an informer. At some point during the story came the annual photograph with members of both sides of the family – senior members on the veranda, younger ones on the lawn, with the exception of Erich who was leaning in the doorway holding a bottle of beer. Finding myself next to Paul, this was my chance to engage him in conversation.

'Erich told me this is your first visit to East Germany.'

'Yes, my family thought I should put in an appearance. Sorry, I don't know your name.'

'It's Lotte,' I replied, offering my hand. Paul shook it and already there was a hint of something not quite right. The grip was firm but not aggressive, no attempt to demonstrate his masculinity. The calloused palm, however, was not that of a person who spent all their time studying.

'How long have you and Erich been going out?' Straight away a casual conversation had turned into an interrogation.

'Just a couple of weeks, although I've known him for over a year, he used to go out with one of my friends.'

'He seems to have disappeared,' Paul said, looking towards the house, knowing full well Erich had already returned to the bar. Sighing deeply only served to make me appear pathetic.

'You're studying at university, that must be exciting. I see on television there's lots of student demonstrations in England.' Something mindless Sabine might have come out with, although it was unlikely she would have dared talk to a foreigner, especially one from a country painted in East Germany as the birthplace of capitalism and imperialism.

'Engineering students tend not to demonstrate, harms their chances of getting a decent job. If I was studying history or economics, it would be different. And it helps to get yourself photographed being arrested at a demonstration if you're thinking of a career in politics.'

While tempting to ask Paul why he was not interested in politics, it was unlikely Sabine would have steered the conversation in this direction. Also, according to Hüber, recruitment and entrapment were not part of my brief. So, at a loss to think what Sabine would say next, there was an awkward silence. Paul used the time to look me up and down and I regretted not wearing something which covered the tops of my legs.

Realising he had been caught gawping like a schoolboy, a slightly embarrassed Paul said, out of the blue, 'Of course, in 1968 the college had its own Che Guevara, but that was before my time. There are still some trying to keep the flame alive, but the middle class tend to abandon Marxism around the time they get the keys to their first house.'

On the back foot again, it was difficult to know how to respond, and I almost blurted out David Cathcart's name.

I was saved by a distraction of sorts. Harassed and irritated, Wilhelm's wife stormed out of the house and demanded her husband helped in the kitchen. On her way back to the house, with Wilhelm in tow, she paused and greeted some of the guests. The exchange with Paul's mother was clumsy and one-sided as the Englishwoman obviously did not speak or understand German. Paul's mother, noticing me watching her, stood up and joined her husband, whispering something in his ear that caused him to look in my direction. He listened to what his wife was saying, obviously about me, then shook his head and returned to the German members of his family. Despite appearing to dismiss what his wife told him, more than once after this I noticed Klaus staring at me.

'Germany, the land of the dominatrix,' Paul said.

'Sorry?'

'Grandes dames, matriarchs.' I then realised he was referring to his aunt.

'That behaviour is common in a generation of German women who lived through the second world war. The Nazis' promotion of manliness had an impact on family dynamics,' I said, forgetting Sabine was unlikely to have read the paper by O J Brandes, published in the December 1950 edition of Social Forces. Professor Pohl and myself had discussed whether my paper on the impact of the war on family life in East Germany should contain a reference to Jean Brandes' research. Eventually it was decided to include it as it might be well received by delegates from the West, should I get to present my paper at the conference in Vienna. Pohl also felt it might provide an opportunity to suggest the Vietnam war had its roots in the imperialist US need to assert its masculinity rather than any political or geopolitical imperative. Pohl's words not mine and I was fearful someone would suggest an alternative explanation: that German men lost the respect of their wives after they failed to prevent them being raped by Russian soldiers. Paul studied me carefully for a moment and then looked away. 'War is so stupid, don't you think?' I said, the most vacuous statement Sabine might have come out with at this point and perhaps why Paul ignored it.

Paul's attention was now on Petra, Hans, and the other younger guests, strolling across the garden towards a gap in the trees and the path that I knew, from studying a map of the area the previous evening, led to a large lake some two hundred metres into the forest. He followed his cousins, leaving me standing alone and feeling stupid.

As presumably Steuernagel and the fat man were still in their car, this would have been the perfect time to slip away and tell them my cover had been blown. But then, just as Paul reached the trees he turned and called out, 'Come on, you'll enjoy this.' Unlikely I thought, but Paul was holding out his hand. Quite why I felt compelled by this simple gesture to follow him to the lake was a mystery. While not skipping hand in hand through the trees, because the path was narrow his bare arm repeatedly brushed against mine. This physical contact, while slight and intermittent, made me feel uncomfortable. Paul must have sensed this because for the next fifty metres he kept his distance, walking through the grass beside the path.

'So, my uncle has been telling you stories about his adventures during the war.'

'You heard?'

'No, I just noticed he was tapping his finger on his glass. During the war he helped a shellshocked first world war veteran defuse unexploded bombs. I guess the sound of ticking is reassuring. He once told me the time to start worrying is when it stops.' Paul sighed, then said, 'So here we are trying to build a perfect world based on the dreams of broken people.' A reference to East Germany perhaps, or just trying to put someone feeling awkward and embarrassed at ease. An ideal time, I thought, to discover what Paul felt about his father having fought with the German army, the question at the top of my list but impossible to ask with the rest of his family present. Unfortunately, it seemed an equally awkward subject now we were alone.

Paul scratched an insect bite on his left hand.

'A run in with the local wildlife?' I suggested.

'Yes,' Paul said holding up his hand, which was still slightly swollen. 'I was sent to the local GP, although it would have probably got better on its own. My father was worried about a reoccurrence of something that landed me in hospital at Christmas. The doctor fixed it with an antihistamine shot.'

'Yes, our health service is very good.'

'But not quite up to the standard of Britain's NHS.'

'Ah, of course everything is better in the capitalist West.'

'Actually, the NHS is an inconvenient illustration that socialism actually works.' The path narrowed as it wound around a fallen tree, and Paul's arm was pressed against mine again. 'I must admit the countryside here makes a pleasant change from London, it's nice to be somewhere quiet, it reminds me of home.'

*Or even Switzerland*, I thought. 'So why didn't your girlfriend come with you?

'She had other plans which didn't involve me,' he replied quickly as if having anticipated the question.

'That's a pity.'

He shrugged. 'Apparently she's met an American studying in Berne and plans to move to New York with him when he graduates.'

'But if she lives in Switzerland and you are in Britain, she was only a pen friend.'

There was a delay before he answered, suggesting this was a key part of his cover story. 'I spent a lot of time studying and earning the money to pay my way through university, so the long-distance relationship suited me. It was fun while it lasted. And why didn't your boyfriend come with you to the party?'

'Erich...' It seemed pointless to continue the pretence. I had been found out and was struggling to think of a half convincing explanation. Luckily one was not necessary.

'It's obvious Erich is not your boyfriend, and I doubt you work in a clothes shop, although I could be wrong, perhaps there is a shelf of psychology books next to the one with those shorts on it which, by the way, really don't suit you.'

The time it had taken to be exposed as a fraud was about as long as it took Erich to become blind drunk. Paul had passed on that message about David Cathcart, although without mentioning the student leader by name. Hüber, Wiedel and Steuernagel would no doubt spend hours, possibly days, attempting to interpret this message. In that case was it really necessary for Paul to make me feel stupid, or was he simply making a point, telling me he understood whatever he said to me would be repeated verbatim to the Stasi? Was that part of his plan? Ironically, I now felt much like Sabine would have done at this point: alone, dejected, insulted and desperate to go home to my mother. In this respect my cover story was still holding up.

It should be remembered Paul was the first overseas visitor I profiled and in future would be better prepared, come across as more convincing and, despite the occasional misstep, never screw up to this degree again. No more total and utter failures. Paul would be the only person in a long list of young men, some who would become leading politicians, journalists and businessmen, whom I made feel at ease while in the DDR and who probably never suspected that everything they said in my company ended up somewhere in the 111 kilometres of files in Normannenstrasse.

Then it was Paul's turn to ask questions. They came in quick succession, mostly about life in the DDR. Despite realising he was now in the presence of someone other than Sabine there was no discernible change in Paul's attitude towards me. Neither did he distance himself, either physically or emotionally, when I told him about Herman who, if he had been here with me, would still be sober and compos mentis although, given that the Anweilers behaved much like the diners at the Luisenhof, we would now be on our way back to Berlin. It was slightly irritating that Paul seemed less interested in me after I told him about Herman's work with Mikroelektronik and the devices it was developing for Robotron.

'I'm working on a robotics project at university,' Paul said, apparently not realising Robotron manufactured computers.

'Herman doesn't work with robots, just microchips.'

'Oh.' Paul sounded slightly deflated, although from his expression I suspected he was anything but.

'Have you ever been to Vienna?' I asked, perhaps feeling inferior in the presence of someone who travelled outside their own country, and, in retrospect, because I wanted him to show an interest in me rather than my boyfriend.

'Yes why?'

'Oh, I've been invited to speak at a conference on psychology there next year.'

'I'll make a note in my diary.'

He was making fun of me again and I felt a mild rebuke was in order. 'You keep a diary? That's surprising.'

'Of course I don't. It's something teenage girls do until they get a boyfriend.' He laughed, then must have realised why I looked down at the ground. 'Oops.' he said.

It felt strange to talk openly about my diary, a confession of sorts, and there seemed no harm in telling someone unlikely to betray me to the Stasi.

From the excited shouts and screams echoing through the trees it was clear the young Anweilers had already reached the lake. There was the sound of a boat bumping against a landing stage and the rattle of oars. But there was no rush on Paul's part to catch up. If anything, he was hanging back, the brisk hurried walk now having become a leisurely stroll.

'Why?'

'Why what?'

'Why do you still keep a diary?'

'One thing you learn when studying psychology is how unreliable your memory is. You'd appreciate this if there was something worthwhile in your life to refer back to.'

He did not even flinch. 'So, you'll be writing all this down,' Paul said. 'And is Erich part of your psychology Phd, or is that when you move on to human physiology? *The subject was immersed in alcohol for two hours and then I carried out a series of simple experiments to assess his ability to string more than three words together and ride a motorbike in a straight line.*' I burst out laughing and we both stopped walking. 'You can borrow my parents if you want a really interesting case study.'

Distracted by the thought of Erich marinating in a vat of beer and schnaps, and the realisation that in a few hours I would be the passenger on the back of the motorbike which he could no longer ride in a straight line, I missed the significance of Paul's remark about his parents.

'So have you been to Vienna before?'

'No,' I replied. 'Have you?'

'I visited Vienna once with my girlfriend.' Did he really have to mention her? 'It was a day trip so we didn't see much of the city, just the usual tourist attractions. We went to the Altstadt but to tell you the truth I can't remember much about it.'

'My point exactly. Now if you kept a diary...'

'Come on,' Paul said and again the offer to take his hand. To my surprise this time his fingers were gently interlaced with mine.

'So, you've never heard of the Frauenhuber Café,' I said, again wanting to appear more worldly wise than the shopgirl I had pretended to be half an hour earlier, perhaps even more interesting than a post-graduate from an East German university.

Immediately Paul let go of my hand and pretended to pat the pockets of an imaginary jacket. 'Frauenhuber Café, you said, I must write that down. Damn, my pen and diary, I must have left them somewhere. Still, perhaps I can commit it to memory.'

We carried on walking, and again Paul took hold of my hand. Reading the account of this exchange it is clear one of us had asked the other out on a date. Which of us did this is still not entirely clear in my mind.

'I'm not sure you would find the conference interesting,' I said.

'I don't know, I'm actually studying psychology.'

'But you said you were an engineer.'

'One of the options is organisational psychology. I think the aim is to teach potential managers how to run rings around trade union officials. In fact I read a paper written by an East German, Kurt Gottschaldt, do you know him?'

'No, I can't say I do,' I lied, now wondering why Paul had mentioned the academic whose name came up during that meeting in Potsdam.

'Of course, I forgot, you only work in a clothes shop.'

'No need to rub it in.'

Reaching the lake, both of us had decided it was unwise to be seen holding hands. In fact Paul took a step to one side so there were at least two metres between us. In front of us a jetty extended out into a lake which was larger than it looked on the map. The boat carrying Petra, Hans and friends was already some distance from the shore.

Hans was pulling furiously on the oars. 'You will have to swim to catch up!' he shouted, and to my surprise, Paul took off his tee-shirt and jeans.

'Sure you won't join me?'

'Definitely not,' I said. 'Hurry up or you'll miss the boat,' I joked, but something caught his eye as I shook my head. It was that stupid pendant around my neck.

There was nothing wrong with Paul's eyesight. He could easily have read the word on the oval shaped piece of metal without his face being so close to mine that I could feel his breath on my chest. There was no need for him to hold the pendant between his fingers, one of which gently stroked my neck.

'Amazing,' he whispered. 'It's very... what's the word I'm looking for? Very modern.'

Why did I find being teased so amusing? Perhaps because it was Sabine, not me, he was making fun of. She, not me, who blushed; she who decided not to stay on the lake shore but follow Paul to the end of the jetty and watch him dive into the water, because of all the mistakes I made that afternoon this one was the most stupid and, ultimately, tragic.

Paul was a strong swimmer and had little difficultly catching up with the boat. On reaching it he placed one hand on the stern and held up the other expecting to be pulled from the water. However instead of doing this Hans used one of the oars to push Paul under the water, leaning on it until all but half a metre was below the surface. 'Take your money belt off and save yourself, you greedy capitalist!' Hans shouted. Some of the boat's occupants laughed; others did not appreciate what I assumed was a joke.

Hans pulled the oar out of the water, holding it as if waiting to strike Paul should he re-emerge, except he did not and the water around the boat slowly settled. At first a few bubbles of air rose to the surface but once these stopped, everyone in the boat, including Hans, fell silent. Already I was feeling faint, aware of the sun on my neck and a dryness in my mouth and throat. There was the feeling, a memory perhaps, of being stood looking across a completely different lake, the one on which my father's body was found floating.

I have no clear idea of the events that followed Paul's drowning, or the order in which they occurred. As soon as I realised what Hans had done, my legs became weak and I started gasping for air as if I too was drowning. Not having suffered an asthma attack for almost a year, I had forgotten the golden rule: never go anywhere without an inhaler. At that moment mine was in my bag, which I had left on a picnic table when Paul invited me to accompany him to the lake.

Which came first – the blow to the head or being pushed into the water? Either way I suspected someone must have followed us from the house and, while I was watching Paul swim out to the boat, crept up behind me.

Next, something in the water was rising to the surface at great speed which, most likely, was my own reflection as I fell from the jetty. Then I sank, deeper and deeper, no matter how hard I struggled.

'Do you think when we die, we meet all those we have lost? I don't believe in life after death but sometimes I think about that.'

Until she mentioned the river, the elderly woman in Dresden had remained composed. During the bombing raid, she, like many other occupants of a city which within a matter of hours became an inferno, sought refuge in the river. Cut off by the flames, she had been unable to return home where other members of her family – her elderly parents and three children – were sheltering in the cellar. Only she survived and, when I interviewed her, still bore the guilt of having done so when others, including her family, had perished.

'Just dust, only dust, all that was left,' she kept repeating, my hand shaking as I tried to remain calm while taking notes. This was the first time I had encountered someone, other than my father, who remained traumatised by things beyond the imagination of a twenty-year-old. Talking to me was supposed to help although I somehow doubt it did. But then came the question she asked herself whenever crossing the Augustus Bridge, when she fantasised about an aquatic afterlife and a reunion with her parents and children. Opening up about this may have put an end to her suicidal thoughts but it also left me with an image of my father's death which has haunted me ever since.

Now it was me under water, and standing in front of me was my father, but only for a few seconds because after that nothing, until a vague recollection of being carried up a flight of steps. 'Please don't, I've done nothing wrong.' Did I just think this, or say it out loud fearing I was on my way upstairs to be beaten senseless by Wilhelm and his colleagues?

I must have passed out again and the next time I regained consciousness was naked, cold and in bed, covered only by a thin sheet. There was a glass of liquid and my inhaler on the small table beside the bed and, on the chair next to the door, a pile of clothes, none of them mine. The room was dark and must have been on the ground floor of the house, because people walking past the window cast shadows on the blind. Someone tried the doorhandle, but the door was locked.

Then voices: 'You're not going in there again, keep away from her. Don't you realise what she is?' *What* as opposed to *who*, and now everyone was speaking openly about a Stasi informer in their midst. Footsteps grew fainter as the two people who had been talking about me walked away. The room where I lay must have been next to the one with tables of food, the television and a bar. Perhaps it was Erich who had tried the door.

'What the hell were you thinking bringing her here?' Petra, presumably talking to Erich. 'I don't suppose you've noticed those two men in the car parked down the road.'

'What two men?'

'My god, you really are stupid.'

'OK, OK I'll take her back to Berlin.'

'When? We can't wait for you to sober up, she's got to go now.'

Then another voice: Hans. 'Look, Erich why don't you go and built sandcastles down by the lake and leave the grownups to sort this out.'

'Ask Klein to come downstairs, he can do it,' Petra shouted and suddenly I was feeling very cold because I assumed Klein was the person who Wilhelm Anweiler had followed upstairs.

'Have you called a doctor?' Hans asked.

'You must be joking.'

'Well, have you given her anything?'

Then another voice, one I recognised although immediately dismissed the idea it was him standing on the other side of the door. 'I've given her some Kaempferol and Chlorogenic acid. That should do the trick.' Then he laughed and there was another argument ending only when Petra insisted everyone shut up and left it to her to sort out. *It* again. I was being regarded as an object rather than a person.

As the key turned in the lock, I reached for my inhaler, making sure to knock the glass over. Its contents spread across the table and dripped onto the floor.

The door open and Petra came in. 'How are you feeling?' she asked, not even pretending to care. She righted the glass. 'Oh dear,' she said under her breath. 'There are some clothes on the chair by the door, yours are still wet. I will dry them, and Erich will drop them back to you.' She picked up the neatly folded clothes – jeans, a man's shirt, socks, bra and panties – and placed them on the bed. The underwear was still wrapped and had been bought from a shop called Marks and Spencer in Britain; the jeans had a label with the word Barney's on it. On top of the clothes was the pendant.

As calm as the Anweilers appeared on the surface, I sensed panic and suspected my fate might be determined by the throw of a dice and it would be Klein who threw it. If he had decided the best course of action was to kill me and dispose of my body in the forest, I would certainly be a well-dressed corpse. Should it ever be found, those who discovered it might wonder why it was wearing a kaftan purchased from a store in London. Perhaps the western clothes were to fool the police into thinking the body was that of someone from the West.

Petra returned holding a carrier bag. She too was wearing a kaftan. 'We are going out this way,' she said, walking past me and opening a second door into a corridor leading to a kitchen. It was now clear the bed I had been lying on for the past hour was in a room which once belonged to a servant or housekeeper, and there was a second set of stairs to the rooms above.

Klein was leaning against the wall at the bottom of the stairs. 'Ready, then,' he said, opening a side door from which I could see Erich's motorbike still leaning against the tree and the van with its side door open.

Petra walked to the front of the van and held the passenger door open, making it clear she expected me to climb in. 'Be with you in a moment, the boys are just bringing something down from upstairs that we need to get rid of.'

'Sorry, would it be possible to have my bag?' I asked.

Petra reached into the carrier bag and took out the shoulder bag which looked fine when I was dressed as Sabine but childishly stupid carried by someone made out to look like a western style hippy. Two deep breaths using my inhaler and I felt slightly better. Still terrified but no longer feeling I was about to faint.

There was a sickening bump in the back of the van then the sound of Klein's boys scrambling in through the side door and slamming it shut behind them. Klein got into the driver's seat while Petra squeezed onto the passenger seat beside me. 'It's still there,' Klein muttered as the van reached the road, obviously referring to the Lada. To my surprise, the van turned left rather than right, driving away from where Steuernagel and the fat man sat watching the house; or were supposed to be watching, because both were leaning forward and listening to the radio the fat man was holding.

Then a second surprise, because after just a few hundred metres the van slowed and instead of disappearing along a track into the forest as I feared it might, Klein brought it to a halt in front of Rethen railway station.

It took time to gather my thoughts – too long for Petra. 'Quick,' she snapped. 'The train will be here in a few minutes.'

Rather than just leaving me alone on the platform Petra stood with me. She checked the timetable and then lit a cigarette and offered one to me.

'I don't smoke,' I told her.

'I'm guessing the two men sitting in the car know that, so just put it in your mouth.' She held the packet in front of me. After I reluctantly put the cigarette between my lips, Petra lit it. 'For God's sake don't inhale otherwise you'll be on your back again.' She glanced towards where the Lada was parked. Even if we could have been seen from that distance Steuernagel would have assumed Petra was merely saying goodbye to a friend. 'I'm afraid Erich can be a shit sometimes. His heart is in the right place, but his brain is somewhere up his arse. There's a few things for you to take home,' she said, handing me the carrier bag.

From the train I watched Petra walking back to the house, waving frantically in my direction; possibly the most insincere goodbye to a friend I have ever witnessed. And totally unnecessary as the two men charged with ensuring I came to no harm had allowed me to be taken away under their very noses.

Putting my Sabine costume on in a toilet at the university, earlier that day, had avoided my mother asking why I was going out half dressed. My everyday clothes were in a box under my desk. The intention was to change back into them before going home. Then only the bananas, oranges, a kiwi fruit, biscuits and coffee would require an explanation. They could have been dropped into a litter bin but why deny my mother a rare treat. So, I made up a story, one Ursula might also believe and, as my sister could not keep a secret, one Herman might find credible. That evening my mother and I shared the gift from a grateful student from West Berlin who needed help with their thesis. The clothes were hidden in a suitcase where they remained for the next 44 years.

Less easy to explain were the shouts from my bedroom during the following week. It hardly seemed fair to tell mother that memories of my father had come back to haunt me big time. Sometimes a problem shared is two people, rather than one, unable to sleep at night.

# 17

# Once in a Green Moon

My account of what happened at the Anweiler party took up three pages in my diary; the report I typed and hand-delivered to Normannenstrasse, for the attention of Hubert Hüber, filled only one side of a foolscap sheet of paper.

Then nothing for over a month, save the arrival of an envelope containing a copy of the Anweiler family photograph taken at Rethen and a book of poems – *Grüner Mond Von Alabama* by Bertolt Brecht – posted to me at the university with a note from Hüber:

*Lotte, Paul Anweiler purchased a copy of this book when he was here. Some poems he took a particular interest in.*

Presumably members of the Anweiler family had been questioned while their memories were still fresh, perhaps the day after their relatives returned to Britain. Their recollections of the party would have been compared with mine and the inevitable discrepancies identified. I was surprised Hüber, Steuernagel and Weidel had not asked for my side of the story but even so, in anticipation they would do so at some point, spent every free moment mentally rehearsing my defence. However, as time passed, I came around to the idea that as the operation had been a disaster Hüber had decided the less said about it the better. Perhaps, following Paul's drowning, the Anweiler affair became too sensitive for the eyes and ears of a lowly academic and part-time Stasi informer.

Life moved on and, as traumatic as the Anweiler party had been, the prospect of presenting my research in Vienna the following year, rather than the drowning of an Englishman, occupied my thoughts. And there was Herman, of course, and speculation by my mother, sister and friends that he might be summoning up the courage to propose.

It was midday on Friday, the 19<sup>th</sup> of September 1975: the diary entry for the previous day included a reminder Herman was spending the weekend in Berlin. So, when approached by a secretary while sitting in the university's canteen and given a note with a telephone number and the word *urgent* written on it, I presumed it was my future fiancé, not Hubert Hüber, who had ruined my lunch.

'Lotte, sorry this is short notice, but would you be kind enough to give us a few moments of your time this afternoon? We are discussing Paul Anweiler's visit. Three pm here in Normannenstrasse. It would help if you could bring all the relevant material you have.'

Hüber had left me insufficient time to return home, collect the relevant material he referred to and still make the meeting. By chance, the copy of Brecht's book was in my desk drawer along with notes I had made regarding some of the poems. The short trip on the U-Bahn was spent recalling and ordering events I had pushed to the back of my mind.

'So, you disappeared midway through the party,' Steuernagel said in a matter-of-fact way as if only mentioning it in passing, as he opened the file in front of him which was now ten millimetres thicker than the last time I saw it. 'Decided not to stay to the end?'

Again Hüber, Weidel and Steuernagel were seated facing me across the table in the conference room next to Hüber's office, only this time empty chairs separated the three men. It was as if Hüber was trying to distance himself from the other two agents.

Twice now, a mere novice had outwitted Steuernagel and the fat man – admittedly both times with someone's help. Humiliating, and thanks to a little research I had carried out – nothing more taxing than checking the sports page of a back issue of the Berliner Zeitung – the reputation of the hapless Stasi agent would take another knock.

'Having gained sufficient information to form an opinion on Paul Anweiler, and suspecting he realised I was not actually Sabine the shop worker, I felt it best to leave. As, due to excessive consumption of alcohol, the person you arranged to take me to and bring me back from the party was indisposed I returned to Berlin by train. I left the party at three-thirty, there was a radio playing and Berlin Dynamo had just scored against Vorwärts Frankfurt. When I walked to the railway station you and your colleague were in a car parked on the road outside, you must have seen me.'

'Actually, Berlin Dynamo hadn't score by three thirty.' Steuernagel said, and I now knew how Bernd Brillat felt when presented with an open goal.

'My apologies Comrade Steuernagel, I was busy at the time and unlike yourself wasn't able to listen to the whole match.'

Wiedel smiled, as did Hüber.

But Steuernagel was not amused. 'Perhaps you would like to talk us through your report,' he said, glaring at me.

'There was something that struck me as odd about the car Klaus Anweiler was driving. The registration, MFS.' I said.

Weidel laughed 'A simple explanation, FS indicates Klaus purchased a car registered in Edinburgh, the M and the number...' he referred to his notes. '...a hundred and forty-two, indicates how many cars were registered in the city that year. So perhaps nothing more than a coincidence.'

'Or perhaps not,' Hüber said. 'Last year, when Klaus decided to take a shortcut when driving from Bremerhaven to Berlin and left the corridor...'

'Restricted corridor,' Steuernagel corrected him.

Seeming slightly annoyed at being interrupted Hüber continued '...how many people contacted us to let us know that an unauthorised foreign vehicle had travelled through their town or village?' A rhetorical question and Hüber did not wait for an answer. 'Even when the Anweiler family stopped for lunch at an inn just outside Templin, where they could sit outside and watch jet fighters taking off and landing at the nearby Soviet airbase? Obviously, their visit attracted the attention of the local population, especially young men who had rarely seen cars other than Wartburgs, Trabants and Ladas. I should imagine the Anweilers now own one of the most photographed cars in the DDR. But only one person contacted us. They were asked to check the car's registration and phone back. They never did. Even the policemen called to break up the crowd after news of the strange car spread, assumed, given the car's registration, that the incident had something to do with us. And so did our Soviet comrades when the Anweiler's car cruised past the main entrance to the airbase.'

Steuernagel found this amusing, the first time he'd laughed since I had cut him down to size. 'What was it the security officer said? *Is this some sort of test because if the Amis do attack, I'm not sure they will turn up wearing sports jackets and summer dresses.*'

Hüber ignored this and adopted a more serious tone. 'The Anweilers' sightseeing trip took in at least two airbases and one Soviet logistics centre, and then there was a stop to stretch their legs on the road between Hammelspring and Vogelsang.'

'Shit. That's not good.' Said Steuernagel.

'Something of an understatement Otto.'

'On the other hand, they could have simply been taking a short cut to Gladowshöhe,' Wiedel suggested. 'It is worth keeping in mind how the British secret service would have responded to Klaus Anweiler's belated decision to return to the DDR. They would have been aware of our attempts to recruit him, and this would have prompted them to do the same. Perhaps he chose the car's registration simply to poke fun at both us and the British.'

Steuernagel spotted something in his copy of my report. 'You can tell us something about the Anweilers' sense of humour because it says here Klaus's brother, Wilhelm, spent most of his time at the party telling jokes.' He had not, but I stretched the truth to cover the time Wilhelm spent in the upstairs room of the house. 'That's when he wasn't talking about Soviet troop movements on the Afghanistan border.'

A simple 'Yes' from me did not suffice.

'These jokes, please enlighten us.'

'Well, there was a silly one about a man having his thumb trapped in a train door.' I repeated it although I couldn't remember the punchline. The second joke I had not forgotten; it was about a young member of the communist party being considered for promotion.

*Would you give up your sports car and forgo your expensive holidays if requested to do so by the Party?*

*Obviously, without a doubt.*

*And the dacha in the countryside?*

*Yes, of course.*

*And your boat?*

*Without a moment's hesitation.*

*And your bicycle?*

*Silence.*

*Is there a problem, Comrade?*

*Just a small one.*

*Please explain?*

*Well, I've actually got a bicycle.*

Only Hüber laughed although Weidel smiled to himself.

'Given where the party was held, I think that was inappropriate. Didn't anyone point this out at the time?' Steuernagel asked.

'Klaus Anweiler made some comment but, other than that, I think most people found it very funny.'

'And did you find it amusing?' Steuernagel was definitely on the attack.

Fortunately, Hüber came to my rescue. 'You said Klaus did not find this amusing. Do you think this gives us an insight into his political leanings?'

'I don't think so, I replied. 'There was a certain amount of tension between the two brothers, personal rather than anything to do with their respective political beliefs.'

'And tension between other family members, the two cousins, for example.' Steuernagel said without looking up from my report. My description of what happened at the lake was one of a group of young people swimming and sunbathing, without any mention of the drowning. 'Did you bring the book and photograph we sent you?' I hesitated as this was the last thing I expected to be asked at that point.

'There wasn't time to return home for the photograph, but I've got the book,' I said, taking the copy of *Gruner Mond Von Alabama* from my shoulder bag.

'Sorry, you're keeping confidential information in your home?' Steuernagel sneered.

Again Hüber was there to defend me. 'With respect, Otto, where else is Lotte to keep it?' .

But Steuernagel's tone of voice was just as aggressive when he said. 'OK then, if all you have is the book, we'll make do with that. You will have noticed, I hope, that the corners of two pages, eighty and ninety-eight, were folded. What did you deduce from that?'

'Well, the poem on page eighty was *Praise of Communism*, perhaps this is how Paul Anweiler sees, or wants us to believe he sees, Cathcart. I'm assuming he knew that we would gain access to the book, given he left it beside his bed in his uncle's house. He is telling us he feels Cathcart was misunderstood. In the man, woman and sixty-year-olds mentioned in the last lines of the poem, he may see his parents and other older members of his family. This is a poem Paul would have chosen to convince us he was considering rebelling against capitalism and embracing communism.'

'And the poem on page ninety-eight?'

'Yes, *Kuppelied*... this I think may be a reference to his relationship with the girl in Switzerland which has now ended. Perhaps for Maria we can read Christina, and the fact the girl in which he invested so much has now taken up with an American has made him realise Christina has been a distraction and this too has caused a reassessment of his political beliefs.' Omitted, for obvious reasons, was the reference to the sight of the red moon on the water, and a man making girls weak at the knees, which reminded me of standing next to Paul on the shore of the lake and fantasising he saw in me Brecht's Maria.

'Excellent analysis from our expert in psychology.' Steuernagel's slow handclap foretold what was about to come, although it was hard to imagine a takedown quite like the one that followed.

'Perhaps Lotte would like to hear our expert analysis.' Steuernagel suggested to no one in particular. 'On the ninth of August, and pay close attention to the date, the Anweiler family, Paul included, set off by bus from Gladowshöhe to Erkner where they caught an S-Bahn train to the centre of Berlin. On its way into the city the train passed through Karlshorst where there were two battalions of soviet tanks. These eighty tanks, again take note of the number, were waiting to be loaded onto trains once another fifteen arrived from exercises on Tangersdorfer Heide. According to interviews with the Anweilers, the first thing Paul did when the family arrived in Berlin was visit a bookshop in Alexandra Platz and purchase a book of poems by Brecht, much like the one Lotte has in front of her.' Given he never made it home I suspected it might well be the same one Paul purchased.

'And what did our visitor from Britain then do?' Steuernagel reached across the table and pulled the book towards him to use as a prop in the piece of theatre which followed. 'He then took it to a café and thumbed through the pages, not looking for poems which chimed with his inner torment but using the book to record two pieces of information: Eighty tanks waiting at Karlshorst on the ninth day of the eighth month: nine, eight. Pages eighty and ninety-eight.' Steuernagel stared at me. I was hoping Hüber would come to my rescue, but he simply sat looking slightly embarrassed. Weidel's thoughts were obviously elsewhere. He lit a cigarette which he stubbed out when Hüber reminded him I suffered from asthma, which only served to make me feel even more inadequate.

It was while watching the smoke curl upwards that I saw there was a nougat bar wrapper in the ashtray, neatly folded by the person who, during an earlier meeting, had been seated where I was now, someone either obsessive or just as nervous as myself.

A triumphant Steuernagel was not finished. It was not enough he had won; I had to be seen to lose. 'And I wonder where all those tanks were going?' he asked, again pretending to search the single page of my report for an answer. 'Ah yes, here it is, the conversation you overheard between Wilhelm and his bother Klaus, Soviet tanks on their way to the Afghan border to put pressure on Mohannad Daoud Khan.'

'It's possible he could have got this information from someone else,' I suggested.

'Who exactly, given the Anweilers were under pain of death not to let the visitors from Britain out of their sight? The only people he talked to were members of his own family. God knows where Wilhelm Anweiler got the information about the tanks, gossip, most likely. But it was obvious Paul Anweiler, or whoever was pretending to be Klaus Anweiler's son, intended to take this information back to Britain with him. I guess when he saw those tanks parked at Karlshorst he couldn't believe his luck.'

There followed a half-hour grilling during which Steuernagel challenged every aspect of my report. Eventually Hüber did intervene. He turned to Weidel whose role at the meeting had been that of observer rather than participant. 'Any thoughts on where we go next?'

Not based on the information to hand Wiedel felt. 'Paul Anweiler seems to be warning us off Cathcart, suggesting he is a spent force, as are his former associates who are still at the university. What was it he said, Lotte? *They give up on Marx when they get the keys to their first house?*

'Something along those lines,' I replied.

'From what Otto has discovered, it appears Anweiler has brought us a story scripted by the British secret service, to turn our attention away from both Cathcart and our contact at the university where young Anweiler is studying. On the other hand, none of the other information, his contact in the wireless monitoring section of the US embassy or details of his employment with the defence contractor, which he was obviously supposed to feed us, was mentioned during his visit.' Weidel shrugged. 'Who knows, perhaps he was just told to muddy the water, get us chasing shadows. On the strength of what I've heard here today I doubt we will be contacting David Cathcart directly. Perhaps I will ask one of our people in London to arrange a meeting with that student who approached us two years ago during the World Youth Festival. Maybe they can provide some clarity, although I seriously doubt it.' Weidel looked first at Hüber and then back at me.

'I must say it would have been helpful if you had spent a little more time with Paul Anweiler and not become distracted by that book of poems.' Which was a little unfair as it was Hüber who had thrown this into the mix, and Steuernagel who withheld key information regarding how Paul Anweiler had used it. But as Steuernagel had already slid my report into the folder in front of him and pushed the copy of Brecht's book back across the table so hard it almost fell in my lap, there seemed little point in trying to defend myself.

Perhaps on the off-chance I had intended to rescue my reputation, Steuernagel provided a parting shot. 'Espionage is not as portrayed in the movies, Lotte. Not car chases around Berlin and romantic encounters with foreign agents. Most of the time it's mundane and, quite frankly, just plain boring.' I was tempted to mention it also seemed to involve a lot of time sitting in a car listening to football matches but thought better of it.

'There was no need to overthink the Paul Anweiler affair, complicate or intellectualise it, and in retrospect it might have been better to leave it to us professionals.' Steuernagel added, then turned to Hüber. 'I don't think we need to detain the young lady further.'

Hüber agreed. 'No, thank you for all your help. I will see you out.' He said and only spoke again when we reached the bottom of the stairs in reception. 'Don't take what was just said to heart, people are merely protecting their backs. Especially those who have been asleep, or even listening to the radio, on the job. You can keep the jeans and kaftan as a reward for a job well done.'

Perhaps one of the Anweilers had told the Stasi how I managed to slip away unnoticed, although it was also possible Hüber, not trusting Steuernagel and the fat man, sent someone else to the Anweiler party. If he did so, they were equally incompetent. 'Erich brought us your shorts and tee-shirt, but I'm guessing you're not interested in having these back.' Hüber smiled and shook my hand. 'Oh, by the way, he added as an afterthought, 'I'll be in touch about the conference in Vienna. You may well get your visit to the café Frauenhuber after all.' This I very much doubted and my chances of being trusted enough to travel to the West seemed remote.

Steuernagel may have had a deep understanding of espionage and was perhaps looked on with awe by colleagues in the Stasi, although this I sincerely doubted, but he was no academic. Rule number one, in my book at least, was never commit the best parts of your research to overhead transparencies or give too much away in the abstract. Instead, hold something back to wow delegates on the day. So it was with my report on Paul Anweiler. The bullet points were all there, but the best bits were in my diary and committed to memory. Had there been time to return home to collect these, the meeting would have played out a lot differently, and I might well have ended up, both metaphorically and literally, digging my own grave.

So, what did Steuernagel miss? Not Wilhelm Anweiler's comment about the tanks on the Afghanistan border, they were in the report. Missing, however, was the observation his nephew Paul, rather than being the recipient of this information, might have been its source. The claim that members of his family had watched over Paul during every minute of his visit was false; he was sent, rather than taken, to the GP for that antihistamine shot. I had telephoned the medical centre at Fürstenwalde and explained I was in Gladowshöhe, had been stung by a wasp and needed to see a GP. Apparently the closest was in Hohenstein, three kilometres away. This was a long walk during which Paul could have met any number of people, including a KGB colonel who was residing in the house next to Wilhelm Anweiler's for the duration of Paul Anweiler's stay in the DDR.

In my report the interaction between Hans and Paul Anweiler was described as antagonistic. Had I got the chance, and felt inclined, I would have mentioned how Hans's mood changed when Paul mentioned he already owned a house, not something a student would have possessed. It had been at this point during the party Hans must have suspected, as I did, Paul was not all he seemed. Not the long-lost cousin but someone come to spy on the family. An interloper who it was better did not return to the West, telling tales of Stasi beatings continuing in secret.

As Paul had realised the story about me being a shopgirl was a lie, very little of what was said during our walk to the lake made it into the report. No mention of the interest in VEB Mikroelektronik or Robotron; why involve Herman in this? The revelation that the corners of those two pages in Brecht's book had been folded before we met, and Maria in the poem related to neither Christina or myself, left me feeling slightly deflated.

Weidel could have told me Paul had studied psychology; had he done so I would have trodden more carefully, and my cover story might have held up. Quite possibly this key piece of information was withheld so that Weidel and Steuernagel could ambush me at the meeting. It was while contemplating this that I imagined, had he survived, Paul being subjected to an interrogation similar to mine. Would this have been at the hands of people just as aggressive as Steuernagel? *'So what was all that crap about Vienna and this café, what was it called, Frauenhuber? Is she going to turn up with an envelope of secret documents from Mikroelektronik or is she just looking to escape from the Soviet shithole which is East Berlin?'*

Even had he not suspected his friend Trixy was not all she seemed, Paul, like me, might have wondered if there was someone hiding in the shadows, someone who had been in the room briefing his interrogators before he arrived. And I kept thinking about that chocolate bar wrapper in the ashtray and the way it was folded neatly into a square.

*'Well, Anweiler, what was she; a defector, a honey trap or a spy? Perhaps you should have asked her out on a date.'*

He did not but instead ended up at the bottom of a lake, or so it appeared at the time.

# 18

# Breakfast on the Elbe

### May 2019

The alarm on my phone woke me at 8:30, the diary for 1975 had fallen on the floor during the night and the one covering the events of 1978 still lay on the bed, open at the page I was reading before I fell asleep. After showering I packed my suitcase and took the lift up to the restaurant with the envelope containing the 5,000 euros in my shoulder bag. I intended the meeting to be short and not include breakfast with Mr Anweiler.

'This is good,' Paul said. 'If I go to heaven the first thing I'll do is order a German breakfast.' Where he was going when he died, the coffee would evaporate before it could be drunk, the cheese melt, and the salami would be black around the edges. Breakfast was being served in a large room on the top floor of the hotel which creaked and groaned each time the building was caught by a gust of wind. Disconcertingly the low cloud moving overhead created the illusion of being on a boat floating above the farmland and forests while tracking the Elbe on its journey to the North Sea.

'I'll get you something from the buffet, what would you like?' Paul asked, getting to his feet.

'Nothing,' I said, slightly more sharply than I intended. 'This won't take long. I'm having breakfast when I get to Wittenberge.' Paul ignored the envelope that landed on the table in front of him and instead bit into a piece of black bread covered with a slice of cheese then washed it down with a mouthful of coffee. 'It's all there, you can count it.' I said.

'I seldom count money. We pay people to do that for us.'

Ignoring this remark I said. 'I'll take my chances with the tabloids.'

'Fine.' He had moved onto the Salami and poured a second cup of coffee which he pushed across the table. Had my mouth not been so dry, as it was most mornings, the result of sleeping with my mouth open according to Herman, a polite way of pointing out I snored, the coffee would have been left to go cold. Instead, the first sip inadvertently confirmed I was prepared to engage with this person, whoever he was or at least was pretending to be.

'If you really are Paul Anweiler your family are a bunch of torturers and murderers. The other possibility is that you are impersonating him and it was Paul I watched drown.'

'Really?' He seemed neither shocked nor surprised by what I said. Then why should he? Even if he was not present at the party, everything that happened that afternoon was in my diaries, copies of which he would have had access to between the two burglaries of my house. And I was at a disadvantage not knowing what happened after falling, or being pushed, into the lake and waking up sometime later, especially if this person sitting across the table from me had met someone who did.

Paul was watching the traffic on the bridge spanning the Elbe. 'If you are going to dispose of a body, that's the place to do it. It will wash out into the sea and never be seen again. Throw it into a lake and one day it will float to the surface, like one of those memories you spend all your life trying to suppress.'

When someone hits you in the stomach you know about it pretty much straight away. But after what Paul said it took at least five seconds before I felt a dull ache in my abdomen and found it increasingly difficult to breathe. Replacing the coffee cup in its saucer hoping the person sitting opposite me would not notice my hand shaking, I said, 'I'll have something to eat after all.' Then got up from the table and walked to the buffet.

Having regained my composure I returned to the table with a tray of food – scrambled egg on toast, a Greek yoghurt and a pot of tea. Paul, now wearing glasses, was reading through the page of instructions which had been in the envelope. The envelope itself, presumably with the 5,000 euros still inside it, was on my side of the table and I moved it to make room for the tray.

'I love these,' Paul said reaching across to take the yoghurt. I rapped him across the knuckles with a spoon, a reflex action because Herman thought it amusing to steal food I was about to eat.

Paul was wearing jeans, there was a waterproof anorak hanging on the back of his chair and a rucksack on the floor beside the table. 'No stick then, and hiking, something of a miraculous recovery since your visit to Lychen.'

'I never thought I needed one but was pestered to carry it.'

'And the pest who was with you in Lychen isn't with you today.'

'Only in spirit, they have booked me into hotels ten kilometres apart instead of the usual twenty. It's going to take an age to reach Berlin.'

'I can give you a lift as far as Templin tomorrow.'

'You're not going home today?'

'No, like I said, I'm on my way to Wittenberge.'

'Well, that's two hundred kilometres in the wrong direction.'

'Not that Wittenberg, if fact my son says his hotel is just one *e* away from being worth a fortune. Although it does well in the summer, lots of cyclists and hikers. I take it you won't be hiking in that direction.'

'No, I'm following the Elbe to Lenzen then heading East to Perleberg.'

'An odd route, why not through Kärstadt?'

'I'm taking someone home.' There were a few businessmen in the restaurant and a group of tourists, but no one dressed for hiking. 'So did you bring the tape?' he asked, removing his glasses and studying my face.

'No.'

'The correct answer was *What tape?*'

He was right and my response had inadvertently conjured the tape into existence.

'Oh well.' Paul sighed as he watched a barge plough through the water on its sluggish journey upstream.

'My son has bought a boat,' I said, rather than talk about the tape, Geoffrey Cathcart or anything written on the single A4 piece of paper on the table. 'He is going to offer cruises along the Elbe to hotel guests.'

'Is the Elbe is deep enough?'

'It's a flat-bottomed boat, apparently, and he is also going to use it for events. Ossie Rock on The Elbe.'

Paul laughed. 'Well, if he books Ramstein I hope he's got fire insurance.'

'Ramstein wasn't an East German band.'

'Til Lindemann was born in Leipzig and was playing in a band called First Arsch in nineteen eighty-six. Richard Kruspe lived just a few hundred metres from your son's hotel and started out in a band called Das Elegante Chaos in the nineteen eighties, so I guess that makes Ramstein a potential signing for one of the Ossie Rock cruises.'

'An expert on rock music or a misspent youth?' Although I should have asked how he knew where in Wittenberge Peter's hotel was located.

'A friend of mine invests in the media industry. I don't suppose your son is looking for a business partner?'

'No, thank you.' I said turning away so as not to be facing him when declining this offer. 'Actually, he has already got someone helping him fit out the boat.'

'I see.' Paul folded the page of instructions and pushed it into the pocket of his jeans.

'What will your friends do now?' I asked.

A disinterested shake of the head. 'Who knows, but it's not your problem. The press won't be camped outside your door because, as you probably know, there are laws preventing that here in Germany.' His tone had changed since our previous meeting. 'Just someone panicking at the thought of having a prime minister who was, and perhaps still is at heart, a Marxist. They'll get over it because so were most Labour leaders at some point during their careers and Britain stayed within the US's orbit. I don't think anyone believes that the day after Geoffrey Cathcart is elected, Putin will sail a nuclear sub up the Thames.' Paul appeared to give this some thought, stroking his neck with his thumb and forefinger causing me to wonder if he realised some men did this when attempting to seduce a woman.

'My guess is it was decided something had to be done and this was that something. The tape was probably just belts and braces because Cathcart will have already been invited for a friendly chat, told the limits to any reforms he might have planned for Britain's security services and warned against doing anything that might jeopardise the country's security.'

'Or its special relationship with America.'

'Which some regard as the same thing. The tape would never have provided a knockout punch. If they wanted to stop him being Prime Minister, a few concocted stories going viral on social media would do the trick.'

'So, you are wasting my time and their money.'

'To a point, but if Cathcart could be persuaded that its contents were about to appear in the German press, he would realise there was more to come and perhaps guess there were other tapes. He might well be forever grateful to an organisation which was able to kill the story. After all, in retrospect it might have appeared statesmanlike to act as an arbiter between the East and West but only his diehard followers believe he was instrumental in bringing down the Berlin Wall. Most people in Britain would regard the contents of the tape as confirmation Cathcart was prepared to surrender to an enemy which was already beaten.'

'I can see how you might get a newspaper interested in the tape. But how do you intend to prevent them publishing its contents once they have it?'

'I must admit this is something of a work in progress.'

'My God, what a bunch of amateurs.'

'Maybe, but Britain's MI5 and MI6 are still there, and the Stasi are long gone,' Paul said, getting to his feet.

'I'm serious about the lift to Berlin by the way. Will you and your friend make it to Perleberg by tomorrow evening?'

'I hope so, I'm booked into the Deutscher Kaiser.'

'You seemed to have lost your friend on the way.'

Paul looked puzzled. 'Sorry?' he said.

'You said *I'm booked in*. Which suggests you will be on your own.'

Paul sat down again and poured me another glass of tea and himself a coffee, then sat staring down at the track running alongside the Elbe, once used by vehicles that patrolled the East German border.

'My father stood down there in May nineteen forty five. A week earlier he was just south of Joachimsthal, part of the mythical Steiner Army, you've probably seen the *Downfall* parodies on YouTube. He'd been on the way to Stettin but the Red Army crossed the Oder and had already reached Angemünde and Bernau so the train was stuck at Eberswalde. The previous December he'd returned from the Eastern front to find the house he helped his father build near Gladowshöhe had been destroyed in a bombing raid.'

'But your grandparents weren't killed.'

'No, they were due to move in the following week and were sheltering in a cellar in the village.' Paul was now looking out of the window at the forest stretching as far as the eye could see to the east.

Eventually he seemed to remember I was sitting opposite him. 'This part of the story, the house in the field, he only told me during a visit to his old home just before he died. Part of his life story which wasn't supposed to end up being mine.

'With the house gone he had spent that Christmas with the rest of his family in the village's mill. *The calm before the storm* was how he described it. The relationship with his mother had always been strained.' Klaus Anweiler's upbringing seemed similar to that of my patient Rolf. 'That was forgotten as he was all that protected her from marauding hordes of Russians headed her way. Although when they did arrive, he wasn't at home but amongst the young boys and old men that now made up his battalion.'

Around the time the Führer was foaming at the mouth and breaking pencils, my father was already heading west. Along the way he ended up hiding in a barn while a column of Red Army trucks rolled past. A tyre on one of them blew just in front of the barn. He knew what happened to soldiers captured in small groups.' Recalling that discussion with Shetlov it was obvious how. 'My father described the thirty minutes it took the driver to change the wheel as feeling like an eternity. He and what remained of his battalion fought their way through the Russian lines just north of Perleberg and surrendered to the US army down there.' Again, Paul was looking out of the window at the east bank of the Elbe.

'It was assumed that once they defeated the German army, the Americans would declare war on the Soviet Union. And that was probably why they had decided to fight in Europe as well as the Pacific. The worldview of German soldiers who had bought into Bismark's and Clausewitz's idea that peace was only a breathing space to prepare for the next war. By summer, Berlin would be free and my father would be home with his parents and rebuilding that house.'

'But obviously that didn't happen. Do you regret that?'

'I've never given it a lot of thought. Perhaps I should have. Anyway, all the rubbish talked about alternative histories is pointless.' He waited for a reaction.' In my opinion,' he added when one was not forthcoming.

'That's a cop-out if ever I heard one.'

Paul ignored the remark. 'The Americans crossed back over the Elbe and handed their prisoners to the British. He was still armed so hadn't given up on getting home. But that never happened. Eventually the British set up speakers and broadcast a warning to their three hundred thousand prisoners that anyone found still carrying a gun would be shot. So he buried his. I should imagine Lüneburg Heath is a metal detectorist's heaven. He was put to work on a farm near Bremen. That's where he was when he got news his mother had died, a combination of malnutrition and pneumonia. On one of our visits to Gladowshöhe we spent a few hours searching for her grave in the forest but my uncle couldn't remember where she was buried.'

'Or didn't want reminding.'

'Perhaps, although ironically, we found the last resting place of the bomber which destroyed the house. Apparently, each year flowers were left on the crash site. Someone's mother must have loved them enough to go through all the bother of getting a visa and explaining to some spotty-faced border guard why they were visiting the DDR.'

'Or simply telephoned Interflora.'

'Now you're being cynical.'

Had Paul been one of my patients, a short note referencing this remark would have been added to my notes. Not when he made it but sometime later, out of his sight, because I suspected he was clever enough to know how to game a session. Confirmation of this came with what he said next.

'Your father was at Stalingrad, wasn't he? Post-Traumatic Stress Disorder wasn't a thing back then. Even if it had been there was no more sympathy for former German soldiers in Britain than there was in East Germany. My father was left fighting his old battles in his sleep every night for the next twenty years.'

'But recovered.'

'Yes, oddly enough when I reached the age he had been when he was called up to fight.'

'Interesting.' I said and was now thinking about my own father and how my life would have turned out had he not died when I was twelve.

'There's a lot that only made sense in retrospect. One was a remark by the person my father and two other German prisoners were billeted with when they were put to work on a farm in Britain. Apparently, he never had to tend his garden for those two years because my father did this in his spare time. My father said he did this rather than sit around moping like his two homesick colleagues, but this was a lie. What he did was co-opt the garden and turn it into a facsimile of the allotment his father owned when the family lived in Adlershof. A hint of what was to come because when freed he set about building a house which, in his mind, was the reconstruction in Britain of the one in Gladowshöhe and no doubt he imagined, when it was finished, his mother would appear at the door and it would be Christmas nineteen forty-four again. Then the guilt which had plagued him since he emerged from that barn after the Russians had moved on, and he decided to continue fighting his way west towards the Americans rather than return to Berlin to protect his family, would simply evaporate.

'The house was finished and, no surprise, my grandmother didn't show. But never mind, just try again. From the age of eight I mixed cement, carried bricks and waded through mud on building sites. My life became some sort of Groundhog Day, trapped with him in a reimagining of those six months between his return home to Berlin from the Eastern front and him hiding in that barn somewhere out there.' The way Paul was looking out of the window at the expanse of trees to the east I suspected he knew where that barn was.

'He was happy with this, less so the rest of us who lived in this make-believe world with him.' Paul's mother came to mind, sitting alone and ignored at the party, and at the time I suspected she filled a void in her husband's life which no longer existed during the family's two-week stay in East Germany.

It then occurred to me why Paul had been so comfortable with that strange long-distance relationship with the Swiss girl. 'Did you ever see that girl again, what was her name? Christine, wasn't it?' This must have seemed to come out of the blue. A sharp stick pushed into an open wound, if this was indeed the person I had spoken with as we walked hand in hand through the trees in Rethen all those years ago.

'Christina,' Paul corrected me eventually. 'Yes, in a manner of speaking, during a trip to New York in nineteen eighty-seven.' I was about to ask what he meant by *in a manner of speaking*. But he recovered and went on the attack. 'Do you resent your father?' he asked. Attacking because he probably felt this was the best form of defence after guessing I understood the role Christina played in his life.

Paul was cornered but I inadvertently allowed him to escape by asking. 'What do you mean?'

'Well, if he hadn't committed suicide, you would have spent the rest of your childhood next to the Weissensee. An upmarket part of East Berlin, and probably why high-ranking members of the Stasi lived there. Perhaps one of them moved into that large house you lived in before you and your mother moved to Biesdorf.' Now, instead of pressing Paul on the similarity between his relationship with Christina and his father's near religious worship of his deceased mother, I was ruminating on the death of my father. Trying to prevent the far-fetched idea Paul had just planted in my mind, that someone in the Stasi killed my father because they wanted our house, from ballooning into a fully blown conspiracy theory. Difficult in view of a diary entry describing a conversation with Herbert Hüber suggesting this might well have been the case.

What I had discovered, however, was how sharp Paul's mental reflexes were when confronted with a problem he was unable to resolve. 'Sorry, do you charge by the hour or the session?' he asked, and we both burst out laughing. The tension that had been building between us was dispelled. Paul tried to pour another coffee from a pot that was now empty. 'I'll get this refilled,' he said, leaving the table. 'Do you want more tea?' he asked but was probably out of earshot when I said *yes*.

Paul's phone was lying next to the envelope. He had only unlocked it once, but this was enough for me to discover the last two numbers which were seven and nine. The first two I remembered from Lychen but it seemed he had changed the code, and why he had been happy to leave the phone on the table.

Paul returned with a tray of tea and coffee and two Danish pastries which I told him would do serious damage too my waistline. 'The idea of a relationship with Christina was always more appealing than the relationship itself,' he said. A confession of sorts, but before I could ask if he blamed his father, he added, 'I discovered this the summer before I came to East Germany. We spent two weeks together. She had been working as an au pair in Ascona and we arranged to meet in Berne. While waiting for her train to arrive I realised nothing would live up to the anticipation of her arrival, but it wasn't until New York that I understood why. Unfortunately, once you start to question one aspect of an upbringing which was unconventional, others become suspect.'

'Such as?'

'Such as how much my decision to go to university was influenced by my father, whose career as an engineer was cut short when he was called up to fight. Gradually more layers were peeled away, and I felt eventually there would be nothing left for me outside this life my father had reimagined. This became a serious issue when he became ill and only had a few years to live. The building became frenetic and intertwined with work I was doing with computers. If my father had built a virtual world using bricks and mortar maybe I could augment it with the help of technology. It also became apparent that without my father the world he created would no longer exist, so neither would I. It became a race against time, which I lost.'

'Did his death hit you hard?'

'That's an understatement. It felt as though it was me who died and he was still alive.' Watching Paul being drowned by his cousin Hans came to mind. 'Some people imagine their limbs no longer belong to them.'

'Cotard syndrome.'

'Well, my whole body felt like that. A physical manifestation of a state of mind. It's hard to explain to someone that you no longer feel you exist. That you're having a twenty-four-hour out-of-body experience, like watching yourself performing in a movie.'

'Did you try?'

'Try what?'

'To explain to someone how you felt. Seek help.'

'You mean have what I experienced diagnosed by a psychiatrist?'

'Given the closed world you lived in with your father, I would have suggested Stockholm syndrome.'

'Another syndrome. For a moment there I forgot what you did for a living.'

'And falling ill on the same day as your father's battalion was wiped out sounds like Ancestor Syndrome.' Something which intrigued me enough to mention it in my diary after the meeting at Stasi headquarters because there were other explanations for Paul's illness which made more sense than a student being attacked with a poisoned umbrella.

'Ancestor Syndrome? Is that even a thing?'

'Some people seem to think so.'

I don't suppose you've ever met anyone suffering from OGS.'

'OGS?'

'Ordinary Guy Syndrome.'

'Very amusing.' Actually, I had and married him but, realising Paul was merely being evasive, kept Herman out of this.

'Oddly enough, I saw you present a paper at a conference in Stockholm in 1985.'

'Very clever, so there are copies of my diary entries on your phone.'

'During the afternoon break you discussed your research with a professor from Upsala University but were interrupted by someone who appeared to know nothing about sociology or criminology.'

'Sorry, that's also in my diary.'

'Then as you left the conference centre you reminded the HVA agent who had the unenviable job of ensuring you didn't make contact with an undesirable westerner, on that particular occasion myself I think, that if she insisted on following you, and listening in on all your conversations, she should be more discreet.'

That was definitely not in my diary.

The cloud thinned and the room was bathed in sunlight. This may have been what caused Paul to become restless, keen to get on his way. He reached down and pulled his rucksack closer to his chair but then looked at me as if suddenly reminded I was sitting opposite him. I suggested a post mortem meeting to divide up every thing he once shared with his father. 'Sometimes it works.' I said, but it appeared someone had got there ahead of me.

'Sometimes,' He said, 'but not if the table is empty when they've left the room. Christina went with him and, looking back, it seemed he had stolen her in nineteen seventy-four. Getting the edge on someone who managed to use identity theft to cheat death took more than a few clever tricks.'

'Techniques is probably a more accurate description than tricks. Speaking as a psychiatrist that is. Even so it would be interesting to know what you have in mind?'

'The barn where he hid from the Russians... If that half hour felt like an eternity, perhaps he was still there. Finding it out there was a challenge but not impossible.' Paul was looking at me rather than out of the window, so it was taken as said that *out there* referred to the forest to the east. 'When the Red Army crossed the Elbe my father took his battalion into Eberswalde to find some guns, and while doing this they ran into Gottard Heinrici who was carrying out a survey for a report he hoped would persuade the high command in Berlin the situation was hopeless. Heinrici felt the encounter was significant enough to mention it in his diary. So, I had a starting point.

'I'm not sure what it is about Germans and diaries, but another person taking notes was one of the regiment's medics. He was wounded and captured during the retreat, close to Fürstenberg. *Dear diary* was not the first thought that came to mind when a rifle was pointed at his head.'

'So, the trail went cold and the rest of the journey was pure guesswork? Thousands of square kilometres and you were looking for a tiny barn.'

'Not quite because apparently the first time my father returned to Berlin by car he decided to take a short cut and turned off the autobahn somewhere close to where we are now. Obviously, a few things had changed since nineteen forty-five. The Soviet airbase at Templin was new and something of a surprise. Only recently I discovered he got away with it because the car's registration began with MFS.'

A tacit acknowledgement, perhaps, that Paul had gained access to my diaries. 'Even so I should imagine there were thousands of barns along the route.' I said. 'How did you plan to find the right one? Knock on the door of all those you passed and call his name?'

'I didn't need to find the actual barn, just a building resembling the one I visualised when he told how he hid from the Russian soldiers. One day I was having lunch at a restaurant close to the Elbe. It had been in the prohibited zone until nineteen eighty-nine. The family which owned it had been moved to a nearby village and for over three decades could only see their former home from a distance. Another place, like my father's home in Gladowshöhe, that for decades only existed in someone's imagination.' Then Paul hesitated.

'Go on.' I said, which seemed to give him the confidence to continue.

'As I started out again, there was the barn, just as I had pictured it, although now partially derelict, untouched since my father hid in it.

Standing on the road in front of it I could even imagine the Russian trucks thundering past.' Another pause.

'And? Was he still there?'

'I didn't have the courage to look. But walking away it felt I was being followed and he was still with me when I arrived here. I can't remember exactly what we talked about. It was probably one of those conversations we should have had when he was alive. Except now I wasn't talking to a grown man but a scared and confused teenager in a ragged uniform. I apologised for not taking him on a trip he wanted to make from the Balkans to Berlin. Only now I realise he wanted to lay some ghosts to rest.' Another reference to something he had read in one of my diaries.

'Paul, is your father ...?' But I never got the chance to finish the sentence, which as it turned out was fortunate.

'Later that afternoon we crossed the Elbe together and somewhere between here and Dannenberg he disappeared. I was talking to him, promising if I ever got the time we could take a walk in the other direction, back to Berlin. Anyway, something in a nearby field distracted me and when I looked back he had gone.

'The next evening I was in Braunschweig. In nineteen nineteen-two we had arranged to meet there when my company was exhibiting in Hannover. He was visiting an old friend who lived in Celle. But I was tied up in meetings and couldn't make it. So, thirty years late I was sitting waiting for him in the café where we had arranged to meet. I stayed until it got dark but, of course, this time it was my father who never showed. That other promise I'm going to keep now. If you do see me on your way home from Wittenberge that teenager walking with me will probably be my father.'

Paul was on his feet again, pulling the straps of the rucksack over his shoulders. 'Keep the money, I'm sure it's a lot less than you usually charge for role playing sessions. Cognitive Behaviour Therapy, isn't that what it's called?' Now I was glad he never gave me the chance to finish that sentence because *Paul, is your father in the room with us now?* Would have sounded as puerile as it was shallow.

*Always remain detached and never, on any account, become immersed in a patient's story.* A rule I had stuck to religiously and would have done well to remember on this occasion, except Paul was not a patient. Had he been I would have simply let him walk away then spent the next thirty minutes clearing my head before the next appointment. Instead, for some reason I still cannot fully understand, I said, holding out my hand 'That piece of paper in your pocket... I will need that.'

# 19

# Of Mice and Men

'What happened, run out of ideas?' I asked, flipping the page over and feigning surprise at discovering the other side was blank.

'No one reads more than an A4 page these days. Perhaps it would be more compelling with a couple of gunfights and a car chase. What do you think?' Paul smiled, no doubt relieved at having won me over.

'I think you're crazy. And so am I for even considering this. A plan which conveniently ends at the bottom of the page has usually been padded out and made unnecessarily complicated. In this case, the thing with the mobile phone.'

'A speed reader as well, is there no limit to your abilities?' This he said while looking past me. I turned around and realised Paul was watching the young couple at the next table, outwardly engrossed with their mobile phones.

'You don't need to worry about them. They are on the other side of the country, probably on one of Hetzner's servers.' Just in case Paul thought I knew nothing about technology, although my knowledge of Hetzner was limited to what I remembered from a PowerPoint on the regulation of datacentres that Herman spent a weekend rehearsing.

Paul leaned forward and said softly, 'Look, you really don't have to do this. Like I said, there are laws preventing the press harassing you or your husband, and Britain's security service won't do anything which might upset their German counterparts, especially with the whole EU thing up in the air.' This might have been intended to test the reaction of the couple, with Paul wanting to see if either of them suddenly strained to hear us or moved their phones to pick up our whispered conversation. On the other hand, he must have been confident I was unlikely to take up his offer. Perhaps he was testing my commitment.

'I don't know, I might be able to fit it in between listening to the problems of neurotic housewives and the occasional trip to the shops.'

'OK.' Paul nodded and leaned back in his chair.

Once again, I found myself considering all the reasons someone might agree to betray their country. The obvious one in this case being financial reward but also a growing emotional attachment to the person who recruited them. Ideology, it was safe to rule out, but what about being made to feel important and the injection of a little excitement into an otherwise boring and mundane life? Paul must have thought enough boxes had been ticked to stop me walking away. Oddly it was not Hüber who came to mind at this point but Rolf clutching his lottery ticket wondering if it was possible to betray a country which no longer existed. The only problem was there seemed more chance of Rolf winning the lottery than Paul and myself making this plan work.

'What makes you think this Günter Hölderlin will be interested in the story?' It was going to be difficult not to sound increasingly negative with each bullet point.

'He used to be the business editor for a national newspaper but has ended up working as a freelance journalist. He writes a lot of product reviews and advertorials; stories only run because the company agrees to advertise on the same page. He grew up in East Germany and writes the occasional story about life in the DDR. A couple of pages and a few grainy black and white pictures in a broadsheet's weekend magazine. But the market for Stasi porn is drying up and reviewing gizmos is a young man's game. So Günter has taken a full-time job with an online publication which started up last year. He's broadened his interests and now covers politics and is having another go at business news. I know this because he turned up at one of our press conferences.'

'So, you think I could interest him in the Cathcart story.'

'Fluttering your eyelashes would help.'

'You mean like this?' Which would have been amusing had one of my contact lenses, which I was only wearing that day because vanity got the better of me, not slipped. 'The mobile phone. I can't see the point. It's your money, I know, but over a thousand euros on a mobile to use just once and then throw away?'

'Only the SIM card, you can keep the phone. Use it to take selfies. Look, let me help.' He reached forward and placed his hand on my cheek and pulled my eyelid down with his thumb. He did this despite me insisting I could fix the truculent contact lens myself. There then came the flashback which I initially thought was that day at the lake when he was making fun of the pendant around my neck. However, I now realise there had been another time his hand might have been on my face and that was probably why I blushed, because on that occasion I was naked.

'The phone has to be powerful enough to act as a Wi-Fi hotspot which Günter's laptop will connect to instead of the router in the café where you arrange to meet.'

'There are too many unknowns. Günter turns up with a pen and shorthand pad instead of a laptop. Or our table is close to the router, so the café's Wi-Fi is at the top of the list.' This I knew because Herman reminded me to guard against having my phone hacked when I visited Berlin. 'And are you expecting me to set up the hotspot while I'm sitting with him?'

'Günter is rather self-conscious and won't do anything that makes him look like an ageing Ossie so no chance he will use pen and paper.

He's never done that in the past so is unlikely to start doing it now. His favourite meeting place is a café in Boxhagener Platz. I'll email you a seating plan showing areas where the Wi-Fi signal is weaker than that of a mobile phone placed within half a metre of a laptop. The network name will be the same as the café's but with *Guest Login* appended to it. When he logs into the fake hotspot, the file tracking software is loaded onto his laptop and then the phone will ring and the hot spot app closes. You turn off the phone telling Günter you are doing this because you don't want to be disturbed. This should ensure he is looking at you and not the screen of his computer when it connects to the café's Wi-Fi.'

'My God, all that for what, exactly?'

'Günter creates a file each time he starts a new story, usually during the initial interview. The people funding this operation want access to that file, probably so they can show Cathcart what Günter has written about him.'

'Well, it appears someone has been meticulous.' Whoever had done this had put the slipshod work of the late and unlamented Otto Steuernagel in the shade.

'Meticulous to the point of fanatical.'

'So it wasn't you, then?'

'Definitely not.' Paul seemed surprised at the thought. 'Life's too short. However, you might want to distract Günter, just to make sure he doesn't suspect something untoward is happening.'

'Any suggestions?'

'Perhaps you could ask him to help you fish your contact lens out of your coffee.' Unfortunately laughing caused the rogue lens to slip again.

A somewhat hesitant waiter approached the table. 'I'm sorry but are you late for breakfast or having an early lunch?' He said and I looked at my watch.

'Is that really the time? My son will wonder where I have got to.'

Paul ignored this and ordered another coffee and tea. 'I shouldn't ask,' he said after the waiter had left. 'But what was a nice girl like you doing in the Stasi?'

If this was designed to throw me off balance again, it worked. 'I think there is a tendency to regard the Stasi as an apparition, an organisation part of the East German political system but somehow separate from it. In reality the Stasi played a part in all our lives, merely by virtue of its existence, and it mattered little if you decided to play an active role within it, fight it or simply tried to ignore it.'

'I'm not sure you've answered my question.'

Which, I had to admit, was true. 'OK, consider all the information on citizens of the DDR the Stasi amassed over the years. The fact that most of the kilometres of files would never be read did not matter. What did was the belief they might be at some point, and that someone close to you, a colleague or family member, might be helping the Stasi collect this information. This fear destroyed traditional bonds between citizens and family members because a society in which no one trusts anyone is easy to control. Not so different from what a handful of corporations are now doing. In some ways the Stasi were the true pioneers of social media, it's just that they rolled it out before we had smart phones, the internet and data centres.'

'I read something like that in a journal a while back. I think it was written by an ex-professor of psychology from Humboldt University. A lot different than the one she wrote during the nineteen seventies.' Well, he certainly had done his research, or more likely got someone to do it for him.

'So, let's see... engineer, banker, builder, spy and reader of obscure journals. Oh, and let's not forget housebreaker and kidnapper. My reward for working for the Stasi back then was a trip to Vienna to present a paper on the treatment of trauma...'

'And blaming Western media for creating a crimewave amongst East German shopworkers, I seem to remember.'

'...So what did the British engineering student get in exchange for spying on his own family in East Germany?'

'There was a difference.'

'It's not apparent from where I'm sitting.'

'I was a member of the East European diaspora, exiles, a fifth column, potential recruits for cold war battles, former enemies even... the British couldn't decide. Poles and Ukrainians made things worse for themselves by creating clubs and associations which were infiltrated by spies from the Soviet Bloc passing themselves off as refugees. We Germans kept a low profile, clubs and cultural celebrations were out of the question for obvious reasons. It was *keep your head down and pretend to be as British as possible*. I spent my school days sitting two desks away from the son of another German. Neither of us discovered our fathers had fought in the same regiment until both had died. Unlike Poles, we didn't get you lot knocking at the door telling us things would be a lot easier for family members back home if we helped further the cause of communism. It didn't take much imagination to realise agreeing to do this would see the British make use of us. According to my father we were regarded as both disposable and deniable.'

'But you ignored his advice. Why was that?' The waiter returned with the tea and coffee, giving Paul more time to answer than I would have liked.

'Someone once suggested my father ought to make more use of his engineering experience and should apply for a job at Cambridge University. So he assumed when I went to London, especially as I would be studying engineering, there was a good chance I would also be approached, either by the British, the Stasi or possibly both. Although nothing happened until I applied for a visa to visit East Germany.'

'And then someone tried to kill you.'

For some reason Paul found this amusing. 'Odd that, because I assumed it was just a manifestation of that Ancestor, or is it Anniversary, Syndrome. It certainly freaked my father out, especially as whatever caused it affected the glands in my neck. I lost consciousness on the same day in December that thirty years earlier the surviving members of his battalion were hammering empty cartridge cases into the necks of Russian prisoners.' Perhaps Paul was expecting me to be shocked, but I was not, having heard this story many years earlier from Nikolia Shetlov. 'I can't see why someone would want to make up a story about an attempt on my life.' Presumably he was referring to Shetlov. 'Perhaps they were trying to impress you.' He paused and looked across the room. 'I kept having this dream about Christina, even thought she was in the room with me one night, but apparently there were no visitors. So perhaps an apparition. Interestingly, only my father visited me in hospital, my mother was too busy, which probably doesn't surprise you.'

It did not. 'How did you end up spying on us for your country.'

'It was complicated.'

'Was it freedom from that make-believe country your father created in the British countryside?'

'That's the part which was complicated because when I left home and moved to London, I found everything and everyone outside the borders of that *make-believe country* both foreign and alien. I was where you would find yourself in nineteen eighty-nine, a citizen of a country which only existed in someone's memory.

'I really must be going; my son will probably have called the police by now.' A lie, as he would not do so without trying to contact me first. I drank half a glass of the remaining tea and left the rest.

Paul said, 'I'll settle up if you want to get on your way.'

As we walked to the lift I noticed he sent a text. *Checking out*, it said.

'When you submitted your paper to that journal, weren't you concerned someone might accuse you of hypocrisy, given the research you carried out for the Stasi?' Paul said as he pressed the button for the ground floor. I pretended to ignore him and instead stared out of the glass walls of the lift as it descended into the reception, because Paul was correct. I did worry, each time I began treating a new patient.

'Perhaps it's worth considering how many of the people on the panel which decided you should lose your job and licence, and not be allowed to practise psychiatry, are now in the pay of social media companies and helping design a high-tech version of Zersetzung,' Paul said as we stepped out of the lift, adding, almost as an afterthought, 'Worth keeping in mind.'

A dismissive wave was all we got from the receptionist as we left the hotel; he was speaking on the telephone, presumably to the person Paul texted. There are people who glide through life never having to interact with people face to face, which probably suited Paul, the person who entered into a relationship with a girl he rarely had physical contact with.

'Nasty scratch on the wheel, hope that didn't damage the tracking.' Perhaps he guessed how I intended explaining my night in Dömitz, or had hacked my mobile phone? Had I not been distracted by the thought that his phone had been lying close to mine during breakfast I would have given more thought to the remark about my article in the journal and being banned from practising.

'What you said about my licence...' I called after him, but Paul was walking away, adjusting the straps of his rucksack as he went.

There is a nightmare scenario I once discussed with colleagues in Berlin. Your patient asks for a glass of water and while fetching it you are distracted. Returning to the consulting room you realise the patient's notes were on your desk. Even if the folder was closed and apparently untouched, could you be sure the contents were not read by the patient and used to game future sessions? This was how I felt after the meeting with Paul. Not only did he have access to my diaries but also extensive research into my background and perhaps even my Stasi file.

The drive to Wittenberge was supposed to clear my mind. Instead, memories of the Anweiler party and the meeting with Hüber, Weidel and Steuernagel came flooding back. Paul had just added a few more pieces to the jigsaw and I was trying to make them fit. It could be a false memory, of course, inspired by recent events, but forty-four years ago, facing the three men in that office in Stasi Headquarters, hadn't I envisaged a similar meeting held in London during which Paul was being debriefed? And at that meeting too a psychological profile was constructed; not of Paul, but me. Then there was that oddly folded chocolate bar wrapper suggesting Professor Pohl had been present at a meeting held in the room before I arrived.

Much of what I was mulling over would be lost after stepping through the door of Peter and Dorothea's hotel and so should be committed to paper before I reached Wittenberge. The place chosen to do this was at a table next to the window of the Kleine Hof café in Cumlosen.

Paul's story about the search for his late father sounded fascinating, but was it true? Perhaps he felt I would warm to someone else mourning the loss of their father. The loss of mine created a scar which was difficult to hide from all but the most casual observer, and Paul had been watching me very closely. Remembering another piece of Hüber's advice, I assumed that hidden within Paul's lies lay a fragment of truth. Later, reading my hastily scribbled notes, one word stood out *Celle*.

# 20

# The Man in Celle

November 1992

An hour was a long time sitting in the cold and dark on an evening in late November. I only stepped outside to escape the constant bickering inside the house, but at some point, inertia, and a strange feeling of inner contentment, prevented my return. 1992 had not been a good year and the consensus amongst the rest of the family was that everything wrong in their lives was my fault. It was me who had decided to leave Berlin and share the fate of a small village which now appeared to be in terminal decline. The children had arrived home from the school they hated and Herman thought his son was wasting his time playing with a local band instead of studying for a place at university.

Inge was becoming increasingly withdrawn, realising studying was the only way she would escape the village. 'There's no one here I can talk to, or feel I have anything in common with,' she told me on one of the rare occasions she left her room, making it clear her mother was one of the people from whom she felt alienated.

Peter was now on the trajectory which in four years would see him drop out of university and along with a group of friends occupy an abandoned warehouse in Berlin. This they used to hold raves and concerts, eventually transforming it into a moderately well-known venue.

'You won't get anywhere without qualifications,' Herman told his son.

'Well, you didn't get anywhere with them,' was Peter's reply.

Herman himself had changed, gone was my substitute father, replaced by a second truculent son.

It should have been obvious I was in a bad place; those trips to Berlin to visit my childhood home in Weissensee were a clue. The house was still there, as was St Joseph's hospital where my father spent his last days and the lake where his body was found. I took walks around the lake, along the path on which my father taught me to ride a bicycle. The ice and snow brought back the memory of him suddenly frozen to the spot halfway through helping my sister and me build that snowman.

Each day it got harder to climb out of bed. No longer was I up and awake in time for lunch, and instead seldom rose until mid-afternoon.

The hospital's shift rota seemed designed specifically with someone with no hope of finding alternative employment in mind. In fact, I should have already set off for another night on the ward, except the cold air had drained what little energy remained from my body. I felt so very, very tired. Perhaps like my father, unable to face the future, I was seeking refuge in a frozen past. A sliver of light escaping through a gap in the curtains illuminated the occasional snowflake and the coffee cup on the table. Then the curtains must have been drawn back because suddenly the garden lit up and the door behind me opened.

'Don't just stand there – help me!' Herman shouted to Peter as if the two of them had been caught mid argument.

'You need to go back inside,' I said. 'You've got a temperature.' Because Herman's hands felt warm on my arms. Perhaps, being carried up the stairs, caused me to recall that party in Rethen, or an incident from my childhood. Tears, like Herman's lips as he kissed me, felt hot on my cheeks. 'You've got a fever.' I insisted as if unaware what was happening to my own body, still feeling I no longer existed.

The last thing I remembered before falling asleep was Inge's voice. 'Is mother going to be alright?' she whispered. A brief display of concern. Later she would accuse me of attention-seeking.

'Of course,' her father replied, although I would have preferred he sounded more confident. 'I'll call the doctor in the morning.'

The house was stunned into silence, no more raised voices, shouts or arguments. Nor was I left on my own. Rather than sleep with me that night Herman sat in a chair beside the bed. The next day he busied himself downstairs, mostly cooking meals but several times I heard him talking on the telephone. Inge took a week off school to stand guard during the day as everyone was now convinced I intended to harm myself.

The doctor probably thought I could not hear him mention the possibility of a breakdown. There was a hint of resignation in his voice and I wondered if, like Dr Rieux in Camus's *La Peste* he believed this was the beginning of an epidemic in the village. Certainly, in the years since, I have discovered my experience of suddenly feeling unable to cope was far from unique.

Ursula visited. It helped to have someone to talk to about my trips back to our old home and reassuring to learn she too made the occasional detour through Weissensee when travelling into the centre of Berlin.

Two weeks before Christmas, Herman sat down beside me on the settee I had been confined to and ordered not to do anything more strenuous or taxing than read or watch television. 'We have enough left over from the sale of our old house to live on until I find myself a job,' he said, and I realised he would regard spending our savings as burning his bridges and the end of the dream of returning to Berlin.

'So, I think you should hand in your notice.' It was not clear this would help, but I was in no position to argue. He took hold of my hand and squeezed it. 'I thought I had lost you,' he said, and seemed shocked when I suggested sometimes people lose each other because they no longer recognise the person they married.

'This year will be better,' Herman said as he climbed into bed after we saw in the new year at the Weissen Ross. I was standing at the window looking down at the garden which, like the field beyond it and the ice on the lake in the distance, was white with frost. Somehow, I found it difficult to share my husband's optimism and expected, at best, 1993 would be more of the same. However, Herman was right. The holiday in Sicily later that year helped, of course, but so too did the telephone call in February.

'Hello Lotte, it's Heinz.'

'Heinz?'

'Heinz Pohl.'

'Heinz! Sorry, I thought... I thought you were my husband calling.' Herman was in the next room, but a small lie was better than telling my old professor that as the Christmas cards had stopped arriving, it was assumed he had died. 'So, what are you doing now?' I asked.

'Well, you probably heard.' I had. At least my role in the Zersetzung scandal was never made public. Heinz, on the other hand, was pilloried in the press. 'Retired now of course, well almost, which is why I've called. Someone asked for your address and telephone number. Given my experience with journalists and such like, I refused to tell them. But they said someone quite important needs help dealing with a mental health problem.'

'I'm not sure I'm in a position to help.'

'I think they are aware of your past. In fact I suspect that is why you were recommended.' Presumably he was referring to my involvement with the Stasi rather than my recent illness. 'If you agree, I'm prepared to act as a go between, and they won't need to know where you are now should you turn this down.'

What did I have to lose? Given this was Professor Pohl, who had introduced me to the Stasi, quite a lot. But I was intrigued enough to at least consider the case.

'I'll put all the details in the post,' Heinz said, and three hours later a motorcycle courier knocked on the door and handed me a large plastic-wrapped package.

Herman had kept his promise and attended a series of job interviews. He was either told he was over-qualified if he aimed too low or his experience was no longer relevant if he aimed too high. He applied for the job as a sales representative for a computer supplier in Wedding, which turned out to be part-time and commission only. The day after the interview a truck arrived carrying a barely roadworthy second-hand car, one of the thousands imported into the former East Germany from the West.

'I was drinking a beer after the interview and I saw it on the forecourt of the garage across the road. It was priced way too low for a Steinmetz. The owner of the garage was on holiday and left his brother, who knew nothing about cars, in charge. He had priced the car assuming it was an ordinary Opel.'

'And you didn't tell him.'

'Of course not. Revenge for what happened to Roland.'

A few weeks after the Wende, Roland was visited by a car dealer from Kassel who convinced him that as his VW Beetle was older than his Trabant, which were now worth practically nothing, his offer of a 1,000 Deutschemarks was generous. As Roland, like Herman, was unemployed, he let his beloved Beetle go. (Recently it came up for sale at an auction and fetched just over 30,000 euros.)

'And will you carry on looking for a job?'

'Definitely,' Herman assured me at the time, although, as I sat opening the package from Heinz, my husband was carrying out repairs on the garage in which he intended to renovate the car, so a more honest answer would have been *No chance*.

Inside the courier's package were two envelopes. One contained a letter from Heinz giving the telephone number of the patient, but no name, and instructions on what to do with the second envelope which apparently contained the notes made by the patient's previous therapist. The envelope was sealed and was only to be opened by the patient prior to the initial consultation which would take place at their home.

'Is that the part I ordered?' Herman asked when he came into the kitchen for a cup of coffee and stood peering over my shoulder.

'No, this is something else,' I said hesitantly, reading the letter from Heinz.

'That telephone number is in the west.'

'Do you mind, this is private.' And, according to Heinz Pohl's letter, *STRICTLY CONFIDENTIAL*.

Herman picked up the sealed envelope. 'What's in here?' He asked

'The patient's notes.'

'My god.'

'I know, either his therapist was rubbish or the patient has a mail-order catalogue fetish.'

Expecting Herman would recommend turning down this unusual and unexpected offer of work, I was surprised when he said, 'Give it a go.' Adding before he returned to work on his car. 'Mind you if those really are his patient notes you'll have your work cut out.'

The mystery patient wanted an appointment the following month, which sounded some way off. When I called the telephone number, the man who answered suggested appointments spread over two days and said a car would be waiting to collect me from Hannover railway station on the 3$^{rd}$ of March. Just a week away I realised after ending the call.

'All very cloak-and-dagger.' Herman said, now concerned after being told I would be away for two nights.

'It will make a nice break,' I replied, avoiding the issue of my health.

'Really? Celle. It wouldn't be my first choice for a holiday.'

This would be my first visit to the West on my own. Vienna, Stockholm and Helsinki hardly counted as I travelled in a cocoon of the HVA's making. 'Of course, I will have to apply for a visa.' I said.

The joke backfired because Herman then insisted on taking me at least as far as Berlin by car. Fortunately, the weather forecast for the following week warned of ice and snow and advised people against making unnecessary journeys by car.

A kiss and a hug at Templin Stadt station. 'There is plenty of food in the fridge and if you decide to eat at the Weissen Ross, remember ogling Claudia gives you indigestion and you end up dehydrated if you sit too long with your tongue hanging out.'

'Says the woman who is spending two days with a mysterious millionaire.'

'I wish.' What I wished was to feel slightly more confident.

As the ICE train left Berlin Hauptbahnhof, I texted its arrival time to a mobile number I had been given. At Hannover a young man with the build and gait of a policeman or security guard was holding up a card with my name on it. The car to take me to Celle was a large Mercedes with darkened windows; slightly disconcerting as I would have preferred to know if anyone was inside it before climbing in. The journey was made in silence, insulated from the flat open landscape outside, and after twenty minutes I was starting to miss the sound of the engine rattling under the bonnet of our Lada.

The car pulled up in front of large metal gates which swung open when the driver pressed the button on a fob.

'I'll show you to your room,' said the elderly maid who took my suitcase from the driver. 'Return here for dinner at seven-thirty.'

*Here* was a cavernous wood-panelled reception area with a round table in the centre of its marble floor and two curved staircases leading up to a mezzanine. Instead of staring up at the ceiling I should have followed the maid, and realised this on hearing a cough from some distance along the corridor in which she stood waiting. This corridor led out into a matrix of wood and glass cubes in the grounds of the house. My cube was subdivided into a bedroom, a bathroom, kitchen and a small study.

There was a telephone on the table next to the bed. 'Well, here I am in Celle in a mansion with my own maid and chauffeur.' I said to

Herman. It was good to have something I could share, recalling that on a tour of the Neues Palais in Potsdam a description of my previous visit would have meant explaining why, when and with whom.

Back in the main reception room at the allotted time, a tall man in his late sixties with a face too tanned for a person who had spent Christmas in northern Europe was waiting for me. 'Lotte,' he said, shaking my hand. 'I believe you have an envelope for me.'

Handing my potential patient the envelope my initial impression was here was a person who did not need my help. Then in his grey eyes I saw something suggesting otherwise. Although, there are some who claim to have detected signs of emotion in the eyes of a shark. He glanced at the seal and then stared at me, as if accusing me of having examined the contents of the envelope. Only much later did I realise he must have assumed I had. He forced his shoulders back as if embarrassed by a slight stoop. 'I'll be with you in a moment,' he said, then left the room via a door beneath one of the staircases. When he returned I was sitting on a high-back wooden chair between two windows, with the fading afternoon sun on my face.

'My apologies, Lotte.' We shook hands for a second time. 'I am Heinrich Reisenberg.' Although the grip was of a man still slightly apprehensive. 'Thank you for agreeing to help. If you would like to follow me, we are about to have dinner.'

What did he apologise for? Not trusting me from the outset?

The dining room appeared to be a recent addition to the house although, unlike the glass cubes, more in keeping with the rest of the building. The view from the floor-to-ceiling windows was of mature pine trees, some with bird boxes attached. The trees were illuminated by lights on the outside of the building. From what I remembered about the last part of the journey from Hannover, the pines were ringed by a wire fence and beyond this were open fields. There was a twinkle of lights through the trees so I assumed the fence was now lit.

'You have a nice house.' I said. Something of an understatement but the first thing that came to mind after Anna Reisenberg introduced herself. She was a short, dark-haired woman, slightly overweight and nervous.

Anna hesitated, glancing at her husband, before replying. 'Yes, in Berlin a house like this would be worth a fortune, but there are disused salt mines here which are now filled with radioactive waste.' For some reason she felt the need to explain the Reisenbergs where not as wealthy as they appeared.

'Don't worry, Lotte,' Heinrich reassured me. 'It's perfectly safe, you won't grow a second head or extra toes.'

'We moved here ten years ago from Frankfurt, that's Frankfurt on the Main, not the Oder,' Anna said, ignoring her husband's interruption. 'Heinrich was planning to retire early but that hasn't worked out quite as we planned.' She purposely avoided eye contact with her husband. 'I think we are ready to start.' She said to the maid.

'I hope you are OK with fish?' The maid whispered as the sauté potatoes and green beans were placed on my plate beside the pike. 'Tell me if not.' I told her this would be fine but, having missed lunch, would probably have said this whatever she had served up.

'You grew up in East Germany,' Heinrich said. 'That must have been hard.' And immediately Herman came to mind as apparently this was usually the opening remark at job interviews back in the days when he was still trying to find work.

*Not as hard as it has been recently,* but I kept this thought to myself. To my surprise, however, this was almost word for word, the answer Anna offered up on my behalf.

'Politicians make promises,' Heinrich said, 'There was a lot of triumphalism following the fall of the Berlin Wall, but too little attention paid to anything which lay more than ten kilometres East of the Brandenburg gate. The biggest mistake was assuming this was a zero-sum game. East Germany had lost, so by extension West Germany must have won. At first the rest of Europe were fearful of how powerful a united Germany might become, but now they realise the former DDR is a millstone around our country's neck. Britain and France must be overjoyed that a third of Germany is now an economic wasteland.'

'What does your husband do, Lotte?' Anna asked, perhaps prompted by the image of him attempting to make a living in that wasteland.

'He used to work in the computer industry, at first with VEB Mikroelektronik and later with the Science and Technology Ministry.'

'Ah, yes under Herbert Weiz.' Heinrich said, adding, before I could point out in 1989 Herman was expecting to replace Weiz as minister. 'And now?'

'Now he is looking for a new job...' More palatable than *unemployed*, which itself sounded better than *unemployable*.

'A case in point,' Heinrich interrupted again. 'Over fifty thousand skilled engineers paid state benefits who could be helping Germany expand its high technology industry. The rest of the world must be amazed at our capacity for self-harm.'

Anna turned up her nose at something she had been served. 'Excuse me for a moment,' she said, picking up her plate and leaving the dining room, suggesting she was going to chastise someone in the kitchen, although it turned out she had something else in mind. She returned sometime later by which time the conversation with Heinrich had moved on from Herman's career to mine.

'That's incredible, the government worries about a mental health crisis and yet withholds a licence to practise psychiatry from someone such as yourself,' Heinrich said after I explained why I had been working as a nurse.

'Really? Is that so?' Anna asked calmly, appearing neither surprised nor concerned her husband was about to receive counselling from someone practising illegally. Rather than wait for an answer she changed the subject. 'Have you and your husband travelled abroad since reunification?'

'No,' I replied as I battled with the fish on my plate.

'We take our holidays on the Mediterranean, Italy, Spain and Portugal, but mostly Greece, Heinrich was there when he was in the army.'

'And you have children?' Heinrich jumped in with an abruptness which suggested his wife had gone off message. From then on, questioning centred on life in the former East Germany which Heinrich appeared to know a great deal about and, for the benefit of Anna, was constantly filling in embarrassing details I would have preferred he left out. He sounded rather like the narrator of a natural history program or the person who produced the taped commentary describing the lives and habits of animals in Berlin Zoo.

We had finished a cherry pie dessert and were sitting back from the table around a blazing fire, relaxing on easy chairs with coffee and biscuits, before the conversation got around to the minutiae of life for those of us living in that strange land east of the Elbe. The disappearance of products from the shops and explosion in high technology. My joke about East German men cursing the growth of DIY stores, because it meant spending weekends repairing the house instead of drinking, amused Heinrich. Anna probed my children's attitude to western fashion, and if it was still regarded as rebellious now it was ubiquitous. Then she pointed out I appeared tired. The fatigue was hardly surprising given the journey to Celle, and that three months earlier I could hardly get out of bed.

Before dinner I had updated my diary while sitting at the small desk in my cube's study. When I had finished, I positioned the pen holder so when the desk light was turned on the shadow cast by the pen pointed to the number three in 1993 on the front of the diary. I thought this might even fool someone clever enough to take a polaroid photograph of the desk before reading the diary. Given this was only the beginning of March and much of January had been spent convalescing – two weeks in Rugen at my doctor's and Herman's insistence – there was little of apparent interest in that year's diary. There was a paragraph on a proposed visit by someone called Lotha who Herman suspected was a contributor to

227

a CompuServe chatroom he had been posting to. Then there were a few notes ahead of my visit to Celle which, as I had no idea what to expect once I arrived, were brief. Even so, the shadow cast by the pen was now nowhere near the three or, come to that, 1993. I suspected the diary was exactly where I had left it on the desk and the mistake Anna made was moving the lamp when she turned it on.

# 21

# The Day Heinrich Shot a Man

The following morning

'It was the middle of the day, sometime near the end of August nineteen forty-four. Hot, I remember that, very hot. We had only been in Greece for a month. Before that I was training in Latvia. I was called up in forty-three, assigned to a Waffen SS regiment which had been fighting outside Leningrad. It lost a lot of men there and I was one of the replacements when it was redeployed in the Balkans. Greece probably lost Hitler the war, if Germany had not been forced to divert troops to sort out Mussolini's botched occupation it could have invaded Russia earlier and reached Moscow before winter set in.' Then, after some thought, Reisenberg changed his mind. 'Well, perhaps not, the whole war was a bankrupt enterprise from the start. Did your father fight?'

'My father died when I was young.' I was determined to block all Reisenberg's escape routes, even those he might not be consciously aware of.

'I'm sorry to hear that. Well, for most of us young recruits this was like a holiday, not much different from our time in the Hitler

Youth, only with real guns and the mountains of Greece instead of the Hartz. And, for us at least, no fighting, just watching and sending radio reports about terrorists.' Then he corrected himself. 'Partisans, ELAS they called themselves.

'We were sheltering under olive trees on the road outside a village not far from Kalabaka. Sixteen of us, on our way into the mountains. There were two men, boys really, teenagers about the same age as us, perhaps a year or two younger, working in a nearby field. At first we couldn't work out where the gunfire was coming from but then noticed these two kids had put down their hoes and picked up guns. There were only two people in our unit who had fought at Leningrad. The rest of us had never seen combat and this was the first time we had been fired at.

'The guns must have been something left over from the previous war, or perhaps the British parachuted them to ELAS who would have thrown them away because there were next to useless. We were well out of range and the bullets were even bouncing off the canopy of the truck. I remember we started playing around, pretending to catch the bullets. Had we not done that the two boys might have run away. Instead, they kept firing and moved closer.'

I would have preferred Heinrich had been sitting on something more comfortable, although he seemed at ease with me behind the desk and himself in front of it on one of the office chairs presumably used by guests. 'You're not taking notes,' he said, but he should have realised why. What he had told me so far sounded rehearsed and like the script of a talk at a regimental reunion, an old soldier's anecdote. Also, I was reluctant to commit to paper anything which might be read during the next search of my room.

'Actually, it would help if I could read the notes I brought with me.'

'I think it is better you start afresh without any preconceptions.'

I picked up my shoulder bag, which was laid on the floor beside my chair, and took out a notepad and a pen. 'Please go on,' I said, although Heinrich did not need much prompting. Had I felt less tired and more confident it might have been possible to puncture a hole in the monologue he was using as a smokescreen.

'There was a machine gun mounted on our halftrack, which we had only taken delivery of a week earlier. The regiment was supposed to be mechanised before it was transferred south but we were still moving weapons and wireless equipment around on mules, especially when we were in the mountains. I think we all wanted to be the first to fire the machine gun in anger. I climbed up onto the truck and pointed it at the two boys. Someone shouted to stop but I pulled the trigger.'

There was a long pause during which Heinrich appeared to be contemplating what to say next while staring at a framed photograph on the wall of the study showing young soldiers grouped around a tent with a radio arial in the background and mountains in the distance.

'One moment he was there, the next he was gone. I think we were all shocked. I didn't pull the trigger again and we let the other boy escape.' Reisenberg remained silent for a while, tugging at the lobe of one ear and still looking at the photograph, perhaps recalling the day the fun stopped and the killing started.

When, eventually, he spoke again it seemed at first he had forgotten about the dead boy. 'My son was doing something stupid as teenagers sometimes do, and I lost my temper.' Another pause during which Reisenberg watched me writing. 'The real reason I was angry was because something about the way he behaved, something he did, I can't even remember what it was exactly, reminded me of that young boy in Greece.'

'Did this change your relationship with your son?'

'Not really, ours wasn't much different from that of most fathers and their teenage sons in those days. They reached an age when they felt the need to rebel. He asked the usual awkward questions you would expect from someone who had discovered his father served in the Waffen SS but there was no great gulf between us.' Then Reisenberg shuffled and fidgeted on the chair, because he was lying.

'No, I think this was probably a one-off incident, and I didn't give the Greek boy much thought again until much later.'

'During one of those holidays in Greece? I take it you have returned to the place where the boy was killed.'

'Yes.'

'And your wife did not know why you did this?'

Reisenberg appeared visibly shocked. 'Of course not, I told her I wanted to take photographs of the mountains and the monasteries nearby.'

'And you still have the photographs?'

'Somewhere, probably.' Now he appeared nervous and I wondered if one of those photographs had been in that sealed envelope.

'What did you feel when you were back there?' No answer, merely a shrug.

'Have you ever thought of writing to the boy, explaining why he was shot and asking him to forgive you?'

'For what purpose? He's dead, a stupid idea. Anyway, I have no idea who he was, just a young tearaway.' I could not understand why the previous therapist had not persuaded Reisenberg to do this. 'Look, the problem we faced was if one of us were hit, or even worse killed, then there would be consequences.' Again, he repositioned himself on the chair, only this time sat himself bolt upright and adopted a more aggressive posture. 'The rule was for every one of us killed, ten Greeks were executed, usually men from a nearest town or village. During our time in Greece our five-hundred-strong battalion lost twenty men, most of those in a single attack, a bomb thrown through the window of a cafe where some of us played cards in the evening. However, we only killed nineteen members of ELAS, and the boy.' He paused awaiting a response, then answered the question he probably expected me to ask.

'Not through any compassion for the locals, although we had no problem with those who hated the communists. It was just that our job would have been a lot harder had we turned everyone against us. We wanted to be able to stand in a village square on a Sunday morning, chatting to the locals while compiling a list of all the young men going to church to receive a lesson from the priest on how to assemble a machine gun or prime explosives. Or perhaps one of us would chat up a local girl and offer to walk her home, especially if she was walking in the same direction as the priest, who hid guns or explosives under his cassock and delivered them to other members of the resistance.' Reisenberg gave a short laugh. 'Operation Orange.'

'Is that what it was called? Operation Orange?'

'No, no that was something else.' He was still smiling to himself. 'Sorry, where was I? Yes, there were those who thought there were better ways to fight ELAS, especially some in the combat battalions. They suspected our watch-and-wait strategy was an excuse for an easy life, which in some respects was true.

'The Americans and British had landed in France, the Russians were advancing from the East and it was only a matter of time before we were pushed out of Greece. There were two schools of thought. Those who had fought on the Eastern front wanted to make sure all that was left when we retreated was scorched earth. There were others, the more pragmatic, including our commander, who thought differently.

'Greece's communists and fascists were fighting each other before the country was occupied. This civil war, assuming Greece was still a functioning country, would erupt again when we left, frustrating the advance of whoever drove us out, presumably the Americans or the British. The thought was this would give us a fighting chance of getting back to Germany without being cut off by the Red Army. Of course, there were those who saw this as defeatist and giving voice to it would probably have got us shot. Even so, a lot of us pinned our hopes on the philosophical divide between capitalism and communism and that America and Britain would join us in a war against Russia. In the event our commander was proved correct and when they arrived in Greece the British Army were forced to pick up the fight against ELAS where we left off.

'If the young man with the pea shooter had actually managed to kill one of us, we would been obliged to report the death and then a battalion from a combat division would have visited the nearby village and killed ten people. They would have worked their way through the list of suspects we had compiled, the most easily identified being the priest. However, by the time he was executed all the other members of the resistance would have escaped into the mountains so the nine other victims would have probably been innocent young boys or old men. Worse, if the squad was commanded by one of the fanatical supporters of the scorched earth strategy, the number of victims would equal the population of the village less those who found somewhere to hide. So one young boy's misguided heroism could end up seeing their village razed to the ground. And make our own lives a whole lot harder.

'The problem was officers such as Lauter...' Reisenberg hesitated. 'My memory, I've forgotten his name, but these massacres became self-perpetuating and we suspected the point of them was to force us to adopt a strategy which was hopelessly flawed.' He may have intended to continue, and I saw no reason to interrupt, feeling that within this stream of consciousness might be something revealing. Perhaps, belatedly, he too realised this and that was why he picked up the telephone. 'Would you like something to drink? Tea, coffee or fruit juice?'

'Tea, green if possible.' Someone, given Reisenberg's tone of voice presumably the maid, was asked to bring a green tea, coffee and biscuits to the study.

'Where was I?' I had already guessed this would be where some blank pages were inserted into his story. 'During the nineteen eighty-eight European Summit in Hannover I was involved in discussions regarding a common currency for Europe and harmonising the economies of EU member states. This is something which is still being worked on, and is challenging as the economies of Germany, Britain and France are radically different from those of Spain, Italy and Greece. Especially Greece, which to some extent is still suffering from the damage inflicted on it by Germany. It is this, and my time in Greece during the war, which makes me wonder whether I can be truly objective and whether my contribution, admittedly small, is influenced by the need to make amends.'

'Is that what you feel?' I asked, realising he was outrunning me. We were talking about politics when we should have been talking about his relationship with his son.

'What is your son's name?' I said, flicking back through my notebook, pretending to search for somewhere to insert this piece of information should he provide it.

'Dieter. He now works for a large bank in Frankfurt,' Reisenberg replied, but then stood up and walked across the room and took a brochure from a bookcase. 'This one,' he said, placing the annual report of his son's bank in front of me on the desk. Another distraction from a man who knew how to cover his back when retreating.

'I'm concerned,' he said, as he sat down again, 'that now Germany is having to deal with reunification, which will require large amounts of money over the coming years, and sacrifices by Germans both in the West and East, people will resent what they perceive as support of less successful economies of southern Europe. We could end up with a situation rather like the one in Germany after the first world war when extremist politicians exploited the economic impact of the Versailles Treaty and the Wall Street Crash.'

The maid entered the study with the tea and coffee. Reisenberg's seemed relieved, like a boxer recovering between bouts. No more talk of war or economics but, instead, the history of the house. It was designed by his father, an architect who, had he still been alive, would have been shocked to discover the house he left to his son was now perched on a subterranean store of depleted uranium. Heinrich would have sold it but when a promotion brought him back to Lower Saxony he decided to extend it and use it as both a home and an office. I could have mentioned that my husband had also moved back into the family home, but this was not the time for the therapist to empathise with the patient. In fact, a moment's silence provided the ideal opportunity to process the information Reisenberg had provided so far. Not quite long enough, so I asked for a break to stretch my legs, which was interpreted as a euphemism for needing a pee.

Back in my cube it took no more than ten minutes to pick Reisenberg's story apart. Compassion played no part in letting the second boy escape. Instead, he was allowed to return to the village and describe what happened to anyone who shot at German soldiers. Like other soldiers who at the end of the war had to adjust to a society in which terror was no longer used as a means of control, Reisenberg, quite naturally, would be keen to put a gloss on this incident. The tomfoolery of his son may have reminded him of the recklessness of the Greek teenager. However, the reason for the sudden outburst was anger at being reminded he killed the boy. This anger was directed at both his son, and the Greek boy himself, for ruining Heinrich's memory of what would otherwise been an exciting adventure in a foreign country.

Possibly Reisenberg was traumatised and perhaps plagued by guilt, morally injured even, but why was still a mystery at this point. Then, sitting at the desk in my cube, a fleeting memory of being in my room at Humboldt University, gone before I could recall what I had been doing there, although unlikely it was counselling an ex-member of the Waffen SS.

During my extended comfort break the patient had reclaimed his leather high-back chair and was seated behind his desk opening and reading letters. As he had obviously decided to stay put, I was forced to sit in the office chair, the victim of a powerplay more revealing of Reisenberg's state of mind than anything he had said up to this point.

'So, you left Greece when?' I asked, beginning the search for another incident which might be troubling him.

'October nineteen forty-four.'

'But the war ended in May nineteen forty-five. So, where to next?'

'We moved north and just before we reached Czechoslovakia most of our battalion was wiped out by the Red Army. There were only twelve or fifteen of us left, and a handful of Russians we had taken prisoner.' I glanced at the photograph on the wall and realised one of the soldiers with Reisenberg looked familiar. I then recalled what Nikoli Shetlov said about the death of his brother.

(Or rather, did not do either of those things because to a degree our past is as unknowable as our future. Memories are edited and updated with contemporary information each time past events are recalled. When prompted, by what Paul Anweiler said during our meeting in Domitz, to read the diary entries for my two days in Celle, it was obvious that when Reisenberg told me about the Russian prisoners, I failed to recall the conversation with Shetlov twenty years earlier. As for recognising someone else in the photograph, this also happened a lot later.)

'Did you discuss this particular incident with my predecessor?'

'No. It wasn't important. It was a fight with Russians. They fought hard but we fought harder. It was tough and brutal but there was no agreement with them under the Geneva convention. Nothing that happened when fighting the Ivans gives me cause for regret or keeps me awake.'

'Not even hammering cartridge cases into the necks of Russian prisoners?' I blurted out. (Because it appears one piece of Shetlov's story may have stuck in my mind after all.)

'Actually... yes... Now I think of it I may have mentioned it.' He looked puzzled and slightly confused. 'Have you read my notes?' He asked staring at me for a few seconds then looking away. 'Of course not, the envelope was sealed.' But he must have wondered if the seal had been tampered with, or a razor blade used to slit the envelope open. 'We will have to finish for today. I have an appointment after lunch and perhaps we can pick this up again tomorrow.'

It was possible, although unlikely, that the previous therapist had failed to consider all the alternative sources of the patient's apparent trauma. More likely the whole therapy thing was a sham and the envelope I handed over on my arrival contained something other than patient notes. My guess was his army records or perhaps his Stasi file. My role therefore was a proxy for whoever was blackmailing Reisenberg, although he must have realised that whoever supplied the document retained a copy. (Another false memory, because at the time, I took all that happened in Celle at face value.)

'We will be having lunch in thirty minutes,' Riesenberg said as we left his study, although when I entered the dining room half an hour later Anna Reisenberg was sitting there on her own.

'Any success?' she asked as I sat down at the table.

'A little progress Frau Reisenberg,' I replied, determined this would be the limit of my breach of patient confidentiality.

'Anna, please. I managed to persuade him to talk with you. After all, you came a long way and it seemed silly not to. Perhaps you are making more progress than you realise and that's why he's run away. I'm sure the meeting at the bank wasn't so important it couldn't wait.'

A thoughtful pause while she poured me a cup of tea and I helped myself to a bread roll and a slice of cheese, then Anna said. 'I'm sorry this is rather spartan, but I thought we would have dinner at a restaurant tonight. Have you ever been to Hannover?'

'No.'

'Of course not, I forgot, this is your first visit to West Germany, although I assume you have been to West Berlin. Well, I'm afraid you'll find a winter's afternoon in Hannover something of a mediocre experience by comparison.' She smiled and out of the shadow of her husband Anna Reisenberg began to bloom.

The chauffeur had parked the car as close to the front door as possible, minimising the time Anna and I were exposed to the pin-stinging ice particles carried from the pine trees by a bitingly cold wind. The sun was already low on the horizon when we reached Hannover. Anna spoke little other than to give a list of instructions to the chauffeur who was to drop us off at The Galerie Luise and book us a table at a restaurant.

'That is the famous exhibition centre,' Anna said as we passed the town-sized collection of grey buildings.

'My husband visited it several times when he worked for VEB Mikroelektronik,' I said.

'Really? It must have been frustrating having to travel back to East Germany every day,' Anna said, seeming surprised when I told her Herman was one of the few people allowed to stay in the West overnight for the duration of the exhibition.

The Galerie Luise was a vast glass-covered shopping arcade and perhaps Anna thought I would be impressed. I might have been had not these cathedrals of consumerism begun springing up in East Berlin and Dresden. Rather than chosen at random, the shops we visited were picked off a list by a woman in a hurry. Much like some elderly bejewelled women wrapped in fur, Anna's mere presence in a shop caused the staff to snap to attention. The difference being she was dressed in a tight leather jacket, jeans and suede boots and wore only a rather plain and well-worn wedding band. She bought a new coat for her husband, and utensils for the kitchen. Everything was to be delivered and charged to an account; we exited every shop we visited as we entered it, empty-handed.

After coffee at a café in the shopping centre's atrium, we were picked up by the chauffeur at one of the lesser-used entrances. There was a short guided tour of the city and then we were dropped outside the Broyan Haus in Hannover's Altstadt. Here, too, it was clear Anna was a regular customer. She gave the menu no more than a cursory glance before ordering a knuckle of pork, potatoes and cabbage. A surprising choice of food given the fuss she made when the maid served dinner the previous evening and it seemed this required an explanation.

'I accompanied my husband on a business trip to New York and we were invited to eat at a restaurant on Long Island, near the Hamptons. The chef came out of kitchen and explained how the special of the day was prepared, the ingredients, everything including where the damn lobster was caught and how old it was. This went on for an age and I was jet lagged and hungry, so I interrupted the chef and asked if he had steak and fries. After all we tell our children not to play with their food and here was this person turning it into a performance.'

'Did you get the steak?'

'Oh yes, eventually, and punished by Heinrich because for the rest of the trip he only took me to diners.' Perhaps the story was true or maybe told to put me at ease.

'I'm not sure his moods have anything to do with the war,' she said. 'Not directly, at least. It would help if he talked about it. Did your father talk about the war?'

'According to my mother, not to her, only former comrades. I think like most of those who fought, much of what he experienced was compartmentalised and he found it impossible to find references to it in peacetime. Perhaps he was frightened doing so would allow the demons he kept locked to escape.' But sometimes those demons did find their way into our world, the one inhabited by Ursula, me and our mother. On cold winter days something once buried was resurrected and returned to haunt him. Turning him from a loving gentle father into a deeply troubled stranger prone to sudden and unpredictable outbursts of rage.

'Heinrich doesn't have any contact with his former comrades, at least not any I have met.' Then she added, as an afterthought. 'Except one, although he lives in Britain. He visited last year.' There were unusual hand gestures before she spoke, a raised finger, or a palm slid along the edge of the table until it reached the corner which Anna then gripped while rehearsing in her mind what she was about to say. This had the appearance of being confected and I suspected she was muddying the waters ahead of my next session with her husband.

'So was Heinrich also a prisoner of war in Britain?'

'No, had he been we would have never married. I wasn't going to wait God knows how long to find out what came back from a POW camp. I felt sorry for all those women who stood on the platform each time a train arrived from Russia and then found out their boyfriend had spent five years in a uranium mine. It's bad enough living on top of a pile of nuclear waste without sleeping with a man who glows in the dark.' We both laughed, but I refused to be distracted by this display of black humour.

'So, he was released quite early on.'

'Yes, he was in some awful camp in Belgium. Some prisoners were transferred to Britain, but luckily, he was not one of them. The British only seemed interested in engineers and radio operators. Heinrich was an economist. Mind you, given the mess Britain is in now perhaps they should have taken him as well.' She laughed again and leant back in her chair while the waiter placed our food on the table and poured two glasses of wine.

'They kept his friend. A pity, he was quite a catch but obviously some English woman got her hooks into him. I wonder if she was worth a lifetime of overcooked vegetables,' Anna said, prodding one of the potatoes on her plate with a fork.

'It was Heinrich's father who got him released. He was a member of the all-party government of Lower Saxony and was working with the British to get the local economy back on its feet, restarting production at the Volkswagen factory and organising the trade show which eventually became the Hannover Fair. He mentioned to a British officer that Heinrich had studied economics at university and might be more use back in Germany than languishing in the camp in Belgium and within weeks my boyfriend was back home and safely tucked up in bed, with me instead of some English woman.'

'And did he ever speak to you about what happened while he was a prisoner? Was he interrogated by the British?'

'Maybe, I don't know.' Then another of those gestures, this one followed by silence. Not surprising as Anna had just run her forefinger across her bottom lip. The conversation turned away from her husband to her children and here we found common ground; the battles between fathers and sons, different in Anna's case to the gulf which was opening up between Herman and Peter. 'The sixties were terrible, that's when stories about Nazi atrocities came out and children questioned what their parents did during the war. The fear was they would hate us, want nothing more to do with us, or worse. We were lucky that didn't happen in our case. Up until then Heinrich had kept his experiences in a closed room. I was hoping when our son was older my husband would open it. Instead, he locked the door and threw away the key.'

It was late when we arrived back at the house. Anna and I sat alone in the living room. Heinrich had not returned from his meeting. We drank Cognac, which Anna claimed would help us sleep. However, sitting close to the open fire, I was already struggling to stay awake. Every so often the pine trees outside shook snowflakes from their branches, which swirled in the wind before landing on the lawn. A shrinking shaft of light across the garden as Anna drew the curtains brought back memories of sitting out in the cold the previous November.

'I must get to bed,' I said, wondering if Herman was still up, because I really needed to hear his voice.

'There is just one thing,' Anna said, perhaps for no other reason than not wanting to be left on her own. 'When his friend from Britain was here, I overheard him say something which did strike me as odd. They were talking about the camp in Belgium and he said, *I would have done the same if it had been me*, or something along those lines.' She drained the last mouthful of Cognac from her glass which was then placed carefully on the table in front of her as, apparently, what she had just told me required some serious thought. 'So perhaps he was interrogated after all.'

At the time I was too tired to pick up on this but on waking the next morning, realised Anna had been hinting at where I should start my next session with her husband.

## 22

# Dying For a Cigarette

Breakfast the following morning was an uncomfortable affair. Heinrich appeared annoyed by my presence but directed his anger at Anna. 'So, what did Lotte think of Hannover?'

'Very impressive,' I replied, despite the question obviously being aimed at his wife.

'Where did you have dinner?'

This time it was Anna who responded. 'The Broyan House.'

'My God, that place. Was McDonald's closed?' Which, after Anna's story about the restaurant on Long Island, had less impact than Heinrich intended. Also, Anna and I shared a secret: this man was regarded as second best because had the opportunity arisen, he would have been passed over in favour of his army comrade.

'I ordered you a new coat while we were there,' she said and her husband was no longer the head of the household but, instead, a little boy who needed dressing by his mother. He left the dining room before I finished my breakfast.

When I arrived in Reisenberg's study I found him, once again, sat behind his desk. 'So...' I began, to throw him off balance, creating the impression what followed would be a recap of the previous day's session, which it was not. 'We got as far as the Christmas of nineteen forty-four. The war continued for another four months. Did you fight again?'

'Briefly. After the battle for Berlin we were surrounded, so fought our way through the Russian lines to get to the Americans. Not much of a fight because no Ivan wanted to die in a war they had already won. They were more interested in stealing watches and raping our women.' He took a deep breath. 'We too wanted to stay alive and help the Americans and British kick the Russians out of Germany.'

'Were you disappointed when it was clear they wouldn't help?'

'In a way, and this is going to sound rather selfish, but my parents' home was not in Russian hands.'

'But still you were a prisoner.'

'Briefly.' The responses were getting shorter.

'When were you released?

'December nineteen forty-six. Home for Christmas.' Riesenberg smiled and had the look of someone who knew he was winning, going through the motions and killing time until I was driven back to Hannover Hauptbahnhof.

'I understood the British kept members of the Waffen SS for at least two years.'

'My father had connections.' Was this what his comrade from England was referring to when Anna overheard him say, 'I would have done the same'?

'Were you interrogated by the British?'

'Questioned. They wanted to know if we were Nazis and if so, how fanatical. Classified us as white, grey or black.'

'And you were...?'

'I really can't remember.'

'Did they ask you about war crimes?'

He sighed. 'Is this important?' He looked past me as if distracted by something behind me, outside the window. I resisted the temptation to turn around and waited for Reisenberg to make eye contact again. 'Lawyers were putting Nazi generals on trial in Nurenberg. One of the cases, the seventh one I think, was called Hostages and concerned the killing of civilians in retaliation for attacks on soldiers. There was talk of collecting evidence from those of us who fought in Greece. But only talk, and then someone pointed out there was a reference to retaliation in British and American army regulations. So only the Russians really wanted to pursue it and relations between them and their former allies were already strained. The situation in Greece was now confused. As predicted, the civil war had resumed, so most of the attention was on so called war crimes in France, which did not involve us.'

'You weren't asked about the boy who was killed?

'Not directly, although I was asked to give an account of what I did in Greece.'

'It must have been tempting to put the blame on one of your comrades, perhaps someone who was killed before the end of the war?'

'No.' He shook his head, but I detected something. My attempt to determine if the guilt felt after the boy's death had been offloaded onto someone else had hit a nerve. But not, as it transpired, for the reason I assumed.

'Why not if it meant you could go home? After all, I've heard conditions in the camp were not good.'

Reisenberg swallowed his voice breaking as he replied. 'Terrible, terrible. We realised it would be bad when we got off the train. It was a ten-kilometre walk to the camp, and in the villages we passed through were people still close to starving even seven months after the end of the war. When we worked on farms in Germany there was always enough to eat, the farmers were obviously sympathetic. There were wild berries and even cattle food when there was nothing else. But in Belgium we were confined to the camp with the same amount of food available to everyone else in the country. Survival rations, so no one should have starved, but some did. The British left the distribution of food to us. Cooks held some back for themselves and others found ways to get more than their share. Those of us who could gave up smoking, swapped our tobacco allowance for food. Those who couldn't, well, they were in trouble.' At last, he was talking again and I felt confident of uncovering the truth. All that was required on my part was a little encouragement, so I nodded sympathetically.

'His name was Karl. Not one of ours, an army orderly, hadn't even seen combat, a bit slow witted. Nineteen, perhaps twenty, came from a village somewhere in Bavaria, worked in his parents' shop before the war. He smoked, was always begging cigarettes. He had the bunk next to mine in one of the metal huts in which we slept. It was a freezing cold night, there had been no sun that day. About two in the morning Karl woke me and asked for a cigarette. Well, he didn't have any food to trade, so I told him to wait until the morning when the daily rations were handed out. An hour later he woke me again saying he would swap his blanket for a cigarette. I can't remember agreeing to do this but must have because I woke up under two blankets. He was sitting upright, his clothes frozen to the side of the hut. He still had what was left of the cigarette in his mouth.' Reisenberg was struggling to finish the story. He took another deep breath, like a diver who had come up for air in preparation for a final search of something hidden in the murky depths from which he had emerged.

'His body was taken away and buried somewhere outside the camp. The cause of death was recorded as Typhus. By now the British knew they had trouble because articles about the camps in Belgium were appearing in newspapers in Britain, but too late for Karl.' Once again Reisenberg was trying to distance himself from the death of a young man, absolve himself of guilt by ascribing responsibility to others.

'Have you visited Karl's grave?'

'No,' he said, shaking his head slowly. *Ambivalent* was how I described his attitude in his notes.

'Or contacted his parents?'

Suddenly he was back with me as if he had just woken up next to Karl's lifeless body.

He took a letter from the top drawer of his desk and handed it to me. The envelope was old and worn. So was the letter inside it, having no doubt been removed and replaced numerous times. My first thought was Reisenberg had written this in attempt to come to terms with Karl's death, that it was a confession and request for forgiveness. Perhaps there had, after all, been a previous therapist, and they had encouraged Heinrich to write this. Except the letter was not to Karl but written by him to his parents, describing his failing health and the fear he would never see them again. According to Karl should the worse happen his *good friend Heinrich* would post this letter.

'The next day I was called into the camp commandant's office, I thought to be accused of stealing Karl's blanket. Instead, I was being sent home.' He was at a loss what to do with his hands but slowly brought them under control, one pressed down hard on his leg, the other rubbing his chin.

'You didn't post the letter.'

'No. On occasions I've thought about doing so. Too late now, I assume both parents are dead, and Karl was an only child.' He looked around the room, anywhere rather than in my direction. 'I'm afraid I have to go, a meeting in Hannover this afternoon.' Reisenberg took the letter from me and placed it back in the drawer from where he had taken it, which he then closed slowly, appearing annoyed I had reminded him it was there. And with that the elderly shopkeepers from Bavaria, and any responsibility he felt for their son's death, were returned to the locked room where Reisenberg had hidden them for the past forty-eight years. 'My driver will take you back to the station.' He said without making eye contact

'Thank you for trying,' Anna said as she walked with me to the car. 'Would it be possible for you to see Heinrich again at some point? Perhaps in Berlin rather than you having to come to Celle.'

'That may be possible,' Although at the time could not see how it would. 'Keep in mind people can change after therapy.' I said.

'Don't worry. I realise that. I know sometimes a couple's relationship is based on the mutual dependence of carer and cared for and if Heinrich no longer feels he needs my support, he will no longer need me. Fortunately, there is a bond between us that would be difficult to break. He likes making money and I like spending it. Which reminds me, this is for you,' she said, handing me a manilla envelope.

I waited until the driver was distracted by a car that was overtaking into oncoming traffic before opening the envelope and pulling the cheque part the way out. 'My God,' I muttered after discovering just how much Anna like spending her husband's money.

'I know,' said the driver. 'Some people shouldn't be allowed on the road.'

'That's generous, Herman said when he saw the cheque, and I regretted not having left Anna's husband in a better frame of mind.

This was not the only surprise to turn up in an envelope that month. Three weeks after my visit to Celle a letter arrived from Berlin explaining the ban on me practising psychiatry had been lifted and there was no longer any objection to me carrying out research in any academic institution that was prepared to employ me.

Herman suggested my first patient's fee was put towards converting a room in the house into an office for future consultations. This was put on hold for two months after I experienced a relapse. Not another near-frozen death in the garden but a sudden and seemingly inexplicable descent into a dark place. At the time I suspected this was triggered by the account of Heinrich's wartime comrade, Karl, freezing to death. But thinking back, more likely it was a connection made in my subconscious between Heinrich Reisenberg and Klaus Anweiler. A clue being the reoccurrence of that dream taking me back to Rethen and that body which, in my imagination at least, still lay at the bottom of a lake.

On the first Saturday in July that year, a BMW turned into our drive as we were having lunch. 'Sorry I forgot to tell you, someone from Munich has come up to see me.' Herman said.

Somewhere in Germany, most likely at the Fraunhofer Institute, there was a machine turning graduates into businessmen like Lotha;

1.8 metres tall; 85 kilos; close-cropped hair; light blue shirt and a grey suit. The fact that Herman towered over this person, and did not have designer stubble, meant he appeared slightly incongruous sitting opposite the automaton from Munich. Not that they were in the house long because, after a brief discussion about the shortcomings of the DDR's electronics industry, the two men spent an hour outside standing next to Herman's partially restored Steinmetz. While there was the occasional petting of the car and lifting of the bonnet so both men could peer at the engine, it was clear the talk was of something other than cars.

Only later that evening did I discover Lotha had invited Herman to a meeting with his employer, Schulenberg Electronics, who were, apparently, taking advantage of a generous government grant to build a manufacturing plant in Brandenburg. Lotha was in Berlin helping recruit former employees of VEB Elektronik and Robotron.

'I didn't tell you because I knew what you'd say. That they will just pick my brains and throw me back on the scrap heap.'

'Only because they are going to pick your brains and throw you back on the scrap heap.' Which sounded harsh to the point of being cruel, so I tried to soften the blow. 'Or they will turn you into a clone of Lotha. That happens, and I'll shave off the designer stubble in the night.'

There was also someone new in my life. Sophie was a tall, slim young woman in her early thirties with doughy brown eyes and freckled cheeks. She had dark shoulder-length hair hanging loose when we shook hands in the reception of her office in Prenzlauer Berg but later tied up and tight to her head when showing me the room where I would practise.

Anna Reisenberg had written to me confirming her request for twelve counselling sessions for her husband, starting in July. So now I needed to find somewhere in Berlin for these appointments.

Making a room available to me would earn Sophie's practise additional revenue and Reisenberg was a moderately high-profile patient. As well, having access to a therapist familiar with

Wende-related mental health issues helped broaden Sophie's client base. My explanation for not practising during the previous four years was the loss of my position at Humboldt, which had been my principal employment. Also that with East Germany gone everyone would be happy and contented so why spend money on mental health.

'Well, that hasn't turn out quite as expected.' Sophie said taking a pen from a cup on her desk as we sat together in her office. She was about to write something on a notepad but then changed her mind. My fear was she might have found some of my old research papers online, including the one presented in Vienna, and realised, this would have been influenced by what the Stasi allowed me to disclose about mental health in the DDR. Her pen hovered over the pad. 'Would you mind if we had a couple of counselling sessions? We could sit and discuss techniques, but I find the best way to discover how a fellow psychiatrist works is a practical demonstration.'

Given recent events I was hesitant but was hardly in a position to refuse. 'That's fine with me,' I said.

'Good,' Sophie replied, a little too enthusiastically for my liking as she took a coin from a tray on her desk and tossed it. 'Heads or tails?' she asked. I won and Sophie would be my first patient in Berlin since 1989.

It was slightly disconcerting to find myself instinctively falling back on techniques, such as causing Sophie to doubt herself and questioning the motives of her friends and family, which had made Zersetzung such a powerful weapon in the Stasi arsenal. I was constantly having to check myself because surely here was a patient who would find me out. But she did not.

'Impressive,' Sophie said afterwards because it was possible I had prised open one of those doors she had rather remained shut.

When it came to probing my mind for any doors that I kept locked, Sophie homed in on the one in Herman's apartment in Leipzig which, had it opened, would have seen me plunge three storeys to the street below. This as an aside when describing how I and my future husband met. 'Is it possible you subconsciously manufactured the incident because you wanted Herman to save you? At that time in your life were you feeling particularly insecure?' Had there been more sessions I was sure Sophie would have pursued my need for a protector all the way back to the loss of my father. 'And of course dreams which involve falling suggest an issue with a person's sex life. Can I ask if you have problems in that respect?' A direct hit, well, almost. The previous November I was freezing when Herman put me to bed and had been frigid between the sheets ever since. Right up to that day in Palermo, a few weeks prior to meeting Sophie, when Herman invited me to join him in that sunken bath.

Heinrich Reisenberg only attended six of the twelve sessions, pressure of work being the excuse for missed appointments. Even so, enough time to determine that the relationship with his son Dieter was not quite as he originally led me to believe. In the 1970s, when children were turning on their parents, sometimes with fatal results, Reisenberg feared he would fall victim to a terrorist attack. I discovered that Lauterbrunnen, the person Heinrich had been reluctant to talk about in Celle and who he held responsible for turning a wartime holiday in Greece into a bloodbath was murdered in Köln. On two occasions Heinrich suggested his son might have had a hand in Lauterbrunnen's death.

# 23

# Peter's Boat

May 2019

Despite not having with me my diary for 1993 it was apparent those sessions with Heinrich in Celle had been carefully choreographed, possibly even scripted with the help of his wife Anna. It was unlikely even the most skilled and experienced therapist would have got to the root of Reisenberg's problem in just two hours. And I was hardly on top form, having recently been wrestling with emotional problems of my own. Little wonder I did not immediately suspect what troubled the businessman and former soldier was not some war-related trauma but the contents of the envelope I handed him when we met. The exploration of Heinrich's past was merely a charade and when the search took me in the wrong direction, Anna Reisenberg pointed me towards her husband's former comrade, whose son I had just breakfasted with on the top floor of the Hafen Hotel in Domitz.

Rather than patient notes did that envelope contain a file on Reisenberg compiled by the Stasi with the help of his former wartime comrades who had returned home to East Germany? It must have been a relief that, after 1989, requests from the Stasi for information on West German and EU economic policy ceased. Reisenberg no doubt suspected, when I arrived at his door with a copy of the file, that the KGB had picked up where the Stasi left off. Given most of our sessions resembled interrogations, Reisenberg perhaps assumed I was his new handler who would pass on instructions and collect information using those twelve counselling sessions as cover. I laughed to myself at the thought and the man behind the bar of the Kleine Hofcafé looked up from the newspaper he was reading.

Was there also in the envelope a request to recommend my services to friends and colleagues so information could be gathered from an ever-expanding network of politicians and businessmen? There had, after all, since Celle, been a constant stream of high-profile patients which increased after the Bundestag relocated from Bonn to Berlin.

Deducting 1993 from 2019, I mentally ticked off all the people who by now would be dead, including Herbert Hüber, Heinrich Reisenberg and Nikoli Shetlov. So, who was recommending me to those businessmen and politicians who were still seeking my help? One obvious answer was Paul Anweiler himself. Did he start doing this as far back as 1993 and if so, what else that happened in my life was he responsible for? The idea of being watched over by a person who, for four decades, I had assumed was dead gave me a strange feeling, especially as just an hour and a half earlier I had been sitting opposite him. Without thinking, I touched my cheek, just below my eye where he placed his hand when helping me with my contact lens.

My mobile phone, which was still switched to silent, vibrated across the table and Dorothea's name appeared on the screen.

'Hello, Lotte, where are you? Are you still having problems with the car?' There were two excited children in the background asking when grandma would arrive.

'Very close, Cumlosen,' I replied. 'Actually, I've pulled over to answer the phone because I didn't realise it was you calling.' This I said a little too loud and the man behind the bar smiled to himself. 'Be with you in just a few minutes.'

'Come and see the boat, grandma,' Marc insisted as he and his sister Tina led me down the long flight of steps from the hotel to where the boat was moored.

'It's not a boat, it's a pleasure cruiser,' Tina corrected Marc. True, it was larger than it appeared in the photograph Peter had emailed to me, taken when the boat was partially covered by undergrowth and the little of the deck visible was being used to store chairs, tables and parts of the boat's engine. Now, standing in what I was assured would eventually be the galley, it seemed *the pleasure cruiser* was almost as large as the barge which had just slid past, the wash from it creating the impression we were at sea.

There were wires snaking down a corridor which ran half the length of the boat then opened into a large glass-sided lounge. Everywhere there were tools, lengths of wood and furniture, most of it still in cardboard boxes. A generator hummed somewhere in the distance.

Peter was at the rear of the boat working on the engine. 'You're late. The car on its last legs?' he asked, wiping his hands on a piece of cloth. 'We'll go into the lounge and have a coffee.' Although I had drunk too much tea and coffee already, it seemed mean to refuse, given the coffee machine appeared the only thing on the boat in working order. Peter removed a box of lightbulbs and a collection of drawings from one of the few tables assembled and we sat down.

'A lot to do,' I said looking out of the window, the glass still covered with the handprints of the person who installed it. 'Will you be ready for this year's tourist season?'

'I hope so. The first cruise is next month, lots of important guests.' The next question, the obvious one: whether he and Dorothea could afford this. But this would carry with it the negativity he had come to expect from his parents, his father in particular, so I said nothing. But even silence had a subtext which Peter was astute enough to spot. 'We've got a backer, he's a businessman and boat enthusiast. He already has a couple like this on the Rhein and one in Hamburg he rents out for parties. He was sailing on the Elbe and called into the hotel for lunch. Apparently, he remembered the club in Berlin. Anyway, we got talking about boats and he said he'd seen this old barge which someone had tried converting into a tour boat and if I was interested in buying it, he would provide the finance. He spends most weekends here helping me and next week is bringing a team of people to blitz it.' He then fell silent and was looking at me the way children do when trying to decide if they have convinced their mother there were fairies at the bottom of the garden. Admittedly the idea now sounded more credible than when explained on the telephone, perhaps because I was now face to face with its proponent without Herman sitting beside me pulling the whole idea apart. Even so, Peter obviously felt it was not me he needed to win round. 'How is father?' he asked.

'OK. Working long hours, away again sorting out something connected to Britain leaving the EU. And he's been asked to represent Schulenberg on some government committee.'

'So, back to where he was in nineteen eight-nine, just in time to retire.' Peter was preparing his defences, perhaps guessing what was coming next because I felt compelled, as always, to at least mention why Herman was disappointed that his son had failed to grasp the opportunities offered to him. However, I had just had breakfast with someone whose father considered him an extension of his ego. Perhaps it was best Peter trod his own path in life rather than trying to fulfil his father's broken dream.

'I think your father worries that you don't seem to settle.' I said because this concerned me too, although most parents I speak to, or rather listen to as they pour out their troubles, would prefer their children's lives were a mirror of their own, forgetting there was a time when they too craved the excitement and unpredictability which, having grown older, they now find disconcerting. 'He had just come to terms with your club in Berlin, when you decided to give it up.'

'The club was no longer viable, too many people wanted a cut. A lot of shady characters as well, some of them former Russian soldiers. People using it to sell drugs who became violent if you tried to stop them. Then there were the property developers who wanted to turn the building into apartments. I still suspect the two were colluding, one trying to give the authorities an excuse to close us down and the other waiting to buy the building on the cheap when they did. We weren't going to wait until they succeeded, so took the first reasonable offer. And it wasn't a bad offer. Enough to buy the hotel outright and cover our costs until it's up and running.' Peter was silent again and I was about to become collateral damage, a not-so-innocent bystander, in Peter's long-standing battle with his father.

'We were the forgotten generation,' he said as raindrops trickled down the outside of the window. 'You were all too busy worrying about what you'd lost during the Wende to realise what the world looked like to us. It was your generation which failed to prevent West Germany tearing the DDR apart. What was the point in me following in father's footsteps if they led off the edge of a cliff? At least people paid to listen to music, they certainly weren't buying Robotron's computers.' That tattooed young racist, sitting in my consulting room, must have felt much the same and I'm only grateful that while it was not what his father wanted for his son, at least Peter had found his place in the strange twilight world he grew up in.

Peter's life had changed immeasurably when his father lost his job, more than it did when the border with West Germany opened. In fact many of his newfound freedoms disappeared overnight and on reflection my decision to move the family to Gehrden made matters worse. The battles between fathers and sons are often territorial and Peter and his father fought theirs in an alien landscape with few resources. It suited Peter to regard his father as a failure, which he was not. Herman did not give up on technology and, as Peter suggested, spend all day tinkering around with an old car. When working for Mikroelektronik he built his own computer from a kit Robotron sold. He did the same when he was unemployed using parts bought from a shop in Templin. It was in this shop he met a young man who, along with a friend, had started an electronics company which designed process control equipment it hoped to sell to the paper producer who had planned to buy Gehrden's sawmill. When that deal fell through, Herman helped the two young men find alternative markets for their product. He also set up an online forum for ex-VEB Mikroelektronik and Robotron employees and it was this that eventually brought him to the attention of Lotha from Schulenberg Electronics. Unfortunately, while Peter had in his own way been equally successful, the gulf between the two men now appeared unbridgeable.

'You remember Joachim from the garage in Gehrden?' I asked, attempting to lighten the mood.

'With the souped-up Trabant.' I could tell from the way Peter smiled he probably remembered Joachim for another reason: the rumour we might have pushed our beds together at some point.

'When I told him you were living in Wittenberge he said you probably moved here because it's the furthest you could get away from your father without leaving the country.'

Peter shrugged and looked out of the rain-streaked window to the opposite bank of the river. 'We get a lot of guests from over there, funny though, I still think of them as visiting from abroad.'

During dinner that evening the children helped the waitress bring food to the table and Peter served behind the bar. Dorothea took orders and supervised in the kitchen. Only when all the guests had finished eating, and the waitress took over behind the bar, were we all seated together as a family, minus Herman of course. The children rarely saw their grandfather, only for a few days each Christmas and sometimes a week during summer. Not last year, however, as Herman had claimed he was too busy, so Marc and Tina had to make do with a week in Berlin with their aunt and uncle. Now it seemed Herman's place had been taken by this man called Max, the person financing the renovation of Peter's boat.

'Mad Max,' sighed Dorothea

'No, fireman Max,' Marc insisted, then ran out of the restaurant and returned with an iPad which he laid on the table in front of me. Swiping through the photographs in the gallery, most of which were of the boat and the hotel, Marc stopped when he came to a scanned newspaper article. The headline read *This Weekend The Rhein Really Was On Fire*, a reference to the boat trips along the river in autumn when the leaves on trees were red and orange.

An accident while lighting a barbeque had resulted in a summerhouse catching fire. The flames then spread to a nearby vineyard destroying grapevines and badly damaging a winery popular with tourists cruising along the Rhein. There was even worse news for Rhein cruise operators when smoke from the fire temporarily halted boats sailing on the river. Total damage was estimated to be over two million euros. According to Maximillian Arndt this was an unfortunate accident made worse by the unusually hot and dry weather. There was a picture of Herr Arndt talking to a fireman, the skeleton of the summerhouse and smouldering remains of the winery behind them. Neither man seemed particularly concerned about the devastation around them. In fact, both of them were smiling, perhaps confirming the widely held belief there is nothing a fireman enjoys more than a particularly spectacular blaze. Max was wearing a tee-shirt emblazoned with *Just Do It, Could Be Good* which both Marc and Tina found amusing. Apparently Max had given the children one each as a present. But it was something else in the picture which caught my eye – a man and a woman, not as jovial as Max and the fireman. Despite being slightly out of focus the man was recognisable as the person who was currently escorting a ghost back to Berlin.

The rest of the evening it felt I was tiptoeing through a minefield, avoiding any mention of visits to my daughter Inge because doing so would require an excuse for not stopping off at Wittenberge on the way home from Hannover.

'Is everything OK?' Peter asked, because I must have seemed distracted.

'Just tired,' I replied. Only partly true, but this sounded more credible than his mother worrying that Paul Anweiler, rather than 'Mad Max', might be financing his boat.

'Max said he wasn't worried about all the damage as he had a friend who would fix it,' Tina said and the conversation turned to Max's other disastrous exploits, of which the list seemed endless.

'Apparently, Max is accident-prone,' said Dorothea.

'There's no such thing,' I said. Later I would discover there was.

After undressing and climbing into bed I read through the notes I had made in the Kleine Hof and came to much the same conclusion as when I wrote them: that Paul Anweiler had been there in the background for most of my adult life. That at the party in Rethen he decided a psychiatrist who worked with the Stasi would be a useful contact. That in 1993, like now, there was something he wanted but instead of throwing a bunch of bananas into my shopping trolley he engineered that meeting with Reisenberg, whom he persuaded, possibly by threatening to make his Stasi file public, to help me reestablish myself as a therapist. What Paul wanted now was clear, to help prevent a radical member of a left-wing party becoming the next prime minister of Britain. But what had he wanted in 1993?

As I drifted off to sleep the whole thing seemed as unlikely as the same six winning lottery numbers coming up twice. So far I had only got one piece of the puzzle to fit and most of the rest were still missing.

Each room in the hotel had a seventies rock band theme; mine was Kraftwerk and there was a *Donnerstag aus Licht* poster on the wall. Recalling Paul's comment about Peter's boat needing fire insurance, I now wondered if this was actually a reference to his colleague Max. I sent Herman a short text telling him I was OK. Stupidly, merely visiting his estranged son felt like an act of betrayal.

An internet search for Max Arndt turned up little beyond what Peter had already told me about his business partner. The Wikipedia entry was second on the list of web pages. This was sparse; born in Munich in 1953, Max owned an electronics design company which was based just outside Bonn, as was the cruise business. The account of the fire however was long and detailed and it occurred to me this might have been intentional, designed to distract, ensuring casual visitors to the site did not delve too deeply into his past. No mention of Paul Anweiler or of the woman standing next to him in the photograph.

Returning to the list of webpages, the fire was the only hint of anything controversial or involving the law until reaching the fourth page of the search results. Then a familiar name, Sonia Engelhardt who had a page dedicated to her on the *Autumn 77 Files* website. Her page came up because the extract read ... *in 1977, Max Arndt, along with Bettina Ansbach, was cleared of* .... As I was reluctant to click on the link what Max and the girl were cleared of, and their relationship with Sonia Engelhardt remained a mystery.

Instead I searched for Peter's music venue in Berlin, and did this on a hunch. There were still a few mentions of concerts and raves, but what I needed was the address, which I cut and pasted back into Google, prefixing it with *property for sale*. This produced a list of apartments, high quality and expensive, some still being marketed by Anweiler Construction. So that explained the generous offer Peter had received for the building. I closed down my laptop, turned off the light and tried to get the person who suddenly seemed omnipresent in my life out of my mind.

It was still dark when I descended the steps in front of the hotel. The rain had stopped and the sky cleared. The moon was reflected in the river as were the lights in the windows of the boat, which had set sail and was crowded with people. This should have struck me as odd but I merely wondered who took the bulbs from the box and put them into the empty light sockets. There were two men in evening dress at the back of the boat leaning on the rail, each holding a glass of wine, surveying the river and sharing a joke. A woman was walking from one end of the passenger lounge to the other shouting something I couldn't make out. She had two children in tow, Marc and Tina. Still shouting when exiting the lounge, she crossed the deck to where the two men stood and placed both hands on the chest of one of them, pushing him so hard he dropped the glass of wine and fell backwards into the water. I turned to climb back up the steps but my way was blocked by Heinrich and Anna Reisenberg.

'We're so sorry, Lotte, but we can't let you go home. Not knowing what you do,' Anna said. Behind me a small boat had been lowered into the water and the woman, with Marc and Tina in front of her, was rowing it towards where I stood.

'I want to go home!' I shouted. 'Let me go home. Herman, help me please...'

At some point Peter must have told Dorothea his mother had nightmares, and during his childhood shouts in the night were not uncommon. Marc and Tina had no doubt only discovered this that morning when Dorothea explained why they heard their names shouted out in the early hours.

'I hope I didn't disturb the guests.'

'I don't think so, your room is soundproofed. We get a lot of guests from our old rock club days who can't seem to get to sleep without music playing.' I suspected Dorothea made this up just to make me feel better.

After breakfast there was another heart-to-heart talk with Peter on the boat. As a mother I felt duty bound to advise my son what sort of people he was dealing with, although as a therapist, I realised this would have been a bad idea.

A patient who had been happily married for over forty years, but blissfully unaware of her husband's infidelity until the day he upped and left her for another woman, insisted, during a twenty-tissue counselling session, that somehow all those years she had been married were now lost.

'OK, he's taken the CD collection and the dog,' I told her. 'But don't let him take your memories or you'll forget that it's possible to be happy.' In our more wistful, reflective and less serious *things are not what they were* moments, Joachim and I sometimes strayed into similar territory when discussing the Wende.

'Were you and Herman happy before nineteen eighty-nine?' Joachim asked.

'Of course we were. Why, weren't you?' I replied.

'Definitely. The thing that annoys me about Wessies...'

'Just one?'

'Oh, there are lots of others. In fact, I've got a spreadsheet here...' He pretended to open a file on his PC. 'No, what I find really annoying...' he said.

'Rather than slightly tedious?'

'Rather than slightly tedious, is not just the assumption we were never happy, but the insistence that if we were it was because we were deluded. Which, given what a miserable bunch they are most of the time, is ironic. Just a thought, now, talking of cheering ourselves up, how about that new Polo?'

Peter may not have realised it but, despite everything, he was still trying to prove himself to his father. Why should I sabotage that? After all, this person Max might be genuine and perhaps I should have used my time in Wittenberge to discover more about him and his connection to Paul Anweiler. There must have been numerous hits on his webpage from the hotel's IP address and maybe even the odd search which snared K and S Investments and its CEO, so who would have noticed a few more from my laptop.

'You know if you need help drawing up a contract with this Max, your father would help.'

Peter bristled at the suggestion. 'I'm OK. I handled the sale of the club, and those people were as hard as nails and just as sharp,' he said, adding as a consolation, 'But thanks anyway.'

Perhaps I should have mentioned that the person in the background in that picture on Dorothea's iPad was someone from both my distant, and worryingly recent, past. That all through his and Inge's childhood it now appeared something dark and hidden from view had haunted their mother.

My contribution to the boat was 1000 euros, taken from the envelope Paul gave me, handed to Dorothea because Peter would have refused it.

My drive home took me through Pritzwalk. Perleberg was probably as far as Paul would have walked in a day and a half. There was no businessman limping along the road with a dishevelled second world war soldier by his side so perhaps they heard my car and hid in a barn.

# 24

# A Woman Called Claudia

The lake to the north of Gehrden was not large, just wide enough for the breeze to create the waves which lapped against the supports of the small jetty on which I stood, the only sound save for the calls of moor hens and geese.

'You bring with you everything you can't leave behind.'

I turned around, for obvious reasons nervous at the thought someone was standing between me and dry land. But it seemed I was alone. For the past three weeks I had been under a great deal of stress, but voices in my head? That was something new.

The day had started with the tape recorder and typewriter set up on the kitchen table. Herman was in Berlin for a meeting and would be back late so, apart from an appointment at eleven o clock I had all day to reproduce, or forge, the page from Geoffrey Cathcart's Stasi file. The tape was threaded through the recording heads, the paper wound into the typewriter and, with headphones on, my fingers hovered over its keys.

*Geoffrey, it is better we discuss this out here ...* the last words lost because the person speaking, Michael Meyer, turned and looked back at the house. He knew, and Geoffrey Cathcart might well have suspected, there were members of the peace movement who could not be trusted. Meyer was looking at Jans M who stood in the doorway with a young girl, and then said to Cathcart, *The garden is a better place to talk*.

The girl surveyed the garden, the fruit trees, ankle-length grass and in the corner a wooden seat which she thought an obvious place for the two young men to sit and talk. But Meyer took Cathcart to the tree with a bird box fixed to its trunk and, tied to one branch, a washing line on which two shirts and a pair of trousers were hanging. The other end of this washing line was attached to a wooden post at the far end of the garden. The bedroom of the house next door had its curtains drawn and in it someone sat operating a tape recorder. The tree under which Meyer and Cathcart stood was weighed down with plums, and chosen because should Britain's future Labour Leader decide he was hungry, crunching an apple would spoil the recording. No one could accuse Stasi technicians of not being thorough. All this I knew because that girl stood in the doorway of the house, a glass of orange drink in her hand, was me.

The tape ran on, but my fingers remained frozen, unable to press the keys. I took off the headphones and went into my office to retrieve the diary for 1978 from the suitcase laid open on the floor. After rewinding the tape I played it again, this time comparing what was said with the account of the meeting in my diary. It was all there: the discussion about the work of Britain's Campaign for Nuclear Disarmament; the support socialists in Britain might offer if workers in East Germany and Poland ever rose up against their Stalinist leaders. Then as the two men returned to the house and were met by Cathcart's girlfriend, a remark by Meyer was lost amongst the background noise, a low droning sound which was present throughout the recording. I rewound the tape and listened again. *Geoffrey, we should....* Twice more I tried but it was impossible to make out what Meyer said. A guess at ... *not discuss this during the meeting*. But according to my diary it was possible they said something else entirely.

There were at least five encounters with foreign nationals after that afternoon with Paul Anweiler at the party in Rethen. Most with people, like Paul himself, relatively unknown during the 1970s. The exception was the West German terrorist whose face appeared on TV and in newspapers in both the West and East. Perhaps if I had forgotten the infiltration of the Peace Group and Meyer's conversation with Cathcart, losing the tape had also slipped my mind. Maybe, as Paul suggested, it had, after all, lain forgotten in my suitcase since 1978.

While I was considering this the doorbell rang and, looking at my mobile phone, I realised it was eleven-o-clock.

The parents of my sixteen-year-old patient had noticed their daughter becoming increasingly withdrawn, to the point where most of her social interactions were via the mobile phone she was glued to for most of her waking day. Her mother had read one of my articles and driven the girl from Eberswalde, promising her this was for an exploratory chat, the idea of six to twelve sessions thought too daunting for someone whose attention span was now measured in seconds.

Growing up is a performance. The response of an audience, made up mostly of a young person's friends, parents and teachers, help them develop the character they play for the rest of their life. Unfortunately, technology companies have locked the doors of the theatre, occupied its stage and are the producers and directors of this performance. The character the young person is now forced to play is no longer one relaxed and confident when interacting with people face to face. Their mobile phone, or rather the algorithm the app on it uses, not their friends and family, provides the applause and the dopamine rush that accompanies it. The result is despite a hundred online friends they feel isolated and marginalised. The teenager seemed mature enough to appreciate this. But apparently, I had underestimated the degree to which those algorithms had arrested her development and left her mind shuttered. Sitting opposite me was a young person who had surrendered to big tech corporations the freedom her parents had won back from the Stasi. A victim of a modern-day manifestation of Zersetzung.

One of the apps the girl thought was particularly *cool* modified selfies. She took my picture then after stabbing its screen with her finger handed the phone to me.

'Impressive,' I said, 'But surely when someone meets me face to face, they will notice there's not even a passing resemblance to Jennifer Aniston,' I said, and gave the phone back to the young girl who was obviously confused as the avatar created when she used the app was merely her ambassador in the virtual world, the only place she and her friends now socialised. The East German Communist Party had fixed ideas regarding the model citizen and turned to people such as Professor Pohl and myself to devise ways to force individuals to conform to this stereotype. Neither of us could have imagined at the time this manipulation would one day be possible using nothing more than a handheld device and a network of computers.

After completing the patient's notes I searched Twitter for references to Geoffrey Cathcart, still not entirely convinced the person on the tape and the candidate in Britain's forthcoming election were one and the same. There were numerous videos of rallies at which the Labour leader spoke and one of these reminded me of something I vaguely remember being discussed in 1978 although perhaps not during a meeting about Cathcart. As my diary might have contained the minutes of this meeting, I decided to read it while having lunch. Then I remembered the tape recorder and typewriter were set up in the kitchen, and rather than sharing a table with tools once used to monitor East German citizens, I decided to eat in the Weissen Ross.

Our house, still referred to by some in the village as Ulbricht Weg Farm, was actually on Wald Weg. I am not sure what the road was called before its name was changed to Hermann Goering Strasse in 1938. Apparently, some Nazi Party members in Gehrden believed that, via a network of tracks through the forest, the road led to the Reich Marshall's hunting lodge. In 1945 the street was renamed

Thälmann Strasse then, later, changed again to Ulbricht Weg as, supposedly, if you followed the road you ended up in Gross Dölln, where the first leader of East Germany died. Herman and I decided to test this theory one weekend and ended up lost in the forest for two hours, finally emerging on the wrong side of the solar farm built on the runway of the former Soviet airbase.

Why the name was changed again, this time to Wald Weg, is not clear, although I suspect it will stay Wald Weg unless the Green Party is designated an illegal organisation. As Joachim once said, a qualified postman is someone with degrees in politics and history.

One piece of history Gehrden managed to hang onto was its war memorial. Until 1945 it stood close to where the roads leading into the village met and listed all the local men killed during the first world war. The tall slab of granite had bullet marks left by a Red Army soldier who sprayed it with machine gun fire because apparently even Germans dead for thirty years were not dead enough. The memorial was hidden, buried at a secret location, until 1989 when it was reinstated and the names of those killed during the second world war added. It was now, however, less prominent than it looked in old photographs, overshadowed somewhat by the new hotel, or at least the tall wire fence surrounding what remained of the new hotel.

The road northeast out of the village passed a former sawmill and ended at what had been a farm but was now just a collection of derelict buildings. Gehrden's manor house was a kilometre outside of the village along a cobbled road which, like Wald Weg, was little more than a footpath at the point where it disappeared into the forest. Lastly there was the tree-lined road to Lychen on which the person in the van lay in wait for me after my meeting with Paul Anweiler. Beside Lychen Strasse, in the centre of the village, was the Weissen Ross, competing, successfully given the number of people who visited it each week, with the church. The pub and hotel was now the principal place of worship for the men of Gehrden, Herman included, who visited it to throw themselves at the feet of its owner, Claudia.

My arrival at the Weissen Ross caused conversations to end mid-sentence. Claudia stood behind the bar serving drinks to farmworkers, employees of Gehrden Motors and a middle-aged woman I did not recognise.

'Hello, Lotte,' said Claudia, surprised to see me at that time of day, and without Herman. No one would describe the self-appointed queen of Gehrden as elegant or beautiful. Even in the photograph on the wall behind the bar the younger Claudia was a shy waif loitering on the periphery of a family dominated by stern-looking parents and confident brothers, half hidden behind an impeccably dressed waiter.

The Weissen Ross had a large room with a stage, used for company presentations and concerts. Before he left the village Peter played with a group called the Hot Cats which he described as a rustic band with unrealistic aspirations and was more famous for on-stage arguments than musicianship. He said it was difficult to play a guitar solo without appearing pretentious. The band's drummer was usually sacked at the end of each performance by either the lead singer, whose preference was contemporary pop, or her bass-playing husband, who was a Beatles and Rolling Stones fan. Rarely did the pair make it to the interval with only minor bickering between songs. A month earlier, having consumed a considerable amount of alcohol during the break, the warring couple only managed three songs before a fight broke out. For some reason things kicked off after a cover of Nena's *99 Luftballons*. Members of Hot Cats ended up brawling in the car park after Claudia ordered them out of the pub. Part of the drummer's kit was thrown into the road where it was hit by a passing car. Despite Claudia insisting *never again*, pressure from regulars meant Hot Cats were due back in two weeks. Someone had modified the poster outside the pub to read *Back by Unpopular Demand*.

Claudia was in civilian dress, jeans and a slightly faded black tee-shirt with *Zelda's Capitola* printed on the front. No white blouse unbuttoned to reveal a hint of cleavage, which in truth was pretty much all there was, or black knee-length skirt with a belt tight around the waist to show off her backside. Claudia's derrière was a work of art, like the Mona Lisa, although in this case it was the eyes of men who came to admire her posterior that seemed to follow it around the room.

'A ham sandwich, small salad and a green tea please. I'll be out the back.' Out the back and not sitting in the bar because I had no intention of discussing Gehrden's past with Claudia's lunchtime regulars or listen to stories about people long dead or who moved away before Herman and I arrived in the village. Perhaps when the last person who saw Roland unloading our furniture from his van had died, the people of Gehrden would forget they had a former city-dweller in their midst. Although given my regular commutes to Berlin it is possible I will always remain something of an outsider.

'And anything to drink?' Claudia called after me as I walked along the corridor which opened out into the courtyard at the rear of the building.

'Green tea, I said!' I did not look back but assumed she was pulling a face for the benefit of her audience.

There were voices and laughter from the windows above as the maids worked their way through the hotel's bedrooms. The courtyard was cobbled with tables arranged in the dappled shade of a tree. The buildings around the edge of the courtyard were used by a riding school and the carpentry business belonging to Claudia's husband, Steven. The story was, and as Joachim was the narrator it might have been embellished in places, that post Wende, the Weissen Ross was in a parlous state, Claudia's mother had died, and her father had all but given up. To earn additional income the hotel's stables were rented to Astrid Seifert who ran a riding school and was daughter of Walter Seifert, the former owner of Gehrden's manor house.

Even the rent from the riding school did little to reverse the Weissen Ross's decline. A foreign paper manufacturer had planned to purchase Gehrden's sawmill and a company based in Eindhoven constructed a hotel just two hundred metres from the Weissen Ross. It was assumed visitors to the factory would rather stay in a modern building than one largely untouched since the 1940s. I am not sure how many hotels have a Eucalyptus tree in the centre of their restaurant, especially one left unattended for two decades and grown big enough to burst through the roof and shade the building. Now surrounded by that wire fence, the new hotel was in a far worse state than the public house it was supposed to replace had ever been. How the Weissen Ross survived had been a mystery and perhaps would have remained one had it not been for that break from transcribing the recording of Geoffrey Cathcart's meeting with peace activists.

Initially I assumed the cup of coffee on the tray with my lunch was en route to Steven's workshop and only remained there because Claudia had decided the noise from the windows above suggested sinks were not being cleaned and beds were not being made. Her voice was sharp and harsh, not the usual cat-like purr with sentences fading into little more than a whisper. The maids fell silent and then Claudia shouted 'Spasibo!' to make sure they stayed that way. 'Who would have thought that Russian we learned in school would ever come in useful,' Claudia said as she parked Gehrden's most admired piece of artwork on the bench opposite me.

It was difficult to see how Claudia anticipated this conversation playing out, bearing in mind all we had in common were two men, one she couldn't keep her hands off and the other she put around the village was my secret lover. 'I hear you've been to Wittenberge.' How did she know that? Then I remembered calling into the garage to fill up with petrol when I arrived back. 'How is Peter?'

'Fine, thanks.'

'We miss him. When he played with the Hot Cats, at least they made it to the end of the evening. I sometimes wonder if cage fighting would suit them better, it would be marginally more dignified.' I was surprised Claudia had aspirations for the Weissen Ross beyond making money. She looked tired, dark below the eyes without her makeup. There were marks on the bridge of her nose from the glasses worn when she was not serving in the restaurant; I had noticed on occasions she squinted slightly when taking money from customers.

I recalled how my own vanity resulted in the incident in Domitz with my contact lenses. A cigarette was lit, then immediately, and somewhat nervously, stubbed out. 'Sorry, I forgot,' she said, perhaps recalling me using an inhaler one evening when the restaurant appeared to be hosting the Brandenburg pipe-smoking contest.

It quickly became clear Claudia wanted a consultation on the cheap, forty-five minutes of therapy for which I usually charged fifty euros, in exchange for a tea bag, hot water, a bowl of lettuce leaves, three tomatoes, a few slices of rye bread, and a slice of ham so thin it was almost transparent.

There was the clatter of hooves, and three horses entered the courtyard, one ridden by Astrid Seifert, the other two by tourists, presumably guests at the hotel. Claudia watched Astrid dismount then asked me 'Do you miss Berlin?' while not taking her eyes off Astrid, who was now helping one of her pupils down from their horse.

'A little but I still get back there every so often. It's changed a lot over the years and I'm not sure I would want to live there again.' I could tell Claudia was not listening, and even when she turned to face me her thoughts were elsewhere.

'I'll be stuck here for the rest of my life.' She said.

'Hardly, you've seen more of the world than me. One trip to Sicily since the Wende. I actually travelled abroad more before nineteen eighty-nine than since. You've been to America. Or did you buy the postcard on eBay and spend three weeks camping in the forest?'

Some of the tension evaporated. Claudia laughed but then cast her eyes upwards at the roofs of the buildings surrounding the courtyard, at the walls of what Claudia seemed to regard as a prison.

'You remember Schmal Schmidt?' she said. This seemed another of those conversations about someone in the village which left me feeling like a Gehrden newbie.

'A little,' I said, the little being that Schmal was only his nickname, *Herr Schmidt* was how he insisted on being addressed, and the clock he once owned, which had stood on the bar since he died, was broken, its hands stuck at midnight. The story was Schmidt threw the antique timepiece against the wall of his room when he heard on the radio that the border between East and West Berlin was open.

'He came to the village before I was born, during the war,' Claudia said, her eyes cast downwards now. 'There had been a big raid on Berlin. His jewellery shop had been destroyed, his wife and daughter were missing. He thought they may have escaped the city, and as they had family in Templin, he came looking for them. I can remember he used to go into town and sit in a café. I think he was waiting for them, never gave up hope they might be alive. Sometimes he went back to Berlin. Perhaps he was still looking for them there as well. He arrived in Gehrden on a bicycle, and all he had with him was that clock. It had stopped when the bomb destroyed his home and shop.'

So much for the story about the fit of rage on hearing the news about the border.

There was a break in the tale because Astrid had stabled the horses and was now standing in the doorway of the carpentry workshop. Claudia was straining to hear what was being said to her husband. Astrid ended the conversation with a laugh more appropriate for a teenager than a grown woman and walked away with Claudia's piercing blue eyes burning two holes in the back of her neck.

'After the Wende, everything here turned to shit,' Claudia said, looking back at me. 'My parents thought my brothers would take over the running of the Weissen Ross, but they went west to look for better paid jobs. My mother died and my father couldn't cope. Then one day Gerhard, that was Schmal's name by the way, suggested I should go with him on one of his trips to Berlin, see what the west of the city was like.' Claudia, who could commit to memory multiple orders for beer and food shouted across a crowded room, struggled to recall the date. 'Nineteen ninety-one, I think, a few months before Christmas. We stayed in a five-star hotel in a street off the Ku Damn, owned by Gerhard's brother as it turned out. When the shop was destroyed, everything left that was of value had been sold and the money helped buy the hotel, so Gerhard owned part of it.'

'Why hadn't he joined his brother? He could have left any time before nineteen sixty-one.'

'I guess because of his wife and daughter. Like I said, he never gave up hope. And guilt perhaps, he had been away on the night of the raid. His family should have been in the basement but that was where the most valuable items in the shop were stored, and it was locked. Gerhard thought they might have been sheltering in a UBahn. Or at least held out the hope they had.' There was a sharp intake of breath, then Claudia continued. 'Anyway, Gerhard sold his share of the hotel to his brother and then told me he had to return to Gehrden but I was to stay in Berlin and learn how hotels and restaurants in the west were run.' She drank a mouthful of coffee and then slowly shook her head.

'When I got back here, everything had changed. I wasn't even twenty but I was running this place. Gerhard was a great help, of course. Gave a lot of encouragement. But there were whole weeks when there were no guests, just a few farmworkers sitting in the bar in the evening. Things got worse when the new hotel was built and the sawmill closed. When Gerhard died I discovered there had been enough money to see us through for another year, but thankfully things improved when all the farms in Gehrden were bought by the Dutch company.'

'So why did you come back here and not find somewhere more exotic like Capitola?' I asked, taking a bite of rye bread and ham.

At first Claudia looked surprise but then tugged at her tee-shirt. 'Oh this, yes California was nice but, well, it's not a real place, just somewhere to visit.' Then added, perhaps not realising it sounded like she was bragging: 'Like Crete or the Adelphi coast, not somewhere you want to stay for more than a few weeks.'

'Not home?'

'No.'

'With all the problems that go with it?' I asked, a reference to the ménage à trois she was part of. She drank her coffee and got up from the table to take her husband his, leaving me to enjoy what I had come for, a few minutes on my own. This was only possible because I had decided against encouraging Claudia to discuss the relationship between herself and Gerhard. She the daughter Gerhard could not accept was dead, and he the replacement for a father who had reserved all his love and affection for Claudia's brothers. Even so, the thought stayed with me and recalled memories of my own father. Perhaps why, instead of returning home, I decided to spend a few minutes by the lake.

# 25

# A Man Called Kellerman

It was not a ghost behind me on the jetty, or some imaginary person in my head, who spoke, but Rene Kellerman sitting in the summerhouse further along the boardwalk – the Dutch accent should have been a clue.

'Sorry, I didn't mean to startle you.' Kellerman got to his feet and strolled along the boardwalk, thrusting his hands into the pockets of his jeans and smiling. 'Sometimes you have to believe in a place before you can go there.' A joke at my expense, not realising at the time who he was quoting. He then turned away and set off along the path back into the village, presumably returning to his office which everyone still referred to as the old sawmill.

Whether I believed in it or not, this place was now part of my life; a world and an age away from the one I shared with people like Paul Anweiler and Geoffrey Cathcart, although the jetty and the lake had brought back memories of the former, despite going there to relax. As for the latter, there was that tape and now the videos of Cathcart on Twitter which I watched before leaving the house. The word *charismatic* came to mind and a reference to Andreas K, by me or perhaps someone else. In the video, Cathcart worked the crowd, repeatedly pointing at parts of it, leaving his audience feeling a close personal attachment to the politician and, at the same time, part of something far larger than themselves. It was a technique used by Joseph Stalin and despite looking somewhat amateurish when coopted by Cathcart, it obviously worked.

There had been a second YouTube video, an interview with a journalist during which Cathcart, while just as passionate, was less eloquent. He reminded me of Beaky Boy, at that party in Leipzig at which I met Herman. Cathcart headbutted each sentence into the interviewer's face. There were also times during his speech when the delivery became staccato, perhaps because he did not get the reaction from the audience he was expecting. This may, of course, have been a limitation of the English language; the structure of sentences not being amenable to blending words into one another to create the smooth, seemingly ever-ascending, mesmerising performances possible in other European languages. After all, also disjointed were the speeches by the politician responsible for persuading people in Britain to vote *yes* to leaving the EU. Tellingly, the Cathcart on the tape was far more relaxed with his audience than the one talking to journalists on YouTube, perhaps because at the meeting with the peace group he believed he was surrounded by like-minded people.

There must have been those, however, who feared Cathcart was merely a voice coach away from, like Andreas K, being able to convert non-believers without resorting to pointing at them, leaving his hands free for the sort of arm waving engaged in by truly charismatic leaders. Some must also have realised that even though Cathcart's head-butted soundbites suggested to a television audience here was someone lacking confidence, the same soundbites had far more impact as social media posts. So perhaps no surprise there were people willing to pay a great deal of money to undermine Cathcart's bid to become Prime Minister.

Walking back through the village, I wondered how much Paul Anweiler had been promised by Cathcart's enemies and whether my share would be adequate compensation should Herman and I lose everything for a second time.

'Lotte, I need Herman's help, they want to take my house.' This was a few months after the 3<sup>rd</sup> October 1990, the day the DDR ceased to exist and we had become citizens of a reunited Germany. Dietmar Bauer stood at our door.

'Can this wait until the morning?' I asked and explained my husband was in bed and I was about to join him.

'Hello Dietmar, what's the problem.' Said a bleary-eyed Herman who was stood behind me in his pyjamas.

'Herman, you know people who can help,' Dietmar said, pushing past me. 'They want to take my house, a woman turned up this evening and said it belongs to her.'

Many of Herman's friends, and Herman himself, were in a similar position to Dietmar except it was not their houses they were evicted from but their place of work. My hairdresser lost both her home and employment when someone from West Berlin reclaimed her salon and the apartment above it. The new owner set the rents for both so high that neither the salon could make a profit nor my hairdresser afford to stay in the apartment. It seemed we were all being punished for not fleeing to the west.

Dietmar's house had been owned by a Jewish family who left Germany in the 1940s either for the West or the East, statistically the latter being the most likely. The house was given to a high-ranking member of the Gestapo who used it as a weekend retreat until the fall of Berlin. Dietmar had heard rumours about someone shot by Russian soldiers and his body buried in the garden. 'Probably the Nazi, because there's always a lot of potatoes and I guess his blood is good for the soil,' Dietmar joked.

'I'm not sure a foreign national can just turn up and take your house,' Herman said.

At first Dietmar looked puzzled but then said, 'They weren't Jewish, although she looked like she was. In fact, she got angry when

I asked if she was the person who'd lived here before the war. No, it turns out she is the wife of the Gestapo officer.'

We had recently received a generous offer for our own house and Herman told Dieter he would telephone the lawyer dealing with the sale. The next day this person, a Wessie I thought given his accent, phoned back asking to speak to Herman and refusing to give his name or leave a message. 'Well, it would certainly make a good story.' The only part of the conversation I overheard, when taking Herman a cup of coffee, because he did not speak again until I had left the room. However, he was right, and it did make a good story, two columns, an eye-catching headline and a photograph in the *Berliner Zeitung*, as it turned out.

What did the woman Dietmar referred to as *the witch from Hessen* hope to achieve when she travelled from Wiesbaden to take away his house? Obviously not to get a picture of her late husband's skull published in the local newspaper, being examined by two policemen, one of them pointing to the hole in the parietal bone with a ballpoint pen. Her son, given he was a prominent member of the SPD, must have been relieved the skull was only identified as belonging to a former member of the Gestapo thought to be Fritz T. He would have realised, should his mother press the claim, that what the T stood for would become public knowledge. So, the last I heard, Dietmar and his wife were still living in their house beside Kleine Müggelsee, although I suspected the days of bumper potato crops were over.

No surprise, given our former neighbour's experience, that I read carefully every piece of paper which came my way during the purchase of our house in Gehrden and even shared them with a friend who understood property law. That remark by Mr Reimann on the day Herman and I arrived in the village regarding moving to Gehrden at an interesting time passed me by. Even when a letter from Treuhandanstalt arrived, informing the owners of Ulbricht Weg Farm there was to be a meeting in the Weissen Ross that all landowners in Gehrden were advised to attend, I was not unduly concerned. After all, as far as I knew, we did not own any land.

It was a mistake arriving at the meeting carrying a folder as the only other person to do this was the woman from Treuhand. Apart from a young man sat by the window in the bar, with a pile of brochures on the table in front of him, everyone else had only brought a copy of their letter.

Ironically, given neither my husband or son expressed the slightest enthusiasm for the village or anyone living in it, I was referred to as either Peter's mother or Herman's wife. Only Ernst Bär addressed me as Lotte as the assembled landowners filed into the concert room and we took our seats around a collection of tables arranged in a large square. Ernst and myself ended up sitting furthest away from the stage on what I suspected were regarded, by everyone else present, as the naughty children's chairs. A surprise guest, seated between Frau Treuhand and Walter Seifert, was the former owner of our house, Edgar Habicht, and I was puzzled why he had received an invitation.

Frau Treuhand introduced herself then launched into the history of landownership in Gehrden during the twentieth century, which sounded rather like a game of musical chairs with the number of chairs, and those sitting on them, constantly changing. 'As you are all no doubt aware, the farmland around Gehrden has changed hands several times during the past fifty years. First there was the land reform between nineteen forty-five and nineteen forty-nine which had little impact as there were no farms larger than a hundred hectares. Also...,' Frau Treuhand raised her voice because Habicht had tried to interrupt. '...the seventy hectares which had been acquired in nineteen thirty-four by a member of the Nazi Party were broken up and parts added to other farms in the village or given to refugee families from Eastern Europe.' What Habicht was eager to say must have been important because he was fidgeting in his chair.

'Then came two periods of collectivisation during which unperforming farms, or those surrendered by their owners, who could not make them pay, were amalgamated with other farms and run as collectives. However, eventually the largest of these was taken into state ownership, hence Treuhand's involvement and the possibility of privatising some of Gehrden's farmland.'

'Very good,' said Habicht, 'Just what we need, someone else from Berlin.' I thought this might have been aimed at me but was wrong. 'I seem to remember the so-called experts from the Communist Party in Berlin decided Stalin's plans for land reform weren't harsh enough and that's why we are in this mess today.'

'I must say, Edgar, that's a little rich coming from you,' said Seifert.

'And what do you mean by that?' Habicht shot back.

'You know very well.' Someone else had joined the fray.

'Gentlemen, please,' said the young man with the brochures.

'And who are you? Habicht asked. 'Someone else from Berlin I suppose,' he added, even though the young man's accent was clearly Dutch.

'I am Rene Kellerman.' The voice was soft and calm. 'If I could explain why I'm here it might save some time.' Everyone fell silent, even Habicht.

'Sometime in the late eighteen hundreds my family purchased almost half of the land owned by the Seifert Family.' Walter Seifert nodded in agreement. 'This is why both the Kellerman and the Seifert farm, now less than a hundred hectares, were left intact during the land reform. However, by the time of this reform my grandfather no longer owned the farm. He was a member of the Social Democrat Party and in nineteen thirty-eight was imprisoned by the Nazis and his farm taken from him and given to a close friend of Herman Göring. As we know this Nazi was himself imprisoned and in nineteen forty-five, as pointed out by our friend from Treuhand...'

'Friend?' Habicht snorted.

'... the farm was broken up into smaller units which the families of some of you present here today worked before and after they were reassembled into a collective.' He waited for a response but there was none.

'My grandfather died in Sachsenhausen concentration camp, but all the other members of our family escaped, first to Holland and then to Britain. After they returned to Holland at the end of the war my father purchased a small farm which has expanded over the years and is now three hundred hectares comprising four separate arable and livestock units.' He held up a brochure briefly then laid it back on the table.

'Well, if you think you are getting your farm in Gehrden back, you're out of luck because the Nazis burned all the records.' Habicht looked around the room, seeking support, and must have been disappointed when none was offered.

Then Walter Seifert spoke. 'Actually, Herr Habicht that's not quite true. I have checked documents my family possess, and it appears Rene is quite correct because there is a record of half of my family's land being sold to the Kellermans.' Most at the meeting, apart from Habicht, must have been astute enough to realise the implications of Walter and Rene being on first name terms and guessed this was not the first time they had met. It meant whatever was about to be offered to the farmers of Gehrden was a done deal. Which made me wonder why Ernst Bär appeared so relaxed.

Ernst was, like myself, a relative newcomer to the village. He and his wife had arrived a few years after Erich Honecker became party leader and young families were encouraged to take over abandoned farms. There was something of the young Andreas K about him and he was still an ardent socialist. At the time I wondered if he realised he now faced the prospect of losing his farm to either Kellerman or Seifert, both landowners and capitalists. Later I discovered he too had, realising in a reunified Germany his small farm was no longer viable, entered into an arrangement with the Dutchman.

'I'm slightly concerned, actually very concerned,' said a person sitting on the other side of the room. 'My father was a cabinet maker in Poland and was expelled at the end of the war because we were ethnic Germans. He was one of the people given a piece of what now turns out to be the Kellerman's farm and the small house that went with it. As he wasn't a farmer, he couldn't make the land pay, so it was taken from him in nineteen fifty-six and became part of the cooperative. He then got a job at the sawmill, which was also where I worked until it closed down. When my parents gave up the farm they moved into a house which had been lived in by a worker on what now turns out to have been Herr Kellerman's farm. This has been our home ever since because when my parents died my wife and I moved in. Now you are telling me we can claim back a piece of land which never paid its way but lose the roof over our head.'

'I don't think anyone need lose their house. From what I have seen there are enough of those empty in Gehrden to go around,' said Kellerman. 'As the sawmill has now closed, and it seems the paper company isn't interested in buying it, we can purchase the buildings and move all the farm's administration from the old manor house to a purpose-built office block and have a new milking parlour and a storage facility on the same site.'

At this point even the slowest-thinking person in the room had caught up. 'Oh, now I see. This is all a stitch up, isn't it, Seifert? You help Kellerman reclaim his farm and then you can move back into the manor house you were chucked out of.'

'Why exactly have you graced us with your presence, Herr Habicht?' asked Seifert, his patience wearing thin. However, Herr Habicht's reply had to wait because Frau Treuhand got to her feet, slid a single sheet of paper, on which as far as I could tell she had written no more than twenty words, into her briefcase, then tiptoed towards the door. She then turned to face us, to ensure we all saw her glance at her watch.

'I have to be in Klein Dölln by one o'clock. If you could let me have a detailed proposal,' she said to Kellerman, 'I'm sure Treuhand will give it serious consideration.' Then she was gone.

Ernst Bär leaned back in his chair and shouted through the door to the kitchen. 'One less for lunch, Schmal!' After which the aging Gehard Schmidt stepped into the room, shrugged and then walked out again to be replaced by Claudia carrying a jug of coffee and cups on a tray, the two of them resembling figurines on a Trenkle weather clock. 'Klein Dölln?' Claudia asked no one in particular, letting us all know she had been sitting in the bar listening. 'Perhaps she has an appointment with Frau Goering.'

Everyone except Habicht laughed. 'I'm here about my land,' he said.

'What land?' Seifert asked.

'The land on Ulbricht Weg, which belongs to me.' Habicht was now shouting again.

'If I understand correctly, Edgar, when you sold your farm to Herman you retained the land?' Seifert had taken a pair of spectacles from the inside pocket of his jacket and put them on even though there appeared nothing to read.

'Only the house was sold,' replied Habicht with a glance in my direction. 'Whatever deal you've made has got to include my land.'

'Perhaps it should also include compensation from yourself for the house you sold which actually belonged to me.' I felt a sinking feeling. Seifert turned to me. 'I'm sure Herman and you will make good tenants and you can even farm that piece of land which Edgar took from my family.'

*Herman and you* because a month earlier Seifert and his wife had invited us to dinner and while the two men talked about the future of agriculture and industry in the former East Germany, Frau Seifert and I were left to make small talk. It seemed I was merely the wife invited along with a man who, despite being unemployed, was still thought to have some influence in Berlin.

'It's me who should receive compensation for that land. I did not sell it with the house and it's still mine.'

'Life in the West doesn't seem to suit him, does it?' Ernst whispered in my ear. It was true Habicht looked tired and his clothes unkempt. 'Are you sure he took the washing machine with him?' I tried, unsuccessfully, to supress a snigger.

'This is not a laughing matter.' Habicht snarled.

'Let's have a short break,' Rene Kellerman said. He had paid for lunch, which was served in the restaurant. What looked like brochures were in fact copies of a proposal for a farming cooperative operated as an offshoot of Kellerman's Dutch-owned agri-business. Ernst flicked through one then quickly passed it to me, clearly already familiar with its contents.

'Habicht is a nasty little man. If he was ten centimetres taller he would have been able to reach the lightbulbs and you would have been sitting in the dark,' Ernst said. Habicht, who was still grumbling about his piece of land, was out of earshot but the remark amused people on the next table. The loss of our furniture was hardly a secret and, according to Claudia, Habicht bragged about *taking the family from Berlin to the cleaners* as he drank away the proceeds in her bar.

'Actually, he may have done us a favour,' I'd told her at the time. 'Herman found woodworm in the floorboards where one of the pieces stood.' A lie, just a little Zersetzung for the benefit of anyone who had a piece of our furniture in their house.

One of the farmers who had overheard Ernst's remark leaned towards me. 'You know why Seifert hates Habicht?' I shook my head. 'During the land reform, his father was one of those who forced Walter and other farmers to give up some of their land. Bricks through the window at night, setting fire to barns... that sort of thing. Then the bastard kept that eight hectare for himself. He must have thought he'd got away with it when he heard those who lost their land between nineteen forty-five and forty-nine wouldn't be compensated.' Then he whispered softly but venomously, 'I think he moved away because he was scared someone would string him up. Everyone knew that like his father he was Stasi.' That someone else disliked Habicht as much as I did was reassuring, but why they did, slightly less so.

Kellerman went to the bar to order a coffee and stayed discussing his plans with Claudia while Gehard Schmidt listed all the benefits of the Weissen Ross over the modern hotel in front of which the Dutchman's 4x4 was parked. One of these was Astrid Seifert's horses stabled on the other side of the courtyard, because Kellerman's two daughters both liked riding and from this point on he, as well as members of his family and visiting employees from Holland, would be booked into the Weissen Ross.

Those who gossiped, as the people of Gehrden did, suggested Kellerman's interest was less in Claudia's hotel and restaurant than the lady herself. Perhaps this was why she was so keen to fabricate evidence of infidelities elsewhere in the village, and suggested there was more to the relationship between Joachim and myself than banter and reminiscing.

As well as sending a steady stream of guests her way, Kellerman provided Claudia with a husband. A young carpenter, resident of Emmerich on the Dutch border, arrived in Gehrden intending to spend a month restoring the boardwalk and summerhouse, built by Kellerman's grandparents in the 1920s. Except Steven fell in love with the owner of the Weissen Ross; although Joachim claimed she held him prisoner while he restored the pub and restaurant and then offered him a warm bed in exchange for a workshop.

Seifert would, by virtue of being the largest landowner, become the major shareholder in the Gehrden branch of Kellerman's farm. However, as most of the new equipment was owned by the Kellerman family who also loaned the money to convert the old sawmill, it was Rene who was very much in control. 'Don't worry about any claim Habicht makes,' he reassured me. 'We can deal with any legal issues. And we won't expect you to put on overalls and harvest wheat with a scythe.' The mural in the Ministry of Finance in Berlin came to mind. 'Actually, I was wondering...' he added as an afterthought, 'I hear your husband works in electronics.' I presumed Seifert had told him this. 'We might call on him for help at some point.' This, I assumed at the time, was Kellerman merely making polite conversation.

Habicht dropped his claim, Walter Seifert refused to let him cross his land to access the fields at the rear of our house and the only other way to reach them was via our garden and this would have meant demolishing the garage in which Herman was restoring the

Steinmetz. The surprise was that the land was now assumed to have been sold to us as part of the *farm* we purchased meaning we too had a stake in *Gehrden Farms GmbH*. This came with certain obligations, as Herman discovered when there was an electrical fault at the dairy. Oddly enough, following that meeting I felt part of the village, less of an outsider, belonging somewhere at last.

There have been many other meetings since, and like that first one, Ernst Bär and myself were usually on the naughty children's table. Ernst represented the interests of Gehrden Farms in his role as its managing director but like Walter Seifert was usually reluctant to participate in meetings. It was Joachim and Claudia who, through mortality and migration, had the roles of village elders forced upon them. Both were members of the generation which, when the flow of money from west Germany dried up and Gehrden was left with partially paved roads and broadband on just one side of Lychen Strasse, realised permission was no longer needed to change things because there was no longer anyone to ask. They had also come to terms with the random and arbitrary nature of free-market economics.

'It's a question of identity,' I suggested at one meeting, regretting straight away opening my mouth, but feeling my experience as a psychologist might help because the talk during the previous three meetings had been of a perpetual crisis. Had Gehrden been a person, one would have suspected it was on the verge of a nervous breakdown. 'We spend too long dwelling on the past. Too many people's memory of what life was like here before nineteen eighty-nine is based on those old photographs in Templin Museum or copies of *Märkische Volksstimme*. This is a false reality...' I was going to add that this was stopping us moving on and, had not Ernst interrupted me, would have probably made an unwise reference to Communist Party propaganda.

'It may well be a false reality, Lotte,' Ernst said. 'But it's the only reality we've been left with.'

However, playtime was over because Claudia was staring at us over her glasses. 'Well, that's the psychology and politics dealt with, shall we move onto the more practical matters of economics and finance?'

Playtime may have been over, but the entertainment continued as it always did when Joachim addressed a meeting. 'Actually Lotte has a point,' he said, but only to save my embarrassment. 'Has anyone seen our Wikipedia page recently or searched for the village on the internet? *Gehrden, population nine hundred and falling. Well known personality, former DDR female Olympic shot-put champion, with links to articles on the use of drugs in sport and transgender athletes. Places of interest, abandoned Russian nuclear missile silo.* That really has the tourists flocking in, doesn't it Claudia?'

And Claudia, not known for her sense of humour, nevertheless could read the room. 'Unfortunately, they usually turn up on their own with a tent and sandwiches. I'm not sure I'll be retiring anytime soon.'

Joachim continued when the laughter died down. '*Within a few kilometres of the biosphere reserve and the Havel*, and a photograph of a group of hikers walking past the sign warning them they are crossing a former military firing range so not to leave the path or pick up metal objects.'

'Hammelspring is doing quite well without promoting itself,' someone suggested.

'So, all we need is a railway station and ten kilometres of track and I guess we will be OK,' Joachim said.

'Well, let's just be grateful for the lake,' muttered Claudia, and it was if she and Joachim had rehearsed this, and perhaps if the DDR had endured, these two would have been a couple. It was clear who Joachim decided was the village's personality of note as, when everyone gathered around his laptop for a preview of Gehrden's new website, there was a brief glimpse of him standing behind the fastest Trabant in Germany parked outside Gehrden Motors.

'I'm sure there is a better photograph of the lake than that,' Claudia said when the homepage was displayed, although what she meant was a photograph of the lake without Fräulein Seifert astride a horse at the head of a procession of tourists. Tourists who, thanks to climate change, after spending two holidays in a Mediterranean resort sitting all day in their hotel rooms due to the sweltering heat, were now seeking somewhere more temperate. With Templin and Lychen packed with tourists from late spring to mid-autumn, and their hotels fully booked, Gehrden was no longer in danger of disappearing off the map. While the decline in East Germany's population continued, there was no longer the suggestion the last person to leave the village should turn the lights off, a comment often made by my children.

Those meetings and my lunch with Claudia early that day came to mind while walking past the Weissen Ross on my way home from the lake. At some point during the previous twenty-eight years, Gehrden had begun to feel like home. Perhaps when my sister, instead of looking on me with pity during her occasional visits, said, 'You are so lucky to live here.' Perhaps envying someone who had not experienced the Berlin of their childhood change beyond recognition.

Like Claudia's, my world had shrunk to the point where it only occupied a few square kilometres of Brandenburg, with everything beyond it a strange and alien place. Just how strange and alien I was about to discover.

Herman phoned as I was typing the final paragraph of the transcript which ended when Cathcart, his girlfriend and Meyer were almost out of range of the microphone and about to walk past that girl still standing in the doorway of the house. 'Anything you want picked up from Lidl? Only I'm just passing through Templin.' Herman said.

I panicked because this was the call he usually made when he reached the outskirts of Berlin. I tried to think of something he would struggle to find in the supermarket and took a guess at smoked mackerel. 'The one without peppers on it,' I said, unplugging the tape recorder and winding the paper out of the typewriter.

'That's a strange noise.'

'Oh that, I'm adjusting my chair. See you soon and remember, the one without peppers and two prepacked salads and a box of eggs,' I said, hoping someone scratches the barcode off a packet of contraceptives and hides it in his shopping.

'Busy?' Herman asked as he stepped into my office and caught me pushing the bookcase against the wall.

'That stupid elephant fell behind the bookcase. Have you been moving it again?' I asked and looked Herman in the eye, hoping he would not see the envelope containing the tape, and the transcript, still lying on my desk.

'Couldn't find the mackerel so got haddock, hope that will do?' he said, holding up the shopping bag.

At ten-thirty I took hold of Herman's hand and told him whatever he was working on could wait because we were going to bed. Making love to me was his punishment for asking me why I seemed so distant. For two hours I had managed to distract myself watching a spy drama with a script almost as bizarre as the one Paul Anweiler had dreamed up. But then the late evening news included an item about the forthcoming election in Britain.

'Where has that guy been hiding since the nineteen seventies?' Herman asked when Cathcart had a microphone pushed into his face by a reporter from ARD. While the translation into German made the politician sound eloquent, the original English was classic Beaky Boy. Suddenly I was dragged back into a world of peace activists, hidden microphones and meetings with Hubert Hüber.

'Sorry, I was somewhere else,' I replied, although an hour later I felt as physically and emotionally close to Herman as it was possible to get, which, if honest, was why I wanted him to make love to me, to feel his arms around me. 'Someone said something today which sounded profound.' I whispered in the dark. 'That you have to believe in a place before you can go there.'

'A pop singer has asked you for help, that must be interesting.' Herman said. Which at the time seemed a strange thing to say and I put it down to him already being half asleep.

# 26

# Practice Run

The next day

'I heard the Bundesarchiv searched for a file but discovered one did
not exist,' Günter Hölderlin said when I told him information from
Geoffrey Cathcart's Stasi file had recently come into my possession.
Perhaps Hölderlin was feigning disinterest to suggest whatever I
possessed was of little value, already starting the bidding process. Best
then to give the impression I was holding something back which was
too sensitive to discuss on the phone or include in an email. This, I
thought, might persuade him we needed to meet face to face, and it
did.

'There is a café on Boxhagener Platz, do you know it?' Hölderlin
asked.

Of course I did, had already looked it up on the map after that
meeting with Paul Anweiler, worked out how to get to it from
Templin station and how long the journey would take. 'No, I'm
afraid I don't,' I lied.

Hölderlin told me how to get to the café from Ost Kreuz Bahnhof
and I asked him to repeat the number of the bus to create the

impression I was making a note of his directions. 'I'm working on something at the moment, so won't be able to meet you until next week,' Hölderlin said. Which was fine with me because, still not satisfied with the transcript, I planned to retype it. Also, it would give me time to prepare for the meeting, purchase the mobile phone, survey the café and recruit someone to assist with the meeting, which was unlikely to be as straight forward as Paul Anweiler suggested. Hölderlin gave me his email address and asked me to suggest some dates and times which would be convenient for me.

The first two days of the following week I had already planned to be in Berlin for appointments with patients and a tutorial with students. However, Herman would be with me for meetings of his own at Schulenburg and the Bundestag. We would probably be having lunch together as Schulenberg's office was close to the university. Keeping a clear head would be difficult if forced to lie when asked what I had planned for the rest of the day. Wednesday was also out of the question as Herman would ask why he was returning to Gehrden to work at home on his own while I stayed in Berlin. Thursday then, midafternoon when, according to Google, it appeared the café in Boxhagener Platz was not too busy and there would be a choice of tables.

Hölderlin answered my email just minutes after I sent it, confirming 3:30 Thursday afternoon would be good for him too. Next a person to act as my bag man during the meeting, or bag person as this would be my sister. So another trip to Berlin, this one within the next two days. How could I explain to Herman the sudden need to meet with Ursula, following on from that seemingly impulsive trip to see Peter? This would have the feel of a family crisis in the making. What I needed was a reason to travel to Berlin other than wanting a face-to-face conversation with my sister. The obvious one was a patient in urgent need of therapy.

This patient would be Thorsten M, an architect who worked in Templin. He lived just a short drive from Gehrden, but not wanting it known locally he had sought the help of a psychotherapist, travelled to Berlin, and paid City rates for my services. He contacted me earlier that year, suffering from depression and experiencing flashbacks. My heart sank on learning he had been seeing a hypnotherapist. 'I went into it with no preconceptions,' he said, almost apologetically, when he came to me for help, so at least he was aware of the pitfalls of hypnotherapy. As Paul Anweiler said, memories are merely stories we tell ourselves, and sometimes our subconscious comes up with fantastic tales. Also, on occasions, communication with the patient's subconscious is bi-directional. My fear was that the first few sessions would be like searching a full wastepaper bin for a screwed-up page of notes thrown away by accident; the cleaner in Sophie's practice muttered a string of expletives when she caught me doing this late one evening.

'As a child I had nightmares. Someone following me while I walked down stairs. There was a voice behind me which I did not recognise. When I woke there was nothing in the dream which, in retrospect, seemed particularly frightening. But I was usually too scared to stay on my own and spent the rest of the night sleeping in my parents' bed.'

'With your parents?'

'Yes.'

'And how long did this go on?'

'I stopped having nightmares when I was about twelve or thirteen but when I was eighteen started suffering from depression which has lasted on and off ever since. Now I am having problems with my work. I am an architect and there is a lot of pressure from clients. And arguments about the designs I submit. I've lost a few contracts recently and my health is suffering.' Thorsten reached down and rubbed one of his legs. 'I have this rash which flares up when I'm stressed. Look,' he said, pulling up his trouser legs. There were red marks on them, just above his ankles.

Under hypnosis, Thorsten seemed to rediscover his childhood nightmare. He had described climbing a set of stairs and on opening the door at the top being attacked by an animal. He was then chased back down the stairs and out of the house. Another time he again described running from something but this time across one of the fields near the farmhouse in which he grew up.

'Tell me about your childhood. Would you describe it as happy?'

'Yes,' Thorsten said after giving this some thought. 'My father worked on the farm and my mother was always busy. I had a lot of time on my own.' Which is perhaps what Thorsten told the hypnotherapist because together they had co-authored a story.

The young Thorsten had been told by his mother to stay downstairs and amuse himself. But, having become bored, he decided to go upstairs and discovered his mother and a strange man doing something he was not of an age to understand. It was his mother who, in a rage, became the wild animal in Thorsten's nightmare and it was the stranger's voice he heard behind him on the stairs because the last thing his mother's lover wanted was the boy running out of the house, assuming correctly he would be trying to find his father. However, as the stranger was not dressed, the pursuit ended when the boy was out of the house, leaving Thorsten to escape across an open field through the stubble left after wheat had been harvested, which caused the welts on his legs, now reappearing as some form of stigmata.

The idea that Thorston witnessed a sexual act fitted with the nightmare not occurring after he reached puberty, and the depression experienced when first entering into a relationship with a member of the opposite sex. So, thanks to the hypnotherapist, the litterbin was full and now all I had to do was find that single piece of paper.

'Do you feel you are good at your job?'

'Yes,' he replied, again sounding hesitant, suggesting a lack of confidence in his own ability. And as far as I was concerned, nothing in the story constructed with the help of the hypnotherapist mattered beyond what occurred at the very beginning. The rejection Thorsten experienced when his mother's affection was shared with a stranger rather than him.

This was where we had been at the end of the last session, and Thorston's homework was to list all his achievements to date. I called him to explain a patient had cancelled and if he would like to bring his next session forward, I planned to be in Berlin the next day. That evening I told the same lie about a patient urgently needing help to both Ursula who seemed pleased I was spending the day in Berlin and Herman who definitely was not.

There was a lot to fit in before Thorsten's appointment. Ironically both patient and therapist took the same train to Berlin, although Thorsten moved to the front carriage when he saw me get on. First, there was an expensive breakfast at a hotel close to Friedrichstrasse Bahnhof, the envelope of cash in my bag had me in a *money no object* frame of mind. This was the sort of place I imagined Herr Anweiler checking into; in fact, I was rather hoping someone would assume he had. Interesting as it was making up exotic and waist-expanding combinations of food from the buffet while surrounded by businessmen and wealthy tourists, the purpose of my visit was to obtain the name and password of the hotel's Wi-Fi connection.

Next stop was the nearby Vodafone store. There was no hiding the fact that here was a sixty-three-year-old woman buying the top-of-the-range Samsung mobile phone, although the young sales assistant tried hard to convince me this happened every day.

'And I'll need a pay-as-you-go SIM.'

For twenty minutes, the sales assistant had been transferring his weight from one foot to another, dancing around in front of me. I was starting to become dizzy but fortunately the weight of the wad of notes I took from the envelope seemed to pin him to the floor.

The next stop was Alexandra Platz to buy a laptop. It was not on Paul's list of required equipment, so I went for something cheap. 'It's not for me,' I said to the salesman, as I prepared to be patronised for a second time that morning. 'It's a present for my husband, something he can use to browse the web. I'm afraid neither of us are very good with computers so perhaps you could set it up.' Then I felt guilty because he agreed to do this for free.

'Your husband's name?'

'Paul Anweiler,' I replied, and that gave me a really strange feeling.

Then back to Friedrichstrasse, to the Starbucks next to the hotel, where I had breakfast, close enough to it for me to still log into its Wi-Fi.

What did I discover in the time it took to eat a croissant, drink half a cup of coffee and begin to find the muzak annoying, suspecting it was chosen to discourage people from using the café as an office? Paul Anweiler was, as he said, CEO of K and S, or Chief Executive Officer of Köhl and Strasse Investments for those of us not in a hurry, a private bank with fifteen billion euros of other people's money invested in building, publishing and manufacturing; mostly in Germany but also in the rest of Europe and the US. Who these other people were was not clear, as evidenced by an article on the Forbes website entitled *K and S's backers, who is behind the secretive trust?* It took the journalist over five hundred words to explain they had no idea. Neither of Max Arndt's companies were amongst the list of investments on K and S's portfolio page. Outside of the bank, Paul Anweiler left no footprints anywhere on the internet.

The screenshot taken while in Peter's hotel had been transferred from my laptop to my own mobile phone and now the web address on it was typed into the browser on the laptop I had just purchased. As in Wittenberge, the resulting search yielded the address of a page on the *Autumn 77 Files* website containing references to Sonia Engelhardt and Max Arndt.

Sonia had come from a wealthy family and in her late teens joined various protest movements, eventually becoming caught up in the steadily increasing violence reaching its peak in September 1977. I had met her in the Autumn of the same year, after she fled to East Germany.

'There is someone I'd like your opinion on.' I wondered who Hüber wanted me to inform on, hopefully not a member of my family, fearing it might be Herman. My husband had just been promoted, and he was now liaising between Robotron and VEB Mikroelektronik and making frequent trips to the West. We were married and living in Erfurt where I worked in the personnel department of the microchip manufacturer.

At that time there was the feeling of being watched. Actually, more than a feeling because one morning as we left our apartment, a man loitering across the street seemed to be looking in every direction save for where Herman and I were standing. It was a cold foggy morning; I remember that because after I pointed the watcher out to Herman and said we appeared to be the target of an unusually clumsy surveillance operation, the watcher, if he was indeed a Stasi agent, seemed to fade into the mist. The man across the street had looked familiar but it was not Steuernagel, who by then was dead. He was thin, so not the fat man either.

Thankfully it was not Herman Hüber was interested in, but the former terrorist Sonia Engelhardt. I was to interview her on the pretext of offering her employment as a secretary; a position for which, I explained as politely as possible, she was not suited. She was confident and arrogant. A typical West German, I thought, and perhaps this stereotyping was responsible for the feeling I had seen her somewhere before. Later I would discover we had met, very briefly, two years earlier.

'Why have you decided to settle in East Germany?' I asked.

'Because the alternative was going to prison,' she replied as if the question was stupid and the answer should have been obvious, even to an idiot like me. However, this at least encouraged her to open up and explain how and why she became involved in the kidnap and murder of Albert Lauterbrunnen, a businessman and prospective member of the West German parliament. 'He was another of the Nazis who still run the country.' And Sonia saw it as her duty to help rid the world of these criminals.

There followed a long discussion about her childhood and relationship with a wealthy father, whom she also felt was an unreformed Nazi. 'It's obvious, he came out of the war with his huge estate and wealth intact. And the imperialist Americans let him keep it.' Worse still, from her point of view, her father's wealth and power denied her the freedom enjoyed by her peers. The material benefits of growing up a rich girl only served to increase the isolation and alienation she experienced as a child. The latter was an observation included in my report suggesting Lauterbrunnen had been a proxy for an overbearing father, who she would like to have killed had it not meant giving up her brand-new Porsche and overcoming the natural aversion to patricide. In conclusion, Sonia's need for a proxy for a father she despised would not end with the death of Lauterbrunnen and she would find many others in a country with a government as paternalistic as the DDR's. Holding back, I thought, from implying our government was overbearing; only when rereading the report after submitting it did I realise this was exactly what I had done.

'Do you think you will have any problems settling here in East Germany, given the way of life is quite different?'

I remembered Sonia smiling. 'I spent a year in London, so will probably cope quite well.' At this point something must have crossed my mind because I then asked where in London. 'A place called Elephant and Castle,' she said and her reply was underlined in my diary. Most likely I had remembered this was where Wiedel suggested Paul Anweiler was headed after he managed to evade the agent from the HVA and whoever else was following him. Whether Sonia's reference to Elephant and Castle was included in my report I cannot remember. Perhaps I assumed Hüber already knew about Sonia's connection to the Anweilers.

Having almost reached the limit of the amount of Muzak a human being can listen to and stay sane and now being stared at by one of the staff in Starbucks who was perhaps hoping to make me feel compelled to buy another coffee, I continued my search of the Internet for traces of Paul Anweiler and Max Arndt. According to the *Autumn 77 Files* website, Albert Lauterbrunnen's body was discovered in the boot of a car parked at a motorway picnic area on the French side of the border between France and Germany. The previous day, Sonia Engelhardt, along with three other terrorists, all four of them with forged British passports and in a British registered car, a Triumph Herald, entered East Germany at the Bergen-Salzwedel checkpoint. They were presumed to be en route from Bremerhaven to East Berlin. This sparked rumours of the involvement of a UK intelligence agency. However, the car was never found, and forged and stolen British passports were readily available in Hamburg and West Berlin. Accompanying Sonia Engelhardt were Karl Ansbach and Jens Steinbrink. Steinbrink spent fifteen years working for the East German TV station MDR and was now a fixture on West German TV and owner of a TV production company. The fourth member of the group had never been identified. Cleared of involvement in assisting the four terrorists were Karl Ansbach's brother Freddie, his wife Bettina and Max Arndt.

As for the spoilt rich girl I interviewed for a non-existent job, according to the website Sonia was shot during a failed escape attempt, a particularly audacious one considering it involved smuggling her into the enclosed village of Rüterberg then attempting to cross the Elbe by boat. Pointless, considering had she waited another five years she could have stepped through the hole in the wall opened up with pick axes on the 29th November 1989 and enjoyed a few days of freedom before the West German police threw her in jail. Her body was never found, something pointed out by the defence during the trial of former border guard Karsten Fischer who was charged with, but later cleared of, Sonia's murder.

Now there seemed a connection, tenuous perhaps but also somewhat disturbing, between a terrorist, Paul Anweiler and the person now embracing my son and grandchildren. And was Paul Anweiler the fourth person in the car? Quite likely as he had met Sonia Engelhardt when she was in London.

From what Paul told me in Dömitz he would have just as much reason as Sonia for using Lauterbrunnen as a proxy for a dominant and overbearing father. Then the connection between himself and the man in Celle, my first patient Heinrich Reisenberg, who blamed Lauterbrunnen for turning Greece into a bloodbath and the population against his battalion.

This must have been how Andreas K felt when belatedly realising he was the victim of Zersetzung; he too must have wondered when the campaign started. In his case the Stasi had begun to close in on him just a month before it became apparent what they were doing. It was now clear Paul had been there in the background for twenty-six years, since my trip to Celle, and possibly longer, maybe since that party in Rethen. This was something I may have suspected earlier had I not assumed he was dead. What about the return of my licence to practise and all the other things dismissed as merely lucky breaks, such as that offer to buy our house in Berlin for way over the market price? Was he the person on the other end of the phone when Herman helped our neighbour see off the witch from Hessen? And what about the generous offer Peter received for his nightclub?

'In your opinion, Lotte...' This back during that meeting in the Neues Palais in Potsdam. 'If Andreas K, realises what we are doing and tries to defend himself what form will this defence take?' Müller, a man who liked the sound of his own voice, asked.

Tapping my pen on the table while considering the question was a mistake as Frau Schmidt, keeper and guardian of Frederick's antiquities, approached me from behind and I could have sworn there was the sound of a grocery van's engine starting. Fortunately, rather than dragging me from the room by my hair, Frau Schmidt settled on snatching the pen from my hand and placing it on my writing pad; lined up perfectly with the edge, I noted later in my diary. This interruption, which Hüber found particularly amusing, gave me time to consider my answer. 'I'm sorry, Comrade Müller, I really have no idea.' Not entirely true, but had I suggested how Andreas might defend himself, and was later proved correct, those sitting around the table might have suspected their target had been warned. Not a casual enquiry by Müller then, but the Stasi officer setting a trap.

Now over forty years later, sitting in Starbucks wishing the coffee was smaller and the croissant slightly larger, I put the finishing touches to my response to Paul Anweiler's attack. As Hüber himself once suggested, I think just before the party in Rethen: 'Let's slap the water and see what swims out from under the rocks.'

First, I created a shortcut on the sparsely populated desktop and called it *Money* which clicking on it would take the user to the website of K and S Investments. Next, with the browser open, I created a series of tags containing the results of searches for information on rifles, hardware shops that sold bolts and nails and where to obtain hairdressing products, in particular anything containing hydrogen peroxide. Then two more tags: one to the *Autumn 77 Files* website, the second to an article about the only surviving relative of Sonia Engelhardt, her sister Helga. Then, with all the tags still open I close the browser and turned off the laptop.

Hopefully the computer would now act as a tracking device. This much I learned from listening to Herman and Roland discussing internet security and privacy: the potential for companies to learn more about us than we should be comfortable with. Herman had suggested it might be possible to build a profile of someone simply by monitoring what they accessed on the internet. Obviously, companies only had access to users of their own websites and not traffic to sites in other browser tags. This was not true of anyone monitoring all the traffic from and to a particular IP address, and there were organisations who did this. This was probably why Paul suggested any research into his background was carried out near a university where the traffic would be lost in a torrent of data, some of it produced by academics researching modern history including the period known as the German Autumn.

Without even looking down I knew the bag containing the laptop had disappeared from between my feet. It was headed at speed towards the escalator leading down to the U-Bahn platforms, although it changed hands before it got there. To be fair, I had been an easy target, my attention divided between the departure board on the first floor of Berlin's Hauptbahnhof and the map in my hand. My portrayal of a confused tourist just arrived in the city must have been convincing.

'Are you OK?' Asked the second young man, with kind sympathetic eyes, who placed a hand on my shoulder to prevent me turning and getting a good look at his two colleagues. 'My laptop, it's gone!' I whined pathetically.

'You should call the police,' the young man said. 'Have you got a mobile phone?'

Really? I suppose some people would have fallen for this and, unfortunately, I had reached that age it was worth a try.

'No,' I said, maintaining the pretence of being borderline hysterical. 'It's in the bag with the laptop.' It was at this point the youth's plan began to unravel. By now he should have grabbed my mobile phone and been headed up an escalator to the S-Bahn leaving me sufficiently confused to give all three thieves time to make their escape. Instead, there was a moment's hesitation.

'Don't worry, I'll catch them.'

No doubt he intended to do just that, suspecting if he missed the U-Bahn train his colleagues intended to catch, the phone might not be in the bag when it came time to share out that day's takings. It was even possible this was the end of a lucrative partnership. For myself there was an overwhelming sense of relief. The feeling I was now in control. This despite guessing when the computer was switched on and its new owner clicked on the shortcut entitled *Money,* the stream of data broadcast would cause Paul Anweiler only minor inconvenience. As it turned out, I guessed wrong.

# 27

# Sister Act

Ursula would have been impressed with that piece of street theatre at the Hauptbahnhof. It was the sort of stunt she would have pulled when a teenager. Just a pity it was not possible to share it with her. My sister texted me to say she would arrive home from work at 5 pm and meet me in the restaurant next to Friedrichsfelde Ost Bahnhof, not far from the apartment where she and Roland had lived since they moved back to Berlin in 1977. The restaurant was also close to where Nikolai Berzarin had died; he was a Red Army general and commandant of Berlin after the end of the second world war. After just 55 days in office his motorcycle collided with a Russian truck. He was posthumously made an honorary citizen of Berlin in light of his efforts to feed the population of the city in 1945, an honour removed after the Wende but reinstated in 2003. I kept thinking about another Russian, also called Nikolai, as well as the young man who had taken me to the Anweiler family reunion and whose demise was, apparently, the result of an unfortunate encounter with a Russian truck while riding a motorbike. Of course, it was possible that Paul had heard the story about Berzarin and it came to mind when he suspected I might contact Erich. What better way to prevent me doing this than convince me he was dead? So perhaps Erich Anweiler was another name to type into a search engine at some point.

Ursula arrived. 'Sorry, have you been waiting long?' she said, still out of breath. Surprising since she had only run from her car which was parked close by on Seddiner Strasse. The result of carrying slightly too much weight.

'No, I'm early,' I replied.

Early because the appointment with my patient had taken less time than anticipated. Rather than list all his achievements, Thorsten had brought along a portfolio of his work. His first projects were renovations and modification of buildings and apartments. Then he moved onto designing offices, and it was in these I identified a pattern, although given the nature of Thorsten's problem it was perhaps obvious my attention would be drawn to the stairs in each of the buildings.

'These all have a turn at the top,' I said pointing at one of the plans.

'It makes something utilitarian appear more artistic.'

'Really?'

'Well, I have to admit, I'm personally not at ease at the top of a long flight of stairs. I know it's unusual for an architect not to like heights. It sometimes proves inconvenient.'

'You are afraid of heights?'

'Not exactly afraid, just not comfortable with them.' There was a long pause while Thorsten waited for the next question. But sensing there was more to this feeling of unease with heights, I remained silent. Eventually he spoke. 'Actually, my mother told me that once, when we were in a large store, I was too frightened to climb down a flight of stairs. I can't remember the incident because I was very young at the time. But apparently she was angry because I would not move and eventually a man in the store carried me down the stairs.' So, there we were and maybe Thorsten was not the only person who should have worried about starting hypnotherapy with preconceptions.

At some point I intended handing Thorsten over to Sophie for Cognitive Behaviour Therapy to convince him nothing frightening lay at the top of every flight of stairs. But for now I booked him in for an appointment when I was in Berlin the following week.

'And how was your day, someone rich and famous pouring out their secrets?' Ursula asked, then lowered her voice. 'You must have plenty of stories which newspapers would pay a fortune for. Enough to retire on.' The conclusion she might have jumped to when asked to help during my meeting with Hölderlin.

'No such luck.'

'Well, you have your old job back, and I've heard Herman is being promoted again, so perhaps lucky enough.' It was as if my brother-in-law Roland was now sitting at the table because there was that hint of the bitterness in Ursula's voice he often displayed towards me. A cloud on the horizon and first hint of the storm which would break later that evening.

'Any progress on getting your old job back?' I asked, steering the conversation onto safer ground.

'Afraid not. It still seems history is best taught by anyone other than those of us who actually lived it.' Ursula's specialist subject had been French History and before the Wende she had lectured on the revolution and written a book on the role of Marxists in the resistance movement during the Nazi occupation of France. The book was currently out of print and Ursula's perspective on the French Revolution was also out of fashion; now viewed by historians as thinly disguised East German propaganda. The idea my sister had been cajoled by East Germany's ministry of education seemed somewhat farfetched given her outspoken and controversial views regarding Guy Debord and the Situationist International. It was also rumoured she was responsible for the comment, often repeated, regarding the reforms introduced after Ulbricht was replaced by Honecker: *OK, so now we have a circus, so where is the bread?*

Unlike the unfortunate Andreas K, Ursula remained untouchable, perhaps because, as she'd demonstrated on numerous occasions, she was adept at making people, mostly men, appear both stupid and impotent. Unfortunately, having avoided even a reprimand, she was, post-Wende, regarded as guilty by association and, at the very least, not sufficiently objective to explain the history of the DDR to the next generation.

'Perhaps I could redeem myself by writing a critique of the DDR,' she said. 'Reinforce the prejudices of those who replaced me and the bullshit they keep spouting. The library is stuffed with books by them. I've taken to transferring anything with *Stasi* in the title to the fiction section. Mind you, those which describe East Germany as some sort of failed Utopian experiment are just as bad, God knows where all these people were before nineteen eighty-nine, because I'm damn sure I never met any of them.' She fell silent and looked away. Perhaps I too reminded her of a past she was trying, unsuccessfully, to put behind her.

She looked around the room and then, catching the waiter's eye, clicked her fingers and shouted, 'Garçon, menu s'il vous plaît.'

The waiter came to the table carrying two menus, stood behind Ursula's chair and put his hands on her shoulders. 'And how is my favourite customer?' he said, looking at me as he whispered in her ear. Here was the male version of Claudia. 'No Roland this evening?' he asked.

'Working late as ever, I'm afraid,' Ursula said casting her eye down the menu. 'I will have a pork chop with sauerkraut.' I ordered salmon and rice and Ursula suggested we shared a salad and a bottle of white wine.

After the waiter had left Ursula took off her jacket and hung it on the back of her chair. The shadows beneath her eyes, prominent the last time we met, had disappeared and her makeup looked fresh as though repaired before leaving work, this was not for my benefit, surely. Also, librarians tended not to dress up to go to work, certainly not those employed by the history and politics department of a university. Tee-shirt and jeans would have been more appropriate than the pale green trouser suit, white blouse and neck scarf with a silver clasp, all which must have made her stand out from her colleagues.

'You said you'd met someone who could help you get reinstated,' I said, although, in truth I guessed she was having another affair.

'It's not that simple,' Ursula replied, but I suspected it would be. The arrival of the bottle of wine provided the excuse she needed to change the subject. Ursula slipped effortlessly into the role of the Parisian west-bank intellectual as she flirted with the waiter, even effecting a French accent. This was something she'd begun doing when we were young and supposed to be focussed on learning Russian and not using illegally imported films to practise other European languages.

'So, tell me about the meeting with the journalist. If you are not ratting on a patient what is it about?' she said when we were alone again.

'Something that happened years ago on a trip abroad,' I lied, because I'd never told Ursula about the Anweiler party or my meeting with Geoffrey Cathcart. Had I done so and she remembered, with Cathcart now in the running to be Britain's next Prime Minister, we would be having a very different conversation.

'Vienna, it's got to be. The guy dead in his room. So, international espionage, that's exciting,' Ursula said a little too loudly and with eyes opened wide. There were numerous reasons why people volunteered to work for the Stasi: financial inducements or other material rewards, coercion, political commitment or, quite often, merely to bring a little excitement into their lives. Anyone recruiting Ursula would have concentrated on the latter. But would she have thought international espionage quite so exciting after seeing Otto Steuernagel lying dead in the bathroom of his hotel room?

Steuernagel had been a man out of his depth at home and proved hopelessly lost abroad. His death, to me at least, came as no surprise. He was chosen to infiltrate a party of East German academics attending a conference in Vienna purely on the strength of looking like a psychology graduate. His brief, I assumed, was to ensure there was no unauthorised contact between me or my colleagues and delegates from outside the Eastern Bloc. In 1976 his death received little attention and was soon forgotten, just another casualty of the Cold War. A search of the internet threw up just a single-column story in an Austrian newspaper. In 1991 there was a longer article in the same newspaper but by then no one, with the possible exception of his parents, was interested in how or why Steuernagel had died.

'Was it a sex game gone wrong? I bet it was, it usually is when a man is found dead in a hotel bedroom.'

'I'm not sure what books you have been reading but I'm guessing there aren't many sex games which result in a person's head being blown off. No, this was a freak shaving accident.' Ursula looked puzzled. 'Someone packed high explosives in his electric razor.'

'Goodness.'

'A slight exaggeration. He didn't actually have his head blown off, just a piece of shrapnel severing an artery. All I heard from my room was a dull thud like a piece of furniture falling over. I only discovered he had been killed while on my way to breakfast. There was a policeman standing in the doorway of his room.' The image of the arc shaped smear of blood on the white bathroom door came to mind, as unwelcome as when it appeared in that nightmare I was having again.

'And you know who did it?'

'Absolutely no idea.'

'So why do you think the journalist will be interested?'

'Because it is a piece of forgotten Cold War history. Everyone who attended the conference was questioned when they returned, me included.' This was not quite true; it was some time before the subject came up, and then only as an aside when discussing the outcome of another manufactured meeting with a visitor from the West. 'It was fairly obvious from the questions I was asked that the Stasi had a good idea who was involved.'

'Given it was a conference on psychiatry, the list must have been rather long.'

'It's because no one was caught the journalist is interested. Nothing they like more than turning a mystery into a conspiracy because these days conspiracies play well on social media.'

'Why do you need my help?' Ursula asked in a matter-of-fact way as the waiter placed her food in front of her and then stepped back and gave a slight bow.

'I hope this meets madam's approval. We endeavour to please.'

'I'll let you know.' Ursula smiled at the waiter, unfolded a napkin and laid it on her lap.

I took the box containing the mobile phone from my shoulder bag and unpacked it. 'I'm using this to make sure the journalist doesn't just run off with the story.' Together Ursula and I followed the instructions Paul Anweiler provided, and studied the seating plan of the café in Boxhagener Platz. The app was downloaded from a third-party website rather than Google Play and when installed and running, the restaurant's Wi-Fi hotspot appeared in the list of available networks.

'Isn't spying on journalists illegal? Not just a little naughty but being thrown in prison for a long time, that sort of illegal?' For a moment I thought Ursula was crying off, but then she said, 'Exciting, all the same.'

Shortly after seven pm Ursula drove me the short distance to her apartment. We passed the travel agent which for many years after the Wende sent me travel brochures. I assumed it stopped doing this when Frau Eppelmann retired. All the buildings in the street where Ursula lived had been renovated since the Wende, according to my brother-in-law to justify increasing the rent. Roland was already in the apartment and about to eat a takeaway picked up on his way home from work. The three of us at around the table in the spacious living room, and I sensed Roland had something on his mind. I suspected not his neighbours being priced out of their homes, but Herman's new job, a subject I was keen to avoid.

It was in that room we had all sat, Ursula, Roland, Herman and myself, four friends having dinner together on the evening of the 9th of November 1989. Someone had shouted from the balcony below that at midnight the border crossings were opening and anyone who wanted to would be free to travel to the West. Roland had laughed and shaken his head, muttering under his breath that his neighbour was talking rubbish. Herman had mentioned the demonstrations in Dresden, but only in passing. As I recalled, Roland thought the crisis would pass, the protestors would cave in, a few concessions from the government and everybody would calm down.

Herman was not so sure although he was keen to avoid an argument with his brother-in-law and friend from his student days. The previous December Herman had told me about a meeting he'd attended with the head of research and development at VEB Kombinat Nachrichtenelektronik, a manufacturer of televisions and radios. Apparently the lignite used to fuel the factory boilers had frozen in railway trucks and everyone in the company, including managers, technicians, even some secretaries had spent a day chipping it out with hammers and pick axes just to keep the building warm.

'If that is true, the economy will collapse by the end of the year,' Herman told me. This from a person who was rarely outwardly pessimistic. 'Something has to change,' he had said.

A year later, at midnight, as Herman and I were about to return home, news of that change was bought to us by our nephew Justus who ran into his parents' apartment and through to his bedroom. 'I've just come back for some money,' he said when his mother asked why the rush.' We are going shopping in West Berlin.' The *we* being Justus and the group of youths revving motor scooters in the street below and calling for their friend to hurry up. Ursula shouted something to her son as he climbed on the back of one of the scooters, exactly what, I had long forgotten.

'It's actually happened!' shouted the neighbour stood on the balcony below. 'The border is open, they've just said so on West German TV.' It was not uncommon to hear fellow passengers on the S-Bahn discussing the plot of a US or West German soap opera, but Ursula's neighbour openly claiming he was watching West German

TV and doing so within earshot of a block warden, who would be obliged to report him to the Stasi, stuck in my mind as the moment the change Herman predicted came about.

Roland was still in denial despite what everyone around him was saying. 'They will turn him back. There is no way they will let young men travel to the West, only people over sixty-five will be let through.' This did little to console Ursula, who was in tears.

'They will,' she said. 'And then close the border again. It's a trick to see who has been planning to escape. It will be like nineteen sixty-one, the only way we will see him again is through the barbed wire.' This from someone who, thirty years later, was quite happy communicating with her son and grandchildren in London via Zoom.

The border did not close again and by the weekend we realised, as guards stood by while people attacked the wall with pickaxes, it never would. Justus arrived home midday on Friday and on Saturday afternoon Roland, Ursula, Herman and I met up to walk together through the border crossing at Friedrichstrasse with our children in tow. Herman, who was familiar with West Berlin, led the way, although the visit to the massive KaDeWe shopping centre was Ursula's idea. Neither Herman nor I waited in line at the cash machines dispensing a hundred West marks to visiting Ossies, having already brought with us the West German marks Herman held onto after visits to exhibitions in Hannover. Instead, we visited a café and acclimatised ourselves to a world containing an endless number of bright shining things to spend money on. In this regard, KaDeWe proved too much to take in, leaving all of us feeling numb. I wrote in my diary the following day that after returning home and putting the bananas in a bowl on the kitchen table, I went to bed feeling neither overwhelmed or underwhelmed, so perhaps just *whelmed* then. This was how many of us felt during the coming weeks until the implications of the Wende and the impact it would have on our lives became all too apparent.

Before crossing back into East Berlin, we visited a car showroom. Roland and Herman crawled over a seven series BMW. 'A few years from now you will be driving one of these,' The salesman suggested, which fitted well with the exuberance of the day.

'Patronising little shit,' Roland commented when we were all back in the street.

'I think there are more computers in that car than Robotron has sold to VEB Sachsenring.' Herman said, the difference between the two men's attitudes an indication they were already moving in different directions. Herman remembered what the salesman had promised and eventually got his BMW, although he would have preferred Schulenberg Electronics provided him with a Mercedes. However, Roland became the other head of Janus, forever looking back while my husband focussed on the future.

It has been suggested longstanding relationships were destroyed during the Wende. That the camaraderie that existed in the DDR ended when West Germans persuaded East Germans to become more competitive, not just with other companies and countries but with each other. But this was not why Herman and Roland, who had been the nearest each of them had to brothers, drifted apart. They had gone their separate ways prior to 1989 when Herman's career took off while Roland's flatlined. Now over thirty years of jealousy and resentment would come to a head. I had forgotten what Paul Anweiler said about closing down the Wi-Fi hotspot app on the Samsung Galaxy when it was not in use, or leaving the phone switched on in the house.

'It seems someone has set up a cybercafé in our apartment,' Roland said after turning on his laptop. My bad luck he worked as a sales representative for a company which sold security software and had a product sophisticated enough to warn overcautious computer users there was an unfamiliar wireless network close by. 'An evil twin.' I recognised this as a reference to the spoofing of Wi-Fi because Herman had used the term. 'In more ways than one,' Roland said, glaring at me. 'I thought you quit that sort of thing years ago. Or are you in Berlin for a Stasi reunion?' He stormed out of the room, slamming the door behind him. Ursula sat examining her hands, only looking up when Roland's car screeched down the cobbled street.

'I'll go,' I said, getting to my feet. Ursula frowned.

'No stay. He'll get over it,' she said, but I was not so sure.

'I was never a member of the Stasi. You know that don't you?'

'Roland thought you were. Isn't that the way it worked? We all suspected each other. You may not have been but must have known someone pretty important who was.'

'What do you mean?'

'That holiday in Lenorenwald when we were nearly all thrown in jail.' Merely the mention of it caused us both to laugh, releasing some of the tension, although I was still forcing back the tears.

'Nineteen seventy-five, wasn't it?' I was trying to place it amongst all the other events I had recently been forced to recall. The four of us had travelled north in the boys' VW Beetle, camping in the woods, evenings spent in Boltenhagen or on the beach, either near Gut Brook or Schwansee. Perhaps because we would have looked more at home in California than in North Germany, and there was a lot of horseplay, we came to the attention of a young member of the border police. He asked why the snorkels, which Herman and Roland were using to go diving while Ursula and I sunned ourselves on the beach.

'Do you really think we are intending to swim to Denmark?' Herman asked after realising the reason for the policeman's enquiry.

'Please hand them over.' By now the skinny teenager who barely filled his uniform had been joined by an older officer, who displayed a mixture of embarrassment and exasperation. His attitude was very much *What have you got us into now?* It was just a pity Ursula had identified a potential target for her not-so-juvenile wit.

'There is something I'd like to ask you,' she purred, rolling her hips and adjusting the strap of her bikini top which was a little too small, given the size of her breasts. 'Does your mother know you are outside of the house playing with a gun?' The boy blushed and the older policeman coughed to disguise a laugh.

'Well,' said Ursula, still finding it amusing after all these years, 'it was either that or asking if he had a torch in his pocket and it was quite clear the poor boy was pleased to see me. His trousers looked like they were about to burst.' Again, we both laughed. 'I'll get another bottle,' Ursula said, because what was left in the one on the table barely filled my glass. 'It's just a pity Roland didn't know when to call it quits,' she called out from the kitchen.

'You know why East Germany is so successful?' Roland had asked the two policemen and then provided the answer himself. 'Because all the idiots who might louse things are put in the border police.' So, we ended up in a police station, facing the prospect of a night in the cells and having to answer for our behaviour on our return to Berlin. There was even the chance we might lose our jobs and, like Beaky Boy, have to work as toilet attendants.

'You do realise you were close to a military base,' the senior officer asked as he waved one of the snorkels in front of Roland's face.

'OK, so now the charge isn't trying to escape, it's sabotaging a Soviet ship.' Ursula was correct and Roland did not know when to stop. With things spiralling out of control, I asked to use the toilet then left the room.

'When the top man appeared and said we could all go I guessed what had happened,' Ursula said. 'It wasn't a call of nature; it was a call to Berlin, to a friend who could get us out of trouble.'

Ursula was correct, but with Roland busy digging a hole and the rest of us wondering at what point it would be impossible to climb out, someone had to do something. Ten minutes after my visit to his office, the chief, having telephoned Berlin, wandered into the interview room with my identity card in his hand.

'*Did one of you drop this?* That was a stupid thing for him to ask considering your photograph was on it.' Ursula's memory was better than mine, because I could not remember that. 'The idea you dropped it in the corridor sounded pretty far-fetched but what really gave you away was his almost total disinterest in what we had done.' Ursula was correct and the chief's impatience had not been with us but the officers who had brought us to the police station. 'And not once did he make eye contact with you after handing you your card.' This was not quite true because as we were being released the chief told me to keep my boyfriend under control. I told him if Roland had been my boyfriend I would have drowned him in the sea. So, we got to enjoy the rest of our holiday and the only punishment was the embarrassment of Hüber introducing me at the next meeting as captain of the Danish Olympic swimming team and having to retell the story of our Baltic adventure for the amusement of everyone present.

Ursula deserved an explanation, so she got one, an account of the meeting in Potsdam and my small contribution to the Zersetzung program although no mention of Andreas K, who she had known quite well.

'More wine?' Ursula asked, topping up my glass then filling her own. 'You remember all that trouble Roland had after he brought car parts from a dealer in Duisburg?'

'Vaguely,' I replied.

'Stupid, really. Roland saw a part he needed advertised in a West German car magazine and wrote to the supplier and arranged to buy it when he was visiting the computer show in Hannover, that one he and Herman attended each year. Anyway, the sale went ahead, and the supplier was interested in the VW Beetle so Roland sent him some photographs of it. A few months later the story telling the history of the car was published, along with the photographs, in the same magazine where the parts were advertised. The dealer sent Roland a copy and Justus took it to school to show his friends. That bitch of a teacher must have reported it because the next thing, we get a visit from the Stasi and Roland had to explain how the magazine got the story. They already knew about him buying parts while he was in Hannover.'

'Hardly surprising, there was always someone from the Stasi in the Robotron sales team,' I said, although perhaps it was a mistake to point this out.

'But then the whole thing was dropped. The teacher said nothing else to Justus, the magazine was returned, and so was the VW Beetle which had been impounded. I guess it was much like that day in Lenorenwald and your friend intervened because I seem to remember it was around that time you were on one of your trips abroad. Not the time to rock the boat perhaps. I'm not sure Roland joined up the dots. In fact I know he didn't.' Another silence. Ursula put down her glass and looked around the room as if taking stock of all she and Roland possessed.

'The next year Roland was not allowed to stay overnight in Hannover during the show.' Ursula said, now sounding more subdued. 'Only Herman stayed, everyone else was bussed back here at the end of each day. And Herman's career took off while Roland was stuck doing the same job, writing software.'

'You can't think that Herman had anything to do with that.'

'No, no, there was something else going on. At least, according to Roland. Of course it may have been him being paranoid. He was under a lot of pressure at the time.' I did not mention that her fling with a colleague may not have helped. Ursula stood up, walked across to the sideboard and picked up a packet of cigarettes. She was about to light one but changed her mind. 'We'll go out on the balcony,' she said.

This was much like the old days when you went outside to discuss something you were afraid might be picked up by a hidden microphone, only now the fear was not being overheard but having an asthma attack. Ursula stood at the far end of the balcony and exhaled a plume of cigarette smoke which was carried away by the breeze. 'You remember all those discussions Herman and Roland had about East Germany falling further behind the West, and something had to be done if Mikroelektronik and Robotron were to survive.'

Yes, I remembered. 'Cars, football and the IBM PC, every time we met, only not always in that order.'

'Something had to be done,' Ursula repeated throwing away the half-smoked cigarette which in the failing light traced an arc on its journey to the pavement below, where it burst into a cloud of sparks. 'And Herman came back from Hannover one year with an IBM PC, only, according to Roland, it had some additional processors in it, more powerful than Robotron could get through other channels. Engineers used them to build a computer for Roland's software. He couldn't see the point as there would be no market for it if Robotron only had a handful of processors.'

'Yes, I think Herman thought the next generation of Mikroelektronik processors would be able to run the software. He posted something about it online recently,' I said, but Ursula shook her head.

'The next time Roland went to Hannover he visited the stands of some of the companies producing graphics software and discovered one marketing a product which translated video pictures into drawings. He said it was very much like the program he had written. After the show he submitted a report to his boss. There was no response, no one wanted to discuss it, and the next year Roland's name was left off the list of Robotron employees visiting Hannover, even for the day.'

'That doesn't mean anything,' I said, despite suspecting it did.

'Then along comes a delegation from a research establishment in the Soviet Union, some place Roland had never heard of. Suddenly he is out of the picture and replaced as project manager. Later he sees a document produced for the Russians, a list of companies in the West which could provide the software they required. On it was the name of the one whose stand he'd visited during his last trip to Hannover.'

'And he thinks Herman had a hand in that?'

'Who knows? We've all made the odd Faustian pact in our time,' Ursula sighed. I'm not sure if this was aimed at me or she had secrets of her own. 'And Roland suspects Herman's rehabilitation is payback from a company in the West he was in contact with while he was working for Mikroelektronik.' I assured her this was not the case but even so, given much of what had happened to us during the past thirty years, some of which I had previously put down to good luck, perhaps there was something in what Ursula was saying.

Not wanting to face my brother-in-law again, especially in light of the conversation with my sister the previous evening, I stayed in bed until Roland had left for work.

'What sort of distraction had you in mind?' Ursula winced as she sipped her coffee. 'My head... we really should have stopped after two bottles.' Actually, I had stopped after one but Ursula had carried on drinking. Despite restraint on my part, there was not much I remembered between anecdotes about old friends and parties past, prompted by a digitised photo album on Ursula's iPad, and ending when daylight streamed in through the window.

'I can't actually remember getting into bed,' I said.

'That's never good, sis,' Ursula said as two slices of toast jumped out of the machine next to the microwave which was reheating a cup of tea I had let go cold. 'I've never been to bed with an ugly man,' she said. 'But, God knows, I've woken up with a few.' Knowing my sister, I quite believed it.

'How about a few bars of Verdi's *La Traviata*.' Ursula launched into the opera but ended up clutching her head. It took me a moment to realise she was still talking about the meeting with the journalist.

'I don't think so.'

'I'll come up with something. Although it would help if I had that plan of the café, and the mobile phone.' I handed both over and Ursula folded the map and placed it in her pocket. The phone she stroked with her forefinger. 'Tall and handsome?'

'Who?'

'The person who persuaded you to do this.'

'No one asked me.'

'Come on, you can't fool me, I'm your sister. I bet you met him in Paris. He seduced you in a five-star hotel.'

'No! It definitely wasn't like that.' Although it sounded more appealing than being propositioned in the fruit and vegetable aisle of Netto.

'It never is,' sighed Ursula. 'So, a grubby little man in a dirty mac and pork pie hat at a fast-food restaurant in Brussels then. Still, at our age...'

# 28

# Where The Dogs Go To Die

What was I supposed to think when Leonard Cohen began singing about waltzing a young lady in Vienna, in a room where dogs went to die? Perhaps the same thing that went through my mind when U2's *No Line on The Horizon* was blaring out of the speakers in Herman's car? That someone was still playing tricks. But Herman played the U2 CD to embarrass me, the lyrics containing those *profound* remarks Rene Kellerman made at the lake. Leonard Cohen's *I'm Your Man* was something different, apparently, chosen at random.

'When did you get this?' I asked.

'It was on the bookshelf, next to that poetry book by Bertolt Brecht, I thought it was yours.'

Well, that figured, no doubt left by the van-driving cat burglar, part of Paul Anweiler's amateurish Zersetzung campaign. Should I be worried people were conspiring against me? Doubting, when he saw me at the lake, Rene really had said the first thing that came into his head? Perhaps, instead, the encounter had been planned, in which case this was in collusion with my husband. And now instead of Bono we have Leonard Cohen so it seems Herman has also been talking to Sophie because the last time I was in Berlin she handed me an invitation for speakers at a conference on Psychology in the Social Media Age to be held in Vienna. 'This was addressed to me, but I think it will be of more interest to you.' She said.

After the initial shock of finding myself now participating in a game whose rules and moves were all too familiar, I had spent five minutes on the conference website, long enough to discover who was organising and sponsoring the event. The Psychology and Sociology Faculty of Köln University was at the top of the list, Köhl and Strasse Investments at the bottom, although I guessed which organisation was putting up the money.

The lyrics of Leonard Cohen's song strayed into the erotic as I struggled to separate coincidence from conspiracy. I was at least able to comfort myself with the thought a firework of my own had been thrown in Paul Anweiler's direction. However, this had only been intended as a warning, to fizz for a while then pop, not explode on TV screens all over Germany.

We had passed through Schorfheide and were heading out into open countryside towards Sarnow when Herman swapped the CD for another by U2. Even so, my mind was still on a dead dog in a room in Vienna, this one called Steuernagel.

My preferred way of travelling to Berlin was by train but Herman loved his car and being in control. In truth, on that day his son kicked off, he had been just as impatient with the train drivers chatting to each other at the Zehdenick crossing. As we were both spending two days in the city, my first in Aldershof, close to Schulenberg's Berlin office on the science park, the car made sense. It was also the easiest way to travel to Herman's hotel of choice on the south bank of the Müggelsee where we would both be spending the night.

'We'll stay with the A10 because there's traffic in Marzahn,' Herman said. True, according to the satnav, but not heavy enough in my opinion to justify a detour to Friedrichshagen, and I suspected he liked the feeling of travelling back towards our old home on Kleine Müggelsee. *Marzahn*, I thought, *now there is a coincidence*, but Leonard Cohen's voice was still in my head, as was my trip to

Vienna in 1976, Steuernagel's death and the half-hearted attempt to discover who killed him.

'Let's go over it again. You said you left the hotel shortly after seven pm but returned thirty minutes later, changing your mind about visiting Altstadt and the Café Frauenhuber. That is where you said you were going?' Hüber asked. The recent rereading of my diaries revealed while there had been just one interrogation, the circumstances surrounding what was referred to as *the incident in Vienna* came up on several occasions between 1976 and 1978, the last time during a meeting to discuss Geoffrey Cathcart's visit to East Germany. Following this there was a consensus of sorts: Steuernagel had attempted to defect to the West, offering his services to the Americans. This advance was rebuffed, possibly because it was assumed he was a plant. A bomb was placed in his hotel room because during the meeting in the Café Frauenhuber, Steuernagel learned more about the CIA than it wished to share with the Stasi. There were numerous holes in this story and analysis of the explosives revealed it was manufactured in East Germany, as was the electric razor it was packed into. However, the idea that anyone attempting to defect to the West faced death at the hands of the CIA acted as a warning to anyone else thinking of betraying their country.

'Yes,' I replied. 'I had a headache and also needed more time to prepare for my presentation the next day so put off the visit to the Altstadt until the following evening.'

'And you were going to the Café Frauenhuber alone?' Weidel asked.

'Yes.'

'Why?'

'Someone recommended it to me.'

'Who?'

As Hüber knew very well who, he did not let me answer. 'Not Steuernagel?' he asked.

'No.'

'Would it surprise you to learn that Steuernagel was seen visiting the Frauenhuber that evening? Are you sure you were not both intending to spend the evening there?' Hüber asked stopping Wiedel pressing me on who suggested the café.

Even so, Weidel was like a dog with a bone. 'And would it surprise you to learn that on the evening in question, two so-called American diplomats were also dining at the Frauenhuber?'

Would it have surprised Weidel to learn that just a hundred metres from the hotel, while on my way to the Aldstadt, a limousine mounted the pavement in front of me and a very large man opened the rear door and said, in Russian, 'Please get in, someone wishes to speak to you'? Would it surprise him to learn everything that happened between then and being dropped back at the hotel six hours later and entering it through a back door next to the hotel's kitchen, which someone had wedged open to ensure my story of being in my bedroom all evening working and then sleeping off a headache was not contradicted by the receptionist?

It had taken almost two hours to reach the small village which, as we had passed through a checkpoint, I presumed was just inside Czechoslovakia. The restaurant lacked the promised splendour of the Frauenhuber Café, and the only diner was Nikolai Shetlov. 'Lotte, so good of you to come.' As if I had any choice. 'Sorry to bring you all the way from Vienna but I thought this would be more discreet.'

I was going to ask if this was an annual reunion but thought if we ended up exchanging jokes Shetlov might get the idea I was comfortable with being abducted a second time, which I was definitely not. He asked me about Herman and our forthcoming marriage and spoke of his son Thomas, but made no mention of Frau Eppelmann. Had I met anyone interesting recently, from England perhaps? Presumably, he meant Paul Anweiler.

'No,' I said and then he mentioned, again, that he had been in Vienna when he learned of his brother's death.

Answers to his questions were brief and as vague as possible, but I remained both polite and guarded as anyone connected to the Stasi would when talking to a KGB officer. His attempt to convince me he was my friend failed. Several times I tried to get him to explain what he wanted, but he responded with either a story or a joke. He was behaving like someone with an hour to kill who preferred not to dine alone. The plate of fish, potatoes and cabbage he was eating when I arrived looked so unappetising I decided to make do with soup and a bread roll. Given the situation it was hardly surprising I was not hungry, and the bowl was still half full when the waiter cleared the table. Shetlov's fish was also largely untouched.

The silences grew longer, and the evening began to resemble a couple's last together before their divorce. Then the waiter approached the table and whispered in Shetlov's ear he was wanted on the telephone. A call he had been waiting for, judging by the speed at which he leapt to his feet. Shetlov listened to the person on the other end of the phone then turned his back on me before replying, perhaps in case I could lipread. On his return he sat with his elbows on the table, mouth pressed against hands folded into fists. 'You must now go back to Vienna, it's late,' he snapped, as if this was an order, then seemed to change his mind and got up from the table again, this time to talk to his driver who was sat by the door. He returned looking less frightened, relieved even. This change of mood concerned me, and it turned out I had good reason to worry, as it was still by no means certain that three hours later I would be back in my hotel room in Vienna, asleep until woken the next morning by a dull thud from a room along the corridor.

Had Hüber and Weidel persisted with their questioning, I might have told them about the meeting with Shetlov, who it seemed inadvertently provided me with an alibi. Once they learned of the KGB's involvement they would have let the matter drop. They would have also removed me from the guest list of the meeting with Cathcart which I had spent months preparing for and was looking forward to.

'Marzahn, another coincidence.' And only when Herman said, 'Sorry?' did I realise I had whispered this loud enough to be heard over the music from the car's CD player.

'That's where they found that terrorist cell that was planning to attack a bank. Something to do with the Red Army faction,' I said.

'They looked more like Islamists,' Herman said. Although I thought what they looked like on the TV news were three young men who had stolen someone's laptop and inadvertently accessed suspicious material via an IP address traced back to their apartment block. A search for similar data had been made earlier that day from a hotel near Friedrichstrasse. There was mention of a bank in Köln and a possible link to the Red Army faction but not of Köhl and Strasse by name or Sonia Engelhardt. Even so, a result far beyond anything I had expected.

Then, two days later, MDR broadcast a repeat of a documentary on the life and death of Sonia Engelhardt, the rich girl gone bad. The final scene was filmed at Domitz, close to where it was suggested Sonia was shot while trying to escape, the camera tracking the Elbe as it flowed north suggesting this was the route her body took on its way to the sea. Someone seemed keen to lay to rest the girl resurrected by the theft of my laptop.

'Are you OK?' Herman asked as we parked outside the Psychology and Sociology Faculty. With good reason, because I had hardly spoken more than ten words during the last part of the journey.

'Fine, honestly. Just wish I was better prepared for today's seminar,' I replied, and received an extra tight hug.

'Research is OK, and teaching would be, were if not for the students of course,' I'd joked to my sister after getting my old job back. While I gave the occasional lecture, most of my time at the faculty was spent supporting colleagues by supervising tutorials: groups of between six and ten students and myself discussing real-world cases, the patient's names redacted of course.

'Today we have a patient with a long history of illness, or actually illnesses because no sooner is one treated than she suffers another.

Her GP would like to review her medication because they suspect some drugs conflict with others, but the patient resists any attempt to do this. She talks of being terrified by the idea of having to go to hospital. However, after being hospitalised there is no evidence of being traumatised by the experience, quite the opposite in fact, describing it as someone might their holiday. The list of her ailments is so long it is amazing she is still alive let alone leading a relatively active life. So, any ideas?'

'Is this a real case or merely hypothetical?' Even when learning back in his chair, Martin came across as aggressive, spoiling for a fight. Perhaps it was the thin lips and chiselled features or the way he dominated a conversation, badgering and cajoling until satisfied everyone in the room agreed with whatever theory he put forward. All this to disguise an inferiority complex because he was at least clever enough to realise he was not the cleverest person in the room. That was Katja.

'Yes,' I replied.

'A starting point would be her childhood of course. Something which happened to her when she was young ...' But then Martin was interrupted by Katja who had been making a show of looking at her watch.

'Thirty seconds before suggesting childhood abuse, a new record,' Katja said. She and Martin were my most enthusiastic students and as usual Katja had let the young man take the lead, providing her with sufficient rope to tie him in knots. It was sometimes easy to forget they were not a couple and rarely socialised outside the university. Katja was the softer, quieter and more ponderous of the pair, her hair falling and hiding her face when she was thinking and then swept aside, like a magician pulling back a curtain, having reached a conclusion. Martin would have done well on this occasion to pay close attention to Katja's left eyebrow which was usually raised slightly when suspecting her adversary had overreached himself.

'Sisters and brothers?' Martin asked.

'Is that relevant?' Katja wanted to know.

'One sister, one brother,' I said, and Katja gave this some thought, glancing at Martin before speaking.

'OK, I accept there may be evidence of childhood abuse.'

'That's obvious,' Martin said. 'The only time the abuse stopped was when your patient was ill or in hospital, which she came to regard as a refuge. Was she hospitalised as a child?'

'Yes,' I replied.

'There you are then. I rest my case.'

'So, if you were providing therapy, what approach would you take?'

'Well, for a start I would ...' Martin said, but Katja jumped in.

'I'm not sure, Martin, that you have enough information to draw up a treatment plan. Is this woman single and living on her own or does she have a husband?'

'Good, Katja,' I said, a reward for her being observant, but felt slightly guilty for holding back a vital piece of evidence. 'Yes, she has a husband, although this is a relationship few of us would recognise as normal. Unfortunately, as a therapist you only hear one side of the story.'

'So, her husband is abusive,' Martin said, glancing at Katja.

'No, the opposite. Very supportive.'

'But comfortable with his wife's illness,' Katja said, not the response Martin was expecting.

'Which suggests?'

'Insecurity. She is dependent on him and is unlikely to leave him while her health is poor.'

Martin was about to say something, but to ensure we kept moving in the right direction, I said, 'Early on in their relationship, he may have become aware she was prone to illness. Then he started, either consciously or subconsciously, triggering her illness by recreating the environment she grew up in.'

'She told you he was not abusive' Martin said.

'Correct' I said. 'But a clue as to what might be happening.' Admittedly a clue introduced in the last chapter of this detective story. 'When I suggested one of her illnesses seemed unusual, she told me her husband had suffered from a mild form of it a few weeks earlier.'

'Was it contagious?' Katja asked.

'No, not in the conventional sense.'

'So, perhaps we should consider psychosomatics,' Katja suggested. 'That if growing up in a family where there was abuse, she may have only experienced it when her sister was ill. Her only defence may have been to become ill herself.'

'That was one of the possibilities considered when devising a treatment plan. There may be others you want to think about. I would suggest before starting your essay you read *Why do People Get Ill?* by Darian Leader and David Corfield.'

'Have you been able to help her?' Katja asked.

'Treatment is ongoing,' I said, which Martin realised meant progress was slow and, ever helpful, suggested a solution.

'They should separate. After all, this is a pernicious and dysfunctional psychological dyad.' Then added with a smile. 'Mind you, then they will find other partners, and there will be two more miserable people in the world.' It was always disappointing when the only contribution from a majority of the group was the occasional burst of laughter.

'Are they miserable?' I asked, despite having decided the case was closed but now drawn into an argument with Martin I would have preferred to avoid.

'Well, she came to you for help.'

'Was referred by her doctor who was concerned about the amount of medication she was taking and suggested some, or possibly all, her conditions were psychosomatic. She sees my role as confirming her illnesses are genuine, which will allow her to continue using medication as a defensive shield, taking them in full view of her husband each day, which I suspect is her way of convincing him she is ill.'

'Wouldn't it be easier to pretend to have a headache?' Martin asked and again the rest of the students laughed.

'Actually, she has asked if there is any medication I could prescribe.' Now I, too, had the students laughing and decided the tutorial should end on a serious note. 'You suggest this is a dysfunctional dyad, but the relationship is functional...'

'But neither she, nor her husband, is happy, surely?' Katja asked, but I merely shrugged and thankfully time was up, so I avoided answering the question which played on my mind at the end of each session with my patient: had I failed because she did not skip out of the room smiling as if having just won the lottery? Perhaps all relationships, the only ones that endure that is, involve a degree of subconscious psychological coercion and one of the participants surrendering their identity and free will.

On my way out of the building, I passed Katja and Martin sitting on a bench in the foyer comparing notes and wondered what messages were being subconsciously passed between the two young people. While considering whether this was the beginning a of a relationship, I recalled what Martin had said about two miserable people in the world being preferable to four and had to tell myself not to be so cynical.

'Let's not argue, I'll meet you halfway,' Herman joked when we discussed where to meet for lunch, and he suggested the Korean Restaurant which was equidistant from his office and the faculty building. He was already sitting at one of the tables, at least I assumed there was a table beneath the large architectural drawing in front of him.

'Don't worry,' I said when Herman folded the drawing revealing the laptop, notepad and mobile phone beneath. 'I'll sit at the next table, assuming that's not where you are putting the filing cabinet.'

'So how was your morning?' he asked, the tone of his voice suggesting he was still concerned about my hour of silent contemplation in the car.

'OK, but I should have chosen a simpler case history. I might have just persuaded ten people to abandon clinical psychology for a career in advertising, or the pharmaceutical industry, or perhaps both.'

'Or in social media.'

'What's this?' I asked ignoring the last remark and taking the drawing and unfolding it again.

'It's Schulenberg's new Berlin Office and R and D centre,' he said, running his hand over it. 'There's lab space to produce semiconductors, although volume manufacture will still be carried out in Leipzig, and there's office space for marketing and a four-storey atrium.'

'And rather odd-looking stairs,' I suggested, realising this drawing looked familiar.

'Yes, that's something we are discussing with the architect.' *The best of luck with that if Sophie and I fail to cure Thorsten of bathophobia*, I thought.

'And why have you got this? Does it mean your retirement is on hold until it's built?'

'It will only take a year,' he said.

'Oh no,' I sighed. 'And what about Brexit and the EU research, are you still expected to work on that?'

'This is part of it. The original plan was to build this in Britain, just outside Oxford.'

'And next year?' I asked, in case Herman got the idea any of this sounded convincing. 'It will be, *Just hold the hand of the new head of R and D until he gets his feet under the table and, by the way we need a few things smoothed over with the mayor's office or the BMWi.* Meanwhile our retirement disappears over the horizon.'

Herman went full puppy dog, or would have done if it was possible to cock one ear while tilting his head. But then what came to mind was the memory of the man broken by the collapse of the East German high technology industry, humiliated by a former employee, whose ignorance was only matched by his arrogance but nevertheless stormed across the border at the head of a conquering army destroying all that lay in its path, my husband's career included. Surely it would be cruel to force Herman to give everything up for a second time. Perhaps this was not the time to discuss retirement and, anyway, the last time the subject came up Herman spoke disparagingly about life as a farmer in Gehrden and the feasibility of buying a small flock of sheep and perhaps an ox to pull a plough.

What Herman did not appreciate, or chose to ignore, was while since 1989 he had travelled extensively across Germany and abroad as far as I was concerned there might as well still be a border between East Germany and the West. It would be nice to discover aspects of life in America Claudia had obviously missed. And to do this with Herman after he had retired and not tagging along on one of his business trips.

'Sis, you should have grabbed it with both hands,' Ursula said when I turned down the chance for a week in New York. She had spent two weeks with Roland in Silicon Valley. 'Highway one, the Pacific Ocean, San Francisco... everything we dreamt of as teenagers. Saw none of them of course, just spent fourteen days on an industrial estate suffering from heat exhaustion and bored out of my mind.' An exaggeration perhaps, but after this my sister insisted on holidays in parts of the world where there was no market for internet security.

A young girl sitting on her own three tables away caught my eye. Perhaps, unsurprisingly, given recent events, the slightest prompt brought back memories of people in my past.

'Did I ever tell you I met Sonia Engelhardt?'

'No,' Hermann replied, giving me a quizzical look.

'Yes, when we were in Erfurt, she came to East Germany. I interviewed her for a job. She was totally unsuitable, of course, and I wasn't surprised she tried to get back to the West.'

'Oh, the girl in that documentary.' Herman had caught up. 'It's a pity you didn't take her on. Her parents' money would have been useful and could have funded Mikroelektronik's new chip.' He joked. 'If she really is still alive, she won't be renting an apartment in Marzahn, a castle on the Rhein perhaps. They say her sister is one of the richest women in Germany. She owns that bank that bought Peter's nightclub, Köhl and Strasse.'

'Köhl and Strasse!?'

'You've heard of them?'

'From somewhere,' I lied, unconvincingly I suspected.

Herman had a spring in his step as we left the canteen, like a young boy who had got away with stealing the farmer's apples. I returned to the psychology faculty and sat waiting for the students to arrive for the afternoon tutorial. This time the case history was a patient unable to come to terms with bereavement. However, perhaps more appropriate would have been someone who believed they were a victim of a gigantic conspiracy, with reference material from the Stasi archive, the file of Andreas K, the Zersetzung project at Potsdam University and a selection of my diaries.

The Müggelseeperle was Herman's home from home when he was in Berlin, although it was difficult to see how he found such a large hotel in any way homely. In truth it was the location which appealed to him, on the south bank of the Müggelsee and just four kilometres from where he grew up and where we lived after moving back to Berlin from Erfurt. As we drove to the hotel I remembered the bus ride from Kopenich to Müggelheim and Herman standing at the end of Odernheimer Strasse, next to his mother's car, waiting to drive me the last one and half kilometres to what would one day be our house. The picture in my mind was spoiled by the thought that, as I got off the bus, like the husband of my patient, Herman might have become aware of a vulnerability he could exploit.

It was working, the game Paul was playing, because I was starting to doubt everything: all that was happening in the present and most of what happened in the past. The trick with the laptop had proved as futile as standing in front of a tank. Now it felt as if Herman was slipping away from me, because the woman behind the reception desk reminded me of my mother-in-law. Fair enough, Herman was the person who decided where Schulenberg held their management meetings. But even so the way he was greeted recalled his mother asking how his day went and suggesting he put his feet up and rest while she prepared dinner.

'And you'll be eating in the restaurant this evening, Herman,' the receptionist said, briefly taking her eyes off him to hand me a key card. 'Sorry for not remembering your name but I didn't expect to see you again.' The receptionist didn't actually say that, but Herman's mother had on my second visit to her house.

'Did Dietmar Bauer manage to hang onto his house?' I asked.

'Yes, he is still there, still growing potatoes,' Herman replied, not caring I had found him out, because he assured me as we strolled beside the lake towards Friedrichshafen that he had never walked in the other direction to the Kleine Müggelsee. It was stupid, and irrational, being jealous of a receptionist satisfying Herman's desire for a little maternal affection. More understandable was the resentment I felt that he, like Joachim, Claudia, the farmers of Gehrden and the Dutchman who had turned their village into some sort of quasi-utopia all had managed to reconstruct their lives based on some make-believe version of their past. Perhaps the reason I felt some affinity with Paul Anweiler was because after a lifetime constructing just such a make-believe world the illusion had been suddenly and dramatically destroyed by the death of its chief architect, his father. Why had my meeting with him had such an impact on my life? Why was there now such a disconnect between me and everyone around me? Paul had managed to rip up the script and tear down the scenery, leaving me acting out my life on the stage of an empty theatre with only a hammer and sickle still visible on the poster half torn from the wall outside.

'The wildlife is hungry this evening,' I said, slapping my hand on an insect drawing blood out of my arm. We had returned to the hotel ordered drinks and were sat on one of the wooden benches beside the lake. The cognac would help me sleep, and the beer would no doubt take Herman back to those evenings relaxing on the veranda of our old house.

'Were we happy?' That was always going to sound wrong, implying we were not happy now.

'Sorry?'

'Back then.' A sip of cognac while considering if what I said next would sound even more hurtful. 'Before the Wende.'

Herman seemed relieved by this separation of our past and our present. I had expected something dismissive, to be accused of being silly. Or worse another attempt to discover what was troubling me.

'It's subjective. Time is like being carried along by the flow of a river and you never get to view the world from the same point twice.' I wondered if he was thinking about that trip we took together in his father's boat.

Moving closer to him along the bench, I rested my head on his shoulder. Herman immediately recognised my less-than-subtle hint that I needed to feel his arms around me. That I had surrendered and was ready to join him pretending we were in his mother's garden watching the sun set over the lake on that weekend in the summer of 1975.

'It doesn't even rhyme,' I said.

'What doesn't?'

'What you just said about being carried along by a river. I'm assuming that's U2 as well.'

# 29

## Escape to Stechlinsee

'So, what are the chances of us both ending up at the same point in time and space nine hours from now?' Herman asked looking at his watch as we left the hotel at the beginning of our second day in Berlin.

'About the same as six lottery numbers coming up twice,' I replied, although it was not Rolf I was thinking of at that moment but the coincidence of the architect chosen to design Schulenberg's new office and my patient being one and the same, and the possibility that in nine hours should Herman and I arrive at the same point in time and space Thorsten might also be there.

'Interesting, but let's aim for five-o-clock in Prenzlauer Berg all the same,' Herman said, assuring me there would be no call at four-o-clock suggesting I got a train back to Templin because the meeting at the Bundestag had overrun.

There was an hour free in the middle of the day, but instead of lunch with Herman I was meeting Ursula in the Forum, which was a short walk from the faculty. These sixty minutes were reduced to fifty by Katja who stopped me in the foyer as I was leaving the building. 'Can I speak to you for a moment?' she said, and while tempted to point out the obvious – that she was already speaking to me – I asked if it could wait.

'Actually, this won't take long,' she said, following me out of the building and walking beside me with her arms wrapped around a folder pressed to her chest. 'Yesterday you suggested happiness is subjective.'

'Did I?' I asked, remembering I only mentioned this was worth considering rather than suggesting psychotherapists put it on their letterhead.

'When you were talking about that couple. The husband and the hypochondriac.'

'She was not actually a hypochondriac, just suffered a number of conditions thought to be psychosomatic.'

'Even so, we were wondering...'

Presumably *we* meant herself and Martin. I thought walking faster might encourage Katja to get to the point but was wrong and there was a danger she would still be stuttering and prevaricating when we reached the Forum. So I stopped, and this seemed to steady Katja's nerves.

'We thought you might actually, when you said happiness was subjective...,' *suggested* I corrected her, '...you might be referring to your experience during the Wende.' Well, that certainly leapt out of the long grass where I had kicked it twenty years earlier. 'I would like to write an essay on the perception, created by West German media, that East Germans were neither happy nor content with their lives before nineteen eighty-nine, and that the expectation they would be after the Wende is at the root of some of the psychological problems they are experiencing.' This poured out in one long breathless sentence, and I suspected Katja must have spent the previous evening rehearsing it. Before I could reply she asked, 'I was wondering if you might help?'

'Yes, of course,' I replied, as this would provide an immediate, if only temporary, escape from a place I would rather not have been in just at that moment.

'Thank you, that would be good,' she said, and for just a fraction of a second, the face which smiled a little too easily betrayed the cold, calculating young woman hidden behind it. Professor material, I thought at the time, and was proved correct.

The essay was never written despite two in-depth interviews with me. However, Katja's PhD thesis was entitled *The East German Patient*. It proved controversial, appearing to reinforce the idea that being an Ossie was a mental condition which could be cured. Consequently, Katja became the go-to academic when the media needed a soundbite on mental health in the former East Germany. Thankfully the thesis contained no references to papers I had written prior to 1989.

Ursula was not alone, and sitting opposite her was a young man dressed in designer jeans, a slim-fit shirt and linen jacket. 'Oh, excuse me,' he said, and getting to his feet, slid a writing pad, a laptop, and a book I recognised, into a bag.

'Let me know how it goes,' Ursula said with a smile which might have suggested, to anyone who did not know my sister, her relationship with this young man was intimate. But as Herman once rather cruelly suggested, if all the men my sister had come on to were laid end to end, he would not be surprised.

'Are you tutoring him?' I asked after the student left the Forum. Although if she was, I was sure the university would turn a blind eye.

'Just helping him with a little French history.'

'And is that a copy of a book on Marxism and the French Revolution by a well-known East German author he is reading?'

'Probably one of the rare copies that weren't burned.'

'Available from second-hand bookshops on Amazon.'

'Yes, slightly annoying how much they fetch these days. But never mind.' Ursula said.

And what happens when he submits his thesis? I assume your book will appear in the references.'

'I should imagine someone will be extremely annoyed.'

'And you will lose your job.'

Ursula shrugged and looked at me over the wire-rimmed glasses she slid down her nose. 'Perhaps you haven't noticed there is something of a truce in academia at present. Not that it will last, but I'm making the most of it while it does. And anyway, that book is over forty years old. As an East German historian, I'm now part of Germany's history myself.' She studied me intently and then asked, 'Is everything OK, you're looking tired?'

Her too. Was there no escape from concerned loved ones? 'I've just been Googled and psychoanalysed by one of my students.' Katja had set in motion a train of thoughts it seemed impossible to arrest. But at least I now realised what prompted that question about historic happiness and contentment, and perhaps even why I had chosen that particular case history to discuss at the tutorial. Well spotted, Katja. Perhaps she had realised I was feeling my way in the dark, crossing back and forth across the no man's land between psychology and sociology.

Towards the end, Andreas K became convinced the whole of society had turned against him. But rather than the monster he had conjured up in his mind, the attack was mounted by just two people sitting in a room in Potsdam University, neither of them as clever nor able as himself. Unfortunately, even the tiniest inconvenience, or what in other times would have been dismissed as a prank, eroded his confidence and made him increasingly suspicious of those around him. There must have been numerous traps waiting for me. Like that Leonard Cohen CD placed by someone who knew about my invitation to speak at the conference in Vienna. Given that Herman put the CD in the car, perhaps because I failed to stumble across it in the house, suspicion fell on him. That is how easy it was to lose trust in those we loved and previously relied upon for support. All those wives who turned to me over the years after discovering their husbands had spent years betraying them. 'Another woman, I could have understood,' one sobbed. 'But the Stasi? My God.'

'I'm turning down the invitation to speak in Vienna.' I said.

'The conference? Why, what's happened? You were so keen last time we spoke.'

Was I? I could not remember being particularly enthusiastic or even giving it much thought. It had only been mentioned to Ursula in passing, the same day Herman was told. Perhaps that was when he transferred the Leonard Cohen CD to the car. It was painful and corrosive to keep thinking like this, suspecting everyone.

'OK, so it's Vienna, but the Cold War is over, no one is going to get killed,' Ursula said.

'But they did, once, the last time I went to Vienna,' I said, and it was as if that line from Leonard Cohen's song was playing in my head.

*Andreas K's current mental state means he is no longer a functioning member of the resistance group of which he was a founding member.* Not quite word for word what was written in my report submitted to Hüber, who forwarded copies to Janowitz and Müller at Potsdam University. Writing that report now, I would suggest the same result could have been achieved using Twitter bots and Facebook posts. And it was odd that my attacker seemed to have dispensed with social media in favour of more dated techniques. Perhaps they were reluctant to leave a digital footprint, or maybe they, too, feared the power of the internet and social media. If so, that trick with the stolen laptop must have given them pause for thought.

'If only there was someone you could talk to, a psychiatrist perhaps. I wonder where we could find one?' Ursula said looking around the room. Belatedly, I realised she was joking.

'They are all so young and look the part,' I said as a group of students and their lecturer descended the stairs after their tutorial on the mezzanine. 'None of those looks like a retired academic on a day trip from beyond the Milky Way.'

'What about the woman with the tray looking for a table, probably only five years younger than you? Her clothes look like they came from Kaufhof. Next week, after you have sold your life story to the journalist, we'll get you dressed for the twenty first century. Oh, that reminds me, you'd better take this.' Ursula took the mobile phone out of her pocket and slid it across the table. Then she retrieved the map of the café from her wallet. It had been amended. 'The person who did the survey was good, but this table is better, believe me.' Ursula pointed to one of the squares which had been ringed with a red felt tip pen. 'Looking forward to this,' she said.

'I'm not.'

'Why don't I believe that?' Ursula said, tapping me on my shoulder as she left.

On arriving at Sophie's practice for my two appointments that afternoon, the receptionist who, in attitude if not looks, reminded me a lot of my sister, said a woman had just called asking to speak to me. I waited to be handed a note which was not forthcoming. Eventually the receptionist looked up from her laptop and, seeming surprised I was still standing there, said, 'Oh sorry, she did not give a name or number, just said she would try again later.' Which the mystery caller did, while I was halfway through listening to a middle-aged woman, whose children had now left home, describing being trapped alone in a relationship with a person she no longer loved. A distraction from all that was troubling me, just not a particularly uplifting one.

'Two messages.' The receptionist peeled one of the notes from the edge of her computer screen. 'Your husband, Herman, called and said he was finishing early and will now pick you up at four...'

'Oh, Herman, that husband,' I replied, teasing her because for some reason she liked saying his name. Waiting for the coffee machine to dispense what its manufacturer claimed was a latte I said, 'Well I may not have finished so he will just have to wait.' It was tempting to remind her to look but not touch while he sat in reception.

'And that woman called again.'

'No message or number I suppose.'

The receptionist shook her head then turned her attention back to the computer. As I was walking back to my office the telephone rang again.

'It's her,' the receptionist whispered, holding her hand over the receiver. 'Do you want to take it in your office?'

No, I will deal with it here,' I replied, taking a sip of coffee.

The coffee machine had a small label stating *Beverages dispensed may be hot*, the same fear of litigation that saw packets of peanuts carry the warning *May contain nuts*. So far we had not been sued, probably because most of what the machine served was lukewarm at best. That afternoon, however, I should have heeded the warning as, having taken hold of the receiver, my mouth felt as though it was filled with boiling coffee. So there was a delay before I spoke during which I could hear a woman humming a tune to herself.

'I'm afraid I have just walked in, could I call you back?' I said as the coffee scalded its way down my throat, causing me to sound as if I was being throttled. 'If I could take your number.' The receptionist pushed a pad and pen across the desk in anticipation. The humming stopped and there was silence. I shook my head and the receptionist shrugged.

As I was about to give up and hand the receiver back, the caller spoke. The number she gave was a mobile. Her accent was both unusual and vaguely familiar; this was someone I had spoken with before – an existing patient perhaps. If so, why the hesitation, and why could I not put a face to the voice?

After returning to my office, it struck me the woman's accent might be unusual because she was attempting to disguise her voice. I called the receptionist and asked her to search the practice's database for the number I had been given.

Closing my eyes and imagining spending ten minutes sitting in our garden in Gehrden was my favoured way to clear my mind between appointments. With five minutes of perfect peace to go, there was a knock at the door.

'Not one of your patients, but they have called before. Do you remember that woman who booked an appointment a while back but cancelled at the last moment?' The chance to play detective had energised a usually somewhat lethargic woman, and she presented me with a computer printout of a patient record consisting of just three entries. An appointment booked, cancelled a week later and then a bank transfer covering the full cost of an initial consultation.

'I certainly do. Thank you. I thought she sounded familiar. I'll call her back after the next appointment.'

'He is waiting outside,' the receptionist said, leaving the door open as she left my office. There followed what I thought would be a difficult forty minutes listening to Thorsten M's assurances that he had finally come to terms with his fear of stairs. Difficult, because twenty-four hours earlier I had seen a drawing of a building which suggested he had not. It was also possible that if the appointment overran and Herman arrived early as promised, there would be an embarrassing meeting of architect and client in our reception.

Fortunately, Thorsten was in a hurry to catch a train, and Herman did not arrive until four thirty. 'Just one quick phone call and I'll be ready,' I told him as our receptionist handed him a coffee, her arms seeming to have shrunk by twenty centimetres because she was standing closer to my husband than she did other visitors.

There had been a text to my mobile on the day the woman cancelled. I'd been in the car with Herman, halfway to Berlin. Had I taken the train back to Templin, and then got a taxi home, I would not have arrived until mid-afternoon. Was this the day our neighbour, Mrs Reimann, saw a broadband engineer's van parked outside our house? If so, its occupants had all day to survey the inside of the house and plan for a second, and much shorter, visit on the day I went shopping in Lychen. So who was Paul Anweiler's fixer? One possibility was the woman standing beside him in that picture on my daughter-in-law's iPad.

'Good afternoon, Kars Travel here. We have some questions regarding a flight booked in the name of Paul Anweiler.' The number I had dialled was the one on the contact page of K and S Investment's web page. My request was too complicated for the person on the switchboard and there was a delay while a colleague was consulted. The consensus arrived at was I needed to speak to Mr Anweiler's PA.

'I'll put you through to Ute Lorenz, she will be able to help you.' The name sounded familiar, and then I remembered hearing it when checking into the hotel in Domitz.

'Good afternoon, Herr Anweiler's office. How can I help?' While the voice sounded slightly different there was little doubt this was my no-show.

'Hello Ute, Lotte here. You just called.' Silence, and in my mind the person on the other end of the telephone was now looking less confident than when standing amongst those firemen on the banks of the Rhein. Maybe Frau, or Fräulein, Lorenze was now shrinking in her chair, struck dumb after being found out. Or maybe I was deluding myself, because if Ute had overseen the minor shit storm which followed the apparent theft of her manager's laptop by terrorists, then surely here was someone prepared for the unexpected.

'I'm glad you called Lotte, it saves me leaving another message with your receptionist. I have the feeling she is busy and sometimes forgets to write things down.' Which translated into, *you are not so smart after all*. 'Mr Anweiler would like to discuss something with you and was wondering if you could travel to Köln next Tuesday. If so, I will book your train ticket and make a hotel reservation.'

'I'm not sure, Fräulein Lorenze.' I had assumed she was not married. 'I think that might be the day we are having our broadband fixed.' I could have sworn she sniggered and that this time the short silence was due to her hitting the mute button on her phone. When she came back online she was humming a tune to herself again.

'Ah, here it is.' Ending the pretence of searching for something. 'The Esplanade on Hohenstaufenring, close to Barbarossa Platz U-Bahn. It's quite convenient for the university.' Was I missing something here? Had I suffered a temporary black out during which I'd agreed to the meeting?

'Do you have any special requirements?' Ute asked, now beginning to sound like an automated help desk.

'I would like the sun to shine through the window at eight am as I don't have an alarm clock,' I said hoping this might call a halt to the stupidity.

'I will arrange that for you,' Ute responded without missing a beat. 'Mr Anweiler will meet you at the hotel between five and six pm on Tuesday evening.' And then before I could answer, she said 'Thankyou' in that singsong voice which she had tried so hard to disguise and hung up.

The receptionist was subjecting Herman to a grilling, reassuringly doing this from behind her desk rather than while standing over him. Her modus operandi was to offer her victims a coffee then loiter close enough for them to appreciate her perfume, the smell of which was strong enough to keep rodents out of the building and required a window to be kept open, even during winter.

'Ready for the off?' Herman said, putting his empty cup on the reception desk. He must have been thirstier than most of our patients; Sophie seemed to have discovered an Ossie nostalgia store with an inexhaustible supply of Kaffee Mix.

My phone pinged as we walked to the car. It was an email from Fräulein Lorenze with numerous attachments, and opening one at random I discovered an e-ticket for a return train journey to Köln, arriving on the Tuesday and back to Berlin on the Thursday morning. This had been booked two days earlier. So, not an invitation but a summons. I would later discover that those who knew her referred to Fräulein Lorenze as *She who must be obeyed*. The hotel booking included the requested time for the sun to shine through the window. That is what I got for being cute. Now, assuming I did go to Köln, the hotel staff would assume I was some sort of idiot. And if I did accept this invitation, as the hotel was *convenient for the university*, here was an opportunity to speak to Mo Fink, so perhaps I would be attending the conference after all. It was tempting to believe fate was lending a hand except it was not; this was someone making sure I returned to Vienna.

I ejected the Leonard Cohen CD from the player and plugged in my iPhone knowing Herman would not object to listening to Cannonball Adderley's *Somethin' Else*.

'These last two days have been like Erfurt, lunch together and you starting work on a new project,' I said as we drove through Bernau.

'In a way, although back then it was Mikroelektronik's new chip for Robotron. Now it's a new building for Schulenberg. Bricks and mortar are not really part of my skillset.'

'Steel and glass, from what I saw. The architect comes from Templin, doesn't he?'

'How do you know that?'

'His address was on the drawing you showed me,' I said. 'Do I take it you knew him before Schulenberg asked you to work on the new building?'

'Yes, I had met him a couple of times.' Herman sounded hesitant, which was a pity because this had started to sound like an interrogation, and there was something more important than a postponed retirement we needed to discuss. Not there in the car on the way home after two busy days in Berlin. Better somewhere he was relaxed and in the frame of mind to open up about part of his past it appeared, after talking to Ursula, he had kept secret from me. And I knew just the place.

'Let's go to Stechlinsee tomorrow for that bike ride we were going to take a few weeks ago.'

'A good idea,' he said, seeming relieved I had changed the subject.

The Rheinsberg nuclear power station was just visible above the treeline as we rode side by side around the shore of Stechlinsee, the lake I always associated with escape, having been sent to stay with an aunt and uncle who lived in nearby Altglobsow during Summer months when the polluted air in Berlin triggered near daily asthma attacks.

'Thinking about what might have been?' I said, tilting my head towards the abandoned building.

'I suppose the switch from physics to electronics was fortunate, otherwise we would be living abroad now. At least something of Mikroelektronik and Robotron survived.'

'Yes, we have been lucky. According to Ursula, Roland is still struggling,' I said pedalling hard to keep up.

'He's got nothing to complain about. With commission he probably earns more than I do.'

'I'm not sure it's money. He is still angry about the way Robotron treated him, stopping him travelling to Hannover.'

'Well, that was his own stupid fault, buying those car parts. With the Deutschemarks he was given for expenses, for God's sake.'

'He thinks it was you who reported him.'

'Well, he is either crazy or his memory is failing. I was the one who replaced the Deutschemarks, so he didn't end up in jail.'

'But that meant you were short of money to give back.'

'I was given foreign currency to buy equipment from western companies exhibiting at the show. I got one of them to add a few hundred marks to the invoice.' I suspected he may have done this more than once and it explained the spending money we took to West Berlin the day after the border opened. 'And there was that article in the West German car magazine,' Herman said slowing down so we were riding side by side. 'Even I started to wonder if he was planning a new life in the West.'

'He thinks you did a deal with a company abroad, swapping his software for advanced microprocessors, sacrificing his career at Robotron to advance yours at Mikroelektronik.' Herman got off his bicycle, appearing exasperated, and I thought he was about to throw it in the lake. Instead, he leaned it against a tree and sat on a large rock at the water's edge. When I joined him, he was channelling his aggression into skimming stones across the glass-like surface of the lake.

'It's a pity rocks are square and our backsides are round,' I said sitting beside him, but the attempt to lighten the mood failed.

'Roland's software was good, brilliant in fact. Even with Robotron's primitive computers, equal to what companies in the west were doing. That's why I thought if we could bring back a computer from Hannover he could use it to produce an even more advanced version ready for when Mikroelektronik's processor was ready.' Herman laughed. 'One of the reasons I got to stay overnight during the show was it justified taking a suitcase.'

'So that was why it always came home empty, you'd brought back an IBM PC. I never did understand how you could lose so many pairs of underpants.'

'Not an IBM PC, a Hewlett Packard with a Motorola 68000 processor. Then later a device called a Transputer. But Roland wasn't satisfied with having the most advanced graphics software in the world. The world had to know he had written it.'

'What did it do?'

'It took video images and turned them into drawings. The idea was to computerise paper drawings which could then be modified with Computer Aided Design software. But one of the people I worked with at Erfurt suggested using something called structured light to turned solid objects into three-dimensional computer models. Roland did this and then wrote a paper on it. I suggested, as did a few other people, the paper wasn't published until it was decided if the technology gave Robotron a strategic advantage we could exploit when Mikroelektronik caught up with Motorola and Intel. But instead of listening to us, Roland persuaded Robotron's marketing department that publishing might help the company appear cutting-edge.'

'And then someone in the West copied the idea?' But instead of answering straight away, Herman stood up and began looking for flatter stones that would bounce further across the lake.

'Yes, and then the Russian engineers turned up. They were trying to design a submarine propellor which was as silent as those use by the US navy. They had managed to purchase machine tools from Toshiba in Japan and CAD software from a company called Kongsberg, and having read Roland's paper, thought if they could film one of the US Navy's propellors they could make a copy of it. Unfortunately the Americans had already come down hard on Japan and Norway for letting companies break CoCom rules by exporting high tech equipment to the Soviet Union.'

'But we could have sold Roland's software to the Soviets.'

'In theory. We did discuss it, and if Roland hadn't published that paper we would have done so, and no one would have been the wiser. But thanks to your brother-in-law, the Americans would know Robotron had supplied strategic technology to the Soviets and might well put pressure on West Germany to stop loaning the DDR money. So instead we suggested our Russian comrades looked elsewhere.'

'Did they get the software?'

A group of hikers was walking along the path and Herman did not answer until they had passed.

'There was a British CAD company which designed software which could be used to create drawings and control machine tools. Someone working for it got hold of Roland's paper and set up a company producing a version of the software which did exactly what the Russians wanted.'

'Did the Americans find out?'

'Eventually, but too late because this company used the technology for lots of other applications. I seem to remember modelling organs in the human body was one of them. But most of their money came from software used in cosmetic surgery, modelling faces. The same sort of software used in those apps which make you look twenty years younger.'

'The company Roland saw at Hannover which he said was using his software?' I suggested.

'Yes, we never heard the end of that. Eventually someone explained what he had seen was the end result of his own vanity.'

'You.'

'No, someone else.' I guessed this someone else worked for the ministry of state security.

Further along the bank there was a couple, close enough for me to see they were about the same age as us. He was in shorts and tee-shirt, she was in a summer dress; the hem slightly too far above the knees given her age. But age did not seem to worry them, and they were behaving like teenagers at play. There was a shriek as the man picked up his wife, or possibly his lover, and threatened to throw her in the water. This could have been us. My fault it was not of course, and perhaps Herman was thinking the same as he took hold of my hands and pulled me to my feet. 'So that's the story of my short and rather boring career in international espionage.' And for a moment I feared he might ask about mine, which was somewhat longer and far more exciting.

We finished the circuit of the lake, arriving at the Luisenhof restaurant, Herman studying the menu as I looked out over the Dagowsee, Stechlinsee's smaller sister. The exuberant couple arrived shortly after us and sat at a nearby table. Like us they spoke in whispers except their conversation was punctuated with the occasional burst of laughter. Again, I noticed Herman's eyes fixed on the woman who was not particularly attractive but, just at that moment, was more fun to watch than the person sitting opposite him. It was the doubt and suspicion making me appear ugly, perhaps even repulsive. As hard as I tried it was impossible to dismiss the idea Herman had been lying. As well, and this was me being hypocritical in the extreme, I was thinking his dealings with the Stasi had been more extensive than he had let on. Was it possible he could have done all he'd said without the involvement of someone from the HVA; someone like Werner Weidel? Perhaps even Weidel himself?

I thought of all the red-eyed people who arrived in my consulting room sometime after they had, for a reason which often defied explanation, requested a copy of their Stasi file. At no time had it crossed their mind what impact the contents of the file would have on their marriage. It was always difficult to know where to start.

'Has anything changed since you discovered the person you loved, and loves you, was a Stasi informer? They are still the same person.

The only difference is your perception of the past, but this should not alter how you view the present. Because the past was a different place. However, when you lived there, did your partner post every aspect of your relationship on social media? Did they broadcast a running commentary on your life to the whole world? No, because in this place there was no internet, so your private life was only shared with the block warden or a contact in the Stasi who noted aspects of it in a file which probably never saw the light of day but instead was left to gather dust. In this place, which we have now left, it was only the collection of information not the information itself, which was employed as a means of control. Today it is the big tech companies such as Twitter and Facebook who hoard this information, for much the same reason. I know you feel hurt and how you view someone very close to you has changed. But did they agree to the Stasi's request knowing the result would be privileges and advancement for both of you, while refusing would put you both at risk?'

Did this help the patient? Sometimes, but not often.

'You seem distant,' Herman said. Which was true, very distant, in a dark place somewhere within one hundred and twenty kilometres of files, one of them containing my account of the party in Leipzig provided during that meeting in Potsdam. Less intimate than the entry in my diary. But even so how would Herman feel if details of our first meeting were, pardon the pun, laid bare to someone with an understanding of psychology who might learn a great deal about both of us? How we interacted with each other at that party, realised it was Beaky Boy who was responsible for bringing us together. My future husband spotting a young woman lost and alone, in a room full of strangers, who was at the mercy of that little shit who'd decided I was an easy target, someone he could bully to impress his friends, reminding her of the violent outbursts of a damaged father.

Now it felt like the person who came to my rescue that evening was slipping away from me, perhaps imagining a future with that woman in the summer dress at the other table.

'You should have spent less time studying human psychology and read up on animal physiology, sis,' Ursula said after I once wondered aloud whether Herman fantasised about air hostesses when we made love after one of his trips. 'OK, so buy yourself a Lufthansa uniform and a pair of those shoes which push your bum halfway up your back. Men are only interested in our bodies for eighteen months, maximum, then their attention wanders. It's all about spreading their genes as widely as possible. We can't fight nature, that's why the Party never tried banning fashion magazines along with everything else that was fun when we were young. Men are willymantics, you may think their hearts are in the right place but in truth its usually between their legs. You just need to reinvent yourself every so often.' I remembered how out of place she seemed during Andreas K's talk on the objectification of women; and, at the same time, how Andreas could not keep his eyes off her.

'They've got rhubarb pie.' Herman was reading the menu, but I was yet to decide on a main course.

'I'll just have a schnitzel,' I said without looking at the menu. A lunch the previous month in Lychen came to mind and not for the first or last time that day, I thought of Paul Anweiler.

'Actually, if Roland and Ursula had been planning a new life in the west, they could have fled any time they wanted to. We could have done the same,' I said.

Herman frowned. 'I don't think so,' he said, So I explained, without mentioning the Anweilers by name, how a family, each member of it arriving at different border posts, managed to leave East Berlin unchallenged.

'If there was a flaw in the border control system, someone from Robotron would have exploited it.'

'There was nothing wrong with the software, you just needed a friend in the border control force.'

Herman scoffed. 'A friend very high up in the Stasi,' he said, shaking his head. 'No, it could never happen.'

As he started eating, Herman said, 'Actually, I'll see what I can do to help Roland.' Perhaps to assuage guilt, or maybe my story about the Anweilers' excursions into West Berlin reminded him he also knew someone well-connected who could open doors.

Stood in the shower, watching the dust wash out from between my toes, my mind was on the summer dress laying on the bed. It had not been worn since our holiday in Sicily all those years ago; bought from a shop in Catania because none of the clothes taken with me were suited to daytime temperatures of forty degrees. At the time Herman thought I looked good in it, although changed his mind when we got back to our hotel room, where in minutes it was on the floor around my feet.

'Look it still fits.' I said stepping through the patio doors and into the garden, and the dress obviously reminded someone else of that holiday.

Gehrden slept during the day and the only sound in the bedroom was the tap of the blind on the frame of an open window each time it was caught by the breeze. If the Stasi had asked the person whose arms were now wrapped around me to provide intimate details of our first night together he would have refused. This was what I believed and could continue believing in the absence of written evidence to the contrary, information I had no intention of seeking out. And I could forgive this man if he had imagined, when making love to me, I was that woman on the beach at Stechlinsee. Forgive him because the tapping of the blind on the window reminded me of water lapping against a boat on a summer's day a long time ago, which was not drifting towards the Müggelsee but somewhere else, on a lake in a place called Rethen, and the person I was imagining lying beside me was not my husband.

# 30

## A Café in Boxhagener Platz

Twenty minutes after leaving Templin Stadt station, the train had a crisis of confidence and whereas during the first part of the journey it had glided over sunlit open fields, it suddenly took fright and sought refuge in the dappled shade of a forest. Like me, it seemed increasingly uneasy the closer it got to Berlin. By now Rolf would have purchased his lotto ticket from the tobacconist on Dargersdorfer Strasse and was about to become one of the richest people in Brandenburg. The tape was safe inside the padded envelope securely stored at the bottom of my shoulder bag. Even so, for a second time, I checked it was still there. The transcript was in a foolscap envelope reinforced with a piece of card to give the impression that the document, the edges of which I had distressed, needed protecting due to its fragile condition and historical importance.

At first I considered telling Günter Hölderlin that, sometime in late 1978, a colleague discovered that the tape and transcript had been retained by mistake. The truth, according to Paul Anweiler, but with a degree of separation between me and this potentially catastrophic error. I had promised to hide the tape for this colleague so it would not be discovered when their office and house were searched after the Stasi realised it was the voice of Sabina the shoplifter, and not that of Cathcart the suspected spy, on the tape. Except, this colleague would have been a very close one indeed for me to risk my career, and possibly my husband's as well. So, much of the train journey was spent going over in my head the series of events Paul Anweiler had dreamed up which led to the tape ending up in the battered suitcase where I hid my diaries and other potentially incriminating mementoes.

Overlooked was my involvement in the recording of the conversation between Cathcart and the peace campaigners. I still thought this was unlikely to come up during my conversation with the journalist.

The train arrived at Ost Kreuz Bahnhof an hour before the meeting with Hölderlin. Plenty of time to reach Boxhagener Platz on foot. As I walked along Gabriel Max Strasse, I passed several cafés and restaurants which seemed better suited than the one chosen for a meeting during which one of the participants was having fun and games with Wi-Fi.

Ursula was already sitting at the chosen table, and on seeing me arrive transferred her cup of coffee and Danish pastry to one on the other side of the narrow aisle running the length of the café. I sat with my back to the wall where, according to the drawing, the Wi-Fi signal was weakest, while Ursula was seated at the table opposite and at ninety degrees to me. Hölderin, when he arrived, would be facing me with his back to Ursula, who would have a clear view over his shoulder.

A waiter pointed out that orders for food and drinks were placed at the counter at the front of the café and then, without waiting for me to explain I was meeting somebody, turned to Ursula.

'And how are you today?'

'Fine, such a beautiful day in a wonderful city,' my sister said in what sounded like broken German. 'Far nicer than Paris, in my opinion. My late husband and I came here on our honeymoon and I have such fond memories. And yesterday I enjoyed my coffee and apple strudel so much I just had to come back.' I'm not sure how many genuine French women the waiter had met but I was certainly convinced, although slightly puzzled as to why the act.

Gunter Hölderlin arrived ten minutes late, appearing slightly flustered. While searching for a woman who had forgotten to provide a description he stood fidgeting and straightening his jacket and the collar of his shirt. He was younger than I expected, and I had been hoping for someone older who, being more at ease with himself, might be less aggressive.

There were only two women in the café sitting on their own: myself and Ursula, who looked as French as she sounded. Also, on the table in front of me was the padded envelope, which Hölderlin would already have guessed contained the tape. 'Lotte, isn't it? I'm sorry I'm late' he said, shaking my hand and effecting a shortness of breath, probably to give the impression of having hurried to get to the café on time, which I somehow doubted he had.

According to LinkedIn, the journalist was a year younger than my son Peter but if, as Paul Anweiler suggested, he was keen to hide his East German roots, the cord jacket, collar-length hair and heavy frame glasses were a poor disguise. He asked me what I wanted to drink and then returned to the counter and placed the order. 'Just coffee.' I heard him insist while shaking his head, after being offered a seemingly endless list of options all available with whole, semi-skimmed or lactose free milk.

'So, Lotte, you have a story for me,' Hölderlin said when he returned to the table. After placing a bag, which I assumed contained his laptop, on the floor, he unzipped it and took out a note pad which had a pen pushed into its spiral binding. This was not going well.

'So, this is the famous tape,' he said, changing his glasses, picking up the padded envelope and pulling out the spool. He paid special attention to the label as if assessing the provenance of an old master. 'Looks genuine. But then it is difficult to tell without listening to it.' Something else I had not considered.

'There's also this,' I said, taking the envelope containing the transcript out of my shoulder bag, which was on the chair beside me. 'It's a little fragile. It has been hidden in an old suitcase for over forty years.'

'Not in bad condition, considering. Better than some of the Stasi files I've seen.' Which I found slightly worrying, not realising Hölderlin was something of a connoisseur.

'Thank goodness for mothballs.' A stupid thing to say to him but luckily he was too engrossed in what was typed on the paper to think of sniffing it.

'How is it you have this?' Hölderlin asked and I repeated the story Paul had come up with during that lunch in Lychen. 'So, in the Stasi archive there is a tape of an interview with this young girl who had been shoplifting?'

'And other people I interviewed,' I said.

'You said there are two other tapes?'

'Yes, one of a meeting between Cathcart and loyal party members, so that he returned to Britain with a balanced view of East Germany rather than the one-sided story told to him by dissidents. And there was supposedly a recording made by the Polish security services during Cathcart's stay in a small boarding house, a copy of which was given to the Stasi.'

'I don't suppose you also have a copy.'

I laughed. 'If I did, I would be in Hamburg talking to a journalist from *Bild*. And planning my retirement.'

'Instead, you are stuck here with me. Still, it's intriguing to think what might be hidden in the Stasi files.'

Ursula raised an eyebrow and pouted, implying she thought I was trying to seduce Hölderlin by suggesting there might be more on offer if he was a good boy. I shook my head, hoping to persuade her to stop playing the fool.

'Yes but as this is all I have so will carry on working for a living.' I thought it was better Hölderlin believed money, rather than political conviction and a desire to wreck Cathcart's career, lay behind my decision to hand over the tape.

'What is your job?

'I am a psychotherapist.'

'And back then, when Cathcart visited East Germany?'

'I worked in the personnel department of VEB Mikroelektronik in Erfurt,' I replied, and Hölderlin frowned.

'So why did you have the tape?'

'Sometimes I was asked to assess whether visitors to East Germany were hostile or sympathetic to the DDR.'

'Aha.' Hölderlin considered this, before asking, 'And was he a friend or foe?'

'There was supposed to be linguistic analysis of the transcription and the recording itself. Obviously, this was not carried out or someone would have noticed the error with the tape.'

'That's surprising.'

'It seems so now, but Cathcart was not regarded as particularly important. The Stasi had wasted time and resources on his brother. Eventually both of them were dismissed as students burnishing their left-wing credentials.'

'Still, I have to be honest with you Lotte, I suspect this is some sort of hoax. The BND, or whoever is keeping Cathcart's Stasi file hidden from the public, has created a vacuum. Some people see this as a chance to cause mischief, or simply to make a lot of money.'

'Are you suggesting this is a forgery.?' I said, taking the transcript back.

'Possibly. How do I know this is a recording of a meeting with Cathcart and not some clever piece of editing?' he said, examining the tape again. 'Audio technology is pretty advanced these days.'

If the tape was indeed a fake then Paul's choice of a journalist was unfortunate. Some of Hölderlin's articles I had discovered on the Web were reviews of high-tech sound systems and recording equipment. Perhaps it was assumed no-one would be stupid enough to try passing off a forged tape as genuine to someone with

Hölderlin's experience. 'For all we know, Cathcart never attended a peace movement meeting,' he said.

'But he did. I was there.' Silence from Hölderlin and behind him a look of surprise on Ursula's face.

'Sorry, you were at the meeting?'

'Yes. On occasions I met visitors face to face.'

This was greeted with a sceptical look. 'But this was a meeting of peace activists. Surely it wasn't possible to just turn up unannounced.'

'I went with a person called Michael Meyer.'

'I've heard of him. Just a moment...' Hölderlin then caught me completely off guard by taking the laptop from its bag and placing it on the table. Ursula also seemed to panic. The moment I dreaded had arrived, although later than anticipated. And I had forgotten to take the mobile phone from my bag.

'I can probably find him,' I said, grabbing hold of the phone, but instead of searching for Meyer, started the evil twin app.

'Don't worry, this will be just as quick,' Hölderlin said, and so, with the Wi-Fi hotspot now active, I placed the phone just behind his laptop.

Ursula had been looking over Hölderlin's shoulder while he typed. Suddenly there was a loud crash as she opened a map of Berlin, pushing an empty cup and saucer and her mobile phone off the edge of the table. 'Oh, no my mobile!' she cried, although seemed less interested in the phone than the two halves of a broken saucer she was picking up. It was left to Günter to retrieve her mobile phone and check it was still working. '*Merci*, young man. It was a present from my late husband. I'm afraid I'm not good with technology. He worked for Atoll Electronique.'

'That's interesting. They make CD players and Streamers, don't they?'

'*Oui*,' replied Ursula with faux excitement. 'You know this company?'

'Yes, I wrote a review of their products,' Hölderlin replied. Obviously my sister's research had been more rigorous than mine. Now it seemed I had been forgotten.

A boyfriend had been lost much like this when I was fifteen. Rainer quickly lost interest in me after I introduced him to Ursula, who told me two weeks later, after dumping him, that she had done me a favour because Rainer was a disappointment from the waist down. Some consolation, considering it was what Rainer had above his neck which had attracted me to him.

Eventually the discussion about Atoll Electronique's multichannel amplifiers came to an end. 'Very nice to meet you, and thank you again, young man,' Ursula said, placing a hand on Hölderlin's shoulder. This gesture, and perhaps being described as a young man, was why he was still blushing when resuming his search for Meyer. By now, however, the evil twin on my mobile phone had done its evil work.

'For some reason it did not connect,' Hölderlin said. Quite possibly it crossed his mind there was more to this than a simple technical error; but then he was distracted a second time when my mobile phone rang and I answered a non-existent call.

'I'm sorry I am in a meeting with someone, I will have to call you back.' I turned off the phone and returned it to my shoulder bag. 'I knew it was a mistake to turn it on,' I told Hölderlin.

The waiter asked Ursula if she would like another coffee and I wondered how that worked because I thought customers were served at the counter, not their tables. Also, the answer was supposed to be *No* or perhaps *Non, mon cheri*, not 'Actually, would it be possible to have a glass of white wine?' This was a deviation from the agreed plan because instead of saying her au revoirs, and then leaving, my sister stayed put, no doubt with her ears straining to hear everything that passed between Hölderlin and myself.

'OK, here he is. Michael Meyer, peace activist jailed for ten years in nineteen seventy and kept in solitary confinement in Hohenschönhausen, in what they called the submarine, apparently.'

A sharp intake of breath, then he whispered to himself. 'Not very nice. Released in nineteen seventy-three after experiencing a breakdown. Are you sure this is the person?'

'Yes, that was what those attending the meeting, including Cathcart, were told, and that I had been helping him after that alleged breakdown. This helped explain my presence at the meeting. But you will struggle to find a former inmate or guard at Hohenschönhausen who saw him there.' The articles appearing in newspapers in the West describing Meyer's trial, imprisonment and breakdown, or at least the one in nineteen seventy-three, were based on information fed to gullible journalists to create a legend. To members of the peace movement, Meyer came across as shy and reserved. He effected a tremor in one hand, and a slight stoop when he walked, the result of numerous beatings, it was rumoured – a rumour the Stasis started on his behalf. The reality was somewhat different; he was a trained Stasi agent, a particularly aggressive one.

'Did Meyer organise the meeting with Cathcart?'

'No, I'm not sure who did that. An informer called Jens was asked to invite Meyer to the meeting because it was thought someone who had suffered at the hands of the Stasi might be best placed to gain the trust of a foreigner.'

'How so?' Hölderlin looked puzzled so I picked up the transcript and pointed to a paragraph on the second page: Meyer asking for support from the Left in Britain for a struggle within East Germany against latent Stalinism. This he claimed would be made easier if East Germany's leaders could no longer use the fact that nuclear missiles were pointing at their country to justify the hard line taken with anyone wanting peace with Britain and America. And if Britain and West Germany ended their close ties with America, there would be less need for an antifascist barrier.

Günter studied the transcript. 'Were you with Meyer and Cathcart when they had this conversation.'

'No. While Meyer had told the group he trusted me, some of them were suspicious of new members. Jens was protecting himself by telling other members to be wary of what was said in my presence. I had been warned he would do this during a meeting with Hubert Hüber a week before Cathcart's visit.'

'Hubert Hüber?'

'My contact in the Stasi.' Hölderlin typed on his laptop again. From the keystrokes, it appeared this was not an internet search and presumably, as Paul predicted, the journalist had opened up a new Word file. At this point I imagined a message flashed up on the screen of Ute Lorenze's computer.

'You said Cathcart had a partner.'

'Yes, a girl. It caused something of a disagreement between me and Meyer. I only found out about her as we were travelling to the meeting.'

'Where was this meeting?'

'A small village to the west of Berlin. We travelled to Stendal by train then the rest of the way by bus. I think Meyer would have preferred making the journey by car, but he was supposed to be a persecuted citizen stripped of privileges, and driving a relatively new Lada would have seemed odd. The host was a pastor and there were between twenty and thirty people at his house listening to what Cathcart had to say. As you probably know, most of the peace groups had links with the church. I'm sorry to sound rather vague but it was over forty years ago and at the time the meeting didn't seem significant. The only reason I was asked along was because some years before I had met someone from Britain who knew people connected with Geoffrey Cathcart's brother David. And I wasn't asked to assist the Stasi again after this, probably because Meyer and I had an argument, and he put in a complaint about me.'

'What was this argument about?' Hölderlin asked when he had finished typing.

'Nothing really. On the train from Berlin, Meyer gave me a copy of the notes on Cathcart's visit. Until then I hadn't realised Cathcart had brought a colleague, a girlfriend. She was black and I suggested

362

Meyer slipped in a reference to Martin Luther King's *building bridges not walls.*'

Hölderlin laughed. 'So, you are responsible for Cathcart including that quote in his speeches.'

'I don't think so. Meyer thought it was a bad idea. When I told him I wanted to see how Cathcart's girlfriend reacted, especially any perceptible change in attitude to Cathcart which indicated this was a genuine relationship, smiling at him for example or standing slightly closer, Meyer said he couldn't see the point. I think he was feeling stressed and was psyching himself up for the meeting. I had already submitted a preliminary assessment of Cathcart based to some extent on what was known about his brother. My opinion was both young men's interest in socialism may have had its roots in competing for the attention of their parents, themselves ardent socialists, and this created in their minds a link between socialism and the receipt of maternal and paternal affection. Seeing how Cathcart now interacts with crowds of supporters, possibly I was right. Anyway, to some extent at least, Meyer went along with this and felt that projecting himself as one of the downtrodden crushed by the East German state would get him close to Cathcart. He regarded any transitioning from a dyad to a triad as an unnecessary complication and insisted he spoke to Cathcart on his own and in private.'

'Then you never actually got to talk to Cathcart.'

'Not one-to-one. I sat in on his talk, next to his girlfriend actually, and gained some insight into her relationship with Cathcart. Which was important because there was a suspicion Cathcart had brought a black person with him for our benefit, to persuade us he genuinely believed in international socialism. It caused some to suspect his visit to East Germany might have been encouraged by Britian's security service to increase his credibility within the country's own peace movement.'

'That would be the CND.'

'Yes, Cathcart was a member. Meyer, for one, felt it all seemed rehearsed.'

'And he still believed Cathcart might be an agent, even after he met him?'

'Why wouldn't he? After all, the Stasi infiltrated him into the East German peace movement.'

'Good point. Now, Meyer, Michael Meyer...' Hölderlin had returned to Google and I waited for the inevitable, having performed the same search the previous day. 'Oh, it appears Michael Meyer is dead.' He was. Suicide, because while obviously not needing counselling after his fake incarceration, it might have helped him adjust to the false reality forced on him during the Wende and the demise of the Stasi for which his fake persona had been created. I was surprised he never contacted me as I was one of the few people he could have trusted not to betray his past. 'What about the Stasi informer Jans, do you know his family name?' Hölderlin asked.

'I'm afraid not. It was redacted from all the reports I saw.' This was not true, but unlike Michael Meyer, Jans was still very much alive and the sort of person who had access to very expensive lawyers.

Hölderlin rubbed his chin then bit his lip. Ursula was staring towards the window looking out onto the street, pretending to be more interested in passers-by than what the journalist and I were discussing. 'Whether this story is true depends very much on the tape being genuine.' He picked up the reel and examined it again, looking for something which might suggest it was a fake. 'I know someone who might be able to help, he is an audio engineer in Magdeburg. Would you mind if I took this to him?'

The perceived value of the tape would have plummeted had I readily agreed to part with it. Admittedly the idea of doing just that was tempting, washing my hands of it having now done everything Paul Anweiler had asked. However...

'I'm reluctant to let it out of my sight.'

'No problem, we can travel to Magdeburg together.'

'As well, I need to know whether this is worth pursuing.'

'Ah, how much we are prepared to pay for the story,' Hölderlin said, looking thoughtful again. 'Do you have any information of that other meeting Cathcart had while in East Germany? Antisemitism in the British Labour movement is a hot subject and in nineteen seventy-eight, when Cathcart visited East Germany, the Stasi was funding anti-Jewish organisations and even printing antisemitic literature for distribution in West Germany and in Arab countries.'

'Yes, I know the aim was to create the impression antisemitism was a purely Western phenomenon and gain influence with oil-producing countries. Not something which required the expertise of a psychologist, so, I'm afraid what you see is all there is.' I reached over the table, took the tape from Hölderlin, and was returning it to the padded envelope when he made his offer.

'I think we might be prepared to pay twenty-five thousand euros,' he whispered, although Ursula heard him and stared at me with her mouth open.

'I was thinking of something closer to seventy thousand.'

Günter feigned surprise and Ursula appeared to go into shock. I then listed the key selling points Paul Anweiler had thoughtfully added at the end of his page of instructions. 'Well, it will be a big story both here and in Britain. I'm sure you won't be throwing it away on a single issue but probably serialise it. Then a deal with a UK tabloid will earn you far more than I'm asking.' Paul listed two other reasons why a journalist might be interested in the tape, but I remembered something Hüber told me before the Cathcart meeting. If something sounds too good to be true it probably is.

'OK, I think we can talk about a figure close to what you are asking. Assuming the tape proves genuine of course.' At this point Ursula handed the waiter a fifty-euro note, telling him to keep the change, and walked out of the café.

With my sister gone, Hölderlin and I planned the next move. I was to bring the tape to Berlin and we would travel to Magdeburg together. 'Would tomorrow be convenient?' He asked.

'Yes.' I said although realised I was in danger of running out of patients in Berlin who needed urgent appointments. With his compromised laptop zipped back into its bag Hölderlin, gulped down what remained of his coffee, stood up and shook my hand. Then, once out on the street, we went our separate ways. As Ursula had turned left when leaving the café I assumed she was heading north to the tram stop on Niederbarnim Strasse. Rather than risk Hölderlin seeing my sister and me together, I caught a tram at Wismar Platz. It was our mother's birthday, and we had arranged to meet at Weissensee.

We were both carrying similar bunches of flowers bought from the same kiosk when we arrived at the grave. 'Do you ever wonder...' Ursula said, her voice trailing away.

'Yes, just a few more months and perhaps a West German hospital might have saved her.' Something we often speculated on when we visited Weissensee cemetery. No physical reminder of my father but when my mother died, she wanted to be buried close to where the grave had once been. And had his grave still been there, there would have been other *if onlys*. *If only* someone had seen him by the lake that evening. If only he had come indoors out of the snow, perhaps they would not have taken him away.

'But they were already treating her, weren't they, western pharmaceutical companies testing their drugs on us and the Party selling us off as human guineapigs.' The bitterness was brief, and the smile returned to Ursula's face. 'What was forty metres long and did not eat meat?'

'I give up.' I replied.

'The queue outside an East German butcher's shop. You should know that. Remember when you were sent to buy meat? The other customers in the shop told you the grown-ups were being served first and children had to wait. So, you stood there all afternoon. Eventually mother went to look for you and when she found out what had happened threatened to report the butcher. We certainly were never short of sausages after that.' Ursula sighed. 'Solidarity, fraternity and everyone helping each other, what a load of shit that was. I wonder what she would think of the world today.'

'At a guess she would wonder why we are wasting our freedom being so miserable. Oh, and throwing away money. A twenty-euro tip, really? And how many times had you been there as Madame Ursula?' She held up three fingers. 'I'll pay you.' I said.

'Don't worry.' Ursula waved the suggestion away. 'Seventy thousand euros, now that's a lot of money. Almost what I earn selling library books on eBay.' It was obvious a serious conversation with Ursula would be impossible until her adrenalin level returned to something close to normal. I took the mobile phone from my bag and removed the SIM.

'This is yours,' I said, handing the phone to Ursula. 'Only delete the app or Roland will stop your pocket money.'

Ursula laughed. 'Thanks, I might wait until Justus is home next and ask him to check it doesn't play a few other tricks, given you seem to have fallen in with some rather dodgy characters.' She took hold of my arm. 'And now some shopping for your trip to Vienna.'

On the way to Alexanderplatz, Ursula insisted on buying a lottery ticket on account of the jackpot being close to the rollover limit. 'My dear, fifty million euro is a fortune *énorme au-delà de l'imagination*, she said, struggling to extradite herself from the role played so perfectly in the café. 'You must have a go,' she insisted.

I struggled to think of six numbers. OK so four, seven and eleven, well, why not? Surely Rolf would not mind sharing some of his luck. With Ursula pestering to move on I turned to our home telephone number for inspiration.

'Geoffrey Cathcart? Really? You met? You weren't making it all up.'

'No,' I whispered, as the man sitting across from us on the tram was listening.

'OK, so what other adventures did you have?' Not receiving a reply Ursula tugged at my arm. 'Well?'

'Let's see. I was kidnapped twice by the KGB. Once they threatened to fly me to Moscow and the second time I was thrown in a car and driven across the border into Czechoslovakia.'

'Well, if you are not going to be serious...' Ursula let go of my arm and the man sitting opposite smiled.

During the train journey home to Templin, with two carrier bags of clothes on the seat beside me, Ursula's account of my visit to the butcher's shop came to mind. This was an experience I could not remember first-hand, but had been recounted on numerous occasions. So many times, I had an image in my mind of the interior of the shop, the counter, the white tiled walls, and could see that five-year-old girl standing in it as if watching myself in a movie.

And a short while ago I played a YouTube clip of a British politician speaking passionately about building bridges instead of walls and imagined I was leaning in the doorway of a house looking out across an orchard. Instead of addressing a large cheering crowd the politician was standing next to his girlfriend speaking to a person he thought was a comrade. What was it Paul Anweiler said about memories merely being stories we tell ourselves?

# 31

# What's That Sound?

This was my third trip to Berlin that week, the second from Templin Stadt station. Although on this occasion the sky was overcast and the weather cold so instead of sitting outside the café I waited in my car. Tired I drifted off to sleep, only waking when the train arrived.

The tape was in my shoulder bag and strangely, given it had increased in value by tens of thousands of euros, there now seemed less need to continually check it was still there. I wondered if Rolf felt as relaxed about his lottery ticket. Had he folded it, pushed it into his pocket where it would stay, forgotten, until a washing machine reduced it to paper mâché?

It seemed each visit to Berlin saw another building demolished and replaced because renovation was deemed too expensive. An exception was a reclad apartment block half-hidden behind a hoarding with *Anweiler Construction* emblazoned on it. Not something I would have noticed a month ago but now shouting at me, a reminder of that encounter with Paul Anweiler and that everyday I dug the hole he pushed me into just a little bit deeper.

Hölderlin was late, only five minutes, but long enough for me to doubt myself. Had he definitely said *tomorrow*? I checked the text sent the previous evening and the reply telling me he would be waiting outside Lichtenberg station. The call to the number on the journalist's business card went to voicemail just as a dark green Sabre arrived and parked in front of me, blocking the path of an expensive looking Audi which was about to leave.

The Audi driver sat with his hand on the car's horn. Hölderlin leaned over and pushed opened the passenger door. 'Someone is in a hurry to get stuck in the traffic at the end of the street,' He said as I climbed into the car. 'OK, OK, were going,' he muttered under his breath as we pulled away from the kerb. 'He should have got himself a Mercedes, then no-one would care if he arrived late. They would realise he was either too rich to give a shit or too old to remember what time he was supposed to turn up.' I told Hölderlin Joachim's joke about the person in a Bavarian car factory fitting indicators that would never be used.

He laughed. 'That's a good one but I am hopeless when it comes to remembering jokes,' he said, and I began thinking of him as Günter, fellow former East German, rather than Hölderlin the journalist.

'The train would have been quicker and easier, but I wanted the chance to talk,' Günter said as we crawled out of the city. We could have talked on the train but I suspected he wanted to discuss the Cathcart tape somewhere as private as a near empty café, although without a crazy French woman eavesdropping. Or perhaps not, because nothing we spoke about related directly to the tape. Instead, Günter was gathering background information on his source, as if composing the introduction to the article he now seemed keen to write. We spoke about our parents' experiences of life in the DDR, although there was little to say about a father I barely knew and a mother who had spent most of her life working as a nurse. 'You may have heard of my father,' Günter said. 'He was a well-known journalist and worked on *Neues Deutschland*.'

'I don't think so,' I told Günter, but soon realised, in a roundabout way, I had.

'It was a difficult life for a journalist in those days, there was pressure to toe the party line. My father was lucky because he had some very good contacts abroad, especially in Britain and Italy. He got information, especially from inside the Italian communist party and the British trade union movement, before anyone else in East Germany. He was once asked to write a profile on a British trade union leader during a strike and discovered this person was helping himself to money donated by East German workers. You can imagine how useful that information was to the HVA. It was things like that got him more freedom than other journalists. He also wrote articles which appeared in *Eulenspiegel*. When Ulbricht was replaced by Honecker and reforms in East Germany moved ahead, his articles about the Soviet Union became even more critical.' The mobile phone Günter had been using as a satnav slipped from its holder and fell into the footwell. Two attempts to retrieve it saw the car swerve across the road so, rather than us colliding with an oncoming truck, I gave directions using the now almost forgotten art of reading road signs.

'There was to be a series of articles on Soviet industry ahead of Brezhnev's visit to Berlin,' Günter said, slamming on the brakes because we had almost missed a turn. 'My father toured Russia to find out what progress had been made with the tenth five-year plan. He interviewed the manager of a shoe factory who had cut costs by spending one year making left shoes and then the next year making right shoes. The problem was for the first year there was a shortage of right shoes and the following year no left shoes in the shops. He wrote a story about this in *Eulenspiegel* using a fictional name for the factory. The problem was he also mentioned the shoe industry in the article for *Neues Deutschland*. He was always slipping jokes into the paper, things which looked like errors but people who were looking for them would know were intentional.' It was tempting to suggest Günter might want to look through the back issues of *Neues Deutschland* for any mention of that week's lottery results.

'He put in some quotes by ordinary Russians, what they thought of the standard of living and whether they believed the ten-year plan was a success. Most of the quotes were genuine but one was made up, a man who felt very pleased with the availability of shoes. He used the name of a Red Army soldier who had featured in a previous article and had lost one leg during the patriotic war. Only someone reading both *Eulenspiegel* and *Neues Deutschland* was likely to get the joke. Unfortunately, a sharp-eyed person in the Stasi had done just that, and wasn't amused. They feared their counterpart in the KGB might also realise the two stories were connected. In Moscow, *Krokodil* had already run their own version of the shoe factory story. There was the prospect of Honecker having to stick his tongue in another part of Brezhnev's body after pushing it down his throat the next time the Soviet leader visited Berlin. Anyway, my father lost his job and ended his career writing children's books.'

'Of course,' I said, now realising Günter's father was both the anonymous character in Rolf's story and the author of books which Peter and Inge had now passed onto my grandchildren. 'My children grew up reading your father's books. *Hoppity*, the story about the boy who could never find both of his shoes.'

'Yes, say what you like about my father, he wasn't one to cave in under pressure. And his books were just as popular after the Wende.'

Then it was my turn to share experiences of life before and after 1989 which, when it came to luck and fortune, mirrored Günter's because around the time I was allowed to practise again he was recruited by a leading business magazine reporting on the growing number of internet companies springing up in Berlin. Except it was not long before Günter's luck ran out.

'There was a lot of money funding technology which was never going to work. I wrote a story explaining this. The editor told me he needed to make some changes and only half of the article appeared in the magazine. In the place of my warning about a rather badly thought-out business model was a full-page colour advertisement paid for by one of the companies I covered. Six months later this internet startup folded and the investors lost their money. In fact I don't think the magazine even got paid for the advertisement. Unfortunately, the PR consultant who had arranged the interview with the company's CEO had already stopped sending me invitations and spread the word I was negative on new technology. Also, the burned investors thought I had promoted a company it should have been obvious was going to fail, so at best I was stupid and at worst I was corrupt. Being an Ossie certainly didn't help. Since then I've been working as a freelancer, reviewing throwaway pieces of electronics, giving five stars to anything that doesn't catch fire when you plug it in.'

Günter fell silent for a moment and I got the feeling I was expected to laugh at this point but instead was reminded of Herman, the man who once helped shape East Germany's industrial strategy, testing pieces equipment free of charge as a favour for a struggling electronics company.

'I guess everything has changed but nothing is different.' Günter sighed then seemed to put pessimism to one side and closed the door on his past. 'The company we are visiting is run by a father and son, Kurt and Klaus. They are specialists in audio and have around forty employees and a recording studio.'

Until we parked in front of a smoked glass cube, the centrepiece of a business park on the outskirts of Magdeburg, I had assumed the tape was to be examined by someone working in their bedroom or garage. The idea there was about to be a forensic examination by a seriously professional looking company was slightly disconcerting.

'Günter, good to see you again. We've got some interesting equipment for you to look at. I take it you are still doing reviews for audio magazines?' Klaus greeted Günter as if he was a family friend. Not so me. 'And you are Lotte,' he said as an afterthought and catching me unawares as I looked at the posters of musicians, some familiar but others looking young enough to still be at school, on the walls of the reception.

Klaus had a firm grip for a man so slight and I realised he and the guitarist on the poster above the receptionist's desk were one and the same, separated by several years during which he had lost most of his hair and dispensed with the piercings in his nose and left ear. 'My son used equipment like that,' I said, pointing at amplifiers in a large glass case, hoping this might put at ease someone who obviously viewed me with suspicion. 'He had a club in Berlin.'

'Would that be Peter, by any chance?' Klaus asked.

'Yes,' I replied, somewhat surprised.

'I thought I recognised your name.' I thought Klaus was about to reminisce about his days playing in a band, but he did not. 'We have just finished working on his boat, installing a high-tech audio system.' He smiled. 'It's the only electronics on it which seem to be working at the moment. Still, I'm sure it will be ready for the launch. But you're not from Wittenberge are you, Templin, isn't it?'

'Hot Cats country.' The elderly man behind Günter said before I could answer. 'I'm Kurt.'

'My father,' said Klaus, in case I had not guessed. 'Yes, tragically, unfortunately, and annoyingly popular with a thankfully shrinking section of the music-buying public in Eastern Germany. That's what I suggested was put on the cover of their CD anyway.'

'Some of the music is quite good,' Kurt said. 'The problem is her.' I guessed the recording session must have been recent as both he and his son exhibited the same combination of despondency and regret when describing their experience with Hot Cats that Claudia did when sweeping up broken glass on Sunday morning after one of their concerts in the Weissen Ross.

'Well, when they play on your son's boat, perhaps someone will throw her over the side,' Klaus said. That image of someone dropped in the Elbe and their body washing out to sea came to mind but was gone again when Klaus clapped his hands. 'You have something for us to listen to, Günter tells me.' I offered him the tape but he refused to take it. 'Not my area of expertise, or something I'm particularly interested in. My father is the specialist in the lives of others.' A reference to Florian Henckel von Donnersmarck's film. 'Personally, I think it's time we all moved on.'

Kurt took the tape. 'I will set this up and let you know when it's ready,' he said. I was reluctant to let it out of my sight but his son, despite being uncomfortable with what his father was being asked to do, still seemed keen to talk.

'Peter tells me his father works for Schulenburg Electronics and is on a government committee for regional development.' I was surprised my son took any interest in what his father was doing. Klaus paused as if giving thought to what he was about to say. 'There is a lot of money being poured into Thuringia. I know Berlin is trying to turn East Germany's high-tech region into a European version of Silicon Valley but it would be nice if Magdeburg was not completely forgotten.' This was probably as much for Günter's ears as mine.

The tape was already running when we were ushered into the studio, the three of us perched on chairs usually used by musicians while Kurt sat in a glass booth adjusting the controls on a recording deck. There was a click and his voice was broadcast over the Tannoy. 'I think what you are hearing is the breeze as it appears the microphone was installed outside.' The sound changed slightly and in the background was a strange noise like the calls of geese. Was there a party somewhere close by?' Kurt asked.

'If there is anybody there, knock once for yes, twice for no.' Klaus laughed having said out loud what had already crossed my mind: that this had acquired the air of a séance with Kurt the person in a trance, communicating with the departed.

He ignored his son's jibe and instead addressed me. 'Günter tells me you were present when this was recorded,' he said, and I could have sworn his son stepped away from me, putting some distance between himself and someone he now realised had links with the Stasi. 'There is a strange humming noise, like someone blowing over the top of a bottle. Can you remember if this was the old trick of putting a microphone in a bird box?'

'I seem to remember it was,' I replied, attempting to paint myself as an innocent bystander. And only *seemed to remember* because perhaps Kurt was helping me construct a scene which only existed in my imagination.

'And a washing line which was actually a wire connecting the microphone to a nearby house where the meeting was being recorded.' Kurt paused for a moment as if allowing this to sink in. 'The person who organised the meeting must have been aware the Stasi were recording it.'

Again, Klaus found this amusing. He turned to me and asked. 'Can you remember how the meeting ended? Was anyone not in the Stasi asked to put up their hand?' A reminder of why some believed the Stasi held back from firing into the crowds during the weeks preceding the opening of the border. They realised there was a twenty-five percent chance a fellow agent would be hit. Once, during their more cerebral moments, when Herman and Joachim were not talking about cars, Joachim suggested the peace movement only gained traction because the Stasi supplied it with manpower and resources.

The voices on the tape sounded different broadcast in the studio than through headphones. And it was a story which had started in the middle. 'It is a pity we cannot hear what was said at the beginning, as they were walking from the house,' Günter said.

Kurt rewound the tape but there was only the whooshing sound of the wind, a clatter of leaves and in the background those strange bird like noises which may or may not have been voices. Each time the tape was replayed there was less whooshing until it was not there at all. Then, with the rustling of leaves filtered out and voices amplified, it was possible to hear Cathcart say 'I agree' in response to something Meyer had said which only became clear after Kurt rewound the tape for the final time.

'Geoffrey, we must encourage the building of bridges and persuade people to stop building walls.' I felt relieved and vindicated in equal measure, recalling Cathcart's girlfriend taking hold of the arm of the person who would refine this phrase and one day use it to inspire crowds of his supporters. A phrase that would lead some in his thrall to claim, admittedly only on Twiiter, it was Cathcart alone responsible for the fall of the Berlin Wall. Klaus merely shrugged, unimpressed by either his father's audio skills or what was on the tape. However, it was obvious Günter was convinced. He gave me a sideways glance and nodded.

Klaus insisted Günter had a late lunch before returning to Berlin. He suggested if I was in a hurry to get away a taxi would take me to the station, and did little to hide his disappointment when I decided to stay.

Mounted on the wall of the canteen was a large TV screen displaying a rolling presentation of the company's products, with the MDR Liveticker running along the bottom. I sat with my back to the screen and noticed Kurt, too, preferred the view out of the window. We were both seated at the same table, some distance from Klaus and Günter, who was scribbling in a notebook.

'I knew your husband.' Kurt said out of the blue. 'We weren't on first name terms, but I met him a few times. He came to the factory for meetings with the boss. That was when he worked with the ministry. Like all companies we wanted more resources but most of those went to Robotron and Mikroelektronik, although things got a little better when we started working with Japanese companies like Toshiba. Even then, sometimes when we needed small repairs carried out, we ended up paying in kind.'

'Sorry I don't understand. What do you mean, *in kind*?' I asked.

'We gave contractors half-built televisions which should have been shipped to the West. I think they made wooden cases for them before selling them on, although I never saw one myself,' Kurt said, but I certainly had, at the Anweiler party in Rethen.

'Wasn't that illegal?'

Kurt shrugged. 'Yes, but the only way to keep the factory going. But of course, in the end...' He said shaking his head and then taking a breath before plunging into the void.

'Klaus was just a teenager during the Wende. I was unemployed but received a letter from Japan, from someone I met during a visit to Toshiba. They were also unemployed, almost unheard of in Japan until nineteen ninety. Would I like to bring my family to visit and I thought, well, I've some savings, so why not. He had started a small company making audio equipment and thought there might be a market for it in Germany but didn't know anyone he trusted. I didn't think I could help but his son and Klaus really hit it off. The two of them went on a tour of clubs in Minato demonstrating DJM mixers. I couldn't see a future in it, a mindless racket.'

'That's pretty much what my husband thought of it,' I said, and Kurt laughed.

'Anyway, we brought one of the units back with us. I didn't know we needed documentation, and customs at the airport wanted to impound it. But Klaus made a big scene.' Kurt smiled to himself. 'Said the customs official looked familiar and thought he had seen him standing in a tower near Oberbaumbrücke border crossing. That got a big laugh at baggage reclaim, and the chief turned up and wrote *sample of merchandise* on a form and the rest is history.' He paused, turned in his chair to look at the screen. 'Except I must admit my part in it was over.' I knew how he felt.

'I was on Peter's boat last week, I think it will be a success, like his club in Berlin. You and your husband must be very proud.'

'Yes,' I replied. Well, at least one of us was.

On the drive back to Berlin the subject of the tape was discussed for a full three minutes. The rest of the time was taken up with Günter enthusing over a piece of electronics for which he had been given an exclusive preview ahead of its launch.

'Let's just hope Cathcart wins the election then we will really have a story,' was Günter's parting remark as I climbed out of the car at Lichtenberg station.

But what if Cathcart's party failed to win the election I thought while texting Herman to say I would be late home and suggest we ate out in Templin? All this effort would have been for nothing.

More worrying was instead of the mystery of a missing tape this would become a story about the person who spied on Cathcart and a banker's relationship with the British secret service. I wondered if Paul had considered this, because it certainly played on my mind.

# 32

# The Key

Had I asked Paul Anweiler to explain what he hoped to achieve, to reveal the endgame if indeed there was one, no doubt he would have lied. However, as with other narcissistic criminals, there was a subconscious desire on his part to be found out – the only way the world would discover how clever he was. This was the only explanation I could think of for a strange piece of theatre on Köln's Hohenzollern railway bridge the day I arrived in the city. A trick hardly worthy of a child's ABC book of magic.

'Engineers are worried the weight of young German's love for each other might cause it to collapse into the Rhein.' Paul said pointing out the locks attached to the bridge as we crossed it on foot from Deutz to Köln's Altstadt.

Perhaps Paul thought distracted by barges on the river or the view of the city I failed to notice him searching for something on the handrail, which turned out to be a small yellow sticker indicating the location of the lock. The lock itself was bright purple and stood out from all the others on the fence separating the walkway from the railway tracks. *Lotte and Paul* the inscription read. 'Seems very noncommittal.' Paul said. Which was true because most of the other locks had, at the very least, a heart engraved on them. 'You probably haven't even thrown the key in the river, but are waiting until you are sure. I'm guessing it's in that shoulder bag you are carrying.'

Mistake one: not saying, *Very amusing. Now let's find that restaurant because I'm hungry*. But instead, taking the keys from my shoulder bag and, dangling them in front of Paul's face, I said, 'Just these I'm afraid, boring old house keys.'

'That one I think,' Paul said, pointing to a key.

'That's for our garage.'

Mistake two: being so keen to make Paul look stupid. I tried the key in the lock which looked remarkably like the one on our garage.

'See,' I said triumphantly. 'It doesn't fit.' But it did, and the lock fell into my hand.

Mistake three: (I would discover later) was losing my temper and throwing the lock into the river then pushing Paul to one side and continuing along the walkway stopping only when realising I had no idea which restaurant we were eating in.

A pointless trick I thought at the time although should have remembered, as I stood glaring at Paul Anweiler, that in 1974 Hüber hoped twelve months harassment of the young activist would cause Andreas K to lash out and behave irrationally.

Paul caught up with me. 'You realise you have just lost me fifty euros,' he said.

Four and a half hours earlier I had arrived in Köln in a relatively positive frame of mind, given that just two weeks earlier Ursula had to talk me into pressing ahead with the conference and the preparatory meeting at Köln University.

'Ah, yes, we have been expecting you. I have checked and the sun shines into your room at eight fifteen am,' the manager of the Esplanade hotel explained.

'Hopefully,' the young girl standing next to the manager added. 'The last thing we need is a dead body in the hotel.' This earned her a frown from her boss. I was shocked that Fräulein Lorenz had decided to pass on something she could have only found out from reading one of my diaries. Although later I discovered she had not, and the young girl's concerns had nothing to do with the death of Otto Steuernagel.

Paul arrived an hour after I had checked in, earlier than expected and rather than come back later, we would both go to his office which was close to the restaurant where we would be dining together.

The offices of Köhl and Strasse Investments took up a whole floor near the top of a blue oval tower on the west bank of the Rhein. From the roof of the building there was a panoramic view of the city, with the cathedral and station to the east and the Rhein Park to the south. Paul pointed out a cheese-grater-shaped building, just visible through the glare of the sun on a glass barrier installed to prevent the suicidal from damaging cars parked below. 'That was the factory where I worked the year after we met at that party in Rethen.' Paul said.

After the windblown roof, the offices below were an ocean of calm. Opposite the entrance was a door with *Senior Administrator Ute Lorenze* engraved on a stainless steel nameplate. Paul opened it and inside the stark minimalist room was an Apple Mac – stood on a chrome and glass desk making it appear the computer was suspended in midair, a grey operator's chair, cupboards and shelves, also glass and metal and for the most part empty. Just a single splash of colour to draw the eye of anyone peering into this monochrome world, a ring of maroon petals around the base of a thin glass vase containing what remained of a single rose.

Paul took a wad of paper out of his pocket and was about to drop it into an otherwise empty in-tray on a cupboard next to the door. He hesitated because even a single sheet of paper out of place would have had the same impact on the aesthetics of the room as emptying the waste basket on Frau Lorenze's desk.

'I threatened to stop doing my husband's expenses because receipts kept turning up like that.'

Paul opened a drawer and took out a folder, placed the receipts inside it and then put this in the in-tray.

'And finally gave up when he started doing that.'

Paul ignored me and his attention moved on to a thick document lying beside the in-tray. He detached the piece of paper clipped to the front of the document and then replaced it, blank side up. Obviously, something I was not supposed to read. Too late, however, because it was a draft of *Dined and Dumped* by Maria Freitag, and the piece of paper clipped to it was a request for comments *Not to be written on the manuscript but on a separate sheet with a reference to the page and paragraph*!

While researching Köhl and Strasse I discovered the bank was particularly proud of its investment in the company which published the novels of Maria Freitag. She was one of Germany's best-selling authors whose success mystified and frustrated literary critics but whose books seemed to have chimed with the public. A common comment was if you had read one of Freitag's books you had read them all; her fans, however, predominantly female with lots of free time and little imagination, did just that. It was gratifying to discover Ute Lorenze had been assigned the menial and mindless task of proofreading one of these formulaic and trashy novels.

The next glass box was Paul's office with a desk someone, presumably Fräulein Lorenze, had made a half-hearted attempt to tidy, knowing full well her boss would quickly return it to its original state. Perhaps I was supposed to avert my gaze at this point because Paul took off his shirt, changing it for one in a cupboard which served as a wardrobe. There was a mirror on the inside of the cupboard door and I was caught staring at the scar on Paul's back.

'Care of a Red Army sentry at a nuclear silo close to where you live. Lucky he was a little worse for drink.' Paul smiled. 'Sounds a little more impressive than a piece of metal falling off a forklift truck.'

'Tedious, would be a better description,' I said, but no explanation was forthcoming for the unusual collection of small scars on his upper arm.

Paul took a folder out of his briefcase and crossed the open space between his office and a row of desks each with three computer terminals on it. He handed the folder to the person sitting at one of the desks, who took it without his eyes leaving the matrix of flashing green and red rectangles on the screen in front of him.

Before I got close enough to see the names of the companies on the trader's screen, Paul led me back towards his office, stopping at one of the wall-to-ceiling windows and looking out at the apartment blocks on the other side of the railway track. 'In nineteen forty-eight, when the British finally released my father, he travelled through Köln by train on his way to visit his former commander in Ingolstadt. He had a girlfriend during the war, but lost contact with her after he was captured. She thought he had died in the battle of Berlin; he assumed she was still in the Russian zone. But she wasn't and had left the East three years after the Red Army arrived and was living here in Köln. He mentioned those apartments and said it was a miracle they were still standing considering the rest of the city was little more than ruins. He couldn't have known, not then at least, that the girl he once planned to marry was living in one of them.'

'None of us can know how our lives would have turned out if our parents had made different choices. We all end up here by chance.' I said, and Paul turned to me and smiled.

'Well, personally, I'd rather have help build a house here, ordered as a flat-pack from Baufritz and assembled on the banks of the Rhein, rather than brick by brick in a muddy field in Britain.'

'And built it for someone who was flesh and blood.' I said. "What happened to her?'

'Who?'

'The woman your father was supposed to marry.'

'Well, we could go over there and ask her, if you are that interested, but according to Ute she's out with friends this evening.'

'Is that why Köhl and Strasse's head office is in this building, by any chance?'

'Well, as Spike Milligan said, everyone has to be somewhere.'

The trick with the lock was not the only surprise that evening.

'Sorry, are you telling me you serve nothing else but schnitzels?' I asked the waiter when Paul and I were finally seated outside the restaurant.

'Well, it appeared some of our regular customers were stuck in their ways.' He looked at Paul and smiled. 'So, we bowed to the inevitable.' Then he relented and swapped the menu for another he was holding. 'This is for normal customers.' I scanned it, a little too hastily and ordered Suurbrode. Paul chose his usual schnitzel and then sat watching a pleasure boat turning and beginning its journey back up the Rhein.

'I'm interested to know why you spent fifty euros on a lock. I think the one on our garage only cost ten,' I said.

'There was the engraving, but you are right it was a cheap lock. The fifty euros was lost betting you wouldn't throw it in the river.'

'A bet with who exactly?'

'Ute. She was convinced you'd want to get rid of it, and it turned out she was right.'

'And why was that so important to Ute? Has she got something else planned for me?'

'Probably. She is basing one of the characters in her next novel on you.' Now I was confused. A regional train purred over the bridge picking up speed and I wondered what I was doing there in Köln, for a moment imagining myself travelling from Berlin Ost Kreuz and Herman waiting for me on the platform at Templin Stadt station.

'So, Ute is an aspiring Maria Freitag?' I asked as Herman gave up waiting, threw the bunch of flowers he had been holding onto the tracks and went home alone.

'Maria Freitag is Ute's pen name.'

'Your PA is the author of all those crappy novels?'

'*Crappy* is probably a word to avoid if she asks if you've read one. Although I'm guessing you haven't.'

'Definitely not.' This was not quite true. The receptionist in Sophie's practice was a Maria Freitag fan and I read the first chapter of *A Bitter Vintage* merely to see what all the fuss was about. Paul was correct; *crappy* was inappropriate. *Easy on the mind, mildly amusing and an unbelievable plot by an author with serious issues when it comes to her relationship with the opposite sex* might have been a better description.

'Ute was married and living in Bremen where she and her husband built up a successful wine distribution business. No children because her husband kept promising the next year they would start a family. Then one night...'

'Don't tell me, let me guess, he had been drinking too much of the stock and drove his car the wrong way along the motorway, collided with an oncoming car at a combined speed of almost three hundred kilometres an hour and was cremated in the resulting fireball. Identification was only possible by analysing the DNA of pieces of tissue which survived the inferno, made difficult by the fact the couple's dog had been on the back seat of the car.' I said, guessing *A Bitter Vintage* was autobiographical.

'A slight exaggeration,' said Paul. 'Ute's former husband was taken to hospital with concussion after his car hit a parked truck. He's still very much alive, although probably wishes he was not because his philandering gets a very public airing every time a Maria Freitag book is adapted for TV.

'A smile a paragraph, a laugh a page and usually something hysterical near the end of each chapter. You can see why media companies queue up to turn her books into films and TV series. But the wife's visit to the hospital, discovering another woman there crying her eyes out and comforted by two teenage children, that really happened.'

'Really? Well, I never got to the end of the first chapter. Obviously I'm one of a minority of women who don't find Ute hysterical or even particularly amusing.' I said, feigning disinterest. Ignoring this, Paul continued.

'The mistress had been given a share of the company, which had debts secured on the family home. Ute ended up broke, unemployed, homeless and emotionally in a bad place. Then someone, one of your lot...'

'I assume you mean a therapist.'

'... suggested committing her thoughts to paper might help. A friend stopped her burning what she had written and persuaded her to turn it into a novel and get it published. The publisher she approached rejected the manuscript but we have shares in Ansbacher Media, who at that time was looking to expand into popular fiction, and by chance we were funding their purchase of the publisher which turned down Ute's book. I went to Bremen with Ansbacher Media's CEO to discover why the publisher was losing money. Lateral thinking got us looking at what it had rejected and discovered they had been searching for a twenty-first Thomas Mann instead of the next Jojo Moye. We were divided over Ute's book so gave a copy to Freddie Ansbacher's wife Bettina.' I was hearing the names of people thrown up when researching the career of Max Arndt, one of these I seemed to remember was a convicted terrorist.

'Bettina was impressed and thought Ute's book would sell well given the me-too movement was gaining traction. I contacted Ute. She was working as a secretary and given up on the idea of becoming an author but obviously changed her mind after the first book was a hit.'

'But Ute is still working as a secretary which I guess means she only gets a pittance while Ansbacher media and your bank takes the lion's share of what she earns. Although someone naive enough not to realise her husband had another family is probably so stupid she still hasn't noticed you are robbing her blind.' The arrival of the food allowed Paul to ignore this embarrassing observation. To my annoyance his schnitzel appeared far more appetising than my Suurbrode.

'It was never Ute's intention to become a famous author,' said Paul. 'That's why she uses a pen name and there's no publicity photographs, interviews or book signings. She says working at K and S suits her, I guess we are her ersatz family. Obviously it's not healthy and you are welcome to discuss it with her, but probably best to wait until she has finished her current book.'

'Because you wouldn't want her to give up while she is bringing the money in.'

'No, because, like I said, you are one of the characters in the next story.'

I had temporarily forgotten this. 'What's wrong with her?' I asked. 'Hasn't she got an imagination?' Paul was engrossed, chasing a particularly elusive French Fry around his plate with a fork, finally relenting and picking it up with his fingers. *Animal*, I could hear Herman mutter in the back of my mind.

'When the first Maria Freitag book was adapted for TV, one of the comments was it contained events which could never have happened in the real world. *Barely credible*, one critic suggested, claiming no woman would be that gullible. There were problems with the CGI that fed the idea some parts of the book were just too fantastic. Ute didn't mind comments about her writing style but in view of what motivated her to write the book, she was sensitive to remarks about its content. She needs to be clear in her own mind while the story is fictitious, everything in the book could have happened. Hence the experiment with the lock.' Paul paused and turned to look back at the bridge. 'Actually, I could deduct the fifty euros from the two hundred and fifty thousand you are being paid.'

'I assume the Cathcart tape is going to appear in the next novel.'

'Definitely not. It was just the suitcase you hid away was a good fit with the storyline of the next Maria Freitag book.'

'And the van I saw parked by the road on the way home from Lychen?'

'If you found your husband had been cheating on you, perhaps your first reaction would be to kill the mistress. You might even lie in wait for her on a deserted road.'

'So, it was her in the van. What was she planning to do, run me off the road?'

'No, I think that was in an earlier book. This time it was a drive-by shooting.'

I laughed loud enough to attract the attention of the couple on a nearby table. 'Well, thankfully she didn't have a gun.'

'Actually, she did, although it probably wasn't loaded.' He paused, noticing the look of astonishment on my face. 'Although maybe it's worth checking that box of ammunition is still in Ute's desk drawer.'

'My God,' was all I could think of saying as I pushed the plate containing the rest of my food to one side and sat with my head bowed, a sick feeling in my stomach after realising I had fallen in with a group of psychopaths.

'Ute was very impressed with the tow truck, by the way. She thought that was inspired. Until then she was worried you might be one of those people who wanders into a forest at night shouting *Hello, is anyone there?*' Paul said, as if this might make me feel better. 'If you read her books, you will see the first attempt on the mistress's life always fails and the heroine resorts to a more complex form of revenge.'

'Is it working?'

'Is what working?'

'Are the books helping her, does she find them cathartic?'

'Well, in book four the husband was pushed into a mincing machine at the family-run meat processing plant, so perhaps she has some way to go. Actually, in that one the police think he has run off with his mistress until they discover her working in a brothel and one of his teeth turns up in a bratwurst at the Munich beer festival.'

'Unbelievable.'

'Really? Because two months from now you will be giving that presentation in Vienna to tech companies whose social media networks create fictional stories from fragments of people's lives. Is that so much different from what Ute is doing? Except of course reality resumes when you finish reading Ute's book, while social media stays with you on an infinite loop, twenty-four seven.'

It had slipped my mind I was in Köln to prepare for the conference in Vienna. 'I hope you are not expecting me to act as a cheerleader for a company you've invested in because I've seen first-hand the damage social media is causing.' I told Paul.

'Transitory problems. Young people who have grown up with the internet and social media will be more at ease with them. Eventually books and printed text will seem as dated as cave paintings and hieroglyphics. People claim we are entering some sort of brave new world but don't realise much of what we regard as intelligence is already artificial and we've coped with its evolution quite well during the past ten thousand years. You might want to read up on Manuel De Landa's theory of self-organising systems before you give that presentation in Vienna.'

'I think you underestimate how difficult that transition is going to be. What Ute is doing is a world away from a teenager opening up about every aspect of their life on Twitter or Facebook, and you know it. Ute's books may well be cathartic but she isn't rewarded with likes or reposts at the end of every sentence. She creates a world as seen through the eyes of her heroine, admittedly a somewhat pathetic one, not the construct of software in a data centre, a stream of consciousness manipulated by algorithms.'

Paul stared at me, and I looked away, across the river at lights coming on in offices, including those of K and S Investments, and the bridge from which I threw the lock. I was still thinking about the trick with the key when Paul finally spoke. 'Interesting,' he said. 'The conference is a long shot. K and S are very negative on high technology. Wooden toys, car parts and components for Leopard tanks are more their thing. It's proving difficult to get them to invest in social media. Not through any high-minded ideals. They got badly burned during the dot-com crash.' Then he fell silent again, folded his arms, and closed his eyes before his head fell forward.

'Was there ever a time when your life changed, and you suddenly felt free?' Paul said when he looked up again.

Much later I would realise, despite appearing to have changed the subject, he was merely attacking from a different direction. I wondered if he was expecting an account of the evening of the ninth of November 1989 from an Ossie point of view; although if this was the case, he was about to be disappointed.

'A boat trip with my future husband Herman. It was the Autumn of nineteen seventy-four, we had lunch in a tourist restaurant called the Marianluste and then the mansion at Schmöckwitz. It was like stepping out of one world into another.'

'And freedom?' Paul asked.

'I'm not sure. But it was like turning a page in a family album and discovering, instead of the photographs being black and white, they were now in colour.' Or the page in my diary where the entries seemed suddenly to betray an optimism previously absent, because Paul had managed, although it was not obvious at the time he had done this, to draw a parallel between Ute's novels and my diary.

'My first taste of freedom, illusory as it turned out, was during the Summer of nineteen seventy-six, my first time here in Köln.' Paul said. 'My father had got me a job in that factory when I left university. An alternative to building more houses. He even suggested I might want to stay in Germany. There was someone he wanted me to contact while I was here, which I put off doing because I had met an English girl who had come to Köln to work in a hotel. After she returned to Britain, I visited my father's friend who, I discovered, was that woman he would have married had he returned home to Berlin. I learned a lot about my father from her, that he had served in the Waffen SS, something else he had kept from me. So not as free as I thought but sent here as some sort of proxy. I should have realised this woman, like his mother, was part of that make believe world I had already spent a decade helping my father recreate.' Paul stopped a passing waiter and

I assumed he was about to order coffee and a dessert. Instead he asked for the bill and, while he paid it, I texted *Manuel DeLanda* to myself before the name went out of my head.

'After that, something changed. Actually, everything changed,' Paul said as we left the restaurant and walked towards the cathedral. 'It was a bad time, a lot of young people were angry with their parent's generation. Like me, frustrated and angry at having to carry the weight of Germany's past. Once we had all got that out of our systems I returned to Britain.' So a single sentence within which was hidden Sonia Engelhardt and the kidnap and murder of Albert Lauterbrunnen.

'Two years later, I was back building houses. Not for some ghost from nineteen forties Berlin but Christina. There was even a point, when each was almost complete, I could sense her presence.'

'Tell me Paul, is Christina here with us now?' Unlike in Domitz I was unable to resist asking and perhaps was punishing him for the trick with the lock. Paul ignored the question, although I now realise the answer was *yes, she is.*

'I would go from room to room showing her what I had built for her,' Paul continued and then stopped walking, pushed his hands in his trouser pockets, looked at me and then down at his feet. 'During one of my visits to Switzerland we went up into the mountains, to this ski hut and restaurant which was closed during the Spring. We spent the morning laying, sunning ourselves, on the veranda, but then I did something only a crazy teenager would do, went for a swim in a lake which was still half covered by ice. Not just in the clear water, but under the ice looking up through it pretending to be trapped. Christina freaked out and started hitting the ice with a piece of wood. Stupid. It was almost an hour before I could breathe again.' There was more to this story and I think Paul was considering whether he should share it with me.

'During my first year at university I ended up in hospital with this strange virus. I lost my sight, had a raging fever and was in a great deal of pain, bad enough to want to die. But I kept replaying in my mind that afternoon in the mountains. The memory of the freezing water seemed to ease the pain. Sometimes the image of Christina hammering on the ice was so vivid it was as if she was in the room.'

These were probably not imagined visits by his Christina but real ones by Shetlov's Rumanian nurse. But, having read my diaries, he would have known this. Perhaps he needed to hang on to this memory, even now. As intriguing, from my point of view, was the similarity between the dream about Christina and the incident at the lake during the Anweilers' party.

'You said she moved to America. Did you ever try to contact her?'

'No point.' Paul looked up again and watched a group of teenagers as they skateboarded in front of the cathedral. 'Although oddly enough, during a visit to the Museum of Modern art I saw Andrew Wyeth's painting, *Christina's World*. Perhaps because my Christina was somewhere in the city, and seeing the image of a girl seemingly lost and alone outside a house, those houses I built with my father came to mind. There's a print of the painting in my office in Britain.'

'Advertising a vulnerability to business associates and potential rivals, is that a good idea?' Paul did not answer. But then here was the person who turned up the corners of pages in Brecht's book of poems and then left it where it could be found. I recalled Steuernagel and Hüber convincing me this was merely a coded message about Soviet tank movements rather than Paul reaching out to someone. The thought of being bait for a honey trap brought home how close the person the Stasi had once hoped to ensnare was now stood.

'Was New York the last encounter with Christina, or has her face appeared on slices of toast?' I asked Paul while stepping back to look up at the cathedral; feeling the need to put both some emotional, as well as physical, distance between us.

'There is still the feeling she is there when a building is near completion although, now understanding why, it is fleeting. Nothing as all-consuming as when I built new offices for a high-tech company we owned in Britain. The design was based on a hotel just south of Hannover, which after standing abandoned for years was being used to house refugees. The idea was to have two identical buildings, one in Germany the other in Britain, and when standing in either imagining I was in its twin. It would induce a mental state similar to the one experienced when immersed in a virtual world. This was at the beginning of the so-called internet Age. There was a large labyrinth on the floor of the office's central atrium with a Foucault pendulum hung over it. In the evenings I would set the pendulum swinging and wait for Ariadne to appear. During the construction of the building I kept a journal, a collection of thoughts and observations, even some short stories.' This, I remembered, was the person who once told me he saw no point in keeping a diary. 'When the building was finished the contents of the journal were fed into software that used Bayesian logic to analyse and classify individual paragraphs, identifying reoccurring themes, much the same as you do with your patients.' It seemed Beaky Boy's prediction at that party in Leipzig forty-five years earlier had finally come to pass and I was about to be replaced by a computer.

'I documented the experiment but found it difficult to do so objectively, even with the use of metaphors and abstraction.'

'Nevertheless, I would be interested in reading it.'

'It served its purpose as a journey of self-discovery, three journeys, as it turned out.' Paul gave a short laugh. 'I'm sure they would not be of interest to anyone else but me.'

'Did you consider carrying out the same experiment with my diaries after you discovered them?'

'Actually, I never thought of doing that,' he said, but as he quickly changed the subject, I suspected this was the first thing he did after scanning them into a computer.

'Two years before he died, my father invited his former girlfriend to Britain and gave her a tour of my new building, obviously he was very proud of it. When I looked down from my office and saw them together at the entrance to the labyrinth in the atrium it was clear I'd spent my whole life helping my father get to where he now stood. All that I had assumed was mine had always been his. Gone too was that freedom I found here in Köln, so too was Christina.'

'So, Christina never appeared in the form of Ariadne to rescue you during one of your trips into the virtual world?'

Paul smiled. 'No, I merely woke the Minotaur.'

'Meaning?' Although I had guessed.

'One evening it was as though something appeared in my peripheral vision. Like a flashback. I was under a lot of stress at the time. Perhaps I felt conflicted about the use of the technology I helped develop. There was the opportunity of making a great deal of money from something I didn't believe in. It had only ever been the means to an end and, as you pointed out, potentially dangerous. I ended up with welts on my neck and marks on my wrist, almost like stigmata.' These sounded very much like the marks Thorsten, the architect with the stairs fetish, got on his legs when under stress. 'Perhaps the ghost of my grandmother had taken it on herself to attack her grandson,' Paul said.

While believing this highly unlikely, I thought again of Thorsten, and that strained relationship between Paul and his mother during the Anweiler party. 'A place of worship, dedicated to a long-departed woman, with a labyrinth in the centre of it. I wonder how many buildings there are like that in the world?' I said looking up again at the spires of Köln's cathedral.

'Actually, the labyrinth was a copy of the one in Chartres cathedral.' Paul handed me his iPhone which was playing a video of the interior of a building with wooden columns and a mezzanine which morphed into a colour one of a high-tech office with a labyrinth on the floor. At the end of the video the original building reappeared with a young boy, one of the refugees housed in the hotel in Lower Saxony, standing centre shot. 'Just in case you didn't believe me,' Paul said.

'I don't want you to take this the wrong way, but is there anything you do which other people might recognise as normal?'

Paul laughed and walked away and for a moment I thought I had been abandoned. My map of Köln was still in my hotel room, the hotel itself on a street whose name I could not remember. Barbarossa came to mind, and I got out my phone to look for Ute Lorenze's email.

'You need to make a call?' Paul stood holding out his hand, just as he had done on that day he had led me through the trees to the lake. We walked side by side into a maze of cobbled streets, some almost as uneven as those in forgotten corners of Templin.

Papa Joe's jazz club was cramped, noisy and sweaty, packed with people all the way from the entrance to the stage. Paul eased his way along a narrow corridor, pulling me after him. A couple were leaving, so Paul indicated we should take their place on the raised seating at the back of the room. I would have preferred somewhere further away from the piano player, but the alternative was sitting even closer to the stage with a trumpet blasting in my ear. Once we were seated, a waiter poured peanuts into a trough in front of us, and we were to drink Kölsch from bottles because, apparently, according to Paul, that was what everyone did in Köln.

'Is something wrong?'

'No, nothing, this is fine. Well, different anyway.' Which was how I intended describing the club to Herman. With this in mind I took out my phone and filmed the bar and stage. As I did so a couple on the other side of the room ceased to be a couple and moved apart.

'Interesting,' said Paul who had also realised the obvious. 'Married, but not to each other.' Conversation was impossible without placing our mouths close to each other's ears. I felt the warmth of Paul's face on mine and his lips on my neck for the second time in my life, the first being when we were together beside that lake in Rethen.

My ears still rang from the noise inside Papa Joe's as Paul and I sat opposite each other on the U-Bahn which I assumed, incorrectly, was headed to the station near the hotel. 'Text me a screenshot of the couple,' Paul said, showing me his phone with the number displayed. After two minutes typing, he handed me his phone, the picture of the couple on its screen but now with text boxes next to their faces. He was a city planner; she worked for a property developer. 'I know someone who would find that very interesting,' Paul said.

'Presumably not a privacy campaigner. And is the software which did this produced by a company funded by your bank?'

'No, a start-up I'm backing with a friend.' Presumably this *friend* was the same one who put up the money to restore my son's boat.

We got off the train, not at Barbarossa Platz but Rudolf Platz, and crossed the street to a café with large windows where Paul and I sat looking to anyone outside like a couple in a Hopper painting. 'I need a coffee, or I won't sleep,' Paul said. 'And in here at least we can hear ourselves think.'

'I was considering putting off any more thinking until tomorrow.'

Paul ignored this and looked out of the window at a fast-food restaurant on the other side of the street. 'That used to be a Wienerwald in the seventies. Margaret and I used to have dinner there at weekends after we had been out for the day.'

'Margaret?'

'The girl from Britain.' Paul continued to stare across the street. 'You meet couples who never exchange a cross word or argue and finish each other sentences. After fifty years together they end up like that. Margaret and I managed it in two months. And then she went, and I made no attempt to stop her. My life would have been a lot different if I had. I still don't understand why that happened.'

'Because she was her own person, strong enough to resist having the image of your Christina projected onto her. I'm not sure you would have been happy staring at a blank screen for the rest of your life. Of course you are over your little Swiss girl now, and I'm sure you only mentioned her every five minutes this evening to make conversation.' There was of course another reason why he'd done this, because I had put up less resistance than Margaret.

'Possibly,' Paul said, the tone of voice the same as my patients use when in denial. But at least he released me and let me be Lotte again. We talked about Peter and his boat and Paul tried to persuade me

Max was a safe pair of hands. 'Just hide the matches and petrol.' He suggested claiming his friend was merely accident-prone, offering up in evidence numerous incidents, including finding himself airside at Hannover airport while searching for a toilet. 'It was during the Hannover Show, and he was taken to the control tower so all the planes that had stacked up while he was wandering on the runway could land.' This sounded too far-fetched to be true but at this point in the evening provided some desperately needed light relief.

Then we moved on to Inge, and perhaps, given what happened the next day, Paul got the impression I felt guilty for not offering her the same help extended to a son who was estranged from his father, that I assumed, being lucky to be living in the West, my daughter was lucky enough.

'Everything went to shit when Margaret returned to Britain.' Paul was reminiscing again as we walked to my hotel. 'It was as if while she was here my life was on hold and the day she left all the bad stuff kicked off. Sometimes I think it would be nice to put those three months of my life on an infinite loop'

The parting was awkward. We stood in silence facing each other and I wondered if Paul was waiting for me to ask him in. Finally, he spoke. 'Well, I think we are there with the tape. Good luck tomorrow and have a good trip back to Berlin.' Then a hand laid gently on my side, withdrawn almost immediately and for a moment I thought I was about to be kissed.

'Just one thing,' I called out as Paul walked away. 'What was the name of the hotel where Margaret worked while she was here in Köln?'

Paul did not answer. He did not need to; I saw him glance up at the neon sign above where I stood before giving a small wave and then continuing on his way back to Rudolf Platz. He was typing on his mobile phone and I assumed this was when in the warped imagination of Ute Lorenze was born the idea of a property developer enjoying an evening out with his mistress from the city's planning department, unaware in the first chapter of a forthcoming

Maria Freitag novel, *Trouble Building*, his body would be discovered encased in concrete and buried under a carpark in Ossendorf.

# 33

# Mo Fink

'Three minutes past eight.'

'Excuse me?'

'The sun... it was three minutes late.'

'Ah yes, according to the radio delayed due to poor weather,' the receptionist said with a grin. Probably true because while having breakfast someone mentioned that most mornings Köln was shrouded in the mist which rose from the river. 'Nevertheless, please accept our apologies and I would be grateful if you kept this failure on our part from a certain person at Köhl and Strasse.' Then he jumped, having reminded himself of another unreasonable request from Ute Lorenze. He passed me a note which had been folded and placed in the mail rack.

*Call into my office at 1:30 pm before you return to Berlin,* the note said; no *please,* but then neither a mention of a cruel and unusual punishment for non-compliance.

The Psychology Faculty of Köln university was a twenty-five-minute walk from the hotel. The idea of a leisurely stroll across the Nagasaki-Hiroshima memorial park had seemed appealing. However, during breakfast I changed my mind – there was insufficient time and a suitcase to consider – and instead took the U-Bahn from Rudolf Platz to Universität Strasse.

Mo Fink was in the reception of the Social Cognition Centre conversing with a student. Shortly after we retreated to her office there was a knock on the door and, without receiving permission to enter, a young woman barged in. This time the exchange was short, sharp and bad-tempered.

'There's a lot of things I will miss about this place,' Mo said after the girl stamped out of the room and slammed the door. 'Students are definitely not one of them.'

Despite Ursula's best efforts I would never pass for a Wessie psychologist, there was always going to be part of me forever rooted in East German academia. If I could work out which part, it might help. Perhaps merely my state of mind, or the seemingly untreatable inferiority complex. It was definitely not, thanks to my sister, the clothes I was wearing. In fact, looking at Mo, who could only have been a few years younger than me, it seemed the jeans, blouse and cravat I was wearing were standard issue in psychology institutions.

'You've presented a paper in Vienna before, haven't you? Before reunification?'

'Yes,' I replied hesitantly, concerned where this was leading.

'And I've read some of your recent articles.' Mo said. 'Some interesting comparisons between the DDR's approach to psychological research and how it is exploited by technology companies today. In fact, that is why I was keen for you to speak at the conference. Although you realise there will be people who will take issue with you, speakers whose research is funded by big tech. I take it most of your income is from practising rather than research.' None of this came as a surprise. A professor at the Humboldt had sat in on a talk I gave to students and made a very public, point-by-point, rebuttal of my paper.

There was another knock on the door. Mo glared at the student who was peering into the office through a narrow window and she seemed slightly disappointed when, suitably intimidated, the young man gave up and walked away. 'You say that social media creates relationships which lack substance, but isn't this due to the current limitations of the technology? Surely it is better to have a relationship with someone which falls slightly short of the real-world equivalent if the alternative is loneliness and isolation?' I hesitated, taken off guard by this challenge, but then realised Mo was prepping me for the conference in much the same way she would one of her students, assuming, that is, one ever gained access to her office.

'It's the algorithms employed by social media companies,' I said after formulating my defence. 'They are designed to exploit rather than overcome the limitations of simulated face-to-face technology. The user is still lonely and isolated but does not realise this as the technology they are increasingly reliant on for social contact mitigates against the development of a robust real-world identity. As a result, there is less of a chance of developing what we, as psychologists, would regard as meaningful relationships.'

'And of course you see this in your practice as you are one of the people expected to repair the damage caused by these algorithms,' Mo said, because I had forgotten to mention this, leaving me feeling slightly apprehensive about the forthcoming battle. 'Well, Vienna should be exciting this year,' she said and perhaps wondered why I frowned. Which I did because the image of Otto Steuernagel bleeding out on the bathroom floor of his hotel room had flashed through my mind.

'Have you been here in Köln for long?' I asked as Mo escorted me back to the reception area.

'Oh, forever. I came here as a student in the nineteen seventies.' Allowing herself a moment's reflection before adding. 'Those too were interesting times.'

'And you know Paul Anweiler.'

'Yes, his bank is sponsoring the conference and a friend from my student days is married to one of his colleagues, Max Arndt.' A change of mood accompanied her reminiscing, and she laughed. 'Life with Toni and Tibo... rather her than me.' I gave her a questioning look but received no explanation. The more persistent of her three students was loitering just a few metres away and eventually managed to get Mo's attention. 'Go to my office, I will be with you shortly,' she said to him, and after shaking my hand walked away with the swagger of someone intending to collect a baseball bat before confronting her student.

The meeting with Mo had left me feeling I could deal with whatever *she who must be obeyed* could throw at me and perhaps was slightly overconfident when stepping out of the lift, ten minutes early for my meeting with Ute Lorenze. At the desk in the office of the head of administration sat a middle-aged woman who was so slight and unassuming I felt merely knocking on the half-open door might send her scuttling behind one of the cupboards like a startled mouse. Hubert Hüber once told me the ideal agent, one he had never actually managed to recruit, would be someone who, after talking to them for thirty minutes, you would be unable to describe after they left the room. Fraulein Lorenze was as colourless as the room she sat in, pale skinned and dressed in a grey suit, her light blond hair almost white. The near absence of anything not transparent or grey made it seem, despite it being early afternoon and sunlight streaming through the window, the small office was still filled with the mist which had enveloped Köln earlier in the day. Perhaps this was why my eyes were drawn to the glass shelf where the rose which died the previous evening had been replaced by another single bloom which, having recently burst forth from a bud, was now dropping bright red petals around the base of the vase in which it had been placed.

'I am looking for Ute Lorenze.' The woman stared at me blankly and began typing furiously. I scanned the open plan section of the office for someone fitting the image of Ute Lorenze fixed in my mind. There was a potential candidate studying the manuscript of the next Maria Freitag novel, although perhaps a little too young for a person in such an important position.

The typing stopped and the keyboard was struck so violently the computer and the table it stood on shuddered. Although not realising this until twelve months later, I had just witnessed the saving to the computer's hard drive of the paragraph which would have me wondering, out loud on some occasions, if I was as plain, overweight and badly dressed as described in the bestselling novel *Don't Bank On It*.

'You've found her.'

'Sorry?' But obviously Ute Lorenze was not a person used to repeating herself. She leapt to her feet, picked up the carrier bag next to the wastepaper basket and positioned herself in the doorway of her office making it clear that entry into what she regarded as her private space was forbidden.

'I have changed your ticket, because you will be staying in Hannover and travelling on to Berlin tomorrow afternoon.'

'I can't do that …'

'There is a house your daughter will be viewing at ten thirty tomorrow morning.'

'I am attending an event in Berlin with my husband tomorrow evening so that's impossible.'

'The Anweiler cruise leaves Friedrichshafen at eight pm and I have booked you on a train that arrives in Berlin at six pm.' Ute offered me the carrier bag, but I refused to take it. Her eyes were as lifeless as those of a shark – not that I had ever been this close to a shark – and almost as grey as her suit. There was an absence of lines around Ute's mouth suggesting here was a person who seldom cried, laughed or expressed any emotion in between.

I took the bag from Ute, hoping this might placate her. It was heavy, containing a folder, books and presumably a rail ticket. 'Are you listening to me?' I asked. 'I'm going to Berlin.'

'I wasn't asked to listen to you. Just to tell you to be in Hannover tomorrow.' There was no obvious answer to this, at least one I could think of on the spur of the moment. The office fell silent, and the young girl who had stopped proofreading to watch the performance quickly returned to the manuscript when we made eye contact, perhaps fearing whatever had made me a target for Ute's ire might be contagious. 'Your train leaves the main station in forty minutes,' she snapped, looking at her watch. She picked up the folder containing her boss's expenses, opened and closed it again then fed it into a shredder which was still whirring when she spoke again. 'Would you like me to call you a taxi?' she asked.

'No thanks, I'll walk,' I said. Ute returned to her computer, not to work on her next novel, but study a spread sheet. She picked up her phone and as I left the office I wondered how long before the person berated for not spotting *first class* on a booking request realised they were talking to a woman who fantasised about turning her ex-husband into sausages.

Punching the button in the lift, I realised my loss of temper had been another small victory for Ute Lorenze and no doubt one long paragraph for Maria Freitag. While crossing Hohenzollern Bridge I checked my phone. There was an email from Ute with a link to the updated ticket. I was about to open it when a second one arrived, this one with *Correction* in the title. It seemed I was the person Ute was upgrading to first class. Even so I was angry and tempted to throw the bag I had been given into the river; but did not because I was probably being watched from Köhl and Strasse's office by a PA hoping to win another fifty euros.

The train was twenty kilometres from Köln when I placed the contents of the carrier bag onto the table. The folder inside contained details of a housing development in a village to the south of Hannover. There were descriptions of the single-storey houses and a map with the showhouse ringed. Prices ranged from 400,000 to 700,000 euros, well out of the reach of Inge and her husband although I suspected *price to be agreed* scrawled next to the showhouse pointed to the possibility of some sort of deal. This would have also proved impossible in view of the houses being sold by Anweiler Construction, the same company hoping to win the contract for Schulenberg's new headquarters. This would be a big step up from a free cruise around the Müggelsee, and should shareholders discover Herman had been bribed, he might even end up in prison.

Neither of the two books was from the keyboard of Ute Lorenze but were those Paul talked about the previous evening, the results of his experiment with virtual reality and journeys of self-discovery. One was entitled *Three Journeys into The Labyrinth* and the other *Fahrenbrink*. There was a press release from 1992 describing how two identical physical spaces might, in the mind of someone who travels between one and the other, cancel each other out. The result would be a simulation of virtual space. This reminded me of something Herman said about staying in Novotel Hotels which all had near identical rooms. Waking up in Brussels after travelling from Nice and wondering why the mini bar had moved across the room while he was asleep. Also of a conversation with Thorsten about East Germany's love affair with the architecture of Corbusier, which it employed to discourage the citizen's bourgeoise attachment to a unique physical space, regarding this as a barrier to collectivisation.

The press release, however, looked to the future rather than the past. It reminded me of the claims high technology companies made about robotics and AI. Here was something so powerful and dangerous governments would want to control it and, more importantly, banks and investors would wish to exploit it. However, there was something else I was reading between the lines. Here was someone experiencing a personal crisis.

Each of the *Three Journeys* was a story made up of social media-like posts which read like streams of consciousness, some appeared factual and others obviously fictional, probably whatever came to mind as Paul sat at the keyboard. All three journeys, *Circles of Conspiracy, Circles of Madness* and *Circles of Friends,* were based on events occurring during the construction of the building and Paul's meditations within it. The book purported to be old but seemed too much of a metaphor for social media to be genuine. The edges of the pages were slightly discoloured but so were those of the transcript of the Cathcart tape I'd forged. When I checked on Amazon, the book was out of print; copies were available from resellers, but this proved nothing, given the resources at Paul's and Ute's disposal.

In our offices in Berlin, Sophie and I had buttons under the desk we pressed if a patient strayed into what we regarded as potentially dangerous territory. It summoned the receptionist who would knock on the door and then enter, pretending to have an urgent message. Initially, on the rare occasions this happened, the receptionist looked terrified, although later she seemed far more relaxed, even in situations I found frightening. Sophie dated the transition to the receptionist's holiday in America and suspected a can of Mace had been smuggled into the country. In Gehrden I worked alone with no one taking on the role of a New York cop if a patient became problematic, so the button triggered the doorbell, providing an excuse to leave the room. Halfway through my lunch, just as the train had passed through Münster, I found my hand searching under the table for that button. In *Circles of Conspiracy*, there was mention of Vienna and a meeting one evening with two Americans Paul suspected of being spies. Innocent enough perhaps, but not so the discovery the next day of an agent from an unspecified country found dead in his room, his injuries consistent with someone having placed explosives inside an electric razor. In one story Shetlov appeared in numerous guises and I was searching for characters who might be based on the KGB officer in the other two when the train arrived in Hannover.

On arrival at Inge's apartment, the books were quickly forgotten. My daughter was preparing dinner and my son-in-law Hans, who had just got home from work, was playing with the children. Realising turning up unannounced late in the day would be a problem, I had found a hotel room for the night. Inge insisted I cancelled the booking, and her son would sleep on a camp bed in the living room. All that remained was to convince the family Grandma Lotte had not gone completely mad, and a drive into the countryside to see a house four rungs higher on the property ladder than the one they owned was the ideal way to spend a Saturday morning.

The next day the sky was clear and the weather warm with only the whisper of a breeze. Perfect weather, according to Hans, for the football match his son was forgoing to accompany his parents on this pointless quest. He muttered as much under his breath as we turned off the road to Hameln and were immediately confronted with a large hoarding with an Anweiler Construction logo on it. At this point I almost lost my nerve and apologised for wasting everyone's time. But Inge's observation that the village looked peaceful reminded me how harassed she seemed in her tiny apartment, so what would be the harm in her dreaming of something better?

There was a small carpark and next to it the house ringed in red in the brochure. A sign in front of it indicated this was the show home. The door was open and inside, on the walls of the open-plan living room and kitchen, was a map and pictures of the other houses on the estate, local attractions and a family about to embark on a cycle ride into the nearby forest. 'I'm sorry, all the houses have been sold,' said the salesman behind a desk in the corner of the room. This came like a punch to the stomach; another of Ute's tricks. I turned to leave and found myself facing someone who had followed us into the house.

'Hello Lotte, we have been expecting you,' said Klein, still recognisable as the person who had driven the van which took me to the railway station at Rethen when I left the Anweiler party.

The man behind the desk leapt to his feet realising his mistake. 'Show Inge and her family the house,' Klein told him and then turned to me. 'Nice to meet you again after all these years. The house will look totally different when your daughter and son-in-law move in, all the office furniture will be gone, and so will the carpark.' Inge and Hans followed the salesman. The children had other plans and were running along the hallway opening and closing doors as they went.

Klein slid open a floor-to-ceiling glass door and stepped outside. Then after staring up at the sky, he lit a cigarette, drawing on it so heavily a third crumbled away to ash. 'There is a lake just a couple of kilometres away at Weetzen if you feel like a swim.' He shouted back into the room. There was a photograph of the lake alongside a description of the nearby nature reserve in the brochure Ute gave me. But I guessed that was not why Klein mentioned it and rather than risk his references to my past being overheard by members of my family I joined him outside.

On the patio was an ornamental cherub, one hand gripping a bow and arrow and the other held aloft with fingers outstretched and between two of which Klein had lodged what remained of his cigarette. He smiled at me while watching the smoke curling upwards and said, 'That stupid thing will be going, we'll probably throw it into the foundations of the next building.'

From inside the house came the cries and laughs of a young boy who had completely forgotten about the football match he was missing, and a young girl adamant which bedroom would be hers. Klein watched the performance through the window. 'To tell the truth, I will be glad to get back to Berlin. By the way, are you going on the boat trip this evening?'

'If I get back before it sails,' I replied, glancing at my wrist where a watch was worn in the days before my mobile phone provided a constant reminder of the passage of time.

'I'll give you a lift if you like.' Perhaps this was not supposed to sound sinister, but it did.

'No, thank you, the train is already booked.'

'Frau Lorenze, I suppose. She who must be obeyed.' Klein said then sighed on hearing behind him the salesman exude the enthusiasm which must have seemed alien to the former East German building worker. It became obvious stood beside me was one of those people from my past who had never quite found their place in the present. I thought of Joachim who, while the company Klein worked for surfed the Tsunami of construction in Berlin, was clinging to the debris of the fast-sinking shipwreck which was the former DDR. Yet Joachim was at home in a world which had changed beyond all recognition while Klein seemed as awkward in his new role as he was in his badly fitting suit. Perhaps, after all, success or failure in the new

Germany was a lottery and the odds of winning where calculated long before the Wende.

Inge was walking through the kitchen, running her hand along one of the worktops and no doubt dreaming of an escape from her claustrophobic apartment. 'Of course, you know this is impossible,' I told Klein, feeling guilty for misleading my daughter.

'Why?' Klein looked puzzled.

'You know why. Anweiler is bidding for the contract to build Schulenburg's new headquarters and my husband is overseeing the project. How would it look if you sold his daughter a house at a knock-down price?'

'My understanding is someone in Munich, not your husband, will make the final decision. And anyway, this particular house is not being sold by Anweiler Construction. It has already been purchased by a property company. They will exchange it for your daughter's apartment which will be rented out, I understand it's in a good location.' This much was true and Inge had told me if there was a spare room they could make a decent amount from visitors to conferences and exhibitions.

'It still seems slightly corrupt.'

'That's capitalism for you, as bent as communism ever was.'

'I can't say I ever encountered anything like that in the DDR.' Klein raised his eyebrows, suggesting I was being naive.

'Perhaps you lived in a different part of it from the rest of us.'

I was about to ask what he meant but the family were being ushered out of the house and assembled in the garden. 'There is an uninterrupted view of open countryside to the front,' the salesman said, and I suspected at some point those living in the house at the rear had been told the same thing. 'And a short walk along the road to the rear will take you into the forest.'

My granddaughter pointed at the smoking cherub and laughed. Everyone looked at Klein and me and not only did I sense a distance between myself and my family, 300km and 44 years to be exact, but a greater affinity with Klein than all these young people.

'There is no point in going back into town because you can get a train to Hannover station from the next village,' Hans explained once we were back in the car. 'And the salesman said there is a hotel and restaurant nearby where we can have lunch.' This I knew because lying in bed the previous evening with pop stars staring down at me from the walls of my grandson's bedroom, I'd found the website of the hotel mentioned in the books skimmed through on the train that afternoon. Only when spotting, next to the Anweiler Construction hoarding, a sign pointing to the hotel did I realise just how close it was to the house which might soon be my daughter's new home.

As Inge, Hans and the children turned right and entered the hotel's cafeteria where lunch was being served, I turned left and walked along the short corridor leading to the main restaurant. The vaulted room with a mezzanine was much as the book described it. So were the Romanesque windows and the view into the forest. Presumably somewhere outside was the small graveyard containing not the body of Paul's grandmother but the family of Adolph Freiherr Knigge, after whom this room, the Knigge Salon, was named. In the eighteenth century, Knigge had been a leading member of the Order of the Illuminati, hardly surprising one of the stories in Paul's book was entitled *Circles of Conspiracy*.

The room did nothing for me, but not having spent my life building houses for the deceased, this was hardly a surprise. There was no feeling of being in two different places or a sensory vacuum in between. Despite having watched the app on Paul's iPhone, the columns and mezzanine did not morph into a high-tech building in another country. But when I turned to leave that refugee at the end of the video on Paul's phone was stood in front of me.

'Mummy was wondering where you were,' my grandson said and then led me into the cafeteria, perhaps wondering why his grandmother had called him Paul. Inge was still coming to terms with the ridiculously low amount the property company was asking for the house. Sitting down beside her, I rehearsed in my head what to say, expletives included, when next I met the person responsible for all these mind-bending tricks.

# 34

# Frau Fish

'The blue dress... I wore it last Christmas.'

'There are two blue dresses,' Herman said, sounding impatient and complaining he was already late leaving home for Berlin.

'I think you'll find one is a trouser suit. I just want something that won't look out of place tonight.'

'Well, as it's Anweiler Construction's party, how about the overalls you wore when we redecorated the bedroom? And I've got a hard hat in the car.'

*Very amusing,* I thought. Perhaps he could bring the Kaftan, jeans and that pendant with *modern* engraved on it from the suitcase behind the bookcase in my office. Or maybe I could buy hotpants and a tee-shirt because this was not the first time I had dressed up to attend an Anweiler party.

'OK, bring both,' I said.

'The dress and overalls?' But my mobile dropped the call as the train for Hannover I had been waiting for arrived at Bennigsen station.

Ursula and I both came of age after Ulbricht's replacement as General Secretary saw a change in the attitude to women's fashion

413

in the DDR. So why did we view clothes differently? *Sophisticated* was how Herman described me after that party in Leipzig. 'You stood out from all the other girls who were dressed in repurposed curtains or dyed bedsheets.' He meant the copies of clothes on sale in the West, hand-made with the help of patterns in *Sibylle*, East Germany's bestselling fashion magazine. My sister also had a friend who intercepted Exportrücklaufe between the factory and Exquisit shops. These clothes were made for West German companies but rejected, either due to manufacturing faults or because they went out of fashion before they could be delivered. Andreas K said the Communist Party should be ashamed having East German women objectifying themselves by dressing in capitalist cast-offs. Honecker probably thought the same but tolerated the obsession with western fashion, and *Sibylle* provided a crumb of comfort for those seduced by what they saw on West German TV.

Within the circles I moved in, the rejection of Western fashion became a fashion in its own right. So that evening would not be the first time I attended an Anweiler party wearing a disguise. Not trusting Herman to bring the right dress or, even if he did, it still fitting me, I visited a clothes shop during my hour-and-a-half wait for the train to Berlin.

'Have you a dress like the one this person is wearing?' I asked, pointing to my phone's screen as I held it in front of a bemused, then amused, young woman. The picture was on the website of a holiday company advertising cruises on Berlin's lakes, rivers and canals. After finding me a black knee length dress which fitted, the assistant assured me I would enjoy my evening. 'Not a chance,' I said. 'Stuck on a boat for over four hours with a bunch of builders is not my idea of an evening out.'

'Well, actually there is a shop in the Galleria which sells inflatable life jackets if you were thinking of leaving early,' she said. A rather bizarre shopping experience although thankfully, unlike the last time I was in Hannover, without condescending remarks from Frau Reisenberg.

There was no time to ponder over a choice of shoes, so I bought the first pair that fitted. As I stood at the cash desk, wearing a left shoe while the assistant found a right one to match, Günter Hölderlin's father and the story about the Russian shoe factory came to mind. Then I thought of Rolf, because his lottery ticket was in that weekend's draw.

There was a rack of Maria Freitag novels stood outside a bookshop in the station concourse and on a whim I bought a copy of *Frau Fish and The Bicycle*.

Having found my seat on the train I dropped the paperback on the table and spent the first fifteen minutes of the journey staring out of the window having already decided Maria Freitag's third novel was eight euros wasted. Book three in the series told the story of a woman who spent fifteen years helping her philandering husband, an international cyclist, build up a thriving bicycle business. On his death she discovered her hard work, devotion and sacrifice had all been in vain. I settled back in my seat and prepared, as the cover of the book promised, to be shocked and amused in equal measure.

*There were three things Bernie Fish couldn't do without the aid of pills: manage his weight, pedal a bicycle up hill and maintain an erection. Frau Fish thought that her openly unfaithful husband would either die in the Pyrenees during the Tour de France or between the legs of a woman. In the event it was the latter and, against all odds, while making love to Frau Fish in their hot tub. The heat was probably a contributing factor, as was the half of a barbequed chicken washed down with a bottle of wine.*

*With the top of her husband's head the only part of him visible above the surface of the steaming water, Frau Fish contemplated pulling Bernie out of the hot tub and hoisting him onto the barbeque. Home cremations are outlawed in Germany but surely a few years in prison would be better than the indignity of having half the tarts and Lycra-clad professional cycling groupies in Bremen turn out to weep at her husband's funeral.*

The suggestion here was that Ute Lorenze might be coming to terms with her troubled past. The body of her husband's proxy remained intact as Frau Fish abandoned the idea of reducing it to ash. Then I realised this was book three and Paul told me Ute had suffered a relapse before starting work on book four.

'They are amazing, I've read them all.' Having now met the author I was deeper into this novel than the one borrowed from our receptionist, so had paid little attention to the woman sitting beside me. She did not seem a typical Maria Freitag reader, being well spoken and presumably well-educated. Although she might well have thought the same about me. A badge with *spoiler alert* on it would have been appropriate because she reeled off the plot of every Freitag novel to date, including the one I was reading.

Frau Spoiler was probably one of those people who camped overnight in front of their local Hugendubel when the latest Maria Freitag novel went on sale. She did not strike me as the sort of woman who usually used foul language in public, but Frau Spoiler was so immersed in the travails of a series of wronged women that twice she said the word *penis* within earshot of other passengers.

Her favourite characters were the Tony and Tibo Mo Fink had referred to, one of these presumably based on Max Arndt, and so perhaps the other a thinly disguised Paul Anweiler. 'When they built that new garden for Frau Fish and it slid down the hill and crashed into the river, Tony and Tibo sat at the table on it drinking beer as though nothing was happening. Did you see it on TV?' I had not. 'And Tibo on the runway at Hannover airport, it was so funny, but a little farfetched I thought.' Which would have obviously disappointed the ever-meticulous Ute Lorenze.

'Well, goodbye then, enjoy the book. I'm really looking forward to the next one,' Frau Spoiler said as she left the train at Wolfsberg. Had I read the last two pages of the manuscript in Ute Lorenze's office I could have saved her the wait.

With not much left of the story of Frau Fish to enjoy, I returned to one of the books Paul had written. This ended with a quote from Plato's Timaeus, a reference to the theory of forms. If this was intended as a conclusion, why the second book?

Paul Anweiler was credited as the author of the second book; he had used the nom de plume Paul Hausman when writing the first. *Fahrenbrink* was set in the hotel I'd visited with Inge and her family. In it, Paul described being surrounded by high-tech equipment including computers and video cameras collecting the data required to create a virtual copy of the Knigge Saal in cyberspace. Sitting in the centre of the room, he was interrogated by characters from the first novel. Periodically, sections of the first novel were fed into a PC and analysed – given the results, I suspected this analysis was carried out using algorithms similar to those embedded in today's social media apps. Except, allegedly, and if the publication date of 1994 was genuine, there was no social media as we know it when the book was written. Instead, this was a physical representation of Twitter or Facebook.

With this foresight, why was Paul now running errands for the British Secret Service and not living in a mansion in the hills above Silicon Valley? Perhaps the answer was towards the end of the book when Shetlov made one of his last visits to Paul. This was the Shetlov I recognised from my encounters with him: benevolent, compassionate, presenting himself as a protector, a father figure. In the book he was never angry but even so instilled in Paul a feeling of guilt when describing the death of his brother. Finally, Paul could no longer face his interrogators but turned to look out of the window at the trees and the graveyard. He reached forward and traced the letter 'S' twice in the condensation on the window, then planned his escape in search of Christina which finally took him to the part of the forest called Fahrenbrink.

Both novels contained characters based on the terrorist Sonia Engelhardt. Missing, however, if these books were forgeries based on my diaries, was their central character: me.

*Fahrenbrink* seemed to be based on a technique used in psychiatry: taking note of the number of times a certain person or an event is mentioned, and the juxtaposition of these references. This often reveals something hidden within a stream of consciousness. The results can be used to construct a three-dimensional version of the diagram devised by Danuta Mostwin, a *Family Life Space* which maps the patient's relationships with members of their family and others close to them. In *Fahrenbrink*, Paul seemed to suggest that not only could computer algorithms create these maps but by reversing the process, and creating false relationships, it would be possible to alter a patient's behaviour and perception of reality.

Hubert Hüber came to mind. 'Lotte, there was something I've been meaning to ask you.' This during another meeting in his office in 1975. 'It's about Andreas K and this Zersetzung programme. Do you think it will really work? What if Andreas realises what we are doing and takes control of the game? What if he gets together with his colleagues and this whole thing is thrown in our faces? Could he start using Zersetzung against us?'

'Think of it like a game of chess,' I replied. 'Andreas is one of the pieces on the board. He could be the king and still not understand the game. Even should he realise the hand which occasionally grips him determines where he moves next, still he would not understand why he is moving to somewhere else on the board. As for taking control of the game, how would he do that?'

Unlike Andreas K, I now understood the game. All that remained was to discover where on the board Paul intended to move me next.

The taxi got me to the hotel an hour and a half before the boat was due to sail. The room was empty and looking out of the window while changing I saw Herman sitting by the lake being mothered by his favourite waitress.

'Sorry I'm late,' I said crossing the garden, hopping on one foot after discovering the right shoe still had a wad of paper wedged in it.

'You always have been a tardy girl, keeping my son waiting.' The waitress did not say this. But my mother-in-law had, on the day Herman and I were married.

'The dress looks nice. Perhaps we could skip the boat trip and spend the evening in the room.' If this was not sufficient warning how the evening would play out, the hand placed gently on my bottom should have been.

'Behave,' I said. 'And if we don't hurry we won't make it. The traffic was terrible on the way from the station.'

'How was the journey from Hannover?' Herman asked, and despite being late he drove slowly, leaving me wondering if he was serious about spending the evening in the hotel and planned to reach Friedrichshafen after the boat sailed.

We took a right turn into a narrow road beside an apartment block.

'Cars prohibited' I read off a sign.

Herman glanced in the mirror. 'No flashing blue lights, I think we'll be OK.' Sometimes he seemed not to appreciate, despite his job at Schulenberg and seat on two government advisory committees, he no longer had the *access all areas* privileges he enjoyed before the Wende. We parked at the end of the road, close to the entrance to the Spree tunnel.

'What do you think, do I look OK?' I asked because my confidence needed a boost.

'Perfect for dancing out of the line,' Herman replied confirming what I suspected, that I was going to look out of place amongst the Anweilers and their guests. 'Don't worry, I've got something which will help you fit in.' He walked to the back of the car and took a yellow hard hat out of the boot. To punish him for teasing me I put the hat on and insisted on wearing it.

As Herman and I walked up the gangplank a ripple of laughter ran through the guests already on the boat. The hard hat might well have been a joke too far but arriving wearing the kaftan and jeans would have been far less easy to laugh off. Fortunately the Schulenberg contingent were amused, with the exception of Lother's wife Heike who appeared to be chewing a wasp. Lother introduced me to his sour-faced partner then walked away with Herman, leaving me fearing I would be stuck with Heike for the evening.

'There's so much graffiti in Berlin, it's terrible and ugly.' Heike's first observation after we had found ourselves a table.

'Well thirty years ago buildings were covered with political slogans, now West German companies plaster them with advertisements.' I said. 'So perhaps some of that graffiti is the work of those who still feel they are denied any form of free expression.' I could tell Heike was not impressed and so thought it best not to mention my son had been responsible for one of the city's iconic urban artworks; a photograph of it hung in the dining room of his hotel. In his case, no deep psychological reason for creating a four-storey high, eighty-metre-long artwork, merely an innovative way to promote a relatively obscure music venue. Had I shown Heike the picture of it on my phone, her reaction would have been much like Herman's when he saw it in *Die Zeit*'s weekend magazine.

A lively talk by Hans Anweiler provided a respite from the combination of misery and despair with which Heike viewed East Germany in general and Berlin in particular. Hans began with the history of Anweiler Construction; brief, but far longer than the few lines in the brochure Inge's husband had studied over lunch earlier that day. 'An East German company,' he'd remarked, sounding surprised, as if expecting the ceiling to collapse a week after his family moved in.

'It was my late father Wilhelm who built the company, just eight people in the nineteen seventies.' Hans Anweiler explained. Dieter Klein, sitting at a nearby table with his wife, appeared as uncomfortable in evening dress as he had been in a business suit. He smiled and gave a polite bow when identified publicly as the company's longest serving employee. No mention, unsurprisingly, of the sideline in beating people to death at the behest of the Stasi. Even so, following a second mention of Erich Honecker, I saw Hans Anweiler's daughter take her brother's arm and whisper something in his ear. My guess is they felt it time their father's reminiscing should end. *The best of luck with that*, I thought, especially as the audience, with one exception, appeared captivated.

The picture painted by Hans was so vivid, for a moment I was standing in the garden of the house in Rethen watching him argue with his cousin, holding a tray to demonstrate how the tens of thousands of apartments in East Germany were built. Perhaps that was why I began looking for Paul amongst the guests and, not seeing him, assumed he must be on the lower deck.

No doubt Hans felt vindicated that East Berlin's apartment blocks were still standing while many of those in Britain had been demolished. Paul, wherever he was, may not have been impressed but Han's monologue went down well with Lother and other employees of Schulenberg Electronics, enthusiastic for all things East German. The company may have arrived later in the city than their competitors but, so far at least, it had proved more successful in exploiting a skilled workforce, my husband being a prime example.

Less excited was Heike who stared blankly over the side of the boat as if planning her escape. The shop assistant's suggestion I purchased a life belt came to mind and I pictured Heike blowing a whistle to attract attention as she floated along the Spree.

The junior Anweiler's patience was being stretched to its limit but Hans ploughed on as the boat sailed under the Lindenstrasse bridge. 'Along the way you will see a number of buildings we have worked on in the past and there are plenty of others you should visit while here in Berlin.' Heike took a mobile phone from her handbag, perhaps intending to log into the Deutsch Bahn website. I imagined the only buildings she wanted to see that weekend were those visible from the window of the train taking her home to Munich.

'And just before my children drag me off the stage...' Everyone laughed as the young Anweilers looked on helplessly and slightly embarrassed. 'You see those apartments on your left.' Everyone, apart from Heike of course, turned their heads and looked upwards. 'Those were built over forty-five years ago. This was where my wife,

Petra, and I lived when we were first married.' Why this warranted a polite round of applause was unclear. But few could doubt the apartments, now refurbished, looked nothing like the grey soulless buildings people expect to see after landing at Schönefeld airport. These apartments, like our lakeside home near Müggelheim, were sold at a premium when the German government moved from Bonn to Berlin. Soon they would become the homes of Schulenberg employees and, as the boat turned and sailed south passing close to where the company's new research and development centre was to be built, this was deemed by Hans a suitable place for the seamless handover from father to son.

Herman and Lother had joined the arc of people standing around the young Anweiler and his sister. 'I'm afraid my hearing is not that good, so I'll have to get a little closer,' I told Heike, looking for an excuse to leave the table. Feigning deafness is one of the few benefits of growing old and on this occasion allowed me to escape someone oozing so much negativity I had to turn on the table lamp to read the drinks menu.

'To the right is part of Berlin which has seen significant development, including the Humboldt campus,' explained Anweiler junior. 'This is becoming the go-to part of the city for any high-tech company.' On the opposite bank of the Dahme was a small single-storey building, Roland's and Ursula's boathouse, now mostly Ursula's, her husband having lost interest in the boat. It was conveniently close to where my sister and the man I suspected she was having an affair with both worked. It was this man who gifted Ursula the expensive Farber-Castell fountain pen I found on her desk one day after we had a lunch beside the river.

'Take it, I don't want it,' Ursula insisted. 'Made by a company whose owner married unwisely and ended up locked in a castle by her husband and never seen again. Given to me by someone I suspect wanted a similar relationship.'

In the crowd around the young Anweilers a familiar face and it should have been obvious the architect would be somewhere on board. Even so it was always a surprise to encounter a patient in the wild. Thorston had already seen me and, unlike some of my other patients, who try to make themselves invisible or pretend there is an item they need on the far side of the shop, acknowledged my presence with a wave of the hand.

'Lotte, I suppose you are here with your husband. Have you seen the plan for the new building?'

'Yes, Herman showed it to me.' Should he have done this? We seemed to have wandered into a hybrid world of client and patient confidentiality. But the conversation was cut short because the architect was asked to describe the more advanced features of the building to the audience.

The rest of the presentation was completed with the haste of people eager to get to the buffet on the lower deck. Once there I loaded a plate with two miniature chicken legs, potato salad and green beans and refilled the glass of wine I had been handed when boarding the boat

'Not quite what I was expecting,' Herman said. I was not sure if he meant the food or the wooden utensils. 'But better than your meal in Köln,' he added. A reference to the screenshot of the trough of peanuts in Papa Joe's texted to him the previous evening; I had almost sent the whole video but realised at the last moment Paul's voice could be heard explaining there was more than one unmarried couple in the club.

'Sandwiches in a tin box and a flask of tea?' I suggested, and he smiled. But Herman had a point because the food fell short of what the Anweilers had served up at Rethen.

Most of the tables on the lower deck were now occupied. Lothar was sitting with the younger members of the Anweiler family, the sister desperately trying to engage with Heike. 'Let's see if there is somewhere to sit upstairs,' Herman said.

While climbing the steps to the upper deck, a woman following me said softly, so only I heard, 'Paul couldn't make it this evening, so if you're thinking of taking a swim, he won't be here to rescue you.'

Glancing over my shoulder I saw Petra Anweiler behind me carrying a tray of food. She was about to say something else but someone called out, 'Welcome to the Ossie deck, the home for retired East German builders.' Two people sat next to Hans Anweiler at the only table occupied on the upper deck: one was Dieter Klein, and I assumed, correctly, the other was his wife. Expecting an embarrassing revelation, I was pleasantly surprised both Hans and Deiter pretended this was the first time we had met. 'We are up here because it was obvious we were getting in the way. But please feel free to join us. Sorry you are?' Hans asked, extending his hand.

'This is my wife Lotte.' Herman said.

'I saw you wearing a hard hat when you came aboard, are you going to be the site manager?' said Hans, shaking my hand. The light from the table lamp lit his face which, like his wife Petra's, wore its age well. His grey hair was receding and had it been combed back rather than cropped he would have born a strong resemblance to his late father Willhelm.

'I don't think so,' I replied, feeling embarrassed and, perhaps unsurprisingly, finding the Anweilers slightly intimidating.

'No, we don't want another Paul,' said Petra, and the mention of his name saw me instinctively look away, and hope Herman had not picked up on something I would have spotted instantly had one of my patients reacted in a similar way.

Petra might have been playing games, but if this was the case, Hans came to my rescue. 'Yes, we asked Paul to lay a foundation stone once because K and S were funding the building. He was still on site when we put the roof on.'

'A slight exaggeration,' Petra said.

'But his wife bought him a cement mixer for Christmas last year,' Dieter said. 'He told me it was the best present he had ever been given.' Of all the questions I had asked Paul, or even thought of asking, missing was the obvious one: *Are you married?* Perhaps not doing so because it seemed so unlikely.

Passengers on a pleasure boat passing in the opposite direction called out. Those dining on the lower deck of ours responded wildly but we made do with a wave of the hand. 'Forty years ago, the only nightlife along here was the midges, now look at it,' Hans said as the boat entered the Langer See. 'You remember what it was like back then?' he asked.

'We lived on Kleiner Müggelsee,' Herman replied, looking at me rather than the person who asked the question.

Hans turned in his chair to survey the north bank of the lake. 'So, you remember the Luisenhof and the butterfly museum. Gone now. Incredible, isn't it, so much of what our parents rebuilt after the war destroyed by vandals or just left to rot.'

'I think the mansion at Schmöckwitz is still there,' Herman said, despite knowing this for certain.

'Really? I will have to hire a suit and tie and pay it a visit,' Hans laughed. The trip down memory lane was giving me a strange feeling which was difficult to pin down. A pity, as had I been able to, an embarrassing incident later might have been avoided.

Hans pointed towards the empty table where Heike and I had been sitting. Her shawl was still hung over the back of one of the chairs. 'Lother's wife doesn't seem very happy. Has someone upset her?'

'My son, I'm afraid,' I said.

'Your son?' asked Hans. Herman also looked puzzled.

'And all the other young people who redecorated buildings in East Berlin.' I described the massive artwork Peter had created on the façade of the warehouse.

'Our children spent a lot of time at that club,' Petra admitted.

'I just hope none of the buildings you suggested your guests visit is near it,' I told Hans.

'I've been to Munich and they have artwork on buildings, especially their churches,' Hans said. 'Perhaps your son should have included the Madonna and her child.' Actually, he had, along with a kaleidoscope of images unlikely to change Heike's impression of the former East Germany for the better.

'When did you visit Munich?' Herman asked.

'A long time ago, wasn't it, Dieter?' Klein nodded. 'Nineteen seventy-one, just after we left the army and were working for a transport company.'

'Tours of Ami airbases,' Klein said and was hushed by his wife. 'So, what does it matter now?' he insisted.

Hans ducked his head and looked under the table. 'It's OK, Dieter,' he whispered. 'No listening devices, it's safe to talk,' although it was he who continued the story. 'We transported goods from factories in Berlin to companies in the West. The truck had a hidden compartment for a guy from the Shield and Sword club. When we drove past Ami airbases he filmed the aircraft.'

'It was a two-day trip,' Klein added. 'One day there, one day back. Wasn't very pleasant for our secret passenger.'

'He had sandwiches and drink, but obviously we couldn't make toilet stops,' Hans said, grinning at his wife. 'By the way, this chocolate pudding is nice.'

'Don't be disgusting,' Petra snapped.

'When Honecker took over, building went crazy, and then we were working full-time helping my father,' said Hans.

'No more trips to Bavaria or western coffee and cigarettes,' Dieter added, although I had a coat and a pair of jeans which proved this was not quite true.

For a second time I heard the story of the bomb falling on the Anweiler house, this time from the point of view of someone whose father was unable physically or mentally, or had the resources, to rebuild it. While Hans described helping Wilhelm, against all odds, set up a small construction company, Dieter began tapping his glass with a spoon. He stopped when Petra made it clear she did not find this reference to her late father-in-law's shell shock amusing.

'Wilhelm went through a lot during the war,' Petra snapped.

'Nothing compared to what happen to him before it started,' Hans said. 'My grandmother was crazy. When she died they buried her in the forest because no one wanted to be reminded of her.' Hans gulped down a mouthful of wine and held up his hand indicating he had more to say about the woman he blamed for damaging his father. 'One day she was walking to the next village to take some flowers to her sister. A young boy riding a bicycle brushed past her. She called him back and beat him around the head with the flowers. When she arrived at her sister's house all that was left was stems. So, she puts them in a vase and sits down like nothing has happened.' We laughed: me, recalling my conversations with Paul, slightly less than others around the table.

'You remember Uncle Klaus, Paul's father.' It was as if Hans had read my mind. 'That scar on his cheek which made some people think he was some high ranking general and got it duelling in Heidelberg? Well, my father said when his mother kicked off he looked for his older brother and hid behind him because she always took it out on the first person she got hold of. Klaus got the scar when his mother threw a bird cage at them, and it hit him in the face.'

'What happened to the bird?' I asked, as if this was even relevant.

'Dead,' Petra said.

The telling of anecdotes is part of the process of assimilation. Herman offered up his father's experience in Russia and his own work with VEB Kombinat Mikroelektronik, Robotron and the government. But only when Herman mentioned his trips to Hannover before the Wende did Hans and Petra finally invite him to join the Anweiler tribe.

'Then you must know Springe, the town close to where your daughter is going to live?'

Herman seemed evasive and non-committal. 'I'm not sure the purchase is possible,' he replied, echoing the doubts I'd expressed earlier when talking to Klein. But this time it was Hans who explained how the transaction would work. I expected Herman to be surprised, shocked even, but he merely nodded and, eventually, appeared reassured. Presumably at some point, many years ago, perhaps while he was still at school, there had been a conversation similar to this one between his father and a member of the party regarding an exception to the rule that sons or daughters of anyone considered bourgeois were at the bottom of the list for a place at university. Perhaps this was responsible for that sense of entitlement and Herman's belief the rules most of us live by do not apply to him.

The boat docked at Schmöckwitz, quite why was not immediately apparent as the tour's itinerary had been vague. The tables were hurriedly cleared and the caterers left. There was confusion below on the pier as a convoy of waiters pushing trolleys ran headlong into musicians wheeling amplifiers in the opposite direction. The situation became more confused after Hans called out to a band member he recognised. The musician, a trumpet player, gave an impromptu performance ending prematurely when the catering manager tapped his watch and shouted, 'Time is money!'

The cruise continued and the party on the lower deck was well underway when the boat reached the Gosener Kanal. 'We'll be down in a short while,' Herman said to the Anweilers and Kleins when they left. It was his decision to hang back and reminisce and so I feel he was partially responsible for what happened next. Admittedly, undoing the top two buttons of my dress, using an unseasonably warm evening as an excuse for doing so, may have had some bearing on how things played out. However, surely in the back of Herman's mind was that boat trip we took during my first weekend at his mother's house. And perhaps as Herman's mother mistook screams during my nightmare for cries of passion, she too, deserved a share of the blame.

It was dark. Schmöckwitz receded into the distance and the lights from the deck below were all that lit the banks of the canal as music echoed in the forest. Herman took a sip of wine, and I put my lips close to his ear. 'When I was young, a handsome young man made love to me in a boat very close to here.' Then I gently bit his earlobe.

'I think we should go below,' Herman said, clearly concerned that something previously in the back of his mind had, with my help, forced its way to the front. I kissed him, pushing my tongue gently between his lips. 'Yes, definitely time to go,' he said with slightly less conviction, and I noticed he glanced down at my cleavage. 'Nice dress, by the way.' He might as well have said 'OK, I give in.'

Herman lifted me and sat me on the table, slid his hands up my legs and began tugging at my panties as I undid his belt. My God we were actually going to do this. *We must be crazy*, I thought.

We were now on the stretch of water where Herman and I first made love. On that occasion I worried the boat might capsize. And being seen of course: in this respect Heike turned up forty-three years late. Not during an afternoon walk along the bank of the Gosener Kanal but after coming up from the deck below to collect her shawl. She might have been attempting to tell me this when I caught sight of her over Herman's shoulder, but while her mouth was moving no sound came out.

'We are not alone,' I whispered in Herman's ear. He was still trying to remove my underwear. I was having better luck with his trousers and presumably it was his naked backside Heike was staring at.

'Shit!' said Herman, looking over his shoulder, by which time Heike had finally managed to process what she had seen and was walking back to the stairs. Herman grabbed his trousers and pulled them up but needed his glasses to find the hole in his belt. I slid off the table and pulled up my panties. I'm not sure how much of this Heike saw as she paused at the top of the stairs for a final look in our direction.

That is pretty much how it happened although I must admit the story has been embellished with each telling. Ursula thought it hilarious, perhaps because until then her impression of me had been of a shy, innocent and rather naive younger sister. Even so, there were implications of this moment of madness which did not strike home until the following morning.

'We'd better get downstairs before Heike starts talking to people,' I said. A good move it transpired because when we reached the bar Heike was whispering in her husband's ear. Lothar glanced in our direction and then gave his wife a doubtful look. It seemed we were in the clear and would remain so unless Heike managed to give a coherent and believable account of what she had seen.

Wine flowed freely and when the boat docked again at Friedrichshafen in the early hours of Saturday morning most of the passengers, myself included, were merry, to say the least. Herman, Lothar and Thorsten, however, were still sober and immersed in a conversation about architecture which began when Lothar asked Hans Anweiler for a copy of that list of buildings his company had worked on. Interestingly Thorsten must have been feeling under pressure because at one point I noticed him reach down under the table and scratch his leg. So much for the supernatural tale about some sort of stigmata.

When Hans's ballpoint pen failed to leave a mark on the map of Berlin, talk turned to the poor quality of Chinese ballpoint pens. This, according to Herman, was due to EU restrictions on the sale to China of the machinery to make ball bearings. I have always considered that my role at times like these, even when slightly intoxicated, was to maintain eye contact with whoever was speaking and nod occasionally. Herman did much the same when I was still talking to Sophie about psychology when he picked me up from the practice.

Heike, however, turned away and stared into space, even while her husband was speaking, and her only contribution to the conversation was the occasional sigh. Lother was obviously used to this and comfortable with having his wife hung on his arm like a lifeless ventriloquist's dummy waiting to be put back in its box. But I was angry with her, perhaps on his behalf but more likely for the obvious reason, the wine having done nothing to dull my frustration.

'Try this, Hans,' I said, taking the fountain pen out of my bag.

'Very smart. Farber Castell, a quality German pen,' he said, waving it like a cigar in front of Lotha and then Herman, who smiled, having been told why Ursula gave it away.

'It has a mammoth-tusk handle, so technically part Russian,' I said.

'I should imagine there are not many of those in East Germany,' Heike sneered.

'There are,' I replied. 'We were all given one in nineteen eighty-nine as a prize for coming second in the battle between communism and capitalism. It even writes on concrete.' Quite where this came from was a mystery, and as puzzling was why everyone found this so amusing, maybe it was because a stony-faced Heike did not. And when my pen was returned I took the map Lotha was holding and drew a ring around a building Hans had forgotten to mark, a block of luxury apartments, barely recognisable as the warehouse my son once owned, apart from the graffiti, of course.

As we all left the boat there was a final drunken jamming session interrupted when one of the musicians tripped on the gangplank and dropped the drum he was carrying into the water. Various attempts to retrieve the instrument failed and while most of the passengers stood enjoying this piece of theatre, Herman and I slipped away, descending the steps into the tunnel. 'This is very Freudian, don't you think,' I said, grabbing hold of Herman, digging my fingertips into his back and then pulling the shirt out of his trousers.

'What has got into you tonight?' Herman said, putting his arms around me, once again his hand ending up on my bottom.

'Well, thanks to Heike, not you, unfortunately.'

Herman smiled at me and gave my bottom a squeeze. 'I think we should wait until we get back to the hotel.'

As we climbed the steps at the other end of the tunnel, the lights over the entrance cast our shadows on the wall and I thought of Plato's story about the cave and then that passage from Timaeus at the end of Paul's book. A train of thought had been set in motion and its destination should have been obvious.

Looking back towards Friedrichshafen, cameras flashed as guests photographed the rowing boat setting off in pursuit of the drum drifting out onto the lake.

The next morning, I asked the woman on reception if the hotel had any paracetamol. 'Oh and if you heard any screams in the night, it wasn't me dreaming, I've given your son a copy of *Karma Sutra* for his birthday.' I did not say this to the receptionist, but seem to remember mentioning it to my mother-in-law many years earlier when my patience with her finally snapped.

We had breakfast sat at a table outside the hotel looking out across a lake almost as blue as the sky. 'I think I can see it,' Herman said.

'See what?' I asked, shading my eyes.

'That drum which fell off the boat last night.'

There was nothing on the lake apart from two sail boats but, anyway, my mind was elsewhere. I was thinking about dressing up in hot pants and a tee-shirt for that party in Rethen and wondering if I had bought that dress in Hannover thinking Paul would be on the cruise around the Müggelsee. And was it him rather than Herman I had wanted to make love to the previous evening?

# Part Two

Magic

# 35

# A Kind of Magic

'Would you like to see some magic?' the magician asked, and then without waiting for an answer, said, 'I'll show you a trick.' So, which was it? Magic or a trick? The cards flew through the air from her left hand to her right then opened out into a fan. A flick of her wrist and the fan closed. The deck was repeatedly shuffled and cut, the queen of hearts always ending up on top. Except the last time. So where was the missing queen? The magician reached across the table and took a card from the shirt pocket of a member of the audience. 'So that is where she is hiding,' the magician whispered.

That was the trick, next the magic.

This time the cards were spread face down in an arc on the table. A member of the audience was asked to choose one, look at it, but tell no one what it is. They returned the card to the pack without revealing it was the four of diamonds. The pack was shuffled and cut twice then squeezed, just as it had been earlier, only this time, instead of taking flight, the cards fell between the coffee cups and glasses of ice cream on the table. The magician apologised, feigned embarrassment and asked the disappointed member of the audience to help her pick up the cards. The young boy did this but then discovered one of the cards was stuck to the underside of the glass table. It was the four of diamonds.

Three days earlier, I had been attempting to understand a magic trick of a different kind, and thinking he might also welcome a distraction, asked Herman if he remembered Oscar, the dog we bought for Inge which took a liking to Peter and kept bringing him a ball to throw. And our son getting fed up with it, because he wanted to do his homework...

'Practice his guitar playing you mean.' Herman replied without looking up from the document he was reading.

... so Peter took the ball and buried it in the forest. But next time Inge took Oscar for a walk he found it and brought it home.

Herman was obviously puzzled why he needed reminding of this obscure piece of family history.

'I'm wondering how far away I'd have to bury that book to make sure you didn't find it,' I said, because all day Herman had been like a dog with a bone, or a well-chewed ball even.

'It's the EU guide to GDPR, General Data Protection Regulations.' Herman held the document up so I could see the cover. 'I just don't understand why I was sent this.' He said, placing the doorstep-sized document on the floor beside his chair.

We were experiencing a period of readjustment as Schulenberg's Brexit project was coming to an end. There was just some tidying up to do, mostly by a junior member of staff rather than Herman. Fewer trips abroad; a relief in a way because I was now of an age when the mind strays to the painful subject of mortality, and the thought that one day the empty chair I found myself looking at when my husband was away would remain empty.

'Perhaps it was meant for one of the government committees you are on.' I said.

'I did wonder, but it was addressed to me personally, here, not at the Bundestag or Schulenberg's office.' He then ran through a list of possibilities; some I was already aware of having overheard phone calls asking people to check whether anything the company had done infringed the data protection act.

Herman phoned Lothar. 'That person who was here doing market research, did she take any customer information with her when she returned to Britain?' Lothar was on speaker-phone, I heard him reassure Herman this had not happened then ask if we had enjoyed the Anweiler cruise. From his voice it was obvious he now realised what Heike experienced on the upper deck of the boat was not a lucid dream based on a suppressed sexual fantasy.

The timing of the document's arrival worried Herman. Heading the Brexit project had been a big step up from the part time EU project manager's job. The next rung on the corporate ladder was a seat on the board of Schulenberg Electronics. He should have felt secure but had not forgotten how quickly in 1990 having a job for life went out of fashion.

'There is another possibility,' he said, then immediately dismissed the idea. 'No, very unlikely.'

'Go on,' I said, as if talking to one of my patients.

'Well, it might be from a whistle-blower. Pointing me in the direction of something they are too frightened to bring to the attention of their manager. That's why it was addressed to me personally.' Someone had thought of a way of throwing Herman off balance, introducing doubt and uncertainty into his life. The list of people who might do that was short; in fact there were only two names on it.

'That looks interesting,' Herman said when I returned to the books Ute had given me, although compared to the EU GDPR guide, a telephone directory would have been a page-turner.

'A patient. Rich and important,' I said, and halfway through the second book, *Fahrenbrink*, scribbling notes and numbers in the margin, I was wondering if I should add Paul Anweiler to my list of clients. Fortunately, *rich and important* was code for *don't ask* and Herman stood up and went into the kitchen to get himself a coffee.

It proved relatively simple, although time-consuming, to repeat by hand what Paul suggested was achieved using a computer. His interactions with characters in *Three Journeys into The Labyrinth* were scored according to whether they were positive or negative, intense or casual, or were displays of affection or aggression. Using this data, I placed each character on a three-dimensional version of a Mostwin's Family Life Space diagram showing how close was their relationship with Paul.

'How long could someone hold their breath if they were under ice cold water?' I asked Herman, having become distracted by the account of Paul's swim in the alpine lake during his holiday with Christina.

'Do I need to lock the door next time I take a bath?' Herman asked as he handed me a glass of tea.

'No, it's just something this person said about swimming under ice.'

'If they were fit maybe a minute without losing consciousness.' Which suggested, while there might have been a swim in the lake, the account of Christina trying to break the ice was part of the dream he had while semiconscious in hospital. There was a similarity, apparent to me and also identified by the computer software, between this incident and Paul's epiphany while standing at the entrance to the labyrinth in his new offices. Perhaps being trapped under the ice felt like being immersed in a virtual world. However, more likely, the computer picked up the similarity between Christina's attempt to break the ice and Paul being attacked by Ariadne as the words *hit*, *struck* and *violently* appeared in both passages. As well Paul described looking up at a labyrinth of cracks as Christina broke the ice. Perhaps, when Paul committed these images to paper he betrayed a belief, borne out by experience, that the pursuit of maternal affection always ended badly.

Returning to the family life space diagram, it was clear Paul was close to both his father and Nikolai Shetlov, who appeared in both books either thinly disguised as other characters – in one case his former maths teacher – or in his own right as a KGB officer. Close enough that they were within a millimetre of each other on the graph. Perhaps at my suggestion, Shetlov had contacted Paul and formed a relationship with him equally as paternalistic as the one he formed with me.

Shetlov appeared alongside Christina in the dream Paul had while in hospital. If this dream was prompted by the presence of his father, and Christina was, in reality, the Romanian nurse, then absent was a character based on Paul's mother. Was she represented by the beating of the ice with the stick, or was I on a similar path to the one trod by Thorsten's hypnotherapist. This aside, the problem discussed with my students, of not having access to all the people influencing the patient's state of mind, was not relevant in this case. Paul's mother was at the party in Rethen and the description of her in my diary was of someone almost pretending her son did not exist. Did the pent-up frustration at being little more than a mere avatar in Klaus Anweiler's virtual world, occasionally explode into violence which was directed at her son? Why had it not occurred to me Paul might have been searching for a mother as the woman his father married refused to take on that role? Perhaps because Steuernagel dismissed this as an explanation for Paul highlighting those poems by Brecht, but more likely because, at that time, I was searching for a father to replace the one I lost.

Then I was back reading for the fourth time the description of that incident at the lake in the Swiss Alps. There was the feeling of being present as Christina struck the ice with a piece of wood. Not because of the quality of the prose, this was no Maria Freitag novel, which mitigated against the two books being, as I initially suspected, the work of Ute Lorenze. This particular passage had such an impact because I had seen Hans Anweiler using an oar to hold his cousin under the water.

While there was a feeling of being an observer in the first book, there was a question mark over my presence in the second, *Fahrenbrink*. An objective analysis of the text was difficult as, a few days earlier, I had stood inside the building in which the story was set. There was, however, an interesting correlation between where characters in the book were stood in the room and their position on the graph I had created. And at the end of the book when Paul set off to look for Christina, the description of his walk through the forest bore a strong resemblance to our walk to the lake at Rethen.

Still at the back of my mind was the same question I asked myself after first reading the two books: what personal crisis persuaded Paul to commit all this to paper? I had presumed it was the death of his father but during my visit to Celle in 1993 Frau Reisenberg mentioned Klaus Anweiler had recently spoken with her husband. The only event which was coincident with the writing of the first book was the Wende. Perhaps as the DDR had been central to Paul's life, his spiritual home, its demise proved as traumatic as any bereavement.

The other mystery was why Ute gave me the books to read and whether Paul knew she had done so.

'I give up,' said Herman picking up the EU guide and handing it to me. 'Want to swap?'

'Definitely not,' I said, putting the books and notes back in a folder, now so full it was splitting at the edges.

'Shall I call Joachim and ask if he and his wife want to have dinner with us in the Weissen Ross?' And I decided this would provide an ideal distraction for both of us.

Joachim was concerned the proposed Tesla factory, and the slow progress Volkswagen was making with electric cars would eventually impact on Gehrden Motors. But then Herman joked that Joachim should build an electric powered Trabant and soon the two men were wallowing in nostalgia. To drag us all back from the 1970s I mentioned Inge's new house.

'It will save you a hotel bill when you visit the Hanover Fair next year,' Joachim said to Herman.

'That's if I go. Looks like I'm going to be tied up in Berlin for a while and the trips to Scotland have ended.'

'A shame, no more Haggis and tartan dolls.' Joachim smiled at me. 'And he never took you to Scotland.'

'I did offer.' Herman said. He did before every trip but there were my patients, students or a research paper to finish. Although no point in mentioning this because Joachim was the one person who knew these were the excuses of someone too scared to drag their suitcase into the tunnel she had helped dig.

'Brexit is crazy.' Joachim decided. 'They say a capitalist will sell you the rope you are going to hang them with, but the British seem to have decided to keep the rope and hang themselves.'

'I must admit I don't understand, but neither do most of the British I've been working with,' Herman said.

'Maybe you didn't meet the right people.' Joachim's wife seldom discussed politics and it was easy to fall into the trap of thinking the Wende had only a positive impact on her life. Outwardly she was, from the outset, one of East Germany's winners, seeming to have fallen on her feet, largely because so many other people voted with theirs. Within a few years someone who only ever expected to be a sales assistant in a village store ended up as a manager in one of Templin's supermarkets. But she was also well placed to pick up on the resentment of customers who now had to travel into town from near deserted villages, to buy products which still seemed alien to then. 'Sometimes it is reassuring to feel in control of your own destiny, no matter where the journey is taking you,' she said.

Our destination, Herman decided, was Rugen and the Panorama Hotel in Lohme for a long weekend in a room with a sea view and a balcony. A little too expensive, according to Herman, but my client, the author of the books I had been deconstructing, had been exceptionally generous. The Cathcart affair was over, and I still 1000 euros left from my expenses.

Herman chose that particular weekend for our short break as it provided an excuse not to go to Wittenberge for the launch of his son's boat. Peter had texted me an invite and I was slightly aggrieved at having to choose between my husband and son. Only slightly because with Max Arndt would come Paul Anweiler, and most likely his PA; two people I hoped never to meet again. True there was still the question of 250,000 euros for conjuring the Cathcart Stasi file into existence. However, I had already dismissed the idea of ever seeing my share of this.

The suitcases were packed, the bicycles were fixed to Herman's car, and we were about to have an early night when the phone rang.

'Peter, a nice surprise. You ready for the big day?'

'Not really, Mutti. Is father there?'

'What's wrong?' I asked, suspecting something disastrous had happened, and from Peter's point of view it had.

'The boat's self-navigating system worked perfectly yesterday, but today it did not. Max tried swapping the controller, but it made no difference.'

I held out the receiver and Herman took it. 'What's the problem?' he asked, then stood listening in silence before beginning what sounded like an interrogation. Apparently, there was no output from a logic analyser because neither Peter or Max had access to one. Perhaps Peter lost his temper when his father asked if Max had remembered to bring a screwdriver, because Herman's tone was suddenly less aggressive, consolatory even. 'OK if the problem is intermittent then it is unlikely to be a fault with one of the processors. Software perhaps, or maybe a connection.' Then another long pause at the end of which the patio door opening out onto the balcony with a view of a white sandy beach and the Baltic beyond was slammed shut. 'We'll be there around midday tomorrow,' said Herman.

'We are running a little late,' Herman said, and whose fault was that? Not mine. He was the one who had spent half an hour talking to the friend who loaned him a logic analyser. I stayed in the car, on the phone to the hotel where I had hoped to enjoy a well-earned rest. Once on our way again, Herman turned on RBB news.

*'Forty-one years ago, the DDR's ministry of industry predicted that in two thousand and nineteen its economy would surpass that of West*

442

*Germany and we will be asking the German Federal Statistical Office why this did not happen.'*

'The person who believed that must feel like a complete idiot now,' Herman muttered under his breath. Which Rolf might well have done although the next item would have lifted his spirits.

*'Brandenburg's mystery lottery winner has still not come forward so it may be a good idea to check your ticket. The numbers are four, seven, eleven, fifteen, twenty, forty-five, and the life ball is thirty.'*

'Sounds like someone chose their telephone number.' Herman said. 'And had relatives in Köln.'

'Why do think that?'

'Four Seven Eleven, Eau De Cologne,' Herman replied, but by then someone from the Federal Statistical Office was part way through a sneering description of 1970s East Germany. 'I can't listen to this rubbish,' Herman said, and then turned off the radio. As we passed the turning to Domitz, I recalled that breakfast with Paul and forgot about the lottery ticket and all the ways acquiring more money than Ute Lorenz earned from her books might ruin my life.

Not, as I had expected, an awkward reunion of estranged father and son, instead more the meeting of two long lost friends, perhaps because Max was standing next to Peter. The three men unloaded the equipment from our car and walked towards the boat.

Enthusiastic to play with his son's toy, Herman forgot to introduce me. Almost as an afterthought, Max Arndt turned around and retraced his steps. 'You must be Lotte,' he said, shaking my hand, adding, 'Paul has told me a lot about you.' Thankfully Herman was out of earshot.

A bright yellow Porsche parked next to our car as I pulled my suitcase towards the side door of the hotel. The driver was a woman the same age as me who stretched as if stiff after a long drive. She was tall, athletic and tanned, with jet black hair pulled back and pinned into a bun at the back of her head. Her lipstick was dark, as was the make-up around the eyes, and she was wearing a short leather jacket, skin-tight jeans and brown calf length boots. If her body was tired after the drive to Wittenberge it recovered by the time she reached the boat. Grabbing the guard rails on the gangplank she pulled herself up onto the deck. Cupping her hands beside her face she peered through one of the windows. It was after she turned and was walking back down the gang plank that we made eye contact. Perhaps because *typical Wessie* sprang to mind, I looked away and pushed at the hotel door. I had encountered women like this before. They arrived in my consulting room with problems and neuroses others would shrug off as minor inconveniences.

The reception desk was unmanned, and the lounge empty. While looking down at the grey waters of the Elbe and watching a group of cyclists ride by, I noticed that the woman in the leather jacket, rather than follow me through the side door, was climbing the long flight of steps to the front entrance. She stopped halfway up, first shielding her eyes, then putting on a pair of sunglasses and scanning the horizon, posing as if she was a model in a fashion magazine.

'Hello, mother.' Peter's wife Dorothea was standing in the doorway of the lounge. *Mother* rather than *Lotte* had me feeling more at home, until Frau Vogue made her entrance.

'Maxine, so glad you could make it,' Dorothea greeted the guest. Hands were shaken and cheeks kissed.

'Well, I still had one set of clothes which didn't smell of diesel so thought, what the hell?'

'This is my mother-in-law, Lotte,' Dorothea said, but Maxine merely stood staring at us.

'She's here, isn't she? I can see it on your faces. That strained look everyone has when the storm trooper from Situationist International turns up.'

Dorothea smiled and said, 'It's OK, Ute is on the boat.' Then she turned to me. 'I have to warn you, Ute is rather odd.' I tried to look both surprised and puzzled, two things I was definitely not.

'I saw her.' Maxine shook my hand. 'Hello, Lotte,' she said belatedly. 'I assume that rather dishy guy working on the electronics is your husband. I hope you like bald men because it looks like the Goddess of Köln has already got him pulling his hair out.' Which proved first impressions can be misleading, and Maxine more closely resembled my sister than the clone of Ute I had expected. 'Now she knows I've arrived it won't be long before she is up here issuing orders.'

Maxine was right and I could see Ute was climbing the steps.

'Good,' Ute said as she stepped through the door. This single word, I discovered, was something of a verbal tic, one on this occasion predicted by Maxine and Dorothea whose simultaneous utterance of it earned them one of Ute's icy stares. 'I do hope your husbands are able to have the boat working by tomorrow.' It seemed Maxine, Dorothea and myself were being held responsible for something beyond our control. I considered explaining this but while Ute may well have operated in two modes listening, as it had been in Köln, was currently disabled.

'Now, Dorothea...' I had disappeared, and presumably Maxine also felt she was invisible, because all Ute's attention was on my daughter-in-law. A sheet of paper on the clipboard the lady in grey had in her hand was removed and handed to Dorothea. 'Tomorrow the caterers will arrive, they will bring the food and serve it. You will only have to prepare the dinner tonight as well as breakfast tomorrow and Sunday morning for those of us staying in the hotel. Lunch tomorrow will be on the boat, assuming it is operational by then, and this will be followed by a short cruise along the river.'

'Actually, can this wait?' Dorothea asked, slowly backing away. 'Only I have to collect my children from school.'

'I will do that.'

As Dorothea was speechless it was left to me to explain teachers did not hand pupils over to complete strangers.

'Then Lotte you will have to come with me.' And it seemed there was no choice because Ute was already heading towards the side door.

Dorothea and Maxine merely shrugged and so I chased after Ute, catching up with her as she climbed into a massive SUV parked four cars away from Herman's BMW. I started giving directions to the school, but its location had already been programmed into the car's satnav. Here was somebody who left nothing to chance. Although the one time she had things did not turn out well for her.

'Grandma!' Tina shouted, her arms outstretched for a hug. Then it was Marc's turn and with that my grandparenting came to an end and the wicked witch took on the role of fairy godmother.

'Hello, I'm Ute. I've come to help with your father's boat. Are you looking forward to sailing on it tomorrow?' Yes, both children were. 'Shall we go for an ice cream? Do you both like ice cream?' Unsurprisingly, they did. There was a pattern to this questioning which I found intriguing as, no doubt, would anyone working in marketing. Predictably Ute had no trouble locating an ice cream parlour although struggled to find a suitable table; soon I would realise why.

Once we were seated around a low glass table under the awning outside the café, and the children had started their ice creams, I suggested we needed to hurry because 'Mummy will worry where we have got to.' Ute took out her iPhone, speed-dialled Dorothea, and the children Facetimed their mother each holding up their ice creams.

'Ute showed us some amazing magic tricks,' Tina told her mother when we finally got back to the hotel. It was left to Marc to explain the details, the Queen of hearts appearing in his shirt pocket and the four of diamonds stuck to the underside of the table. Dorothea gave me *a told you so* look. Ute herself still had the fading crow's feet beside her eyes because while at the ice-cream parlour I saw her smile for the first time. However, she reverted to her default subdued state during the drive back to the hotel when Tina asked if she had any children.

'So, what progress have you made?' Ute asked when the men entered the dining room.

'Don't worry, Ute, it's all under control,' said Max.

'If I had a euro for every time I've heard that I could afford to rebuild the summer house you burned down.' Which everyone present, even Maxine, found amusing. Herman, Peter and Max took their food back to the boat, to carry out a few *minor adjustments*, suggesting not everything was quite as under control as Max suggested. The children pestered Ute to perform more tricks, which she did, most involving coins and other objects disappearing from one hand and appearing in the other or from behind one of the children's ears. Here was a chance to watch and learn and already I wondered if Ute could perform some of these tricks when wearing a short-sleeved blouse.

After dinner Ute was keen to try out some of her more sophisticated magic tricks on us adults. 'We should play poker,' she suggested and, taken by surprise, no one objected. The worst that could happen, I thought, was an account of the game taking up a couple of pages in her next book.

'Only with a sealed pack of cards,' Maxine said.

'We have some cards for guests,' Dorothea said, then left the room, returning with a new pack. She also brought with her a jug of coffee, a bottle of cognac and four glasses, presumably guessing we might be drowning our sorrows by the end of the evening.

As if Ute could read my mind, she rolled the sleeves of her blouse up to her elbows leaving her arms bare save a woman's Rolex watch. 'It's warm this evening,' she offered as an unconvincing explanation.

My limit was one hundred euros, after that I would admit defeat and walk away. I had, after all, helped more than one patient successfully overcome their gambling addiction. But I would have done well to cast my mind back to the ice cream parlour: the trick and the magic and the role distraction played in each.

The game started in much the same way as the performance put on for my grandchildren. Like Tina and Marc, we all looked on in awe as Ute juggled the cards. 'Where did you learn to do that?' asked Dorothea.

'She used to work in a casino,' said Martina, before Ute could reply.

'Not true,' Ute said. 'When I was young some boys kept teasing me and one of my friends. Pestering us to do all sorts of stupid things. One day they suggested we played strip poker with them. Well, neither of us had brothers and so hadn't seen a boy's penis and thought, why not? Another card please.' Dorothea was laughing, so was Maxine who slid a card off the top of the pack. Ute picked up the card and continued with the story. 'We got a book on card games from the library and practised for almost a month. Eventually we took up the boy's offer. Another card, please.'

'Did you win?' asked Dorothea as both she and I asked for another card.

'Naturally, another card please Maxine, although a big disappointment, actually, two very small disappointments.' True or not, the story was amusing; Dorothea laughed out loud, despite that last card putting her out of the game. Another card and Maxine, still smiling, folded. My hand looked like a winner, but Ute's was better.

Ute's first trick. Creating the impression she did not make a habit of engineering kidnappings, breaking into people's houses or lying in wait for them on a deserted road with a gun in her hand but instead was a shy, vulnerable, and somewhat naïve, young woman defending herself in a world of predatory men.

'Anyone want more coffee?' Dorothea took the coffee jug back to the kitchen.

While she was gone Ute studied the hotel's menu.

'You need a better selection of wines, these all seem rather cheap.' Ute said, still reading the menu when Dorothea returned.

'We are only a small hotel.'

'That doesn't matter. I suggest you offer at least two wines over fifty euros, a Morlet Late Harvest and a Barbaresco, and a few reasonably priced wines such as Chateauneuf du Pape.'

'We wouldn't be able to sell them.'

'The more expensive ones, it would not matter. You might get lucky and have a rich cyclist stay overnight, but the point of stocking something expensive is to make the other wines look cheap by comparison. You might even be able to add a few euros to the lower priced wines. And if you do start selling a few bottles between thirty and fifty euros you may want to consider increasing the price of your evening meals.'

'I'm not sure that would work,' Dorothea said, looking at me, perhaps hoping I could discourage her tormentor.

But Ute persisted. 'I will have a case prepared and sent to you next week. Maxine, are you still in?'

Where had that shy young teenager gone? Suddenly Ute was in control, dictating how my daughter-in-law ran her hotel. One could appreciate how impotent those two naked boys must have felt.

At the end of the next game Maxine quit, leaving her hundred euros on the table with Dorothea's fifty and the hundred I had already lost.

'So, Lotte, it's just us then.' Which I now realise was what she had planned from the start. Maxine and Dorothea had merely been collateral damage. Erasing from my mind the image of Ute as the innocent teenage girl defending herself against a pair of misogynists, I thought again of the psychopath with a revolver in her hand.

The last of the money Paul had given me, nine hundred euros, was all I could put up. Dorothea gasped and Maxine shook her head then mouthed *no* while Ute searched in the bag hung on the back of her chair, eventually finding sufficient cash to match my stake.

Ute was arranging the cards in her hand when her phone rang. She took the mobile, which was still ringing, from her bag and laid it on the table then, after answering it and plugging in earphones, began a one-sided conversation in English.

'Thank you for calling back,' Ute said, studying her hand following the addition of yet another card. 'I was expecting your call earlier, but forgot *Cosmopolitan* went on sale today so presumably you have been busy.'

Ute rearranged the cards. 'No, we are not expecting Paul tonight. Tomorrow morning, just before lunch.' Ute listened then pursed her lips.

'Well, you will just have to change the booking. I hope you are not expecting me to do it?'

Dorothea returned with more coffee and stood behind me long enough for Ute to glance up at her face and, no doubt based on what she saw, decided there was no need to pick up another card.

'He's taken his wife to London for the day.' Ute's voice now slightly softer. She was multi-tasking and with her free hand poured herself another cognac which, like the two others she had drunk, was swallowed in a single gulp. 'Picking Paul up in Cambridge when he and his wife get back would not be a good idea. It's their wedding anniversary and they might have other plans for the evening.'

Ute looked at me then up at the ceiling.

'The whole point of using a private jet is to avoid Paul landing at an airfield in the middle of nowhere at three in the morning.' Ute whispered to the put-on secretary in England, 'If you are worried about spending ten thousand euros then by all means book him on Ryanair, although you might want to make sure your CV is up to date first.'

It was hard to tell, looking into Ute's eyes, whether she was holding a winning hand. All I needed was one more card to guarantee she was not.

'No, not Luton.' Ute sighed. 'There is an airport at Cambridge, have the car pick him up at 6:30 am. No, actually, I have a better idea. You spend the rest of the evening with your magazine, and I'll sort this mess out.' With one hand Ute snatched the earphones from her head and with the other laid her cards on the table. A royal flush. Had I been one of those teenage boys, my penis would have now been a good three centimetres shorter.

Ute got up from the table and walked to the window, still holding her mobile phone, but now without the earphones attached. 'Is everything working now?' she asked, looking down at the boat below. 'Good, I will come down later.' Returning to the table she gathered together all the money on it save a single fifty-euro note over which she placed her left hand. When Ute turned her hand palm upwards there was no note under it. She then held her right hand above the table. It was squeezed into a fist but when opened held the fifty-euro note.

'This is for the coffee and Cognac, Dorothea.' Ute then dropped the note on the table and walked out.

'Should we warn them she is on her way?' Dorothea said, picking up her phone.

'No,' said Maxime. 'Why should we have all the fun?'

During the Wende there was a story about an Ossie and Wessie standing beside a fountain in Berlin. The Ossie threw a mark in and then made a wish. The Wessie, not to be outdone, threw in two marks and made their wish. The Ossie then threw in five mark and the Wessie bettered this by throwing in ten. This went on until neither had any money left at which point the Wessie asked the Ossie what they had wished for.

'That one day East Germany would be as prosperous as West Germany.'

'Well, I wished...' The Wessie started to say, but the Ossie interrupted him.

'I know what you wished. You wished you had realised it was only my old Ost marks I was throwing in the fountain.'

This was amusing at the time, but less so when it became apparent how much reunification would cost West Germans. I wonder what Dorothea thought while watching me throw away 1000 marks. The money meant nothing to me, payment for something I never wanted to do. That aside, being out-manoeuvred yet again by Ute was humiliating. No one contacted her from Britain; the call was initiated while she pretended to search her bag for money, probably using an app similar to the one I used to trigger the false call during my meeting with Günter Hölderlin. Then the call itself, scripted to distract with those references to Paul and his wife, their wedding anniversary and the idea *they may have other plans for the evening*. The idea was to make me jealous and I dwelt on this while sitting alone at eleven pm on the steps in front of the hotel.

'Have an early night,' Herman told me, because I had complained of feeling tired. 'I'll be there later after we've tested the boat.' But how could I have slept with both my son and husband on a boat in the middle of the Elbe with the man-hating psychopathic Fräulein Lorenze?

Occasionally the boat's engine speeded up and then slowed down again. This, I was told, was to ensure the boat remained in the same position. It was the technology making this possible which had failed and presumably Herman had managed to fix. At first the boat was in the centre of the Elbe but then its engine raced and it moved closer to the bank to avoid a barge sailing north. This, apparently, it did without human intervention. Herman thought the technology was impressive and questioned why Peter had not put his mind to something like this earlier instead of entertaining headbanging punks in a Berlin warehouse.

The sound of people cheering carried over the water and someone had popped open a bottle of champagne, so presumably the trial had been a success. A crowd gathered at the back of the boat. Someone was leaning on the rail, and Ute was walking through the lounge, appearing at one window after another. This was a replay of that nightmare I had during my previous visit to Wittenberge. Then someone tapped me on the shoulder, except it was not Frau Reisenberg.

'I'm Magda Herbstrudel from Ganderkersee, it's a small town near Bremen. I was called as a witness in a court case brought against the mistress of the German Cycling champion during which it emerged that I had sex with him in a yellow Mercedes in a Lidl car park. The evidence was my footprints on the rear windscreen, which was removed from the car so it could be examined by members of the jury.' Then Maxine gave me a glass and filled it with red wine from a bottle she was holding. 'I thought you might need this. It's not Morlet Late Harvest I'm afraid,' she said, imitating Ute's accent. 'Actually, be honest, do I look to you like someone who shops at Lidl?' She did not; the bracelet on her wrist was probably worth more than the combined wealth of half the population of Gehrden. Maxine did not wait for an answer but sat down beside me and poured herself a glass of wine.

'Given the display in there this evening, she must have something special in mind for you in the next Maria Freitag book. You may even be the arch-villain. Have you noticed anything odd happening recently?'

'Are you kidding?' I laughed, then described all the tricks Ute had pulled, those I knew of and those I suspected. Omitted were any that hinted at my former life, the van in the carpark in Lychen and the swapping of coffee and soap powder. Despite what Paul said I still suspected a character in the next book would have a Stasi connection. I told Maxine about the trick in the ice cream parlour, which like me she assumed involved a second deck of cards.

'What about the disappearing fifty-euro note? How was that done?' I asked.

'No idea, but I'm guessing it reappeared from under the strap of her Rolex,' Maxine said. 'Although I don't know how she keeps a clear head after knocking back all those Cognacs.' So I told her how Claudia managed to drink the copious amount of Courvoisier her admirers in the Weissen Ross bought her, or more likely only pretended to, as it seemed to have found its way back into the bottle by the following evening.

My head was in my hands again, as I wondered what Herman and my children would think when Ute's book was published. 'How do you cope with it, being Magda Herbs whatever?'

'Herbstrudel. Admittedly it was a shock finding I was a prototype for one of her characters, especially as the only reason Frau Herbstrudel was in the book was to show that Bernie Fish was also cheating on his mistress. And I've been in every book since. Always humped in a car, usually while it is in a carpark.' Maxine smiled to herself. 'I take it you've never had sex in public.' She said.

'No, er, no definitely not,' I replied, shaking my head, but with the image of Heike standing holding her shawl still clear in my mind.

'You don't sound very sure? My god, have I just given a glass of wine to a recovering alcoholic?'

Finally, after we stopped laughing, I asked. 'So, what do people say to you?'

'*Hello, Maxine, how are you today? Max OK? Has he set fire to anything recently? Your garden not slid into the Rhein?* Once someone asked if I'd seen the latest episode of Frau Fish and The Bicycle on TV the previous evening, because there was a car in it like mine.' Maxine shrugged. 'I just told them the car was being sold once I got the footprints off the window, and they laughed.' She drank a mouthful of wine. 'Despite my more than passing resemblance to Magda Herbstrudel, they don't make the connection. That's because twenty-four hours after the book hits the street newspapers are full of people claiming the character is based on them. Ansbach thinks Maria Freitag taps into the *MeToo* movement but as far as I can see, most of her readers are members of the *LookAtMeToo* club. If you are expecting fifteen minutes of fame, you'll find yourself at the back of a long queue of narcissists, the sort of people who send a picture of their husband to *Bild* claiming he looks like Adolf Hitler. Personally, I blame social media.'

'I can't believe her former husband has never sued her.'

'I should imagine he kicked himself for not doing so after the first book was published. Especially as by then his business was experiencing financial difficulties. Instead, along comes a private bank from Köln offering Herr Lorenze and his former mistress who, by then, was his new and already somewhat disillusioned wife, a huge loan on very good terms. The only catch being the bank insisted on a controlling share of the business and appointing a director to the board. Take a wild guess who that director was.'

Maxine poured us both another drink. 'I'm sure you've discovered how unpleasant the grey witch can be, and her troubling attitude towards members of the opposite sex,' she said. 'Imagine how her husband felt waking up one morning and discovering he was handcuffed to Ute for the rest of his life.'

We sat in silence for a moment, watching the boat. Ute had crossed the lounge again and was remonstrating with Max. Maxine said, in a near whisper, 'Still, it will be interesting to see what she has planned for her ex, and the both of us, in her next book.'

'I've a feeling it might be something related to the DDR,' I said.

'I doubt it, that's a sensitive subject for Ute. Have you read any of her books?'

'I've listened to the audio versions,' I replied, then told Maxine about my encounter with Frau Spoiler on the train from Hanover to Berlin.

'Handy person to know. You don't have her address by any chance?' Maxine asked.

The boat came to life again. It moved to the other side of the river and I found myself willing it back. Maxine said, 'In book five there was mention of a grandmother who was in Berlin when the Russians arrived. She gave up her baby daughter to a couple from a Christian group that saved children from communism. They raised the child in Denmark. Then three years later the grandmother arrived in the West and was reunited with her daughter. Have you noticed Ute's accent?' I admitted it struck me as odd and was difficult to place. 'Well, I think her mother's first language might have been Danish,' Maxine continued, 'and Ute's grandmother was actually from East Germany. About two months before book five was published, Max overheard Paul and Ute having an argument. Not just a difference of opinion but an airborne paperweight, full-blooded, tooth and claw fight. Paul was saying there were some things which are best forgotten and Ute accused him of airbrushing inconvenient truths out of his family's history. So, the story about her mother got only a passing mention, and if Max hadn't told me about the row I wouldn't have paid it any attention. My guess is, like the burning down of her summerhouse and the vineyard, Ute's East German connection is off limits.'

'I thought the garden sliding into the Rhein was based on the fire.'

'No, unfortunately they were both two of Max's more spectacular accidents. Max decided cutting the grass on the side of the hill was hard work and we needed a terrace. I'm not sure if he realised what would happen to the tons of rock when it rained. One afternoon during a storm it slid down the hill and demolished our neighbour's house. Luckily, he was away in Turkey, would you believe he was a geologist. The fire will definitely not be mentioned in a Maria Freitag book. There was someone with money invested in K and S who was particularly unhappy when the bank's name appeared in the press. So, there have been a few changes since the fire and Paul is being pressured to retire. As Ute is regarded as the only adult in the room, I suspect a promotion is in the offing.'

'And Paul and Max are happy with that?'

'Max has never worked for K and S, he has his own company, playing with boats and other toys, as you can see.' Maxine nodded towards the boat. Ute was now talking to my son, who was sitting on one of the tables in the lounge.

'Are Paul and Ute in a relationship?' Somehow the word *lovers* did not seem appropriate.

'What have you heard?' Maxine asked and I repeated the story Paul had told me about a struggling author in Bremen who started writing as a form of therapy.

At a guess there were few people Maxine could confide in and maybe approaching the subject as I would when talking to a patient encouraged her to speak openly. 'Paul's relationship with the truth is much like Einstein's theory on light, it bends when coming into contact with physical objects. Yes, everything he told you actually happened but, not necessarily in that order. Ansbach owned that publishing company long before it started publishing Ute's books. There was no therapist, and it was Paul who suggested Ute would feel better if she wrote things down and he originally suggested she locked the manuscript away and forgot it. Ute was already working for K and S before she started writing. She was a wreck back then, bursting into tears all the time, and only avoided getting sacked because Paul had got her the job. Freddie Ansbach was visiting the bank one day and found a few pages of the book in Paul's office and he suggested it was published.' Maxine was watching me, perhaps to see how I would react. 'I don't think Paul stumbled across Ute. I think he sought her out.' There was only one piece of information Maxine needed to solve this puzzle but it seemed Paul had never told her the story about his father's train ride through Köln in 1948.

'Mo Fink said you studied together,' I said, because it was time we talked about someone other than Ute.

'You've met Mo..., God that takes me back.' Maxine smiled. 'Mo was Max's girlfriend until I stole him and made a dishonest man out of him. Still, as Max is accident prone and Mo's parents had an enormous collection of valuable Dresden porcelain, I'm not sure they would have made an ideal couple.' It was now apparent we had drunk too much.

'Seriously though,' I said, having temporarily managed to stop giggling like a teenager. 'Don't you and Max get fed up with Ute's stories, even if no-one realises they relate to you?'

'Sometimes the best place to hide an inconvenient truth is amongst a collection of unbelievable lies and better people look for it in a Maria Freitag novel than something written by Stefan Aust.' There was not time to ask what Maxine meant by this because the boat had docked and our husbands, along with Peter and Ute, descended the gang plank. As Ute led the party up the steps Maxine hid the bottle and glasses behind us; we sat up straight and tried not to laugh.

'Well, the boat seems to be working,' Ute said. Maxine saluted, we both said 'Good' and then had another giggling fit.

'I'm glad you've enjoyed your evening,' Ute snapped as she walked between us, looking down, shaking her head and sighing after accidentally kicking over one of the empty glasses.

'Next weekend we will be in Rugen,' Herman said as I drifted off to sleep. Yes, I thought, and thanks to Ute we would be taking sandwiches and a tent.

The following morning, I pulled back the curtains and watched the last of the mist drifting off the river. I was thankful for a dreamless sleep but thinking again of that nightmare during my previous visit and how it seemed to predict what I saw while sitting with Maxine on the steps in front of the hotel. Except of course it was not a premonition. That nightmare had been so disturbing I buried it deep in my subconscious with the recollection of the boat on the river the previous evening now acting as firewall. Memories are merely stories we tell ourselves, in this case to block out something I was still unable to process.

# 36

# Schnackenburg

The table, covered with a white cloth and stretching half the length of the boat's lounge, seemed excessive for the small group of us having lunch. But this was a rehearsal and there were already thirty places laid for dinner that evening. Max, Paul, Herman and Peter were sitting closest to the large TV screen showing the boat's location on a digital map. I was sitting opposite Maxine with Dorothea beside me. Instead of the children being seated next to their mother, they were at the far end of the table with Ute; the only person without a prepacked lunch. She was too busy to eat, and her current obsession was ensuring the caterers remained unobtrusive to the point of being invisible when serving guests. 'Remember there is a world of difference between a takeaway in a box and a three-course meal,' she said, explaining the limitations of the props used during the preparation for the main event.

Ute was also trying to pacify the window cleaner who, taking longer than expected to remove hand marks from the lounge windows, was still on board when the boat sailed. This meant a shopping trip to Perleberg that afternoon had to be cancelled. 'Don't ask,' I heard him mutter into his phone when breaking the news to his wife.

Also on board were members of Hot Cats setting up their equipment on the small stage at the far end of the lounge. This went relatively smoothly until the lead singer, whose two-and-a-half-hour drive from Templin was a long time for a member of Hot Cats to go without a drink, approached the table. A collective gasp coincided with Ute spotting the singer opening a bottle of wine with his penknife.

'Let's get a few things straight,' Ute said, snatching the bottle back. 'No drinking, and you spend time when not performing sitting there.' She pointed at the small table next to the stage.

'Are we allowed to visit the toilet or do we pee over the side of the boat?' Not one to quit while he was ahead, this was followed up with a simulation of someone relieving themselves which saw Maxine shielding her eyes in anticipation of what was coming next.

'Have you got the playlist I asked you to bring?' Ute asked, then snatched the scruffy piece of notepaper Herr Hot Cat offered up. 'Totally unsuitable,' she said, screwing it up and then detaching an A4 sheet from her clipboard. 'This is what you will play and pay special attention to the times, no improvising.' Then, because he was not paying attention, Ute turned to the singer's wife. 'I understand you have recorded a CD and hope you realise the people who will decide if it is worth promoting will be here this evening.' At the time I did not dwell on the idea there might be a connection between K and S Investments and the audio company in Magdeburg, distracted instead by the thought of sending a video of this performance to Claudia at the Weissen Ross to prove it was, after all, possible to herd Hot Cats. Satisfied Frau Hot Cat would now keep her husband under control, Ute returned to the table and sat down next to my grandchildren.

Dorothea seemed as perplexed as me, puzzled as to why Marc and Tina were so engrossed in whatever was on the screens of the iPads Ute had given them. Initially I thought they were playing computer games but then overheard Ute suggest if guests spoke to them to point out something of interest on the banks of the Elbe. Promising they would act as unofficial tour guides seemed rather cruel as Tina and Marc would be spending the evening in the hotel with a babysitter.

Meanwhile at the other end of the table Max was demonstrating the boat's *self-navigation system*. Maxine had, given her husband's reputation, persuaded him to avoid using the phrase *anti-collision technology*.

'There we are on the opposite side of the river to Wahrenberg,' said Max, indicating the boat's position on the screen with a cursor.

'I'm not sure we need a computer to tell us that,' said Paul, turning in his chair and looking out of the window.

'OK, so let's zoom in and get a closer look,' Max said, ignoring Paul and dragging his fingers across the screen of his phone. As its engines sped up, the boat turned and moved to the other side of the river.

'Very impressive,' said Paul, and it was plain here was a well-polished double act, or triple act even, as I assumed Ute was standing by with a fire extinguisher.

Peter looked at me across the table. 'Rather symbolic, don't you think. Neither in the East nor the West,' he said. Paul smiled to himself, but Ute, not quite as immersed in what the children were doing as it appeared, glared at Peter and me.

'What was the problem which ruined Lotte's and Herman's weekend in Rugen?' Maxine asked her husband.

But it was Herman who answered. 'One of the pins on a chip wasn't connected to zero volts. Can easily happen on a prototype.' *Easily* no doubt to save Max's feelings.

'Should have been obvious,' Paul said, looking at Max.

'Hey, no problem. It's working now.' Max shrugged as he chewed a mouthful of bread roll. The lunch was chicken and potato salad, take it or leave it, with no accommodation for people with particular dietary requirements, such as the inability to eat anything other than schnitzels. 'You remember that graphics board for Reuters.' The fork in Max's hand was pointed at Paul. 'Now that was a stupid mistake someone only spotted at the last moment.' Peter looked from one man to the other, keen to hear more.

'Yes, that was an intermittent fault,' Paul said, and I had the feeling this one was down to him rather than Max.

'An ungrounded chip?' Peter asked.

'No, something had got onto the film we used to make the circuit boards in those days, a hair or small speck of dust, and two tracks were shorted together,' Max said. 'Unfortunately, it was a multi-layer board and this was the middle layer. The courier who was taking the graphics board to Heathrow was sitting in reception. A salesman was booked on a flight to New York leaving in three hours. There was a demonstration to Reuters the next day. So, what did you do Paul? Call a friend with a logic analyser like we did yesterday? No, you see Paul here is a builder.' Max put his hand on his friend's shoulder. 'So he drills a hole through the board, just like a builder would if you asked him to put up shelves in your kitchen.'

Herman winced. 'And that actually worked?'

'Well, the board worked long enough to get it through the demonstration didn't it.' Paul said. 'Mind you the timing could have been better.' Which both he and Max found amusing.

'The board displayed video in a window on a computer screen so traders could watch Reuter's TV news feed while buying and selling shares,' explained Max. 'Nothing revolutionary in the age of YouTube but this was October nineteen eighty-seven...'

'A week before the meltdown on Black Monday,' Paul interrupted. 'After which, financial institutions stopped buying trading terminals...'

'It was another twenty years before video on webpages took off.' Max picked up the story again and I could see Peter was puzzled why both Max and Paul found it so amusing. 'Still, all was not lost. We had a piece of graphics software that helped us sell the board to cosmetics companies.'

'And hospitals,' Paul added although Max's version of history won the day.

'It meant beauticians could let their clients experiment with makeup without trying it on. It was also used by cosmetic surgeons. Both big markets, especially here in Germany and Switzerland. How many million did that make us?'

'It was a stupid idea,' Paul replied.

Maxine agreed. 'A machine to promote the objectivization of women, how clever or ethical was that?'

'Well, we did stop doing it,' Her husband replied.

'Eventually, and not because you got bored with all those super models on your exhibition stands,' Maxine said.

'Didn't uncle Roland work on a piece of graphics software like that when he was working for Robotron?' Peter asked his father. There was silence, suddenly the joking was over. The question had caught Herman off guard. It was Paul who spoke, a response which was calm, measured and flawless.

'Before we set up the company I spent a few months at the CAD Centre in Cambridge. It was a joint venture between a computer company, ICL, and the Government, so employees had access to information collected by trade attaches around the world. I remember reading papers written by researchers at Robotron, so it's possible that's where the idea came from.' My eyes were not on Paul while he said this, but on Herman because I wanted to see how he reacted.

My husband suddenly appeared more interested in his lunch than the well-rehearsed cover story by a spy who was protecting his source. I recalled the man who had stood behind Rolf outside the supermarket in Templin, and Huber's description of the kiss, information passed between two men with the outward appearance of strangers. In the case of Herman and Paul, no leap of imagination was necessary; the relief on Herman's face at the end of Paul's story told me everything I needed to know. Another coincidence came to mind, one which had been troubling me of late, the logo on the sign outside the hotel near Inge's new house. The same one was on one of the matchboxes Herman brought back from a trip to Hannover in the 1980s.

'And we didn't end up as rich as Wozniak, Gates or Ellison.' Max was goading Paul again and it was odd, given the experiments with social media, that Zuckerberg had been left off the list.

'That was never going to happen. Remember how Robert Maxwell reacted after he saw the trading terminal. We were the smallest kids in the playground with a biggest bag of sweets. As well being too early with an idea can be as disastrous as being too late, after all, there were electric cars before petrol engines caught on.' This, I felt, was aimed at Peter as well as Max, because Herman had already told me he believed his son's boat was being used to test self-drive technology for use in cars.

Maxine placed her hand over her mouth and pretended to yawn. 'That's a nice jacket you are wearing, Ute, where did you get it?' Only later did it become apparent why Maxine asked this, or why Ute obviously found the question annoying and refused to answer. Even so the tension which had been building at our end of the table dissipated.

The Pied Piper of Köln was quizzing the children on Höhbeck and the countryside beyond. Tina gave an account of the controversial storage of nuclear waste at Gorleben.

'Well done, Tina.' Ute rewarded the young girl with a smile. 'I'm sure there will be people here tonight who are interested in that.' Dorothea was about to say something, but Ute chose that moment to declare lunch over, telling Max to type the coordinates of the hotel into his toy as guests would be arriving for a private meeting preceding the dinner and party. I sensed an argument between Ute and my daughter-in-law would erupt when we reached dry land.

Dorothea caved into the inevitable, cancelling the babysitter and agreeing to let Marc and Tina spend the evening on the boat. The occasional shriek of recognition from the wives of old acquaintances punctuated the murmur of businessmen as the boat set sail for a second time. Guests who either now understood the boat's self-navigating technology or found it too confusing split away from those transfixed by icons moving on the screen and gravitated to the boat's windows. It was there that Marc and Tina were acting as tour guides, the wives of the visiting businessmen proving the most attentive. Omitted by my grandchildren were mentions of Cumlosen or Lenzen and no explanation of the former role of the abandoned watchtowers. Only what passengers saw on the West bank of the Elbe was deemed worthy of note even if it involved protests over the storage of nuclear waste. *Intelligent children*, was the impression Ute wanted the guests to take away with them, children who only looked west and it was inconceivable their father, responsible for the technology they had come to Wittenberge to see demonstrated, was an Ossie. Pragmatic perhaps, but as insulting as it was hurtful.

Dorothea and Maxine supported their husbands. Herman stood at his son's side. I was all alone listening to my grandchildren dismissing the country I grew up in as an irrelevance. 'Hello, I believe you are Peter's mother.' A small man I vaguely recognised shook my hand. 'Do you live in Wittenberge?'

'No, in Gehrden, a small village near Templin,' I replied

'Then you must know Joachim.' Of course, that is why I recognised him, he was the engineer from Volkswagen standing next to *the man with a two-hundred-kilometre-per-hour Trabant* in one of the press cuttings on the wall of Gehrden Motors. 'When he visited Wolfsburg with his Trabant it caused quite a stir.' A recollection which caused the engineer to rock on his heels and laugh. This should have made me feel better but did the opposite. It brought to mind Joachim reborn as a Wessie, calling back down the tunnel, mocking me for being the last one to leave. Three decades of inertia, suitcase filled with clothes from the Anweilers' party that I only got to wear once, diaries full of fading memories and that stupid Cathcart tape.

The Hot Cats were well into their set when Herman finally remembered he was married and decided to dance with his wife, even then I only shared his company until Peter mentioned the engineer from Volkswagen wanted to talk to him. Once more I was on my own, but finally, a reference of something on the East bank. Marc explaining the building towering over Domitz harbour had not always been a hotel. Now I was looking around the room for Paul.

The boat turned and began its return journey to Wittenberge coming to a halt twenty minutes later and holding its own against the flow of the river. Unlike during previous demonstrations, Hot Cats kept playing. At first I suspected the lead singer was doing this in defiance of Ute, but then noticed she was watching everyone dancing to a rendition of the Beatles *I Saw Her Standing There*. She approached me and said, 'I think Tina and Marc are tired so I sent them to the wheelhouse. Would you mind checking they are OK?' A strange request but one it was impossible for a grandmother to ignore.

The children were indeed in the wheelhouse, talking to a friend of their father charged with taking over control of the boat should the automatic navigation system fail.

'We were being followed,' Tina told me.

'I think it was the police' Marc suggested and Tina told her brother the boat was not travelling fast or on the wrong side of the river. 'Then maybe the problem is we are not moving at all,' Marc said.

Then I noticed Paul was sitting on a bench just below the wheelhouse. When the motorboat came alongside, he helped a late-middle-aged woman up onto the deck. She was slim with wavy silver hair which the wind was blowing across her face. There was the briefest of embraces then Paul handed the woman a glass of wine and the two of them sat down next to each other on the bench. The discussion, businesslike with no trace of intimacy, lasted no more than fifteen minutes.

What would the young terrorist I interviewed for a job at VEB Mikroelektronik look like had she lived? Was this the woman people had gone to great lengths to convince the world she was dead after references to her were found on that stolen laptop? If so, why was she being paraded in front of me now?

Paul kissed the woman on both cheeks before she climbed back into the motorboat which, after it had been untied, raced upriver. The woman's hair trailed behind her as the motorboat turned in a wide arc and headed back towards Domitz with its engines roaring and a plume of spray behind it. Was I the only person aware of this clandestine meeting? I suspected not as less than a minute after resuming our journey upriver the door to the wheelhouse opened. 'Oh, good, you found the children, Lotte,' Ute said, then lured Tina and Marc away with the promise of supper in the galley.

Peter had given into temptation and joined the Hot Cats on stage. The fact that his guitar solo earned a round of applause from Herman was a measure of how much the events of the previous two days had done to heal the rift between father and son. As we were having the last dance of the evening Herman asked where I had disappeared to, and I wondered if he had noticed my absence coincided with Paul's. But then he smiled and whispered, 'Lother didn't bring Heike, so if you've found somewhere private, I'm still up for it.'

# 37

# #ItWasAScam

Whenever I see the hashtag trending on social media I am reminded of the morning after my son's inaugural Rock on the Elbe cruise. This began with the sun streaming through the bedroom window after Herman drew back the curtains. 'Max wants to discuss something before he returns to Köln. I'll be back after breakfast,' Herman said, kissing me before I pulled the bed covers over my head.

Breakfast was almost over by the time I got up, although Maxine was still in the lounge sitting with only a cup of coffee in front of her. 'Some evening,' she said. Then watching me collect three slices of rye bread, some cheese and a glass of orange from the buffet, added, 'I think it went well.'

'In Gehrden, any event which passes off without Hot Cats wrecking the place is regarded as a success.' I said.

Dorothea brought a jug of coffee from the kitchen, filled my cup and topped up Maxine's, then joined us around the table. 'Personally, I'm exhausted,' she sighed. 'I'm not sure how I would have managed without Ute.'

'Where is she?' I asked.

'On the boat with Max's friend Paul,' Dorothea replied. 'By the way, did you see that motorboat which pulled alongside us last night?' Either Tina or Marc must have told their mother about Paul's brief liaison with the mystery woman.

Maxine's response to Dorothea's question was interesting. 'Missed it, probably too busy dancing.' Then she performed a waist-up version of the twist while singing the Beatle's song the Hot Cats were playing when the boat carrying Paul's guest arrived.

My mobile phone rang. 'Could you repeat that?' I asked then, once I understood what the caller was telling me, abandoned my breakfast, walked out of the hotel and, after descending the steps to the towpath, climbed onto the boat.

'Hello, Mutti.' Peter was tidying the galley. 'Is everything OK?' he asked, seeming surprised to see me.

Bursting through the door into the boat's lounge, I saw Paul at the far end, standing by one of the windows and looking out over the river. The room look much like it had the previous evening although the stage had been cleared of the Hot Cats' equipment. One of the tables which had been removed when the floor was cleared for dancing had been put back and Ute was sitting at it typing on a laptop.

'You complete shit!' I shouted while still only halfway across the room, pointing the mobile phone I was holding at Paul. 'I've just had a call from Günter Hölderlin.'

Ute closed her laptop and stood up. 'I'll come back later,' she said while walking past me on the way to the door.

'Never would be too soon,' I shouted after her then turned back to face Paul. 'He tells me it will not be possible to publish his story about Cathcart's Stasi file because the magazine's computer system has been hacked and someone is demanding a large amount of money to unlock all their files, more than they can afford. Apparently, they are negotiating with a bank, presumably the one you work for, hoping to raise a loan, but for now Günter is out of a job.'

'I wonder who put ransomware on his computer?' Paul had got his revenge for the trick with the stolen laptop and, as a bonus, made me look stupid. A diary provides only the gist of what is said in the heat of the moment, which often differs from what you wished you had said at the time. But as I had stopped committing my thoughts to paper in 1993, what follows is, to the best of my recollection, my feelings towards Paul Anweiler finally finding a voice in one long and very loud rant. A rant which later I discovered could be heard by Peter at the other end of the boat and was probably decipherable to anyone able to lip read who might have been watching from the front window of the hotel.

It was now clear how Paul was able to promise whoever was putting pressure on Cathcart that the story about the missing Stasi file would only be published if the politician refused to do what was asked of him. And overhearing the conversation between Ute and Frau Hot Cats, it now seemed quite likely Kurt Kohnen was keen to make Hölderlin believe the Cathcart tape was genuine because his son's company had a hand in forging it.

'You know damn well who put the virus on Günter's computer and I'm tired of being used. Not just to help you sabotage the career of a politician but as an avatar in the fantasy world you and Ute have created. I want you to leave me and my family alone, pack up and go back to Köln, Britain or the hole you crawled out of. You can't go around messing with people's lives.'

'Really? That's interesting,' he said, and my suspicion this was a reference to my work on the Stasi's Zersetzung program was confirmed when he added, 'I suppose you had a conversation like this with Hubert Hüber?'

By now I was pacing the room like a caged lion; better this, I thought, than Paul continuing to see me as prey. 'Do you even understand what gaslighting is? This isn't some sort of stage,' I said, looking around the boat's lounge. 'And my family aren't actors in a bizarre story made up by you and your psychotic side kick.'

'If you are referring to Ute, I'm not sure she is psychotic, just struggles a little with interpersonal relationships.'

'A little? My god.' I was now standing next to Paul who refused to look me in the eye but instead was staring at something on the opposite bank of the Elbe. 'You are just another Wessie, standing there in your Amani suit, thinking you can rewrite the history of a country which only exists in your imagination. Well, it's time to bring the curtain down on this performance and let us get on with our own lives.'

'Hugo Boss, actually,' Paul said, examining the label on the inside of his jacket.

'What?!' I shouted.

'The suit. It's not Amani, it's Hugo Boss.'

'Well that just about sums you up. Morally bankrupt, devoid of ethics and no appreciation of history.'

Paul flinched and I wondered if this was how he reacted when his mother had lost her temper, and it crossed my mind he might have engineered this confrontation with that in mind.

Turning away and, despite my legs feeling weak and my whole body seeming to shake, I walked calmly out of the lounge and along the corridor where Ute was standing, as poker-faced as ever. From the towpath I looked up and saw Maxine and Dorothea looking at me from the hotel's dining room. Standing beside them was Tina. My granddaughter turned to her mother, perhaps expecting an explanation for what she had seen. Deciding against climbing the steps to the hotel entrance, I walked along the towpath, feeling slightly more at ease after putting some distance between myself and the boat.

A barge was headed north; there were two bicycles behind its wheelhouse, reminding me Herman and I had planned to spend that weekend cycling in Rugen. 'Mutti, are you OK?' Peter had followed me and looked genuinely concerned.

My hands were still shaking so I thrust them in the pockets of my jeans. 'Fine,' I replied.

'Do you know Paul?' I did not answer and to my relief he took a guess. 'Is he one of your patients?'

The thought of this made me laugh. 'Even if he was, I couldn't tell you. But you need to be careful when dealing with these people, even Max and his wife,'

'They seem OK. Ute seems short of cups in the cupboard. Max said he would throw her overboard but she would probably grow fins and attack the boat. We would end up pushing a gas cylinder in her mouth and shooting at it.' This time I did laugh. 'Although Paul did say something strange when Max was rewiring the computer. Something like *I hope you've given us long enough to get clear this time.* I guess they might have played around with explosives when they were younger.'

'Who knows?' I shrugged as it appeared Peter's research into the background of Max Arndt had got no further than the statement about the privacy of EU citizens at the bottom of a single page of results.

'Don't worry, Mutti, I can look after myself.' He could; after all, when two former Russian soldiers turned up at his club with knives and iron bars offering to act as bouncers in exchange for a fifty percent share of the business, Peter and his partner put one in hospital and persuaded both they would be safer back home in Moscow.

'When these people strong arm you, they don't resort to violence, not the physical sort, anyway. You don't owe Paul and Max money, do you?' I asked.

'No, Max put up the money to restore the boat and will get it back selling self-navigation technology to those people at the party last night. Father says there is a good chance car companies will be interested.' Once again that feeling of being a mere observer, watching a play as an audience of one, ignored by those on the stage who probably would neither notice or care if I got up and left. 'Come on, Mutti.' Peter took hold of my arm. 'What is it they say? Everything will come right in the end. And if things are not right yet ...'

'Then it's not the end.' I completed the quotation often recited to my son when he was young, trying to persuade him there might be a future for him in a rapidly shrinking village in rural Brandenburg. That did not work out well, but at least it seemed to have turned him into an eternal optimist.

'Why were you shouting at that man, Grandma?' The question I had been dreading.

'You'll find when you grow up, shouting at men is one of life's rare pleasures,' Martine told Tina. But it was Ute who, inadvertently, came to my rescue. A large limousine had pulled up alongside the boat and its driver stood waiting while Ute remonstrated with Paul and Max, neither of whom were taking any notice of her. Tina and Marc had forgotten their grandmother's violent outburst and were now concerned their fairy godmother might leave without saying goodbye.

'Can we go down and see Ute?' Marc asked his mother. The request was denied.

Paul was holding a chequebook given to him by Ute, he took a pen from his jacket pocket and unscrewed the cap. But there was a delay in signing the cheque because Max said something to distract his friend. Chastised by Ute, Max sought refuge on the boat and Paul signed the cheques and three pieces of paper, none of which he gave more than a cursory glance. Then something strange seemed to happen to Ute; her arms dropped to her side and for a moment it seemed the clipboard she was holding might fall to the ground. Her shoulders sagged and her head bowed. At first, I suspected a *little girl lost* style seduction on Ute's part. Then I remembered that manuscript in Ute's office, another Maria Freitag novel completed, as cathartic as all those that had gone before, but maybe not cathartic enough.

I imagined the phone call that might have preceded the beginning of the strange relationship between the two people now stood on the towpath.

*Hello, Paul,* the caller was a woman with a heavy Danish accent. *How is father? Mother tells me he was looking well when they met during her holiday in Britain.* An absence of the words *your, my* or *our* when describing this father. *By the way, mother said those offices you built were impressive.* Then the reason for the telephone call. *Paul, if you happen to be in Bremen at some point... And this weekend would be good because Ute is having a terrible time. Her husband has left her, she has lost her business and home and, with all your contacts, perhaps you could help ...*

Max re-emerged from the boat and the symbiotic relationship between the three people on the tow path was gradually and painstakingly repaired. Ute got her two ersatz children back. Paul his make-believe mother and Max still had someone to liaise with the emergency services next time disaster struck.

Was Paul aware Ute had given me those two books, which together inadvertently revealed fundamental vulnerabilities he might have preferred were kept from a psychologist? It was possible, of course, she realised Paul needed help and now expected me to provide it. But then again Maxine had suggested a promotion at the K and S bank was in the offing so perhaps Ute was attempting to sabotage Paul's career. In that case all that I had witnessed on the towpath was, on Ute's part at least, a very convincing act.

Paul reached out and took hold of Ute's arm, looking concerned, and said something. At a guess *Are we good*? Max appeared to assist with a stupid or irreverent remark and Ute was, once again, *good!* This I know because it was the first word she used on her return to the hotel's dining room. Although I was beginning to suspect *good!* marked the end of paragraphs Ute was mentally composing for her next Maria Freitag novel.

'Here is payment for our stay in the hotel, and something I would like you to give Tina and Marc for all their help,' Ute said, handing three sealed envelopes to Dorothea.

'Oh yes, wait there, I will get those two iPads you lent them,' Dorothea said.

'No need, Dorothea, we cannot use them again for security reasons,' Ute said, glancing in my direction to remind me how malware ended up on Günter Hölderlin's computer. 'And that wine we spoke of will arrive shortly.'

'I'm really not sure we can afford it.'

'I insist, I've arranged a special discount, and shipping is being organised as we speak.' I should imagine Ute took great pleasure in getting her former husband, and his new wife, to go into work on a Saturday morning to give away wine for free.

'You will be coming back,' Tina insisted, as Ute turned to leave.

'I'm very busy, but perhaps you can come to Köln. We can go to Fantasia Land. Would you like to visit Fantasia Land?' Ute asked. Yes, unsurprisingly, they would. Then she left, not through the front door and down to the towpath, where Max and Paul were saying their goodbyes, but the side exit leading to the car park. The children followed her, and it flashed through my mind Ute might take them with her. Eventually, however, they both returned. Neither looked happy and Tina whispered something in Marc's ear.

Martine left in her Porsche driving back to Köln ahead of Max who was still loading tools and equipment into his 4x4. Paul stood talking to the driver of the limousine, only climbing in when it started to rain. I stayed near the edge of the window hoping he would not see me watching him but need not have worried as he left without looking up.

Hikers and cyclists began arriving at the hotel for an early lunch and to shelter from the rain. Herman and I sat with Dorothea and Peter at one of the tables in the lounge. 'My God, look at this!' Dorothea said, showing me the contents of the envelopes Ute had left for Tina and Marc. My grandchildren had been gifted the money won from me during the poker game. The pain of this final twist of the knife dulled after overhearing Tina ask her mother why Ute had been sat in her car crying before driving away.

The three-hour journey back to Gehrden was in the pouring rain, and Herman dropped me at the house before returning the borrowed logic analyser. In view of what fell out of my bag when I upended it on the kitchen table it was fortunate I got to unpack it while on my own.

'Is That All There Is?' I said, staring at the horizon where the sea and sky seemed to merge. We had made it to Rugen, a week late and spending a long weekend in a five-star hotel – not a tent.

'Sorry?' Herman asked after the voice of Hildegard Knef, trapped in my head since the previous Wednesday, escaped.

'It's from a song a patient had stuck in his mind. Unfortunately, now I can't get it out of mine.'

'Oh, your rich guy,' Herman said, leaning back in his beach chair. An easy guess because the rich guy he referred to had been my only appointment that week. Until recently I assumed this patient was a member of the network of businessmen and politicians of which the late Heinrich Reisenberg had once been a part. Now I suspected he moved in the same circles as Paul Anweiler. He paid well, but not well enough to cover the cost of our weekend on the Baltic coast. Even so, I had come home from Berlin on the day of the appointment over 5,000 euros richer.

'I don't know whether it is remembering the song which makes me depressed or the other way around; that I think of the song when I'm feeling low,' Herr Richguy said. 'The song triggering, or recalled during, his rumination was made famous by Peggy Lee and based on Thomas Mann's short story, *Disillusionment*. I am all for patients researching their own condition, but suspected Herr Richguy had gone off at a tangent. But that week we focussed on the number of times, while sitting in my consulting room during the past year, he had said, 'I would give up everything if only ...' Apparently there were numerous things he would rather have than money and political influence, things which, apart from his youth of course, only existed in an imagined past. He was another child whose parents reinvented themselves after 1945, and the censorship of their own youth had a detrimental impact on their son's. Despite his wealth and power, or perhaps as a result of it, he became increasingly disillusioned following the death of his parents. So perhaps his research was not so wide of the mark after all.

As was the case with many people in Herr Richguy's position, few suspected here was a person who needed therapy or, if they did, would risk the impact seeking it would have on their company's share price. 'He looks just like that person they interviewed on TV a few nights ago,' Herman remarked after catching sight of him when picking me up at the practice one evening. Even our receptionist failed to make the connection between my patient and the person standing next to Frau Richguy in one of the fashion magazines she read.

The appointments were irregular as he spent very little time in Germany and was an infrequent visitor to Berlin. So far, I had been able to remain objective; there was nothing in his lifestyle I could relate to. But that changed after Paul Anweiler, the uber-Wessie, gate-crashed my life. At one point during a recent session there was some inappropriate empathising. In some respects here was a person whose disillusionment was similar to mine, and perhaps not so much different than that experienced by other East Germans my age. Three decades on from Wende, how often did we ask ourselves: *is that all there is?* But for myself, it was a question that only became relevant after the Cathcart affair was over.

It was possible, of course, that rather than the song's chorus it was the first verse which played on my mind, the account of the family home burning down. The argument with Paul may have put paid to Inge's chance of a new house and funding for Peter's boat. Pride before a fall on my part, and I was examining my motives and regretting my stupidity when my mobile phone rang.

'Lotte, hello. Sorry to disturb you while you're on holiday. Maxine here. I'm just giving you a quick call about your visit next weekend.'

'Sorry, that's news to me.'

'Me too until I saw an email Max sent Herman yesterday evening. I trust Max with my life, just not our diary. And matches, of course.'

I leaned forward in the beach chair and looked at Herman who must have guessed it was Maxine who called. 'Ah, yes, I meant to tell you...' he said.

'Yes, Maxine, I see what you mean.' Together we filled in the gaps our husbands had inadvertently left out of the itinerary, small details such as how we would be travelling to Köln and where we would meet.

'You can stay with us in Königswinter, and best if you come to Köln by train. We will pick you up in the city and do some sightseeing before we leave.'

The call over, I got up and strolled onto the beach.

'Where are you going?' Herman called out.

'Swimming to Denmark, remember,' I replied and was then chased down to the sea. We didn't get more than fifty metres from the shore and despite Herman insisting we were no longer teenagers I hitched a ride on his back when we returned to the hotel.

'Are you sure we can afford this?' Herman asked when I enquired whether the hotel's restaurant had a bottle of Morlet Late Harvest, although not realising I would have to play the part of winetaster when the bottle was bought to the table. What was I supposed to say? 'I'm detecting something both sweet and sharp, citrus maybe, is this 7-Up by any chance?' I'm not sure Herman found this amusing. 'After what Ute Lorenze said I wanted to see what all the fuss was about' was my excuse, but as service in the hotel seemed to improve after ordering it I regretted not asking for a bottle when we arrived. In fact, as Herman thought a fat fee from my patient was paying for it, I could have got away with a bottle on all three evenings. However, it was Rolf we should have raised our glasses to.

When, on our return from Wittenberge, I emptied the contents of my bag onto the kitchen table, falling out of it, along with the two toys I forgot to give Tina and Marc because Ute magicked my grandchildren away, was the lottery ticket bought in Weissensee. My fear two people in Brandenburg were about to share a fortune and spend it all on lawyers, proved unfounded. I missed the jackpot by several million euros. A disappointment, yes, but only because I would have rather the 5,270 euro which came my way by chance had been won in that poker game with Ute.

After our long weekend in Rugen, Herman and I spent four days in Berlin. Most of my time was taken up with research as Mo Fink wanted a draft of my presentation ahead of the conference in Vienna so an extract could be included in the program. I also had five appointments with patients; the first of these was on the Wednesday afternoon. With this over I was about to turn off my computer when a message from our receptionist appeared on the screen. *'Strange woman with accent phoned.'*

Presumably the receptionist meant *'woman with strange accent'* although it was possible she was more perceptive than I realised. Someone on the switchboard of Köhl and Strasse Investments put me through to Fräulein Lorenze; I decided against calling Ute's mobile, fearing this level of familiarity might end up with me using *du* instead of *Sie*.

'Lotte, you got my message, good! I understand you are coming to Köln on Friday. Please could you call in our office at two pm to meet someone from our London office? I am presuming you haven't bought tickets so I will purchase these for you now.'

*'Please?* Does that mean I have a choice?'

'Of course, there are trains arriving from Berlin at twelve fifty-eight, thirteen fifteen and thirteen thirty-nine. Text me which would suit you best and I will make the booking. I understand your husband is travelling with you, so tell me your seating preferences.' Then Ute hung up.

The assumption until then had been that my row with Paul would feature in the final chapter of Ute's next book. However it now appeared this story was no further along than I had got with *Frau Fish and the Bicycle* when I left my copy on a beach chair hoping a Maria Freitag fan would relieve me of it while Herman and I swam in the sea.

# 38

# Königswinter

July 2019

'I think we've had a famous guest,' Peter said when he called to thank his father for fixing the boat. 'A Maria Freitag novel Dorothea put on the shelf in reception has been signed. Maybe someone did it as a joke, because I can't remember seeing anyone who looked like a writer recently.' Perhaps if Ute arrived in my consulting room wearing an anorak, jeans and hair which looked like a home for nesting birds, I might have guessed here was someone who only communicated with the outside world via the printed page. So, it must have been easy for Max to keep Ute's pastime secret from Peter, and sensible in view of his portrayal as a buffoon in the Maria Freitag novels.

It was what that very private book signing told me about people's subconscious desire to betray even their most closely guarded secrets which came to mind as the lift took me up to K and S Investments' office.

'Lotte. Good! Follow me, please.' At this point a normal person might have asked a visitor if they had had a pleasant journey, but presumably Ute had checked the train was on time and probably hacked into various web cams along the route, so why bother with unnecessary pleasantries?

'I understand your grandmother lives in Köln,' I said as we walked together towards the glass-walled meeting rooms at the far end of the trading floor.

'And what makes you think that?' Not a denial but Ute's attempt to cast doubt on the story I felt most credible after decoding Paul's lies and Maxine's assumptions.

When Ute ushered me into the small meeting room, a young man sitting alone at the table got to his feet. 'This is Mr Phillips. He is an analyst from our London office and would like to discuss social media with you.' I suspected Mr Phillips may have wanted to tell me this himself had Ute given him the chance.

'Would it be possible to have another coffee?' Mr Phillips asked Ute as he shook my hand.

'Lotte, I take it you will have green tea,' Ute decided on my behalf while seeming happy letting Mr Phillips die of thirst. The Ryanair ticket next to the folder on the table indicated that, unlike Paul, the person sent from London was not important enough to make the journey by private jet. As Ute walked back to her office, she confirmed what I had suspected with the briefest of glances out of the window in the direction of her grandmother's apartment.

'This shouldn't take long,' Mr Phillips said, looking at his watch. 'I'm actually due back in London this evening.' So not even important enough for an overnight stay in Köln. 'It's regarding the paper you are presenting at the conference in Vienna. I'm not sure if you have been told, but one of the companies attending the conference is about to go public in both London and Frankfurt. K and S are considering underwriting the issue ...'

'If you are suggesting I modify my paper to suit K and S Investments, I'm afraid I won't do that.'

The young girl who had been proofreading the next Maria Freitag novel during my last visit came into the meeting room carrying a tray. 'Frau Lorenze thought after breakfast on the train you might want something else to eat.' Along with my tea were a croissant, a selection of cheeses and a Danish pastry. Mr Phillips got his cup of coffee but only a small packet of biscuits to make up for any shortcomings in Ryanair's catering.

'No, I read your paper on the flight and it's fine. Well, as far as I understand it. My job is to identify risk associated with any deal. K and S have had some unfortunate experiences with high technology companies in the past, especially during the dot-com era,' Mr Phillips said, adding quickly, 'Although that was before my time.' He drank half the cup of coffee in two gulps. 'In the case of social media, the risk of financial loss in the current climate is low. It is the possibility of reputational damage which concerns the bank. Normally, I would be discussing this with someone in a UK university, but Paul suggested I come over here and speak to you given you studied the subject in depth. Also, it is within the EU this company is likely to experience problems.' Perhaps Paul was not someone to bear a grudge after all, or maybe after the way I behaved, he assumed I would not do anything else to upset him given the impact this might have on Inge and Peter.

However, while Paul might be worrying about K and S Investments' reputation I was thinking of mine and the growing number of troubled young people seeking my help.

'From what Paul tells me you believe social media is responsible for some of the mental health problems young people are experiencing? The CEO of the company we are taking public claims their software is different, therapeutic and an aid to wellbeing. More likely to help people build a network of likeminded friends and lessening the chance of social isolation.'

'Really?' I asked, trying not to laugh. 'I hope they have evidence.'

'They have. A study carried out by psychologists at a well-known UK university.'

'You have a copy, I assume?'

'It is due for publication later this year,' Mr Phillips said. 'Just after the conference in Vienna.'

Why did the timing not surprise me? 'As a therapist I might attempt to alter a patient's emotional response to certain stimuli but do this for their benefit not mine. To repair a relationship or help someone cope with stress, not to create a dependency or sell a product.' I said and Phillips leaned back in his chair and ran his hand over his mouth, perhaps he had intended to say something but, not believing it himself, saw little point in trying to persuade me it was true.

'Good,' he said eventually, Ute's verbal tic seemed to be contagious, then added a paragraph to a mind map in his A4 notebook. Most of the other bubbles contained formulae and numbers followed either by the letter $m$ or a percent sign. 'I think that covers it.' But it did not, and after closing his notebook and finishing his coffee he bombarded me with questions, mostly about my research at Humboldt and other papers I had published. I in turn tried to discover the identity of the company K and S Investments was taking public but Phillips refused to say. He did let slip, however, that someone from this company would be a keynote speaker at the conference.

As we walked back to Ute's office, Phillips asked why I was visiting Köln. I joked that my husband and I were planning a holiday in Bavaria and were spending a weekend acclimatising ourselves to people who were borderline certifiable. Philips found this amusing but from the look on Ute's face, I suspected laughing out loud was prohibited inside the building.

'Would it be possible to order a taxi to take me to the airport?' Phillips asked Ute.

'It would but the S-Bahn will get you there in twenty minutes and leaves from the Deutz exhibition centre, which is just over there,' Ute said, pointing out of the window. 'Walking distance,' she added, then turned to me. 'I have prepared something for your stay in Köln, a list of places you might wish to visit, including the Cathedral, the Ludwick, Wallraf Richartz and some nice restaurants in the Altstadt.'

'Actually Ute, I think Maxine and Max have arranged something.'

'The chocolate museum and kart racing I should imagine, so you won't be needing this,' she said, and threw the folder into a wastepaper basket.

While we waited for the lift, Phillips was lamenting his early start that morning and how little time he got in the numerous places he had visited. In his three months with K and S Investments he had been to Silicon Valley twice and Paris four times but only seen the inside of offices, hotels and airports. It could have been this that made me think of that guide to Köln in the wastepaper basket and the look of disappointment Ute had tried, unsuccessfully, to disguise. And Tina asking why the woman who seemed so happy pretending to be her mother had been sat crying in her car.

If, heaven forbid, Ute had been a patient, my approach would have been to provide the tools to help her cope with the hurt caused by her husband, not stick a knife in an open wound. Although few Maria Freitag fans would thank me should this prove successful.

Ute looked up from the keyboard of her computer after I knocked gently on the half open door of her office. 'Yes, have you forgotten something?' she asked.

'Actually, I will take this,' I said, retrieving the itinerary. 'I think we can make time on Monday to see the city.'

'Enjoy your stay,' Ute said, and there was just the faintest hint of a smile. 'Oh, and when you see Tina and Marc again, say thank you from me for their letters.' Well, both the patient and I seemed to be making progress.

'You're the international traveller and technical genius, I'm the country girl lost in a strange city, so you decide where we meet.'

'In front of the cathedral, that tall building with the spiky bits on the top,' Herman laughed. Then there was someone else talking in the background and when they had finished Herman said, 'Actually, according to Max that won't work, limited vehicular access, apparently.' So I texted the name of the restaurant that only sold schnitzels and continued walking across the bridge.

Herman was sitting in the passenger seat of the 4x4 which was already parked outside the restaurant when I arrived. 'Max wants to show us something before we leave for Königswinter.'

'Wouldn't be something to do with kart racing, by any chance?' I said after climbing into the back of the car and sitting next to Maxine.

'How did you know?' Max asked.

'An inspired guess.'

'I think I know who provided the inspiration,' Maxine said, taking the folder containing Ute's tour guide and flicking through the pages. 'Looks comprehensive but she's losing her touch. The timings are rounded up to the nearest minute. Perhaps she forgot her stopwatch when she was planning your tour.' Oddly there was a temptation to come to Ute's defence.

'This building used to be owned by a company which made batteries.' Or at least that is what I thought Maxine shouted as we were sitting beside the refreshment kiosk in the centre of Le Mans Go-Kart Track watching our husbands racing around us between walls of blue and yellow painted tyres.

'Paul was working here for Daimon batteries and had spent a week trying to install a machine but getting too much unwanted help from people who weren't engineers.' Maxine was no longer shouting because Herman and Max were now at the far end of the building. 'Come Friday, the job was still not finished and Paul's boss asked him to come into work the next day. Paul asked Max to help so he would finish in time for whatever the two of them had planned for the afternoon. As they left the factory, they saw a car parked in the street with a man lying beside it. A heart attack, or possibly he had fainted. Anyway, the wife was hysterical. Max phoned for an ambulance and Paul tried some first aid. The ambulance arrived and took the guy away. Then on Monday as Paul was leaving work the wife was waiting with an envelope with a thank-you letter and five hundred deutschemarks in it. She asked for Paul's address and so began his long and lucrative relationship with the Strasse family.'

'Come on you two, give it a try,' Max shouted over the noise of the go-kart engines as he and Herman drew up in front of us. Maxine and I declined the offer and the go-karts roared into life again.

'It's not easy growing up, that's why men don't bother,' I said.

Maxine waited until the noise of the go-karts subsided and then continued with her story. 'After Paul returned to Britain, Herr and Frau Strasse stayed in touch and when he decided to set up a company, they helped with the finance. They had plenty of money, were the sort of people who were driven out of Prussia at the end of the war with all their possessions loaded on handcarts and a few years later were driving around Germany in Mercedes and living in castles. Paul's business did well and the Strasse family asked him to find other companies to invest in.'

'Why Paul?'

'They say these days you will find traces of cocaine on practically every banknote in circulation, but in those days it was blood. The Strasse family fortune wasn't any different. In Germany few people cared, but abroad it was different so an upstanding British businessman proved useful.'

'What happened to Köhl?' The question took Martine by surprise, perhaps because most of what she was telling me was a lie. The evidence was lying on the table in front of me.

'Köhl?'

'The other half of Köhl and Strasse.'

'Oh, Köhl, yes. God knows, probably died,' Martine said, saved from further embarrassment by the return of the two wannabe racing drivers.

'You girls ready to go?' Max asked, he and Herman as excited as two children who had discovered the four of diamonds stuck to the underside of a glass table.

'I'll take a souvenir.' I said picking up one of the flyers advertising the go-kart track.

As we made our way out of the building Max added substance to his wife's story. 'See those.' He said, pointing to a random pattern of holes drilled into the floor. 'Six people spent a week trying to install a power press. Paul and I finished the job in just three hours.'

Perhaps Maxine noticed I seemed lost in thought when studying the Le Mans Go-Kart Track flyer. Or that my eyes lingered a little too long on a street sign attached to the traffic lights at the junction with Hugo Eckner Strasse. It had crossed my mind to say, 'That's a coincidence.' But thought better of it because Maxine already seemed sullen and was avoiding eye contact.

We were saved an embarrassing silence during the drive to Königswinter by Max and Herman, whose visit to the former Daimon factory sparked a debate about the decline of battery manufacture in Germany and what it said about the future of car manufacture if the market for electric vehicles expanded. Meanwhile I studied Ute's Köln travel guide – missing was any mention of Pappa Joe's jazz club.

The hills to the west of the Rhein were visible from the patio at the rear of the Arndt's house but the river itself could only be viewed from the far edge of the terrace. The description in the Maria Freitag novel of tons of rock sliding down the hillside played on my mind as Herman admired the view.

'It's OK, Lotte.' Maxine had noticed my tight grip on the handrail. 'Our neighbour helped us out with the second attempt at building a terrace. After all, he had a vested interest in making sure it stays put.'

'I'm not surprised, his house must have cost a fortune,' Herman said, leaning over the railings to get a better look at the sprawling chalet further down the slope.

'It did, and we paid for it,' Max replied, and then led the way back to the Arndt's own house.

'We decided to rebuild rather than renovate after buying this place,' Max said. 'It's factory built, and Paul helped us put it together.'

'Helped?' Maxine laughed.

'OK, Paul did it,' Max admitted. This was revealing and recalled how Paul thought his life would have turned out had he been born in Germany rather than Britain. In front of me was the house he saw himself living in had his father disembarked from the train in Köln in 1948 and sought out his former girlfriend amongst the ruins of the city. Max was yet another avatar in one of Paul's alternative realities.

'This is like an art gallery,' I said to Martine as we stepped into a lounge resembling an open-air exhibition because the walls were the same brick used on the outside of the house and the floor tiled like the patio. Most of the paintings were modern and abstract, some original and others prints. There was a Richter and a collection of Rheinshagen's scriptural works.

Out of place was an unsigned watercolour of a tree-shaded square in a small town; French, I assumed, as one of the shops had *Boulangerie* above it.

'That is by the famous impressionist painter Maximilian Arndt during his exile in France,' Maxine said as I looked for a name on it, not realising straight away, as she had used Max's full name, that this was her husband's work

'Does he still paint?' I asked.

'Not even the bathroom ceiling I'm afraid,' she said. Almost as incongruous as Max's sole contribution to the world of art was the collection of photographs on the top of a white grand piano. Prominent were the couple's wedding photograph and their children's graduation portraits. Behind these were photographs of parents and grandparents with most of the men in uniform, and another of a group of young people sitting around a table in a café. Max was easy to spot, a younger Maxine less so. One couple had been more interested in each other than the camera; the boy was Paul, the girl with him not Sonia Engelhardt so most likely Margaret from England, the Frau Anweiler not to be.

The last time I had seen a black and white photograph of sixteen young soldiers, with radio ariels, a tent and mountains in the background, it was on a shelf in Heinrich Reisenberg's study during my visit to Celle. Perhaps the one on the Arndt's piano would also disappear overnight now I had spotted it.

Dinner was in a small restaurant in Unkel during which Herman and Max exchanged anecdotes mostly about the high technology industry and overcoming the inertia of managers in big corporations. 'Of course, in East Germany you could just force them to use your equipment.' Max said and Herman found this amusing.

'True, managers always achieved targets for the number of robots installed in factories each year.'

'Really?'

'Yes, we were surprised too. But then we discovered they were simply reclassifying everything, from vacuum cleaners to forklift trucks, as robots.'

'Lotte, your profession must have seen a lot of changes since re-unification,' Maxine said, realising we were being excluded from the conversation.

'How the party viewed the role of psychology in the DDR changed several times before the Wende, but by and large, social norms were determined by the state. So since it has been a case of adjusting to the idea these are now arrived at by consensus.'

'But not exclusively.'

'Sorry?' I asked, somewhat confused.

'In the marketing and media industry computer software and analytics shapes social norms and began doing so long before nineteen eighty-nine. So East Germans have exchanged one political system which restricts freedom of thought and expression for another.'

'And now politicians have joined you,' Max said.

'I'm not so sure, they have merely noticed people in the former DDR are rejecting our social norms and are exploiting this, offering up as an alternative those which shaped Germany before nineteen forty-five,' Maxine said to her husband, then turned to me. 'Isn't that so?'

Whether by accident or design Maxine had nudged the conversation towards the rise of right-wing politics in the former DDR which, as we were only halfway through our entrées, would have made for a long and, from my point of view, uncomfortable, evening.

Max must have realised this. 'Have you ever seen that open-top Triumph Herald, two tone red and white, driving around Berlin?' he asked Herman.

'Someone brought a car liked that to the club in Templin a while back,' Herman replied, surprised by this handbrake turn taking the conversation in a totally different direction. 'Fully restored and owned by a strange guy, very cagey about how he came by it.' I recalled this being discussed in the Weissen Ross one evening and Joachim having his own theory about the car; now I was about to hear Max's.

'So, he should be,' Max said. 'In nineteen seventy-seven Paul was travelling to Berlin with friends and just after they crossed the border into East Germany, the car broke down. They put it in a barn and told the farmer they would come back for it, but for some reason that wasn't possible, so there it stayed. Then a year before reunification...' (As the demise of East Germany obviously had little impact on the lives of Max and Maxine, both used the term *reunification* rather than *Wende*) '... Paul was returning from a visit to East Germany and the border guard searching him discovered he was carrying a large amount of cash, Deutschemarks, French Francs as well as Swiss and German chequebooks. Anyway, it turned out the guard was a car enthusiast, and he spent more time examining the photograph of the Triumph Herald in the barn than asking what Paul was doing with the money. So, Paul writes the address of the farm on the back of the photograph and gives it to the guard, who lets him go. Well, a week after the wall comes down, I take a tow truck to the farm and guess what?'

'The car had gone.' Herman was not alone in guessing the end of the story.

'The farmer said a few days earlier someone from the border police turns up and tells him the car is being impounded and he's lucky not to be thrown in prison for aiding a foreign agent.'

All the time her husband was telling the story Maxine was watching me, trying to assess how much of it I believed or had heard from another source. Or maybe trying to work out whether I knew that amongst Paul's friends in the car on that trip to East Berlin was a female terrorist called Sonia Engelhardt. *What date was this?* I wanted to ask, now suspecting that the person sitting in the park outside our apartment when we lived in Erfurt was not a Stasi agent checking on Herman prior to him being allowed to make business trips to the West, but Paul Anweiler spying on me. Given the amateurish surveillance, this seemed quite likely, but why, and what did he want from me? I already suspected Maxine knew.

Fortunately, having returned to their favourite subject, Herman and Max lost interest in politics and sociology and spent much of the rest of the evening talking about cars. Even the mention of Peter's boat was another excuse to discuss the future of self-drive cars. Then Herman let slip that he knew the person who drove the two-hundred-kilometre-per-hour Trabant, and it was as if Joachim had arrived at the table disguised as the waiter and shouted, *Surprise!*

'So, you know this guy?' Apparently Max had been one of the Wessies who made an offer for the most famous car in Brandenburg.

No other mention of Paul that evening, save Maxine mentioning he seemed to be in good humour recently, which at first I suspected might have been a veiled reference to me re-entering his life.

'I think having the bullet removed from his backside may have helped,' Max muttered under his breath. A turn of phrase peculiar to this part of Germany, I thought, but then remembered the walking stick Paul was carrying in Lychen and the reference to an operation.

The reason for the lack of sleep that night was blamed, when Herman asked, on too much coffee and a chocolate cake dessert. In truth it had been Sonia Engelhardt keeping me awake. 'Did you really believe that story about the old couple and Köhl and Strasse Investments?' I whispered to Herman at some time just after three in the morning. I cannot remember him answering, most likely he was asleep.

'I'm going for a bike ride with Max and Maxine,' I vaguely remember Herman saying after he got up. He returned at eleven, by which time I had finally managed to crawl out of bed and get dressed.

'The boys are playing with their toys in the office,' Maxine said. She was sitting on a sun lounger wearing a tee-shirt and jeans and reading *Der Spiegel*. 'Take a seat,' she said, getting to her feet and dropping the magazine on the ground. 'I'll fetch you some breakfast.'

She returned with a tray and placed it on the patio table, which was shaded by a parasol buffeted by the warm wind blowing along the Rhein valley. 'During my first job interview they asked if I wanted tea or coffee. I said tea because coffee kept me awake. They must have thought I was trying to be smart, or didn't really want to work for their company. I think it was a bit of each. Anyway, I didn't get the job. But at least I made an impression on the guy who interviewed me, and I was head-hunted when he set up on his own.'

'That was in marketing, not psychotherapy?' I asked.

'Yes, I'm afraid my psychology degree ended up being wasted,' Maxine sighed, then quickly changed the subject. 'So, you have known Paul for quite some time?'

'Yes, on and off.'

'And it was you he travelled to East Germany to see in nineteen seventy-seven. By the way, the car didn't break down, Paul abandoned it. At the time he didn't intend coming back. I can understand why you weren't interested, marrying someone who would always be suspected of being a spy wouldn't be a good career move.' This still came as a shock despite it having been in the back of my mind for the previous two weeks.

'I was already married to Herman by then.'

'But you stayed in touch with Paul.'

'Not really, he has just reappeared.'

'Yes, people have an annoying habit of doing that. Sonia Engelhardt came back from the dead a few weeks ago. Rose up from the depths of the North Sea or wherever her body ended up. I take it you know that Sonia Engelhardt's parents owned Köhl and Strasse?'

Maxine looked out across the terrace, shielding her eyes from the sun. 'I'm sorry about the story and Paul and the bank. When I saw you looking at the address on the Le Mans Kart Track flyer, I guessed you had found us out.'

'The street sign, Köhl Strasse, was a bit a giveaway as well.' Maxine remained silent, despite me giving her the opportunity to explain why the deceit. 'I met Sonia Engelhardt when she defected to East Germany,' I said, and now she seemed surprised, which was the point, ensuring Maxine did not simply substitute one lie for another.

'What did you think of her? I take it you didn't offer her a job.'

My explanation was more detailed than the one Herman had received but still fell short of the one given to Herbert Hüber. 'Sonia enjoyed a degree of notoriety in Britain where the protest movement, unlike in Germany, was non-violent and consequently, she was feted by activists who fantasised about taking direct action against the state. Unfortunately, in West Germany Sonia could not shake off the image of the spoilt rich girl. And I doubted whether she would be content in East Germany once her defection was no longer news.'

'Very perceptive,' Maxine said. 'The German Autumn has been mythologised to death. Considering this came just two decades after the second world war it was somewhat muted, to say the least. Baader and Meinhof, especially Meinhof, knew how to work the media and in Stefan Aust the movement had its inhouse member of the commentariat. There's no shortage of books and movies to keep the story alive or surviving members of the group to drag out and parade in front of the public. Which was why Sonia's recent resurrection a few weeks ago had us worried.' Clearly Paul had not told Maxine this was my doing.

'It was a strange time. Who the terrorists targeted now seems as random and arbitrary as those the police chose to punish,' Maxine said wearily. 'Even back in the days when there was a Wanted poster in every railway station there was the feeling some of the alleged fugitives were chosen because they needed an even number of photographs.'

The number of times over the past thirty years I had opened a newspaper and discovered another obscure Stasi officer or informer had been outed and realised that one day this might also happen to me. I should imagine that was exactly how Maxine and Max had felt when Sonia Engelhardt's face appeared on their TV screen.

'Max was worried if Herman knew about his past, he would persuade Peter to pull out of the project.'

I laughed. 'Sorry, the thought of Peter taking any notice of his father...'

'Everything Max told you happened, he and Paul put those holes in the floor of the go-kart track in nineteen seventy-six, some physical evidence to add credence to the story.' Then Maxine smiled. 'Unfortunately, none of us are a match for Ute Lorenze. And I forgot you are a psychologist and were once a member of the Stasi so can tell when someone is lying. I'm sorry... I didn't...'

'That's OK, I wasn't a member, I was asked to provide psychological profiles of visitors from the West,' I said to save Maxine's embarrassment. 'It was why I ended up interviewing Sonia, and how I met Paul.'

Maxine appeared relieved her observation had not received an angry response. 'So, not a femme fatal sent to seduce Paul.' The first time this had been implied, during that meeting in Stasi headquarters a long time ago now, the idea was instantly dismissed. I tried to do the same now but sounded less convincing than Steuernagel and Hüber had.

'Well, even if not, Paul certainly fell for someone and intended to give up everything and live with them in East Germany.'

My cheeks were burning and I hoped Maxine would think this was due to midday sun on my face. 'I doubt if he would have done that,' I said.

'Well, a few years back there was a corporate event in London, and I went along with Max, a chance to do some sightseeing and shopping funded by K and S. Paul gave a presentation at the dinner in the evening, and I was sat next to this English woman. It was only when Paul joined us I discovered this woman was his wife. Not once in the half an hour we had been talking did she make any reference to a person I recognised as Paul, no common friends, interests, places visited. Even after telling her I was married to Max and lived in Köln. It was apparent she had never heard of us or even knew what Paul did while in Germany. Never get attached to anything you cannot put on a handcart and wheel to the border, or anyone you aren't prepared to leave in fifteen minutes without a second thought. That's what he told Max once. It seems his life is made up of separate hermetically sealed compartments, so we can't rule out one of the compartments being in East Germany and containing people we know absolutely nothing about.' If that was true it was obvious why both Hubert Hüber and Britain's intelligence service took such a close interest in Paul.

'Presumably he learned that from his father.'

'Quite likely. There were issues with his father, he's always seemed to be searching for something. Perhaps he had found it in East Germany,' Maxine said, giving me another of her quizzical looks.

The story about his late grandmother sounded too farfetched to repeat. 'I'm fairly sure he hadn't found it in me.'

'*Fairly*, but not *completely* sure.' Maxine may have only been teasing me, but she was right and it was time to change the subject.

'So how did you become involved in terrorism?'

'That was Sonia's doing. Until she arrived in Köln it was not much more than a game, a performance, a group of weekend radicals. Max and Paul, the Toni and Tibo of urban terrorism. Put it this way, if you are planning to blow up a building with a home-made Panzerfaust, best not to be inside it when you pull the trigger. They almost got themselves killed and were lucky not to get caught. They at least had the intelligence to dress up as gas engineers when they did it. Even so, the police started to suspect Max might be the Red Army Faction's bomb maker, and from time to time, members of the group hid in our apartment. So, Friday evening we would unscrew the hinges on the door to limit the damage when the police kicked it in as they did every

Saturday morning. Although in those days almost every student was a suspect, the police were clueless and resorted to checking electricity bills assuming a sudden increase meant you were hiding someone. You could get raided simply by buying a bigger cooker. When I caught Max turning an electric razor into a bomb, I suggested it was time he moved back in with Mo Fink.' Maxine must have seen me go pale. 'Are you OK?' she asked, getting to her feet. 'I'll fetch some more tea.'

'Water will be fine,' I called after her as she walked towards the house. My throat suddenly felt dry. Had Max actually built the bomb which killed Otto Steuernagel in his hotel room in Vienna?

Maxine adjusted the parasol as I poured the water from the jug she had placed on the table into a glass. 'It's hot today, best to keep the sun of the back of your head,' she said, and I was grateful for this explanation as to why I suddenly looked faint.

'You were saying about Sonia,' I said.

'Yes, until she returned from Britain, we were just a group of friends. It was family connections which brought us together rather than any desire to overthrow the state. There was Paul, Bettina Harzer, she later married Freddie Ansbach, and Dieter Reisenberg. Their fathers all served with Max's during the war. Klaus Anweiler, Paul's father, used to come to Germany and meet up with his former comrades, which is how Paul and Max met.' Maxine smiled. 'In fact, Klaus still visited Max's mother long after my father-in-law died. I got to know them all through Mo Fink who was going out with Max. All of us except Paul were studying at Köln University, he arrived from Britain during our final year.'

'And Paul brought Sonia with him?'

'No, he arrived with an English girl. Marline, or Margaret, I think her name was. They were close, really close. At first, we thought they had been together for years but it turned out they met on the train from Britain. She didn't join in with the rest of the group and if it was a choice between going somewhere with us or her, Paul went with Margaret. Then one day she left and returned to Britain. According to Paul she was in a relationship with someone else. After that everything changed.' Not for the first time, Maxine gazed into the distance, lost in thought, but this time it seemed recalling the past caused her pain. She pulled her feet onto the chair and was hugging her legs, having adopted a foetal position. Struck by the change in Maxine's body language, I took note of mine, and instead of sitting bolt upright fearing the next revelation, I was reclining in the wicker chair and Maxine must have realised she was now talking to someone who was far more relaxed.

'You know Paul's father had a friend in Köln?' A rhetorical question because Maxine did not wait for an answer. 'Well, he spent a weekend with her after Margaret left. That was when everything changed. Paul seemed angry, what about was difficult to tell, everything, it seemed, but his father especially.' It seemed unlikely Paul never told Max what he discovered that weekend: that his father had served with the Waffen SS. Even more improbable, given Max would have then realised the same was true of his own father, as well as those of his circle of friends, that this information was not shared with Maxine at some point. 'This anger seemed to infect everyone, Max, Dieter and Bettina mostly. Nihilism replaced hedonism in a matter of weeks,' Maxine said, and maybe it was the memory of the fear she felt at the time which had her curled up in a ball. 'Things might have calmed down again but then along came Sonia. She had stumbled across a group of young people easier to impress than the demigods in the Red Army Faction. Perhaps more to the point, some of us were just as eager to impress Sonia.

'Suddenly Dieter came up with a plan to kill his father. He knew Max had a gun. We would all drive to Frankfurt and knock on Herr Reisenberg's front door and when he opened it, bang.' Maxine extended two fingers and mimicked the pulling of a trigger. 'It was Paul who was the voice of reason, although it was him who inadvertently got Lauterbrunnen killed.' Not *murdered*, I noticed. 'There was a small theatre in Hohenlind, a kilometre or so from the university, where a group of actors sometimes performed Avant Garde plays. Pretentious crap, according to Max. Afterwards we would have a picnic in the Lindenthaler Tierpark. Well, one evening Dieter was still in a rage about his father when Paul pointed to a house at the edge of the park and said if Dieter was looking for a real Nazi that's where he would find one. The house belonged to Lauterbrunnen. There were rumours he had been involved in massacres in Greece, wiped out whole villages. He had been due to give evidence at Nurenberg after the war but the Americans and Soviets were no longer on speaking terms when the case came to court. Now Lauterbrunnen was campaigning to get elected as an MP even though his political views hadn't changed much since the Nazi era.' Maxine still seemed disgusted by the thought of a former Nazi entering the German parliament.

'No-one took much notice of what Paul said, or so we thought. He, Max and myself went to Nurenburg and then on to the Munich beer festival with Max's parents. While we were there, we heard that Lauterbrunnen had been kidnapped. Hardly surprising, I thought, since he had been spouting his vile views the week before. Only when we got back to Köln did we discover that Sonia, Dieter and Bettina had Lauterbrunnen imprisoned in an apartment on the outskirts of Köln.' Maxine was now sitting upright, both feet back on the ground. She pushed her glass and plate with a half-eaten piece of cake to one side. The involuntary reconstruction of a mental process; with her side of the table cleared, so too was Maxine's mind. Clear enough to continue with a story which, I suspect, she had kept to herself for at least as long as mine had remained secret.

'As far as I was concerned, we had an alibi. This was Sonia's problem so let her take the rap. But Bettina was involved and Freddie begged Paul and Max to help even though they had nothing to do with the kidnapping. They agreed and were gone for a week. The next I heard from Max he was somewhere in France, painting that picture hung on our living room wall. Paul was in Britain getting UK passports for Sonia, Bettina, Dieter and Jens Steinbrink...'

'Steinbrink? I remember he defected to the East, but I never realised why. He used to present a news program on East German TV,' I said.

'And now he appears on West German TV,' said Maxine. 'Part of Freddie Ansbach's media empire, and almost as rubbish as Ute's books. The last one I watched had a blindfolded member of the studio audience guessing the colour of a rabbit by touch.' Maxine seemed grateful for a moment's levity however brief.

'Paul called from Britain saying I should stay put in Köln and tell the police where Max was and what he was doing. I was to get a message to the others to meet him in a hotel in northern Germany, somewhere near Hannover.

'Max came back from France three weeks later. Told me Paul was in East Germany and had given him keys for three left-luggage lockers in Köln Hauptbahnhof. Each locker contained a Samsonite suitcase stuffed with money. One was care of the Engelhardt family, a guilt-ridden father wanting to make sure his estranged daughter continued to enjoy the luxury she was accustomed to during her exile in East Germany. Quite how this was going to be possible wasn't apparent at the time. The second suitcase contained the ransom for Lauterbrunnen's release, fortunately non-refundable because his body was discovered in a forest near the French-German border a week later. By then Paul was back, the lady of his dreams having turned him down.' Maxine waited for my response, and a blank stare was probably not what she expected.

'The third suitcase, what was that for?' I asked.

Maxine shook her head. 'Who knows? We are into conspiracy theory land with that one. It could have been the second half of the ransom. But also, possibly, rather than trying to rescue Lauterbrunnen, someone felt it was better he was dead. Had he lived, and become an MP, it would only been a matter of time before his Nazi past became public knowledge. The Greek government was already pressing for compensation for what Germany did to their country and would have probably insisted Lauterbrunnen was put on trial. Then there was East Germany portraying the parliament in Bonn as a den of fascists which, considering they had replaced the Gestapo with the Stasi, was as hypocritical as it was ironic.' Having temporarily forgotten who was sitting opposite her, Maxine leaned back in her chair and waved her hand across her face in attempt to brush this slip of the tongue away.

'Either way, we had a pile of money, somewhere near two million Deutschemarks, stashed in my apartment.' Maxine smiled and shook her head. 'When Paul saw it he asked me how long will it take to wash the blood off it. He found a way to get some of Engelhardt's money transferred to East Berlin. The problem was what to do with the rest of it. Then Max came up with the idea of setting up a company somewhere abroad. Paul suggested one with branches in London and Köln. So was born Köhl and Strasse, not a bank at first, merely a holding company which could transfer money to Britain.'

'I think that's called money laundering, isn't it?' This time Maxine laughed out loud. 'Our journey from socialism to capitalism was as short as it was rapid, I'm afraid. I'm pretty sure we wouldn't have got away with it today.' Maxine poured herself a cup of lukewarm coffee then offered the jug to me.

'No thanks.' I said shaking my head.

'Then, about a year later, Sonia Engelhardt's parents asked for a meeting.' Maxine paused for a moment, taking a sip of coffee. 'They wanted to know how much was left of the money they had given Paul to pass onto their daughter. So, we arrived at their palatial chateau with the record of currency transfers. They saw there was more money left than they had given us and wanted to know where the rest came from. Paul told them it was profits from the company we had set up. Now the Engelhardt family had a problem not dissimilar from ours. They also had a heap of money, an embarrassment of riches, so to speak, much of it accumulated during the second world war, earned with the help of slave labour. As on paper our company was generating a huge return, would we be interested in investing some of the Engelhardt's fortune? Max refused to have anything to do with it. I also thought it immoral but Paul was in an awkward position being the one who smuggled Sonia into East Germany. He agreed to using Köhl and Strasse Investments to manage Engelhardt's money and applied for a banking licence.'

'You've certainly done very well,' I said, turning to look at the house, but then, in view of the comment about Engelhardt's money, realised this might be taken the wrong way.

'Really?' Maxine said, examining her hands. 'I left university, like you, expecting to go into research or practise as a therapist. Max wanted to work for Siemens and maybe by now he would have a seat on their board. Instead, I'm working in marketing and Max is playing with boats because no one was interested in employing someone suspected of hiding a terrorist who might well have had a hand in gunning down one of their directors. That, thanks to Sonia and Paul, was our punishment.'

Up to that point I had never regarded myself as fortunate. Since the Wende, Herman and I had measured our careers against what might have been. But here was someone who, despite outward signs of wealth, regarded themselves as less fortunate than us. I felt stunned and slightly embarrassed.

After a moment of reflection, Maxine said, 'If the protest movement had not resorted to violence we might have changed things, made West Germany a better place. Perhaps even one that would have met East Germany halfway after reunification instead of crushing it to death.' Maxine was now doing what I advised my patients against, ruminating.

'I'm puzzled as to how Paul could enter East Germany at will and move around freely while he was there,' I said.

'You probably know as much about that as I do. He obviously had a contact with some influence, maybe a member of his family.'

'Most of them were at the garden party where I met Paul, and apparently some could leave the country and return at will, but my impression was this was a privilege granted to them rather than one in their gift.'

'He had an ID card,' Maxine said. 'Forged, most likely. And he told me he passed himself off as an agricultural inspector and if challenged would claim to be carrying out spot checks on farms. The name on the card belonged to a genuine official, apparently, someone who was having an affair and used visits to farms as cover for days away with his mistress. Obviously, this inspector didn't tell anyone in his office which farm he was visiting. How Paul found this out is anyone's guess. As for getting in and out of the country there was a rumour about a route through Friedrichstrasse rail station you could use if you had a special pass. And Max said Paul had once crossed the Elbe at Rüterberg, that village in East Germany you could only enter if you lived there. Apparently, kids had tunnelled under the wire because there was a ten pm curfew. It was unlikely anyone would break into the village to cross the Elbe so guards didn't pay a lot of attention on that stretch of the border. According to what Paul told Max, the best time to cross was after a storm. Get someone on the west side to throw in lots of tree branches up stream and the patrol boats eventually got tired of checking. It seemed farfetched but oddly enough it was where they say Sonia Engelhardt was shot trying to escape.

'Do you think Paul was helping her escape?'

'Helga Engelhardt does, she blames Paul for her sister's death. After her parents died she insisted Paul brought back what remained of the money he had transferred to East Germany. I think she hoped Paul would be caught and thrown into jail. I'm not sure bribing the guard with the car is what got him out, I think that was down to his guardian angel.'

'Was the incident with the boat two weeks ago something to do with Sonia's death?' I asked, but assumed, wrongly, Maxine would stick to her story about being too busy dancing to notice anything happening on the river.

'Paul has always felt guilty about Sonia's death. He was responsible for her being in East Germany. He wouldn't accept she was killed due to her own stupidity and a lucky shot by a trigger-happy border guard. I think he may have seen the cruise as an opportunity to reconstruct the escape, show it had been possible and assuage some of that guilt. What I do know is that woman in the boat, whoever she was, was definitely not Sonia Engelhardt.' Maxine had already constructed one very elaborate lie that weekend. I suspected she had now told me another.

'So, what are you ladies plotting?' Unnoticed, Max, with Herman following him, had crept up on us and placed his arms around Maxine. 'Choosing somewhere to have lunch, I hope.' I missed out on a similar display of affection and instead my husband flopped into the chair beside me. Our weekend in Köln was supposed to have been a break from work; despite this Herman seemed to have acquired another doorstep-sized document, which he placed on the table.

'A restaurant close by,' Maxine replied.

It was. We ate both lunch and then, after a walk beside the Rhein, dinner on the patio. And as the day came to an end, with insects gathering around the awning lights which swung in the breeze, and wine, beer, and finally schnapps, flowing as easily as the conversation around the table, something strange happened. Suddenly it occurred to me: *Here I am in the West,* not just physically but emotionally as well, and Joachim came to mind. He reached down and lifted me out of the tunnel. *My God, Lotte, thirty years*, I imagined him saying as I brushed the sand off my knees and out of my hair and handed him my suitcase. *What took you so long?*

# 39

# The Dance of Death

'It's not as if you haven't been to Vienna before,' Herman said, having insisted on carrying my suitcase onto the platform at Berlin Hauptbahnhof. This observation neither inspired confidence nor put me at ease.

Of course he could have said, 'This time it will be different.' And he would have been right. My previous visit to Vienna had been organised by the Stasi who sent along a minder, not a very competent one but even so someone to watch my back. This time I was there at the behest, or connivance, of Paul Anweiler, who I suspected had a hand in killing that minder. Paul may also have decided to dispose of a West German politician for any number of reasons, that number equating to how many suitcases it took to hold the money he used to found the company sponsoring the conference I would be speaking at the next day. Unfortunately, much of this only occurred to me as the train was speeding out of Berlin.

A room had been reserved for me in the hotel hosting the conference, so it seemed the view from the bedroom window would be, as it had been in 1976, all I would see of Vienna. The evening was spent making final edits to my presentation: deleting a paragraph dealing with a topic not covered in my research paper after deciding it was too controversial and, as it was near the end, might be interpreted as an unsubstantiated concluding remark. Then after drinking a bottle of cognac from the minibar I phoned Herman. 'Knock them dead,' he suggested, realising my confidence needed a boost. A slightly inappropriate remark on this occasion. Unfortunately, there was not a second bottle of cognac in the minibar.

There were three friendly faces in the hotel restaurant the following morning – and a particularly hostile one. Mo Fink was talking to a group of delegates while Mr Phillips, from K and S Investments, was sitting alone at a table next to the window, more interested in the street outside than anything happening in the room. Günter Hölderlin joined me in the queue for breakfast. 'Lotte, good to see you again. I'm sorry about the Cathcart article,' he said. 'We have got our systems up and running again but will hold back on publishing until after the British election. If he becomes Prime Minister it will be news but putting it out before looks like we're campaigning. It puts us down in the gutter with the tabloids, not somewhere I think we should go. Have you been paid yet?'

'No,' I said, and in the circumstances, did not expect to be.

'Don't worry, I will tell our accounts department to make the payment.' This did not seem like something a freelance journalist could do.

'Are you still working for the publication?'

'Yes, full time now.' He handed me his business card; Günter was now the Editor in Chief. 'Email me your bank details ...' He said before being interrupted by Edouard Monget, that hostile face appearing even more unfriendly up close.

Monget was the CEO of a social media startup called Companion which, after a little detective work, I discovered was the company K and S Investments was taking public. It was the only French company with a speaker at the conference, and I remembered four of the overseas trips Phillips said he made since joining K and S were to Paris. Monget was the first speaker in the social media stream, I was the second; this I only discovered after receiving a copy of the conference program.

'Here is the information on our IPO you requested.' Monget was thin but obviously fit and most likely had been in the hotel gym since sunrise but still had enough energy left to bombard Günter with a stream of financial information, the second time he had done this, apparently. He pushed his way in between Günter and me, then turned so I was left staring at his back.

'By the way this is Lotte, she will be presenting a paper this morning,' Günter said, clearly annoyed, but Monget merely glanced at me over his shoulder.

'Ah, the enemy,' he said with the stone-hard stare of a gunslinger.

'Would it be possible to have a printout of your paper,' Günter asked when we reached the end of the buffet; thankfully by then Monget had joined Phillips, who appeared even less comfortable than Günter or myself in the presence of the Frenchman.

'It's an early draft, I'm afraid.'

Günter thumbed through it, frowning when he reached the final page and the paragraph with a line through it.

'Personally, I would have left that last bit in. It's a good point.' I had thought this too but decided to show a little restraint and if Günter was intending to use it in his conference review, he might discover there were limits to his editorial freedom. 'Actually, don't you think it odd that a social media company gets to give a keynote address at a conference like this?' He looked again at the first page of the presentation and something else caught his eye. He lowered his voice and whispered, 'I do wonder whether someone's vanity has got the better of them.' For a moment I thought he was referring to me. 'It would make more sense for an IT company to speak at the end and address some of the things you are saying here,' he said, folding the draft of my presentation and placing it between the pages of his notebook. 'Let's talk later, after your presentation.'

Monget gave a barnstorming performance which, in my opinion, seemed out of place at an academic conference. Unfortunately, my paper would now appear dry by comparison and give the impression I lacked both enthusiasm for the subject and confidence in what I was saying. I was about to become the Ossie hit-and-run victim of a speeding Wessie. I took a deep breath and recalled Herman reminding how well my presentation to a packed auditorium at the Palace of the Republic was received in 1986.

It is unnerving being ignored while presenting a paper; members of the audience talking to each other or playing solitaire on their mobile phones. On the other hand it can be just as disconcerting when delegates either stare at you intently, as if hanging on every word, or furiously take notes. Given that the audience's adrenaline rush during Monget's presentation had dissipated by the time I started speaking the applause at the end of my presentation was a pleasant surprise. Surprised too was Monget, who leapt to his feet and was ranting even before he was given a microphone, and even when he got it did a passable impression of the mime artist Marcel Marceau until a technician showed him how to switch it on. Once audible, Monget made it clear to everyone in the room he thought my presentation was typical of how social media was portrayed by mainstream broadcasters and newspapers. This remark was presumably intended to intimidate members of the press, but I could already see it had alienated Günter.

Monget then set about reinterpreting the case histories in my presentation. It would be his technology which would overcome social isolation, would enlighten the user, extend their horizons rather than corral them into silos. Finally, in a flourish, he even doubted whether my patients even accessed social media.

'Well,' I said, and then took a deep breath, and the fact this alone caused a ripple of laughter amongst the delegates suggested Monget had misjudged his audience. It also gave me the confidence to expand on my presentation with a step-by-step account of my teenage patient's gradual withdrawal into a dark, lonely and frightening corner of their virtual world. Then I listed the type, and probable cause, of the psychological damage incurred as she doomscrolled each day further away from anything resembling a meaningful relationship. Despite more furious scribbling by delegates and members of the press, Günter in particular, Monget prepared for another attack. Never did I imagine I would draw inspiration from a woman whose only achievement in life was a series of rubbish books, but suddenly it seemed Ute Lorenze was standing behind me whispering in my ear. *Remember that ace up your sleeve, Lotte, play it now and let's see what Monget's got in his underpants.*

Abandoning even the pretence of rational argument, Monget was now ranting again. 'The problems experienced by a very small number of your patients are transitory and society will adjust to social media in the same way it did to other leaps forward in the way information is communicated, such as print, radio and television. Social structures are self-organising and adaptive. You would do well to read ...' I had heard this somewhere before, in a restaurant in Köln after being made to feel a fool by someone who tricked me into throwing a lock instead of a key into the Rhein. With time to think I would have realised this was not a similar game but an extension of the same one. However here was an opportunity not to be missed, rather like standing in front of a goal with a ball at my feet and realising the keeper had his bootlaces tied together. (Actually, that metaphor is care of someone watching television in the Weissen Ross one evening, an edited version, without the expletives.)

'If the self-organising system you are suggesting is the one described by Manuel DeLanda, who used as an example the erosion and reformation of sedimentary rock, then how many young people will be crushed under the weight of an ocean of information before society has advanced to the point where your software is no longer considered a threat to their mental health?' And in case this was not sufficient to cause a shrinking feeling in Monget's trousers, and because I had spotted Paul Anweiler in the audience with Phillips sitting next to him, I took another swipe at Monget. 'I believe the received wisdom amongst advocates of social media is that here is an alternative to some sort of conspiratorial deep state. Unfortunately, that alternative seems to be a shallow state, a thin slice extracted from the richness of interpersonal communication, a labyrinthine virtual world from which neither your users, or yourself for that matter, seem able to escape.'

Paul said something to Phillips, who glanced at his watch and then stood up, grabbed his briefcase and coat then left the auditorium, Vienna becoming another of the cities he would only remember for a hotel and the airport. Paul followed him without making eye contact with me. All this while the audience applauded. I was hoping Monget had given up, but he had not, and afterwards Günter suggested he would have continued until the battery in the microphone was flat. Fortunately, I did not have to wait that long because Mo Fink, who was chairing the session, decided then would be a good time to have a break.

Most of the exhibitors in the hotel lobby were disseminating the results of research projects, funded by the EU as part of either its health or technology programs. An outlier resembled a video installation, so predictably was attracting a great deal of attention, and not just during the breaks between sessions. The floor of the stand was marked out in one metre squares. A large screen displayed various segments of moving images dependent on which square the viewer was standing in. Waiting my turn to try it out gave sufficient time to work out that the images became increasingly violent as a person moved towards the centre of the stand.

Walking around the edge of the stand caused videos of children playing in a meadow and then a young couple walking beside a lake to appear on the screen. A circuit closer to the centre of the stand invoked images of people arguing and the final round of a boxing match. Another circuit and police were breaking up a demonstration with clubs, dogs and a water cannon. Standing on a square in the centre of the stand caused first the iconic image of an execution during the Vietnam war to appear on the screen followed by that of police searching a forest and finally the bloodied face of Albert Lauterbrunnen.

'What are you trying to achieve?' The young man handing out information sheets was asked by a delegate. The woman standing beside him answered on her colleague's behalf.

'It is a comment on social media. We are presenting the results later this afternoon,' she said, pointing to the time and room number printed at the bottom of the information sheet.

'Have you read a book called *Fahrenbrink*?' I asked. Which, despite being met with a blank look from the young man, I thought was a sensible question, for two reasons. Firstly, because the three cameras set up above the stand to triangulate the position of the person performing the so-called *Dance of Death* were reminiscent of those in the hotel mentioned in Paul Anweiler's book. Secondly, in the absence of a ring of yellow stars on a blue background, this experiment, and I assumed this was an experiment because the woman mentioned results, was funded by someone other than the EU. Thirdly, the image of Albert Lauterbrunnen's body narrowed the list of potential sponsors to one person.

Mo Fink followed me on to the stand, moving from one square to another, slowly at first then faster as different images appeared before she gave up and after a *so what* shrug, moved on to the next stand. 'Will you be attending our session?' the woman with the information sheets asked me.

'I'm not sure, it clashes with a talk on OCD,' I replied.

A table behind a column in the dining room seemed an ideal place to hide during the break for lunch. Neither my sister nor I had considered, when choosing how I should dress for my trip to Vienna, the possibility the woman in the Forum that day might also attend the conference. This woman was called Hildegard, Hilde to friends, of which for obvious reasons I was not one. She was fielding inquiries from delegates who mistakenly thought it was she who savaged Edouard Monget. After discovering where I was hiding she pointed people in my direction, her smile less convincing each time she did so. Eventually, to my relief, she realised that what at first seemed an embarrassing inconvenience provided an opportunity to promote her own presentation and the stream of delegates to my table dried up.

'Well, that was quite something,' Günter said, sinking into the chair on the other side of the table. 'So, this is where you are.' He peered around the column, and I suspected he too was hiding, not from a doppelganger but Monget. Having looked up Companion on the internet I had arrived at the conference with a basic grasp of how the company's technology worked. I had also checked a few key facts with Herman given Mo Fink felt the suggestion I was technically illiterate might be the big tech faction's line of attack. He was intrigued how a social media start-up priding itself on the use of its own IT infrastructure handled its users' data and intended mentioning this during the next parliamentary committee meeting on GDPR. It was also something I was planning to discuss with Günter, had not Monget discovered where we were sitting.

Günter was laughing when Monget got to our table as I had suggested he checked his clothes for a tracking device. Maybe this was the reason I was addressed first, even before Monget sat down and pushed my coffee to one side to make room for his glass of water, responsibly-sourced vegan salad and sourdough roll. 'It is always possible to find isolated or rare instances where social media has been used inappropriately but you have to realise there are millions of users for whom our software is empowering,' he said.

'But as yet no users in Europe,' Günter responded on my behalf. 'I mention that because our readers are mostly based in Germany.'

'Yes, in Europe,' Monget was becoming agitated, perhaps suspecting Günter's negativity meant he shared my scepticism.

'Really, I'm sorry but...' Günter searched back through his notebook. I noticed he was not using his laptop, which remained in the bag on the floor by his feet. Perhaps he belatedly realised how the ransomware found its way onto the magazine's network. Unfortunately, without the computer he appeared clumsy and unprofessional. Eventually he found what he was looking for. 'Ah, here it is.' He put on those heavy-framed glasses and read from a page headed *Press Release*. 'Apparently the money raised during the IPO will fund the building of a data centre to serve European subscribers. So, you don't yet have a data centre in Europe.'

'No, obviously.' Monget was sneering at Günter in the same way he had at me during my presentation. I now regretted that trick played in the Café at Boxhagener, taking advantage of Günter's naivety. As I watched him writing, slowly and deliberately, that visit to Magdeburg came to mind. It was only after Paul revealed the Cathcart affair had been a hoax that I suspected both Günter and I had been duped. Of course Kohnen Audio certified the tape as genuine; they produced it. 'And when you have a data centre in Europe, you will use it to do all that clever stuff you mentioned during your presentation.'

'Of course.' Monget said, then added as if he was talking to someone who was stupid. 'That's where we will do *all that clever stuff.*' There was something about Monget that reminded me of Beaky Boy, although somehow I doubted he would end up cleaning toilets in a Berlin hotel.

'That's an interesting experiment,' said Günter as we entered the lobby, and until then I had not noticed a fourth camera on the stand, this one filming people queuing up to take part in the *Dance of Death*. We watched as Monget performed a manic dance, perhaps hoping to crash the software. 'Oh well, more interviews. Don't forget that email,' Günter said and then walked around the edge of the dance floor, careful to stay out of the line of sight of the cameras, on his way to speak to the couple manning the stand.

Sitting on a low wall in the small garden at the side of the hotel, I studied the guide to Vienna with a map attached, supplied as part of the conference information pack. This fell a long way short of Ute's minute-by-minute tour guide of Köln. Although even that, in Herman's opinion, had a glaring omission and he'd insisted on setting aside time to visit the chocolate museum, his excuse being when we got home to Gehrden, everyone would expected us to have done so – and because he liked chocolate. Unfortunately, Vienna had hundreds of similar must-see attractions.

'The Café Frauenhuber is in Himmelpfortgasse.' I looked up and Paul was standing in front of me holding a cup of coffee in one hand and a shortbread biscuit in the other.' He studied me intently then said, 'It is Lotte, isn't it? Only I keep confusing you with your twin sister.' I pushed the guide to the city into my pocket, annoyed at the reference to how I was dressed and because he had guessed why I was looking at the map. Paul placed the cup and saucer on the wall, sat beside me, and after he had eaten the biscuit said, 'I think it's time we talked.'

'We have talked.'

'And shouted, I recall.' He picked up the coffee cup and took a sip. 'I'll meet you in the hotel lobby at seven thirty.' Perhaps he was angry about my implied criticism of Companion's business model, the attack on Monget and the impact this might have on K and S Investments' reputation. However, there was something else and I was reminded of what Maxine said about Paul moving from one compartment of his life to another and becoming a different person as he did so, because the man sitting beside me, brushing crumbs from his trousers, screwing the wrapper into a ball and dropping it into the empty cup, was not the same one I'd shouted at on Peter's boat.

The room where the talk on OCD was about to take place was almost empty, so out of curiosity I looked in on the *Dance of Death* presentation. Mo Fink saw me lingering by the door and pointed to the seat beside her, one of the few in the room still empty. The woman who had been on the stand first described the technology used to create the *Dance of Death* and then explained the purpose of the experiment.

'Violence, there is a difference in how it we perceive it depending on whether it is an individual or a shared experience.' Her colleague pressed a button on the remote control he was holding and the screen above the stage came to life. A window in the top corner displayed the same images which appeared when I moved around the stand in the lobby. The rest of the screen was filled with a computer graphic of the stand itself. The animation began with matchstick figures dancing around the stand, each represented one of the delegates who had earlier performed the dance of death. At first the delegates were distributed across the stand and the video images in the window appeared at random. However gradually, a black mass of matchstick figures formed at the centre of the stand and the images displayed alternated between the Vietcong's execution and Albert Lauterbrunnen lying dead in a forest. 'This is a composite of all of you who performed that dance of death this morning.'

There was silence as everyone stared at the screen. 'That is so damn spooky,' I whispered.

'It is,' said Mo, 'when you realise each of us is one of those figures.'

But there was more because then came the explanation for that fourth camera. 'The speed with which you converged on the centre of the stand was determined by how long you waited your turn in the queue,' the woman said and the young man on the other side of the stage brought up graphic representations of the stand during the break, when it was busy, and in between when only one person was waiting their turn. 'Watching those on the stand you learned how to invoke the most violent images, and this saw each of you move to the centre of the stand more rapidly than the person who went before you. This begs the question whether our fascination with violence is an individual or a collective experience, and should be of concern to anyone designing a social media service.'

I looked around the room but could see neither Monget, Phillips or Paul Anweiler.


'Himmelpfortgasse,' Paul told the driver as we climbed into the taxi, then turned to me and said, 'In case you thought we were headed for the Czech border.'

'Cute,' I said. 'Of course, I forgot, you've read my diaries.'

'No, I've got computer software that did that for me.' Then Paul turned away and looked out of the window of the taxi, sightseeing like a tourist as if seeing Vienna for the first time, one hand holding onto the laptop bag on the seat between us.

'Did you see the *Dance of Death* presentation?' I asked.

'No, I was in the OCD session, or CDO, the same thing only with the letters in alphabetical order as they should be,' he replied. 'Coincidentally CDO also stands for Collateralised Debt Obligation, which probably explains some of the deals our traders have been making recently.' It was clear Paul was not going to make any sense with the taxi driver listening.

'So here we are, only forty-three years too late. I hope they held our table,' Apparently, Paul had made a reservation and pretended not to notice I was finding his presumptuousness annoying.

'Would your fancy software tell me if Max killed Otto Steuernagel?' I asked. While Paul had told me, a long time ago, he did not keep a diary, he had written those two books. There had been an account of a death in a hotel room in Vienna in the first one, and a reference to a politician kidnapped and killed by terrorists in both.

'Steuernagel?' Paul asked. 'Oh yes, the guy who contracted that fatal shaving rash. No, I'm not sure it would.' Despite making light of the Stasi agent's death, he seemed on edge.

'There is schnitzel on the menu if that's what's bothering you.' I said, but Paul ignored the remark.

'So, what did you think of the *Dance of Death*?'

'Well, I suspect it was someone trying to convince us violence is a collective experience, initiated by the crowd, rather than the individual. Perhaps they once did something they now regret and are confusing an explanation with absolution. And an odd thing for a person financing a social media company to do.'

'What is it they say? Keep your friends close but your enemies closer. Difficult to do if you don't know where your enemies are hiding. And there seem to be a lot of them hidden in the psychology departments of European universities.'

'I spoke to Maxine when Herman and I visited Köln.' I said, although guessed Paul already knew this. 'Max put the explosive in the razor which killed Steuernagel, didn't he?'

515

'He did, but Max isn't, and never was, a killer. It's not in his nature. You're a psychologist, you understand disassociation. Max was always too intrigued by the logistics, fascinated by the technology, and never gave a thought to how it would be used. Had he done so, Steuernagel would still be alive.' I sincerely doubted this; Steuernagel was not one of life's survivors and there was another twelve years of testing potentially lethal surveillance equipment before the Stasi was disbanded.

'So, was it you who planted the razor in Steuernagel's room?'

'No, Sonia did that,' Paul replied. Which explained why she looked familiar when I interviewed her. She was the hotel maid who eyed me suspiciously when she came to clean my room in the hotel the day before Steuernagel's death. 'Someone was going to die in Vienna, or at least return home and face a very long time in jail. Although weren't the Stasi still executing traitors in the nineteen seventies?'

'Me? Are you suggesting I intended betraying my country?'

'A young woman taking advantage of her first trip outside of East Germany to meet up with someone already suspected of being a British spy. The young man she met at a party, fell in love with and even suggested this place as somewhere they could meet during a forthcoming visit to Vienna.'

I burst out laughing. 'Me, in love with you? You must be joking.' The couple on the next table glanced in our direction. 'I'm sorry, but I really wasn't,' I said softly.

'That was how it was made to appear by your friends in the Stasi. The how and why only became apparent when I got hold of your diaries. Had I not been bitten on the hand by an insect before the party you might well have ended up in Hohenschönhausen or been hanged and your ashes spread in a forest somewhere. Missing, gone without trace, if your mother and boyfriend had even dared ask. It was a man called Shetlov who explained what the Stasi had planned for you.'

Paul chose a goulash soup as a starter followed by the inevitable chicken schnitzel and perhaps to humour him I asked for the same.

As the waiter took our order Paul asked him for the Café's Wi-Fi password then took out his laptop and placed it on the table. 'What do you know about Shetlov?'

'That your father's regiment killed his brother.'

Paul raised one eyebrow and then typed. 'A pity there wasn't Wikipedia in nineteen seventy-five.' He said then turned the laptop around so I could see the screen. 'That's the entry for Nikolai Shetlov. Born nineteen twenty in Petrograd, died in Moscow in two thousand and seven.' Paul paused as if giving this some thought. 'I wonder if Frau Eppelmann and his illegitimate son turned up at the funeral. I'll have to ask Ute if she thinks there's a market for Maria Freitag novels set in Russia. Anyway, click on his brother, Vitaly Shetlov, allegedly brutally murdered in nineteen forty-four outside Tar in what was then Yugoslavia.' I did this and a page with a picture of a late middle-aged man appeared on the screen. Vitaly Shetlov was described as an advisor to the State Planning Committee and there was a photograph of him stood next to Nikolai Baibakov and Yuri Andropov. 'Looks rather healthy for a person with a spent cartridge case hammered into the back of his neck.'

'So, the story about your father's regiment killing Russian prisoners was false.'

'The regiment killed prisoners, and the Red Army did the same. No soldier was safe if they surrendered on their own or in a small group. My father did a lot of screaming in the night when I was growing up. Not sure it related to the killing of prisoners, more likely it was the realisation he could just as easily have been a victim. Perhaps he was having nightmares about hiding in that barn.' Paul poured himself a glass of wine, then surveyed the room before his attention returned to the computer.

'Go back to Shetlov himself.'

'And?' I asked after clicking *back* on the browser.

'Doesn't it seem odd he was stationed in Berlin for so long? You would have thought at some point he would have been recalled to

Moscow. Which would have been unfortunate since he was in love with Gerde Eppelmann, and presumably she with him.'

'Sorry, I'm not with you.' Although I was catching up, slowly.

'So wouldn't it be convenient if he developed a network of agents in the West, former members of the German army and in a position to be useful to the Soviet Union. There must have been any number to choose from as they questioned families about sons who were being held prisoners by the British, French and Americans. Even so, I'm guessing questions were asked regarding the absence of anything useful coming from this mythical network of agents.' Paul said, then his mind appeared to wander.

'You visited Frau Eppelmann's house, what did you think?'

'As far as I remember modern and luxurious. Certainly compared to my mother's house.'

'Care of Anweiler Construction. They worked for various companies, but also for factory bosses and other members of the Communist Party. That's how they managed to survive as a small private company. Party officials diverted scarce materials for use on their own properties. Anything left over was used on other jobs. They also worked on Soviet military bases, which is probably how Shetlov got to know them. You remember my uncle Wilhelm, very talkative and sometimes indiscreet, which may be how Shetlov discovered I was studying engineering. And why when I set off on that walk to get a doctor to look at that insect bite I was followed and came face to face with a colonel from the KGB holding a gun.'

'My God, what did you do?'

'Pointed a gun at him. I'd seen him, sitting in the garden of the house next door to where I was staying. Sometimes he was nursing a revolver so it didn't take a leap of imagination to figure out what was on his mind, and I took a gun with me.'

'How did you get it through the border?

'I didn't. It was my uncle's, or rather it had belonged to one of the soldiers he helped bury after the battle of Berlin.'

'What happened? You obviously didn't shoot each other.'

518

'I think we discussed the implications of either of us pulling the trigger and came to an arrangement. As far as I remember the only casualty was someone's postbox because neither of us believed the other's gun was loaded.'

'But why the lie about his brother?'

'He guessed as a student I would have left-wing views and guilt might amplify any sympathy I felt towards the Soviet Union. He was right.'

'Tell me, Paul, how did that make you feel?' An ill-judged and inappropriate joke.

'That was supposed to be funny?'

If he had received counselling after his father's death, then pity the person who provided it. I had just alienated Paul and thought a little empathy might win him back. 'Perhaps he was attempting to drive a wedge between you and your father and offer himself up as a substitute, he came across to me as paternalistic. Perhaps a personality trait, but I suspect he knew I lost my father at an early age and played on this.'

Odd that I'd never thought of this until saying it out loud. 'Have you heard of Danuta Mostwin's Family Life Space diagram?' I asked.

'Yes, it is possible to create one using entries from your diary.' Paul turned the laptop around so he could type on the keyboard. Moving to the chair next to him I watched a diagram, similar to the one I'd created by hand back home in Gehrden, appear on the computer's screen.

Here, finally, was proof of what I had suspected, that between the two visits to my house by people pretending to be broadband engineers my handwritten diaries were in Köln being scanned and converted into text which was then analysed by the same software Paul had used to produce his computer-generated book *Fahrenbrink*.

Feigning surprise, I said, 'That's a little intrusive.' In my diagram of Paul's relationships, it was Shetlov almost overlapping his father. The one on the screen in front of me now had Hubert Hüber and Herman depicted as father substitutes. Strange though was the distance between myself and my sister. My brother-in-law was even further away, at the edge of the screen amongst a scattering of people such as the members of the Stasi: Steuernagel, Weidel, Janowitz and Müller. Not quite so remote was Professor Pohl who was almost as close as my son and daughter.

'Interesting, isn't it?' The goulash soup arrived, so the laptop was moved to the edge of the table.

'I don't understand this,' I said. 'I knew Hüber, and met him a few times, but how is it the software thinks he was as close to me as my husband?'

'The software didn't think, it merely analysed your diary entries. There were similarities between the description of your encounters with Hüber and those with Herman. There is a button at the bottom of the screen with *Connection* on it, click this and then the names *Hüber* and *Herman* to find out how and why they are connected in your mind.'

I did this and the screen was filled with windows containing short extracts from my diary with various words highlighted in red. Words I had used to describe someone coming to my defence. Herman intervening when Beaky Boy set about me and Hüber at the meetings with Janowitz and Müller in Potsdam and later Weidel and Steuernagel at Stasi Headquarters.

'Both men, one by accident, the other I suspect by design, projected themselves as father figures. Which given what happen to you when you were young ...' Paul seemed unwilling to finish the sentence, so I did this for him.

'I would feel an affinity with anyone who did so,' I said, realising neither Paul or Shetlov appeared in the diagram. 'I notice it is possible to edit certain people out of my life. Or do I think so little of them they are off the edge of the screen?' The diagram I created using Paul's books showed Shetlov and his own father were the only two people close to him. Perhaps Paul excluded Shetlov from the analysis of my diaries because it revealed my affinity with the Russian. I even wondered if there was some form of subconscious sibling rivalry at play.

Paul offered no explanation for the omission. 'That from just your diary so imagine would happen if all those Stasi files were accessed using AI software. Germany would probably be transformed into a totalitarian dystopia overnight. This might have been to prepare me for what came next. 'Would you like to discover how your Professor Pohl got so close to you, and his relationship with all those Stasi goons?' he asked.

Paul clicked first on the *Connection* button and then on *Hüber* and *Pohl*. Numerous windows appeared on the screen; one described a meeting in Hüber's office and a second Pohl and myself having lunch together in Mahlow after our visit to Potsdam. Highlighted in both was *Schicht Nougat* because there was a bar in Pohl's pack lunch and also a wrapper in the ashtray in Hüber's office. Also highlighted in each window was the word *obsessive,* my description of the folding of the wrappers on each occasion.'

'Interesting,' I said, something of an understatement given here was evidence Pohl had been at a meeting with Hüber prior to the one I attended. Also extracted from my diary was a comment after a practice counselling session with Professor Pohl while researching psychotherapy techniques, regarding what might happen if the information I disclosed ended up in the hands of the Stasi. 'I should have realised what had happened.'

'I think you did but simply refused to believe it.' Paul said sympathetically. 'The Andreas K experiment was merely a distraction; you were the real target.'

'Apparently,' I sighed, and Paul closed the screen of the laptop.

'Nothing is more important than schnitzel,' he said as the waiter cleared away the soup bowls and placed the main course on the table. But while the screen was no longer visible, the questions posed by the software still hung in the air.

'But why?' I asked.

Paul shrugged. 'I think it started here thirty years earlier. In your diary, you described Hüber as being in his fifties in nineteen seventy-five, so born around nineteen twenty. And he was in Vienna after leaving university. How old would he have been then?'

'Between twenty-five and thirty, perhaps.'

'Which means he was enjoying coffee and apple strudel in here somewhere between nineteen forty and nineteen forty-five. Must have felt slightly uncomfortable, an ardent communist surrounded by all those German uniforms.' Paul swallowed a mouthful of wine. 'My guess is he wore a disguise, dressed himself up as a member of the Gestapo.'

'I can't believe that.'

'In your diary you mentioned a conversation with Shetlov.'

'Yes, in Werneuchen, he made out he was taking me back to Moscow.'

'And you believed him?'

'At first,' I said.

'You wrote in your diary he was here in Vienna when he heard his brother had been killed.'

'He lied about his brother being dead so he might have also lied about being here.'

'Possibly, but assuming he didn't, it would mean he was in Vienna when Hüber was a prisoner of the Red Army. And Hüber has form when it comes to switching sides, so perhaps a deal with Shetlov, handing over the Gestapo's records rather than ending up with a bullet in the head. Given the speed with which he rose through the ranks of the Stasi, he probably also helped round up his former comrades in Berlin.'

'I find that difficult to believe.'

'I think you need to revisit the idea Hüber and Shetlov had your best interests at heart. At some point both realised their lives would be a lot easier if you were dead.'

'No, you don't know that,' I protested, then we sat in silence while I thought about what Paul had just told me and what the software on his laptop had discovered about Heinz Pohl. 'Are you sure?' I asked.

'Hüber's position in the Stasi, and possibly his life, depended on the goodwill of Shetlov and he would sleep a lot easier at night if the KGB officer was forced to leave Berlin in disgrace. He would also feel safer if my family were locked up. I'm not sure how he found out Shetlov had a mistress and was using KGB funds to pay a private building company to renovate her house.' I wondered if Paul realised the hold Hüber had over his late cousin Erich. 'Anyway, he obviously thought he'd found a way to do both.'

'Shetlov told you that?'

'Oh yes, we had a long conversation. After the gunfight at Karl Marx Corral he insisted on walking with me to the doctor's surgery. Apparently there were some dangerous people wandering the countryside and he wanted to make sure I didn't come to any harm. I thought the chance of two gun-toting members of the KGB being on the loose in Brandenburg seemed remote but went along with it. He never actually referred to me as *English* but I got the idea he based his persona on Len Deighton's Colonel Stock.'

'Sorry? Who?' I asked but Paul ignored the question.

'According to Shetlov you were central to Hüber's plan, which began with your visit to Gerde Eppelmann. He assumed this was merely to get his attention and trick him, successfully as it turned out, into contacting you. Hüber was attempting to create a link between Shetlov and the British Secret Service. Hence your presence at the Anweiler party, a guest of the people Shetlov employed to work on his mistress's house. Alarm bells would ring in Moscow when the KGB were told you had attempted to defect to the West during your visit to Vienna. Which Steuernagel would have claimed you were doing while sitting here in this Café with me. For Hüber, rounding up the Anweilers and throwing them in prison would have been a bonus and may have seen him promoted to the head of the Stasi. Neither of us, nor Shetlov, were going to come out of this well. The easiest way to make the problem go away was to remove one of the key links in the chain.'

'By throwing it in a lake,' I joked, but Paul looked away. 'My god, he considered having me killed. Did he ask you to do it?'

'No, I assumed he had spoken with my uncle and found some way of dealing with Hüber.'

'I can't see how that would have worked.'

'The Anweilers weren't without influence. Remember they did a lot of work for members of the party. They may not have known where the bodies were buried but they knew where the mistresses slept. Anyway, I returned to Britain and I didn't give the matter any more thought. It was my last year at college and after that my father got me that job in Köln.'

'And you forgot all about me.' I pouted and gave Paul the sad eyes.

'A month after I arrived in Köln my father forwarded me a postcard from someone in Ostbevern asking me to contact them. Shetlov sometimes hitched a ride with SOXMIS, travelling to West Germany to take part in officially sanctioned surveillance missions. We met and he asked me if I had any plans to travel to Vienna. Oddly enough, I did.'

'Why?' I asked.

'To attend the conference you were speaking at.'

'Really, you are joking.'

Paul appeared embarrassed. 'OK, don't tell me that if you had presented that paper, you wouldn't have been looking for a familiar face in the audience.'

'Hardly. I thought you were dead, remember,' I replied, hoping I had not mentioned in my diary the possibility of meeting someone in Vienna who might throw some light on the identity of the young Englishman I thought had drowned during the Anweiler party. In retrospect, possibly the most dangerous thought I had ever committed to paper.

Paul sighed and stared at me until I blushed. 'Shetlov had come up with a plan even Ute would have dismissed as impossible. He discovered Otto Steuernagel, who would be accompanying your party, had attended a meeting in Moscow and stayed in a hotel for foreign visitors. There were hours of film of him doing all manner of things, the least embarrassing of which was shaving. It meant Shetlov knew the make and model of his electric razor and bought one with him to Ostbevern. All Max had to do was add a detonator and a small amount of explosives.'

'Why didn't he get someone in the KGB to do that?'

'East Germany had supplied a batch of explosives to terrorists in the West. Using some of this would make it look to the Austrian police as if the Stasi had killed one of their own. Max, Sonia and I travelled to Vienna. After we arrived, I visited the British Embassy and asked them to pass a message to someone I knew in London telling them a Stasi officer attending the conference wanted to defect. I assumed if Shetlov was right and you were being set up, that comment you made about the Frauenhuber Café was relevant and someone had suggested it to you as a meeting place.'

'I was so naive,' I said, wishing instantly I had kept this thought to myself.

'Don't worry, I've had my moments,' Paul said. If this was an attempt to make me feel better, it failed. 'Shetlov arranged your little trip into Czechoslovakia, Max was waiting until the car picked you up and Steuernagel, who had been following you, went back into the hotel. Max caught up with him and asked if he was with the East German group because he had arranged to meet you here. Steuernagel presumed this was where you were headed. I was already here with Sonia when Steuernagel arrived, and had brought a camera with me. We acted like tourists and took photographs of each other during the meal – and one of Steuernagel when he was approached by two men. He played the part of a potential defector well, looked nervous, possibly because you hadn't turned up. The only thing which didn't go as planned was the British Secret Service deciding any potential defector in Vienna was best handled by the Americans. Shetlov was over the moon when he saw the photograph but London less so, and their American cousins weren't happy when news of Steuernagel's death broke and fingers were pointed at the CIA. Once I had the photograph I waited until Steuernagel had returned to the hotel and was safely back in his room then phoned the restaurant where Shetlov was providing you with an alibi.'

'Except he didn't trust you, not fully, did he? He was not convinced you would keep your side of the bargain and prevent Steuernagel returning to Berlin.' I remembered how terrified I had been while sat in that near-deserted restaurant as Shetlov listened on the phone. Listened for a long time, perhaps wondering if the person on the other end was telling the truth and thinking if I disappeared so would any possibility Hüber would get him sent back to Moscow. I thought of the disastrous exploits of Toni and Tibo in Ute's books. And that one evening in 1976 my life was in the hands of the two people on whom Ute had based a pair of clowns. 'He lost his nerve, didn't he?'

The waiter cleared the table and left us with the dessert menu. Paul said, 'I think Shetlov may have given the impression you were in danger but that was for my benefit not yours. He must have realised one day I would discover his brother was still alive and he would lose his hold over me. It also must have been obvious there was another reason I didn't want you hanged as a traitor.' With the suggestion Paul might have been in love with me began a train of thought which would become increasingly corrosive during the coming months.

There was no outward sign Paul had detected my sudden change in attitude towards him. 'Shetlov was already feeding information to me via my uncle. Unfortunately, some of this was lost in translation, or, more worryingly for Shetlov, added to before reaching me,' Paul said, and I found myself staring at his lips without fully listening to what he was saying. 'The story about tanks destined for the Afghanistan border, for example.' Now he had my attention again and I recalled Brecht's book of poems. 'There had always been the possibility we inadvertently passed on something which got either the KGB or Britain's secret service overexcited. But now Shetlov had access to someone who he assumed was in direct contact with the security services in Britain. Whether that was responsible for you getting back to the hotel alive I don't know.'

'How many of Britain's secrets did you betray to keep me alive?'

'It didn't work like that.'

'Is that why you didn't stay in East Germany with Sonia Engelhardt and the other terrorists?' I was hoping Paul would explain why he had been sitting outside our apartment in Erfurt that morning, but he did not.

'I was told the same thing as those young idealists who thought East Germany was a socialist eutopia, that I would be more useful to the Stasi in the West. That's how I met your friend Hüber.' Paul said, although I suspect Hüber had other reasons for not wanting him in East Germany with the rest of the Anweilers. He must have suspected Paul helped derail his plan to remove Shetlov. And Paul had brought into the country the terrorist who killed Lauterbrunnen, a politician the Stasi would have preferred lived and become an embarrassment to the West German government.

'And did Hüber find you useful?'

'Never heard of him again. He left me and my family alone and at a guess it was the fear Shetlov might exploit the death of Steuernagel to his advantage that kept them safe.'

'But you and Shetlov stayed in touch.'

'Wilhelm must have mentioned to Shetlov, or Gerde Eppelmann, that I was working for a high-tech company because I received a letter posted in Hannover but written on the sort of paper used in East Germany,' Paul said. 'It was anonymous, but I now suspect it was written by Gerde on her lover's behalf. Apparently, someone wanted to meet me at a café in the forest close to Springe, a place called Köllnischfeld. In time I got used to Shetlov's theatrics, but finding myself surrounded by Red Army soldiers in uniform came as a bit of a shock. This was on the edge of the area around Celle which SOXMIS was prohibited from entering. But Shetlov was playing cat and mouse with a Captain Coulson who was in charge of a Cymbeline radar system which was set up about a hundred metres from the café.

Apparently, this game had been going on for a year, long enough for Shetlov and Coulson to end up on first-name terms and exchange Christmas cards. It was that sort of thing which probably prevented Europe ending up a pile of ash. Anyway, it seemed *the crazy Russian*, as Coulson referred to him, was still using SOXMIS as cover. Shetlov sat down at a table with me while the rest of his team searched for Coulson and explained he needed my help. He updated me on your family and career, his way of telling me he'd kept his side of the bargain. Subtle he was not.'

'What did he want?'

'What he only ever wanted, something which would justify his presence in East Berlin. He had been at a conference in Moscow and heard talk that the navy were trying to design a propellor which didn't make so much noise it could be heard halfway across the Atlantic. He joked the Politburo was worried about the impact it was having on whales. So I suggested there might be a way of finding out how the British navy's silent propellors were made.'

'And risk the British throwing you in prison.'

'The British knew the Soviets were two thirds of the way to catching up with the West. What they didn't know was who was working on the remaining third.

'Shetlov arranged for my company to exhibit in Moscow and got engineers and scientists who were working on the design of the new propellor to visit the stand. We came away with a list of names of people working on the project, their qualifications and the institutions where they were based. The British then came up with a plan to disrupt the project. During a discussion between us and the Ministry of Defence regarding other work we were doing, a scientist mentioned an experiment with specially shaped objects which could act as passive microphones. I mentioned it to Shetlov, who thought, like me, it was rubbish that had been fed to me, but felt his superiors in Moscow would find it amusing. Unknown to us Britain's Foreign Office had been giving miniature reproductions of Henry Moore sculptures to visiting Soviet diplomats.' Paul laughed. 'Members of the politburo had always suspected modern art was part of a Western conspiracy to undermine the Soviet Union, now they started to worry it was being used to bug their offices. Overnight those engineers and scientists who had been working on silent propellors were wasting time bouncing soundwaves off rocks. By monitoring any contact we had with Soviet institutions, the government's export-control department could assess how effective this scam had been.'

'There must have been repercussions for Shetlov when it was discovered what the British had done.'

'Don't forget Shetlov's brother was very well-connected.'

'What happened to Shetlov after the collapse of the Soviet Union?'

'He morphed into a businessman with offices in both Berlin and Moscow, It was an ideal arrangement although it meant hanging up the uniform and putting away the medals.

'I lost contact with him after Gorbachev paid a visit to a university in Moscow and waved a computer graphics card in front of TV cameras to show how advanced Russian technology was. You had to look very carefully to see it was one designed by Max. Just our bad luck that some people in America still paid close attention to all things shown on Russian television. I guess there was still a lot of ill feeling regarding that incident here in the Frauenhuber, especially as the press and conspiracy theorists believed Steuernagel's death was a CIA hit.'

'I wonder what he would have thought of Russia today?'

'I know there was a huge argument between Shetlov and the KGB office in Dresden because they wanted to fire into a crowd of demonstrators just before the wall came down. He said it was lucky Putin got back to Leningrad alive. So perhaps he wouldn't have fitted in too well with the new regime.' Then Paul sighed and, displaying a lack of self-awareness, whispered softly. 'But he died, a year before my father.'

'Where are we going?' I asked, because a taxi had driven past, and Paul ignored it and kept walking so it appeared I would not be returning to my hotel.

'It's not far. The Kursalon Hübner. You'll enjoy it.' Although when we arrived the doorman explained the party going on inside was a private event.

'That suits us,' said Paul. We are very private people.'

'Sorry, you don't understand...' But after examining the invitation Paul took from his inside pocket, the doorman stood to one side.

'I'm not really dressed for this,' I protested, hanging back as we approached the ballroom.

'We could go back to the hotel and ask your twin sister if she has an evening dress?' Before I could respond we were descended on by a tanned woman with greying wavy hair, a lock of which had fallen across her face. She curled the errant hair around her finger then tucked it behind her ear.

'Paul, glad you could make it.' A kiss on both cheeks for the man now holding my arm. Paul eventually realised this physical contact meant my presence needed explaining.

'Oh yes... Lotte, this is Tina, an old friend from my college days. Tina, this is Lotte, an old friend from Berlin.'

'Not so keen on the old, Paul,' Tina said, shaking my hand. I held hers just a little too long because she looked familiar. Why became clear when a man approached and handed her a glass of champagne.

'Trixy, Emily would like a word when you are free.' So, this was the person who supplied the information on Paul, and a list of books in his college room, which both found their way into his Stasi file along with the picture of her sitting next to him in one of London's parks. Despite having gained access to my diary, and obviously now being aware that Tina, or Trixy, was the person who informed on him, the conversation between the two ex-college friends was cordial, jovial even. And who in their right mind uses their Stasi code name as a nickname? Maybe Paul and his college friends had been playing games with the Stasi and Weidel had been almost as hopeless at his job as Steuernagel.

'So how is the apartment?' Paul asked Trixy. 'I can see from the suntan you are making the most of the balcony.'

'It's wonderful Paul, thanks for your help.'

'That's OK. Perhaps you could have a word with the people who got you your OBE. Ask them if I could have one.'

'Yes!' Trixy shrieked. 'That was a surprise.'

'Order of the British, sorry, what does the *E* stand for again?' Paul asked, 'Oh yes, I remember now, *Empire*. Wasn't that written on the banner you hit the policeman with when you were demonstrating with Cathcart?'

'You're terrible. Look, let's catch up later. I've got to have a few words with Emily, it's an embassy bash after all.'

Paul introduced me to a businessman who exported electronics to the Middle East, mentioning my husband was a director of Schulenberg Electronics. Conversation dried up after just five minutes so when the businessman suggested we danced I accepted the offer. Occasionally I noticed Paul looking in my direction, perhaps wondering why my dance partner was attempting to stamp out an imaginary forest fire. Both he and Trixy were talking to Emily. Trixy seemed pensive and none of the trio smiled. Perhaps, come the morning, the Viennese police might find another body in a hotel bathroom. Eventually Paul broke away from the two women and walked over to speak to one of the musicians, who in turn conferred with the female singer. His request agreed, Paul then saved me from further punishment. One hand held mine and the other was on the small of my back. I guessed the orchestra was warming up to play a waltz, just not that one. But Leonard Cohen's *Take This Waltz* was obviously a popular choice as soon the dance floor was filled with couples.

What could have been more romantic than gliding around a glittering ballroom with the taste of champagne still on my lips and a man so close I could feel his breath on my neck? But the references to rooms where dogs went to die invoked the image of matchstick men crowded into one square metre of the stand in the conference hall lobby and that of a dead body in a forest playing in a continuous loop on a video screen. I would have liked to think it was the hypocrisy of people like Paul and Trixy which was troubling me, but there was something else. Perhaps Paul chose the wrong moment to look into my eyes, and the image of his mouth on the dew of my thighs was just a little too vivid in my mind. Had this not been followed by the continual repetition of the word *death* I may not have felt compelled to press my hand on Paul's chest.

'I'm sorry.' I whispered. 'But I'm afraid now is when the woman says, *I'm not comfortable with this.*'

Almost instantly there was half a metre separating us. 'Do you want to leave?' he asked.

'No, no, it's just... I'm sorry.'

'It's OK, I understand.' But I felt he did not. We had not argued, and it was unlikely anyone else in the room noticed the abrupt distancing of ourselves from each other. And we did stay, in part because of the genuine interest people showed in the presentation I had given earlier in the day. Emily, Trixy and I all had different but overlapping views on social media, perhaps not surprising given our areas of interest. Emily the diplomat regarded anything which influenced the citizens of one country but was ultimately controlled by the government of another as a potential threat. Trixy, her OBE having had little impact on her political views, was troubled by the growing influence of big tech companies. The only person with a positive view of the technology was the manic dancer who had bruised my feet and was now determined to do the same to my ego. Never trust a man who repeatedly uses the word *hysterical* when arguing with a woman. While I felt increasingly confident as my audience grew, Paul seemed to fade into the background. How, in such a brightly lit room, had someone managed to disappear into the shadows?

In the taxi taking us back to my hotel, Paul seemed tired and dejected. I had wanted to apologise for the conference session, to explain I felt compelled to tell the truth about the impact the technology was having on my patients. And say sorry for pushing him away during that waltz. Perhaps a simple squeeze of his hand would have stopped his slide into an abyss. From years treating patients with depression, I suspected the descent into darkness began when I stopped playing the role of his Christina, because that was who he'd imagined he was dancing with.

'Please wait,' Paul told the taxi driver. 'I'm staying at the Biedermeier Hotel.' So, no presumption of being invited to stay for a nightcap or asked up to my room. Merely a curt goodnight and a promise to be in touch next time he was in Berlin. Giving in I extended my hand but his remained by his side. 'Goodnight and thanks for a lovely evening,' he said and there was the same sinking feeling in my stomach I'd felt when we parted that evening in Köln.

Sitting in bed like a lovestruck teenager, I found the Biedermeier Hotel on a tourist street map of Vienna. Although even as a teenager I'd never felt as conflicted as I did that evening.

I took my mobile phone from the bedside table. 'Hello, I hope you are feeding yourself?'

'Of course.'

'That's not the television I can hear, is it?' I said recognising a familiar voice in the background. 'Unless Joachim is on RBB again.'

'No, I thought rather than cook I'd have something at the Weissen Ross,' Herman said.

'Well, I hope you're keeping your eyes on the food and not Claudia's backside.'

'I'll take you off speakerphone.' Now there was laughter in the background. As I talked with Herman I lifted my laptop out of its bag, switched it on and opened the browser. 'I can hear you typing,' he said. 'You're not still working?' I was not. There had been something playing on my mind all evening, which I was reminded of again when I heard my husband's voice.

'No,' I replied. 'Just checking something before the panel session tomorrow.' Which was untrue. 'Have you ever heard of a place called Köllnischfeld?' I asked. 'It's near Hannover.'

'No, why?'

'Inge mentioned it,' I said as a pin was dropped into the map of the forest close to the hotel in Paul's book, the one where Inge's family took me for lunch. Herman should remember it because on two occasions when he attended the exhibition in Hannover, he'd brought back receipts from the Köllnischfeld Café. I zoomed in on the small group of houses, but no café so perhaps the receipts were forgeries to cover Roland's purchase of car parts. Even so, as Herman made small talk, I began to suspect there might have been a third person sitting at the table during Paul's meeting with Shetlov – my husband.

# 40

# Return to Rethen

February 2020

While it was Ute who suggested I was not the sort of person who wandered into a forest at night, torch in hand, shouting *Hello, is anyone there*, it was her responsible for me ending up doing just that. Although there was no torch, instead the light on the mobile phone shone on the tree lined path while searching for a pair of glasses dropped after taking them out of my bag. And despite snow sliding from the branches of a nearby tree and thudding onto the ground there was no calling out to an imaginary attacker. Instead, I was pondering the attraction of danger and what compels us to revisit the scene of a traumatic incident. Something which occupied my mind on occasions when sitting on the terrace of the Michhäuaschen café looking down on the Weissensee where my father's body was found floating.

Not the Weissensee this time, but another lake and perhaps the sound behind me was Ute Lorenze setting up a camera and tripod to capture the iconic image of a woman standing alone at the end of a jetty for the cover of her next book. It was not, and neither was it more snow sliding off the branches of spruce trees at the edge of the lake. Dressed not for the cold but in just a shirt and trousers, as on that summer's afternoon a long time ago, was that ghost from my past. He walked towards me, slowly and deliberately, like an animal about to pounce.

Britain's Labour party had lost the general election, so interest in Geoffrey Cathcart's Stasi file faded, as did any chance I would receive those 250,000 euros. Günter Hölderlin, however, kept his word, and 65,000 euros arrived in my bank account three days after my return from Vienna. Surprisingly, in view of the reputational damage my presentation inflicted on Edouard Monget's company, Köhl and Strasse Investments paid me well for attending the meeting with Mr Philips. A clear winner to emerge from what the press described as a social media meltdown was Günter's magazine; the print version launched with an exclusive on Companion's disastrous IPO.

In contravention of EU privacy laws, Monget's social media platform was sending German citizens' personal information to the US where it was processed in a data centre outside Boston. For a week in September Günter seemed a permanent fixture on TV news, a steady hand on the tiller during a panic over mass surveillance by US Big Tech. His name, and that of his magazine, scrolled across the bottom of the screen when a second tsunami of bad news hit Monget's fast sinking ship. Günter wrote a follow-up article containing revelations about the use of social media during Britain's election and expressing fears there would be similar interference with the democratic process in Germany at some point.

Backing up Günter's articles were the results of a project by a group of my students. They had  created an animated version of Danuta Mostwin's Family Life Space diagram only this time the members of the family were not mine or Paul's, but Cathcart's supporters and detractors during the UK election. And the data came not from a diary or a book, but Twitter and Facebook. The diagram illustrated how close, or distant, a social media user's opinions were to

Cathcart's own at any one point during the campaign. It also showed the influence of various types of comments, including some posted by bots. Intriguing was the impact of automatically generated posts used by both sides in the contest, along the lines of *I'm not a great fan of Cathcart but on this issue I think he's right,* and, *On most things I agree with Cathcart, but on this occasion he's hopelessly out of his depth.*

It had proved difficult keeping my students focussed on mechanics and techniques and prevent them being distracted by politics. However, Martin and Katja, now an item, proved competent project managers. My only concern was that I might be training the next generation of psychologists employed by IT companies.

It was to a meeting with Martin and Katja I was headed, after having finished a session with a patient, when the receptionist put a call through to my office. 'It's Ute Lorenze for you.'

'Did you have a good Christmas?' she asked.

'Yes and thank you for the presents you gave my grandchildren.'

'No need, they have already sent me very nice letters.'

'Very good. Is that it?' Admittedly this came across as a little harsh but no doubt bounced off Ute's armour-plated business suit.

'Could you meet me for lunch at the InterContinental Hotel on Budapest Strasse?' she said, and I found myself sitting up in my chair after realising Ute was not in Köln but worryingly close to the office.

'Isn't that in the West?' There was something about Ute that brought out the worst in me.

'Yes, close to the Zoo. You will need one of those maps without a large blank space this side of the Brandenburg gate.' And I brought out the worst in Ute.

'I'm afraid I have appointments this afternoon.'

'Nothing you cannot cancel, I'm sure. It is important we meet.' This made me suspect she had either hacked into Sophie's IT system or was standing at a window in the building opposite holding a pair of binoculars. As this was Ute, neither could be ruled out.

'Perhaps we could discuss this on the phone.'

'Yes, we could but won't. I will see you at one-thirty.'

Ute was correct; there was nothing that afternoon I could not cancel. In fact, two students would be relieved at not having to explain computer graphics to a digital novice and my sister would no doubt prefer to be curled up in her boat house with a colleague from the library.

'That's a nice coat, did you buy it here in Berlin?' Something Maxine has told me since is that questions like these preceded *seriously strange shit happening*. Hence her comment about Ute's jacket when we were on Peter's boat.

'It was from a shop in Templin,' I said. 'A branch of Prada, or it could have been Delikat.'

'That's interesting,' she said. 'So, let's have lunch.' And a long and very expensive lunch it was, three courses and half a bottle of wine with coffee and fancy chocolates to follow. I was quizzed on every detail of the Christmas Herman and I spent in Wittenberge, at least those details which involved my grandchildren. Between the main course and dessert Ute's eyes lingered on a family sitting at a nearby table. Unusually there was a hint of makeup, foundation under the eyes which did little to disguise a reddening of the skin which I suspected was the result of Ute crying herself to sleep. I then remembered her book was with the publisher; a somewhat worrying prospect for one of its principal characters, but also for an author left with nothing to distract her.

'So, what was important enough to drag me into the British Sector?'

Surprisingly, Ute found this amusing. 'Actually, it was Paul who wanted to meet you, but he's delayed by the weather and still on his way back from Poland. He will be at a hotel outside the city, in a village called Rethen. Do you know it?' She knew I did and probably noticed my pupils delate.

'Yes, I do and tell him there is no way on earth I'm going back there.'

'I believe Paul made you a promise a few months ago and he is anxious to keep it.' An obvious reference to the payment for my part in the Cathcart scam. The phrase *not for all the money in the world* sprang to mind.

'I'm definitely not interested,' I said emphatically, then stood and put on my coat. 'If that's all, I've got a busy afternoon.' Then added as an afterthought, 'Thanks for lunch.'

Ute did not respond and instead remained silent as we walked out of the restaurant and across the hotel lobby.

'A pity,' Ute said as I fastened the top button of my coat, the breeze now colder than it had been earlier in the day.

'What is?' I asked, making no attempt to hide my irritation and hoping to make it clear I was not about to change my mind. But Ute merely shrugged. 'Everyone needs closure,' she said, then walked off towards the queue of waiting taxis.

Why, instead of taking the S-Bahn to Adlershof after my train arrived at Ost Kreuz, did I end up on platform 8 waiting for the train to Kostrzyn? Perhaps I noticed one of the stops along the way was Müncheberg, where I arrived an hour later. By that time, I now know, Ute had hired a Silver Polo like mine and was headed towards Templin.

Rethen railway station was much as I remembered it except there was now no ticket office. There was also no Lada parked across the road with Steuernagel and the fat man sitting in it. The house where the Anweiler party was held looked more welcoming than it had done in 1975. It now had an entrance looking out onto the road, a porch with two large glass doors and a sign with *Rethen Guesthouse* in green gothic lettering above it.

'I am supposed to be meeting someone here. A Herr Paul Anweiler.'

The elderly lady stared down at the leather-bound hotel register laid open on the counter. Her hair was white, pulled back tight and tied in a knot with a large pin pushed through it. She ran her finger down a column of names then turned to the previous page. It seemed improbable, in the middle of winter, the hotel had that many guests.

Eventually she looked up and shrugged. 'It's no good, I'll have to fetch my glasses,' she said, and then retreated into a small office.

Hung on the wall of the lobby were enlarged photographs of the building. In one, First World War soldiers, some bandaged, were sitting on the veranda flanked by two rather stern-looking nurses. Several others taken between the 1920s and 1940s contained men dressed for hunting trips with guns hung over their arms. Then the Red Army arrived and there was an officer pictured behind a large desk and Russian soldiers swimming in the lake. After this a long gap and the next photograph showed the building in 1990, in a worse state than during my visit, with weeds on the paved driveway and bushes covering much of the garden. Five more photographs, all taken since showed the evolution of the old hunting lodge into the hotel it now was.

Behind me something metal was dropped onto the counter. 'Your room is at the top of the stairs,' the receptionist said.

'I think there has been a mistake; I'm not staying.' The receptionist looked towards the glass doors. What, fifteen minutes earlier, had been the occasional snow flake floating out of an almost clear blue sky was now a blizzard. Aware of how dark the room had become, she flicked the switch on the wall behind her.

'Where is Herr Anweiler coming from?' she asked.

'Poland.'

'Poland? I think you will have a long wait,' she said picking up the key and dangling it in front of me. Even so, I did not intend to stay and would not be going upstairs.

'I'll wait in the dining room.'

'As you wish,' the receptionist muttered under her breath while studying the register as if, now having found her glasses, she realised there were other bookings which had been overlooked. 'There is tea and coffee in there and dinner will be served after seven.'

'I was here in the nineteen seventies,' I said, hoping this might prompt an explanation as to why several decades of the hotel's history were missing. Instead, the statement was met with surprise.

'Interesting,' the receptionist said, raising one eyebrow and giving me a questioning look before returning to the register.

The room in which I had recovered after the incident at the lake was now part of an extended dining room. But the door which I remembered opened into the corridor leading to the kitchen, and through which I had been escorted to the waiting van, was still there. Outside the window the snow had already covered the veranda. It had also settled on the branches of the pine trees, making more vivid the gap where the path entered the forest. After helping myself to tea from the buffet in the corner of the room, I sat at a table next to the window where the warmth of the room and the hypnotic effect of falling snow made me feel sleepy.

'Still not arrived. You might be more comfortable in your room.' The woman's voice jolted me awake. The snow had eased, and the sun was shining again. The garden looked less daunting, inviting even.

'I'm just going outside for some air,' I said. 'It might wake me up.'

A picnic bench covered in snow recalled stepping through a patio door into a frozen garden and being sat there until my husband rescued me. I heard a young child's voice in my head, asking her father to build a snowman. At this point I should have returned to the dining room but instead walked across the snow-covered lawn towards the gap in the trees.

Paul had not pounced, and I was still trying to determine whether the person standing in front of me, holding out one hand, almost blue with cold, was a figment of my imagination. Then he said, 'Walk towards me very slowly.' It was then it occurred to me the snow was hiding the fact that the renovation of the hotel in those photographs had not included repairs to the jetty. And that the sound I could hear was the creaking and groaning of rotted wood.

Retracing my steps was a mistake as my foot slipped on frozen snow and the handrail I grabbed broke loose at one end. The weight of my coat, once wet, would pull me to the bottom of the lake and there I would stay until weeks later my bloated body floated to the surface. Holding my breath I waited for the impact with the ice-cold water which never came.

Paul grabbed hold of my arms and held me until I had steadied myself. 'We need to get off this thing,' he said, releasing my arms and then taking hold of my hand.

'You're freezing,' I said, cupping his hand between mine.

'My coat and jacket are in the car. I saw you walking across the garden as I arrived and, well, thought ...'

'Thought I intended to do something stupid.'

'Well, facts seemed to have borne that out,' he said. I gave his arm a playful punch at which point he lost his footing. Fortunately, the section of handrail he grabbed stayed in place. Rather than shake my hand loose, Paul kept hold of it as we walked back to the hotel. After we climbed the steps onto the veranda he stood staring back across the lawn to the gap in the trees.

'Let's get you inside,' I said. 'Before you freeze to death.'

'Really? Don't you want me to build you a snowman?' he said. It was as if I had been punched in the stomach and my knees felt weak. I tugged at Paul's hand, gently at first, but then more violently as I pleaded with him. However, it was not Paul I begged to come out of the cold. It was someone else standing frozen like a statue.

'I should have helped him. Done something.' My face was now pressed against Paul's chest and his arms were tight around me. At one point he released me briefly to stroke my hair and kiss my forehead. 'It was not your fault. It was never your fault.'

'I know, but still, if I had just managed to get him into the house, then perhaps he wouldn't have collapsed, they wouldn't have taken him away, he wouldn't have ended up in the lake. I resent him for being so weak. Then I end up feeling guilty and the whole thing keeps going around in my head.' This was something I'd held back during the practice therapy with Professor Pohl, although I suspect he worked out for himself what was troubling me and passed it onto

Hüber. Paul had also got me beyond the point I reached with Sonia many years later.

'Shouldn't there be a box of tissues on here?' Paul said when we were back in the warm, facing each other across the table in a still-deserted dining room. Levity was just what I needed at this point and the next tearful outburst was punctuated with laughter. He shuddered as if this was the first time he felt the cold. 'I'd better get my things from the car.'

After the hotel's front door slammed shut the building fell silent. Even so it seemed from the garden came the sound of voices and looking around the dining room I recalled how it was in 1975. Remembering Erich stood at the bar and the other young Anweiler's crowded around the television, and that abundance of food and the pile of Western clothes, none of which would have looked out of place now.

When Paul returned from his car he was wearing a sweater and jacket, carrying a coat over his arm and pulling a suitcase.

'My suitcase is still in a hotel in Berlin,' I said.

'I've got a spare pair of pyjamas.' And a thought flashed through my mind, one I had been trying to suppress since Vienna.

'I won't be staying,' I said a little too quickly. Now even I was not convinced.

'Well, looking at the weather, I'm not sure either of us has much choice. And there's more bad news, apparently the chef is snowbound in a place called Oberbarnim so it looks like its self-catering. On the bright side, we have full use of the kitchen.'

There were two things I learned about Paul Anweiler that evening. One, he did a passable impression of Michael Caine, and two he made the worse omelette I have ever tasted; so bad he used his as the filling in a bread roll. As we stood side by side in the hotel kitchen, memories of my father came back in waves. Tearful again I felt Paul's hand on my back and, just once, received another hug. He found a candelabra and a bottle of wine and made a dessert out of a can of fruit and pots of yogurt. The snow began falling again and the evening seemed just a little too romantic. It forced me to step outside myself and warn patient Lotte she was not in the right frame of mind to make a rational decision.

*No jumping in bed with Paul, Lotte, and do not even think of entering into a relationship with him. This man has found a way to break you. True, he is picking up the pieces, and putting you back together, but you know deep down he hopes to reconstruct you in the image of a girl called Christina. And should he succeed, and you try to break free and become Lotte again, or he decides you are a flawed imitation of this imaginary woman he idolises, well, just remember how coercive and manipulative he can be.'*

'How did you know what I felt about my father's death?' I asked. 'I don't think I mentioned it in my diary.' The only clue might have been my lunchtime walks to Weissensee, but these only started in 1993, by which time I was no longer keeping a diary.

'You referred to it on the first page of the exercise book you wrote in when you were twelve. Or rather drew it. That picture of the snowman, and you hand in hand with the man standing beside it. It was Ute that noticed you weren't holding his hand but pulling at it. Pulling him towards the house.' That made sense. After all, Ute must spend a lot of time fantasising about a child pulling her out of the cold place she has found herself in.

'How did you remember I kept a diary?' I asked.

'I didn't, someone in Britain's security service was trawling through their archives looking for a person who might be able to shed light on what happened during Cathcart's visit to East Germany and came across my file. They asked if I could help and when I told them it was a long time ago and they should know all I did was visit my family, they reminded me I mentioned you kept a diary.'

'Why on earth would you have told them that?'

'Maybe when asked whether I thought you were a member of the Stasi, I suggested the mention of a diary was part of your cover story, one you were comfortable with because it was close to the truth given you would be writing an account of what happened at the party.'

This sounded farfetched and I suspected Paul was lying. 'The other possibility, of course, is you did remember me telling you about my diaries and needed access to them for some reason unconnected with Geoffrey Cathcart. But when Ute borrowed and scanned them Cathcart's name cropped up and you saw an opportunity. You told your friends in the secret service that you had located Cathcart's Stasi file and they could use it to put pressure on the politician. You could even hide the story behind a firewall for release when it was most embarrassing. All you needed was a large amount of money to take control of an online magazine.'

Paul smiled and seemed relieved. 'That sounds plausible. They say Robert Maxwell had help from Britain's Secret Intelligence Service to set up a company called Butterworth-Springer believing it would provide access to a wealth of German scientific research. And I'm pretty sure if Shetlov hadn't got to him first, Hüber might also have made a deal with the British.'

At this point I should have questioned why Paul had changed the subject and pressed him on the real reason he needed access to my diaries. But because of the reference to Hüber I did not. 'Is that what you meant in Vienna when you said Hubert Hüber had form when it came to switching sides?'

'When East Germany collapsed he collected as many Stasi files together as he could and did a deal with West Germany's BND. He even had a few left over to finance his pension. There was a black market for files which could be used to put pressure on someone with a questionable past.'

'Like the one I delivered to Heinrich Reisenberg in Celle.' I suggested. 'Although I don't understand why the pretence of needing therapy, and Reisenberg paying me for it.'

'Possibly he wanted to know if you'd read the file. Telling you lies about his war record and seeing if you gave yourself away by contradicting him. Pointless really, as he was obliged to make sure you got your licence back. Perhaps he just wanted peace of mind, or genuinely needed therapy, did you think of that?'

'I suppose I should say thank you.'

'For what?'

'Getting hold of Reisenberg's file when Herman asked for your help.' I was guessing my husband had been calling in a favour.

'Not me, I'm afraid.' Paul put his hands behind his head and stretched. 'Maybe Shetlov, he was in a position to persuade Hüber to part with any files useful to him.' Paul appeared to give this some thought then leaned forward. 'When was the last time you saw your Stasi friend?' He asked.

'I really can't remember.'

'In your diary you mentioned meeting with him in nineteen eighty-eight. What did you discuss?'

'Sorry, it was a long time ago.'

'About Cathcart and Weidel wasn't it?'

'I think it might have been about a comment Cathcart made when he was a member of parliament. Something about that visit Köhl and Reagan made to a cemetery where SS soldiers were buried, fascism and American Imperialism. Hüber was under a lot of pressure. Hardly surprising if what you said about him and Shetlov is true. Weidel was becoming more influential within the Stasi. He was the golden boy of the HVA and the next step up would see him promoted above Hüber's head. Weidel was claiming the Cathcart speech illustrated how much influence the HVA had in Britain and made sure it was covered in newspapers and on television. Hüber thought if he could show that Weidel was exaggerating and taking credit for something his own department had done, it might clip his wings. All Hüber wanted to know was if there had been something said during Cathcart's meeting with peace activists which wasn't recorded or passed on by an informer.'

'And was there?' Paul asked casually, but even so appeared concerned. With good reason because if there had been it would prove the tape he had given me was a forgery.

'Have you ever wondered what happened to our files?' I asked.

'Hüber probably shredded them as they both implicated him in the operation which got Steuernagel killed. If so, then the ultimate irony.'

'Which is?'

'The machine matching strips of paper to rebuild the Stasi's files uses a modified version of that software your brother-in-law claims was stolen from him,' Paul said. 'It's all one big game of chance, isn't it? Individual decisions which seem insignificant at the time but ...' He reached across the table and put out the candles by squeezing each flame between his fingers.

'But what?'

'The week before that party in Rethen I was on a bus from Erkner to my uncle's house. There was a girl sitting across the aisle and we caught each other's eye. When she left the bus just outside the village, she looked at me and smiled. I watched her walk away from the bus stop along a track that led to a farm. There had been times when working on a building site with my father I'd seen a tractor pulling a plough across a field and thought, that would do me. Instead of helping someone recreate some crazy dream in wood, brick and plaster, I would settle for my only mark on the world being a small scratch on its face with a plough. So, while the rest of my family kept banging on about East Germany being some sort of prison, I saw in it the chance of freedom, and that insect bite on my hand provided an opportunity to seek it out. On my way to the doctor I intended to visit the farm. If it hadn't been for Shetlov, well, who knows?'

It somehow did not seem fair to suggest the girl who caught his eye may have been returning from Erkner with fabric to make a hot air balloon. And, had he wanted to spend the rest of his life with her, he simply had to wait until she floated across the border or made a flight to the West in her uncle's crop spraying plane.

'Well, if you hadn't been at the party I might have drowned.'

'Or not ended up in the water.'

'You pushed me?'

547

'No, I was already in the water. You know that because in your diary you said Hans was pushing me under with the oar. Actually, I was holding onto it because that was easier than swimming to the bottom of the lake. I saw you standing on the jetty and came to the surface in front of you like the shark in jaws. I expected you to find it amusing, not faint and land on top of me. Then you grabbed me and pulled me to the bottom. You weren't struggling, just holding onto me. At first, I thought you were trying to drown me but you weren't being aggressive. Somehow, I couldn't see you as a professional killer.

'I had taken a gulp of air when I surfaced and remembered you had an inhaler so guessed you would need to return to the surface before me. But you just stayed put, looking at me. Then I thought of that image that kept going through my mind when I was in hospital. Being trapped beneath the ice which someone was trying to break.'

'Christina,' I prompted because Paul now seemed reluctant to tell me how the story ended.

'Eventually, I got you to the surface and Hans and Petra pulled us into the boat. I got my breath back but you just lay there, so I carried you back to the house. Someone suggested you had gone into shock. We knew you had some connection with the Stasi and had seen two people sitting in a car further down the street. Petra thought if you just disappeared, we could say you left early and didn't go anywhere near the lake.'

'And the poison? Was that part of the plan?'

'Poison? You've got a vivid imagination.' Then he must have realised what I was referring to. 'Oh, that poison. Yes, I did try to get you to drink some but you spilt it. Had more luck today though.'

'What do you mean?'

'That cup of tea you drank this evening it had chlorogenic acid in it.' Which did not make sense because I still felt fine. 'Tea, constituents Kaempferol and chlorogenic acid.'

'So, just a silly student prank.' I sighed. 'And misguided, considering the trouble I could have caused your family.' But Paul shrugged this off.

'Time we turned in.' Perhaps I read too much into this. Would he have chosen just then to suggest we sleep together, after making me feel a fool? Then I recalled him inspecting the pendant hung around my neck, putting his face close to mine and at the time suspecting he was about to kiss me; perhaps even willing him to. What if I had remembered this incorrectly, that this did not happen at the lake but while I was in the house, in this room where we were now sitting. Was it Paul, not Erich, in the room with me and now into my head came the image of lowering the bedclothes slightly in a clumsy attempt to seduce him. Humiliating, and perhaps why it had been so easy to convince myself he had drowned. Was it possible, despite what I was told by Hüber and Steuernagel, that this was what was expected of me? That it was a honey trap after all? More likely a false memory; how I felt at that moment rather than the way I behaved in the past.

'I'm spending the night down here. There's a settee in the lounge and I'll sleep on that.'

At first Paul looked puzzled but then appearing embarrassed said. 'Oh, no, I'm sorry, I didn't mean... I've booked two rooms.'

'Even so, I'd prefer to stay down here.'

Again, he looked perplexed, a shake of the head as he stood up. 'Well, you are missing a rare treat. The rooms are a piece of East German history.' Which seemed a strange thing to say. 'Some of Anweiler Construction's best work, a masterpiece in brown and beige.'

'What are you talking about?'

'You were here when the work was carried out. The whole point of the party was to drown out the noise of the building work and disguise the coming and going of Anweiler employees. This place belonged to some party official. He wanted it restored and Wilhelm obliged. An exciting day, what with you trying to drown yourself and poor Uncle Willi breaking two of his fingers.'

'What?' I said still trying to catch up with the idea the rooms above were not used to torture people.

'A bath was being replaced. Nothing wrong with the old one apart from it being a bit small. Anyway, the new one was really big, and Willi had to help get it into the room. He got his hand trapped between the bath and the wall.'

We climbed the stairs and I hesitated before opening the door to a room that, in the worst of my dreams, I had entered before. Maybe I still feared inside, tied to a chair, was a man with broken limbs and a bruised and bleeding face. Paul must have misinterpreted this hesitation because after opening the door to his own room he stood looking at me. Had I realised this was the last time I would ever see him, perhaps I would have walked along the corridor and stood beside him, waiting to be invited into his room.

Giving in to temptation would have changed everything, especially given the pillow talk which would have followed. First a whispered apology for my conference speech in Vienna. Then the suggestion a person close to him could not be trusted, because someone sent a document on EU Data Privacy Regulations to my husband knowing full well I would have discussed Monget's company with him. Did Paul know Mr Phillips had been invited to Köln to speak to me by someone who no doubt guessed how I would respond to the suggestion I became another psychologist in the pay of the social media industry? And had Maxine told him she believed Ute might be in line for his job? Not a particularly romantic way to end the evening.

Instead, I was considering filling the famous bath and lying in it, but somehow I could not pluck up the courage, fearing... Well, who knows what I was afraid of? Everything and nothing. On any other occasion I would have called Herman. Instead I sent a text, *Trapped in the snow, marooned in Berlin*, it said.

*Nightmare here in Munich too, hope Deutsche Bahn get their act together and we see each other again one day*. Herman replied. Not the most reassuring text he had ever sent me. I stared at it wondering what nightmare would interrupt my sleep that night, and really not wanting to wake on my own.

The person standing in front of me while I fought for breath was my father. But looking different from when he lay in the mortuary. His face was not white but tanned and his mouth, rather than just a black hole in his face, was smiling. But then I had to leave him there at the bottom of the lake because someone dragged me to the surface. A young man pulled me out of the water and then lay beside me as the boat drifted. There was silence save for the sound of water lapping against wood and birds singing in the trees on the banks of the canal. The sky was clear, the sun shone in my eyes. The boy leaned over me; he tugged at the pendant around my neck, then we kissed and made love. The dream ended halfway through our lovemaking, frustratingly before I reached a climax.

Perhaps it is my imagination, or maybe my memory of that evening in Rethen has been clouded by all that happened in the months that followed, but I am sure the person I dreamt made love to me in that dream was not my husband.

Breakfast was on my own because according to the middle-aged man now on the reception desk, Paul had already checked out. My room had been paid for, and a taxi booked to take me to Templin.

'I wonder, do you know who owned this building in the nineteen-seventies?' I asked when handing over my room key.

'A man called Mielke,' was the curt reply.

'Erich Mielke?'

'Yes, that's the guy, head of the Stasi, but don't worry, we've checked all the rooms for any strange wires. Supposedly he came here to fish in the lake and hunt in the forest, but I think it was mostly used to entertain ladies.' This explained the strange response the previous day when I mentioned my visit in 1975. Oddly, this final twist in what had been an increasingly strange affair was not uppermost in my mind when I finally got home.

While I had been eating breakfast in Rethen, in Templin Ute Lorenze had already left the hotel in which she spent the night, bought a red coat from the clothes shop on Am Markt, and driven to Gehrden. She even waved back at Joachim when he thought it was me driving through the village, and to Frau Reimann when my neighbour looked puzzled by the brevity of the visit. But then Ute held up the box she was carrying, and Frau Reimann was satisfied this contained something I had forgotten when leaving home the previous day rather than a reel of tape. What Ute had not realised, however, was that Herman had, once again, turned the elephant on the shelf in my office to face away from the door.

It was Herman I thought about while sitting alone looking out of the lounge window and across the frozen fields. He seemed further away than a snowbound train somewhere between Munich and Berlin. It would have been better not to have returned to an empty house because there was the feeling of no longer belonging there, or in the village I had outgrown, or even in the country which in my mind had belatedly ceased to exist. And I still could not get out of my mind the voice of Hildegard Knef singing, *Is that all there is?*

# 41

# This Page Is Intentionally Left Blank

October 2024

March last year was spent in Cambridge researching cognition. Most weekday mornings I took a walk from Downing College to a café in one of the city's cobbled courtyards, perhaps chosen because it reminded me of Templin. There I had breakfast with the person who helped me write this book and, like Paul Anweiler, had been a visitor from Britain I met in East Germany during the 1970s. He would take one of my diaries and a recording of our conversation then work on the first draft of a chapter in the reading room of the local library. When we met up again in the same café that evening, I would read through the day's work while we drank coffee and ate apple strudel.

On completing the account of my visit to Celle, he handed back the diary for 1993, the last one, ending prematurely in the June of that year. 'What do we call the next chapter?' he asked. 'This page intentionally left blank?' Then followed a philosophical conversation about life for people our age being very much like a diary with just a few empty pages to fill. An observation which came to mind again when what was supposed to be the final draft of the book arrived by post. To fill these pages what follows is a snapshot of the five years since my return to Rethen.

Few relationships would survive someone forcing their way into your life and turning you through a hundred and eighty degrees. After that day in Lychen it seemed the future was a place I was returning from and the past a dark road stretching into the distance. Over the coming months, my perception of the person I leaned on since the age of twenty changed. Observations made by patients over the years came to mind; *life is not a rehearsal* was one I found myself repeating when Sophie offered to help.

What did I say when suggestions, along the lines of imagining you have just met the partner you had suddenly tired of after forty years of marriage and try courting them all over again, fell on deaf ears? Usually that it was time to call a halt to the prevaricating. *OK then, make the break and find someone new.* Sometimes it forced the patient to face reality and ended the fantasy that there existed some mythical lover missed the first time around. Sometimes it did not, and Sophie and I often pondered the tally of relationships saved and those destroyed during our careers as therapists.

My someone new I met in the autumn of 2022, while running on the beach near Half Moon Bay early one morning during a holiday in California. He was ahead of me but flagging slightly, or perhaps I was putting in the extra effort to draw level with him.

'So, you've caught up,' he said. I suspected he slowed on purpose. *Where have you been all my life?* I half expected him to ask. Breakfast together was not as romantic as I expected and he made it clear neither the coffee, waffles, eggs, nor even the cutlery met his expectations. I was reminded of that visit to the Marianlust. Unfortunately, we were a long way from the mansion at Schmökwitz. 'There is the Ritz Carlton, further along the coast,' He suggested.

'Can we reach it by boat?' I asked.

That evening, while sitting watching a Pacific sunset, I thought there ought to be another postcard from America pinned on the wall behind the bar in the Weissen Ross, this one not of Capitola but the Golden Gate Bridge. For Claudia's benefit I wrote on the back '*Herman and I are camping in the forest near Ahrensdorf but found this postcard on eBay.*'

That is not to say this was some second-time-around romance. It was hard work. Even now I look at our wedding photograph and see two strangers; they stare at me from a world which seems as unimaginable to me now as this one would have been to them. There are still times I dwell on what might have been. One evening after making love, my mind drifted back to Rethen. 'You OK?' Herman asked, catching me unawares and part-way through that pillow talk with Paul that never was.

'When you went to Hannover, did you ever go to a café called the Köllnischfeld?' I asked.

'You asked me that once before,' Herman said.

His memory of me doing so confirmed in my mind he had indeed been there and, in the expectation of a full confession, I repeated the story Paul told me about his meeting with Shetlov, only this time with Herman also present at the table outside the café in the forest.

'So, what you are saying is that I conspired with this Englishman and someone from the KGB to help the Soviet Union steal secrets from East Germany.'

'Well, now you put it like that...' I said when laughed out of bed.

'Maria Freitag makes a fortune out of crazy stories like that – why don't you give it a try?' Herman said. So here we are, although Ute usually manages to unburden herself in a mere three hundred and fifty pages.

Two years ago, there was an incident at Aldershof S-Bahn Station, which resulted in the train I was waiting for entering and leaving the station without stopping. An ambulance arrived and then the police, who seemed in two minds whether to evacuate the station or keep everyone on the platform. Within a few minutes crowds formed around the top and bottom of the steps leading up from the street. The next train stopped, but the doors remained shut, save one in the front carriage. Out of this stepped the giant of a man who must have got a phone call every time a film company was casting the part of Leonid Brezhnev. Shetlov's son walked the length of the platform, stopping occasionally to talk to a member of staff or a police officer. Even when only listening it seemed he was issuing orders. Eventually, the remaining doors of the train opened, and Thomas Eppelmann climbed aboard. As the trained pulled out of the station, and the crowded platform cleared, there was the feeling I had just witnessed a fifteen-minute re-enactment of the history of East Germany between 1945 and 1989.

By then, of course, both Thomas's parents were dead, and presumably Hüber and Professor Pohl had also passed away; as far as I know there were no obituaries of either. Hüber perhaps because of a change of name care of the BND, and Heinz Pohl because he had become a non-person within his chosen profession. I suspect my own passing might also go unnoticed. Half a page in a broadsheet was given over to the death, following a heart attack, of Werner Weidel, an excuse perhaps for an article about Stasi operations in Britain during the 1970s and 1980s. An Austrian journalist revisited the death of Otto Steuernagel for no other reason than the discovery of a grainy photograph of the Stasi officer talking to a pair of CIA agents in the Frauenhuber Café. In the years since Steuernagel's death, the archives of both the CIA and the KGB have been opened, closed again, hacked and leaked, so the photograph could have been found in either. It might have even been supplied by Paul Anweiler. Although, of course, Paul is no longer with us, which sounds as if he has merely left the room halfway through a meeting; but that is how the news was broken to me.

'I'm sorry, I thought you knew,' Maxine said, mentioning it in passing during a stay in Gehrden with Max. One of the four jobs Herman has acquired since he retired is the director of a company Max set up to market self-drive technology to car companies. As during these frequent visits all four of us eat in the Weissen Ross, it was inevitable Max would meet Joachim, so I expect one day to read about a self-dive Trabant.

There was a lot I learned that day when Maxine, seeing the news about Paul had come as a shock, suggested we left our husbands talking business while we walked into the village.

Köhl and Strasse Investments lost a small fortune in Germany when Edouard Monget's company crashed and burned; however, the bank's London office was more fortunate. Mr Phillips placed a large bet on Companion's IPO failing, shorting its shares. This was done with the full knowledge of some of Köhl and Strasse's investors, who were promised a tax loss in Germany offset by a profit in the UK, much of which Britain's government, now free from EU regulations, let them keep. Helga Engelhardt had been kept in the dark about the deal as this was Paul taking back control of a fortune he felt was rightfully his, or at least two billion euros of it, which made the 250,000 I had been promised look like small change.

However, Paul seemed to have forgotten what he told me about people whose wealth and power survived even the most dramatic geopolitical upheaval. It was hardly likely Helga Engelhardt would let her fortune fall into the hands of a working class grifter. Even so, Paul's plan was both well thought out and inspired. He knew I would lash out at Vienna, my attack on Monget as predictable as me throwing that lock in the river and losing my temper on Peter's boat that morning after discovering the Cathcart affair was a scam. That was magic which only worked because I had been distracted by a trick. I struck out because Paul, with the help of Ute, made me feel powerless. Realising this caused me to revisit those tricks the Stasi played on Andreas K.

Heinze Pohl was right when he suggested Hüber's interest in Zersetzung was half-hearted. His intention all along was not to break up groups of dissidents but provoke a violent reaction. He took his lead from the West German state which marginalised radicals like Sonia Engelhardt, engendering in them a feeling of impotence which would inevitably cause them to resort to violence. Tricking Andreas K into taking direct action would have enabled Hüber to convince the Stasi physical force was the only way to suppress dissent amongst the young. Except of course Andreas K bided his time until the Stasi had alienated a large majority of East Germans.

Today within social media resides the ghost of Zersetzung. Herman tells me at this point I am back on my hobby horse. But really, to what end are we alienating people to the point where they feel so isolated and powerless they end up driving a truck into a crowded Christmas market? What reaction does the state hope to provoke?

It was through an act of violence Helga Engelhardt got what she wanted. It had all the hallmarks of a Ute Lorenze stunt gone wrong, life's imitation of art a little too convincing for the police. A man was shot dead in a hotel – that hotel, the one Paul Anweiler created a facsimile of in Britain, and it was surprising I only belatedly learned of his involvement, given Inge's accounts of roads blocked by the media when she took the children to school. Apparently, according to Maxine, there were sufficient mentions of Paul in his capacity as CEO of Köhl and Strasse for Helga to convince the board that it was time he left the bank. He was appointed to the board of a company near Dannenberg and bought a house just outside Perlberg. Most days he travelled to and from work across the bridge at Domitz but one evening returned on the Pevestorf-to-Lenzen ferry. While his car was on the boat when it docked, Paul was not. Maxine thought he never managed to assuage the guilt he felt over Sonia Engelhardt's death. I recalled what he had said during that breakfast at the Domitz Hafen Hotel about a body in the Elbe being lost forever when it washed into the sea.

Ute's grief, if she truly felt any, was poured into a Maria Freitag novel called *The Man on the Bridge*, too dark for most readers and, ironically, panned by critics for being too improbable, which must have hurt. A year later, Ute, by then on the board of Köhl and Strasse, married the widowed owner of one of Germany's largest retailers. Less a wedding, more a corporate takeover, was how some described it. Herman and I were not invited to the wedding although all four of our grandchildren were co-opted as bridesmaids and pageboys.

Moving on from the sublime to the ridiculous, 2022 saw the broadcast, in eight episodes, of *Don't Bank on It*, the TV adaptation of the Maria Freitag book of the same name. The trailer had shown a clip of the police searching a garage which was home to a restored Trabant. This guaranteed at least two people in Gehrden would be watching, one of them being Herman. Having read the book I tried, unsuccessfully, to persuade him we did something else other than watch television on the evening the final episode was broadcast, I had even tried to coax him into bed. Unfortunately, while men seem obsessed with cars and sex, it is strictly in that order. For seven weeks I feigned disinterest in what, in my opinion, expressed several times, was too farfetched to be credible. The mistress hitching a lift on a breakdown truck to avoid being gunned down on the way home was considered inspired by Joachim, who recalled that this resembled something I had once done.

So why did no-one realise the woman having an affair with the owner of a private bank, which came to light after he was suffocated to death in the bank's vault, was based on me? That I was the woman Ute had in mind when she wrote about a mistress framed for the embezzlement of her lover's fortune? Because the story was not set in Templin, but Vechta in Lower Saxony. If even my son Peter, who came of age after the Wende, saw a foreign country when he looked across the Elbe, it seemed my secret was safe.

The story fitted the Maria Freitag template and I could visualise venom and tears splashing in equal measure onto the keyboard as Ute wrote it. After the quick thinking which saved her life in the first episode, things rapidly went downhill for the hapless mistress. 'Idiot,' Herman muttered when the lock was thrown into the Rhein. 'She must have realised it wasn't the key which was copied but the lock. Now she won't be able to prove it.'

Well, I certainly missed that, and I'd had the lock in my hand. The reason the mistress threw the lock in the Rhein was because it had her name and that of her lover on it. I did it because Paul had made me angry. But any comment on my part would have needed explaining, so none was made. For that reason, when the last episode was broadcast, there were things that urgently needed doing in the kitchen. These were closing my eyes, praying and, to drown out what was on the television, feeding fruit and vegetables into the blender.

The police suspected the *G* on the tag attached to the key, which fitted the lock now consigned to the river, indicated it might be for a garage and escorted the mistress back to her house. 'If the police took the plywood off the wall of our garage all they would find is Habicht's rubbish brickwork,' Herman said as I poured the smoothie into two glasses.

'It must be a few years since these fitted her,' said one of the two policemen standing over the battered suitcase while holding up the jeans. As Maxine said, Ute just never gives up. She herself had sold her yellow Porsche as now, whenever cleaning it, neighbours asked if the imprint of her backside had gone. In Ute's book, Maxine's alter ego had been made love to on the bonnet in the carpark of Frankfurt Airport, photographic evidence provided by a passenger on an Emirates flight to Dubai.

'And look at this,' the second policemen said, picking up a notebook. 'She keeps a diary, so I think we'll find everything we need to know in this.' A magazine article about the series mentioned Maria Freitag took a keen interest in how her books were adapted for TV, the director suggesting she was a pain in the butt. So, intrigued how the next scene played out, and wanting to see Herman's reaction, I peered into the lounge.

'There's something else under here,' the first policeman said. 'My god look at this.' He was now holding up a wad of banknotes. 'How much do you think there is here?'

'Must be at least two hundred and fifty thousand euros.'

The first policeman looked into the camera, and I got the strangest feeling he was talking to me when he said, 'I wonder what she had to do for that?'

'I thought so,' said Herman and my heart stopped, my mind racing through all the explanations dreamed up for having come into possession of such a large amount of cash. The money Paul promised, which after reading *Don't Bank on It*, I realised Ute left in the suitcase when retrieving the Cathcart tape. Some of these explanations had been almost as bizarre as the plots of Ute's books.

'Herman ...' I said, regretting making up the story about a rich American patient who experienced an emotional crisis, paid for our first-class flight to San Francisco and whose fee easily covered the cost of our holiday in California. We were in Pink Panther territory, another of the film's the Stasi confiscated from Roland's apartment after the party in Leipzig, and Inspector Clouseau claiming, when asked how a policeman's wife could afford a mink coat that she was very frugal and saved out of the housekeeping.

But thankfully Herman was not listening but instead studying the photograph of the TV screen he had taken with his mobile phone. 'Joachim said a TV company hired his Trabant a while back. That was it in the garage. 'Look,' he said, zooming in on the car in the background of the shot of the policeman holding the wad of notes. 'It's definitely Joachim's.'

Someone else in receipt of a large amount of money was a couple from Eberswalde. 'We were on holiday in Spain so we left our numbers with my father,' the middle-aged woman said. Presumably the delay in coming forward was the time it took to think up an explanation as to how she and her husband inherited this large slice of pre-Wende luck. Inherited because their father, not being a young man, wanted to ensure thirty percent of this fortune, in trust to East Germans since 1978, did not fall into the wrong hands, in this case those belonging to West German tax collectors. How did I know the father in question was Rolf? I did not, but the insistence all the woman's father wanted as a share of the lottery prize was enough to pay for a two-week holiday in Rugen and a tractor for his sister's farm was a clue.

With only half a page still blank the diary has been in my bag for several weeks in anticipation of something coming to mind. And it just has, a thought which if not committed to paper now will be forgotten when the train arrives in Templin and Herman, who is waiting there, puts an arm around me, gives my shoulder a squeeze and explains why *preparing dinner* as promised ended up as booking a table at the Weissen Ross.

*The train was approaching Zehdenick and out of the window I saw a tractor in a field, scratching the face of the earth with a plough. Perhaps, when the person driving it finished work, waiting for him in a farmhouse was a woman content in her role of his Christina. I wondered how my life would have turned out had that woman been me.*